DEAD RECKONING

The Third Cameron McGill Mystery Thriller

JENNY ROBERTS

First published 2005 by Jenny Roberts,
an imprint of Millivres Prowler Limited, part of the Millivres Prowler Group,
Spectrum House, Unit M, 32-34 Gordon House Road, London NW5 1LP
www.divamag.co.uk

A catalogue record for this book is available from the British Library

ISBN 1-873741-97-9

Printed and bound in Finland by WS Bookwell

Distributed in the UK and Europe by Airlift Book Company,
8 The Arena, Mollison Avenue,
Enfield, Middlesex EN3 7NJ
Telephone: 020 8804 0400

Distributed in North America by Consortium,
1045 Westgate Drive, St Paul, MN 55114-1065
Telephone: 1 800 283 3572

Distributed in Australia by Bulldog Books,
PO Box 300, Beaconsfield, NSW 2014

To my sister Edith

Author's note

All the events and characters in this book are fictitious. Many of the places where the action takes place exist, but some are entirely fictional. In particular it should be stressed that, although there are various taxi firms in (or close to) Manchester's gay village, Lavender Taxis is not one of them and is purely a figment of my imagination. Chow City and the Golden Snapper are also entirely fictitious.

I would like to thank Chris Barton for his help on the legal background to the story. Any mistakes or inaccuracies are mine entirely.

Finally my special thanks to Dorothy Lumley of Dorian Literary Agency for her inestimable help in reading the first draft and for giving me valuable insights into the various ways in which the story could be improved upon.

About the author

Jenny Roberts's debut thriller, *Needle Point*, the first Cameron McGill Mystery, was published by Diva Books in 2000, and her second, *Breaking Point*, in 2001. She is also a contributor to various short-story collections.

Her website is www.jennyroberts.net, where you can read extracts from her books and some of her short stories. She also welcomes feedback from readers via the website.

One

The rain rattled against the car roof like tintacks from the sky, beading down the glass in front of me, shimmering briefly in the dirty amber street light, then dying in the blackness of the road.

Jesus.

I rubbed my belly, trying to ease the cramps. The clock on the dashboard blinked over to 18.33. I'd been sitting here for over an hour. Watching, thinking.

I'd promised myself, hadn't I? Eighteen months ago. I wasn't going to be the kind of sleazy PI who spent her life spying on sad old men and their lovers. Oh no, not me. Not Cameron McGill.

Yeah, but here I was. Still doing the kind of work that made me feel dirty, dishonest.

I pulled the rear-view mirror round and studied my face for something to do. Bad move. I looked like I felt. Dull grey eyes stared back at me. My once-black hair was getting greyer by the day, and it needed cutting. Then there were the wrinkles. Another two years and I'd be forty. Life was passing me by.

I should be doing the jobs I enjoy. The ones I'm good at.

I pushed the mirror away in disgust and turned my attention back to the house. Every room in Number 27 was lit up. The bedroom lights had gone on just minutes after Elaine Wilson's husband had got there. I'd watched his ladylove pull the curtains and I'd got a good close-up with the zoom as she looked out of the bedroom window. An older woman, with a craggy face and a slightly uncomfortable expression.

1

Yeah, that surprised me. The man's wife was in her late twenties. Cute, blonde, sexy – a good fifteen years younger than her husband. A sad middle aged man's fantasy. Yet here he was, playing away with an older woman.

I closed my eyes and ran my fingers through my hair as the dull ache in my belly reasserted itself and I wondered why my body couldn't stick to some kind of routine any more.

Jesus, thirty-eight years old. Could I be menopausal already?

The clock winked at me again and flipped over to 18.34. A lone cyclist pushed on past, head down against the weather, his torn waterproof flapping cheerlessly behind him. For all that I could tell, the house might just as well be empty. Since that first sighting I'd seen nothing I could use. I wondered if they'd spotted me and left by the back way, leaving me sitting here like a fool.

I pushed two more ibuprofen from the blister pack, and washed them down with a swig of cola, shifting in my seat, desperately hoping that both my tampon and my bladder would hold out.

How come fictional heroes never have bodily functions? When was the last time anyone saw Tom Cruise breaking off for an urgent shit? Or one of Charlie's Angels nipping behind a bush on some fucking exotic island to change her tampon?

I looked out into the road again and took a deep breath.

When I'm doing the work I like, it's a breeze. Finding people, interviewing witnesses, researching evidence for solicitors. Building a case for someone, or uncovering evidence that leads to an acquittal – or a conviction. I like that. And I'm good at it. Trouble is, there's never been enough.

I looked up as the light changed. The bedroom was in darkness now. They were settling in – or they were coming back downstairs. Please, God, let them come out of the door and drive into town – to a nice restaurant, perhaps, where I could leave them for a while, find a toilet, stop the leaks and get comfortable again.

The man's wife had phoned me the previous Friday afternoon. I'd had a good week. I'd just finished digging around for evidence in an assault case. I hadn't tailed a lousy adulterer for days, my bankroll was in the black and the in-tray was empty. I had my feet up on the desk, a big mug of coffee in my hand, a *Guardian* in front of me. Peaceful, just me and the gentle murmur of the street market outside the office window.

Yeah. Then the phone rang.

The woman attempted a classy Home Counties accent, but there was no disguising the flat Northern vowels beneath.

'Cameron – it is Cameron, isn't it?' She said it as if she knew me, 'I need your help. It's my husband.'

I put the coffee down on the desk, my good mood crumbling to dust. 'Your husband.' I repeated, searching my head for some clue.

'Yes, he's cheating on me. I need your help.'

I pushed the newspaper away and reached out for my notepad. Whoopee-doo!

'Just a moment – first of all I need your name and address.'

She paused and sighed impatiently. 'Mrs Elaine Wilson.' She put the emphasis on the 'Mrs' as if it were some kind of trophy, 'I live at 43 Barkington Road, Bury.'

Bury? Jesus, that's the other side of the Pennines.

'The thing is, he goes out every Monday night and never gets home until the early hours. Then when he does, he smells of cheap perfume, and—'

'Excuse me, Mrs Wilson,' I interrupted, 'but you need someone local. I'm nearly two hours' drive away. How come you've rung *me*, anyway?'

'Oh,' she said dismissively, 'your friend, Bernice Nolan – she said you'd be pleased to help.'

I winced the moment she said it. Bernice Nolan – Beano. The PI with the van and the Sanilav, the woman who persuaded me to turn detective in the first place.

'She said you'd sort it out for me right away. I need him followed on Monday. I need video evidence, Cameron. It *has* to be this Monday, though, I can't wait any longer.'

3

My stomach sank to my knees. 'Look, just a moment, Mrs Wilson—'

'Call me Elaine. You *do* do video, don't you?'

'Yes I do, Elaine. If you've spoken to *Bernice*, then why isn't *she* helping you?'

I asked the question carefully, trying to keep the cynicism out of my voice, waiting for the all-too-plausible explanation.

'Oh, she was going to.' She sighed, a hint of disappointment creeping into her voice. 'I rang her last Thursday. She would have helped, but she was on her way abroad.'

'Oh, really?' I gritted my teeth; this sounded like classic Beano. 'And where has she gone this time?'

'Well, India, of course!' She snorted a little, as if I must be dim. 'I thought you two were friends. She goes every year, to see her spiritual mentor and sort out her karma. She's *so* spiritual. I admire that in a woman, don't you? It's not the sort of thing *I* would do, but I think it suits your friend. Anyway, she told me – get in touch with Cameron, she said. She's the best, she said.'

I took a swig of lukewarm coffee and kicked the desk.

'I'll see you Monday, then – say one o'clock?'

I stared up at the ceiling. Beano was always doing this to me. Dumping her least favourite clients under the pretext of helping me build up my business. And the bigger the lie, the more easily her clients seemed to believe her. I couldn't think of anyone less likely than Beano to have a spiritual leader, and I knew for a fact that she never went further than Brighton.

'I'm sorry,' I lied, 'I just can't do it. Not just now, I'm too busy.' Beano's cast-offs were always trouble. The last one was a woman with an imaginary stalker. I spent three days trailing her before I realised that she actually *wanted* someone to follow her.

'No, I'm sorry, Mrs Wilson, Bury's too far away. I only work around York.' Untrue. I work anywhere that pays. But, hell, give me a break – I didn't want another matrimonial. And definitely not one of Beano's.

'But Bernice said I could rely on you, Cameron,' she simpered, her voice quivering with despair.

Yeah, I bet she did.

I tried to put some finality into my voice, 'No. It's too far. I'll be too expensive. You need someone local.'

'I don't want just anyone, Cameron. I want a woman to do it. Besides, I know I can trust you: Bernice said so. There's no problem with money. What do you charge?'

I told her, doubling my normal daily rate in the hope that it would put her off. As a ploy, it wasn't one of my best.

'Good!' she chirped. 'So that's settled, then. One o'clock Monday. I'll tell you everything then. OK?'

So I'd agreed. The money was good and, even if the job was a pain in the neck, I figured that I'd nothing else to do. One night's easy surveillance, then I could drop in on Beano. Pin her to the wall. Tell her what a rat she was.

Yeah. Then, this morning – Monday – my period had started. Five days early.

Some movement caught my eye and, when I looked up, the front door was opening. I wiped the condensation off the side window again and lifted up the camcorder. Thank goodness I'd be able to move soon. And, wherever they were going, there'd be a toilet. There had to be.

I pressed the record button as the door opened and the woman I'd seen earlier stepped out of the house. She glanced nervously up and down the street, then opened up a flowery umbrella. I blinked. She wasn't dressed for a night on the town at all. Her long, grey hair was uncombed and she was wearing a baggy jumper and a pair of old jeans with slippers on her feet.

She turned back and nodded at the silhouette of a big broad-shouldered woman with an ample bosom standing just inside the house. I aimed the camcorder again as she stepped out of the house and stopped on the path, glancing nervously up and down the street. The grey-haired woman passed the brolly across, and seemed to pause for a moment. Then she patted the bigger woman on the arm and retreated back into the house.

The big woman hobbled out through the gate and across the road, making for Charles Wilson's car, juggling with keys, brolly and handbag as she went, looking awkward, uncomfortable and panicky.

I kept the video rolling and zoomed in for a closer look.

She was a long-haired, brassy redhead – a tall, wide and ungainly figure, wearing a dark green jacket, a white blouse and a very short red skirt.

A woman with a big handbag, three-inch heels and a walk that John Wayne would have died for.

Two

The traffic was light as I drove towards the city centre. Rush hour was long gone and the evening trek to the city's nightspots was only just beginning. My favourite Never the Bride album was kicking in on the CD player and my spirits were lifting as Nikki and her band belted out the loud rock music. Charles Wilson was a couple of cars in front, and undeniably eager to get on with his girlie night out.

There was never any doubt about it, even under yellow cast of the street lights: the walk, the height, the broad shoulders and the face – despite several layers of pancake – clearly belonged to Elaine Wilson's husband. The woman with the grey hair might be a friend, but she certainly didn't seem like a lover.

So there *was* no other woman. Charles Wilson was a transvestite. His Monday night socials were just harmless fun. The perfume was his own. End of story. All I had to do now was follow him to his destination and record a little more video, then I could drop off the tape with my report, collect my money and go home. For just a moment, I considered what a relief the news might be to her.

But it was a very small moment.

She would be furious. I could have called Elaine Wilson many things but broad-minded would not have been one of them. Quite apart from the acute embarrassment that the news would cause her, she'd also feel severely cheated. I doubted that cross-dressing qualified as grounds for divorce.

The tracks changed as Charlie-girl stopped at the lights, three cars ahead. Nikki began belting out 'Surprise, Surprise' and I smiled for the first time that day. Maybe there is such a thing as natural justice after all.

OK, so I didn't like Elaine Wilson. Why would I? She was vain, self-centred and obsessed with her own status. She'd been nice enough on the phone, but when I arrived at her house she'd treated me like some kind of lackey. If I hadn't spent two hours getting there, I would have walked off the job right there and then.

I'm not much drawn to transvestites, either, but I felt sorry for her husband. She talked about him as if he were a failure – a boring little man who had gone to seed and just didn't cut the ice any more. Now he was cheating on her, and she wanted him nailed. Jesus, she'd been married to the poor guy for only three years, and it didn't need a detective to see through her little-girl-hurt routine.

The subtext was that she wanted out, big time, on her terms, with a nice big wad of his money to take with her. Call me cynical, but she'd probably drawn up a list of objectives the day after she met him. As I say, matrimonials depress me.

She told me that Charles was a restaurateur and that he left work around 4.15 p.m. every Monday – his night out with the boys, she said, looking at me sideways, as though she despised him for using such an obvious lie.

From the way she spoke about his business acumen, I'd been expecting a sleazy rundown café. But when I followed her directions I found myself across the road from a swanky bar/restaurant, just off Albert Square in one of the most sought-after areas of the city. Chow City it was called – a big white palace with a pale-green glass frontage that stretched nearly twenty feet from pavement to ceiling. It didn't look like the business venture of a failure to me.

Behind the restaurant, down a backstreet, a small concreted yard housed a couple of big silver rubbish bins and a pile of wet cardboard. His wife said that he always used the back entrance, so I pulled in some fifty yards away and hunkered down in my seat to wait.

I studied him carefully as he walked past. He seemed a lot bigger than the photograph, and better groomed, too. A tall, weighty man with a round face and kind eyes. His grey suit was more Austin Reed than Burton, his hair was thinning but neatly cut, and there was just a touch of eagerness in his face and in his walk. As if he was going to a party, and it was his own.

He turned left at the end and strode briskly through the side streets away from the city centre. Following in the car, I lost him when he turned down a no-entry street, but I made a lucky guess and picked him up again on the other side as he made his way into a multistorey to collect a two-year-old, midnight-blue Mondeo.

As I followed him out of the centre, through the thick lines of rush-hour traffic, I wondered about that. His wife had said that he was a partner in the restaurant, so I might have expected him to drive a more expensive car – maybe a Merc or a BMW. But then later on, knowing his plans, I guess it made sense for him to drive something more ordinary.

We crept out of the city, up Oxford Road and through university land, past the big teaching hospitals, the art gallery and the seemingly endless curry houses of Rusholme.

It had been after five by the time he pulled up outside the house in West Didsbury. Now, driving back through the university again, it was nearly seven. Three hours of sitting in one place and my legs and my backside were joining the list of other discomforts. I flipped open the glove compartment at some traffic lights and stuck a tampon, the ibuprofen and a handful of tissues into the left-hand pocket of my leather jacket. The video-cam went into my right pocket and clicked neatly into the custom spy hole.

Charlie-girl signalled a right as he passed the BBC. I followed as he cut into the side streets just beyond the Mancunian Way, threading his way through the Umist buildings, towards the gay village, where, I guessed, he'd be meeting some other 'girly' friends for a night on the town.

Poor guy. I couldn't help but feel sorry for him. He'd get hell after I told his wife – and I *would* have to tell her.

I drove past his car and pulled around the corner onto the big surface car park by the canal, paid the fee and hoofed it back to the corner, my heart pounding in case I'd lost him. But I needn't have worked up a sweat. When I glanced down the street at the Mondeo, Charlie-girl was still sitting in the driver's seat, adjusting the hair and applying even more makeup.

The rain had stopped now and the wind had dropped. It was a pleasant, warm October evening and the village felt washed and clean after the downpour. People were coming out to play and the streets seemed surprisingly busy for a Monday night. A few dykes passed by, laughing and shouting to each other, on their way to Vanilla. A knot of leathermen were gathering outside the Rembrandt. Up the street the *Big Issue* seller was standing on the corner wearing a silly hat and charming passers-by, then bowing to them dramatically whether they bought or not. Ahead to my left, a gang of students were making their way noisily down Canal Street. I smiled as I noticed that some wag had whited out the C again. A cliché, I know, but who can resist it?

Outside the fried-chicken place, there was a guy in a too-tight suit, holding forth at the top of his voice to anyone who would listen, which in this case was nobody. I crossed over the road away from him, trying once more to ignore the squelchy feeling in my pants and my painful bladder, and leaned against the side of the bridge, pleased that, as always, I was wearing plain black jeans. The preacher with the loud mouth was a gift. I could keep a discreet eye on my quarry, wait for him to make a move, while I leaned against the canal bridge bleeding quietly.

The man started in surprise when he saw me – I guess I must have been the first audience he'd had in weeks – then his thick lips turned up a little and he turned around, face-on, giving me an exclusive. Maybe it wasn't such a good idea after all.

'Bless you, young lady. Bless you,' he said, softly now. 'The Lord is ready to forgive your sin.'

He looked like a cat that had cornered a vole. I stared back coldly, willing him to turn away again.

He was an untidy, overweight man in his sixties with a lined, ruddy face that looked as if it were two sizes too big for his skin. His greasy slicked-back hair glimmered under the orange street lights. His eyes seemed twice as big as normal – big and white and wild. For a second, I felt like a rabbit caught in headlights.

I dislike religious fanatics, anyway, but there was something even more uncomfortable about this one. He wasn't pleasing to look at, that was for sure. Every time he opened his mouth a drop of saliva ran down his chin and dripped onto the lapel of his jacket, turning it a kind of blotchy grey. But it was his tone of voice that got to me the most. Barely hidden beneath the pious rhetoric, there seemed to be real anger. And it was rolling across the street at me in waves.

I caught my breath and looked away, willing him to turn his attention elsewhere.

He paused momentarily until I turned back. Then he held my eyes and took a step forward, extending his arms towards me.

'Come,' he said. 'Allow the Lord to embrace you.'

I folded my arms and gave him the death stare. The Lord could embrace whoever he wanted, but I wasn't going to be in the queue, and certainly not with him standing in as proxy.

But the man was undeterred. For all my obvious hostility, the preacher never let his gaze falter.

'You have sinned, have you not? Sinned – as so many have in this poor godless place.' He was darkly serious now and there was true menace in his voice. 'God frowns upon carnal joy with your own sex. He punishes those who defy the natural order. You know that, don't you?'

I turned away as a shiver of anger rippled through me, fingering the video-cam. Down the road, Charlie-girl was still in the car.

The preacher's voice softened again and a generous smile slid back across his face. 'But, there is a way out, my dear. If you repent your sins – if you embrace the teachings of the Bible – the Lord God Almighty will forgive you.'

I stared back, ready to take issue. This bigot, with his twisted morals was lecturing *me* on what was right. I opened my mouth to speak, but before I said a word a couple of baby dykes brought me back to reality, waving across at me as they walked behind the man, pointing at his back and then sticking their fingers down their throats. I relaxed and pulled a face at them instead.

The bigot didn't seem to notice. 'Take comfort, young lady: it is never too late for repentance. The hand of the Lord will show you the way back to a wholesome life. Given his help, you can be wholesome again. You can seek a husband with great joy. You can procreate.'

I looked away in disgust. Down the street, Charlie-girl was finally getting out of the car, swinging shiny tan legs out onto the pavement in a pastiche of feminine deportment, standing up, adjusting the skirt and jacket, primping the big hair one last time, then locking the car and mincing bow-legged up the street towards me. I turned to face down the street and clicked on the camera. Elaine had said she needed as much evidence as possible, so I was going to provide it – even if it wasn't quite what she'd anticipated.

Someone took hold of my arm and squeezed it. It was a woman. A very proper woman in a tweedy green three-piece, with a blue rinse and a sad smile. She was looking at me as if I were a small abandoned child.

I stared back and pulled my arm away, shaken by the intrusion, and kept the video pointing in the right direction. Charlie-girl was stumbling up the street in his heels. A small, distracted part of my brain had an unaccountable urge to shout at him, to tell him to keep his knees together. The rest of me wanted to know why this stranger had just walked up and squeezed my arm.

'Take some information, dear,' she said, pushing a small printed handbill into my palm. I turned to face her as Charlie-girl minced past, then kept on turning to film his continued progress up the street.

I think she said something about the *minister* helping me to redemption, but I wasn't listening. I was far too distracted watching Charlie trying to avoid the preacher, who, by now, was standing coldly silent, glaring across the street at Elaine Wilson's befrocked husband.

Charlie-girl pointedly looked the other way and walked faster, stumbling in the three-inch heels as he attempted to get past the preacher.

'All the information you need is in this leaflet,' the woman twittered, like someone selling double glazing.

The preacher lunged forward and Charlie-girl tried to run for it. But the three-inch heels were hardly made for flight and, before he'd managed two steps, his adversary had him by the neck and was dragging the painted face close to his. Charlie pulled back in terror. The madman held on even tighter, first staring into his eyes, then spitting heavily into his face.

'Sinner, adulterer!' He raged. His eyes were as big as eggs now and saliva was streaming across his chin. Charlie-girl was shaking and screaming at the old man to let go. He did so, but followed through, striking the transvestite hard across the face.

The woman with the blue rinse looked over her shoulder and froze. 'Oh, no!' she mouthed. 'Dear God, Ernest, no!' Then she turned and scurried towards them.

The force of the blow knocked both men off balance. Charlie-girl staggered backwards, losing a shoe in the process. The preacher lurched drunkenly to one side but recovered and lunged out again at his victim. As Charlie-girl attempted to retrieve the shoe, the red-faced assailant pounced again, spinning him round, and shouting a string of obscenities into his face. For a moment Charlie-girl stared back helplessly. Even with the makeup his face was white as death.

'You will *die*! You will go to *Hell* for your sins.' The preacher was shaking from head to foot. 'You will not be spared. God will have his reckoning. '

Everything seemed to stop and, for just a few moments, an eerie silence fell on the street. I shivered. It sounded like a curse. The woman with the blue rinse took hold of the preacher's arm, pleading, attempting to restrain him. Charlie-girl took his chance and hobbled off, shoe in hand, down a backstreet. The preacher turned sharply and stared at her with contempt. Then he pushed her away and stormed off past me and on down the street.

'You're wrong, Ernest,' she shouted as she caught him up. 'I wouldn't. I couldn't... You've got to believe me. I was doing the Lord's work, I swear to you.'

The preacher brushed her away and stormed on towards an old maroon estate.

I set off after Charlie-girl, but glanced back before I turned the corner. The man was in his car, pulling out of the parking spot and roaring angrily down the road. The woman was left in the middle of Sackville Street, wailing helplessly.

I sighed and shook my head as I turned into the backstreet. I felt sickened. I've never regarded myself as any sort of believer and I don't profess to know anything about religion.

But none of that had seemed very Christian to me.

Three

I stopped as soon as I turned the corner. After the bright lights of Sackville Street, the backstreet was poorly lit, unfriendly and empty. Charlie-girl had gone.

I checked the bar near the corner first. It was almost empty and there wasn't a frock or a wig in sight. Further on, two men stirred in a doorway as I approached, the whites of their eyes shining out in the darkness. They caught me unawares and I faltered for a moment, drawing back and scowling at them as I passed. It took less than a moment for them to decide that I was no threat and they slipped back into their frenzied embrace before I even looked away.

Halfway up, a large sign flickered brightly through the gloom, spilling red neon across the dirty wet road, warming the puddles and flushing the night away. CHLOË'S BAR it said, and a flashing green arrow pointed repeatedly at a door in the wall below. It was the only other bar in the street, so I guessed that Charlie-girl had to be inside.

Yeah. Maybe that's why I'm a detective.

When I pushed on through the metal-clad door, the fresh air of the village gave way to the musky dampness of a poorly ventilated bar. A Gloria Gaynor track pierced through a humid cocktail of warm body odour, cheap perfume and cigarette smoke and I blinked hard, trying to focus in the half-light.

I was standing at the top of a short flight of steps. Below me, about thirty hazy figures were sitting on settees around the sides of the room, with another dozen sitting at the tables in the centre. The bar was at the far end. It was too dim to make out either Charlie-girl or the toilet, but both of them had to be there somewhere.

A sudden, uneasy silence fell across the room before I'd even closed the door. Heavily made-up faces came into focus in the half-light, staring up at me, inspecting me as I walked down the steps and threaded my way through the tables. I could almost hear them thinking, A stranger; no, worse: a lesbian.

I swallowed hard, forcing myself to stay cool, glancing around the room as casually as I could, trying to find the man I'd been following, and feeling more out of it with every step I took. Everywhere I looked, eyes stared back at me, openly curious as to why a woman like me would walk into a bar like that. They were mostly people of a certain age – in their forties and fifties. A few men, in men's clothes, were scattered around, and a handful of straight-looking older women. But all the other occupants of the room were, unmistakeably, men in frocks.

As I pushed my way through the tables, conversations struck up *sotto voce* behind me and I could feel the eyes burning into my back. Ahead of me, new faces turned upwards and examined me as I approached. I smiled back as pleasantly as I could, looking directly into the eyes of the counterfeit women, daring them to keep on staring, but, all the time, wondering how the hell I could preserve my cover now.

Right then, I couldn't think of anywhere on this earth where a dyke like me was less likely to melt into the scenery. It was like some kind of bizarre film set, a sea of wigs and heaving plastic bosoms, a room full of men exposing their feminine side to one another. Quite suddenly I was desperate to be somewhere else, somewhere bright and wholesome, somewhere gentle and clean, a room filled with real women, a place full of people like me.

It was then that I saw her – just as I was approaching the bar. The woman behind it – a genuine woman – was standing, arms folded, grinning at me, gently amused at my discomfort.

She was a little smaller than me, around five seven. Her long black hair framed a pair of big, dark eyes that shone out from her pale face like rescue beacons. I was drawn to her straightaway. Maybe it was the heady mixture of her half-Chinese, half-Caucasian features or, perhaps, her pretty, almost boyish, face. It could have been the way she wore her clothes – the simple body-hugging top that accentuated her small breasts and suntanned shoulders. Or her attitude, her good-natured self-assurance. There was no doubt about her being a woman, but I wondered if she was a lesbian as well. She had a kind of style, a way of being, that set my gaydar blinking.

'You look like you need a drink,' she observed, her voice husky and pleasurable. Her flat Northern accent was half mocking, half sympathetic, and she leaned casually on the bar, her big grin lighting up the space around her.

'Yeah.' I raised my eyebrows and made a show of looking over my shoulder at the rest of the room. 'Sometimes, don't you just wish you'd chosen another bar?'

She studied me with some care, then smiled back ruefully. 'Mmm. I better make it a strong one, then.'

'Yeah, I guess. I'll have a Campari and tonic – and go easy on the tonic.'

She pushed the glass up against the optic and allowed the deep red liquid to fill almost half before she added a splash of tonic and a little ice. When she put the glass down her eyes looked straight into me. 'The words "fish" and "water" spring to mind,' she remarked, looking me up and down, as she pushed the drink across the counter. Then, raising a pair of neat eyebrows, 'What brings someone like you into a tranny bar?'

I grinned back sheepishly, totally disarmed, and rubbed my belly. 'I'm, er, just desperate to use the toilet – if you know what I mean.'

I could see from the look in her dark eyes that she did. She cupped her hands around my drink and jerked her head towards the door to my left. 'Go ahead, I'll keep this safe for you.'

For all my desperation, I paused for an instant, taking her in – one of those rare people that you make immediate contact with. I could trust her, I was sure of it.

'Um, I'm looking for a friend,' I began, a little awkwardly, 'A redhead, I, er, thought I saw him – her. He was wearing a green jacket and a red skirt. He – she – came in here just before I did.'

She stood there silently, watching me squirming.

'I'm sorry. I'm not very good at this, am I? I feel a little, you know, awkward.'

Her eyes flashed in something like disbelief.

'Yeah, you do, don't you? A tough-looking woman like you. And you're blushing as well!' She studied me with amusement, then took pity on me. 'Ah, you don't need to worry.' She smiled. 'They're nice people, y'know. And don't feel awkward about the pronouns, either – if they're dressed as women, you say "she". That's what they like.'

I rubbed my forehead and tried again, still feeling out of it. 'Yeah, OK. Is *she* in here?'

'You must mean Penny.' She grinned, nodding towards the other side of the bar. 'She's over there on the settee, sitting next to Aunt Emily – the one in the flowery dress.'

I looked across the room. Charlie-girl, a.k.a. Penny, was perched on the settee, knees together, face still strained, hanging onto a glass of wine and listening intently to a Margaret Rutherford lookalike who was holding forth, scarcely pausing to take breath. Charlie-girl didn't look as though he – or she – would be going anywhere for a while.

'Thanks,' I said, feeling easier again. 'Don't say anything. I'll go over and say hello just as soon as I've sorted myself out.'

Dark Eyes nodded conspiratorially and I made for the toilet door before my bladder, or my tampon, called time.

It was a small room with two cubicles, a large mirror, one wash basin – and three people already fighting for space. One of them, a small dumpy person with too much green eye shadow, was leaning against the wall fighting a pair of tights with his feet – and from where I stood it looked like the tights were winning. The second, tall and wigless, was blinking as he applied the mascara. The third, standing behind him, combing a short brown bob and wearing the makeup well, could have been for real. The guy was genuinely pretty – it was only the voice that gave him away.

'Don't mind us, love,' he grinned, as I made for a cubicle, 'we all share everything round here.'

I hovered for an instant by the door and smiled back. 'You look good,' I commented, surprising myself. He looked back at me as if I'd just made his day and I closed the door quickly before I got involved in a conversation.

I knew that I was in a state but, without going into details, it was a whole lot worse than I'd expected, and I was in there much longer than I'd intended. Maybe ten minutes, maybe a little more. When I came out of the cubicle, the toilet was empty, and I washed my hands quickly, drying them on my jeans before pushing my way back through the door.

Out in the bar, the party was in full swing again. The music had changed to a Shirley Bassey show number and now quite a few of the customers were joining in, agreeing that they were what they were. This time no one seemed to notice me at all. I thought that I'd finish my drink, then make some excuse about mistaken identity and wait outside until Charlie-girl left. But, when I got back to the bar, I saw that the settee across the room was occupied by a big blonde in a wedding dress and a tall beanpole in a skimpy black number. There was no sign of Elaine Wilson's husband anywhere.

My first instinct was to head for the door and, if I had, maybe things would have turned out differently. But the woman behind the bar was looking at me, holding out the drink and smiling. So I stalled. Hell, there weren't too many bars in the village. I'd find him again soon enough. In any case, I'd already discovered what Charlie's little secret was – the hardest job now was breaking the news to his wife.

'You feel better?' Dark Eyes flashed a smile as I approached and shouted above the singing. Sort of flirty, kind of nice. I grinned back and she held my gaze. Something in my belly did a quick somersault and I took a mouthful of the deep red drink and closed my eyes for a moment in sheer bliss.

'Penny's gone,' she said. 'I'm sorry. I was going to ask her to wait, but you said not to say anything.'

'Penny?' I repeated, frowning. I moved closer, thinking I'd misheard her.

'You know, your friend – Penny,' she said, right into my ear

She means Charlie-girl, Cameron.

'Oh – yeah.'

'She left with Aunt Emily.'

When I frowned, she raised her eyebrows and sighed at me, pulling me across the bar and shouting into my ear again.

'The tranny in the flowery dress? The one who was sitting next to her?'

Yeah, I remembered: Margaret Rutherford.

'They've only just gone,' she shouted helpfully. 'If you're quick, you'll catch them.'

'It's OK,' I shouted back, looking straight into her eyes with a message that I hoped was unmistakeable. 'I'll find her later. I'm Cameron, by the way.'

She hesitated for a moment, almost as if my reciprocal flirting made her feel uncomfortable. She looked away and began to wash glasses. I took a sip of my drink and sat back on the bar stool. Sometimes I can be a little too pushy.

The singing abated as the Diva sang a verse that few people knew, so I tried again – in my normal voice this time. 'So how come you work here, rather than a women's bar?' I asked eventually, certain now that my gaydar was right.

She dried her hands and shrugged, 'Good money. Plus, this is just one night a week, which is all I want. Anyway, trannies don't get into fights.'

'And dykes do?'

She held my eyes. 'I bet you've had your share.'

I opened my mouth to protest, but the woman was peering over my shoulder. 'You're in luck,' she said, 'Aunt Emily's just come back in.'

The big tranny stooped down by the settee where she'd been sitting, retrieved a brown leather handbag and then hurried across to the bar tut-tutting and shaking her head giddily.

'Oooh, I don't know, Lin! What *am* I like, love?' she twittered, holding up the bag. 'All my worldly possessions and the housekeeping are in here! Tsk! Forget my own head, wouldn't I?'

The barwoman shook her head good-naturedly and, before I could stop her, began to introduce me. 'Actually, we're glad you came back, Emily. This lady is a friend of Penny's; she was hoping to say hello.' She looked around the bar. 'Where is Penny, anyway?'

Aunt Emily seemed to hesitate a little, then sighed. 'She's walking on down to the Bridge, love. I said that I'd meet her in there.' She smiled guiltily, 'I know, Lin, I know. I did tell her that she shouldn't go off on her own, what with all these attacks – but that woman is so headstrong. You simply can't tell her anything.'

The music reached the next chorus and nearly everyone in the room joined in. The portly figure turned to me, clutching her handbag to her full bosom and shouting above the racket. 'You can walk with me if you want, dear. I'll take you to her – I hate that dark street. It'll be nice to have someone with me.'

It was more of a decree than a request. I smiled to myself and paid for the drink, wondering what I was letting myself in for. I'd no idea what I was going to say to Charlie-girl when I was introduced, but I was sure that I'd think of something. Besides, it was a chance to confirm that his Monday nights were every bit as innocent as they seemed.

I downed the rest of my drink and leaned across the bar towards Lin, the barwoman. 'You here all night?' I asked, giving her my best soft smile. She glanced down shyly and then looked up and nodded, breathing in sharply as if she'd missed a breath or two.

'Would you mind if I came back and had another drink?' I

shouted as the singing reached the final crescendo.

'Yeah – I mean no,' she shouted back. 'No, I don't mind at all.' She looked almost embarrassed, but there was no mistaking the light in her eyes.

My belly did a half-dozen backflips, then I pulled myself together and raised my eyebrows at the sight of Aunt Emily standing by the stairs, waiting. 'I better go.'

She smiled easily at the unspoken joke and I turned and pushed through the tables. The music changed to a Billy Joel number and the room relaxed, glowing with pride. I smiled to myself, pleased that they at least felt good about who they were, and caught the flowery dress as it mounted the stairs.

I felt relaxed and happy right then. I was clean and dry again. The drink had lifted my spirits. The job was almost over. And, for the first time in an age, I felt that I might have connected with someone I really liked.

Then, as Aunt Emily and I walked out into the alley, everything changed.

The neon sign still flashed its red and green light down the grimy backstreet, glinting off the puddles and filling the darkness with cheap colour. But, around us, the damp night air was heavy with the smell of burning rubber – and of something else. Something unpleasant, something human. Tyres squealed round the corner on Sackville Street, and we both instinctively turned towards the sound.

It was then that we saw it – just a few yards down the street, to our right. A body dressed in a red skirt and a green jacket. Smashed against the wall. Bleeding heavily into the gutter.

Four

I stared in dismay at the mangled heap that had once been Charles Wilson. Aunt Emily leaned forward and threw up beside me, splattering my jeans and boots with her vomit. The smell made my own belly heave. I left her retching against the wall and ran to take a closer look.

The sight of him made my guts turn even more. His body was lying, grotesquely twisted, right up against the brick wall of an old warehouse. His white blouse was soiled and dirty. Blood and ordure were still oozing out of his abdomen, and through the torn fabric. His nylon-clad legs were twisted and broken behind him and the shoes lay smashed on the road a few feet away. The wig was askew and his face horridly grazed. Pink foundation congealed with fresh blood. Blood still ran in profusion from his nose and mouth. Wide eyes stared up at me, still oozing terror. The smell of death and shit and ruptured guts overwhelmed me.

I caught my breath and wrapped my scarf around my face, trying to control the nausea in my throat and the heaving in my belly.

A trail of still-wet blood glinted on the wall, tracing a steep arc that rose upwards and backwards from the bloody corpse to a height of four or five feet, then suddenly stopped, confirming – if any confirmation were needed – that this was no ordinary hit-and-run. Charlie had been upright and on the pavement when he was hit, perhaps trying to get out of the way. The driver of the car, whoever he was, must have deliberately smashed him against the wall – and then dragged him to a bloody death.

My belly heaved again at the thought. I turned away from the body and I threw up as well, in the road.

When I recovered I turned to see Aunt Emily scuttling away up the alley, her ungainly figure swaying to and fro as she tried to break into a run. Coughing and choking, I yelled at her to stop. She glanced back momentarily, but then disappeared round the corner without even stopping.

I pulled out my phone, running my tongue round the bitterness in my mouth, and called the cops. By the time I'd finished, the bar door had opened and two matronly transvestites were stepping out. They stopped when they saw my face and backed off in horror when they saw the corpse.

'Take it easy,' I said, standing in front of them, blocking the view. 'There's been an accident. Just stay calm and, please, go back into the bar. The police will be here soon and they'll need to take statements from everyone.

The two cross-dressers looked at each other and turned back without saying a word. But scarcely had the bar door shut than it was open again and, led by my messengers, the customers hurriedly took their leave, some heading off up the alley, glancing back at me and the crumpled heap at my feet, others skirting tentatively around us, staring goggle-eyed as they passed, then hurrying away, down the dark backstreet and into the bright lights of the main village – and anonymity.

Lin, the barwoman, was the last out. She hovered in the doorway at first, looking pale and confused, then jolted visibly when she saw Charlie's body, bringing a hand up to her mouth.

I ran across to her and turned her face away from the distressing sight. For some reason, I felt that I needed to protect her. But she resisted, and turned back, staring straight-faced and white-eyed at the mangled corpse. Somewhere in the distance a siren sounded.

'The police and an ambulance are on their way,' I began, stating the obvious, trying not to breathe my foul breath on her. 'It's Aunt

Emily's friend. I think you called her Penny.'

She turned and looked me straight in the eyes, her voice quite steady. 'Is she dead?'

I nodded, trying to stay calm, attempting to control the sledgehammer in my chest.

Lin opened her mouth to speak, but nothing came out. Then she glanced back at the body and began to tremble. She shook her head in dismay and glanced from me to the body and back again as a second siren joined the first and both grew louder.

'What...? I mean, was it... an accident?'

I put my arm around her and led her back towards the bar door. 'No, I don't think so. He's obviously been hit by a vehicle of some kind. But no, I'm sure it wasn't just an accident.'

'But... who would do such a thing?' she asked, incredulously.

'I don't know,' I admitted, 'perhaps, he – she – crossed someone. Did... Penny have any enemies that you know of?'

Like the preacher man, maybe.

She shook her head and sighed. Now there were three sirens wailing loudly, a disturbing, discordant melody of death.

Lin raised her voice above increasing noise. 'I didn't know her that well. I don't know. She seemed like a really nice person. I can't believe that she went off by herself like that. What with all the threats and queerbashings lately, most of the trannies are really careful about walking down this alley alone.'

A squad car turned into the alley from Sackville Street, its blue light bouncing off the warehouse windows on either side. The noise stopped abruptly.

'You think it was a kind of extreme queerbashing, then?'

She shook her head wearily and sighed. 'Why not? You must have heard what it's been like round here lately.'

The squad car had stopped a good few yards from the other side of the body and one of the cops was already taping off the area.

'No.' I frowned. 'Except for the madman with the bible, I'd no idea at all.'

A second cop approached us then and, after asking a few basic questions, she sent us back inside to wait. As we left the street a second squad car – a Land Rover this time – entered from the top end.

Once inside Lin turned the lights up and doused the music. I hadn't liked the place much when it was poorly lit. Now the brighter light revealed a totally characterless room, with nicotine-stained walls and shabby furniture. I watched Lin as she walked back towards me, a couple of drinks in her hands: a Campari and a red wine. A stylish, classy woman, working in a dump like this. I still couldn't get my head round that.

'So what happens now?' she asked, handing me the Campari and pulling a sad face.

I took a swig and let the bitter red liquid wash around in my mouth, hoping that it would take away both the taste and the smell of the vomit. 'Well, now we'll get questioned interminably, I'm afraid. This could take quite a while.' I toasted her with the glass and attempted a smile. 'Thanks for the drink.'

She smiled weakly back, shaking her head gently at me. 'That's OK. I guess we both need it. You must be devastated.'

I frowned, trying to grasp the significance of her remark. I was shocked and sickened all right – but devastated? I'd hardly known the man.

'Were you close?' she asked, laying a hand on my arm and studying my face.

I screwed up my eyes some more. I still didn't understand the question.

Lin tipped her head to one side and gave me a curious look. 'You and Penny – you said you were friends.'

Oh, shit!

I closed my eyes. Then I turned and walked away from her, sitting down heavily on the arm of the nearest settee. There was no way of breaking it gently. Whatever I said, however I tried to dress it up, she'd despise me.

Lin followed, looking anxious – and a little scared.

'Are you all right?' She tipped her head to one side and tried to smile encouragement.

I looked back at her and groaned inside. She was lovely. The beautiful dark eyes. The way she looked. The way she held herself. The strong Manchester accent, her forthrightness, her softness, her shyness. She was a genuinely nice woman. Now it was over before it had even started.

'I didn't know him.' I sighed, bracing myself. 'I lied to you. I'm a private investigator. His wife hired me to follow him.'

She didn't react at once. But I saw the truth register in her eyes. She froze for a second before drawing back as if, suddenly, I were contagious or something. Then she tossed her head angrily and turned and walked away.

Jesus, I felt like crying.

Five

I slumped back against the settee feeling beneath contempt, staring out across the dingy room and trying, half-heartedly, to convince myself that it wasn't my fault. I was doing my job, that was all. OK, so I lied to her. It's an occupational hazard, that's all.

Yeah, and the man you were supposed to be following is dead. Where were you? You might have prevented it. He could still be alive.

Over in the centre of the room, Lin was wiping tables and clearing half-empty glasses. Her face was drawn and she was making a show of avoiding my gaze. I was a pariah. A dirty shoo-fly who'd been out to gather evidence against one of the people she approved of. Me of all people. Cameron McGill, who always defended people's right to be who they were – their right to privacy and respect. I felt sick.

The door opened with a creak and two uniformed officers, a man and a woman, came in, their eyes taking in the room, then alighting on me. I produced a sad kind of smile from somewhere, as if I were pleased to see them, but inside I was already running away. We have a history, the cops and me. And it's not an entirely happy one.

I directed them to Lin, who, by now, was leaning on the counter, her head in her hands. The female officer led her over to a settee and sat down beside her, her face all soft and sympathetic. The guy ambled over to me, dropped his hat on a chair and pointed at the table next to it.

I've never understood the term 'friendly witness'. Every time I've been interviewed by the cops, they've made me feel as if I were the culprit. Maybe I just overreact. Maybe it's the way I look. Anyway, today was no different. The cop started with the assumption that I had something to hide, and the interview went downhill from there.

It was the usual package of questions. Who are you? Can you prove it? Why were you here? When did you arrive? Where did you come from? How? What were you doing in the backstreet?

He raised his eyebrows and smirked when I mentioned that I was a private investigator. Then, of course, he wanted all the details. Name of client, address, phone number, why she hired me. And all the time his eyes were commenting on the coincidence.

Well, well. The day she hires you to follow him is the day he gets topped.

'I should ring her and tell her what's happened,' I said. I didn't sound convincing, even to myself.

He shook his head, firmly. 'Sorry, love. You need to speak to CID first. They'll be here soon.'

To my shame, I felt relieved. Right now, Elaine Wilson was the last person I needed to talk to.

Over by the bar Lin was going through a similar, but presumably more sympathetic, routine. She looked strained and bewildered by it all. Like most people, she probably hadn't been interviewed like this before. But I had. And I knew what was coming next – who was coming next. And how much of my time it was all going to take.

The suits arrived fifteen minutes later, five minutes behind the scene-of-crime officers, who took a cursory glance inside and then got on with the job in the backstreet. Bright light and the bustle of activity spilled in through the door when it opened again.

The senior officer appeared first and acknowledged me curtly on her way to where Lin was sitting. Seconds later the door opened again and a tall, wiry man – her sergeant – advanced down the stairs and joined her. After a brief conference, he sat with Lin. Detective Superintendent Dyson headed over towards me.

She was tall for a woman – around five ten – and in her mid-forties, with short, neatly styled, brown hair and the kind of smile that might cut through glass. You could tell from her manner that she'd come up the hard way. She carried the scars around her like a defensive shield. It was still there in her eyes, in her abrupt manner – the need to prove herself, and the ever-present fear that she might not.

The superintendent sat down opposite me, taking her time, laying her red silk scarf and her beige raincoat neatly on a chair, watching me out of the corner of her eye. She arranged her pale-green cardigan around her, straightened the white blouse and smoothed her skirt. If that was a ploy to wind me up, it was working.

Over her shoulder I could see Lin, sitting with her back to me, talking to her sergeant. Something like a lead ball dropped down through my belly and I closed my eyes at the unfairness of it all. When I opened them again, Dyson had her notebook open and her pen at the ready. She held me with her hazel-coloured eyes.

'Thank you for your time,' she began, brusque and coldly efficient. 'I'm Detective Superintendent Dyson and I'm the officer in charge of this incident.' She glanced down at her notebook. 'Now, you are Cameron McGill. Is that Mrs, Miss or Ms?'

She was well spoken, but with just a hint of a Northern accent. Her voice was cool rather than cold, factual and unemotional, rather than hostile. But there was a hardness to her that I guessed would serve her well.

'Ms.'

She glanced down at her notes again. 'I gather that you're a... private investigator,' She said it as if she'd just sucked a lemon. 'You were following this man prior to his death, I understand.'

'Yes. His wife hired me – she thought he was having an affair.'

She glanced at her notes again. 'Mrs Elaine Wilson, forty-three Barkington Road, Bury?'

I nodded and she copied the details onto a separate piece of paper.

'I really should ring her,' I said, hating myself for bringing the subject up again. But I needn't have worried: she was already on her feet, handing the slip over to the uniformed policewoman, talking quietly to her before sending her off.

'Now, where were we?'

'I was asking if I could ring my client and tell her what's happened.'

She smiled weakly. 'Ah, yes. You can talk to your client in due course, Ms McGill. For the moment I've arranged for an officer to go and see her, break the news and then stay with her, until I arrive.' She looked at me out of the corner of her eyes. 'You will understand that I need to question her before you see her.'

I nodded graciously. 'Will you say anything about her husband's cross-dressing?'

She drew breath and held it for a moment. When she spoke it was with care, weighing each word. 'We have guidelines – you probably know that. We're obliged to respect an individual's privacy. Unless it becomes material, we simply stick to the facts and we don't pass on personal information.' She paused, twirling her pen around her fingers. 'However, since you ask, I can tell you that I do consider, in this instance, that the victim's transvestism *is* material, since he was wearing women's clothing at the time of his death and he was killed outside a transvestite bar.'

'You think he was killed *because* of his cross-dressing? You think it's a hate killing.'

She shook her head stiffly. 'I've no idea at present, Ms McGill. I've told you the basis for my judgement.'

'So you'll be telling his wife?'

'Yes, I've already told you that. Is that a problem for you?'

I shook my head, relieved. At least that was one dilemma out of the way.

Dyson watched me for a moment. Her lips twitched. 'So, we've saved you a difficult job. I hope you're grateful.'

I shrugged. *Go to hell.*

She paused, letting the silence wash over me before she asked the next question, the one I was waiting for.

'Don't you think it's something of a coincidence that this man gets himself killed on the very day that you are following him?' She said it in the same slightly weary tone as before, but this time her eyes were staring at me, watching for a reaction. I leaned back in the chair and looked back with loathing. It was just like that time in Hull. You hang around, you do your best to help them and they immediately treat you like a suspect.

I went through exactly what had happened that afternoon step by step. When I got to the end the eyes were the same but the voice was icily cynical.

'So you were following the victim because his wife – your client – badly wanted a divorce. You don't take your eyes off him for hours, then you turn your back for a few minutes and he's killed.'

I sat up and leaned across the table. 'What are you trying to say, Superintendent?'

She looked straight back at me without even blinking. 'I tend not to believe in coincidences, Ms McGill.'

I grunted sarcastically and leaned back in the chair. In truth, there was something in what she said. It seemed kind of strange to me as well.

'Did you recognise any of the other people in this bar?'

I wanted to be helpful, but suddenly she was getting to me. 'No. I've told you – I haven't been around here for years,' I snapped.

'Did any of them say anything as they left?'

'No. Should I call my lawyer?'

Dyson paused momentarily and seemed to drop her guard a little. 'Don't be so sensitive. I'm not accusing you of anything.' I might be wrong but I thought I saw her eyes flicker in amusement. 'I'll let you know in good time if I change my mind.'

I shifted uncomfortably in my chair. *Yeah, thanks.*

'Now, please tell me what you know about Mr and Mrs Wilson, would you? Particularly the man's movements this afternoon.'

I told her everything I could: the apparent state of their relationship, the place where Charlie worked, the house he'd visited in West Didsbury, the violent episode with the preacher and the rest.

She painstakingly wrote it all down, glancing up from time to time with the whites of her eyes. When I'd finished I remembered the handbill that the blue-rinse woman had given me and I dug it out of my jerkin. I made her wait a moment while I read it myself. 'Come back into the arms of the Lord,' it said. 'Penitence expiates the sinner, the Lord blesses the redeemed.' Underneath was a name, Ernest Winterton, Pastor, Church of the One God, Walton Street, Stockport.

I passed it across, memorising the name and address.

'I'll also need your videotape, please.'

I dug the video-cam out of my pocket and flicked it open. She smiled a little as she took hold of the cassette and dropped it into an evidence bag, but instead of thanking me profusely for my help she got up, moved to the far corner of the room and talked into her radio.

She returned a few moments later without comment and continued with the interview.

Did Charles Wilson have any enemies? Apart from the preacher? I don't know. Was I sure that no one else had been following him? Yes, I was. I'm a professional. I would have noticed. Who was the woman at the house in West Didsbury? Oh, come on, Superintendent. I'm a PI, not a fucking oracle.

When we finally got to the end she leaned back and read through her notes. Her cool manner excepted, we'd not done too badly. Better than I expected, anyway.

'Your client lives in Bury.'

'Yes.'

'You said it was unusual for you to work so far away from York?'

'It is. Well, on matrimonial cases, anyway.' I shrugged. There was no point in lying about Beano: if I didn't tell her how I got the job, then Elaine Wilson would. 'A Manchester colleague passed my name on. The victim's wife tried to hire her first. My friend was unable to do the job, so she suggested me.'

'And your colleague's name?'

Over her shoulder, I could see the younger detective writing up his notes. Lin was getting her things together. I tried to catch her eye, hoping that she might wait for me.

'Your colleague's name?'

'What? Oh, Bernice Nolan. She's a private investigator as well. She lives in Stretford.'

I was distracted but, even so, I noticed Dyson's eyes register something. And her shoulders twitched unaccountably.

'Her address?' she asked levelly, a little too controlled now.

I tipped my head and frowned. 'Twenty-three Burley Street.'

I watched, intrigued, as she wrote Beano's address down in her book, taking her time, as if she was thinking. Then she snapped the notebook shut and grunted dismissively.

Lin slipped into a black raincoat and slung her bag on her shoulder. She made for the exit, glancing across briefly at me as she passed. I looked up and tried to catch her eye. But she turned her head away and hurried up the stairs.

'Thank you for your time, Ms McGill. We'll need you to sign a statement and I may need to interview you again, so I would be grateful if you could remain available.'

I had to know. 'Superintendent, before you go...' She stopped and looked across at me, waiting. 'You seemed to recognise Bernice Nolan's name.'

Dyson made a face and thought for a moment. 'Well, it's in the public domain already, so there's no reason why I shouldn't tell you.' She pulled her mac over her shoulders and straightened it around her, watching me curiously. 'Your friend, Bernice Nolan. She's also known as Beano, I believe?'

I nodded, puzzled. How the hell would she know that?

'Well,' she said, picking up her scarf and bag, and turning to go, 'your friend is in prison.'

'What?'

'Yes.' She grimaced, as if the recollection left a bad taste. 'She's on remand. Last Friday. She tried to kill someone.'

Six

I followed them up the stairs when they left. It was someone else's case and Dyson couldn't – or wouldn't – go into detail. Beano was in jail. On remand. Full stop.

Bitch.

Outside the bar, a big halogen spotlight shone down from the top of the Land Rover, bathing the backstreet in a clear bright light that shone off the SOCOs' white boiler suits as if they were extras in some corny soap powder ad. A large, white, tentlike structure had been erected around the body and it flickered periodically with bright blue-white light as the police photographer recorded the grim details of the murder scene.

I watched dejectedly as the superintendent and her oppo conferred with a middle-aged man in a white boiler suit. They walked into the tent and a police officer guided me through the crime scene to the police tape. I ducked underneath and pushed my way through a large group of rubberneckers into the blackness beyond, heading back down the alley towards the brighter lights on Sackville Street.

I guess that I'd planned to call it a day. Maybe have a quiet drink or two, then report back to Elaine Wilson once the cops had finished with her. But, when I turned the corner, the woman from the bar was just down the road, standing on the corner outside Napoleon's, talking to a man. I stopped and leaned against the wall in the shadows, waiting for her to finish.

Beano in jail. I couldn't believe it.

I took a few deep breaths, trying to push away my anxiety. People were still wandering around as they had earlier in the evening, but now there was real tension in the air. Up the road, even the *Big Issue* seller had stopped his antics and was standing forlornly by the car park, simply holding out a copy of the mag to passers-by. I looked across the road to the corner of Canal Street, and pictured the preacher, standing there only half an hour ago, telling Charlie-girl that he was going to die.

I played the scene again in my mind. The fear in Charles Wilson's eyes. The preacher's look of pure hatred and the venom in his voice. His abusive, violent behaviour. His threats, and the way he'd treated the woman.

The man was undoubtedly ill, but, even so, something must have happened between the three of them to trigger that kind of scene. And it didn't take much figuring out what it could be. Every cop in Greater Manchester would be looking for him by now.

Down the street Lin and her friend were hugging, as if they were finishing their conversation. I pushed off from the wall as they parted and set off after her. She saw me coming and took off, past Napoleon's and round the corner. The guy gave me a funny look as I ran past, his ginger beard twitching with concern. I could still feel his eyes on my back as I ran down Bloom Street after her.

When I caught up and touched her arm, she spun round and scowled at me.

'Look, I know that you're angry with me,' I began quietly, 'but let me explain. Please.'

She glared back for a moment and then brushed me to one side, fumbling around in her bag as she walked. I caught up with her again as she crossed the road, heading towards a red Ford Escort, keys in hand.

'I thought you'd have to stay and lock up,' I said, trying a different tack.

She threw me a black look and kept on walking. 'You're joking, of course! The police are going to be there all night. Besides, they rang the owner.' She stopped suddenly and turned on me, spitting the words in my face. 'I needed to get away. I needed some space.' She eyeballed me. 'I still do.'

'I'm sorry,' I said quietly. 'I guess you must be feeling lousy.'

'Yeah, I guess I am,' she retorted bitterly. 'And you're not helping very much.'

She strode away in disgust, as though the whole thing had been my fault.

'Look,' I persisted, keeping up with her, 'I don't feel too good about it either.'

'Oh, don't you?' she muttered, looking straight ahead. 'Well, that makes it all all right, then, does it?'

I sighed, and overtook her, spinning on my heels and stopping in her path. She sidestepped and carried on down the street. I spun round and set off after her again, trying to stay calm. Failing badly.

Today hadn't been one of my best. I felt bad about Charlie, I was reeling from the news about Beano, and I still had to deal with bloody Elaine Wilson. Now my belly was hurting again. Basically, I was in no mood for pissing around.

'Look, just hold on a moment,' I shouted, grabbing her shoulder. She spun round to face me, furious at the intrusion. 'What the hell gives you the right to set yourself up as judge and jury?' I demanded. 'You earn money behind a bar. I make it by helping people sort out their problems. Is that so bad?' She grunted at me and began to turn away again. I stopped her again, more forcibly this time. 'I was just doing my job, that's all. I didn't *know* the man. I wasn't *judging* him. And I'm really sorry he's dead.' I stopped, my anger suddenly dissipated by my own remorse over the poor man's fate. 'It *wasn't* my fault,' I added, more quietly than before.

She tensed and glared down at my hand until I removed it. A few yards on, she stopped by the ageing Ford Escort, and put the key in the lock.

'Look, give me a break, will you?' I pleaded. 'We were getting on really well.'

'Yeah,' she snorted, 'until I found out that you were spying on one of my customers. Worse – that you'd lied to me about it!' She looked down at her feet for a moment, breathing heavily. 'And now he's dead. Then again, why should you care?'

That tipped me right off balance. 'Jesus, what makes you think that?' I asked, stung to the core.

'Oh, come on!' she retorted. 'Don't pretend that you're not doing this just for money, because I don't believe you. Anyway,' she said as she looked me up and down, 'people like you disapprove of transvestites on principle – everyone knows that.'

'People like me?' I said, crestfallen. 'What makes you think I'm so bigoted?'

'Oh, come on! You *right-on* lesbians, with your Doc Martens and your fuck-you attitude. You just think you're the best. And people like Penny – they're just a bad joke, aren't they? You and your precious political correctness!'

I looked away for a second, smarting.

'Jesus! And what makes you so fucking precious? You serve drinks to a bunch of blokes who spend their time taking the piss out of women. How do you think that makes some of us feel?'

She snorted in disdain and looked me over from head to foot. 'It's no worse than you. You're wearing *men's* clothes, aren't you?'

I closed my eyes and took a long deep breath. When I opened them she was still there, waiting. 'Look,' I tried, 'we're both upset. This has been a terrible night. It's just unbelievable what happened to Penny. But please... don't take it out on me. I feel bad as well – and I'm not like you think.'

She sniffed. Her eyes were wet. She took out a tissue to wipe away a tear.

'C'mon, we both need to calm down.' I said it as kindly as I could. 'Maybe it would help both of us if we talked. Let's have a quiet drink somewhere. Please.'

She hesitated, gazing out over the top of her car, still sniffing.

'Is everything all right, Lin?' The man she'd been talking to earlier laid a protective arm across her shoulder and threw me a disapproving look. I shrugged and turned away.

'It's OK, Lewis.' The woman turned and shook her head. 'We were just having a slight disagreement.'

'You want her to leave you alone?' he asked, fixing me with his eyes.

I turned and looked at her. She looked straight back, more calmly now.

'No, it's OK, Lewis, thank you. I'm going to buy her a drink. I guess I've been taking my feelings out on the poor woman. I should set things straight. You want to join us?'

The man smiled and shook his head. 'No, it's OK, thanks. I've got a lecture to prepare. I just wanted to make sure that you were OK, that's all.'

The woman kissed him on the cheek and he smiled again, turning to go, pointing a stubby finger at me. 'Just handle her with care, OK? She's had a rough time.'

'Yeah,' I agreed, 'I know.'

When he'd gone, we looked at each other for a while, uncertain of how to proceed.

I broke the ice by asking the obvious. 'That guy, Lewis – your boyfriend?'

She laughed lightly and shook her head. 'No. Just a special friend. He works at the university.'

I looked back, uncertainly. 'You think that maybe we can be friends as well?'

She took a deep breath and looked up into the dark sky, rolling her eyes. 'Yeah, well, a drink's one thing, but I think I might need to take a rain check on friendship, Cameron. We haven't started off too well, now, have we?'

'Yeah, I know. Maybe we should try starting over again,' I said carefully, eyeing her kind of sneakily.

She leaned back against the car and shook her head in disbelief. Her long black hair was blowing in the breeze, brushing the shoulders of her raincoat. A little colour was returning to her cheeks. Her eyelids flickered as she wet her lips with her tongue, watching me, weighing me up.

'Maybe we should start by introducing ourselves properly,' I suggested.

She nodded quietly, biting her lip, her wet eyes shining in the glow of the street lights. Then she stood up straight, pulled a face, and stuck out her hand.

'Yeah OK, I'm Lin – Lin Lee – and I get a bit rat shit sometimes. I'm sorry.'

I smiled, taking her hand and holding it for a moment.

'Yeah, well, who am I to criticise? I'm Cameron McGill, and sometimes, I guess, I need taking down a peg or two.'

Seven

I guess we both felt a little awkward. Things get said in the heat of the moment and they sting like nettles. I hoped that a drink would soothe our wounds and that maybe, just maybe, I could still retrieve something from such a lousy day.

It was half past eight as we walked through the backstreet towards the Bridge Inn, an hour and a half since the murder. And the reality of that, and the news about Beano, was still sinking in.

It was a pleasant, dry evening now. Small groups were standing outside the bars in Canal Street, talking quietly. Music still spilled out over the canal, but the atmosphere was tainted and, for once, there wasn't a cross-dresser or a drag queen in sight. The Bridge itself, a big place and once one of my preferred drinking spots, was about a quarter full. The barman was serving a customer at the other end of the room when we reached the back bar.

Lin took out her purse. 'I suppose that the tabloids will be onto this already. Those people outside Chloë's – you think they were reporters?'

'Could be. But it's a little soon even for them. Probably just a bunch of ambulance chasers.'

She pulled out a ten-pound note and handed it to me with a bashful smile, then went over to claim an empty table in the corner, away from everyone else. I followed her with my eyes. She had real style, real poise. Yet there was nothing forced or girly about her.

The barman coughed behind me and I turned round to see him grinning. 'You on a promise, luv?'

A queen with a fruity Lancashire accent. Nice combination.

I shook my head and smiled back. 'Mmm, I wish.'

He grinned amiably and I ordered a Campari and tonic for me and a glass of red wine for Lin. As he poured the drinks, I thought of Beano again. She liked her beer; she liked her space. I wondered how she was coping. I wondered where the hell they were keeping her.

'Bit of a shock, tonight,' I remarked, as the barman put the drinks on the bar.

He pulled a face and exhaled loudly. 'Ee, you're not kiddin', luv! Used to be nice and friendly round here a few years ago, but I dunno, these days...'

I handed him the tenner. 'Yeah, you'd think things would be even better now, wouldn't you? Now that we've made such progress, I mean.'

'Aye, you would, but ah reckon it's a backlash.' He cashed the money at the till and walked back with the change. 'Thing is, we're winning the fight for equality – and there's people who don't like that one little bit.'

'You mean like the old preacher up the street?'

'Aye, that silly old bugger. He's just a daft old fart – but there are some real troublemakers as well nowadays. Fuckin' Nazis, luv. I've never known so much gay-bashing. We've had a real spate of it these last few months.'

'Why, though?' I asked, surprised that things had got so bad. 'I thought the police were really cracking down on hate crime now.'

'Aye, well mebbe they are, but there's a nasty political element these days. The BNP and the like, right-wing fundamentalists – and now we've got a bunch of skinheads who've jumped on the bandwagon. Good excuse for a fight. They're round here regular like, scaring the shit out of people. Course, the fuzz, bless 'em, do their best, but they never seem to be there when they're needed.'

'So you reckon they had something to do with this murder?'

He nodded sadly. ' Well, yeah. I mean that's how it goes, in't it? A bit of tauntin' for starters, then real abuse, then t'violence. Heaven knows, luv, any of us could be next. You just tek care, luv.' He met my eyes for a moment and then broke into a broad smile. 'Hey, listen to us! If we go on like this, we'll end up topping usselves. Fuck 'em, I say.'

I smiled and picked up the drinks. I was grateful for the information, but I found it depressing all the same. The last time I was here, the place felt safer than anywhere.

'Yeah, well, thanks for the warning.'

He leaned on the counter and grinned lasciviously at me. 'No problem, darlin'. You have a nice evening. Go and chat that lovely woman up – you never know where it might lead.'

When I reached the table Lin was staring absent-mindedly out of the window. I put the glasses down and then sat on one chair with my feet up on another. Suddenly I felt exhausted.

She turned and smiled a little, raising her drink. 'Here's to the police. Let's just hope that they get this killer – whoever he is – and before he has a chance to do it again.'

I clinked my glass against hers, nodding in agreement. 'The barman was just telling me about the skinhead gang – he seems to think they did it.'

She nodded despondently. 'I agree with him. I can't see why anyone would want to harm Penny. Some of the other trannies can be quite bitchy at times, but Penny – she was just so nice, she never fell out with a soul.' She took a sip of her drink and sighed. 'Anyway, that's what the police think as well. That sergeant said that they've been dreading something like this happening for a while. I can see why. The village hasn't felt safe for months.'

We sat in an awkward silence, neither of us ready to discuss the subject further. I took out the pack of ibuprofen from my jerkin. Lin watched as I washed a couple down with a mouthful of Campari. She smiled sympathetically and I looked out across the room. Three straight women, clearly on a night out, were being entertained by a some gay men in the far corner and a few dykes were sitting around chatting or staring into their beer. The rest of the tables were occupied by men. Nobody looked as if they were having a great time. When I looked back, Lin was gazing out of the window.

'Do you spend a lot of time in the village?' I asked, feeling instantly embarrassed by the variation on the do-you-come-here-often? cliché.

She didn't seem to mind. She threw me a tired smile and relaxed a little.

'I used to – five, six years ago, when I first started at uni. Four nights a week sometimes, clubbing, eating out with friends.' She looked at me very directly as she talked. 'It was great: no straight men, lots of nice *women*.' She hesitated a fraction, putting extra emphasis on the word, as if she were reassuring me about her sexuality after her earlier tirade about political dykes. 'It felt so safe round here then. You hardly saw any straight men, let alone the kind of thugs you see these days.'

She stopped suddenly and stared into her wine. 'I still can't believe it.'

'I know. It's horrible.'

We sat quietly for a moment, waiting for the cloud to pass. She stared out into the night. I shredded my beer mat into small pieces and tried to push away the guilt that was still gnawing at my guts.

'What about you, Cameron? You seem to know your way around?'

I smiled a little, relieved to be back on safer ground. 'Yeah, I've had some good times here – round about the same time as you, funnily enough. I used to come over with my friend, Becky. We'd go clubbing till early Sunday, then have breakfast in the twenty-four-hour café near Follies.'

She leaned back in her chair and smiled nostalgically. 'Mmm, yeah, I remember that! Bacon butties at three a.m. – and the place would be packed.'

'Yeah, well, I'm veggie, so I had eggs, but I remember the bacon being a strong temptation' – I raised my eyebrows playfully – 'as was the bare-breasted woman who served it.'

Lin's mouth dropped open and her eyes lit up. 'Yeah!' she exclaimed, suddenly chirpy again. 'All she wore was a pair of leather hot pants!'

We looked at each other for a moment and broke out into laughter at the shared memory.

'Strange that we never ran into one another,' I remarked. 'We must have been in the same places on the same nights.'

She shrugged, glancing away uneasily for a moment, then smiling dismissively. 'Oh, it's a big place, Manchester. You probably wouldn't have noticed me anyway.'

'Oh, I think I would,' I persisted, puzzled by her sudden embarrassment. 'Someone as attractive as you.'

She blushed. 'Well, when I was younger I stuck mostly to student bars like Manto's. Afterwards we'd sometimes go to one of the nightclubs in the village, or that dive in Ducie Street – what did they call it?'

I laughed. 'You mean the Beehive.' So *that* was the reason. She used to hang out with gay men.

'Yeah, that's it, the Beehive. They had karaoke every night, and cheap beer.' She shrugged. 'I was a student, those things were important.'

'And you've always enjoyed being around gay men?'

She coloured up at once and glared at me. *Me and my big mouth.*

'Sorry.' I held my hands up in contrition. 'Yeah, Becky and me went there a few times as well. Good atmosphere, and some of the gay men could be outrageous.'

It didn't work – she just scowled at me all the more. 'Cameron, unlike you, it seems, I try to accept people for who they are. OK?'

I breathed out heavily and took a swig of my drink. This wasn't the time to get into an argument.

'So what do you do the rest of the week?' I asked, sweetness itself.

She glared at me a little more and then shook her head and let it go. 'I told you, I'm a student, uh… I was, anyway. I finished in June – got a first, I'm pleased to say, in accounting and finance.' She looked pleased.

'You're going to be an *accountant*?' I asked in disbelief.

She eyed me critically. 'There's no need to look like that, Cameron. I like figures. It's a window into a different world. Besides, we did a lot of work on corporate fraud, embezzlement, tax evasion – all that sort of thing. You wouldn't believe what goes on behind big business and finance. That's what I really want to get involved in.'

'So you're job hunting now?'

She pulled a face. 'Mm, sort of. Actually, I'm moving back to Singapore, where I was born, in a few weeks. My grandfather has business contacts there. He's finding out what jobs are available.'

'Oh. I'm sorry it's so soon,' I said, genuinely disappointed. 'I'd hoped to get to know you better.' I looked straight into her eyes as I said it – gently, carefully, testing the boundaries.

She looked away and shifted awkwardly in her seat, changing the subject. 'Uh, look at us, will you? We're sitting here talking trivia and... poor Penny.' She stopped, suddenly flustered. I wondered if it was the killing that was still getting to her, or me. Maybe I was still taking things too fast.

'What exactly happened tonight, Cameron? You still haven't told me.'

I told her about Charlie's argument with the preacher and related what had happened when Aunt Emily and I left the bar. But I found it impossible to keep the scorn out of my voice. 'I can't believe him and the others ran off like that. Jesus! Some friends! Don't they have *any* sense of community?'

Lin looked at me sharply. 'Oh, come on, Cameron! Emily must have been scared out of her wits! The others as well.'

'Yeah, OK! But for God's sake! Emily's the one person that might be able to help the cops – I can't believe that he didn't even try!'

She glared at me angrily again, her chest heaving.

'What?' *Jesus what is this woman's problem?*

'You're just like so many other people, aren't you?' she declared.

I sat back in my chair, furious at being spoken to like that. 'Just hold on a moment, will you, Miss Lee? What the fuck are you talking about?'

She looked away and grunted scornfully. 'You know very well what I'm talking about! You've been making snide remarks about them ever since you walked into that bar.'

I looked at her open-mouthed. 'Oh, I get it! We're back on the "people like you disapprove of transvestites on principle" kick, are we?'

Her eyes flashed with indignation.

'Look, Lin, what is it with you? I'm a dyke. I know damn well what it's like to be different; I know how hard it is to fit into a society that doesn't even try to understand – so don't go lecturing me about disapproval or exclusion.'

She sighed and closed her eyes. For a moment I thought that she was going to burst into tears. I took another mouthful of the Campari and pushed the ice cubes around with the stirrer. When she opened them again, she looked me straight in the face.

'OK, I'm sorry.'

I breathed out in relief. She looked as if she meant it so I nodded as graciously as I could.

'It's just that...' she continued. 'Well, it can be really hard for trannies. I mean *really* hard. I know that that being gay is difficult – but it's even worse for them. Hardly any of them are out – I mean out to *anyone* except each other. Even then, they don't talk about their male lives because they're so scared that their wives or their children, or their friends, or their employers will find out – and that they'll lose everything. So, when people start to criticise them I get really mad. I'm sorry.'

'Yeah, OK, I understand that completely.' I lowered my voice and tried to sound like a mature human being making a rational point. 'But, all the same, Aunt Emily was supposed to be his *friend*, wasn't he?'

She shifted uncomfortably, rubbing her brow. 'Look, I'm sorry Cameron, I can't get my head around the *his* bit. I mean... OK, I *know* they're all men really, but I only ever see them in their female role, so

I don't think of them as anything else. So can we please keep to the right pronouns.'

I turned away. *Jesus, and she'd accused* me *of being PC.*

'I thought I *was* using the right pronoun,' I replied evenly. 'You just said it – they *are* men, aren't they?'

She rolled her eyes at me and sighed, clearly struggling with her anger. Then she began talking quietly, patiently – as though I were a child or something.

'When they're dressed – when they're in the village – they identify as women. We should respect that. If we met Aunt Emily in her male role, then it would be "him" – of course – but otherwise I would prefer us to stick with the female pronouns if that's all right with you.'

I grunted some kind of reply and stared out blankly across the room. Lin shook her head at me and pushed her glass around the table. I sipped at what was left of the Campari. Maybe this was all a waste of time. I liked the woman all right but there didn't seem any way that we could hit it off. Dyson would be at Elaine Wilson's house now. By the time I got there, she'd be finished. I could see my client and then get the hell out of this city.

Lin looked up at me and smiled kind of sadly. Maybe she felt the same as I did. Maybe I should give it one last try.

'Tell me about Aunt Emily, then.'

She looked at me with the whites of her eyes, clearly wondering if I was serious. When she saw that I was trying, she set her glass to one side and leaned across the table.

'Well, she's almost like a fixture round here. She's one of the village's characters. Lots of people know her. I met her around five years ago. I wouldn't describe her as a friend, but she's OK – and she's always been nice to me. She comes into town every Monday afternoon – she hangs around in the village, eats in certain "safe" restaurants, and shops a couple of the more exclusive dress shops. She does her rounds every week, but that's where it ends. The rest of the time she lives as a man. I told the police that she once mentioned living in Altrincham but that's as much as I know about her other life. I do know that she's really scared of being outed, though, so she's always been very careful.'

'But would you have disappeared like that if you were in Aunt Emily's place?' I asked carefully.

'No, of course not. And you wouldn't either, but this is different.' She shook her head, as if she might be about to give up on me. But she didn't. And, this time, she didn't get angry, either. Just passionate. 'Listen, Cameron.' She fixed me with her big dark eyes. 'You probably think that men oppress women, and I'd mostly agree with that. But what you may not realise is that they oppress each other just as much. And, if one of their number doesn't conform, there can be hell to pay. You can see it in the way that some of them make fun of gay men. You can see it in all the innuendo and the queerbashing. It's exactly what those skinheads are doing. Being different isn't allowed.

'Cross-dressing – serious cross-dressing – is even worse. Transvestites aren't taking the mickey – they're not drag queens – and they're not usually interested in having sex with anyone. They're nearly always straight and they identify very strongly as *normal* men most of the time. If you're in that position, then wearing women's clothes and makeup is just about the last big taboo – and, however "out" they are here, most of them just can't handle it in their personal or work lives. Even some of the more understanding wives would draw the line at admitting their partner's obsession to anyone else. Can't you see? They're nearly always uneasy with what they do, and, whatever ground women might have gained in the fight for equality, most straight people – of either gender – still expect men to be bloody and brave. Look what's happened to poor Penny if you need any proof of that.' She leaned back in her chair. 'Being seen wearing pretty undies and makeup isn't just difficult for them – it can be downright dangerous.'

I shook my head. 'So what the hell makes them want to pretend they're a "woman" for a few hours every week? I'm sorry – I can understand transsexuals. I can understand men and women feeling that they were born wrong. But men dressing up? And, if they really like being men, well, why?'

She leaned forward, staring aggressively straight into my face. 'What makes you a lesbian, Cameron?' She held up her hand and sat back again. 'Oh, and don't give me any of that shit about it being your choice – you, and thousands like you, couldn't be straight if you tried.'

I ought to have been really angry but instead I was having to suppress a smile. It felt good to meet someone with fire in her belly. I like passionate people, even if I don't always agree with them. And I was beginning to like this woman more and more – she wasn't turning out at all like I'd expected.

Lin looked at me anxiously, as if it were important to her that I took the matter seriously, as if it mattered that I understood. Yeah, well, maybe I did – or at least maybe I was beginning to. I nodded. 'OK, that helps. I guess that, like most people, I only ever see the sensational stuff in the tabloids.'

She winced noticeably. 'You mean like the sort of stuff they're all going to print about Penny.'

'Yeah, sorry. Me and my big mouth.'

She reached out and touched my arm. 'It's all right, Cameron. It's been hard for both of us tonight. I'm sorry if I flew off the handle. I guess I'm still emotional. Thanks for listening.'

I smiled back, a little embarrassed. I was pleased that we were ending on a good note anyway. 'I'll have to go, I'm afraid. I have an unpleasant job to attend to before the night is over.'

She looked at me and frowned.

'I have to go and see... Penny's wife – make my report. The police said that I could call after nine thirty, once they'd interviewed her.'

She looked at me anxiously. 'How do you think she'll react?'

'She'll be upset that he was a cross-dresser, but otherwise...'

'You mean she won't be upset that he's dead?'

I shrugged. 'I wouldn't expect her to be – not after what she said about him earlier on.'

She slumped back in her chair and sighed. I got up and put my leather jerkin back on, hoping that my assessment was going to turn out wrong.

'I guess I'm might have to pick up a few pieces. What you told me tonight about cross-dressing might help me to explain it to her, at least.'

She grunted just a little cynically as she picked up her raincoat. I guess I wasn't the perfect envoy.

'Yeah, well, I don't expect you to like it.' I paused and zipped my jerkin up. 'But please try to understand my side of it. Whether I approve of her or not, she *is* my client and I have an obligation to see her through this. She might need my help. Whatever she thought of her husband, this is going to raise all sorts of practical problems for her.'

Lin nodded with resignation.

'At least I can tell her that her husband wasn't being unfaithful. Maybe that will help, I don't know.'

Lin breathed out sharply and pulled her mac round her shoulders. I hesitated. I wanted to ask for her phone number, but I didn't want her to think that I was coming on to her again. So I handed her one of my cards instead.

'Ring me if you hear anything, won't you?'

She smiled nervously. 'Yes, I will. Wait a minute. Would you do the same for me?' She took out a pen and wrote her own mobile number on a beer mat and passed it to me. 'Please... I would be very grateful.'

I nodded. We both stood looking at each other – for just a fraction longer than necessary. When I finally broke the connection, she smiled gently.

'Watch out for reporters,' she cautioned.

'Yeah.' I looked back, a little embarrassed, 'Well, see you around, maybe.'

Suddenly I felt like a five-year-old.

Eight

The traffic was light as I left the city. I should have been thinking about my meeting with Charles Wilson's wife. I should have been rehearsing what I was going to say. But, as I drove towards Bury, I was obsessing over two other women.

I'd felt a bit weird when I'd left Lin. I liked her a lot but there was something about her that made me uneasy. She'd seemed like a straightforward, uncomplicated woman at first but, looking back, I'd kept picking up signals about something else. Like the way she'd kept pulling back every time the conversation turned personal. In the end I brushed the concern away. After all, it was highly unlikely that I'd ever see her again.

Besides, I was concerned about Beano.

I just couldn't believe that she'd tried to kill someone. Hell, Beano was no angel, but violence wasn't her style at all. I needed to know what had happened, I wanted to help her. After I'd crossed the M60, I pulled into a side street and rang my friend Becky.

'Oh, hiya, Cam!' Becky sounded pleased, her voice lilting with the strong Liverpudlian accent. 'I was going to ring you. There's a concert on Wednesday, at York Uni. You want to go, then stay over?'

Becky feeds my cat when I'm away. She's a solicitor as well. She puts various jobs my way and encourages colleagues to do the same. A nice arrangement, you might think – and at first it was. Lately, though, it had started to become more than a little claustrophobic. Nothing to do with the jobs, I might add. The problem was that we'd been lovers once – fifteen years ago – and then friends ever since. But lately, for some reason, Becky seemed to think that she was in charge of my welfare.

'Come on, Cam, what do you think?'

'Well, yeah, possibly.'

'Oh, come on, flower. They're doing Górecki's Number Three – you know how much you enjoy that!'

She was right, I love the piece. But I didn't think I was up to yet another argument over how I should be leading my life. 'Actually, Becks, this isn't really a social call. I'm in Manchester, on my way to see a client, so I can't talk for long. It's just... Well, I've got a slight problem. I hoped you might be able to help.'

'*Only* if you come with me to the concert, Cam.' She was half joking. But only half.

Oh, Jesus.

Sometimes I am *such* a coward. But then I suppose I realised just how many brownie points I was going to need to get through this conversation unscathed.

'Yeah, OK, I'd love to.'

She laughed, pleasantly. 'All right, then, flower, shoot. What can I do for you?'

'Well... Ah... It's Beano, she's been... um... arrested.'

'Oh...' The sudden drop in temperature was unmissable. 'Well, I hate to say it, Cameron, but are you surprised? Trouble follows that woman around. I've told you before: you should stay away from her.'

I could picture her at the other end, arms folded, face set. 'Aw, come on, Becks. I know you two don't get on, but she's a good friend. I have to go and see her.'

Silence. Then, reluctantly, 'What's she up for?'

'Um... I'm not too sure,' I lied. 'I just heard she was on remand. I wondered if you could find out where.'

Silence.

'Please, it would mean a lot.'

'Mmm... Well, I suppose I could.' She stopped suddenly and drew breath, 'Christ, you don't want me to *defend* her, do you?'

I reeled at such a preposterous thought. 'Probably not, Becks, but if you could check the lists I'd be really grateful. She was in court in Manchester at the end of last week.'

'And you'll come to the concert Wednesday with me?'

Shit. 'Yes, of course.'

'All right then, flower. I suppose I can check first thing. I need to be in the office for half past eight, anyway. I'll do it then.'

'Thanks, Becky, you're a star.'

'Huh! Cam?'

'What?'

'Don't forget the concert, will you? It's Wednesday – *that's the day after tomorrow.*'

'No! Of course not!'

I put the phone away with some relief and stared at my face in the mirror.

Jesus, I'm thirty-eight years old, my parents are both dead, I'm supposed to be an assertive adult. Why don't I just say no?

My belly started again and my head began to fuzz over, so I took two more tablets, washing them down with a swig of flat Coke from the half-empty bottle on the passenger seat. Then I started the car again. Periods, they're no fucking good to anyone – well, except for would-be mothers, perhaps. Of which I'm definitely not one. There should be a multiple-choice question when you're prepubertal. A tick if you want babies, a cross if you don't. Simple, see? Then all this pain and nuisance could be avoided.

I drove on up Bury Old Road, past rows of dilapidated houses and shuttered businesses, past takeaways and through endless sets of traffic lights. When the road broadened out and the housing stock improved I turned off the main drag and threaded my way through the streets of more prosperous-looking Victorian housing at the posh end of Bury.

Barkington Road is as posh as it gets. A wide, tree-lined street of elegant late-Victorian houses with big gardens and high hedges. The Wilson house was about halfway down, standing proudly in its own extensive gardens, surrounded by rhododendron bushes and large, neatly cut lawns. The walk from the road to the front door was a good twenty yards of smooth tarmac drive, lit by its own street lamps, and easily accommodating Elaine's sporty BMW – and the two police cars that were still parked behind it.

In truth, it was more of a mansion than a house and, like many of its kind in this part of the world, it harked back to the cotton boom of the late nineteenth century, when mill owners had both the money and the inclination to beef up their despised *nouveau riche* status in high society. Thinking of my client as I rang the bell, I reflected that nothing much had changed over the years.

Elaine Wilson answered the door with poison in her eyes. I was going to say something supportive, but, sensing her mood, I kept my mouth shut and made a half-hearted attempt at a sympathetic smile instead.

'You'd better come in,' she said tightly. Her blonde hair was gathered back off her forehead as neatly now as earlier in the day; her mascara and her lipstick more perfect than I would have believed possible. She'd changed her dress since this morning. Now she was wearing a simple mid-green classic, which fitted her beautifully, and round her neck was a string of small pearls. I looked at my watch. Nine thirty. Had she been out already, or had she been about to leave when the police called?

'Come into the lounge.' She snapped. 'The police are still here.'

I followed her through the spacious hall. On my right an antique-looking pew took up most of the wall and on my left a huge polished mahogany staircase led to the upper floors. Elaine's stilettos tapped unevenly as she traversed the ornately tiled floor. Her body swayed just a little too much. She glanced back as she reached the lounge door, her blue eyes cutting through me, her delicate blood-red lips curling in contempt.

Three faces looked up at us as we entered. Superintendent Dyson and her sergeant were sitting uncomfortably close on a settee that was slightly too small and a fraction overfriendly. The pretty young policewoman whom I'd seen in the bar was almost buried in one of the large chintzy armchairs. Dyson stood up as we entered.

'Your timing is perfect, Ms McGill.' Her voice was loaded with irony. 'My sergeant and I were just leaving.'

'Oh,' I replied overpleasantly, 'that's a pity.'

We held each other's gaze for a moment. I couldn't quite work her out. As a woman I respected her. She held her own, she'd done well for herself. But she was still a cop and she hadn't been even the slightest bit helpful over Beano.

She ignored my remark and moved to the door. The sergeant and the constable followed her.

'You'll be going back home to York now, will you? After you've spoken to Mrs Wilson.' It was an instruction more than a question.

I shrugged it off. 'Any sign of the preacher yet?'

She looked across at me coldly, as if it were none of my business, and left the room without uttering another word. Lady Ego trailed after them, working hard at being the little lost widow and enunciating every syllable with an almost impeccable accent.

I stayed by the door straining to hear the hushed conversation in the hallway.

'Well, goodbye, Mrs Wilson. You're quite sure that you'll be all right on your own tonight? I can still arrange for a family liaison officer to be here if you wish.'

I heard the widow say that, no, she would manage, in a quiet, cultured voice.

When they'd gone Elaine took me into a large, expensively fitted kitchen. I stood by the door waiting for the onslaught.

She didn't speak at first, just folded her arms under her breasts and walked slowly away from me across the shiny floor. I leaned against the door marvelling at the not-so-subtle shift in her mood. When she reached the units on the far side she swung round and glared at me, spitting venom.

'I can't believe the idiot would do this to me!' she hissed. Her accent was pure Manchester now. Her face had turned hard and her body language was graceless and aggressive. 'For Chrissake, McGill!' she screamed. 'You were there – *and you just let it friggin' well happen!*'

I held my hands out. 'Hey, hang on a minute! I feel as bad about this as anyone but I hadn't even left the bar, so how could I have prevented it?'

'You *could* have followed him out! I *thought* that that was your job!'

I tried to be patient – the woman was bound to be traumatised. 'If I'd followed him straightaway, Elaine, he would have noticed me, especially in a place like that.'

She stared hard, then turned her back and poured a neat whisky from a half-empty bottle of Glenfiddich. Not the first glass of the evening by any means, nor, probably, the last. Then she turned back, leaning against the unit, and took a big slug, her face set. I stared back at her, pushing away the nagging guilt in the pit of my stomach.

'They told you about his cross-dressing?' I asked.

She slammed the glass down onto the work surface and nodded her head over and over, like one of those dogs on the back shelves of cars.

'Yeah, they fuckin' told me all right.' She laughed bitterly. 'Christ! All I wanted was a friggin' divorce. Now I've got all this shit to handle.'

I tried to think of something reassuring to say. But all I could think of was, At least you'll get the money now; or maybe, even more cynically, Look on the bright side: you'll save all the legal costs of a divorce and get everything, not just half. Neither seemed very suitable. I guess that she needed a scapegoat – someone to dump her own guilt on. I suppose I fitted the bill perfectly. Best thing was to just take it, collect my fee, and then leave without reacting too much.

She must have read my mind, because, when I didn't respond to her invective, she picked her drink up and walked towards me, swinging the glass by her side, spilling whisky all over the blue and white tiles. She stopped really close and stuck her face right in front of mine, breathing alcohol up my nose and into my eyes.

'You think I should be pleased, don't you?' she drawled. 'You think that Charlie's killer has saved me a lot of trouble? That he's saved me a job and landed me in the money?'

I turned my face away from her and waited. I wasn't going to say another word.

She backed off a step and took another slurp of her drink. A smile flitted across her sad, sad face. 'Well, you're quite wrong, McGill – because there *is* no fucking money!' She raised her glass to that, and broke out into an empty, desolated laugh. 'That's good, don't you think? My husband was skint. Broke. Penniless.'

She reached out her hand and tweaked my nose, joylessly playful. 'And you wanna know something even funnier?'

'Go on.' A shiver ran down my spine. Something told me that I wasn't going to be amused one little bit.

'I don't even have enough to pay your fee.'

I looked her up and down. Everything she was wearing shouted money. The kitchen I was standing in must have cost a fortune.

'I don't believe you.'

She glared at me and took another mouthful of booze.

'I told you, my husband was broke, and, ipso-fucking-facto, so am I!'

Shit.

'I still don't believe you. What about Chow City? His business looks really successful!'

She grunted scornfully. 'Too damn right, sweetie. The place is raking it in – but my poor pathetic husband wasn't!'

I narrowed my eyes. 'But you said he owned half of it.'

'*Used* to own half of it, McGill. They sidelined the poor sod long ago. The money's all going to someone else. Charlie was told to accept it, or get out. And, like the spineless creep that he was, he just hung around and took it. I told you this afternoon – he was a loser. Huh, the sad bastard couldn't even be a real man.'

I watched her drain the glass and help herself to another, feeling sorry for the poor guy. How in God's name had he ended up with someone like her?

'But you must have access to some money?'

She shook her head as if she didn't care. 'Nope, sorry, Cameron. He stopped my allowance and cancelled my cards two weeks ago. Even the damn car goes back Friday.' She assumed that I was thinking of my fee, rather than her precarious situation. But then she would, wouldn't she?

'But you have the house – it must be worth a good bit.'

She walked back over and waved her glass in my face. 'Oh, it is! It's worth a *huuuuge* amount of dosh.' She assumed an exaggerated accent. 'But it used to belong to Mummy and Daddy – and little Charlie wouldn't sell.'

'Well, all right, but it'll be yours now. You should be very comfortably off.'

'Yeah, like hell I will be!' she snorted contemptuously.

My brain began to hurt – wasn't this what she'd been after all along?

She stared at me hard for a moment, then emptied her glass. 'What I'm saying, McGill, is that I don't get the house either. Charlie's left me half of it in his will, but it's useless. *I can't sell it.* The other half belongs to his sister – and she doesn't like me one little bit!'

His sister? Oh yeah, of course.

'The sister that lives in West Didsbury?'

She pointed a manicured finger at me and burped in my face.

'You got it, sweetheart. Now, on top of everything else, I've got to deal with that bitch as well.'

Nine

After I left Elaine Wilson's house, I drove back into the centre and booked into the Overnite Inn, a low-cost, low-frills hotel standing next to a high bridge, just off Deansgate. There was a kind of inverted multistorey next door, which went three floors down to the river level, making parking easy and relatively secure – even if it did cost nearly as much as the damn room.

I was still simmering nicely when I slumped down into one of the bar's lumpy armchairs with a large Campari and tonic, angry at the way I'd let a client dump me like that, but even more upset by Elaine Wilson's self-centred response to her husband's murder.

I finally crawled into bed around midnight, after a few too many drinks. And, even though I was exhausted, my head refused to close down, replaying blurry, anxious clips all through the night: Charles Wilson's twisted, bleeding corpse, Aunt Emily throwing up as she ran away, Dyson pinning me against a wall and accusing me of neglect, Beano sitting unhappily in a dark prison cell, Lin's smile, the way she'd looked at me when we parted.

At some point I drifted off and the images drew back, replaced by a wretched and fitful sleep, which seemed to go on interminably. When I awoke it was with a start, blinking in the bright morning light. My mobile was playing the theme from 'Ride of the Valkyries' at full volume.

I rolled over and flipped it open, grateful that the morning had finally arrived.

'Hi.' I picked my watch up off the cabinet. *Nine o'clock. Damn.*

'You still in bed?' Becky's voice was sharper than I'd expected.

'Yeah,' I groaned, still not connecting. 'Late night.'

'Mmm, well it's all right for you, Cameron, out all hours enjoying yourself. Some of us have to go to work in a morning. And *some* of us have to go round and feed your damn cat before they can even do that.'

'No, Becky. I was working, really.'

'Oh, yeah? You sure that you weren't out painting the town with some young dyke?' Her weak attempt at humour was completely ruined by the bitterness in her voice.

I rubbed my belly, then my head, and reached for the ibuprofen. 'Becky, what's wrong?'

Silence. A cold, hostile silence.

'You lied, Cam. You lied to me.'

Oh no, here we go. 'Becky, *What* are you talking about?'

'Beano! You *knew*, didn't you? You *knew* what she was in for all the time – you just didn't want to tell me.'

I gritted my teeth. 'And why would I do that?'

'Because you knew damn well how I'd react. Cameron, *wounding with intent* – do you know how serious that is?'

'I knew she was in trouble, Becky, but I didn't know what the charge was.'

'Bollocks! You knew damn well that I'd blow a fuse! Stay away from it, Cameron! This is Beano's problem, not yours.'

I took a deep breath and snapped back. 'Look, don't start that again, Becky. I told you last night, she's my friend. You came over to Hull and bailed me out when I was in trouble, remember?'

'Yeah, exactly! That's what I'm worried about.'

'What?'

'You're becoming obsessive, Cameron. Your sister's death I could understand. But that woman on the bridge in Hull. You had no good reason to get involved. Now you're going to do it all over again, this time with Beano.'

Jesus!

'What's the matter with you, Cam? Why can't you be satisfied with a steady job, like everyone else? Why the hell do you have to go looking for trouble?'

I drew breath and tried to stay calm. 'For Christ's sake, Becky, stop being so bloody dramatic, will you? All I want to do is give the woman a little support!'

She grunted cynically. 'Yeah, well that's what you say now. But I know you, Cameron – and I know her as well. You know what a manipulative bitch she can be.'

God, I hate these conversations.

'Becky – will you please stop trying to run my life?'

She went silent for a moment. I could almost hear her gathering herself together again. 'I just care about you, that's all. I don't want you to go and see her. It gives me a sinking feeling.'

'Yeah, well, that's because you don't like her.'

'No, it isn't that at all.'

'All right, then, where is she?'

Silence.

'Come on Becky, tell me!'

She exhaled impatiently. 'She's in Styal, next to the airport, in the remand wing.'

For once I didn't have any pleasantness left. 'Thanks.'

'You're welcome.' Becky was equally cold.

I'd got dressed as soon as I put the phone down, grabbed some cereal bars and another bottle of Coke from the hotel lobby, collected the car from the riverside multistorey, and got on the road – all within half an hour.

Now I was nearly there, driving through the mist, past the airport, past the plane spotters, who always seem to be at the end of every runway, onto the Styal Road and out into open countryside.

In truth, I'd rather have done anything than visit Beano today. Whatever I'd said to Becky, I wanted to help if I could; I wanted to know what she'd done, to whom, and why. But what I didn't want was to see her in the visiting room of some dingy prison.

I nearly missed it. I'd been expecting a bleak Victorian building to loom out of the mist at me, but in the event the entrance was simply a small double gateway in the hedge to my left. As I drove through and turned into the visitors' car park, the immediate buildings came into focus and, far from being grim, the Victorian mock Tudor seemed almost welcoming. It wasn't until I got out of the car and walked along the access road to the main entrance that I realised the mist had been playing tricks with me. Ahead, looming through the grey fog, was the real boundary to the prison.

A strong, twenty-foot-high, wire fence, topped with large coils of shiny razor wire, marked the perimeter. And, as if that weren't enough, it was reinforced by a ten-foot concrete wall on the inside. Beyond, new and old buildings huddled together depressingly in the grey morning light.

The visitors' entrance was a wire door set into the fence, with a small reception office behind. When I approached it, one of the three warders came forward and asked for my identification. A cold hand twisted my guts, bringing back the memory of the police cell in Hull: the smell of disinfectant, the stink of stale urine.

I'd rung before I'd set off, to check the procedures. Good job, too. Becky must have known, but had omitted to tell me, that visiting ended at 11.30 a.m. If I'd missed out, I would have had to wait until Thursday for the next chance to visit. They also told me that I wasn't on Beano's visitor list so, they said, they couldn't allow me in. It was only when I got really pushy that the officer agreed to speak to Beano and allow me on the list if she agreed. I set off anyway but I had to stop the car and ring them twice more before I'd finally got the go-ahead. Even then, I had to crawl to the bastards.

By the time they let me through and into the building, my belly was churning. The officers were more pleasant than I expected, and the surroundings were clean. Even the all-pervasive smell of disinfectant was absent. But there's still something about places like this that makes my blood run cold, and, by the time I was sitting at one of the Formica-topped tables in the big visitors' hall, I was a bag of nerves. I knew that I should try to relax or I'd be of no use to Beano at all, so I leaned back in the chair and looked around me, breathing deeply, trying to ease the tension in my neck and shoulders.

The big room was well over half full, with around thirty visitors – mothers, fathers, husbands, friends and relatives, talking to their loved ones under the constant gaze of four screws – two men, two women. I wondered how Beano was taking it. Then I wondered why I was being so anxious about her. I knew how resilient she could be. The woman would probably walk in grinning all over her fat face.

But I was thrown when she finally came in with her escort. The woman walking across the room wasn't the Beano that I knew: the one who constantly told tall stories, the woman with the incorrigible spirit and the indefatigable sense of fun. Beano's wide, generous mouth was turned down at the edges, her usual fuck-you walk had turned to a slouch and even her short black curly hair had lost its bounce. The big woman in the cargo pants and the baggy khaki jumper looked tired. But, worse than that, she looked defeated.

I held out my arms, vaguely wondering if physical contact was allowed. Vaguely not caring. She walked right up to me and put her arms around my neck, holding me silently.

One of the screws yelled at us to sit down. I ignored him and kissed her on the lips. Just a normal sort of greeting, but now all the warders and most of the other visitors were staring.

Lesbians. Yeah.

A female screw with short hair and an attitude danced through the tables and chairs towards us, barking something about touching not being allowed. She was pointing to a big notice on the wall, which said that prisoners had to remain seated at all times. We let go.

Beano sat down without a murmur. I stared at the screw and then at the rubberneckers all around the room. Instantly all eyes turned away. The warder instructed me to sit down, so I did, pulling out a chair on my side of the table and staring intensely at her as I did it. She stared straight back until I was seated and only then did she turn away.

When I looked at her, Beano avoided my eyes. I'd never seen her give in to authority so easily.

'You took some tracking down,' I began, not quite knowing what to say. She looked back at me, but said nothing, her face set. 'Why didn't you tell me?'

She shrugged and I could see now that she was struggling to keep control.

'Beano, you know I'll do all I can to help, don't you?'

She shook her head, smiling painfully, trying to look cool, as if she didn't give a shit. But I could see the tears filling her eyes. Damn, I could feel my own beginning to burn.

'Yeah, thanks, Cam.' She coughed to cover up the catch in her voice, then she looked away again, gathering herself together. When she eventually turned back she seemed a little more composed, but I guessed that it was only anger that was keeping her other emotions at bay.

She shook her head. 'No one can help me – I'm in too deep this time.' She paused and tipped her head to one side, trying hard to sound upbeat. Failing. 'Anyway, what the hell are you doing this side of the Pennines? Who the fuck told you I was here?'

I sat back in the chair, remembering that first telephone conversation with Elaine Wilson and how I'd promised myself that I'd strangle Beano for recommending me.

'It's a long story; I'll tell you later.'

She waited. I wasn't going to get away with that.

'Becky told me,' I conceded.

She grunted contemptuously. 'Well, thanks, but you're wasting your time. Go get a life, will you? Leave me be.'

I bit my tongue and waited. This wasn't like her.

She shifted awkwardly on her seat, rubbing her eyes.

'You're not getting rid of me, Beano. Not before I know what really happened.'

She threw me a weak smile and shook her head. 'I'm in it up to my neck, Cam. And there's nothing that you or anyone else can do about it.'

'Aw, come on,' I objected. 'That can't be true.'

Silence.

'They say you nearly killed someone.'

She leaned forward and covered her face with her hands for a moment.

'Yeah, well, *they* are wrong.'

'You didn't do it.'

'As I live and breathe, Cameron, I didn't even touch the guy.'

Silence.

'*You think I did?*'

I shook my head. 'No, you can be a stroppy bastard, but you're not a thug.'

She pushed the hair away from her eyes and snorted. 'Uh, thanks, pal. You're too kind.'

That was better. 'So how come you got charged?'

She sighed heavily and closed her eyes, letting her head fall back for a moment. 'Basically, I've been a stupid cow.' She shook her head. 'You won't believe it.'

'Try me.'

She looked at me out of the corner of her eye and grunted, 'There's a woman involved.'

She waited for a reaction. She didn't get it.

'Erm, well, I've had this... *relationship* for around four months... well you know me, Cameron, I'm kinda shit at the hearts-and-flowers stuff. Uh... but Hannah, mmm, well... she's sort of special – and I was kind of taken with her.

'Anyway, we were getting on fine. She came out a couple of years ago, had a few flings and by the time I met her she was looking for something more settled.' She shrugged. 'Well, normally I'd have run a mile, but this time, huh, I just thought, Fuck, this is it.'

She stopped and looked up as if she expected me to take the piss or something.

I shrugged and smiled at her. 'Sounds OK to me.'

Beano shuffled in her seat, embarrassed to the roots. 'Yeah, but what I didn't count on was the jealous ex.'

'I thought you said she'd only had flings before.'

'Yeah, that's right – flings with women. This ex was a man, Cameron – her ex-husband, Mark Taylor. Mad Mazza, they call him, and I can see why now.'

Oh, shit.

'We'd only been going out a month when he started pestering her again, asking her for money – she's got a kid, a six-year-old girl, and he'd got access at the time, so there was nothing much she could do. But Susie was just an excuse. Hannah said he'd been a crap father and never bothered with her until they split. The truth of the matter was that he was skint – well, that and the fact that he resented being replaced by a woman. I think he saw it as a slur on his manhood.

'So you got into a fight?'

'I told you, I never touched the bastard. Hannah said she could handle him, told me to keep out of it, or I'd make things worse. So I kept away from him as much as I could – which was difficult, seeing as how he was always hanging around her place. Every fucking time I went to see her he'd be there, either when I arrived or when I left. Usually I got away without getting involved but once or twice we had a real dingdong.

'But I never hit him, Cameron, you gotta believe that. I swear to you on my mother's grave, I never touched the guy.'

'I believe you.'

She looked up at me, as if surprised. 'Anyway, the more I saw of her, the worse it got. He started calling round at all hours, banging on the door and shouting through the letterbox in the middle of the night. He was usually pissed or stoned or worse. We got abusive phone calls as well. All the time he kept saying that he'd stay away if we gave him some money.'

'And you did.'

'Yeah, it was stupid, I know, but we did. We thought that we might be able to pay him off. But, of course, he just spent that and came back for more.' She paused, fidgeting. 'Well, there's only so much you can take, and Hannah was getting really worried about Susie. She didn't want him to see her any more, let alone take her out anywhere. She worried about the effect he was having on her – the poor kid was getting really frightened. Hannah went back to court to get the access rescinded.'

'Did she get it?'

'Yeah, three weeks ago. She got an injunction as well, and we both hoped that would be the end of it. It was. For a week. Then he was back after the folding stuff again. Said that if we gave him enough, this time he'd stay away for good.' She shook her head. 'I can tell you, Cam, I'd have done anything to get rid of him, but he was talking crazy money.'

'What the hell was he into?'

She grunted contemptuously. 'Crack, probably, judging from his cough and his massive mood swings. But the guy's a slaphead – he probably does anything he can lay his hands on.'

'So you refused to pay him off and got into a fight?'

She rolled her eyes in disbelief. '*No!* For fuck's sake, Cameron! You really think I'm that stupid?'

'Sorry.'

'Yeah, well maybe I *am* stupid. I went to see the guy, last Monday, thinking that I could reason with him, try to make some sort of human contact, then maybe he'd relax a bit. That was Plan A, anyway, and if that didn't work Plan B was to tell him to just fucking well get off her back.'

She sighed and rubbed her forehead. 'I guess I should have known better. Sometimes, Cameron, I can be so bloody naïve.'

I shrugged. 'Can't we all? But it's always worth trying to negotiate.'

'That's not what I meant. The stupid bit was that I went to see him at his flat – he lives on the Cardogan Estate.' She looked at me and shook her head at herself. 'Can you believe that? Even the fucking cops go there in fours.'

'And you went by yourself?'

'Huh, worse than that. I went round after dark and when I got there there was some kind of power failure on the fourth floor. I just put it down to crap public services.' She looked at me ruefully. 'But it gets worse. His door was ajar, and there was the sound of scuffling inside – you know what I mean, the sound of flesh being beaten. I could hear whining, crying. It was Mazza. Someone was beating the shit out of him.'

She stopped and looked at me for a moment. 'I know, I know. I should have run. I should have got the fuck outta there. But I just stood there, wondering how I could help the poor bastard. Can you believe that? After all the crap he dished out to Hannah?

'Anyhow, the next thing I knew, I was coming round on the floor with a broken bottle in my hand and a police torch shining in my eyes. Good old Mazza was on the floor next to me in a pool of blood.'

Jesus!

She closed her eyes a moment and let her head drop. 'When he came round, the bastard told 'em it was me who'd cut him up.' She shook her head angrily. 'Can you believe that? I try to help the bastard, and he sets me up like that.'

I ran my fingers through my hair, stunned, 'Christ, Beano! I mean, shit, you want me to go and try talking to him? See if I can get him to come clean?'

She grunted sarcastically. 'That's really nice of you, Cam, but he's hardly likely to change his story, given that he probably wants to stay alive.'

'You think he was being worked over for not paying his drug debts.'

'Yeah, I do – and the payoff is that he fingers me, rather than them. Anyway, since I was the one who was seeing his ex, he's probably very happy that I'm taking the rap. It gets me out of the way, which is what he wanted all along.'

I didn't know what to say.

Beano shook her head sadly. 'Let's face it, Cam, I've been stitched up real good. I've got the motive – the bastard was really getting to me – and I was found next to him with the weapon in my hand and his blood on my clothes.'

'But, surely, someone – a neighbour maybe – must have seen the guys that did it.'

'Yeah, sure – and you think anyone from the Cardogan Estate is going to stick their neck out for me?' She shook her head slowly. 'Forget it, sweetheart! They're all scared witless.'

'Well, what about Hannah? Can't she testify for you? Surely she can say—'

'Say what? That I was furious with her ex over the way he'd been bothering her? That I went round to see him, to sort him out?' She sighed in exasperation. 'Just tell me how that's gonna help, 'cos I just can't fucking see it!'

'Yeah, OK, OK. Just calm down, will you?'

She shifted in her chair and put her face in her hands.

'Can I at least go and see Hannah, make sure she's OK?'

Beano looked up again and smiled. 'Yeah, that would be nice. Mazza's in no condition to bother her, that's for sure. It would be great if you could just look in.' She paused and studied the table. 'I saw her yesterday. She's really cut up. She could do with some support.'

'So, any idea who really beat him up?' I tried to sound offhand, but she glared at me fiercely and grabbed my arm. The screw with the attitude stepped forward as if she were wound up and ready to go. Beano let go but her expression didn't change one iota.

'Don't even think about it, Cameron! These guys aren't playing games. If they catch you sniffing around, you'll be dead meat, no fucking question.'

I stared back at her without a word.

She leaned forward and held my eyes. 'Do me a favour, love: just make sure Hannah's OK. Then go home, will you? Leave it.'

'I can't – I can't just walk away.'

She stared at me intensely. 'You can – and that's exactly what you're going to do.'

I left with a heavy heart. The screws called time before I could argue with her, but it would have been pointless anyway: Beano seemed determined to carry the whole damn load on her own shoulders. Some people might say that that proved something; but I know my friend, and I believed every word she'd told me.

I sat in the car park for a while, turning her account over in my mind, trying to see a way out. To be honest, the more I thought about it, the worse I felt. It was bad enough visiting. Being told what to do and when. To be locked up in there must be hell.

But she was probably right: the guys who beat up Mazza Taylor didn't sound like small-time villains. So what could I to do? Have a cosy chat? Get them to explain that it was all a mistake? Or maybe Mazza himself would retract his statement. Yeah, as Beano said, just so long as he was ready to die.

The situation looked impossible. Worse, it looked *dangerously impossible*.

I rang the Overnite Inn from the prison car park and booked myself in for another night, then I thought about ringing Becky. However much she disliked Beano, I knew that she'd help her if I asked. She was a good brief. She knew all the angles. Yeah, but she'd never believe that Beano was telling the truth, and, even if she did, it wouldn't alter anything. Some situations you can change legitimately, some you can't. Besides, in the circumstances, I could do without another lecture about not getting involved.

I started the car and flicked the wipers on, pushing a thick layer of water from the windscreen, then I tuned the radio to the local station. Eleven thirty-two. The fog was lifting but the day was still dull and depressing. I needed to find a chemist and replenish my supplies of tampons and painkillers, then I'd go and see Hannah – make sure that she was all right, and that her ex really was staying away.

After that – well, I didn't know. Maybe I'd pay a visit to the Cardogan, anyway. Nothing heavy, just a recce to get the lie of the land, get some idea of what the hell I might do next – uh, if anything. OK, I know, I was grasping at straws. But – still – I needed to do something, whatever Beano had said.

Traffic was backing up by the time I reached the M60 and it took me over twenty minutes of stop/start before I reached the sliproad for Hannah's house. The news jingle played on the hour and, not surprisingly, nearly the whole bulletin concentrated on the murder, and the attendant fear of further hate killings in the gay village. There was reaction from a number of gay men and lesbians, and much speculation on the part that skinhead hate gangs may have played. The only new information they gave was that a man was, as they say, helping the police with their enquiries. They didn't give details, but I guessed that it must be the old preacher.

I was sitting at the traffic lights on the exit roundabout wondering about him when my phone rang.

'Hi, Cameron! It's me – Lin. Remember?'

'Um, yeah,' I joked, my heart leaping. 'I kind of remember someone with that name hurling abuse at me last night.'

She laughed lightly. 'OK Miss Detective, you don't need to rub it in. How did it go with your client? I've been wondering all morning.'

'You mean my ex-client.' I told her the story.

She commiserated, then suggested that she might buy me lunch to cheer me up. I thought about it for at least a millisecond before I said yes – I would still go and see Hanna, but tonight would be fine.

Ten

The ornate red and yellow lettering confirmed that this was indeed the Golden Snapper. There was even a large shiny fish in the middle of the name, sitting on its tail and blowing bubbles, just as Lin had said. This had to be the place – just a few yards from the big arch in Chinatown – but it wasn't anything like I'd been expecting. For a Chinese restaurant, the menu was way pricey – in fact, the whole place oozed the kind of class that was well above anything I could afford.

Lin had given the impression that she was hard up: she'd just finished her degree, she drove a beat-up old Escort and she worked for pin money in a seedy bar. So what the hell was she doing inviting me out to lunch in a ritzy joint like this where even the starters run into double figures?

I took a deep breath and walked through the big doors into an opulent lobby. The walls on both sides of me were clad with large flawless sheets of marble, each inlaid with different red and black carvings. Fiery dragons, noble warriors, peasants working in the fields, children, emperors and concubines. The floor was of deep shiny-black tiles, each inset with white, anemone-like flowers. Straight ahead, the open doors of a small lift beckoned.

I stepped inside and punched the only button on the console. The lift whirred smoothly upwards for a few seconds, then shuddered to a gentle halt, opening onto a small jasmine-scented anteroom. I stepped out onto a deep burgundy carpet to be greeted by an old man in a black monkey suit. He approached me, bowing slightly, welcoming me with a heavy Chinese accent.

'Miss 'Gill, I believe?' When he smiled, his small, creased eyes twinkled.

I nodded, both impressed and a little scared by the reception. When he offered to take my jerkin I shook my head. It was still wet and clammy from the rain outside, but I needed something to hang on to and, right now, my battered jacket was all I seemed to have.

'Miss Lin is here already. Please follow me.'

He scurried off, leading me out past the bar and into the main restaurant – a big room that covered the entire floor of the building, yet its décor and design lent it the intimacy of somewhere much smaller. It was expensively appointed, but in a pleasant, understated way. Plain cobalt-blue paper hung on the walls, setting off a collection of beautiful, traditional tapestries in golds and reds and yellows. Overhead, the high ceiling was draped with fabric woven in rich patterns of green and gold.

But it was the pond that dominated the room. Richly decorated with gold leaf and traditional Chinese sculpture, it covered almost a quarter of the floor area at the very centre. At its heart, an elaborate golden fish reached up almost to the ceiling, sitting on its tail, just like the sign outside, gushing foamy water from its mouth, down the sides and into the pool, where big orange and silver koi swam languidly around, in and out of the water lilies, under and around the luxuriant green weeds.

There were no more than forty tables in all, some round, some square; all well-spaced, divided by tall hedges of graceful bamboo and fig. The restaurant wasn't full, but a good many of the tables were occupied, mostly by men, both European and Chinese, all smartly turned out in their business suits. There was a scattering of expensively coutured women sitting quietly in among them, conspicuously out of place. I fingered my leather jerkin awkwardly as I followed the old man round to the far side of the pond. My black jeans were fading and my DMs needed polishing. What the hell was she playing at? There were loads of restaurants in Chinatown, every one of them more comfortable – and much cheaper – than this one.

I almost didn't recognise her at first. She was sitting in a quiet alcove next to the pond. Her hair was fastened back, leaving wispy ebony strands tumbling over her bare shoulders. Her black strappy top skimmed the curve of her neat breasts but then clung tightly underneath, accentuating and following their every movement.

A silver-haired man was sitting at the same table directly opposite her, his back to me. Lin looked up and smiled nervously at me. I frowned back, feeling my stomach pitch.

She registered my concern at once and her eyes spilled reassurance. I smiled back automatically but, in truth, I felt angry. I'd been expecting a one-to-one.

Funny how certain moments in your life stand out, how time slows for just an instant and you can remember every detail, every texture from those few seconds. But it's not until much later, when you look back, that you really begin to understand their significance. And then the small gestures and the gentle courtesies take on a different interpretation altogether.

Lin stood up as I approached the table, stepping forward and kissing me formally on the cheek, then pulling away, directing her gaze towards the man. When I turned around, her companion was already standing. He smiled too, then held out his hand, holding my eyes. I looked back calmly, pushing back the knot of anger in my guts, wondering who he was and why the fuck he was gatecrashing my date.

He was old, very old, but he stood straight, like someone much younger; his eyes were bright; his face was full and mostly unlined. It was only the pigmentation of his skin and the loose folds around his neck that gave his years away. A more distant observer might have placed him in his fifties, but close up it was clear that he was into his eighties.

'Cameron, this is my grandfather, Mr Lee. Grandpa, this is my friend Cameron.'

Grandfather?

He was shorter than either Lin or I, with a full head of silver hair, cut neatly around his ears and into his neck, not too long, not too short. And he wore a conventional mid-grey suit, expensively tailored, complemented by shiny black slip-ons with gold buckles and leather tassels on the front.

She'd talked about him last night. He was helping her to get a job in Singapore.

His grip was firm and dry and, as he shook my hand, he looked into my eyes as if he were taking my brain apart and examining every thought in my head. Maybe that was why he started with an apology.

'Forgive me for intruding on your lunch like this, Cameron.' He smiled and bowed slightly. His English accent was almost perfect. 'I get so few chances to meet my granddaughter and, when she talked about you, I suggested that maybe I could entertain you both.' He inclined his head politely. 'I hope that you don't mind.'

I gritted my teeth and smiled back. I said I was pleased to meet him and we sat down. But I was lying. I did mind. I'd been hoping to get Lin on her own. I wanted to get to know her. And, after the trauma of the last twenty-four hours, I needed to let my hair down a bit, flirt a little. Maybe even get slightly drunk.

But, for all my disappointment, I found myself taking easily to the man. He was friendly, relaxed, urbane – someone who puts you at your ease without even trying. Yet he was as distinguished as anyone I've ever met. A man with natural style and impeccable manners – the sort of class that comes only to those with money. And a lot of it.

'Lin tells me that you are a private investigator.' I thought I detected a note of amusement in his voice, but his eyes were on me again, judging my reaction. 'I don't believe that I've ever met a *lady* PI before.'

'You still haven't,' I chanced, 'and for my part, Mr Lee, I don't believe anyone has ever called me a lady until now.'

He paused for a second and then broke into a deep, pleasurable laugh. Then, he lifted his arm and the old waiter appeared again as if by magic.

'We're ready for the food now, Chen, if you please.'

He smiled with his eyes again and bowed, before hurrying away. Mr Lee gazed pleasantly across the table at us. 'I hope that neither of you will mind, but I've taken the liberty of choosing the food myself. I've ordered a selection of both vegetarian and meat dishes. Lin tells me that you're vegetarian, Cameron. Is that all right?'

'Thank you, that's very kind.' It sounded like another politeness but, actually, I meant it. I was beginning to feel relieved – and impressed. The man had real presence. Jesus, I almost called him 'sir'.

He chatted easily for a few minutes, choosing his subjects carefully so that I felt more at ease. He talked about York and the people he knew there, about Lin's degree, and her forthcoming trip to Singapore. We discussed food, and the weather in Manchester. He complained about the aches and pains he suffered every time it rained.

Around us, waiters in white mess uniforms and waitresses in blue and gold sheaths were gliding in and out of the dining areas serving food and clearing tables: smiling, deferring, speaking to the diners only when they were spoken to.

I looked across at Lin and caught her eye. She smiled back warmly, but still offered no explanation. She'd said little since my arrival and I wondered who'd invited who to this meal – and why. I hardly knew the woman. We'd had words, then we'd had a drink to make up. Now I was meeting a close relative and being treated like royalty. It all seemed a little sudden.

'This is a fine restaurant, Mr Lee. I've never seen anything quite like it.'

He smiled modestly. 'Thank you, Cameron. It is the one achievement that I value above all other.'

I looked across at Lin. I was surprised: she'd told me that her grandfather was well off, but I didn't think she meant *this* well off.

'It's yours? This is *your* restaurant?' I asked, clearly impressed.

He inclined his head graciously. 'Yes, I spend a lot of my time here. It's become very special to me. I think that maybe as I get older I appreciate quality more.' He swept his arm around the room. 'My parents would have been amazed. We were very poor when I was a boy in Singapore, before the invasion. After the war, I spent many years building my business. But I have been lucky. I have done well. I own a number of, shall we say, less ostentatious, restaurants in the city, a shop or two and various other business interests, so I can afford to indulge myself a little.'

'Don't you believe him, Cameron.' Lin laughed and leaned across the table, taking hold of the old man's hand. 'My grandfather is being modest. He is *hugely* successful, filthy rich as well! And I'm very, very proud of him.'

Grandfather beamed back at her affectionately, clearly thrilled with her company and not embarrassed in the slightest by showing it.

We paused while two of the women laid out a variety of dishes on our table and spooned rice into our bowls. Another brought a large pot of green tea and filled our porcelain cups. She was about to withdraw with the pot, but Lin's grandfather motioned to her to leave it. She smiled affectionately at him, then bowed almost imperceptibly before leaving.

At Mr Lee's invitation I spooned out some black bean tofu into my dish and picked up my chopsticks. When I looked up Lin was helping herself as well, but she was also exchanging furtive glances with her grandfather. I watched them, wondering what was going on. Mr Lee noticed, put the spoon back in the dish and sat up straight.

'We have all been very polite and sociable, Cameron, but I know that you must be as shocked as we are over the murder last night. Charlie was a good man – he deserved better.'

I must have looked confused. I certainly felt it. Suddenly the old guy was talking about the dead man as if he knew him.

Lin leaned forward, eyes wide. 'They keep on talking about it on the radio – we've been listening to the reports all morning, but they never give any real details. All they keep saying is that the police are treating the death as murder, and that a man is helping them with their enquiries. What's going on, Cameron? Have you heard anything?'

Mr Lee stared at me, waiting for a response. His breathing was erratic now, as if he were trying to retain his composure. A cheerless silence descended over the table. I glanced at Lin and then at him and put my bowl down.

'I don't know any more than you do,' I said, treading carefully, wondering how well Mr Lee knew Charles Wilson, 'but I assume that the man they've arrested is the street preacher. Like I told you, Lin, he and Charles Wilson had a fight last night, but whether he actually killed him...'

I looked across at Mr Lee, wondering how much he knew about his granddaughter's acquaintance with transvestites, how much he knew about Charles Wilson and his alter ego.

The old man breathed in deeply, and held onto the table with the palms of his hands, as if trying to steady himself. He saw me staring and shook his head in sorrow.

'I'm sorry Cameron, I should...' He coughed a little, composing himself. 'I should explain that Charlie was a friend of mine – a very good friend, as a matter of fact – as well as being a fellow restaurateur. I – I find his murder deeply distressing, as you may well appreciate.'

I looked down for a moment, remembering the grim scene in the alley, the crushed body, the efficient, almost callous, way that the authorities moved in to take care of the scene of crime. It occurred to me then that they were probably conducting the postmortem as we spoke. I pushed the thought away and wondered vaguely whether the old man shared his friend's weakness for women's clothing.

'I'm sorry, Mr Lee. I hope I haven't been insensitive in any way.'

He shook his head, his chopsticks hovering over his bowl. 'No, of course not. In any case, you weren't to know. Charlie and I go back many years. I helped him get started in this business.'

'Did you know of his, erm, indulgence?' I looked at Lin out of the corner of my eyes, wondering whether the question was inappropriate.

He looked straight back, unfazed by the question. 'I had no idea until this morning – how would I? But coincidence is a funny thing. When I spoke to Lin earlier, I realised that we both knew him' – he smiled weakly: the irony was not lost on him – 'even if it was in very different ways.'

Lin had gone pale and was picking at her rice. Her grandfather noticed at once and let the subject drop.

'Now, Lin, tell me all about your plans. When do you leave? Where will you be staying?'

Lin's eyes lit up again and the focus changed almost immediately.

'I fly in a few weeks' time,' she told him. 'I've got a friend there who I met at university, and I'm staying with her parents for the first few months, until I get somewhere of my own. They're nice people – I'll be all right.'

He sighed and shook his head in the slightly bemused manner of older people who don't understand. 'I wish you'd let me arrange things so that you get to the front of the waiting lists. You know how long it takes to get housing over there.'

'No, Grandpa, it's very kind of you, but you know that I'd rather do it my way.'

He shook his head in dismay. 'Lin, I've told you already, you could use my house. Please. It's empty for months at a time. You would be doing me a favour – and it's much nicer than those awful tower blocks. In any case it's still very difficult for a single person. You might not get anywhere permanent at all.'

Lin smiled and touched the old man's arm. 'Thanks, Grandpa, but I'll be fine. I'd rather be with people I know, and they'll put me up until I sort something else out – even if it takes a very long time.'

Lin looked across at me and grimaced. 'He worries about me all the time – you can see that, can't you?'

He reached across and took hold of her hand, shaking his head in complete bewilderment. 'Darling, of course I worry when you talk about involving yourself in politics the way you do.'

I looked puzzled. 'I thought you were going to Singapore to be an accountant.'

She turned and smiled brightly at me, relieved to have a distraction. 'Oh, I am. I have to – I need to earn a living. But that's not the only reason I'm going back.'

She took a sip of tea, glancing at the old man over the rim of the cup, then dabbed her lips with the serviette. 'You may not know it, Cameron, but Singapore is one of those countries where it is still illegal to be gay. There's a liberation movement, though, which is making some progress. I intend to join it.' She shrugged and looked directly at her grandfather, tapping him gently on the nose. 'That's all. It's no big deal.'

Mr Lee held up his hands in horror and looked to me for support. 'Tell her, Cameron, will you? You're a sensible woman; please make her come to her senses.'

I busied myself scooping up another mouthful of the delicious black bean mixture and pretended not to hear.

When I didn't react, he sighed and turned back to Lin. 'Singapore is a model, young lady. The laws may be strict but they are for the good of all – and they work. You shouldn't go stirring things up.'

She shook her head in affectionate dismay. 'The laws might work for the majority, Grandpa, but if you're gay then life can be hell – and you know it! Someone has to speak up, someone has to make a start with changing attitudes. The government outlaws everything that is inconvenient – litter, chewing gum, jaywalking. For goodness' sake, you can even be fined for not flushing the toilet!' She folded her arms, her eyes sparkling with resolve. 'Well, gay people should be treated with respect – and they should have real rights. There are others already speaking out. It's my country too – and I want to join them and help to make a difference.'

He shook his head sadly at me and tried again. 'Cameron, you see what I have to put up with? Can you not talk her out of this folly?'

I shrugged; he was asking the wrong person. 'I'm sorry, Mr Lee, I agree with her. If I was in Lin's position, I guess I might do the same thing.'

Lin threw me a grateful look. Mr Lee eyed me in dismay and shook his head. 'Hmm, so you disappoint an old man as well, young lady. Does *neither* of you understand how much trouble this could cause?'

Lin leaned across and stroked his face with the back of her hand. 'Times are changing, Grandpa – the *world* is changing – and your beautiful island is being left behind. I have to do this; you know I do. *Please* don't be angry with me.'

He took her hand and kissed it, then shook his head. 'You know I can't be angry with you, but all the same' – he looked sternly at her and wagged his finger – 'you'll get yourself locked up. You know that, don't you?'

She grinned at him mischievously. 'Only if it's absolutely necessary.'

He shook his head and frowned, but I could see from his eyes that, whatever she said or did, he would always be inclined to indulge her.

We continued chatting over the meal. None of us mentioned the murder again and the atmosphere grew increasingly relaxed and sociable as we ate. Nonetheless, I still felt a little uncomfortable. Mr Lee was a nice old guy, but I still wondered what the payoff was. I'd clearly been invited here to meet him. What I couldn't grasp was why.

But I was soon to find out.

Two of the waitresses came across and began clearing the table and, as if on cue, Lin folded her napkin and stood up, smiling across at me reassuringly. Then she left and walked around the edge of the pool in the direction of the toilets. I watched her go. She was wearing combats pulled up above her waist and fastened with a wide brown belt. They should have been passion killers. They should have hidden her figure completely, but instead they exaggerated her small bottom and slender hips in a very appealing way. She looked good – all the way from her head down to her Doc Martens. I was impressed how the woman broke rules and mismatched her clothes so attractively.

Mr Lee watched me watching her and filled the moment with a

pleasant smile. I sat back in my chair, feeling anything but reassured.

The old waiter appeared again with three large glass goblets and a bottle of red wine, already uncorked, wrapped in a white serviette. He poured a few drops into Mr Lee's glass and the old man swirled the deep red liquid around, breathed in the aroma and then sipped a little, moving it around his mouth several times before swallowing. Finally he smiled at the waiter in approval and signalled to him to pour.

When he'd gone Mr Lee looked across with obvious satisfaction and turned the bottle around showing me the soiled and worn label. When I didn't react, he raised his eyebrows. 'You don't know much about wine, I see.' I smiled back uncertainly, shaking my head. He picked up the glass again, savouring the bouquet. 'Then, my dear, you are in for a very special treat. This is one of the last bottles of a 1978 Châteauneuf-du-Pape – it's from my personal stock and it is just about at its very best. I laid down two dozen bottles in the 1980s. Now, it is as perfect as wine can be.'

I inclined my head in his direction. 'You're very generous, Mr Lee.'

He smiled back. 'And you're very personable, Cameron.'

I held up my glass to him and took a sip. I'm a *vin ordinaire* fan myself – it's cheap and it does the trick. But I can tell quality when I taste it – and this outclassed anything I'd ever drunk in my life. Smooth and complex. So good that it caressed my mouth and made love to my throat on its way down.

Nineteen seventy-eight? My God, every mouthful must be worth a fortune. And he hardly knows me.

Mr Lee took another sip, held it in his mouth for a moment and then set his glass down. The smile slipping from his face.

'Cameron, I have an admission to make.' He looked at me for a moment, his eyes searching mine. 'I'm afraid that I have an ulterior motive in asking you here today.'

At last.

'It's to do with Charlie.'

He paused, gauging my reaction as he pulled a packet of cheroots out of his inside pocket. I met his gaze head-on and declined the offer of a smoke. He didn't look so upset any more and there was a steely look about his eyes.

'You won't be surprised to learn that I am a traditionalist. I believe in authority and I believe in law and order. I support the police in every way I can – they are the fabric that holds our society together.' He pulled a small gold lighter out of his pocket and lit up, exhaling a cloud of pale grey smoke out over the pond. 'You may not believe this, Cameron, but, rich though I am, I consider that there is more to business than simply making money. I have been a restaurateur for many years and made many good and loyal friends. Charlie Wilson was one of them.'

'And?'

'From what I understand, the police are operating at a disadvantage with this case and I feel that I should give them a little discreet help.'

I frowned.

'For a start, I know that they want to interview this so-called friend of Charlie's – "Aunt Emily", I believe she calls herself. But how are they going to find her? Lin has already told me how secretive these people can be. I understand you watched her desert the scene, so you'll know what I mean.' He leaned back in his chair and took another pull on his cheroot.

This is bizarre.

'But what about the preacher? Isn't he the prime suspect?'

He shrugged. 'I don't know him, but I understand from my sources that he may not be. We won't know for certain, of course, until they find the vehicle that killed Charlie. In the meantime, I understand that they are anxious to trace this Aunt Emily – and indeed, any other people who knew my friend. Any one of them might provide a vital clue.'

I must have looked uneasy, because Mr Lee leaned back in his chair and considered me for a moment.

'Cameron, you have to trust me on this. I have close friends in the police. I served on the Authority for some years. Without putting too fine a point on it, I know for certain that they are struggling with this one.'

'So you want to hire me. You want *me* to find Aunt Emily for them?' I was gobsmacked.

'Exactly.' He licked his lips and put the cigar down on the ashtray. 'The police can't possibly hire you, so I want to.'

I took another sip of wine. 'You obviously haven't spoken to the officer in charge of the case – she made it quite clear that she doesn't want the slightest interference.'

He smiled, giving nothing away. 'No, I'm not familiar with any of the CID case officers. My contacts are much higher up the chain of command.'

I shifted in my seat. I wasn't too sure whether I was comfortable with this. Being hired to do a job was one thing. Being hired by proxy – Jesus, I couldn't even get my head round that one.

'Cameron, please, do not look so sceptical. I am a rich man. Your fee means nothing to me, but my debt of honour to a friend means everything.' He regarded me intently for a moment. 'Forget what I said about the police, if that makes you uncomfortable. That is irrelevant in any case. My chief concern is to see the murderer – whoever he may be – brought to justice. And, to be sure of that, I need to make sure that the police are given every assistance in this matter.'

'But why me?'

He leaned back in his chair and picked up the cigar again. 'Because you have the kind of access which they can never have. You're a woman; you're gay. People who would run a mile from the police – or any other private eye – may talk to you. You can uncover things others cannot. I want you to find Aunt Emily, Cameron. I want you to find him and persuade him to talk to the police. They believe – and therefore, I believe – that he may have information that will help the case.'

I looked away. I still had Beano on my mind. I didn't know if I wanted to get involved with something else.

'Indulge me, please, young lady. I'm an old man. My friend's death has come as a big blow. I need your help.' He looked down sorrowfully and then sat back, taking another sip of wine, cupping the glass in his hand, waiting for my response.

I stared out across the restaurant. What he said made sense. People might talk to me. And, yes, I liked the idea of finding Aunt Emily. It was exactly the sort of work that I was good at.

The old man pulled a roll of notes out of his pocket and set them down in the centre of the table.

'I don't know what your fees are, Cameron, but here is one thousand pounds – enough, I imagine, to cover a few days' work. If you are the woman I think you are, then that will be more than enough. All I'm asking is that you make a few enquiries, find the man who is Aunt Emily and any other friends, and then get them to talk to the police. That's all.'

I hesitated.

'Cameron, I have known you for less than two hours, but I sense that we have a mutual respect. I can't think of anyone else whom I could trust with this.' He pushed the bundle of notes towards me. 'Please, take it. This is good work for you and the money means nothing to me. I'll pay all your expenses and your accommodation on top of the fee. You will also be doing Lin a favour. She doesn't show it so much, but I can tell that she is also distressed by all this.' His eyes softened again. 'You are a little fond of her, yes? I can see it in the way you look at each other.'

'Yeah, I guess I do like her. She's a nice woman.' I think I probably blushed. That wasn't a question a granddad should be asking. 'Excuse me for saying this, Mr Lee, but you seem very relaxed about Lin's sexuality.'

He sat back in his chair and laughed, suddenly relaxed again.

'Yes,' he nodded, 'I suppose I am. But, then, I've been through a lot of bad times in my life, Cameron – and so has Lin. It would be cruel of me to deny her happiness now, when she has finally found herself.'

Mr Lee picked up his cheroot and took a long pull. For all my unease earlier, I understood now why Lin had arranged the meeting. And, in all honesty, I was impressed with the man. Rich or not, he had a good sense of values. I liked him. I liked him a lot.

'So what do you say, young lady? Will you do it for me?'

I pulled a face; there would have to be conditions. 'I would need to do it my way. I would need your assurance that all confidences would be maintained. There are people out there who are very sensitive about their privacy.'

He inclined his head. 'But of course.'

I thought about Beano again. I needed to help her too. And £1,000, plus expenses – Jesus, that was more than two weeks' fees. It would keep me bankrolled while I found out who'd framed her.

'OK, Mr Lee, you got a deal.' I scooped the roll of notes up off the table and stuck them inside my jerkin.

He smiled and proffered his hand. When I took it, he held mine tightly for a moment and looked at me intensely.

'One more thing, Cameron.'

'Yes.'

'Since I am paying the bill, you must promise to keep me informed before anyone else. And I too expect total confidentiality. I wouldn't like the chief constable – or the media – to find out that I was helping the police from behind the scenes. I think it might just be a little embarrassing for my friends in the force.'

'Don't worry, Mr Lee,' I assured him. 'I understand the extreme delicacy of the situation. You can trust me completely. I'm a professional – and confidentiality comes as standard.'

Eleven

The old man didn't refer to our conversation once Lin returned. She eyed me quizzically for the rest of the time, then, when we took our leave, she stared at me expectantly all the way to the lift.

'Well?' she prompted as I pushed the button to take us down.

'Well what?'

Lin sighed impatiently. The lift shuddered to a halt and the doors opened into the lobby.

'Come on, Cameron, what did he say? Are you going to do it? Did you agree?'

I didn't say a word until we were back out in the drizzling rain again. Then, as she unfurled her umbrella, I stared at her reproachfully.

'What?' She looked baffled.

'You could have warned me.' I was teetering on the edge between playfulness and anger – I was pleased to be hired, but still irritated by the method.

She shrugged, as though it didn't matter, and lifted the umbrella over both our heads. 'Yeah, but, if I'd told you, you might not have come.'

'Maybe not,' I countered, 'but at least the choice would have been mine.'

She linked arms and pulled me to her, going all wide-eyed and playful. 'Yeah, but look what you'd have missed. That was his favourite wine, Cameron. He only has a few bottles left. He paid you an *enormous* compliment.'

I grunted. 'Mmm, well, maybe he did, but I still hate being manipulated.'

She raised her eyebrows at me. 'Well, you lied to me back in the bar!'

'Yeah, well, I was just doing my job, wasn't I? I gather evidence on people – if I went round telling everyone the God-honest truth, I'd never get anywhere.'

She shook her head in good humour and moved closer, so that our hips brushed as we walked. Drips fell off the umbrella and landed on our shoulders. I should have felt pleased at her forgiveness, and excited by her intimacy. But instead I felt sore and edgy.

Lin wasn't having any of it and pulled a stupid face at me. 'Aw, come on, Cameron, don't be such a drama queen! I didn't mean to deceive you. Look, I called round to see Grandpa last night before I went home. I'd no idea he knew Penny, but, as we talked, it soon became clear that his friend Charlie was the same person.'

I was implacable. 'You *still* should have warned me.'

'Yeah, I know that really. But Grandpa said not to. He wanted to talk to you one-to-one. He was worried that you already had a client and that you might not feel you could help him. You can't blame him for wanting to persuade you personally.'

I sighed heavily, my objections waning. 'No, well, maybe not.' Jesus, what did it matter anyway?

She stopped suddenly and turned to look at me. 'I would have rung you anyway, you know.' She looked down, blushing at her own candour. 'I enjoyed last night. I was worried that I might never see you again.'

I smiled in spite of myself – totally charmed by this unusual, unpredictable woman. 'Yeah, OK,' I conceded. 'Just don't do it again, that's all.'

She bit her lip and smiled right back, flirting openly and, for a moment or two, we stood there taking each other in. As she held me with her eyes, the last remnants of my crabbiness dissolved in the rain. There was something so good about her, a radiance that shone out from her face. A strength that seemed to come from deep inside.

Well, something like that. Anyway, I envied her. She seemed to know who she was, and what she wanted to do. It must be good to be so sure about your life, to be so content with who you are.

She put her arm through mine again and pulled me along, down the street past the big arch and round the corner. 'So come on, then, gumshoe, tell me what he said.'

'Apparently everyone wants to find Aunt Emily.'

'Yeah, I know *that*. What else?'

I shrugged. 'Not much. Your grandfather seems to think that I have a better chance of finding Aunt Emily than the cops.'

'He's right, you do.' She pulled me a little closer, smiling mischievously. 'Especially if I help you.'

I stopped in my tracks and pulled free of her. 'Hey, just hang on a minute. Something tells me that Grandpa wouldn't want you mixed up in this. You've already said that he worries about you.'

She tipped her head and dropped the umbrella back behind her shoulders, just like in those old Hollywood movies. 'Yeah, you're probably right – but so what? I live my own life. If I want to help you, then I will. Anyway, I'm not likely to get into any real danger, now, am I? All we're doing is looking for poor old Emily – and she wouldn't hurt a soul!'

I closed my eyes and sighed. I'm not too good at sharing my work, especially with the granddaughter of a client, specially with someone I like a lot. It's a sure-fire recipe for disaster – and this was one promising relationship that I didn't want to mess up.

When I opened my eyes again, Lin was striding purposefully towards the main road. I caught up with her standing at the traffic lights, waiting to cross. She turned and threw me an impish look, then moved closer and held the umbrella over both of us again.

'Y'know, this could be a tough one, Cameron,' she opined. 'Aunt Emily must be scared silly right now – she might not surface again for years.'

'Yeah, I guess.' I shrugged. 'Still, lots of people must know the guy. I'll find him, all right.'

'*We*, Cameron.' She turned and held my eyes for a moment '*We'll* find him.'

I smiled sneakily and cocked my head. '*Him?*'

She coloured up, embarrassed by the slip. '*Her.* I mean *her*. See, you've even got *me* doing it now!'

I laughed, making the most of such a small but significant victory, pulling her back from the kerb as a passing bus spattered water across the pavement.

'Why the hell would you want to help me, anyway? I'm getting paid for it. You aren't.'

She shrugged and leaned towards me, serious now. 'I like you, Cameron. Isn't that enough?'

The lights changed and the traffic stopped. We stepped off the kerb and crossed the road in a scrum of other people, dodging the oncoming umbrellas. Lin was great for my ego but, all the same, I wasn't too easy about her motives. For all I knew Grandpa might have asked her to keep tabs on me. Maybe she even wanted to *stop* me finding Aunt Emily. Maybe they were bosom buddies.

When we reached the other side Lin turned sharp left and headed towards Sackville Street. Quite suddenly, I realised I was being led.

'Hey, where the hell are we going?' I demanded, catching her arm.

She looked at me as if I was thick or something. 'The taxi office, of course! Isn't it obvious?' I screwed up my eyes at her. 'Look, Aunt Emily never used her car. She used to come and go in a taxi every week. If we want to find out where she came from, that's the most obvious place to start, isn't it?' She glanced at me out of the corner of her eye and smiled sneakily, as if *she* had got one over on *me* this time.

I sighed and tried to pass it off. 'Yeah, OK, smartarse, that's where I would have started if I hadn't been so damn busy trying to fend you off.'

She laughed in my face and tweaked my nose. 'Yeah, I bet!'

Jesus.

The offices of Lavender Taxis were tucked away round the corner in Richmond Street, on the first floor of an old building, a few doors up from the back of the Bridge Inn. When we reached the top of the dingy staircase and pushed open the door, the guy behind the counter looked up briefly from his phone conversation, then turned away and carried on talking. As I leaned against the doorjamb and waited, dripping all over the floor, Lin took the only chair available and played with the Velcro on her umbrella. As in most taxi offices, the surroundings were neither comfortable nor appetising, but at this time of day they were at least quiet. By midnight there'd be a queue outside that would last through until the early hours.

It was only minutes before the guy put the phone down and got up, looking like someone pissed off by life in general and us in particular. I nudged Lin and nodded towards him. She smiled weakly and bit her lip. 'You do it,' she mouthed.

I eyed her caustically.

'You want a cab?' The voice was deep and rich. The guy was like someone you might find in any taxi office in any city in the world – hacked off, and cynical. Except, in this case, he was almost certainly gay. He was also very big and muscular. I weight-train a little myself, so I appreciate a well-honed body – even if it is on a man.

'Hi.' I smiled, real friendly. Private eyes have one big disadvantage when it comes to investigation: nobody *has* to tell us anything, so we need to rely on whatever skills we can muster at the time. Sometimes it's threats or blackmail that gets the goods; sometimes it's being pushy or pathetic. Right now I thought of Mr Lee's comment. Today I was being personable.

'Yeah, I'd like your help,' I began, handing my card across. 'I'm trying to trace someone. A man – a tranny. You might know as him as Aunt Emily. I need to talk to him – her – in confidence.'

His face hardly changed. 'This somethin' to do with the dead transvestite?'

'Yeah, sort of. Aunt Emily was with him just before he was killed.'

His eyes didn't move, but he shook his head slowly and pushed the card back across the counter, as if he wasn't even going to run it through his brain. I left it there, and tried again, this time describing what Aunt Emily was wearing. Lin joined me, chipping in from time to time with some of the detail. The big guy shook his head as if he'd never met anyone in his whole life.

'So you won't help,' I said, personable melting into slightly stroppy.

He looked at me very directly and shook his head.

'Can I ask you why not?'

He pulled himself up to his full height and glared straight back. 'We're a gay taxi company, sweetheart, that's why. I'm telling you exactly what I told the fuzz. We respect our customers' privacy; we don't keep records.'

'Or memories?'

He wrinkled his nose at me. 'Look, babe, we get a lotta people in our cabs every night. Our drivers don't even notice who they're driving most the time. Anyways, who said he took a cab?'

'My friend here knew him.' I nodded at Lin. 'He took a cab every week, believe me.'

The man looked at me as though I were a fly that he was dying to swat.

I eyeballed him for a moment, then tried again. 'Look, I'm not about to out the guy or anything. Whatever you tell me will be treated in confidence.'

He turned his back and walked over to the desk and sat down, picking up a copy of the *Sun* and burying his head in it. I waited. After a few moments, he swung lazily round in his chair.

'OK, I'll talk to the drivers when they come in Monday night.'

'Thanks, I appreciate it. You'll ring me if you find anything out?'

He shrugged. 'Sure thing.'

Yeah, sure thing. He wasn't going to lift a finger and we both knew it.

I turned to go, but Lin was leaning over the counter, almost shouting at him.

'How dare you?' she shrieked, banging the counter with the flat of her hand. 'One of *our* people has been murdered, and you just shake your head and act like it doesn't matter!'

The Big Man looked up unconcerned. 'I can't do any more than ask my drivers, sweetheart,' he drawled, then turned back to his newspaper.

I pulled Lin out of the door and down the stairs. We stopped just inside the doorway and she slumped against the wall, fuming.

'Can you believe that guy?'

I shook my head at her. 'Look, just wise up, will you?' This was exactly why I preferred to work alone. 'You think people are going to hand us this on a plate? You think that all we have to do is ask, and someone will lead us straight to Aunt Emily's door?'

She stared at me wild-eyed. 'But he's got no bloody intention of asking his drivers, Cameron. You could see that by his face.'

I breathed in deeply. 'Yeah, I know, but screaming at the guy isn't going to alter a thing. You have to rely on goodwill in this job. If you can't get information one way, then you have to try to get it in another.'

She stared back at me resentfully, fidgeting with her bag. 'Oh, yeah, and how might you manage that?'

'You might manage it by talking to the drivers yourself, one by one. Here's some of Grandpa's money. If you really want to help, take a few taxis, ask a few questions; if you work hard and you have just a little luck, you might just get somewhere.'

She swallowed hard. 'Me?'

'Yeah, you. It was your idea, so you can follow it through.' I grinned smugly. 'Remember? You insisted on helping.'

She looked out of the door into the rain and opened her mouth to protest. When I stared back at her she grunted disdainfully and turned away again.

I smiled to myself and pulled out my notebook, flicking through the pages until I found the address that I'd copied off the preacher's leaflet.

'And what about you?' she asked petulantly. 'What are you gonna do while I'm traipsing all over Manchester?'

'Me?' I retorted. 'Well, while you're conducting *your* investigation, Miss Lee, I am going to church.'

Twelve

Church of the One God.

It sounded impressive, as if it might be a big imposing building with stained-glass windows and flying buttresses. But, in reality, it was little more than a shack, squeezed into a gap in a terrace of houses. A dull single-storey affair built of wood with rusty, corrugated roofing and a single three-paned window at the front. The middle sheet of glass had been clumsily replaced by a rough sheet of chipboard, which was swelling in the damp air. And the boards on the front of the building, once a deep maroon, were turning mossy green as nature began to reclaim her own.

I pulled my collar up against the incessant drizzle and rubbed a circle of grime off the bottom pane of glass. Inside, a dull brass cross stood on a bare table at the far end. A few chairs littered the floor, some upright, some lying on their sides. The room looked dirty and little used, except for a bunch of bright yellow carnations in a vase next to the cross, splashing unexpected colour among the dirt.

A sign pinned to the door and protected by an old opaque polythene bag confirmed that this was the preacher's 'church', but there were no service times, no contact phone numbers. Round the back was no different: another decrepit door and a small yard, but no sign of life.

I was looking up and down the cobbled alleyway, wondering what to do next, when I noticed the curtains twitch in the house to one side. Too good an opportunity to miss. So I wiped the rain from my hair and knocked on the door.

The old woman who answered had the slightly vacant look of someone who has lived alone for a long time. She eyed me nervously, peering through the gap, chewing on her gums.

'I'm sorry to bother you.' I flashed my driving licence at her, just long enough so that she could see my photo, then withdrew it before she had a chance to read anything. 'I'm from the council – Environmental Health. I was supposed to meet a lady here this morning.' I scratched my head and tried to look lost. 'It's a vermin problem. I've, erm, come along to lay some poison. Only she hasn't turned up and I really need to get on with the job. These things have a habit of getting out of hand if they're not tackled straightaway...'

She leaned forward and opened the door a little wider, forgetting her initial nervousness. 'Vermin? What kind of vermin?' she asked, chewing faster. 'You mean mice?'

I hesitated and wiped the drips away from my forehead. 'Well, I'm not sure. Could be mice – or even, well, rats.'

She brought her hand to her mouth and looked at me with big fish eyes.

I sighed dramatically and looked around in despair. 'Look, you don't know where the key holder lives, do you? Only stupidly I forgot the file. I'll get hell if I go back without doing the job.'

She opened the door completely now and shook her head sympathetically. 'Eeh, ah'm sorry, love; ah can't help! They were here durin' t'night, both of 'em. Bur ah doubt you'll find 'em 'ome now.'

I feigned surprise and wiped the rain from my face. She beckoned me into the shelter of the doorway and whispered theatrically into my ear.

'They've bin arrested, duck. Bobbies came in t'middle o' t'night and found 'em inside. Woke me up with all t'bangin' and shoutin', they did. Took 'em both off, they did. I heard it were sommat to do wi' t'murder down in t'town, in that gay village place. Y'know, one weer t'nancies go.'

'Really?' I looked back at her wide-eyed.

She nodded sagely and leaned closer. 'Oh aye. Ah've nowt against 'em, mind. T'nancies, ah mean – they can go do what they like, long as it don't hurt others. But that so-called *minister*...' She shook her head sagely. 'Well, if you ask me, he's a bit... well...' She tapped a finger against her temple and pulled a face at me. 'Ah think that t'bobbies think he did it, an' personally ah wouldn't be surprised. He's a right funny bugger, that one! And that poor wife... ee, ah don't know how she copes...'

'They don't live on this street, then?'

She laughed. 'Ooh no, bless you, duck. They're far too posh. They live miles away, up on t'Park Estate – Duke's Road, ah think. One of them big old Victorian jobbies, I 'eard.'

I smiled gratefully. 'Well thanks, er...?'

'Marjorie.'

'Thanks, Marjorie, that's a big help. You might have just saved my bacon. I'll nip up there now. Maybe they've let them go.'

'Ee, well, ah 'ope so, duck. He deserves all he gets, that one, bur ah feel right sorry for her. She ollus seemed such a nice sort. Friendly, ollus ready to pass t'time o' t'day. Poor thing, she were ollus trailin' round after him, and he'd ollus be goin' on at her.' She clicked her tongue sympathetically. 'And now she's got bloomin' rats to contend wi' an' all.'

Duke's Road was just as Marjorie had described it, and, though she hadn't known the number, the exact location wasn't hard to find. Five men and a couple of woman were standing around by the gateway, looking wet and miserable in their sodden waterproofs. They came to life as soon as they saw I was heading for the house and began firing questions about the preacher and his wife. I looked straight through them and hurried on up the potholed driveway, thankful that they were at least respecting the boundary. Reporters. Everybody was one step ahead of me today.

The dirty redbrick house stood out like a sore thumb in the neat, middle-class street. The neighbouring properties stood comfortably in well-tended gardens. This one rose three floors up above a jungle of dead vegetation. The windows were clean and the house looked lived in, but the black paintwork and the damp confusion of the garden lent it a bleakness that would be depressing in any weather. I wondered whether the preacher ever let sunlight into his life. I wondered whether he ever stopped ranting about God and virtue long enough to understand the value of living.

The main door was set at the side of the house, up a half-dozen moss-encrusted steps. I pushed the bell, wondering whether she would be at home – and, if she was, what my chances might be. The noise rattled around the hall but the only response was from the sparrows, squabbling in the tree next to the drive. That and the insistent ticking of an old clock just beyond the door.

I stepped back a little as water from a leaking gutter dripped onto my head, then rang the bell again, for a little longer this time. Down the driveway, the reporters were watching me, stamping their feet on the pavement. They would have been trying to talk to her all day. No wonder she wasn't answering.

I hammered on the door with my fist this time. I wasn't going to go away without some kind of an answer. A moment later there was a shuffling; the door opened slightly on the safety chain and the blue rinse appeared fleetingly in the gap.

'Go away!' she shouted crabbily. 'I've told you – I've nothing to say.'

I stepped back under the drip and held the door, stopping her from closing it.

'Please, I'm not a reporter. I want to help.'

She stopped pushing and one suspicious, bloodshot eye below it appeared above a down-turned mouth.

'I'm a private detective. I think I can help.'

The eyes studied me suspiciously for a moment. A large drip fell down my collar and a shiver down my spine. The door began to shut again.

'I might be able to help the minister.'

The gap opened again and she fixed me with her eye. I pushed a card through and she took it. 'We met last night, by the bridge. You gave me a leaflet, remember?'

She took the card and read it. Her lips twitched, then the woman closed the door, slipped the chain and let me in.

She eyed me suspiciously as she led me through a dingy hallway into a room at the front of the house. I blinked as I entered, adjusting to the gloom of a large lounge, taking in the faded brown velvet curtains, which were almost drawn across the big windows. It felt as if she were in mourning.

The woman switched on an antique table lamp and invited me to sit down on a battered Chesterfield, then she stood looking expectantly at me, her back to an ornate wooden fire surround, fidgeting with her pearl necklace, clearly distraught. She was still wearing the same outfit as yesterday; her hair was untidy and her makeup faded. She looked as though she hadn't slept.

'You said you could help.' She eyed me uncertainly.

'I hope I can. I'm a private detective. I've been hired to find a friend of the deceased, someone who might help prove your husband's innocence.'

She nodded vacantly, as if she hadn't really been listening.

'When did they arrest your husband?' I asked, as kindly as I could.

'Early this morning.' Her voice was cracked and throaty. 'In the church. We'd been there all night. We were praying for him. They took his car.'

She turned suddenly and sat down in a high-backed wing chair, her head in her hands.

'You were praying for the dead man?'

She looked up, dry-eyed and weary. 'Yes, for *Charlie*.' She bit her lip. 'My husband was seeking repentance for the terrible things he said – but we didn't know that Charlie was dead, not until the police came.'

There was something about the way she said the name. With warmth, and pain, and affection too. I looked across at the drawn curtains and my mind went back to the night before. The scene in the street. The argument between Charlie, the preacher and herself.

'Look, I'm sorry to intrude, Mrs...'

'Winterton, Dorry Winterton. Call me Dorry.' She dabbed her eyes with a small cotton hanky, then sat up straight again, looking at me wide-eyed. 'How can you prove that you're not one of those reporters?'

'I can't,' I admitted, 'but you saw me yourself in the village last night. I was following Mr Wilson. I was working for his wife – she suspected that he was having an affair.'

'Oh!' she grunted cynically, obviously believing me now. 'Oh, another one.'

'I'm sorry...?'

She waved her hand in the air. 'It's no matter. Forgive my rudeness – I feel, like, besieged. First the police, now the press. They keep on ringing the doorbell; I don't know what to do.'

I took off my sodden leather jerkin and laid it down on the settee. 'You knew Mr Wilson?' I asked.

'Charlie? Yes.' Her voice caught in her throat as she attempted a sad smile. 'Maybe this is my punishment. I've lost a good friend – and now my husband is accused of his murder. I—' She stopped suddenly. 'You said that you could help. How?'

'Someone else was with him last night just before he was killed – another cross-dresser. If I can find him, then there is a chance he may have seen something that could help the police.' I saw the hope rise up in her eyes. 'I can't make any promises, Dorry, but if I can find this friend, it might just help.'

She swallowed hard. 'Oh, I do hope so. But why...?'

'I'm working for an old friend of Charlie's. He doesn't believe that your husband was responsible, either. He's asked me to try to help. I can't tell you who he is, but I can tell you that he is very anxious that I find out the truth.'

She nodded and glanced down at my card. 'Well, whoever it is, I'm grateful. I'm at the end of my tether with worry.'

'I'd like to ask you a few questions. Is that all right?'

She smiled at me wearily and shrugged. 'Ask me whatever you wish, Miss...'

'McGill – but call me Cameron.'

'Ask me whatever you want, Cameron – I've got nothing to lose, have I?'

'How long did you know Mr Wilson?'

She screwed the handkerchief up in her hands. 'About two years.' She looked down momentarily. 'I expect you think I'm a terrible hypocrite, after what I said to you on the bridge.'

It had occurred to me. But this was hardly the time to go into that. 'I saw you arguing with your husband in the street last night. Was that over Mr Wilson?'

She laughed. Counsellors call it a coffin laugh. There's no humour, only pain and sadness.

'Ernest was convinced that I was having an affair with Charlie; and, even worse, he was disgusted that I should do it with a man who wears women's clothing. Uh, someone who was "possessed by the Devil", he said.' She paused and shook her head gently. 'The truth is, once I got to know Charlie, I saw nothing wrong with it. I liked him – as a man, anyway. He had a kind of sweetness that made me feel good. And, despite what Ernest thinks, there never was any kind of sexual involvement.'

She looked away and swallowed hard again, fighting the tears. 'Charlie was safe, nice to be with. It's Ernest, my husband, who's the problem. It's hard, coping with someone like him – someone you once loved for their good humour and companionship.'

She looked away, staring out through the gap in the curtains. I waited patiently for a minute or more. When she turned back, her voice was still shaky, but her eyes were clearer.

'Do you know, I feel almost relieved that he's been locked away. Isn't that terrible?'

'Maybe not so terrible. I heard what he said to you; I saw how he treated you.'

She shook her head. 'It's not his fault. He's a good man, you must believe that. He's worked hard for the church. Next month is our fortieth anniversary. We married just after he got his first ministry. A little village near Lancaster. The church was empty the first Sunday but, together, we built a thriving congregation.' She paused, smiling wanly. 'It's been a good partnership. He used to be so popular as well. He was the sort of man who seemed to understand everyone.'

'When did he become ill?'

She shook her head and her eyes filled with tears. 'He was accused of a terrible thing – about five years ago, when we were in the Wirral. It involved...' She stared away helplessly for a moment and took a deep breath. 'It involved... children. He was innocent, of course – the case was never even brought to court. But the press said a lot of wicked things about him – and poor Ernest had a breakdown. He never really recovered.' She looked down at her hands, twisting and pulling on the handkerchief. 'And now he's been accused again. Well, I don't know how he'll bear it. Dear God, I don't know how *I* can bear it.'

A tear gathered on her lower eyelid and then trickled down her cheek and onto her chin. I knelt down by her side and took her hand, wiping the wetness away with a tissue, thinking of my mother, all those years ago. I'd always hated her. I thought she'd hated me. No one ever told me that she had Alzheimer's. I'd never realised it until a few months before she died.

I squeezed her hands. 'You've stayed by him through it all, Dorry. You should be proud of that.'

She sniffed hard. 'I couldn't desert him. I know he's ill and I know he's not going to get better.' She stopped and looked me in the eye. 'I also know that what he preaches isn't really right, but it makes him happy, it gives him some purpose in life. You can call me an hypocrite if you like, but it's all he has. What else can I do?'

I nodded to show that I understood, but I avoided replying. It wasn't the time or place to make judgements. 'Do you mind me asking, how did you meet Charlie?'

She smiled ironically. 'Strangely enough, it was through Ernest. He was holding Bible classes. He gave free counselling to people with all sorts of problems. He wasn't as ill then, but he genuinely believed that he could help cure people like Charlie.'

'But you didn't?'

She shook her head. 'I did at the time. But Charlie taught me so much. I always met him as a man, but I came to understand his needs and I liked him for who he was. We would meet on an evening in the park, in a pub – anywhere, really. We never had – you know – an affair. I don't think Charlie wanted anything like that. I suppose that was one of the things that drew me to him. Anyway, we became close friends. He was nicer than any man I've ever known. And he liked doing a lot of the things we women like so much, like gossiping, or window shopping. In the end it was I who was converted, not Charlie. I think my husband knew that, and – of course – it made him deeply angry.'

'Did Charlie ever mention a friend called Aunt Emily?'

She looked back at me blankly and shook her head. 'No, I'm sorry. I don't know the name.'

Damn.

'Did he ever talk about any of his cross-dressing friends?'

'No, I'm sorry, Cameron. We talked about his needs, but we didn't discuss his other life. I think Charlie understood and kept off the subject.'

'OK, what about other friends?'

She thought for a moment. 'No, I don't remember him ever talking about anyone. He was a very private person. I got the impression that he didn't have many friends. Oh, he recommended a solicitor once. I was thinking of drawing up a new will, in view of my husband's illness, you see. Charlie offered to make an appointment for me.'

My eyes lit up. 'Can you remember his name?' I asked, eagerly.

She shook her head. 'No, we never got that far.'

'So he never made the appointment for you?'

'No, there was no point. It was a kind enough thought, but the man's office was miles away. I don't drive, so it was very impractical. I used a local solicitor instead.'

'Miles away? Where exactly?' My spirits sank; I felt like I was grasping at straws.

She stopped and thought. 'It was fairly near to the city... No, I'm sorry...'

I gave up on that particular line of enquiry. 'Was there anyone else that Charlie mentioned? Please think very carefully, Dorry – it's really important.'

She paused for a moment or two. 'No, sorry dear, no one. I'm not being much help, am I?'

'You're OK, you're doing fine.'

I let go of her hands and sat back on the leather settee. 'Did you tell the police about your friendship with Charles?'

She shook her head. 'I didn't have to: they knew already. His wife told them that we'd been having an affair.'

'His wife? Elaine? You mean she knew about you?'

She laughed at my surprise. 'You think you were the first private detective she hired? Oh, no. I'm sorry, my dear, but she's had him followed before – you get to know the signs, you know. She knew all about our friendship, all right. But she couldn't prove anything sexual, because there wasn't anything.'

'She'd had him followed *before*, you say?'

She shrugged. 'Mmm, off and on for... well, two months, I suppose. We noticed a man in a car following us the first time. I was really angry, but Charles was so good-natured that he just took it all in his stride.'

'So you think his wife knew about his cross-dressing as well?'

She looked me straight in the eyes. 'Oh, I'm certain she knew about that. How could she not?'

'So she hired more than one person?'

'Oh, yes, two or three. Charlie and I made a joke of it. "Spot the stalker", we called it.' She turned away and brought the handkerchief up to her mouth. 'He knew very well that Elaine wanted a divorce, but he didn't. So he just put up with it. I suppose he hoped that she'd eventually see that he was faithful and then he would win her round.'

I shook my head in disbelief – amazed by Elaine Wilson's deceit.

'And your husband – you say that you were with him last night. What time did he come home?'

'About eleven o'clock. He'd been wandering – he does that when he's angry. He drives off to some desolate spot on the moors and walks, raging at the sky as he goes. Then, when he's spent all his anger, he comes back to me full of remorse and I take care of him. That's why we went to the church – to ask forgiveness.' She looked up at me, her eyes wide with dismay. 'The police told me that the murder happened around eight thirty last night. He has no alibi. He can't even remember where he was.'

'Has he got a solicitor?'

'Yes, our family lawyer. He's with him now.'

'And your husband's car?'

'The police have that as well. They won't find anything there because he didn't do it. What worries me sick is that it won't make any difference. It's just so... ridiculous!'

I made all the right noises. About finding the vehicle that really did kill Charlie, about paint fragments, fingerprints and other forensic evidence. I didn't say so, but I knew from personal experience that the cops sometimes got it badly wrong. I also remembered her husband's abusive behaviour and the violence that I'd so innocently recorded on my video-cam.

Dorry looked across at me and nodded sadly. There was nothing more that I could say.

Outside, the rain had stopped but the mist was setting in and darkness was falling. My spirits sank as she closed the door behind me. The conversation had been mildly informative, but I had no more idea of Aunt Emily's identity than I had before.

As I threaded my way back through the suburbs I went through the conversation over and over again, trying to find the spark of a lead. Something I'd missed, maybe. Anything. By the time I reached the Overnite Inn and parked the car, I still hadn't found a thing.

Except...

There was one question that kept gnawing at the edges of my brain. A question that had nothing at all to with finding Aunt Emily.

If Elaine had known all along about her husband's cross-dressing, if she'd already known about his friendship with Dorry for the last two months, then why had she hired me?

And, more to the point, why had she lied?

Thirteen

When I left Dorry's house, I went back to the hotel to dry out. I was anxious to talk to the dead man's sister at the house in West Didsbury, but I hadn't been into my office for a couple of days, so I needed to check out my answering machine. I'd been putting this off all day and now I didn't dare leave it any longer. When you work for yourself, you either get back to clients or lose them.

There were four calls. A Mrs Courtney-Jones wanted some "help with a matrimonial matter". She'd been referred by one of Becky's colleagues and wondered if I could take the job on straightaway. A debt-collection agency that I did occasional work for wanted me to trace a missing debtor for them. A corporate client wanted me to check out a competitor. And my landlord wanted to talk to me about the leak in the roof. It was just past five and I managed to get back to all three within ten minutes. I agreed to pay my landlord a contribution to the repairs; I persuaded the debt-collection people and the corporate client to wait for a few days; and, very politely, I told Mrs Courtney-Jones to go and get lost.

From now on, I wasn't doing matrimonials. I'd rather starve.

As I drove back up the ramp out of the riverside multistorey, I thought about Lin and smiled. It was a lousy job trailing round talking to taxi drivers, especially in the rain. But she was right. If she could get a lead from one of them, then we were probably home and dry. I hadn't said so at the time, but Lin's thinking had really impressed me. Maybe she was going to be a help after all. As I drove out towards

Stretford I crossed my fingers and hoped. I'd give her a ring and see how she was getting on – just as soon as I'd seen Hannah.

Thinking of Beano's partner made me wonder again about Mazza Taylor. From Beano's account, it sounded as if there was a high-powered drug dealer involved. Someone with real muscle and the power to scare the hell out of the punters. It occurred to me again that, if I was going to help Beano, then I needed to get to the guy who was threatening Taylor. There didn't seem to be any other way.

I put the thoughts aside as I turned off the main road at the edge of Stretford and worked my way through the streets of terraced houses until I found Burley Street. It was nearly six by now and cars were lined up along both sides of the narrow road. I found the last space in the next street, and walked back, scanning the dismal lines of two-up/two-downs for Number 42.

Hannah's house was on the opposite side, halfway along.

She had to be a remarkable woman, this Hannah. Beano was someone who just didn't have serious relationships. In the eighteen months I'd known her, she'd always displayed a cavalier attitude to other women, the sort of casual just-for-fun approach that waves a big red flag at any hint of involvement. It was almost misogynistic sometimes, and it was the one thing about her that I'd never been easy with. And now she'd fallen in love. And, like many others before her, my strong, self-sufficient friend had suddenly stopped thinking and let her emotions do the talking.

The lights were on in the house, so I rang the bell and waited. Unlike many of the others, it looked well cared for, cherished even. The front door was freshly painted in a deep red colour that reflected patches of yellow street light. On the sill, a matching window box still overflowed with white nemesia and slightly weary red geraniums, bringing a little faded colour to the hardness of the street. Poor Beano, poor Hannah, they'd probably stretched their finances to the limit buying this. I wondered how the hell they were going to keep up with the mortgage now.

I was about to ring the bell a second time when I heard them: the little girl's voice ringing through the house; her mother's heavier footsteps on the stairs. When the door opened on its security chain, two faces peered at me from different levels, the smaller one wide-eyed and curious.

'Hi, I'm a friend of Beano's,' I began, trying to sound as reassuring as possible. The woman looked at me askance. 'She asked me to look you up, make sure you were OK.'

Hannah blinked, narrowing her eyes.

'Cameron, Cameron McGill, from York.'

She relaxed a little but still nodded uncertainly. She shut the door, removed the chain and then opened it properly, studying me carefully.

She was older than Beano, around forty. A big woman with a presence that had an attractiveness all of its own. Her hair was long – a faded amber that suggested it had once been bright and fiery. She looked at ease with herself, kind of natural and, though she was neatly dressed, there was something slightly dishevelled about her that appealed to me a lot. She had a round friendly face, a weathered complexion and an appealing lack of pretence. A little old-fashioned too in her long patchwork skirt and big warm jumper. I could already see why Beano would be so taken with her.

'Oh, I'm sorry,' I said, digging in my pocket to find Beano's note. 'She wrote you this.'

She read the brief note and dropped her arms to her side, smiling broadly now. 'It's lovely to meet you, Cameron. I'm sorry to be so rude.' She stepped back, mocking herself. 'I'm just a little paranoid about visitors.'

The little girl appeared from behind her legs, clutching her mother's skirt. For a moment she looked up at me, self-assured, almost grown-up, standing in her red dressing gown, chewing on her lip. But then her courage failed and she buried her head into her mother's skirt.

I smiled back. 'You're quite right to be careful.'

I followed the two of them through the lounge into the back

room, then Hannah turned and studied me in the light. 'Mmm, I remember your face from the photograph now. You look just as nice in real life.'

I glanced down at my damp leather jerkin and creased black jeans, slightly embarrassed. 'I'm flattered.'

'You should be.' She smiled – a clean open smile that put me instantly at ease. 'Beano talks about you a lot. I feel like I've known you for ages.' She looked down at her daughter, who was listening to every word, and continued cautiously. 'You've... er, seen her today, then? Is she all right?'

'Yes, she's...' – I shrugged – 'well, coping.'

She shuffled a little self-consciously and then, when she noticed her daughter tugging at her, she smiled again. 'Oh, and this energetic little person is Susie. Say hello to Cameron, Susie.'

The little girl froze and stared at me shyly, edging in towards her mother's side again, fiddling with her dressing gown belt. 'Hello, Cameron.'

It was a good twenty minutes before we got to talk. Hannah made me a drink, hung my sad, damp jacket on a coat hanger, and then finished getting Susie's tea ready. I sat on the settee in the small, neat back room, sipping the coffee. The *Evening Post* lay discarded on the side, so I picked it up.

The headline almost covered the whole front page: HATE KILLING SHOCKS GAY VILLAGE. Though the picture next to it was poor and out of focus, it was, without doubt, Charles Wilson – seated at a table in his restaurant.

Police are treating last night's vicious hit-and-run incident in Manchester's gay village as murder. Manchester restaurateur Charles Wilson was leaving a transvestite bar when he was deliberately killed, they say, by the driver of an unidentified vehicle. Police are currently interviewing a retired vicar who is believed to be an acquaintance of the victim, but both they and the man's wife remain tight-lipped about the situation.

Charles Wilson was a well-regarded member of the local community and a part-owner of the newly opened Chow City bar/restaurant in the city centre.

Neighbours said they were shocked by the news of his murder. His wife Elaine was too ill to give interviews but, in a statement, a friend said that she was distraught and still hadn't come to terms with either the suddenness or the manner of her husband's death. They had only been married three years, he told reporters, and she was finding the situation 'very difficult'.

At a press conference early this afternoon, a police spokeswoman confirmed that they were treating the death as murder but would not comment on a possible suspect. However, they appealed to the public to come forward with any information they might have on the vehicle involved or Mr Wilson's movement's.

They are particularly anxious to interview the man who was with him a few minutes before the incident so that they can eliminate him from their enquiries. They would also like to interview anyone else who was in Chloë's Bar in the hour before the murder. They promise complete confidentiality to any witnesses who may come forward.

Asked about the likelihood of further incidents, the spokeswoman said that, like everyone else, the gay and transgender community should always take care over personal security. It was accepted that the level of assaults had increased in the gay village recently and that this was not acceptable. Extra police would be drafted into the area from today as an extra precaution. She insisted that the investigation was proceeding well, but she wouldn't confirm whether or not the man being held for questioning would be charged.

Hannah appeared through the kitchen door with Rosie and a plate of scrambled eggs and toast.

'Come on, Susie, you can eat your tea in the front room while you watch television.'

The little girl pulled a face as she looked across at me, no longer shy. 'Aw, Mummy, do I have to? Can't I stay in here with you and Cameron. *Purleeezze?*'

Mother raised her eyebrows at me, impressed. Eating in front of the television was obviously a privilege and I was honoured that she'd rather be here.

'No, young lady, Cameron and I have grown-up things to talk about.'

Susie hesitated, standing on one leg and pulling an awful face.

'Cam-er-on...?'

'Yes?'

'Will Auntie Beano be coming home soon? She's been away *ages* and she *said* she was going to take us to Blackpool.'

I looked up at her mother, who shook her head almost imperceptibly.

'Not for a while, Susie. She's really busy, I'm afraid, but she sends her love and says she'll get back as soon as she can.' I looked up at Hannah, hoping that I'd said the right thing.

Hannah smiled back, grateful for the big white lie.

'Come on, young lady,' she said, ushering the little girl through the door again. 'You can watch the cartoons as long as you promise to be good and let Cameron and Mummy talk.' Susie hovered in the doorway, looking at me and considering the deal. In the end, the cartoons won.

I picked up the paper again and thumbed through the pages. There were several background articles to the killing, including a summary of the 'politically motivated' skinhead attacks on gay men in the village over the last few months. There had been seven, it said, ranging from a barracking of a man in Sackville Street to the hospitalising of another in one of the backstreets about two weeks ago. It speculated that the police still hadn't ruled out a connection and that they wanted to interview four men in their twenties. Then there was a brief description, which could have applied to thousands of men in a city like this. My immediate question was whether similarities existed between earlier abuses and this killing – and neither the police nor the paper seemed to be making any comment on that.

Another article explored the more sensational elements of the case and I skipped that and discarded the paper just as Hannah came back through the door.

'You've been reading about the murder.' She was shaking her head in dismay. 'I'm so tired of all this violence, Cameron. Beano said that it was getting bad in the village these days. I just thought she was exaggerating – as usual.'

She closed her eyes and let her head drop. I stood up and pulled a tissue from the box on the coffee table and handed it to her. I wasn't going to tell her about my involvement – the woman had enough of her own problems.

'I'm sorry.' She dabbed her eyes and looked up again, her face flushed with anxiety. I can't say much when Susie's around, but I'm *really* worried about Beano.'

'Yeah, me too.'

'We were getting on so well!' She bit her lip and stared tearfully up at the ceiling. 'It was just *so* good. For the first time in Susie's life, she had a family – a proper family. Like I always wanted for her. Now...' She shook her head in despair, trying to compose herself. 'Now I don't know what's going to happen. Beano could be in there for years. I don't know how she'll survive, locked up like that.'

'That's just what I was thinking. She's like a wild animal – put her in a cage and she'll fade away. She needs space and freedom like most people need air.'

Hannah smiled sadly and we both sat down on the settee. 'Thank you, Cameron. Thank you for understanding. I'm at my wit's end.' She sighed wearily. 'I just don't know what to do. When I saw her yesterday, she just kept on telling me that everything would be all right – but I know it won't be. She's just trying to make me feel better. I'm certain that she's innocent. She's got more sense than to hurt someone like that. My ex-husband is a bully and a coward – somebody's put him up to this.'

'He's still in hospital?'

She grunted with contempt. 'No, the social worker told me he was being sent home today. He's still very ill, so she said I wasn't to worry. They've put an injunction on him, though, so if he does bother us, all I have to do is ring the police. Even so, Mark will be milking it for all it's worth. He hates Beano. He can't stand it that a woman can make me happy, when he couldn't.'

'You have his address?'

She turned suddenly, apprehension in her eyes.

I shrugged. 'I'd like to go and talk to him, that's all.'

She tensed and opened her mouth to speak, but I stopped her. 'Look, don't say it, Hannah. Beano's already refused to give me any details and told me not to get involved. But I'm not going to just stand by and watch her get locked up.'

A glimmer of hope skimmed across her face, quickly followed by consternation and uncertainty.

'I've no idea what I can do,' I insisted, 'but I have to try to do something.'

She put her hand on my knee, clearly frightened. 'Cameron, you mustn't. These are bad people.'

I took hold of it and held it in mine. 'I know. But Beano's a friend. You have to give me the address. Please.'

She hesitated, clearly torn between a desire to help Beano and concern for my safety. Inevitably, Beano had the edge.

'You will be careful?' She still looked doubtful, but I was winning.

I nodded. 'Believe me, I will be *very* careful.'

'Well…' – she hesitated – 'I don't know…'

'Hannah, I can't promise anything but I might just be able to help. You do want her back, don't you?'

'Yes, but she said that—'

'That's just her,' I replied. 'She wants to protect everyone. And you know how independent she can be.'

Hannah smiled in spite of herself. I squeezed her hand and let it go. 'I won't tell her that you gave me his address – whatever happens.'

She turned away for a moment, fighting with herself. When she swung round again, her mind was made up. 'All right. It's Brook House, Flat 426. It's on the Cardogan Estate, though, you know that?'

'Yes – she told me.'

'And did Beano tell you what kind of place it was?' I nodded. 'Well, be careful, then. I don't know how I'd live with myself if you got caught up in their violence as well.'

'Yeah, well, don't worry. I won't.'

We sat and chatted for while. About Beano, about Susie. The likely date of the trial and the thought of leaving the house that they'd just bought together. I talked to Susie for a while as well – before she went to bed. When she was settled, Hannah insisted on cooking us a meal and we sat eating and talking like old friends.

It was just after nine when my phone rang. It was Lin. I'd been so caught up that ringing her had slipped my mind. She didn't seem to mind; in fact she sounded quite excited. She'd spoken to just about every taxi driver in the city, she said – and she had some information that might be useful. I pressed her for it, but she held back, saying that I owed her a drink and it was time to collect. To be honest, regardless of any reservations, I was pleased that she was so eager to see me again.

I put the phone away and got up. 'I'm sorry, I'll have to go. Work, I'm afraid. '

I wasn't sure whether I should shake her hand or give her a hug. In the end it was no contest: she came to me and held me tightly, burying her face into my neck for a moment. I could feel her warmth. I could sense her great sorrow.

'You will be careful, won't you?' she asked as she pulled away.

'You can count on it.' I dug into my pocket and pulled out the roll of notes that Mr Lee had given me and peeled off half of them. 'I just got paid cash for a job,' I explained, 'Look, count this as a loan, until things are sorted out.'

She drew back. 'No, Cameron, I couldn't.'

I took hold of her hand and pushed the notes into her palm. 'Don't be so proud, Hannah. I'm a friend, and friends should help out when they're needed. You can pay me back, but there's no hurry.'

She closed her hand on the money and put her arms around me, hugging me briefly again. 'Thanks. Beano's lucky to have such a good pal.'

'Yeah. Well, it's mutual.'

She let me out, back into the damp night air, then stood and watched from the door as I drove off down the street.

My heart went out to her – and to Beano. Jesus, I meant it when I said that I wanted to help. All the same, I hadn't a clue what I was going to do.

Fourteen

An hour and a half before closing time, the Bridge Inn was buzzing. Lin couldn't keep still while we waited at the bar. Her eyes were bright and her face had an eagerness about it that betrayed her excitement. I was desperate for her to tell me what she'd found out, but, in the meantime, she made me laugh.

'What?' she asked, wide-eyed and innocent.

I shook my head, good-naturedly. 'You! You're like a cat on a hot tin roof.'

She pulled a face. 'Well, if you're going to make fun of me, McGill, I won't tell you what I've found out.'

I went all serious and put a hand on my heart. 'Humble apologies, Miss Lee. You should know that I have the greatest respect for you.'

She stuck her nose in the air. 'Well, I should hope so – otherwise I shall demand a share of your fee, Miss McGill!'

I paid for the beer and we went over to a quieter part of the bar. Lin sat down next to me, wriggling about on the bench seat till she was comfortable. Close enough for me to feel her warmth and sense her smell. She was still wearing the strappy top and the combats and she still looked as good as ever, but, beyond the excitement in her eyes, she looked tired.

'You've been working hard.'

She breathed out sharply. 'My God, Cameron, I never realised that investigating was such hard work. I must have talked to nearly every damn taxi driver in this city.' She smiled wryly. 'Not exactly a

117

beautiful way to spend an afternoon and evening, I must say.'

I agreed: I'd done it myself, many times.

'So come on, then, what did you find out?'

She grimaced. 'Well, let me tell you, I spoke to maybe five guys and a couple of women drivers from the Lavender taxi firm. I have to say that they were all less than helpful – a couple were just plain rude.'

I frowned. 'But you said on the phone that you'd found a taxi driver who knew Emily.'

She gave me a schoolmarm's stare. I drew back in mock alarm. She nodded approvingly at my silence, then continued.

'OK, I know that taxi drivers aren't big on interpersonal skills, but it seemed really odd to me that none of the drivers at Lavender Taxis recognised Aunt Emily's description. There wasn't a flicker, not even a raised eyebrow from the whole lot.' She leaned forward, getting into her stride. 'I worked it out, Cameron. If Aunt Emily's been coming to the village every Monday for, say, the last five years, then that's around two hundred and fifty trips here and two hundred and fifty trips back home.

'Well, that got me thinking.' She looked at me meaningfully. 'The people at Lavender Taxis were either doing a really good job of covering up for her, or they knew Jack Shit. And I tend to the opinion that taxi drivers aren't generally very good actors.'

'Go on.'

'That's when I started asking around the other taxi businesses. But this time I didn't mention the killing. I just said that Emily was a friend. I'd been away and I'd heard she was ill. I needed to contact her urgently. Could they help?'

I grinned across at her, impressed. The woman was a natural.

'Yeah.' She smiled modestly. 'And it worked. I found a taxi firm on the edge of Chinatown just a few minutes' walk away from here. She used it regularly and usually got the cab at the office door.'

I leaned forward eagerly, waiting for her to go on. 'So come on, Lin, *where – does – she – live?*'

She paused for just a little too long and her face fell. 'Ah! Well, I have to say... that's where I come unstuck.'

'You mean they didn't give you her address?'

She grinned cheesily. 'Erm, well, not exactly.'

I slumped back into my seat. Damn!

'But there is something. Thing is, from what they told me, she always phoned for a taxi around seven o'clock every Monday night – and always asked to be picked up ten minutes afterwards.'

'Yeah? Where from?'

She watched my eyes. 'It was always the parish church in Salford. She always waited just outside the main doors.'

Damn! I took a swig of beer and sighed.

Lin leaned across the table. 'Hey, come on, Cameron! That's something, isn't it? I mean, I know it's not an address, but it has to be useful!'

'Yeah. Yes, course it's useful.' I tried hard to sound pleased.

She leaned back and eyed me critically. 'So, what was it you said to me earlier?' she demanded. 'Something about not expecting information to be handed over on a plate?'

I gave her a sideways look. 'Yeah, OK, smartarse.'

She was right, of course. I suppose I'd hung onto the hope that, by some stroke of luck, she had found Emily's address straightaway and that I'd be able to move on to the next stage of the investigation.

Silly, really. Nothing is that easy. Nobody was going to lead me straight to Aunt Emily. Lin's information was excellent. She'd done a remarkable job and it was the best start we could hope for. I told her so – then I started doing my job.

'All right, then, Emily was ready to be picked up ten minutes after he rang, so it figures that he must have changed somewhere within a ten-minute walk of the parish church.'

She shook her head. 'More like a normal five-minute walk, I'd say – she'd be slowed down by the big heels. Hell, I would be!'

'Yeah, so he must live somewhere round there. Maybe if we talk to some other trannies, they might be able to give us another clue, like whether he talked about his house, the local shops, anything like that. If we can find out even some small details we might be able to narrow it down.'

Lin sighed. 'I dunno, Cameron. There's a hell of a lot of high-rise flats and housing estates round there. It could take a lifetime to—'

She put her drink down with such force that some of the liquid splashed out of the top. 'No, that's not right, anyway. Emily once said something about living in Altrincham. It was ages ago, something to do with not taking the tram because someone on it might recognise her.'

Damn.

'He might have moved,' I suggested. 'Maybe he wanted to be nearer the village.'

She bit her lip and scowled. 'Mmm, I doubt it – she's such a snob, I can't imagine her moving to Salford. She was always making such a big thing about living in a "particularly good area".' Lin did a passable impression of the transvestite, deep voice, hand movements and all.

I laughed at her. She turned and grinned at me. Maybe it wasn't so bad having a partner after all.

'Yeah, very good, Lin, but we still have a mystery on our hands.'

She nodded and her eyes sparkled. 'I like that, Cameron – the *we* bit, I mean.'

I think I probably blushed a little.

'Look, are you sure that they never picked her up or dropped her off anywhere else?'

'I'm damn certain, Cameron. I really grilled the poor guy. He said that it was regular as clockwork – every Monday. It was even the same driver more often than not. They got to know her quite well – but she never gave anything away. I believe him as well. Aunt Emily lives in a little fantasy world. She spends all her time talking of the clothes she's bought, the famous people she's met, the experiences she's had – and how people never even realise that she's a man.'

'Really?'

Lin raised her eyebrows. 'Yeah, really!'

'Is Emily married?'

She frowned. 'I'm not sure. I think so.'

'Would he be out to his wife?'

She shrugged. 'Mmm, I doubt it: most of them aren't.'

'So, in that case, he probably doesn't get changed at home anyway.'

Lin's face brightened up momentarily. 'Yeah, you're right. But how does that help? We still don't have an address.'

'No, but it's a start. Maybe he gets changed at a friend's house, or a relation's – like Charlie did. He could be renting a room in Salford. Maybe there's a small hotel that he uses every Monday night, for instance. If the worse comes to the worst, I could always put on a pair of three-inch heels and walk from the parish church in each direction.'

It was a half-serious suggestion, but Lin looked at me and laughed out loud.

'What?' I protested.

Lin shook her head. 'Cameron, that just conjures up an image too ridiculous to even consider!'

I scowled indignantly. 'You might well laugh, Miss Lee. I can get dolled up! I can wear skirts – and makeup. I can do all that stuff!'

She shook her head and wiped the tears from her eyes. 'Cam, I just think you're great the way you are. I don't think I'd take to you at all in a pretty skirt and a pair of fuck-off heels.'

'No, well, I think I'd probably fall over, anyway.'

Lin smiled again at the vision. 'You're right, though – about the five-minute walk, I mean.'

'Yeah, you've made a good start and I'm grateful for all your work, Lin. Now we have to hoof it some more and talk to anyone who might know Emily.'

She looked at me kind of wearily and rested her head on her hand. 'What's with this *we* that you're referring to all of a sudden, Cameron?'

But she got up and came with me all the same.

Fifteen

We tried the Bridge's bar staff first. The guy I'd spoken to the night before was there again and smiled at me when I approached him.

'Now then, love, I see you and your lady are making out after all.' He nodded towards Lin, who was talking to another bartender.

'We're doing OK.' I handed my card across. 'She's helping me on a case. I'm working for a friend of the man who was murdered. We're trying to find the tranny who was with him that night – calls herself Aunt Emily.'

He scanned my card and his smile slipped away. 'Aye, so are t'fuzz, they've been asking questions all bloomin' day. Why can't you all let t'poor woman be?'

I shook my head. 'She might know something. And that could make the difference.' I stared straight into his eyes. 'You seemed concerned about the violence round here last night. Now you have a chance to help do something about it.'

He breathed out and shook his head. 'Aye, mebbe. Mebbe not. All I know is that she's been coming in here every Monday night for years. All I can tell you is that t'word hereabouts is that she scarpered 'cos she were worried about being outed – she's definitely not going to reappear in these parts for some time, love, I can tell you that for nowt.'

'Well, maybe you'd give me a ring if you hear anything?'

The barman shook his head. 'Aye, I will that, luv, but I wouldn't hold your breath.'

Lin drew a similar response from the other barman.

We tried the snug bar next, a tiny room on the canal side of the building, which Lin said was popular with trannies as a stop-off point on their weekly promenade around the village. Not tonight, it wasn't. In their place there was a lone drag queen in a big wig and a sparkly frock, holding court with few gay men. When I approached them, they neither knew nor cared about anyone called Aunt Emily.

Outside in Canal Street, three uniformed officers with clipboards were interviewing all and sundry. I'd already seen the mobile incident room on the Richmond Street car park and there were at least half a dozen other cops doing the same job around the rest of the village.

A young woman officer stopped us as we left the Bridge and we each had to explain that we'd both already given full statements. After she took a note of our names and apologised, we continued with our own questions in every bar on the street. We started with the door staff, then split as we went inside, talking to anyone who looked remotely helpful – dykes, gay men, straight couples, bar staff. But there were no transvestites and, though a few regulars thought they might know Aunt Emily by sight, none of them knew anything else about her.

Lin was looking depressed by the time we reached the top of the street. I was feeling frustrated. We both stopped and leaned on the railings for a while, watching the cops. They were probably having as much success as we were.

'This isn't working, is it?' I observed. 'None of the gay men or the students are likely to know her. We really need to talk to some other transvestites – you think we should take a look at Chloë's next?'

She pulled a face. 'Well, you can go and try if you want, but count me out. It's only a tranny bar on Mondays. The rest of the time it's a men's leather bar – they probably won't even let you through the door.' She regarded me with her big eyes. 'And somehow, Cameron, I don't think you'd really want them to.'

'Yeah, all right,' I conceded, 'you could be right.'

'But there are other places – no night is as good as Monday, but there are usually a few trannies around. You just have to look for them, that's all. Besides, we still haven't tried the three most popular meeting places.'

I looked at her for a moment and pushed myself off the railings. 'OK then, where next, oh wise one?'

She took my hand and led me round the corner. We stopped at the end of the back alley as we passed and looked up the poorly lit street. The tent and the police tape had gone. The neon sign outside Chloë's still flashed out its welcome. Everything was back to normal.

In the next road, Paddy's Goose was full and noisy, a traditional pub with a varied selection of customers – queer and straight – but, again, no cross-dressers, and nobody who knew anything useful. The Hollywood Show Bar raised our hopes again. The man and the woman on the door didn't know Emily by name but recognised Lin's description of her. That might have been useful, except they hadn't seen her for over a week. Inside it was nearly empty. A blonde drag queen was on the turntables, desperately trying to persuade a small group of gay men to get up and dance.

She persisted. We gave up and went back outside.

We left Napoleon's until the last. It was after eleven when we paid our money and walked into the cosy, comfortable bar – one of the village's oldest and most popular clubs. Not the biggest by any means, but what it lacks in size is more than made up in comfort and intimacy. A comfortable bar downstairs with squashy leather settees for intimate tête-à-têtes, a small dance floor up above where – if it turns you on – you can watch yourself dancing all night long in the big full-length mirrors. Not a dyke hangout, I know, but, from my memory anyway, it had always been a popular spot for transvestites.

The downstairs bar was busier than I expected, given that it was still relatively early. The place wasn't full, but there was a reasonable crowd for a Tuesday evening: gay boys, leathermen, a few queens and a couple of fag hags. The bass notes from the disco were already thumping through the ceiling above us and people were moving up and down the stairs. But, when I looked around the room, there wasn't a cross-dresser in sight.

I thought about Charlie again. It was little more than 24 hours since I'd been following him. He'd been headline news all day. Every billboard carried some lurid caption or other about Charlie's transvestism, linking the murder to the village and the newly resurgent homophobia in the area. Poor guy. I'd hardly known him, but it seemed to me he'd had a lousy deal.

I thought about Elaine Wilson, the way she talked about him, especially last night. I thought again about the way she was dressed and the feeling I'd had that she'd been planning a night out herself while he was away. I wondered what the woman was doing now. Not grieving much, I bet.

Lin returned from the bar with a couple more beers and chased my blues away with a broad smile. I sat up straight again and clinked my glass against hers. She smiled a lot, this woman. And, every time, a kind of warmth washed through my body, making me feel good and wholesome again. I didn't really care any more why she was so keen on helping. I just liked her being there. And, for now, that was enough.

Lin put her glass down and touched my arm, glancing meaningfully at the door.

A youngish woman in a navy raincoat had just walked in. She pulled off a cream headscarf and shook her blond bob as she walked past the doorman, heading for the bar. I stared back at Lin, baffled.

'Your turn – I got the drinks,' she prompted.

'What?'

'Your turn to talk to the tranny – the one who's just walked in.'

'You mean...?'

Lin threw her head back and laughed at me. Soft, husky, sexy.

Feeling a little unsure, I started to get up. But, before I could make a move, another woman emerged from the corner of the room behind us and beat me to it. She was quite small, in her twenties, with short, jet-black hair. Her neat, black dress was cut against the weft of the fabric, so that it clung to the contours of her body, accentuating her hips and her breasts. She was already draping her arm around the pretty young transvestite, smiling with sugary affection. He leaned forward and kissed her briefly, lipstick on lipstick, then the two of them retired to a settee in the corner.

I let them get settled, then stood up again. But this time Lin grabbed my hand and pulled me back down.

'Don't!' she hissed. 'There's no point.' There was something like panic in her eyes and her whole body was shuddering.

'What's wrong?' I asked, bewildered by her sudden change.

She sank back into the settee, still holding onto me, talking through gritted teeth. 'That woman – the one with the low-cut dress – that's Natalie. She's a bitch. Stay away from her.'

I frowned at her uncharacteristic behaviour and glanced across at the woman. She was leaning back into the settee with a glass of wine in her hand, sitting close and listening sympathetically to the blonde, who seemed to be spilling his heart out to her.

I frowned. 'She looks all right to me.'

Lin shook her head firmly. 'Yeah, well, she's not! She gets off on men in dresses. She always goes for the new ones. The ones who don't know any better.'

I shrugged. 'OK, so you don't approve of her. But, all the same, she looks like she knows her way around.' I started to get up again but she grabbed my wrist.

'Leave it, Cameron.' She squeezed so tightly that it hurt. 'Please!'

I stared back angrily now, unsettled by the sudden change in her mood. I hate being told what to do at the best of times. It's even worse when it gets in the way of my work. 'Let me go,' I demanded, more coldly than I meant to.

She released me and turned her head away. I got up feeling confused and a little upset. She'd struck me as someone who was easygoing and sorted. Now, as I took the empty seat opposite the couple, I was beginning to fret about her all over again.

Natalie looked up and eyed me uncertainly. The transvestite smiled, thinking, I suppose, that I was a friend.

'I wonder if you can help me.' I'd said the lines so many times that they were beginning to sound like a cliché. 'I'm trying to find someone called Emily. She's often referred to as *"Aunt* Emily". I wondered if you knew her.'

The transvestite didn't react, but Natalie blinked when I mentioned the name. Her eyes were a beautiful pastel green with pupils that seemed just a little too small. Her complexion was pink and didn't quite go with the ebony blackness of her hair. It occurred to me that she might be taking something. Or maybe she was just very warm and very drunk.

'You know her,' I prompted.

'Yeah, I *know* her, all right.' She eyed me intently. 'What do *you* want with her?'

'Let's just say I need to talk to her confidentially.'

'You're another cop,' she grunted and started to turn away.

'I'm a private detective.' I handed my card across.

'Oh!' She blew through her nose at me. 'Same difference. If it's about the killing, I've already been stopped three times out there already.'

'Yeah, well, this is different.' I tried to hold her eyes, but she turned away and looked at her companion instead. 'I understand your reluctance to talk to the police and I understand Emily's concern about being outed. If you can help me, I can handle everything discreetly.'

Natalie turned back, smirking unpleasantly, and glanced down at my card. She curled her lip. 'There's no need to labour the point with me... McGill. For all I care, you can out the bitch to the whole friggin' world.'

'You don't like her, then.'

She tossed the card back at me. 'You're very perceptive.'

'Can I ask why?'

Her eyes strayed back to the young transvestite, exploring his body – from the nylon-clad legs right up to the acrylic hair – as if she were mentally undressing him. He smiled back, slightly bemused by our strained conversation.

I persisted. 'Why don't you like her?'

She turned back impatiently. 'Emily and I have an arrangement. She doesn't approve of me – and I actively hate her.'

She turned away again, but I wasn't going to let it go. 'If you dislike her that much, you must know something about her.'

She sighed theatrically. 'All I know is that she's a vicious old gossip with a big mouth.'

'So why don't you help me find her?' I suggested, sensing an opportunity. 'The police are really keen to interview her.'

She stopped and thought about that one.

'If you want to get back at her, then this would be as good a way as any.'

She made a face and nodded. 'Yeah, well, maybe. Someone once told me that she was a lawyer or something, in her male life. I thought that figured since she was so fucking pompous.'

'Have you any idea where he might work?'

She glanced at her companion, then turned back to me, indifferent once again. 'That's it. That's all I know. Now get lost, will you?'

I shook my head at her rudeness. 'Yeah, well, thanks for your trouble.'

She smiled falsely. 'Pleasure.'

I glanced over my shoulder at Lin, thinking that she was right about the woman's character. She sensed my looking and turned and met my gaze with anxious eyes. My reassuring smile wasn't returned, and, when I turned back to Natalie, *her* eyes were smouldering with amusement.

'So you're with the Chinese girl, then?' she said, mocking me.

'Yeah, I am, actually,' I retorted, a little angry now. 'And *she's* someone else who doesn't approve of you.'

Natalie's eyes sparkled with something close to pleasure.

'Yeah, well' – she eyed me sneakily – '*ex-lovers* don't always admire each other, do they?'

I started, shaken by her statement. 'You were lovers?' I exclaimed. 'You and Lin?' I looked at the transvestite sitting quietly next to her. 'But you're straight.'

Natalie snorted with undisguised amusement. 'What I am is a matter of conjecture. But what interests *me*, McGill, is what *Miss Lee* has told you about *herself*.' She stopped and raised one neatly plucked eyebrow. 'Or maybe she hasn't told you anything at all.'

I glowered at her. 'What the fuck are you talking about?'

She smiled maliciously again and peered over my shoulder, at the settee where Lin was sitting. 'I think that maybe you need to have a serious chat with our little Chinese girl, don't you?'

I took one last cool, silent look at her, wondering what the hell was going on.

And, when I turned to look behind me, Lin had gone.

Sixteen

I pushed my way out of the smoke and the noise back into the cold clean air of Sackville Street. Lin was already at the junction in her beat-up old car, accelerating out into the traffic on Portland Street like some kind of maniac.

I felt sick. Clearly, Natalie had it in for her, but I couldn't believe that she thought so little of me that she'd just leave like that. Did she really think that I'd let a bitch like that poison our friendship?

I wrapped the scarf around my neck and zipped up my jacket, then headed across the main road and through Piccadilly Gardens. The late-night trams were thundering and creaking their way down the road. The pavements were full of young people – women in strappy tops, men in shirtsleeves, all impervious to the cold as they sauntered between clubs and bars. A small knot of people stood outside the chippy by the bus station, pushing steaming food into their mouths. They all seemed to be enjoying themselves. Sometimes other people just piss me off.

I'd taken to Lin because she seemed so guileless. OK, so there was something deep about her that I couldn't quite fathom. But, then, most of us have our hidden sides. Yeah, and most of us have exes who – given the chance – would exploit them.

'*But what interests me, McGill, is what* Miss Lee *has told you about* herself.'

Told me what? That she'd had a relationship before? That she was into S&M? That she'd worked the streets? Been heavily into drugs?

Jesus, I could get paranoid if I kept on thinking like this.

But there *was* something, I knew it. There had to be a reason for her reticence, the way she kept changing the subject every time we started to get close. Her obvious discomfort whenever I started to come on to her.

'... ex-lovers *don't always admire each other much, do they?'*

If Natalie and Lin *had* been lovers, it did no more than confirm that Lin was lesbian – or bisexual, anyway. Or there was another possibility, one that had crossed my mind more than once before. Yeah, OK. Except that one seemed plainly ridiculous. And, given the way I felt about the woman, very unlikely.

Fuck, all this was making my brain hurt.

By the time I got back to the Overnite Inn, I was very confused as well as very angry – and I was certainly in no mood for sleep. So I took the steps down to the bottom level of the car park and sat on the wall by the riverbank throwing pebbles into the river and kicking myself. I'd wasted half the day trying to work out how the hell I could help Beano, and the other half trying to find a cross-dresser who had a reputation for talking incessantly but never actually said anything. We must have buttonholed more than a hundred people tonight and the only thing I had was that he *might* be a lawyer.

Yeah, big fucking help.

I'd let the man I was tailing get murdered, failed to hang onto a key witness and been dumped unceremoniously by my client. Now the only person in Manchester who seemed to have anything in common with me had jumped ship as well.

I threw another pebble as hard as I could and it landed with a crack on the stone shoring over the far side of the river. I guess that, more than anything else, I felt sore about being taken for a pushover by Lady Ego.

I kicked my heels against the wall and wondered about her again. Elaine Wilson was a style freak. She probably wore makeup in bed. But nobody wears the kind of outfit she had on last night just to sit around the house. *And* she was drunk and *very* upset. But not about her husband's death. It was almost as if there was something else going on in her life – something that was far more pressing than the mere murder of a man she'd never much liked anyway.

I threw one last pebble into the water and went to my car.

I don't know what I expected to do at twelve thirty in the morning. I was crabby, upset and still a little drunk. I think I had some weird notion in my head that I was going to talk to Elaine Wilson. That I'd knock on her door and demand some answers from her when she least expected it. Jesus, I don't know. Maybe I just wanted to get my own back – maybe I just wanted a good fight.

As I drove through the quiet streets of Bury, I thought back yet again to my conversation with the preacher's wife. According to Dorry, I wasn't the first PI Elaine Wilson had hired. She already knew very well where her husband went on a Monday night. So why had she hired me? Was it in the hope that I might discover something that the other investigators hadn't? And, if so, why had she lied about it? Surely it would have been more productive if I'd known the facts.

I slowed down as I approached the house, watching for reporters lurking in the shadows around the big stone gateposts, but there was no one. Still, they'd probably finished with 'The Widow's Story' – time for something else. A deranged minister being held on suspicion presumably sounded like a better angle. I drove past and parked up the road, thinking of Dorry and wondering if she was still besieged.

Elaine's drive stood empty, but the four street lamps that stood along one side were lit and the hall light was on. I leaned on the doorbell, willing the bitch to open the door and talk to me, listening with relish as the racket from the buzzer resounded through the big house. But there was no response. No footsteps, no voices, not even a face at the window.

I rang it again, intermittently and banged hard on the door. Nothing.

After a couple more minutes, I gave up and walked around the side, peering through a window into the garage. The smart BMW sports car was parked snugly inside. Round the back of the house, the curtains in the kitchen were drawn back, but the room was in darkness. The woman was out. And, since her car was still here, it was reasonable to assume that she was out with someone else.

I zipped up my leather jacket and crept in among the shrubs, sitting in the shadows opposite the front door, behind a large rhododendron bush. I wasn't in any hurry and, even if it took an hour or two, I wanted to see if this woman, who had been so determined that her husband was having an affair, was playing fast and loose herself.

The wind had dropped and the weather was dry. But, by half past one, the alcohol was wearing off and I was beginning to shake with cold. I thought about Lin again and cursed quietly to myself. I used to consider myself a good judge of character; now I wasn't so sure. Eighteen months ago, I'd trusted another woman. Someone who'd smiled in my face and lied. Angel had very nearly got me killed. I'd never quite trusted my judgement the same again.

So I could have been wrong about Elaine as well. She might be staying with relatives, away from the media. The cops could have put her up in some hotel while the fuss died down. Maybe they'd find me in the morning, frozen to the fucking spot. I checked my watch again and then stuffed my hands back into the warmth of my pockets. Shit, I'd give it another fifteen minutes, then I was going to bed.

Less than ten minutes later I heard the faint purr of a car engine up the road and I slid back into the depth of the bush, as blue-white headlights swung into the drive and lit up the garden around me.

The dark blue Jaguar S-Type stopped almost opposite, and, when the lights went out, I crept forward, close enough for me to hear their voices – a man's and a woman's – murmuring inside. I couldn't hear what they were saying, or even see them through the smoked-glass windows, but, when the driver's door opened a few minutes later, a man got out and walked around to the passenger door. He was a tall and, by most people's standards, good-looking. He was in his mid-forties, with dark, slicked-back hair and a slightly Mediterranean appearance. Not quite Italian, not really English. He looked fit and smooth, cultured even, and he wore his clothes – a tailored azure blue suit and a plain white open-necked shirt – with style.

When he reached the other side of the car, he leaned over and opened the passenger door, stepping back to help Elaine Wilson out. She swung her legs over the sill and emerged with a grace that seemed completely at odds with the woman I'd met the previous evening. But it *was* her, pulling her fur coat around her shoulders and cooing provocatively in the ear of the man who was now closing the car door behind her.

When he stood up straight she moved in close and slid her arms around his neck, giggling and rubbing her body up against his.

'Are you coming in?' she asked, her classy accent now rediscovered. 'We don't have to worry about you-know-who any more.'

The man pushed her gently away and shook his head at her. His voice was soft and, despite his Latin appearance, he sounded like a true Northerner. 'Have *some* respect, Elaine. Charlie did his best. It wasn't his fault he was so boring.'

Elaine stroked his arm and reached up and kissed him on the mouth. 'Maybe it wasn't, but let's forget him, eh?' she breathed. 'There are far more important matters to attend to.' When they separated, they stood a moment, looking into each other's eyes, their breath white and hungry, in the chill night air.

The man broke away first, retrieved his coat from the back seat, and pointed his remote at the car. The doors locked with a dull clunk and the orange lights winked a brief goodnight.

The hall light went out almost as soon as they got inside. Then the lights along the drive. Suddenly I was standing in pitch darkness, but the images in my head were bright enough. Charles Wilson's widow was excelling herself. The man was clearly wealthy, but who was he?

The car doors were locked and the little red light on the dashboard was flashing a warning. So no point in picking the lock. I crept behind the car as the bedroom light came on for just a few minutes. When everything went dark again, I took out my torch and walked around, running the tiny beam over anything that might give a clue to the driver's identity. A car park permit, a monogrammed gear change, an envelope on the back seat maybe. But, damn it, there was nothing.

I crouched down by the boot, switching my torch back on and shining the beam across the number plate, picking out the name of the dealer and then the personalised registration, letter by letter.

B A P 0 0 3

It was clearly owned by a man with money behind him. And it wasn't hard to make the connection between Elaine's fine clothes on the evening of her husband's murder and this new lover. Had she been waiting to go out with him then when the news of the murder came?

I wondered whether Dyson had made the connection.

And I wondered who the man in the azure-blue suit could be.

Seventeen

I pulled the sunglasses out of the glove compartment and swallowed another two ibuprofen. The sun was out this morning, low in the sky, glinting at me through the houses like a giant strobe. It wasn't my belly any more. Today it was my head and shoulders – the result of skulking around in shrubs during the early hours of a freezing autumn morning and, once again, too little sleep.

I'd mapped out my day in the early hours – a chat with Charlie's sister, a quick recce of his restaurant, and then maybe a walk round the streets of Salford. So far I had next to nothing to go on in my search for the elusive Aunt Emily. I could only hope that some small clue might present itself at some point during the day, but I wasn't holding my breath.

Meanwhile, up ahead, the high-rise towers of the Cardogan Estate glowered at me over the rooftops, just beyond the edge of Stretford. Seeing them depressed me even more. This journey, too, seemed doomed to failure. Both Beano and Hannah had told me that Mazza had a grudge against them. And, even if he hadn't, even if he was the nicest guy on earth, he would need a death wish to finger the man who really beat the shit out of him.

I rubbed the back of my neck and tried to think of a way to get him to withdraw his evidence. Asking nicely was a nonstarter. And any threats I could make would be nothing compared with those from the real thugs.

Yeah, so the situation called for some smart thinking, and right now – at 9.30 in the morning, with a thumping headache – I wasn't at all sure that I was up to the task.

I took a left just past the traffic lights and parked the car out of the way on an industrial estate just a few minutes' walk away from the Cardogan, sitting for a few moments, toying with the phone, and thinking about Lin – wondering for the hundredth time why she'd left like that.

'*But what interests me, McGill, is what* Miss Lee *has told you about* herself.'

However much I might dislike Natalie, I couldn't deny that her words had disturbed me. I went to sleep with them echoing in my brain, I dreamed about them all night and I woke up with them running around in my ears. I kept telling myself that the woman was poison, but all the while I knew that there must be something in what she'd said. The way that Lin had suddenly left only confirmed that something wasn't quite right.

In the end I put the phone away and locked the car. I made my way back to the main road on foot, then I cut off and walked the last quarter of a mile through the side streets, trying to concentrate on the job in hand. In the near distance, the four towers of the Cardogan dodged in and out of the rooftops, larger and more forbidding than ever.

Most people think Moss Side when you mention crime and Manchester in the same breath. But there are other areas, other estates in the city, where poverty and exclusion run rife too, where there is fertile ground for sowing fear and planting hate. Places where even the police don't get out of their cars unless they're in fours. The Cardogan is one of them.

Built in an age when architects and bureaucrats were infatuated with dreams of a cheap housing Utopia, the four towers were now struggling to make their fortieth anniversary. A few years ago the council had done its best, painting them in nice bright pastel colours with big wistful names on the top. But I doubted if they'd ever fooled anyone, and now the ugly concrete structures looked dirty and neglected again.

Each of the four, fifteen-storey tower blocks stood on one side of a large square. Each had its own car park at the front and, in the common ground between them, they shared what had once been an extensive recreation area. Now the thin covering of grass was crisscrossed by muddy, rutted tracks, scarred by earthy mountain-biking ridges and strewn with old pram wheels, bike frames and other junk. Bits of old bin liners flapped noisily from the branches of near-dead trees at each of the corners and, in the car park nearest to me, a burned and rusting vehicle rested on its axles like the shell of some long-dead animal.

I could smell the place before I even got there: the scent of decay, dereliction and hopelessness. No wonder people turn to crime.

I walked on past the first block and through to the edge of the grass. Brook House was directly opposite, so I took the short cut across the common ground, stepping carefully around the puddles, the dog shit and the wind-blown rubbish that littered my path. A motley pack of dogs was milling around outside the flats to my left. They pricked up their ears when I was hardly halfway across and bounded towards me, yapping and cavorting. I stood my ground as they circled around, sniffing the damp air. When I shouted at them, they leaped off again, chasing and pushing one another across the grass.

I saw the kids long before I reached the other side, lolling against the bonnets of two cars, eyeing me lazily. When I was three-quarters across, they started moving en masse, across the car park, ready to intercept me when I left the grass. Eight of them altogether; six of them boys. The youngest would be no more than nine years old, the eldest maybe fifteen. He rode his bike in front of the others, tracing out a figure of eight with his arms folded. Yeah, tough guy.

I lengthened my stride a little, smiling grimly to myself. The germ of an idea had begun to sprout and grow. By the time the leader reached me and slowed to a halt across my path, it was in full and glorious leaf.

The kid didn't say anything, just stared at me as if I were vermin.

I thought of Beano again and a little ball of anger flared in my belly. OK, so if my plan was going to work, *vermin* was what I would have to be. I stared back, cold and hard. A mean bitch with a bad attitude.

'You in charge round here?' I demanded.

He paused a moment checking to see if I was taking the piss; then, reassured, he put his shoulders back and smirked a little.

'Yeah. Yeah, that's right.'

'Good. Then you'll know if Mazza's in.'

The boy sneered at me, trying to take control. 'What's it to you, lezzer?'

I grabbed his shirt collar and pulled him half off the bike. 'He made me a promise, *shithead*. Over a week ago, and I'm mad as hell, 'cos he never fuckin' delivered.'

When I pushed him away, the kid shuffled about regaining his balance and his composure while his small gang watched him silently, waiting to see how he'd deal with this indignity. I watched just as closely, hoping that my impersonation was having some effect.

It was.

'Mazza's not seein' anyone,' he snorted, but more defensively this time.

'Says who?' I demanded.

The kid smiled nervously and shrugged his shoulders, clearly wondering who the hell I was. 'No. No, he just ain't,' he said, trying to sound tough, even though his eyes were popping. 'Word's out, that's all. The guy's off limits. You might get hurt *real bad* if you try to see him.'

Perfect. Just what I wanted to hear.

'Well, now.' I spoke slowly, taking a step forward and peering right into his pimply face. *'I'm – really – fucking – scared.'*

The kid lifted up his head in defiance, as if he might have one more go at stopping me. Just for the sake of his ego. But, if my plan was going to work, he had to be impressed.

I looked straight into his eyes. 'Get out of my way, *sonny*.'

His expression stayed defiant but he swallowed hard, and his hands started pumping the brake handles. 'We've been told not to let anyone see him.' He looked round the group of fellow truants for support. None of them looked too sure.

'Who by?'

'That's none of your business – dyke.' His voice trailed away uncertainly on the intended insult.

I grabbed him again, harder this time and pulled him right off his bike.

'You call me dyke or lezzer again in that tone of voice and I'll rip your fucking head off. You understand?'

The kid backed off when I let him go, but, just in case, I glared at him until he turned away and started to pick his bike up. Then I gave the death stare to the gathering of startled faces around him.

'Anyone else feel like arguing?'

Nobody moved, so, with some relief and legs that were beginning to feel like jelly, I pushed my way through and walked, bursting with adrenalin, across the remaining tarmac and into Brook House.

I took the stairs. I avoid lifts – all too often they stink of stale urine or else of the disinfectant they use to cover it up. Like prison cells. Besides, I spend too much time sitting in cars; I miss too many sessions at the gym. Every bit of exercise counts. The stairs also gave me time to think, time to calm down. I had only one shot at this. It had to work first time.

The door to Mark Taylor's flat was halfway along the fourth-floor balcony. A lace curtain twitched as I emerged from the stairs, a door opened quietly behind me as I passed and, ten doors on, a woman stopped to watch me as she put down her shopping and searched for her keys.

I knocked on Mazza's door. No response.

I knocked harder with the side of my fist and breathed deeply, squeezing my fear into a tight little ball and burying it deep in my belly. The door rattled noisily. When I stared at her, the woman with the shopping looked away and went inside.

I hammered again until I heard him yell out in irritation.

'All right, all right, I'm fuckin' coming!'

But I kept right on knocking until the door opened and a thin, patched-up face peered around the edge.

'Yeah? Whadyouwant?'

'I hear you can fix me up,' I replied, nice and casually.

He started to shut the door, but I shoved my boot into the opening and threw my shoulder against it hard. It swung open and I fell through into the hallway. Mazza stepped back in panic, raising a single fist.

'Get out! Fucking get out, will ya?' he shrieked, backing off, shaking, as I walked towards him. A man on the edge, a man missing his regular hit.

But I wasn't too scared of him – standing there in his bare feet and a pair of old training bottoms. He limped when he stepped back. His right arm was in a sling and his chest was bandaged. He had a plaster over his left eye and a two-inch-wide graze on his right cheek. His nose was busted and he had two spectacular black eyes. I didn't expect he'd want to get into another fight, not just yet.

I shut the door behind me and walked down the short hallway, concentrating on looking cool, controlled. He stepped back, and let me past.

Bullies, they're all the same.

'OK,' I said, walking into what passed for a lounge. 'I just wanna talk, that's all. Let's sit down. Let's be real nice to each other, huh?'

Like him, the room was a mess. It looked as if it might have been decorated once, but it was difficult to tell when. It certainly hadn't been cleaned in a good while. There was a faded brown settee along one wall and two dark-blue, torn armchairs stuck against the other. Piles of old magazines littered the floor: *Auto News*, *Loaded*, *Rally Driver* and several well-worn copies of *Playboy* and *Swank*.

I lifted a plate of mouldy, half-eaten food off one of the armchairs and sat down, wondering how the hell Hannah could have got involved with such a creep. He was still standing by the door, looking bemused.

'Take a seat, Mark,' I said quietly, smiling at him. 'Chill out. Take it easy, man.' He edged his way to the settee, keeping his distance, pushed aside some dirty clothes and lowered himself painfully down, fumbling for a fag with his one good hand, and awkwardly lighting up. I kept watching him, taking my time before speaking. His eyes were everywhere and his hand could hardly keep hold of the cigarette. He was really scared – maybe not of me, but he was filling his pants all the same.

I let the silence hang in the air for a while before I spoke again. Pleasant, relaxed like an old chum – the kind of friend who might have a gun up her sleeve and was dying for an excuse to use it.

'I'm sorry to barge in like this, Mazz. Thing is, I have a big, big problem. And, from what I've been told, *you* are just the guy to help me.'

He narrowed his eyes and played nervously with the cigarette. 'Huh?'

'Fact is, I've been let down by my regular man.' I shook my head and grunted. 'It's fucking embarrassing. I mean, I've got customers waiting, and I can't supply. They get restless – if you know what I mean.'

He pushed back into his seat as if trying to disappear into the settee. His eyes were big and white and his voice went up a couple of octaves. I do like it when people are responsive.

'I can't fucking help you, man!'

'That's not what I heard.'

He shook his head wildly, pleading with me. 'No, man. Honest. I used to deal but not now, not any more.' He swallowed hard. 'Just get the fuck out, will ya? Leave me alone, for shit's sake!'

I shook my head and swore obscenely, making a drama out of my disappointment. 'Yeah, all right, but give me a name at least. You gotta have contacts. I don't need any of this small-dealer shit. I'm talking in bricks and kilos, you savvy?'

I thought his eyes were going to come out on stalks. He tried to laugh, but his face was too tight. 'I don't know nobody, I... I can't fucking help you, man – honest to God.'

I was right: the guy was scared out of his mind. Someone out there had got to him and there was no way on God's earth that Mazza was going to give anyone an excuse to finish the job off.

I'm a reasonable woman, so I got up and walked to the door. 'OK, you win.' I smiled sweetly. 'I'll ask around.'

He'd told me all I needed to know. The rest was up to the kids outside.

I saw myself out and walked back down the stairs. When I reached the car park, the gang were taking it in turns throwing stones at an old petrol can, except that the older youth seemed to be taking every other turn for himself. As I stood and watched, they stopped one by one to look at me. I jerked my head at them and stood my ground. They waited a while until the older boy made up his mind. Then when he walked towards me they all followed.

'Why the fuck didn't you just tell me, man?' I asked him, pleasantly, one hard case to another.

'What?' The kid looked mystified.

'The guy's a fuckwit!' I made quotation marks in the air and quoted him: ' "Mazza's not seein' anyone." What the fuck was all that shit about?'

The kid still looked puzzled, but was clearly relieved. I glared around the sea of faces. Then, when I had their attention, I eyeballed him again. Like maybe I could take him into my confidence, like maybe he was *the man*.

'Hey, c'mon, you gotta help me, man,' I confided. 'I got customers waitin'. Mazza promised to help me, but he never delivered. You know some fucker who can get me some *merchandise*?' I held his eyes. 'You understand my drift?'

The boy straightened up again as if he'd got his dignity back and the gang breathed out in relief. The two young girls looked at me as though I were some kind of hero. Jesus, I didn't like that.

'Gimme a few hours,' he replied. Tough guy again. Even the swagger came back.

I pointed my finger at him. 'Don't screw around with me, kid.'

He shook his head and his eyes almost revolved in their sockets. 'No shit. Honest. Just gimme time, will ya?'

I nodded and glared at him for a moment, then took out my pad and wrote my mobile number down. 'I'm here overnight. Ring me real soon, huh?'

'Yeah, OK. I need a name, though – he's gonna ask.'

I turned and stared at him hard, playing for time, casting around in my brain for something suitable.

'Candy. Tell him it's Candy from Leeds. If he's anyone, he'll know the name.'

The kid looked impressed and stuffed the paper in his pocket.

I turned and walked quietly away, over the grass, past the tower block and back to my car. The setup seemed to be working. He was going to do exactly what I wanted.

I just hoped that I could handle it, that was all.

Eighteen

I stopped for a coffee at a small café on the way back into the city. I needed a little time to settle down. Time to get my head together and work out how the hell I was going to handle the process that I'd just set in motion.

Beano would go crazy if she knew what I was doing. But I couldn't think of any other way. I shivered and pulled my jacket around me, cupping the hot drink in my hands, soaking up what comfort I could from its warmth. After this morning, it was unlikely that Mazza's dealer would ignore me. I'd get the call pretty soon, then I'd set the whole thing up. Three days max, it should be over.

My thoughts were interrupted by a bleep from my mobile. When I flipped it open, there was a text message: 'Sorry I panicked last nite. Cn we meet 2day n b friends? Cn I xplain? PLEASE!'

I tried to ignore the sudden lurch in my belly and got up to pay the bill. The woman at the counter smiled amiably at me as she took the money and chatted about the weather and yesterday's rain – the kind of pointless conversation you have with people the world over. She was nice and I liked her, but she was a businesswoman. And, beyond the pleasantries, her friendly smile didn't mean a thing.

Was it the same with Lin? After the initial misunderstanding, we'd made friends a little too easily. She'd worked hard with the taxi drivers, though whether that was for my benefit or Granddad's remained to be seen. And she'd gone out of her way to be friendly – perhaps even a little more than that. Then, the minute I started talking to her ex, she'd run.

'*But what interests me, McGill, is what* Miss Lee *has told you about* herself.'

When I got outside I took another look at the text message. Whatever was going on, it was clear that there was something that scared the life out of her – and she was clearly convinced that Natalie had told me what it was.

A voice inside of me started to sound a warning again. *You've been here before,* it said. *You remember Angel? You remember how much you trusted her? You remember what she nearly did to you?*

But I rang Lin's number all the same.

She answered almost at once, as if she'd had the phone in her hand. 'It's Cameron. I got your message.' I was offhand and distant. After the way she'd acted, I didn't want her to think that she only had to snap her fingers and I'd be there.

'Oh, hi.' Her voice was quiet, reticent. 'Thanks for ringing.'

'Yeah. You asked for a chance to explain.'

'I know. I'm sorry, Cameron, I... should have told you.'

'Told me *what?*'

Silence.

'I thought... I mean, I should have told you that I'd had an affair with her.'

'She implied that you had some kind of secret, Lin – she didn't say what it was, but from the way you acted it's obviously important.' I paused and took a breath, trying to push back the bitterness that was rising in my gullet. 'You going to tell me, or what?'

'Cameron, I... Can we meet up again?'

The voice in my head told me to leave it. To walk away, forget her. Another voice said go ahead – this is different. I hung back for a moment, my head spinning off in all directions. Lin was a million miles away from the sad damaged woman that Angel had turned out to be. And I liked her, for God's sake! No. It was more than that. I respected her as well. She was a strong, gutsy woman. There had to be a good reason for her walking off as she did.

'Cameron, are you still there?'

'Yeah. Look, I'm not making much progress on this job. I'm kind of running out of ideas. I was going to take a look at Chow City to see if anything clicks. I know it's a long shot, but...' I stopped myself. My sudden nervousness was making me ramble. 'You could meet me there if you want. Maybe we could have lunch – or something. I can't go on like this, Lin, you really upset me last night, walking out like that.' I stopped myself: there was no point in recriminations.

'Thanks, Cameron. I really appreciate it.' She paused, breathing into the phone. 'Cameron?'

'Yes?'

'Please try to trust me.'

My stomach lurched as I put the phone away. Hell, that's exactly what Angel had said.

I stood for a moment, gathering myself together again, looking across at the newsagent's next door to the café. A red *Evening Post* van had pulled up onto the forecourt and the driver was taking a bundle of newspapers into the shop. As he came out, he lifted the wire cover on the billboard and pushed a new sheet in.

TRANSVESTITE KILLING, it shouted. VICAR RELEASED.

Nineteen

I arrived at Chow City just after noon. The place was almost deserted when I walked through the small glass lobby and into the vast white and mint-green restaurant with its high ceiling and scented air. Above me, large white fans turned lazily. Four banks of theatre spots met in the centre of the ceiling, dropping bright pools of light all around the room.

I walked through an avocado-green carpet to the long shiny-white bar and pulled out one of the elegant chrome stools, feeling just as scruffy as I had when I had met Mr Lee in the Golden Snapper.

Though I knew it had been open for some months, the restaurant still felt pristine, as though it were wrapped up carefully and put back into mothballs each night. The thirty or so tables were all neatly laid out with starched white tablecloths, shining cutlery and mint-green serviettes. Only two were occupied.

I put it down to the time; it was still barely midday. All the same, the place felt too neat, too perfect, too quiet. I could be on some film lot, waiting for the cast to show.

It was over three minutes before the waiter appeared. I know, because I counted them off on the clock above the bar. Not a real clock: it was a four-foot wide image, projected onto the wall from somewhere among the theatre lights above. And it changed colour every time the second-hand passed twelve.

White. Green. Lilac...

It was pastel blue when he finally pushed his way through the swing doors and into the bar, pulling on his white tuxedo and straightening his bow tie as he went. If I'd expected Chow City to be staffed with polite Easterners, then I was disappointed. This guy was Caucasian, about six feet tall. He also had close-cropped hair, a broken nose and a face that would put zombies to flight.

'You have a reservation?' He tried to smile, but it sounded more like a threat.

I looked around the near-empty restaurant and laughed. 'I'm waiting for a friend. Do I *need* a reservation?'

White Tux shrugged his shoulders, feigning offence. 'No, I was just asking, lady. This is a restaurant. People sometimes book tables.'

I shook my head and apologised; there was no point in rubbing the guy up the wrong way – I'd find out nothing.

'I'll have a Campari and tonic, please.'

He grunted and turned away to pour the drink. I stared at the clock again, feeling irritated. I was still cut up over Lin's behaviour and, if I'm honest, more than a little apprehensive about our meeting. I'm a cut-and-run sort of girl. I like relationships OK, but I hate the confrontations that always seem to follow.

When White Tux eventually turned back and pushed the drink across, he made a reasonable attempt at conversation.

'You waiting for a friend, then?'

'Yeah, among other things.'

He frowned at my remark, but I didn't elucidate.

'This place looks pretty new.'

He eyed me a mite uneasily and nodded. 'Yeah, we been open only a month or so. Place has been completely done over. Used to be a real dump.'

I tipped my head on one side and smiled, attempting to be personable again. 'Is that why it's so quiet?'

'Takes time to build up business. We'll be busy soon.'

I wasn't sure whether by 'soon' he meant in half an hour or two months, but I didn't push the point. The guy didn't seem to know too many words, and I didn't want to stretch his brain too far.

'You want I should add the drink to your tab?'

I nodded and he punched something into the computer.

'You must still be in shock.' He turned back to me, but didn't react. 'The murder. The victim was a partner here, wasn't he?'

'Oh, yeah. The hate killing. Bad situation.' He stopped and stared at me intently.

'You'd know him, I suppose?'

The man backed off and squinted at me. 'Hey, what's with all these questions, lady? You a reporter?'

'Nah, relax.' I pulled out the fake letter of introduction that I always carry and flashed it in front of him. 'I'm representing Commercial & Collateral Insurance.'

He peered down at the writing as if his reading wasn't too bright either and I pulled it away again.

'We don't need no insurance, lady.'

I shook my head and smiled, handing him one of my cards. 'No. I'm not selling any. I'm a private investigator. I'm just doing a routine check into Mr Wilson's death – for my clients. They insured his life. I need to interview various acquaintances – including his business partner – prior to the company releasing the monies.'

He hesitated, suddenly unsure of what to do.

'Could you ask his partner if he'll see me, please?'

He grunted as I took the paper back. 'Yeah, Mr Keane will be in soon. I'll tell him you're here.'

I smiled in acknowledgement and he turned away and busied himself filling small glass bowls with big peanuts, then arranging the contents with his big fingers. I watched him idly, wondering when he'd last washed his hands.

He slid a bowl over in my direction. I smiled back and pushed the dish away again. I remembered the survey that someone did a few years ago with bar titbits. As I recall, they found traces of urine and human faeces in every single sample. Several types, too, in every bowl. I've never touched peanuts since.

By the time I finished my drink the clock had gone through its entire repertoire more than five or six times. My mind was flicking through the events of the last two days in much the same way.

Flick. What kind of moron beats the shit out of Mazza, then quietly sets Beano up – someone he's never even met – for maybe ten years in jail?

Flick. If the preacher had been released, who was next on the suspect list? The skinheads? And was it really a hate killing as everyone assumed?

Flick. And Aunt Emily. Was he just scared – or did his disappearance signify some deeper involvement?

Flick. And Lin – what was it with her?

I looked around me while I waited, trying to relax, trying not to get neurotic, trying to rein in my more extreme thoughts. A number of people had drifted in and one of the larger tables was occupied now by four besuited, middle-aged men. Two waitresses – a young, too-thin blonde and an older, dark-haired woman – were fussing around them serving drinks and changing cutlery, under the careful gaze of an older man in a black tuxedo. The women looked very smart and Continental in their white shirts and long black wraparound aprons. But it was the men in suits who grated on me, the way they were acting, as if they'd never heard of respect.

Damn, but they felt good. They had cash in their expense accounts, they had power in their pockets and they had women crawling all around them, stroking their egos. Making them feel like big important people.

The dark-haired waitress saw me staring and I raised my eyebrows at her by way of a comment. For just an instant she stopped, the trace of a smile on her lips – as if same thoughts were going through her mind as well.

Across the room, the glass door opened and Lin walked in, glancing nervously around the tables. I raised a hand and got down from the stool. She half-smiled as she waited for me to come across.

My belly did a somersault. My brain as well.

She looked stunning, and, for all my reservations, my heart still skipped a beat as I walked towards her. Her shiny black hair was pinned up with small red sticks crisscrossed at the back. She was wearing silky black trousers with a bright-red, embroidered, Chinese-style top and just a touch of makeup. She was really trying to make an impression. I wasn't sure whether I liked that or not.

'Hello, Cameron.' She blinked self-consciously and stepped forward a little. I touched cheeks with her, more formally than the day before. She noticed and I could see the disappointment in her eyes.

Black Tux appeared before we could speak and showed us to a table in the middle of the room, pulling the chair out for Lin and holding it while she sat down, leaving me to seat myself. Then he handed us two large menus and a wine list. When he'd left, she leaned over and touched the back of my hand. I looked back impassively, but my skin prickled with delight.

'I'm sorry about last night.'

'Yeah, me too. I thought we were doing OK.'

She hesitated, rubbing the back of her neck, and looking down, as if she didn't quite know how to bridge the chasm that had opened up between us. Under the makeup, her face was even paler than normal and there was a blotchiness about her eyes that suggested that she might have been crying.

'Natalie said that you used to be lovers. Why didn't you just say?'

She looked away. 'It was a long time ago, Cameron. I'm still touchy about it. It was a *big* mistake.'

I waited a moment, hoping that she'd tell me more, without prompting. She was trembling and she was still having trouble meeting my gaze.

'What is it that you need to tell me?' I asked, gently.

She looked down at her hands, swallowing hard and licking her lips. She breathed in deeply and forced herself to look up, meeting my eyes, clearly trying to calm herself, trying not to turn away again.

'That's all there is...' She faltered, and looked away for a moment, then continued unsteadily. 'I'm sorry. I just panicked last night when I saw her staring at me. Those eyes, those evil eyes. I'm sorry, Cameron, I just couldn't take it.'

I nodded. 'Yeah, well you were right: she isn't a very nice person. But you seemed to think she'd told me something when I phoned you.'

She looked away for a moment. 'Yeah, I know, and I'm sorry. I get paranoid about her, I suppose. She was my first sort of lesbian affair and I'm not proud of what happened between us. I just assumed that she was trashing me and that you'd never want to speak to me again.'

'You think I'm so easily manipulated?' I asked.

She looked across at me and smiled sadly. 'This isn't about you, Cameron. It's about me. There are some things about my life that I'm still having to deal with – and Natalie's one of them.'

But what interests me, McGill, is what Miss Lee *has told you about* herself.

'But she implied that there was something that you hadn't told me – like there was some kind of skeleton in your cupboard.' I watched her reaction carefully.

She shuffled in her seat, and for just a moment, she looked all at sea.

'We all have pasts, Cameron. There are things in mine that I don't particularly want to talk about at the moment and I'd like you to respect that. '

I looked away and sighed. Lin stared feebly after me, a tear forming in her eye.

'Please, Cameron, Natalie is a vicious bitch; you must have realised that. She's just trying to make trouble.'

I sighed and tried a smile. 'Yeah, well, I'm sorry. I just like you, Lin, and it upset me when you ran out like that.'

She bit her lip and nodded, but I could still see the pain drifting around in her eyes. I was certain that there were things that she was keeping back, but, hell, maybe she was right: I'd only known her for three days, so the least I could do was respect her privacy.

Black Tux returned and we both sat back, trying to act normal again. 'Would you like to order drinks from the bar, sir?'

I made a show of looking around me, but there was no doubt that he was talking to me.

Lin came to my rescue. 'I think *Miss* McGill and I would probably like some wine.' She looked across at me and I nodded. Black Tux looked as if he wished the floor would swallow him up. He coughed politely and then turned and left. Glad of the distraction, Lin watched me for my reaction.

I shrugged. 'I think it's called the heterosexual imperative. They see an attractive, feminine woman like you, then automatically assume that the short-haired, butch-looking person with her must to be a man. It happens all the time. You get used to it.'

She shook her head and almost smiled. 'You don't look anything like a man, Cameron.'

I raised my eyebrows. 'Yeah, well, I'm pleased about that.'

Silence.

'I'm sorry I ran off.'

I shrugged. 'Well, thanks for getting back to me anyway. Maybe we can pick up a few of the pieces, at least.'

She smiled quite sadly. But it was the most I could offer.

I watched her as she studied the menu, wondering why I was so drawn to her. Wondering why in God's name I was being so patient, when every fibre of my body wanted to shake her, and make her tell me whatever it was that was bothering her so much. It wasn't just that she was pretty. OK, I liked that. But it was more than good looks. Beyond the clothes and the beautiful hair there was something else. Something very distinctive that I'd never come across before. And, try as I might, I just couldn't pin it down.

The dark-haired waitress who'd made eye contact with me earlier put the wineglasses down on the table and winked at me as she opened the bottle with practised ease. She was in her early thirties, with an easy style that probably betrayed a long career of waiting at tables. She didn't act like someone who conformed too readily and I wondered how she got on here.

'Would you like to taste the wine?' She looked at us both in turn and raised her eyebrows.

I shook my head, as I always do. So did Lin. Maybe if I had been Mr Lee with a real appreciation of fine wine, it might make sense. But, hell, this was house red. If it was off, we'd send it back. If it wasn't, then we'd have to drink it anyway.

The woman broke into a smile and poured us half a glass each.

'You get a lot of customers like that in here?' I asked, jerking my head in the direction of the businessmen.

'Yeah, more than I'd like.' She screwed her face up in good-natured distaste, then froze, looking towards the door and the man and woman who had just walked in. 'Hah,' she exclaimed, 'here comes the press again. Watch this!'

Over on the other side of the room, the woman reporter made a beeline for Black Tux, smiling charmingly as she approached. Her colleague broke away and started taking snaps of the restaurant. The maître d' didn't respond kindly at all and began pushing her back, shouting at both of them to get out. The barman almost leaped over the bar to his assistance and frogmarched the photographer out onto the pavement. Black Tux shoved the woman through the door after him, ignoring her shrieks and her threat to report his violence against her. Within seconds the disturbance was over and a roll of film was swinging from the barman's hand.

The waitress watched them leave and grunted contemptuously. 'Yuck! Reporters! They just don't know when to give up, do they?' She shook her head, then put the bottle down on the table.

'To do with the murder?'

She swallowed hard. 'Yeah. It's kind of hard – at the moment.' She had real difficulty getting the words out.

'Mr Wilson would be your boss, I suppose.'

She smiled ironically. 'Yeah, once upon a time. Poor guy.'

I watched her eyes as she spoke. There was something there. Regret, but a touch of anger too. It looked as if she had an opinion and, suddenly, I wanted to know what it was.

She cleared her throat and stood up straight. 'You want some water to go with this?'

'Please.'

She smiled at us as she left, as though she approved. I liked her too. I liked her style.

When she'd gone, we turned to the menus. There was an excellent choice, a selection of European, Oriental and South Asian dishes, all with tasty vegetarian alternatives, and I settled into my seat pleased to have such a variety to choose from. Black Tux was watching calmly now from near the kitchen door and, as soon as we put the menus back on the table, he came over and took our order. I went for an Eastern-style vegetable risotto, Lin chose the salade niçoise. The man wrote it down on his little pad, and then almost smiled at us as he took the menus back. Maybe I'd been a little hasty in my judgement. The place was growing on me.

The waitress returned with a jug and two glasses.

'You worked here long?' I asked, as she made space for them on the table.

She checked to make sure that nobody was watching and then pulled a face.

'Since we opened.' She said it as if it left a nasty taste in her mouth.

'And you don't like it much,' I prompted.

'Mmm. I don't usually bitch to customers,' she muttered conspiratorially, 'but, hell, this isn't really my kind of place any more.'

She poured some water and ice into each of the glasses then glanced round at Black Tux, who was watching her from the other side of the room.

'As a matter of fact,' she whispered, 'I leave at the end of the week.'

I remembered the way she had reacted a few minutes earlier. And I took a chance. 'You're upset about the way they treated Mr Wilson here?'

She stopped suddenly, jug in midair, and studied me, narrowing her eyes, talking slowly.

'Yeah, I might be.' Then she put the water down abruptly, as if I'd thrown her. 'I... I better go, or Monkey-Man over there's gonna tell me off for being too familiar with the customers.'

When she'd gone Lin frowned. 'That was odd – she seemed really uncomfortable when you said that.'

I shrugged. 'Maybe she's just upset.'

'You don't believe that, do you? I can tell from your eyes.'

I smiled and shook my head, dropping a note into the pending folder in my brain.

Lin asked if I'd got any further with finding Aunt Emily and I told her that I was still drawing blanks. I filled an awkward gap in the conversation by telling her about Beano, Hannah and little Susie. I didn't mention my visit to the Cardogan. *That* was strictly between me and the birds.

The waitress brought the food much sooner than we expected and set it down on the table. She looked at me as if she was about to say something, but didn't.

Lin smiled at her. The woman looked at the two dishes kind of doubtfully. 'Well, I hope you enjoy it,' she said, without much hope in her voice.

We didn't. Lin's tuna was tinned and the salad was limp. She pushed the plate away after picking at it for just a few minutes. My risotto fared no better. It was too sticky by far and, well, tasteless. At their prices, it should have been excellent. No wonder the place was half empty.

When we sat back, the waitress came over and cleared the table.

'You didn't like it,' she observed, without a hint of surprise.

Lin smiled regretfully. 'No, I'm sorry.'

The woman shook her head. 'Hey, don't apologise to me – I only serve the stuff.' Then she raised her eyebrows at me. 'You mentioned Mr Wilson earlier. You sound like you knew him.'

'No, not really. I just read about him, that's all. Tragic.'

She lowered her eyes, her sociability suddenly subdued. 'Yeah, he was a nice man, I can tell you that. Good restaurateur as well.'

I nodded at the plates. 'And the place is already going downhill without him.'

She sniffed and closed her eyes a moment as though struggling a little. 'Naw, they never let him run this one. If they had have, then you would have eaten wonderful food. Like when I used to work for him years ago.'

'I'm sorry, it must be hard for you.'

She threw us a bogus smile and grunted amiably as though it didn't matter. 'I better get your bill.'

She turned to go, then stopped, swung back round and raised her eyebrows in surprise. 'You must be important,' she remarked, her manner full of irony. 'The big bossman is coming over to see you.'

She smiled a little too broadly at the man as she passed. He nodded back solemnly, unaware that she was gently taking the piss.

He stopped at the table, looking carefully from Lin to me and then at the business card that I'd left with White Tux. 'Miss, erm, McGill?'

'I'm Cameron McGill. And this is Lin Lee, an... associate of mine.' I glanced at Lin. I hoped that was all right.

I extended my hand and he took it, shaking it firmly. He was quite small as men go, maybe five eight or nine. He had a sharp voice, laced with an east London accent. He wasn't thin, or overweight. But smart. He wore a well-tailored navy suit over a neat white shirt and a flecked gold and blue tie. He was in his forties, with slicked-back brown hair and a small, sharply featured, clean-shaven face. And, though his body language and his measured smile seemed pleasant enough, there was an edge in his voice and a staring quality about his eyes. He wasn't friendly, either. I guess that that's the way insurance investigators and taxmen are received the world over.

'Mr Palliachelli tells me that you were asking about Mr Peterson.' I frowned.

'Joe Palliachelli,' he repeated irritably, 'the bar manager.'

'Ah, yes.' I smiled at him broadly and took out the letter again, flashing it briefly in front of him. 'It's purely routine. In cases of natural death, my client pays out on life policies at once. In this case, well, obviously, we have to satisfy ourselves that everything is in order. I need to talk to the late Mr Wilson's business partner or partners, before I can finalise my report. You are...?'

'I'm John Keane, the chief executive.' He stared at me for a moment, clearly annoyed at being disturbed. But clearly more than a little curious as well.

'Maybe we could go somewhere private to talk?'

Keane looked at his watch, irritably, as if he really wanted to tell me to get lost, but didn't quite dare until he knew what I wanted to know. 'No, not now. I'm busy. You'll have to make an appointment.'

'Later today, then? It won't take long.'

He paused for a moment and blew down his nose. 'I'm busy all afternoon.'

'That's OK,' I replied pleasantly. 'This evening will be fine.'

He stared at me coldly, and yielded. 'Yes, all right. I'll be here until ten. I can see you any time after eight – but I can't give you very long. I'm a busy man.'

I smiled pleasantly. 'Thank you very much. That's very kind.'

He eyed me resentfully, then walked away, past the kitchen door and up the stairs.

The waitress returned with the bill and I pulled out some notes.

'I'll see you tonight if you're still here.' I smiled.

'You're coming back?' she asked incredulously.

I couldn't help laughing at her reaction. 'Yeah, I just have a little business with Mr Keane.' She looked at me anxiously. I shook my head. 'It's OK, you don't need to worry about me. I don't even know the guy.'

She looked relieved. 'Yeah, well, I'll still be here. I expect you'll eat beforehand this time.'

I smiled a big 'yes' and dropped a more-than-decent tip on the table. When we got outside, neither of us spoke at first. We'd avoided going back to the original conversation all through the meal. Now Lin's continuing uneasiness and my remaining misgivings hovered over us again, casting clouds across the sunny, late-October afternoon.

'I didn't know you worked for an insurance company as well.'

I shook my head. 'I don't. It's a ruse. A lot of people distrust private eyes, but nearly everyone will talk to an insurance assessor.'

'And the Commercial and Collateral?'

I smiled. 'It doesn't exist. I just had a few letterheads die-stamped. As long as I don't let anyone keep a copy, nobody ever checks.'

She tried to smile, but didn't quite make it.

'Why do you want to speak to him, anyway? That man, I mean.'

I ran my fingers through my hair. 'I don't know. I'm just fishing. Since we haven't been able to get a lead on Aunt Emily from the village, I thought I might try to work from another angle. Someone here might know something relevant, you never know.'

'You want me to keep on helping?' The dogged insistence that so irritated me yesterday was gone. Now she expected a negative answer.

I didn't disappoint her.

She nodded quietly and looked down at her feet. The breeze wafted some loose hairs around by her ear. The sun shone onto her face and highlighted a tear track on her cheek.

'Will I see you again?'

A small part of my brain was still ringing warning bells, but I took hold of her hand anyway and kissed her on the cheek. 'Yeah, I guess.'

She smiled kind of sadly and took a pen and a small notebook out of her bag. 'This is my address. It's in Salford. Will you at least come and have dinner with me tomorrow night?' She bit her lip. 'Please – I want to make everything all right before I leave for Singapore next week.'

I nodded and squeezed her hand. 'Yeah, all right. I'll give you a ring.'

I stood, gazing after her, as she walked off disconsolately down the street. I still didn't know what to make of her. Hell, I didn't even know what to make of myself. A few hours ago I'd sworn never to see her again. Now I'd virtually agreed to another date.

When I looked back into the restaurant, most of the other diners had left and the two waitresses were resetting the last remaining table. I thought about Keane again, replaying the brief conversation in my mind. There was something about him that made me uneasy.

Maybe I'd find out what it was tomorrow.

Twenty

I was halfway to West Didsbury when my phone rang. It was Mr Lee, wondering how the investigation was going and whether I was any nearer to finding Aunt Emily.

On the one hand, I was pleased to know that he wasn't using Lin as a conduit for his information after all – at least that dealt with some of my unease over her. On the other hand, it always grates when a client dogs me for details. Still, he *was* paying me generously, so I guess that he was entitled. I filled him in with what details I had and assured him, diplomatically, that I would be in touch just as soon as I had a result – and in the meantime he shouldn't worry.

When I pulled into the kerb outside her house, I was quite apprehensive about meeting Charles Wilson's sister. It was only thirty-six hours since the killing, and I had no idea what kind of state she might be in – or whether she would even talk to me. In the event, the woman with the grey hair was very defensive when she opened the door to me. She looked older now, her eyes were tired and her face drawn. She was dressed in a simple knitted jumper with a long flowing skirt, both of them plain and black. Her hair was tied back and her feet were bare.

'I'm sorry, I don't talk to reporters.' She recited the words as if she'd used them a lot recently.

I tried what I hoped was a sympathetic smile. 'I'm not a reporter. My name's Cameron McGill. I was in the bar with your brother just before he was killed. I'd like to talk to you about him, if I may.'

The scowl on her face evaporated and her eyes flickered with something more positive. 'You're... a friend of Charlie's?'

I didn't answer. There was no point in lying unless I really had to.

She looked me up and down – my short hair, my face, the black leather bomber jacket, my black jeans, my DMs. I guess that she believed me, because she opened the door wider and invited me in, leading me into the hall and then to the front room.

I stood in the doorway while she bundled up a long-haired Abyssinian from the nearest armchair. When she put him down, he wandered around resentfully, his tail in the air, then walked haughtily out of the room. Magazines and books were strewn in untidy piles on the floor, and sewing littered the worn-out chintzy settee. Two old armchairs stood at either side of the high Victorian fireplace, each covered with a throw. One was brown with a flowery cream design, the other a tie-dyed blue.

'Do sit down, Miss er... McGill, did you say?'

'It's Cameron, call me Cameron.'

I was wearing black jeans so I brushed at the white cat hairs on the seat. She noticed and switched seats at once. The other armchair was almost as bad but, since it was covered in black hairs, I could live with it.

'Have you known Charlie long?'

'I have to be honest with you, Miss Wilson—

'Please, Martha.'

I made an effort to smile: if I was going to get thrown out, then at least I could be graceful about it. 'The fact is, Martha, I'm not actually a friend of your brother's.'

She leaned back a little and eyed me warily. 'But you said that you were with him the other night.'

'Yes, I was. I'm afraid that I was following him.'

Her mouth dropped open. I handed her a card.

'I'm a private detective. I've been working for his wife. I was in the bar when he was killed.'

She stared hard at me for a moment. Anger flitted across her face, then she reached over for her glasses and studied the card.

She looked up, openly suspicious now. 'You were *following* Charlie? You're working for *his wife?'*

I shook my head. 'No, not any longer, I'm not.'

She put my card down and thumped the arm of the chair. 'That bloody woman!' she exclaimed, closing her eyes and clenching her fists together.

'I'm sorry. I know it's not very nice.' I almost got up to go right then.

She opened her eyes again and stared accusingly at me. 'Huh! I suppose she doesn't need you any more now. She's going to get what she wanted anyway, isn't she?'

I shook my head 'Look, Martha, I'm sorry about what's happened. Your brother seemed like a really nice man.' I paused for a moment wondering how much I should say. 'Let's just say that Elaine and me didn't exactly hit it off.'

'So *why* are you here?' she asked, holding my eyes.

'I'm working for one of your brother's friends. I can't tell you who he is, but he's concerned that the police may never catch the killer. There's an important witness, someone who was in the alley with your brother just before the attack. He ran off afterwards. My client's hired me to find him.'

She looked at me curiously now. 'You think this man may be involved?'

'I don't know, but the police want to interview him. He may have seen something. He met your brother every Monday.'

'Ah.' She nodded, relaxing a little. 'You must mean Aunt Emily.'

My heart missed a beat. 'You know him?'

She smiled weakly. 'No, I don't. The police asked me the same question. I know *of* him, that's all.'

I shook my head in disappointment. Martha noticed and tried to be helpful.

'Charlie talked about him – I mean her – a lot, but I've only met her – him – once.' She rubbed her forehead in frustration. 'Oh, I get so mixed up. I never know whether to say she or he – Charlie was always telling me off for getting it wrong.'

'It's OK, Martha, you're not the only one.' I smiled, encouraged by the way the conversation was going. 'I think we all have problems.'

Her face brightened a touch. 'Well, I must say, even after so many years, I never quite got used to it. I'm a little old-fashioned, I suppose, and men dressing up as women just doesn't seem quite right. Even Charlie found it a burden. Poor dear, he's thrilled when he's doing it, he comes alive—' She stopped suddenly, dismayed at her choice of words. 'Oh dear, what an unsuitable thing to say. I'm sorry, it still seems unreal. I keep expecting him to walk through the door whistling, like he always used to.'

'I know, Martha, it's really hard. My sister was murdered two years ago and it took me a very long time before I could accept that she was really gone.'

She studied me silently for a moment and her eyes changed. 'Your sister? Were you close?'

I nodded. My skin began to prickle with grief. 'She was a journalist. She was investigating a drug ring in Amsterdam. He killed her.'

'Oh, poor you.' She leaned towards me, her eyes big and soft now.

I shuffled uncomfortably in my seat at the memory, and changed the subject. 'Your brother didn't have an address book, did he?'

She smiled at me more kindly now. 'No, I'm sorry, the detective asked me that too. He and his friends were always worried about what they did. They had an agreement, he said, never to ask each other personal details. So I'm pretty sure that he wouldn't have put anything down on paper. All I know is that Aunt Emily was a really good friend to my Charlie. They seemed very close – closer than two men usually get.' She stopped suddenly and looked up in horror. 'Oh, I didn't mean...'

I smiled at her. 'It's OK, I know what you mean – you seem to have been very fond of your brother.'

She bit her lip. 'He was a lovely, kind man. He deserved better than this.'

She looked away, wiping her eyes with the back of her hand. The defensiveness had slipped away now, laying bare a desolation which hung in the air between us and wrapped itself around every word.

'I hope you don't mind me calling on you like this.'

She turned again and held me with her pale blue eyes. 'No. No, not now. Not when I know why. As a matter of fact, I think it helps to talk to someone. I've been sitting here moping for far too long.'

She stared off into the distance.

'Would you tell me about your brother, Martha? I'd really like to know and it might just help.'

She nodded. She even smiled a little, and I felt instantly guilty. She was interpreting my need for information as kindness.

'He's the nicest man I've ever known... er, Cameron. Gentle and kind. He always was – even when we were children. He's – I mean he was – a few years younger but, even so he always took care of me – protected me.'

She smiled affectionately. 'He started "dressing" when he was thirteen. He used to come to my room and borrow my clothes and makeup. As he got older, I helped him choose his own things. When he got married I just carried on helping. Betty, his first wife, never knew.'

'You don't *have* to tell me all this,' I cautioned. I felt like an intruder.

'No, it's all right.' She smiled wanly. 'It helps really. I'm sure Charlie wouldn't mind now. Do *you* mind?'

I shook my head. I felt quite privileged and I said so.

'The one thing that's always puzzled me is why he took up with Elaine.'

'Well, maybe it's not my place to say, but she doesn't seem very upset.'

'No, I know. I've just spoken to her on the telephone. I knew from the start that she was up to no good. Charlie just wouldn't listen. He was so besotted. I think he was trying to be somebody he wasn't –

trying to keep up appearances.' She shook her head sadly and explained. 'His business partner is... well, a bit of a playboy, I suppose. I've only met him a few times. Not a bad man – but certainly a spendthrift and a philanderer. Still, at least he's single, he never makes any pretence about wanting to settle down.'

'You mean Mr Keane?'

She looked at me, slightly startled. 'Oh no. Goodness no! I don't even know that man, and, from what Charlie told me, I don't think I'd like to. No, I mean Barrie, Barrie Peterson. They started the restaurant together – about five years ago. They were good friends at first, in fact they were always joking with each other – I remember that Charlie used to tease him. He'd call him "Bread Bun" because his initials were BAP and he knew that it really annoyed—'

'And he drives a blue Jaguar?' A shiver trickled down my spine as the innocently offered information jumped up and slapped me in the face

She blinked and drew back, startled at my sudden reaction. 'Oh, I wouldn't know about that, dear.'

Suddenly I was back on Elaine's drive watching Charlie's wife making out with the driver of the blue Jaguar's license plate. The implications began to bombard me. Charlie's business partner was Elaine's lover. I pushed the vision away and shook myself back to the present.

'I'm sorry, Martha, I didn't catch that last bit – what did you say?'

She looked at me with some concern. 'Are you sure you're all right, dear? You've gone very pale?'

'It's OK, I'm fine. Just a little under the weather, that's all. You were telling me about their restaurant.'

'Oh, yes. They've worked together for years. I rather think poor Charlie felt he needed to keep up with Barrie.' She smiled affectionately. 'He was fine before – while his first wife was alive. They were well suited. She was a little old-fashioned, but he was more settled then.'

'So when did he start going out "dressed"?'

'Six years ago – a few months after Betty died. He came round here more often than before – there's a room upstairs which I let him use. He often wore her clothes, though they didn't fit him very well. It was almost as if that brought her closer again. Anyway, after a few months, he began to get restless. He kept saying that he wanted to go out and walk around West Didsbury.'

'And you didn't like that idea.'

'I'm not a prude, Cameron, if that's what you're thinking.'

'It never crossed my mind.'

'I just know how cruel people can be. I didn't want them laughing behind his back, so I did some research and found out where people like my brother meet. I went with him the first time. That's when I met Aunt Emily – she befriended him and, for a while, he seemed happy enough.'

'But it didn't last?'

'No, he soon became morose again. He said he didn't feel like a real man and that he wished he didn't have to do it. It was about the time that he took up with Barrie. So I'm not sure whether Barrie's machismo was what depressed him or whether teaming up with Barrie was his way of trying to escape from his needs.'

She paused and gazed across the room, collecting herself together again. I waited, thinking how hard it is when you don't like who you are. When you take on society's paranoia and direct it at yourself. I was in my late teens when I first had to face up to my sexuality and it drove me to drugs. If it hadn't been for my sister and Becky, I would never have survived.

Martha went on to tell me how her brother was supremely happy when he dressed up – as though something inside him had been allowed out for a while. But then, afterwards, he always felt bad. As if he'd let everyone down – himself most of all.

'I suppose Elaine made him feel like a red-blooded male,' she mused. 'Maybe he even believed that his problem would go away if he married someone younger.'

'It must have been difficult for you, too.'

'Yes, I admit it, I've had my moments – but I've never been ashamed of him, Cameron. He's my brother.' She held her head up and steeled herself. 'He *was* my brother – and I loved him.'

'Yes, I understand.' And, for once, I think I really did. 'We're all different. We should all be allowed to be ourselves. It's nice that you helped him.'

We sat for a moment in a comfortable silence.

'This partner – did he know about your brother's cross-dressing?'

She blanched. 'Oh, goodness, no! I'm certain he'd never have breathed a word of it to Barrie, of *all* people.' She stopped suddenly and looked up at the ceiling, her voice catching in her throat. 'Goodness, I can't imagine what Barrie must be thinking now. He's such a man's man.'

I thought about the scene on the drive again and felt sick inside.

'So where does this Keane man fit in? I was in the restaurant today and he told me that *he* was in charge – he didn't even mention a Barrie Peterson.'

She shook her head and made a face. 'It's a very long story – I don't want to bore you, dear.'

'No. No, I'm interested.' I leaned forward. 'Really.'

She nodded and lay back in the chair, clasping her hands in her lap.

'Well, they used to be good friends. But for the last two years there's been a lot of bad feeling between them. Money problems, I think – to do with the business. The Cheshire Grill – that's what Chow City used to be called – got into a terrible mess. They nearly went bankrupt. Charlie blamed it all on Barrie, said that he was irresponsible.'

'Did he say why?'

'No. All I know is that, while Charlie looked after the kitchen and front of house, Barrie took care of the money side. Charlie told me that he felt very badly let down, though.' She hesitated. 'Well, if you want my honest opinion, I think the man was cooking the books.'

I frowned. 'You mean he was stealing from the business?'

'Well, maybe *borrowing* would be kinder, Cameron. Charlie didn't say it in so many words, but reading between the lines I'm sure that's what he was hinting at.' She sighed. 'Anyway, it's water under the bridge now. Whatever it was that happened to the business, Barrie did the right thing and found some investors. They were willing to put up a lot of cash into the restaurant for a half-share.'

She sighed heavily. 'I'm sorry, I'm probably talking rubbish – these things are beyond me – but Charlie told me that the business was expected to do well after the relaunch. Secretly, I think he harboured some notion of buying the rest of the business back again one day. And now this.' She looked away, crumbling.

'But Elaine told me that your brother was broke.'

She shook her head in disapproval, fire rising in her eyes again. 'Huh! What she meant is that she's spent all his savings. That woman's nothing but a gold digger!'

We sat around for a few moments after that, in a gloomy, reflective silence. I wanted to see the room that Charlie used, but I wasn't quite sure how to introduce the subject. In the end I didn't need to worry: Martha suggested it herself and took me up there.

The front bedroom was almost like a shrine dedicated to the late Charlie Wilson's feminine side. Ten or more cuddly toys nestled together on the flowery pink cover of the bed. A big old dressing table stood in front of the window, littered with every kind of cosmetic that you could imagine, all neatly arranged on the polished surface. No wonder that it took him so long to get ready.

On a side table nearby there were two wigs on polystyrene heads: one short and blond, one long, black and curly. A third stand stood bare and empty next to them.

Martha sat on the bed turning a white shirt over and over in her hands, fingering the fabric as if it were a rosary. She saw me watching.

'He left it when he got changed,' she explained. 'It still smells of him.'

I just nodded. There was nothing I could say.

I moved over to the chest of drawers and glanced across at Martha for permission to look inside. She mouthed a silent 'yes' and I continued with my search.

One of the two smaller drawers was bursting with a miscellany of knickers in bright reds, blues, oyster, black and white, many of them decorated with lace. The other held a collection of tights, stockings and a single black suspender belt. In the other drawers I sorted through the miscellany of cardigans, jumpers and leggings, with a sinking heart. When I'd followed him that first evening, I'd turned my nose up at his cross-dressing. Now, poking about among his possessions like this, I felt as if I were violating his memory. And all for what? I didn't even know what I was looking for.

I turned to the clothes rack, pushing the garments along the one by one. Blouses, plain and embroidered, hung neatly on plastic hangers. Five or six skirts hung from grippers. But most of the freestanding tubular rack was filled with dresses. A floral shirtwaister, a brown corduroy, several chintzy prints and an assortment of summery numbers. Nothing unusual at all – except that they had all belonged to a man.

I asked Martha where her brother bought his clothes.

'I bought them at first,' she admitted, smiling wanly. 'But after he met Aunt Emily, he started going round the shops himself. He liked wearing different outfits, though he never wanted to wear wedding dresses, thank goodness – like one or two of his friends did. That would have taxed me *too* much.'

When we'd gone up there, she'd brightened a little and now she was sitting on the bed leafing through a photo album. When I joined her, she moved it across between us and continued to turn the pages without comment. Every one featured Charlie in different outfits, some alone, others in groups. Several included Aunt Emily. I asked her if she had recalled anything else about her brother's friend.

She shook her head and turned the page again, sighing. My brother once asked if his friend could come here and get changed with him.' She turned and looked at me. 'Charlie told me he couldn't do it at home because his wife and family didn't know. He wouldn't get changed in the toilets at the bar, either, because people would see him as a man and might find out who he was.'

She pulled a face. 'If I'd been a better sister I would have agreed. But I said a very definite no. Helping him was one thing, but I wasn't going to become a community resource.'

'I think you did more than enough, Martha. Did your brother ever say where Aunt Emily *did* get changed?'

She shook her head and turned another page. 'I don't... No, wait... I think Charlie said something about him doing it at work. That's why he was so uneasy about it. He was worried that one of his staff might come back and catch him.'

'Did your brother say where his friend worked?'

She shook her head. 'No, I'm sorry. I didn't encourage him to talk about his friends. I didn't mind helping him, but...' She turned back to me again. Her eyes were wet and a tear was running onto her cheek. She closed the album and began to weep. I took hold of her hand and sat quietly until the sobbing passed.

'I think you've been an exceptional sister, Martha. You did everything that you could to accept him; he must have been very proud of you.'

She turned and smiled weakly at me, her lips pressed tightly together, still sniffing. Then the phone rang in the hall downstairs.

'You want me to answer that for you?' I asked.

She shook her head and sniffed, 'Thank you, dear. You're very kind, but I'm expecting a call – I'd better go myself.'

I moved out on the landing and listened. Downstairs Martha's voice was tense and reproachful and most of what she said was monosyllabic. She was wound up like a spring when she returned to the bedroom and walked right past me to the window, where she stood with her back to me, staring into the street and huffing indignantly.

'I'm sorry Cameron. I'm normally calmer than this. It's... it's just *that woman*!' When she turned her hands were fidgeting and her face was flushed and unhappy. 'Her poor husband isn't even been buried yet, and she's *already* worked out how she can get her hands on his share of the house!'

'That was Elaine?'

'Yes. The cold-hearted...' She stamped her foot and dissolved into bitter tears.

'All this – that phone call and half a dozen others before it – they're all to do with Charlie's half of the house.'

'She wants to sell his share?'

She snorted angrily and her grey hair trembled. 'Oh, it's worse than that – she wants to sell it now – this week! Can you believe that? I was hoping I could buy Charlie's share – my parents wanted us to keep the house in the family – but, *really*, she could have waited.'

'What did you say?'

'I told her yesterday that nothing could be done until the will was published. But she rang back again last night. She'd "taken advice", she said. There was "a way", she said. We could make some kind of a contract and I could pay her a large percentage as deposit. Then, when the will was published and the conveyancing was completed, I could pay her the rest.' She waved her hand irritably, 'Something like that.'

'Is that possible? Is it even legal?'

'Apparently – her solicitor said so. Anyway, mine has confirmed it as well.' She ran her hand across the back of her neck and sighed again. 'Apparently, they draw up something called a *conditional contract*. I can hardly believe it but Elaine's adamant that everything can be finalised by tomorrow. Tomorrow! That's not even three days after Charlie's death!' She shook her head. 'That's what the call was about. Anyway, for all my anger, I'm going to do as she asks – my solicitor strongly disapproves, of course.'

'*Tomorrow?* Are you sure?'

'Yes, I've got some money put by, and my credit's good at the bank. They've agreed to lend me the rest.'

For a moment I couldn't quite take it in. I'd never heard of anything like this. 'So it's all set, then?'

'Yes, It seems like it. Her solicitor is sending the papers to my lawyer tonight. If I sign tomorrow, the deal can be processed straight away. She's dropped nearly twenty-five thousand pounds off the valuation to get my agreement.' She shook her head in frustration. 'To be honest with you, Cameron, I think I would have agreed even without that. That woman's been driving me mad! I must confess, I can't take much more!'

I said a few words of reassurance and she promised to contact me if she came across anything that might help to trace Aunt Emily. When we reached the front door she stopped and smiled warmly. 'Thank you for listening to me, dear. Thank you for your understanding.'

I tipped my head. 'It's OK. Like I said, I know what it feels like.'

She opened the door and stood back to let me past. The two long-haired cats emerged from the back of the house at the sound of our voices, arching their backs and circling testily around the hall, clearly waiting to be fed.

'I hope that it all goes through without too much upset. Maybe you should tell Elaine to go through her solicitor from now on. There's no reason why she should ring you direct.'

She shook her head and snorted. 'I've already told her *that* – but it doesn't seem to make any difference. Her lawyer seems to let her interfere in whatever way she wants.'

'And who is her solicitor? Do you know?'

'Oh, he's just some small-time lawyer.'

'Do you have his details?'

She looked puzzled by the sudden edge in my voice. 'Why, yes, of course.' She went back to the hall table, pulled a note out from under the telephone, and read from it. 'It's Perkins and Gill – a Mr Pritchard. They're on Chapel Street in Salford.'

She stared at me in confusion. 'Why? Does that mean something to you?'

I smiled properly for just about the first time that day.

'It means a lot, Martha. I think we may just have found Aunt Emily.'

Twenty-one

By the time I drove out of Martha's street, it was nearly half past four and, though Salford was a mere hop, skip and jump away, the rush-hour traffic turned the short, hurried journey into a major headache. For the first time since the summer I missed my Harley. I missed the big black machine underneath me, the freedom it gave. Cars were OK, especially in this weather, but, damn, they were so fucking *slow*.

The solicitor's office was on the main road, on the first floor of what was once a bank, back in an age when banks still had local branches, and cared about being part of the wider community. Now it was a florist's with trendy aspirations and little real style. I turned right into a small back road beside the building, parked on a double yellow and then hoofed it back past the wilting irises and gaudy chrysanthemums to the office entrance.

I stopped briefly to check the polished brass plate at the door: HORACE PRITCHARD LLB, SOLICITOR, it read. Then I took the stairs two at a time. Four minutes to five. I'd made it just before closing time.

The receptionist, a mean-looking stick insect wearing a grey twin-set, looked up in surprise when I walked breathlessly into the dingy, neat little room. 'I'm sorry... er, *madam*.' Her mouth twitched patronisingly. 'We're about to close for the day.'

I smiled back, ignoring her sourness. 'I'd like to see Mr Pritchard, please.'

She stared back at me, openly assessing my value, silently

175

cataloguing my faults: my untidy hair, my leather jerkin, my black jeans, my boots. Then she forced a disdainful smile. No, not client material at all. No need to be concerned.

She looked at her watch and shook her head, hesitating slightly. 'I can make you an appointment for tomorrow, if it's an urgent matter, but there's absolutely no question of—'

'It's a personal matter,' I insisted, leaning across the counter and raising my voice just a little. 'Tell Mr Pritchard that I'm here to talk to him about his *aunt* – Aunt Emily, that is. Tell him that she's in trouble and he's the only one who can help her.' I stood back and relaxed. 'I think you'll find that he'll want to see me.'

She eyed me uneasily and disappeared through a door on the far side of the room, reappearing a few moments later.

'He says you may go in,' she conceded, tight-lipped. 'Through that door, second on the left.' She waved her hand haughtily towards a short corridor.

I smiled back sweetly. 'Thank you so much.'

Ah, the power of words.

Pritchard met me at the door. He attempted a formal smile and led me into a tidy and spacious office. I could tell from his awkwardness that he remembered me, but he was trying hard to keep his composure.

I certainly recognised him – his size and features were the same with or without makeup. But his demeanour was very different from the oh-so-flowery woman I'd met in Chloë's Bar. His small round face looked scrubbed and clean now, and though his hair was thinning it was slicked back, neatly combed over the crown of his head. He wore a smart charcoal-grey suit with a starched white shirt and a blue, regimental-type tie. White double-cuffs, fastened with gold cufflinks, peeked out from his sleeves. On his left hand he wore a single plain wedding ring. His nails were the only giveaway: slightly too long for a man, but now unpainted.

He took refuge behind the desk, looking distinctly uncomfortable, and gestured for me to take a seat. As I sat down he stared at me apprehensively and toyed nervously with a silver paperclip holder.

'How did you find me?'

'With difficulty. I must say you cover your tracks well.'

'Yes, well, it's very hard, you know.' He was awkward, embarrassed.

'Yes, I suppose it is. But Penny was your friend. I would have thought that you might want to help the police to find her killer, however hard it might be.'

He looked away for a moment, shame-faced, but, before he could respond, the phone buzzed and he picked it up. 'Yes, yes, Mrs Evans, I'm fine. No, I'll be here a little while. Family business. If you put the door on the latch, I'll lock up when I go.'

He put the phone down carefully and breathed in deeply through his nose. 'If you want to know the truth, I'm devastated.' He offered, wretchedly. 'I suppose you think I let her down?'

I didn't reply.

'Well, I didn't. I saw nothing unusual, so there was little point in risking everything by talking to the police. I couldn't have helped them.'

He took a tissue from the shiny silver holder on the desk and dabbed his eyes. I looked at the photograph in the nice polished frame next to it. A respectable-looking woman with two young boys standing in front of her.

'Young lady, this is very difficult. I know that you were in the bar that evening, but may I ask what your interest is in all this?'

I handed my card over to him. 'I'm a private detective. I'm working for one of Mr Wilson's other friends. The police want to interview you.'

He hesitated and then jerked his head in irritation. 'I've told you – the backstreet was empty. There was nothing to see! How can I possibly help them?'

'Are you sure there wasn't something – a parked car, someone watching from the top of the street, a noise of some kind?'

He shook his head. 'There was nothing, I promise you. The alley was deserted when I went back for my handbag. I *told* Penny to come back in with me, I *told* her it wasn't safe being out there alone.' He wiped his forehead with the crumpled-up tissue and then began to twist it in his fingers. 'She just laughed! She said that I was only going to be a minute or two, and it was a nice night, so she'd walk on and I could catch her up.'

He stopped and looked at me appealingly. 'I can't be of any assistance to you or the police. Please, just forget me, will you?'

I stared back evenly at him, totally unmoved by his pleading. 'I can't do that, Mr Pritchard. Even the fact that you saw nothing is relevant – the police will still want to interview you.'

Pritchard's cheeks were flushed and his breathing was irregular, panicky. 'Please, it will ruin me, if...' – he swallowed hard – 'if my other life comes out.'

I nodded towards the photograph. 'I suppose your family doesn't know.'

He looked down at my card again and reached inside his jacket, 'Miss McGill, I don't suppose you could see your way to—'

I glared back. 'Don't even ask!'

He nodded and let go of his wallet, glancing across at the photograph. 'All right. But do you think the police will respect my situation?'

I shrugged. 'They told the press that they would. I think that's a chance you have to take, don't you?'

He cleared his throat. 'I don't suppose I have a choice now, do I? All the same, I would take it as a favour if you could check for me.'

I nodded and pulled out my mobile. The switchboard put me through to Dyson straightaway and she answered in the same usual curt and efficient manner as always. I told her the news and asked if I could bring her lost witness along straightaway. There was a short, slightly stunned silence at the other end.

'Just one thing.' I looked across at Pritchard, who now seemed as if he might burst into tears at any time. 'He has concerns about confidentiality. I've told him that you'll do your best to be discreet.

Can he rely on that?'

'I'll do my best within the normal rules of evidence,' she answered, somewhat uneasily. 'I can't give him any long-term guarantees. The media are almost certain to pick up on it, even if no one else does.'

'Yeah, that's more or less what I told him. We'll see you shortly, then.'

'Right. I'll be waiting. Drive through into the yard at the back. I'll clear it with the duty sergeant and have someone meet you.'

I ended the call and smiled at Pritchard. 'She says no problem – shall we go?'

He stood up, still fidgeting, if anything more nervous than ever. 'I need to ring my wife. She'll be expecting me. Could you give me a few moments – please?'

The request – and his concern – seemed reasonable in the circumstances, so I walked out and left him to it, thinking that, whatever he told his wife now, she was bound to find out in the end, in court, if not before, and in a very *public* court where just about every tabloid would be represented. I almost felt sorry for the poor guy.

Yeah, almost.

I left the door slightly open as I left, then made a show of letting the door into the reception office slam shut, before stopping and straining my ears to catch what I could of the conversation.

His voice was so soft that I hardly caught a word. But there was no mistaking the urgency of his tone and the panic that was mingling among the despair. After a few seconds I abandoned what respect I might have had for his privacy and crept back to the office door.

He was standing in the far corner of the room with his back to me. But, even out there in the corridor, I could still hear the barking discordant voice that was haranguing him from the other end of the phone.

If it had been his wife, then it might have been understandable. But it wasn't. Without any doubt at all, it was a man. A man with a very threatening voice. A man who was clearly scaring the shit out of Charlie Wilson's 'best' friend.

Twenty-two

While Pritchard sweated it out in his office, I sneaked back into reception and rang Mr Lee. He was delighted at the news, of course, but declined the chance to meet Pritchard himself before our visit to Bootle Street Police Station. He was busy getting ready for some business meeting or other, he said, so we talked only long enough to arrange a final debriefing the following day.

When Pritchard emerged, he was wearing a neat black overcoat, with a deep-blue woollen scarf around his neck. He looked tense but resigned, an honourable man, prepared to give evidence, if he really had to. If I hadn't heard him on the phone, I might have missed the small signs of culpability. The restless eyes, the pink tinge to his skin and the way he couldn't quite manage to stop his hands from clenching and unclenching by his sides.

'I'll follow you in my car,' he said stiffly, opening the door for me.

I shook my head firmly. There was no way I was going to risk losing him now. Besides, there were still questions that I wanted to ask him and this might be my only chance. 'I'm sorry, Mr Pritchard, but you come with me. I'm sure that the police will get you a taxi back.'

He looked at me in surprise. 'I beg your pardon?'

'I think you heard. If you'd rather I asked them to send a squad car, then I will.'

He blanched, locked the door, then followed me downstairs like a lamb.

As I pulled out onto the main road and slotted into the traffic, I broke the gloomy silence. 'I met someone who knows you last night,' I said – pleasant, conversational. 'A woman called Natalie – in Napoleon's.' His head swung round. 'She tells me that you don't like each other.'

He looked at me, sullen-faced. I changed down and slowed in the heavy, city-bound traffic.

'She doesn't like anyone,' he retorted, tight-lipped and bitter. 'Unless they're rich, pretty and male.'

I wondered again about Lin and her, but pushed the thought away.

'You make it sound like she uses people.'

'She does. She's a drug addict; she needs money, and that's the way she gets it.'

'Did she hate Penny as well?'

He sighed and threw me a black look. 'Yes. Penny used to warn newcomers to keep clear. She detested the way Natalie led them on.'

The car in front slowed and I dropped into second, then braked to a stop as the traffic log-jammed again. 'Natalie wouldn't be very happy about that, I don't suppose'

He grunted disdainfully. 'No, she threatened Penny more than once.'

'Threatened her? With what?'

'She said she'd out her if she didn't stop it.'

'She didn't threaten violence, then?'

He turned in his seat to face me, clearly angry at my constant questions. 'No,' he snapped, 'she didn't. And why are you asking me all these questions?'

I shrugged. 'I'm just interested, that's all.'

He slumped back in his seat and looked out at the cars passing by on the other side of the road. Way ahead of us the lights changed to green and little by little the line of traffic began to move forward again.

'All the same, do you think Natalie could have killed your friend?'

'No, I don't think so. I'm not sure she even drives.'

'How about the preacher, then?'

'The police let him go. I thought you'd know that,' he snorted contemptuously.

'Yeah, I know,' I replied, 'but he seems to be the only person with a motive.'

Pritchard didn't reply. I changed up into third, picking up speed as the traffic eased, crossing the river and heading for Deansgate.

'Do you think that Charlie and the preacher's wife were really having an affair?'

He looked at me as if I were simple. 'Huh! It was hardly a secret, was it? Everyone was laughing behind the old man's back. He was out there shouting at us all about eternal damnation and, all the time, a transvestite was bedding his wife.'

He smiled smugly at the thought.

'But what did Charlie say? Did he admit it?'

'No, he didn't.' He scowled. 'Questions, questions – why are *you* so interested in what was going on?'

I shrugged. 'I told you, Mr Pritchard, just making conversation. Besides, the preacher's wife told me that Charlie and her were just friends.'

He snorted derisively and I wasn't sure whether the snub was intended for me or for her. 'So, who do you think did kill him?'

He shook his head and cursed quietly through his teeth. 'For God's sake! It was the skinheads! They're thugs, *everyone* knows that. It's been obvious for weeks that someone would get badly hurt – or killed. Besides, who else is there? Penny didn't make enemies.'

I glanced across at him as he pontificated. 'Except for Natalie, of course.'

He grunted and stared straight ahead, nicely wound up now with my constant questions. I pulled round the corner onto Deansgate. Bootle Street was only a short distance away but, before we got there, I had one more question that needed an answer. The main question. The one I'd been working up to.

'I've been talking to Charlie's sister,' I said, giving each word due emphasis. 'She tells me that Elaine's selling Charlie's share of the house.'

His eyes swung round to meet mine and his face turned a deeper shade of pink.

'It seems odd, doesn't it? Charlie was your best friend – yet all the time you were acting for his wife. Isn't there what you might call a conflict of interests there?'

Pritchard stared at me hard, his face set.

'I've *no* idea how you know about that,' he snapped, 'but, no – there was no conflict. I'm a professional man – and an honest one too.'

I turned left up Bootle Street and then pulled through the archway and into the station yard. 'So what about Charlie's shares in Chow City? Is Elaine selling them as well?'

He looked at me blankly. 'I've no idea, Miss McGill – and, even if I had, it would not be ethical for me to discuss it.'

I smiled grimly. 'Yeah, ethics. Well I guess you'd know all about them.'

Twenty-three

Dyson didn't keep us waiting long. Pritchard was greeted with real courtesy, taken to an interview room and no doubt plied with tea and biscuits by the sergeant. The superintendent took me to a different room and dispensed with the niceties.

'I should be annoyed that you're still around.' She threw me a curious look and pulled up a chair on the opposite side of the table.

I smiled back at her. 'Yeah, but how could you be? I've just found your star witness for you.'

'Yes, so you have.' She chewed on her tongue and stared back at me. 'But why? That's what I'm asking myself.'

I leaned back and clasped my hands behind my head, relaxed, affable, secretly pleased that I was winding her up a little. 'I'm just a good citizen, Superintendent. I saw a chance to help the police and I took it – isn't that what you always hope for?'

She eyed me carefully. 'Mmm, well, I've been in this job long enough to have caught a healthy dose of cynicism, McGill. And you know something?' She drew closer. 'I don't believe you.'

I shrugged. 'I can't help that, but you could at least be grateful.'

She stared back at me and sighed, unwilling – or unable – to let her own defences down that far. 'All right, then, McGill, so tell me, how did you find him?'

I told her about Martha and the sale of the house, and Pritchard's involvement with Elaine Wilson. I told her that Lin and I had asked around and learned that Aunt Emily was a lawyer. I didn't mention

Natalie specifically or Dorry's remark about Charlie's having a solicitor friend. I also kept quiet about Pritchard's phone call. Some things I wanted to keep to myself. At least until I spoke to Mr Lee.

When I'd finished she nodded and led me to the door

'I heard that you let the preacher go. Does that mean you're back to square one?'

She stopped, considering me again. 'We're continuing with our enquiries.'

I smiled. 'Aw, come on, Superintendent! I've helped you out a lot – the least you can do is fill me in on some of the detail.'

She stared at me silently for a moment. 'There were no fingerprints on the murder car, in fact there was no worthwhile forensic anywhere. This wasn't the work of a deranged old man. It was carefully preplanned. Mr Wilson could well have been just a chance target. We'll perhaps feel able to confirm that once your Mr Pritchard has made his statement.'

I nodded and half-smiled. 'You want me to go looking for skinheads now, then?'

Dyson blew down her nose. 'Do I detect a note of sarcasm there, McGill?'

I pulled a face. 'The hate-crime angle just doesn't feel right, that's all'

She tipped her head and glared at me irritably, 'Well, I'm sorry about that, but real detectives have to work on the facts – we can't allow ourselves the luxury of intuition.'

I ignored the jibe. 'So you don't have any other suspects?' I persisted, as she eased me out into the corridor

Dyson gave me a long hard look and held out her hand. 'Thanks, McGill. I'm much obliged to you. Now *go home* will you – *please*?'

I was going to make some final comment but my phone rang. Dyson threw me one last warning glance and took her leave.

I didn't recognise the number on the screen and, when I answered, the voice was deep and strange. Mid-European.

'Candy?' He rolled the name around on his tongue, making it

sound rich and dirty all at the same time. 'You want speak with me, yes?'

My brain flipped for a moment then I made the connection. The dealer. It was the dealer from the estate.

'Yeah, you got me, man. But I'm busy,' I hissed, playing for time. 'Can I ring you back in five?'

The voice on the other end laughed coarsely. 'No, I ring *you*. Five minutes.'

Twenty-four

The call came as I got back into my car.

'I hear you want buy?'

'Sure.'

'Where are you?'

'In town. Near Deansgate.'

'Good. There is bar, yes? Moon Under Water, at top end Deansgate, yes? Buy Budweiser and bottle of water. Sit near main door, leave drinks on table. I recognise you. Ten minutes.'

Click. The phone went dead.

I started the Clio and drove back into the street. Traffic was lighter now and I made the short hop back across Deansgate to the hotel in three, taking the ramp down to the second level and nipping into a vacant lot as a Volvo estate pulled out. It took me another ninety seconds to get up the stairs back to street level, ninety more to walk round the corner. Dead on time, I paid the bartender and carried the drinks to one of vacant tables just inside the double doors of the big café-bar.

The place was half full. Busy enough for him to hide in. Not so busy that I might be missed. I looked around, studying the faces, my belly churning at the thought of the confrontation. He'd be here somewhere. The unshaven man upstairs, leaning against the balcony and idly watching the bar below. The sharply dressed twenty-something sitting alone three tables up. The older guy touching up the platinum blond at the table across the room. Or any one of the other sixty or seventy men who were standing around by the long bar.

It was what I expected. He'd be weighing me up, checking that I was alone, making sure that I was legit. So I leaned back in my chair and waited, hands in pockets, gazing casually, uninterestedly, around me.

A young man strode in through the door, looking around him as if he owned the place. But his eyes passed over me and he joined his mates further up the bar. An older man, boozy and unshaven, crept in past the bouncers and was immediately retrieved and thrown out again. A gang of young women burst in singing and chattering among themselves.

I waited twenty minutes, then I left and took a walk down Deansgate, making a show of my displeasure, still feeling certain that he'd be watching me. He was playing a game. He'd make contact when he was ready, I was sure of it.

I stopped and gazed idly at the colourful displays in Kendal's, watching the reflections in the glass. Pedestrians hurried past like spectres among the *haute couture* dresses and suites. The hazy reflection of the black guy singing reggae in the doorway across the street. Ethereal traffic pushed slowly past in front of the plastic mannequins. A big old Bentley stopped momentarily, a Mini reversed into a parking space.

I set off again and crossed over the main road, doing my Green Cross Code on the kerb, checking the street carefully on either side. No show. No obvious tail – either on foot or in a car. The guy was good. Either that or he just hadn't shown. I hoped not. I had this one chance of helping Beano. I didn't want to blow it.

I thought about Dyson as I walked. After I'd put the phone away in the station, I'd fleetingly thought about sounding her out on my plan. But only fleetingly. She wouldn't approve, I knew it – at least not until she was in a position where she had little choice.

I glanced back as I cut left at a main junction, then crossed over again, taking another long, casual look behind me as I stepped off the pavement. The roads were busy, as always. There were plenty of vehicles that could have been tailing me. Small cars, vans... The hairs on the back of my neck prickled. There was the Bentley again, the one that pulled into the kerb near Kendal's. It was waiting at the lights behind me, ready to turn in my direction.

I took another casual look as I crossed the road, telling myself that I was imagining things. Why would a drug dealer be driving around in a Bentley, for Christ's sake?

At the end of the road I cut off onto Albert Square, stopping by Albert's memorial in the centre. From there I could see it all. The big Gothic town hall stood massively illuminated at the far edge, way across the cobbles. The roads and pavements running around the three other sides were busy enough, but the square itself and the benches around it were empty. Except for Albert and the four other statues, I was alone, in the heart of the city. Even the Bentley slid past up Princes Street, seemingly uninterested.

Calm down, Cameron. You're so jumpy you're beginning to imagine things.

I walked diagonally across the big open space and sat down on one of the benches facing into the square, tapping my feet impatiently. The black look on my face was no longer an act. I was tired of playing this game, and more than a little pissed off at being given the runaround. Either he wanted to deal or he didn't.

All around the vast square, people were scurrying about their business. Some were going home from work, others on their way out for the night. A well-dressed young woman hurried across the cobbles towards me, an eager, anxious look on her face as if she might be on a first date and unsure of what to expect. A businessman ambled past to my right, cradling an old leather briefcase to his body as if it might be full of cash, or precious documents. An old couple sat down wearily on a bench fifty feet away. A mother tripped past on the far side of the square, her two small children dragging colourful balloons behind them.

All so very ordinary. All so clean and wholesome. Right now I wished that I were one of them, going about a normal life, looking forward to a normal evening. If this guy was who I thought he was, he'd probably kill me if he found out what I was doing.

I shivered with cold and leaned back against the bench, pushing my paranoia away. Letting go. Stretching out my legs, feeling the tautness of my muscles, sensing the adrenalin beginning to bite, closing my eyes, clearing my mind. Drifting, drifting...

Suddenly all my senses were on alert.

He was there behind me. I smelled the sharp acidic bite of male sweat first. Then a finger tracing a pattern on my head, then his warm, fetid breath brushed the back of my neck as he started to sing, very badly, his heavy, mid-European accent rasping in my eardrums.

'It's the *Candy*-m-a-n, it's the *Candy*-m-a-n...'

I opened my eyes without moving a muscle. 'Very funny,' I muttered, without turning. 'Why don't you come round here where I can see you?'

He ruffled the hair on the back of my head and then walked around the bench and into my line of vision. A thin, mealy-looking guy, wearing a blue fleece, jeans and dirty trainers. His dark, lanky hair was overdue for washing and he probably hadn't shaved for at least two days. He looked as if he hadn't eaten for a long time, either. But what struck me more than anything was the long, white, hairless scar that divided the right side of his face. That, and the deranged, dangerously playful look in his eyes.

I stayed quite still, stretched out, eyeing him coldly while my heart tried to fight its way out of my chest and make a run for it. But I breathed steadily and focused on his eyes. The worst thing I could do was look scared.

He stood right in front of me, weighing me up, a smirk playing on his scaly lips. Then he lifted his right leg and put it in between my thighs, pushing it up into my crotch. Smiling curiously. Waiting for a reaction.

I sat up, pulling back. 'I came to do business,' I remarked, cold as ice. 'Touch me again and I leave.'

He smirked and sat down silently next to me, fouling the air.

I moved away a little. 'You should get a fucking bath, man. You stink.'

The smile slipped and a sneer took its place. 'Yeah, and you should get zip fitted on mouth. Johnny say you was gobby cow.'

I looked back at him belligerently. 'So what the fuck happened to you, man? I busted a gut to make the bar and you never even showed.'

He grinned kind of scarily and winked. 'You know score, Candy. You trust people you never know, eh?' He shook his head and smiled kind of sneakily. 'I think maybe not.' He stared at me for a moment and the smile faded to a scowl. 'Johnny say you see Mazza.'

It was very nearly a threat.

I raised my eyebrows. 'Johnny's a very observant boy.'

'He says you maybe copping off him.'

'Yeah, well, Johnny's wrong. Mazza's nothing but a big mouth. I get talking to him in Leeds and he gives me a load of bullshit. When I come to fix up a deal, some snotty kid tells me he's not home any more.'

'Yeah, well, he not deal. You stay clear, OK?'

I held him with my eyes. 'And just *who* the fuck are *you* when you're at home?'

He drew back. 'I deal you baggies, maybe few ounces rock or some E, lady, but you keep nose out, yes?'

I turned in my seat so that I was facing him and shook my head.

'Look, man, you don't get it do, you? I'm not talking a few pathetic wraps, or a bag of skunk. My regular guy took a fuckin' powder. He ran off, yeah? I got my people waitin', man. They got punters. Jesus I'm gettin' all kinds of fucking verbal. Look, I need a half-brick of shit and a K of rock – minimum – an' I need it soon.'

He looked back at me coldly, as if not too impressed. But his eyes blinked and his hand jerked.

'Look, man,' I persevered, ' I don't know you, either, right? You could be any fucker. At least gimme your name, then we're equal, right?'

He eyed me warily, but he was biting.

'Yeah, what about you… Candy? I not hear that name around.'

'Maybe you haven't been listening in the right places. Next time you're in Meanwood, you ask. You'll hear plenty of shit then, I promise.'

I watched him as I said it. Chapeltown, he'd know. He might even have contacts there. Meanwood – Jesus, who the hell ever went to Meanwood?

He sat thinking for a spell – the guy was clearly no geography expert.

I started to get up. 'OK, so you're a nobody, and you're wasting my time.'

'No, wait.'

I glared at him and stood my ground.

'You chill, lady. I get what you want, all right, but I need time, I need sign of good faith.'

I eyed him cynically. 'How big sign?'

'Two hundred.'

'Two hundred quid?' I ran my fingers through my hair. 'Jesus, you think I'm some kind of bubblehead, man? You could be some fuckin' tramp on the make, for all I know.'

His eyes suddenly jumped in their sockets and his face twisted angrily. I guessed I'd hit a tender spot.

He pointed his finger in my face. 'You show fuckin' respect, yes?' he hissed. 'You ask any person here in city. They tell you not mess with Vinko – OK?'

I pushed his hand away, pleased that, at last, I had a name. 'Yeah, OK, Vinko, just so long as we understand each other. I'll go to fifty quid – just to show my respect.'

He snorted derisively. 'One hundred – then maybe I see what I do for you.'

'Yeah, OK.' I dug in my jacket pocket and pulled out what was left of the wad, then, keeping the money hidden between us, peeled off five twenties.

'OK, I need two days. It is big supply you want, all right? I am in touch, forty-eight hours. You have plenty money, yes?'

We haggled for a good ten minutes about quality and price. He assured me that the resin was top grade and that the crack was as pure as a nun's knickers. They always start off like that; they're almost always lying through their teeth. So we negotiated. And, eventually, we agreed both price and quantity. I stuck in my own proviso about quality. No one I'd ever known would do a deal like this without it.

'I want notes. Twenties, tens, fives. Five thousand, unmarked.' He stared at me with his strange eyes. 'I check money before I let you go. You make monkey business, I kill you. You are smart bitch. You understand, I think.'

'Yeah, no probs, man.' I pointed my finger at him. 'But don't you try to fuck me, either, Vinko. I know what's what. If the stuff is crap, the deal's off. Do you understand that?'

A greasy smile slipped back onto his face and he leaned back, his hand on his heart. 'I have reputation, Candy girl. Like I tell you, ask around.' The smile slipped again. 'But maybe while you ask, you check what happen when people fuck *me*, yes? In case you feel like talking out of your turn.'

'Is that why Mazza isn't seeing anyone?'

He shook his head and sneered. 'He good example for you. I give him credit and he not pay. I not forgive easily. Yes?'

I smiled grimly to myself. 'That's funny, I heard it was some woman that beat him up. They said she was fucking his ex-wife and your friend Mazza took exception.'

He leaned back and shrugged, the same crazy glint in his eye. 'Well, if that what they say...'

The wind was getting up now and the square was suddenly icy cold. I pulled my leather jacket round me and stared at him silently until the smile was replaced by a scowl and he stood up.

'I will get in touch, yes? You take care, Candy. I watch you.'

'What's your number – just in case? It didn't show up on my phone.'

'You want me – see Johnny. If not, I ring in two day with time and place. You come alone, yes?' He looked at me as though he didn't trust me an inch. 'Now where you stay? In case I need you.'

He looked at me as if I had no choice. These bastards are all the fucking same. They always have to be on top of the game.

'Overnite Inn, just off Deansgate – and don't start following me, I don't like it.'

He smiled like someone pleased with himself. I threw him a black look. 'Don't fuck with me, Vinko.'

He grunted and an evil grin spread across his face as he turned to go. 'No worries, Candy,' he scoffed, 'you safe as house. I *never* fuck lesbian.'

I gave him the finger and watched my hundred quid walk away along the front of the town hall. The guy thought he was so damn good. Jesus, he made me feel dirty.

I was so preoccupied that I didn't notice the big guy in the suit, and the gold-rimmed glasses. The one who'd just walked up beside me. When he touched me on the arm, I almost jumped off the seat.

'Miss McGill?' he asked pleasantly – a real gent.

I looked up at him, then at the receding figure of the dealer, a little anxious in case Vinko turned and saw me talking to someone else. But he didn't. He just sauntered round the corner of the town hall as if he were the fucking lord mayor or something.

I looked up at the big guy and frowned.

'Yeah, that's me,' I responded, still in character. 'What's it to you?'

The man leaned forward and proffered a hand to help me up.

'Please be good enough to come with me. Mr Lee is waiting.'

Twenty-five

Mr Lee was sitting in the Bentley, a small figure almost lost in the vastness of the car's plush interior. He smiled warmly through the open rear door as I approached. I was less than courteous back. In fact, I was bloody furious.

'You've been following me.'

He waved his hand with good humour and moved over to let me in. 'I'm impressed, Cameron. I thought you hadn't seen us.'

I glared back, irritated by his bonhomie. 'Yeah, I saw you, all right. In Deansgate and then around the square.'

Mr Lee blanched at my sharpness, pursing his lips and then gently shaking his head. 'Forgive me, young lady, I'm an excitable old man. I was returning from an appointment and I saw you walking down the road.' His eyes flashed disarmingly. 'Well, I just couldn't wait. I was so pleased that you'd found this Aunt Emily. I just couldn't resist talking to you at once.'

'Yeah, well, OK,' I conceded, 'but you could have rung me. I might not have wanted to see you just at this particular moment.'

He regarded me soberly for a moment and his eyes flashed. 'You mean while you were talking to that man Cuzak?'

I stared back, stunned. 'Cuzak?'

'Vinko Cuzak – the man you've just been talking to.'

'You know him?'

Mr Lee leaned across and held my arm. Suddenly there was fire in his eyes and an edge to his voice – as if he were *my* grandfather; as if, suddenly, he were responsible for me.

'I've been around for a long time, Cameron. I may only be a restaurateur but I know how it is in this city. He's a criminal. He's Serbian mafia. That man is dangerous. Stay away from him.'

I stared back, speechless.

He smiled a little and withdrew his hand, raising one grey eyebrow. 'I see that you are surprised that an old man should know such things. Remember, I served on the police authority for many years, I count senior police officers as close friends and I still keep my ear to the ground – even fancy restaurants like mine get frequented by scum like that. My friends in the force have been trying to put Cuzak away for some time.' He paused a moment and regarded me curiously. 'He's a drug dealer, Cameron. Why would you be talking to him, of all people?'

I leaned back into the soft leather upholstery, reminding myself that he was my client, fighting the impulse to tell him to mind his own fucking business.

'I appreciate your concern, Mr Lee,' I replied tightly. 'But it's a different job, for a different client, and I have to respect their confidentiality too.'

He held his hands open in contrition, clearly concerned that he'd upset me. 'I just thought you should know, that's all. This city can be a dangerous place.'

I acknowledged his apology without much grace. 'Yeah, well thanks. I can't say that I relish dealing with the man, but in my job I sometimes have to do things that I don't like.'

The chauffeur pulled out, joining the line of traffic moving into Princess Street, then made his way to Chinatown. Mr Lee seemed to forget the incident straightaway, making pleasant conversation all the way there. Inside I was still smarting, but there was no point in falling out with a client. Besides, I still liked him and – for all my indignation – he'd done nothing more than express concern over my safety. People are always telling me that I can be too sensitive.

Mr Lee's private apartment was directly above the Golden

Snapper. I was expecting something grand, but what I saw took my breath away and erased all memory of the confrontation. He used his private key to take the lift right up to the top floor and then led me in through an intricately carved, antique door, over soft white carpeting and past beautiful Chinese wall hangings, into a room overflowing with stunning antique furniture, china and some amazing pieces of art.

He smiled proudly at my gasp of admiration and invited me to sit down on a beautifully upholstered divan, before ringing down to the restaurant for drinks. While we waited he related the colourful history of some of his treasures.

The waiter arrived within minutes and deposited a large glass of Campari and tonic on the lacquered table beside me, bowing slightly to us both before leaving. Mr Lee leaned back into the wing chair and raised his fruit juice. 'To you, Cameron. Congratulations on a successful investigation.'

I smiled back, totally relaxed again. The old man could charm a snake.

'So, the transvestite lawyer has agreed to help the police. That is excellent news!'

I put my glass down onto the coaster and leaned forward, rubbing my hands, still choosing my words. 'Yeah, I suppose so. The police are pleased, and the lawyer – Pritchard – has promised a full statement.'

'And you didn't mention my involvement?'

'No, not at all.' I smiled. 'I told Superintendent Dyson that I helped out of a sense of public duty.'

'Good, so do you think that the police will find the killer now?'

I shook my head. 'No, Mr Lee, I don't believe they will.'

He threw me a curious look.

'The thing is...' I tried to collect my thoughts into some kind of logical argument, but the trouble was, most of my feelings still lacked any real foundation. 'The lawyer is adamant that he neither saw nor heard anything when he left the victim in the backstreet. The police found nothing worthwhile on the murder vehicle. And, as far as anyone can tell, nobody had a motive for killing your friend – aside from the preacher, who has been ruled out anyway.'

'So, what are the police saying?'

I sighed testily. 'Everyone – including the police now – seems to believe that this is a hate killing, maybe the first of many.'

'But you don't?'

'I have strong doubts, Mr Lee. I just think that's a little too easy.'

'But if the lawyer saw nothing and the religious fanatic is vindicated; if, as you say, there appears to be no motive...'

I ran my fingers through my hair and sighed. I knew exactly what he meant. I'd been through this a hundred times already.

'Yeah, I know. The hate-killing scenario makes sense. But when you look closer, there are inconsistencies.'

'Like what?' Mr Lee eyed me with interest and took a sip of his drink.

I wondered for a moment what he'd think of my distinct lack of openness with his beloved police force.

'I have to be honest with you, Mr Lee. I didn't tell the police everything that I found out. I wanted to talk to you about it first.'

He waited.

'There *are* people with possible motives, apart from the preacher. There's at least one person in the village who really disliked Charlie. Then there's Charlie's wife, Elaine – my previous client. She never made any secret of her desire to make a lucrative divorce settlement. She wasn't the least bit upset about her husband's death. And it also turns out that Horace Pritchard – Aunt Emily – is acting for her. There may be life insurance as well. She could do very nicely out of his death. She certainly has a credible motive.'

Mr Lee looked dubious. 'You're saying that she was capable of killing him?'

'I'm saying that she was capable of *having* him killed. Perhaps with someone else's help.'

'And you have that someone else in mind?'

I nodded. 'Charlie's old business partner, Barrie Peterson. They're having an affair. It wouldn't be the first time that a wife and her lover had conspired to bump off the husband.'

'And you haven't talked to the police about all this?'

'I haven't mentioned the affair. I'm sorry, Mr Lee, but I don't think it's up to me to do their job for them.'

I suppose I expected him to be critical of my lack of cooperation with Dyson, but there was no sign of displeasure. Instead the old man shook his head slowly and swirled the drink around in his glass.

'You make an interesting case for further investigation, Cameron.'

I picked up my Campari and sank the last of the fiery red mixture. 'There's one more thing.'

He turned and gave me his attention again,

'I have no hard evidence but I suspect that Pritchard is lying, or at least not telling the whole truth. I overheard him making a phone call. I can't be sure, but I think that someone was putting pressure on him.'

Mr Lee held my eyes for a moment and then pressed the restaurant intercom again. I could see from his manner that he was still concerned. I hadn't known him long, but it was already clear that he had a well-developed sense of fair play. He wanted his friend's killer caught – and there was no way he would be happy with a convenient fudge.

'You will have another drink, Cameron?'

I nodded and he ordered another Campari for me and a mineral water for himself.

'I envy you your age, young lady,' he beamed as he sat down again. 'My doctor has given me strict instructions. Whenever I eat or drink, it is always a value judgement. Do I value extra years – or quality of life? Sometimes it is a difficult choice.'

I smiled sympathetically, wondering how it might feel to be old. Knowing that death could come at any time. I wondered if it made you relish your life, your loved ones, that little bit more. 'You seem very fond of your granddaughter, Mr Lee. It must be nice to belong to a big family. I never had anything like that.'

He shrugged. 'It is good when it is good. But heartbreaking when it is not.'

I frowned.

'I should explain, Cameron. It is true that Lin and I belong to a large family, but the sad fact is that we have only each other. She may not have told you, but – for very different reasons – we both have difficulties with our family.'

The waiter returned with the drinks, bowed respectfully and left. The old man waited until he had gone and then looked at me apologetically. 'I'm sorry, I was beginning to indulge myself. I'm sure that you are not interested in my family issues.'

I shook my head, the man wanted to talk to me and I wanted to listen. 'No, it's all right. Actually, I feel privileged to have met you, Mr Lee. You're a remarkable man. You're rich and successful. You must have had to work very hard to get where you are. Yet you still have a sense of respect for others – I admire that.'

He inclined his silvery head. 'Thank you, Cameron. This may surprise you. I'm a man who has everything other people yearn for – wealth, power, influence. I mix with important people from all around the world – ministers, politicians, celebrities, top businesspeople. All of that is important to me – of course it is. But, in the end, nothing matters more than Lin's happiness.'

He got up and walked over to the window, silently gazing out over Chinatown for a few moments. When he turned to face me again he was silhouetted against the light. I wondered if he'd done that on purpose – so that I could no longer see his face. At any rate, as he continued, there was a noticeable shakiness to his voice.

'Lin is far more than just a grandchild. I saw her on the day she was born. A tiny bundle not much bigger than my hand. I sneaked into the hospital when her father left. Even then, when she was only a few hours old, she looked exactly like Lee Soo May.'

I murmured an acknowledgement, wondering, frankly, what the hell he was talking about. He paused for a moment and then came back to the seat looking deeply reflective. His eyes were damp and his face softer than I had seen it before.

'Circumstances meant that my late wife and I only ever had two children. A small family for wealthy Singaporeans. But I loved them both with a passion. My daughter and her husband – Lin's parents – became a problem for me in later life. My other daughter, Soo May, never had the chance to become anything. She died when she was only two – and, rich though I was by then, there was nothing I could do to save her.'

'I'm sorry.'

He looked up at me and smiled thinly. 'It was a big loss and, forgive me, it still is. We had the best doctors, the best care.' He paused for a moment, swallowing hard and looking down into his glass. 'Many years later, after I had fallen out with my son-in-law, after I had learned to cope with the despair, my daughter had her first baby...' He paused again, choosing his words carefully. 'Well, let me just say that the baby was beautiful. And, quite magically, it was as if my precious daughter had somehow been reborn.' He looked down briefly.

When he lifted his eyes again, they were wide with wonderment. 'Can you imagine what that meant to me, Cameron? Can you imagine the way it felt – if you believe in ancestors as strongly as we do? The child was the *exact* image of my little girl and, incredibly, I knew that the gods had given her back to me.

'So you see, that's why we are closer than you might expect. That's why I defend her and why I take a more than usual interest in her wellbeing. It is the reason that I indulge her – yes, even in her scatterbrained desire to help with this... "gay liberation" in the Straits.'

'Are you really worried about her getting jailed?'

He raised his eyebrows and pulled a face. 'If she and her friends cause too much trouble, they will not be tolerated. That much is true. But, of course, as long as I am around, I will see to it that she is all right.' He leaned forward and pointed a finger at me. 'But you are not to breathe a word of that, do you understand?'

I smiled and nodded. Maybe Mr Lee was a champion for human rights too and he just didn't realise it. All the same, I could understand how much Lin would disapprove of any interference.

He sat back, a little pink, slightly embarrassed by his own sudden candour. 'Forgive me. We should get back to the matter in hand. You were talking about motives. It seems that you have got a good deal further than the police have. Would you consider continuing with the investigation?'

I smiled in response. I thought he'd never ask.

'I'd like to, Mr Lee, but I can't guarantee anything. I could be wrong.'

He stood up, nodding sagely, and led me to the door. 'You're a good woman, Cameron. I like you. And – much more important – I respect you. If anyone can find out what really happened that night then I'm sure you can. I will pay you generously, I think you know that. All I ask is that you keep me informed and report to me before you hand anything or anybody over to the police. Is that clear?'

'Of course. I've already told you, it's standard practice.'

He stopped in the doorway and then turned back uncertainly. This rich, urbane old man who had seen and done so much was hesitating, as if unsure of his ground.

'I hope that you won't take this the wrong way.'

I smiled, trying to put him at his ease. 'Try me.'

'I'm sorry to bring this up again, Cameron. That man – the one I saw you talking to in the square...'

'Please, Mr Lee, I've already told you...' I sighed, trying hard to remain affable. 'It's to do with another case. I really can't talk about it.'

He put his arm round my shoulders and led me down the stairs into the empty restaurant. Staff were running around busily preparing for the evening shift. Through the open door to the kitchen, I could see a team of chefs and kitchen assistants preparing food and sauces, laughing and joking noisily with each other as they worked.

'I'm telling you this as a friend, Cameron. I like you very much and I don't want you to get hurt. Stay away from him – he is a bad person.'

I held out my hand and he took it. 'I wish I could, Mr Lee. But, like I told you earlier, it's what I do.'

He nodded soberly and pushed the button for the lift. 'Maybe. But sometimes we can all take our work too seriously. Whatever the job is, it is not more important than your life. Whoever is hiring you and whatever they are paying you, the risk is not worth it.'

The lift opened and he held the door back.

'Thanks for the advice, Mr Lee, but this is one case where I don't have a choice. Vinko Cuzak has framed a good friend of mine and this is the only way I can help her. It won't interfere with your investigation, I promise you.'

He touched my arm, looking genuinely troubled. 'Listen to an old man. Please.'

I shook my head and brushed past him into the lift, more than a little rattled by his persistent intrusion. 'I'm sorry, Mr Lee – this is a private matter. I don't want to talk about it.'

He opened his mouth to reply, but before he could say another word the lift doors closed and I was on my way down to street level.

Twenty-six

It was well after nine by the time I reached Chow City and, by then, I was so hungry that I was beginning to feel a little sick. Or maybe it wasn't just hunger. I thought about Lin as soon as I walked through the door and my spirits sank again. She'd said that I should go round for dinner the following day and part of me was still inexplicably excited by the invitation.

Black Tux nodded at me when I walked in and appeared mildly surprised when I asked to see his boss. I sat at the bar while he went upstairs with my message. The place was no busier than at lunchtime. Only four tables were occupied and there were a couple of smooth-looking guys drinking at the bar but, even for midweek, business looked slack.

'*But what interests me, McGill, is what* Miss Lee *has told you about* herself.'

Lin had been circumspect this afternoon, to say the least. She hadn't admitted to a secret, but she hadn't really denied it, either, and I was left with the strong suspicion that I was being strung along.

The barman, whom Keane had referred to as Palliachelli, sauntered over as if he were about to throw me out, but instead he asked me what I'd like to drink. When I declined he pushed a half-empty bowl of peanuts over to me and grinned. I swear that he was winding me up.

Was Lin doing the same? Was I really being taken for a ride? Angel had seemed like a sweet woman too, at first. Attractive and vulnerable.

I'd trusted her. Jesus, I'd even slept with her. And all the time her killer boyfriend was watching me from the sidelines.

Black Tux returned few minutes later and interrupted the depressing train of thought. Mr Keane couldn't see me: he could be busy for the next hour. He said it as if his boss hoped I'd go away and I sensed that, if I just came back in an hour, the man would have left. I looked at the clock on the wall. I needed to wait. That way I was certain of catching him. But, by the time I'd finished, most of the other restaurants would be closing. It had to be Palliachelli's peanuts or another Chow City meal. I thought of the survey again and asked the guy to show me to a table.

I ordered a beer and asked for a cheese omelette in the hope that something so simple might at least be palatable. He looked thrown and said that it wasn't on the menu. I agreed with him, but suggested that every chef in the whole damn world knew how to make an omelette. He grunted and said that he'd see what he could do.

My friendly waitress brought the beer and smiled a greeting, as if she really was pleased to see me again. 'So you kept your promise,' she said, eyeing me wickedly. 'You're a brave woman, eating here a second time.'

I laughed. 'Yeah, well, I tried to get out of it, but your boss can't see me yet and I can't wait. I'm starving.'

She put the drink down on the table and smiled wryly. 'Yeah, well, I hope you realise that you've put Monkey Man into a flat spin asking for something as complicated as an omelette. Jeez, no one's ever asked us to *cook* anything before.'

'I know, I saw the panic in his eyes.'

She smiled and her eyes danced. 'Yeah, well you're in luck – he's offloaded the job onto me, so I'm gonna disappear into the kitchen right now and see what I can do.' She winked and headed for the door at the far side of the room.

It was only ten minutes before I saw her again. She came out bearing a plate of crispy chips and one of the fluffiest omelettes I've ever seen. I watched her approach, genuinely impressed.

'Ever heard of a restaurant where they don't employ a chef?' She pulled a face. 'Yeah, well, you have now, sweetheart. See, our monkeys can operate a microwave really well. Next week they're gonna learn how to boil an egg. Omelettes! Jesus! I think that's a few years away.'

I smiled as she put the plate down. I liked the woman, she had style. I decided to stick my neck out.

'That's really kind of you. I... um... wonder if I could ask another favour.' She cocked her head and waited. 'I'd like to talk to you when you finish, if that's OK. In confidence. I'm a detective. I'm compiling a report on Charles Wilson for an insurance company.'

She looked a little startled.

'It's all right. It's just routine.' I quickly reassured her. 'I just have to talk to a few people who knew him and write a report, that's all. That's why I'm seeing Mr Keane.'

She pulled a face and looked round behind her. Black Tux was standing by the desk, watching. When she turned back she hesitated, moving her eyeballs in his direction.

'I... er, I think I better go.'

I put my hand out and stopped her. 'I'd rather you didn't mention this to anyone.'

She nodded slightly and moved away, making a show of laying a recently vacated table.

I enjoyed the omelette. It was light and cheesy. Even the chips were good. When I'd finished she came and collected the plate. After I'd thanked her I tried again.

'*Will* you talk to me? I promise you absolute confidence.'

She frowned. 'You said it was something to do with insurance. What the hell does that mean?'

'Mr Wilson had a life policy with the company I work for.'

Lying gets easier the more you practise – and I've practised a lot. Even so it bothers me sometimes, especially when I lie to someone I like.

'They always ask for an independent report in cases where there's been a violent or unknown cause of death. You know what these big businesses are like – they aren't keen on paying out even if everything is above board.'

'And you think that *I* can help?' She raised her eyebrows and feigned confusion.

'Yeah. I'm just looking for background, that's all.'

She pulled a face 'Well, let me think about it, will you? You want a coffee?'

When she returned with the cappuccino, I pressed my case.

'There's nothing heavy – just a few basic questions. It won't take long, it's confidential and my clients will pay for your time.'

She looked more interested then. I wasn't sure whether it was the reassurance or the money that had done the trick, but whichever it was she never got to answer because Keane appeared at the bottom of the stairs and walked right on over, brushing the woman aside.

'I can see you now.' He didn't look at all sorry for keeping me waiting – in fact he looked decidedly sour. 'I can give you a few minutes, that's all. Follow me.'

The waitress and I exchanged meaningful glances, then I walked after him, up the stairs to the first floor. At the top we turned right onto a short, windowless corridor that ran across the back of the restaurant, over the kitchens. The only doors were on the left. The first two were toilets, the third appeared to be Keane's office.

It wasn't what I expected. The room was spacious enough, maybe fifteen feet by twenty, with a wide, uPVC window that looked out onto the back of the restaurant. A table stood in the middle of the room with a computer screen and keyboard on top and little else. Two of the walls were lined with metal utility shelving, most of which held a collection of dingy-looking box files. A grey filing cabinet and a table occupied the other wall. For a swanky restaurant, it was a very basic office, almost a storeroom. In other circumstances, I might have been impressed with the lack of pretension – except that, in Keane's case, it didn't fit. The man wore expensive suits and loud ties. His every action spoke of a well-developed sense of self-importance – he'd never have an office this lowly, I just knew it. Besides, there were no personal effects, no individual touches. Even the plastic wastepaper basket was empty.

Keane sat down behind the table, taking in my short hair, lack of makeup, flat breasts and check shirt and jeans all in one glance, then he pulled a face.

Not his type. Now there's a relief.

I took a moulded-plastic chair from near the passage wall and scanned the room as I sat down. There was no PIR and I couldn't see any plates on the door when I came in. It looked as if the place wasn't alarmed. However, the window looked impregnable. Not an easy point of entry, especially on the first floor.

He made a show of looking at his watch. 'I hope this won't take long.'

I gave him my most professional smile and handed him a card.

'As I told you earlier, Mr Keane, I'm working on behalf of Commercial and Collateral. Mr Wilson had a life policy with my clients and, as is normal in unfortunate circumstances like these, they've asked me to compile a routine report on his death.'

He eyed me suspiciously. 'I thought that the police had already done that.'

I took out my notebook and crossed my legs demurely, hamming it up a little. 'I'm sure they have. But you know what these big insurance companies are like.'

I smiled pleasantly, but he just kept on staring through me as if he wasn't quite connecting. It wasn't cold in there, but a shiver ran down my spine all the same

'Not surprisingly, the beneficiary is concerned at any delay in payment, so I'd like to tie things up as soon as—'

'And *who*, exactly, is the beneficiary?'

I shook my head, trying not to let his intense staring faze me. 'I'm sorry. I can't say, but... well, I'd like to submit my report as quickly as possible, so that the insurers can get a cheque off.'

He grunted and finally looked away. But I could see his brain turning over and I wasn't too sure that he believed what I was saying.

'I'd like to ask a few questions about his business interests first, if I may.'

He leaned back in his chair and screwed up his face. 'Look, girlie, you can ask all you like. Whether I answer is a different matter.'

I stared back silently for a moment and then decided to ignore his rudeness. 'That's your prerogative, Mr Keane, but please bear in mind that my clients need this information and, if you won't tell me, I shall have to spread my net much more widely.' I smiled sweetly. 'It would be in everybody's interests if we could tie all this up tonight.'

He grunted some sort of acknowledgement and I continued. 'First of all, I'm a little concerned about Mr Wilson's changing business interests and the whereabouts of his original partner – Mr Barrie Peterson, I believe he's called. I need to talk to him as well.'

Keane shook his head sharply at me. 'Our takeover of the restaurant is private information, Miss McGill. As for Mr Peterson, well, he doesn't come in much now since we took over. Besides, he's rather traumatised in the circumstances – I think it would be respectful if you left him alone at this difficult time.'

I blinked at the obvious lie and began to get even more interested.

'Even so, Mr Keane, I'd appreciate your help. I know that Mr Wilson and Mr Peterson sold a significant part of their holding in return for a share in the new venture. I simply need to establish the facts – just to confirm that there is nothing in Mr Wilson's business dealings which could have contributed to his death. '

He sniffed angrily and turned a little red. His eyes looked through me, resentfully again. 'If Charles Wilson chose to spend his leisure time with homosexuals and perverts and then got himself killed because of it, I don't see how his business dealings could be at all relevant.'

'It's just routine, Mr Keane,' I reassured him, gritting my teeth and trying to remain as charming as possible. 'The police think that it was a hate killing. I'm simply trying to confirm that. You know how it is.'

He paused and scowled at me for a moment. Clearly he didn't

know how it was, but I stared back anyway, determined not to concede defeat.

'Very well,' he snapped, 'it's hardly confidential. We bought shares from both of the original partners. They kept a significant stake, but gave up control. I run the business now.'

'And Mr Wilson and Mr Peterson, did they both continue working here?'

'Only for a few hours a day.' He eyed me coldly.

'So they became kind of sleeping partners?' I persisted.

He looked away in contempt, then continued sourly. 'Yes, you could say that. I'd prefer to call them nonexecutive shareholders.'

'What about Mr Wilson? I'm told that he wasn't too happy about that arrangement.'

Keane looked at me sharply. 'It doesn't matter whether he was happy or not! He and his partner sold us a majority interest and we invested over a million pounds into a failing business. A deal is a deal. It is pointless complaining after the event.'

'Yeah, I guess so. What now then? I'm sorry to be so direct, Mr Keane, but will you buy the dead man's shares or will his wife become a "nonexecutive shareholder" in his place?'

His eyes flickered briefly and I knew that I'd touched a nerve. Maybe both the old partners were something of a problem. Or maybe it had just been Charlie. Whatever it was, he sure as hell wasn't going to tell me.

'If I may say so, girlie, I don't think that's any of your concern.'

I hate it when people play the 'little woman' card, but I managed to ignore the fury that was welling up inside and just shrugged pleasantly. 'Ah. Actually, I think it is my concern, Mr Keane, but, like I said before, if you don't wish to tell me, then that's your choice.'

'Yes, it is.' He stood up, signalling the end of my interview. 'Now, if you'll excuse me, I have work to do.'

I stayed where I was. 'Before we finish, can we just clear up one, rather important, point?'

He sat down again and blew impatiently through his nose.

'You said that *we* bought the shares. Who is *we*?'

He sighed impatiently and laid his hands flat on the desk. 'I'm the chief executive of the Three Seas Business Group. We buy and reposition failing restaurants' – he eyed me patronisingly – 'if you know what that means. Now is that all?'

I nodded graciously and stood up. 'You've been a big help, Mr Keane, and I'm very grateful for your time. Just one last thing: I need to talk to Mr Peterson. Could you give me his address or phone number please?'

He looked at me as if I were a bad smell and walked over and opened the door for me. 'I've already told you, girlie. I don't want you bothering Mr Peterson just now. I've tried to help you – even though I'm a busy man. Now please have the decency to stay away – from me *and* my colleagues.'

I stopped as I drew level and looked him in the eye. 'You almost make it sound like a threat.'

He faced me off. 'Take it how you wish – only leave us alone. The last few days have been difficult enough.'

I smiled and thanked him anyway, then walked off down the corridor. When I heard his door close, I turned back and slipped through the door into the women's toilet. Inside, a small lobby led to a single cubicle with a toilet on one side and a small wash basin fixed just beneath a small uPVC window. The top section opened. It was just a little wider than my hips, with the usual lever fastening. I reached up and opened it – just enough so that it wouldn't be obvious, then I did my ablutions and returned to the table downstairs.

The coffee was cold by now, but my friendly waitress brought me another one almost as soon as I sat down. She eyed me up quizzically as she approached, the steaming liquid warming her face. 'You OK? Only, you look kind of pensive.'

I smiled. 'I'm fine, thanks. I was just thinking about what your boss said. I must say, he wasn't very easy to talk to.'

'Mmm, well, that figures. The man certainly is no great conversationalist.'

'And are you?' I looked at her directly, making no secret of my need for information.

She hesitated. 'Yeah, I guess I can be. It depends. You mentioned that your clients might pay a fee.'

I shrugged. 'Yeah, it's usually a straight twenty-five quid,' I lied.

'Can you make that fifty?'

I hesitated just a little. 'Yeah, I guess I can swing it – I didn't pay your boss a bean, so you can have his share.'

She smiled. She liked that. 'OK, then, you've got a deal. But not tonight. I'm bushed. I'll meet you in the Willows – it's a café, near the bus stops in Piccadilly Gardens. Tomorrow, before work, around eleven?'

'Thanks,' I said, passing her my credit card. 'What's your name, by the way?'

'It's Rita.'

I smiled back. 'Thanks, Rita – for everything, especially the omelette.'

Twenty-seven

One a.m. and there was still a smattering of people and cars moving around under the glow of the sodium street lights. A drunk lurched down Deansgate talking to some invisible friend; a down-and-out huddled in a shop doorway shivering as I drove past. Two young women in strappy tops and tight skirts hurried down Bridge Street, hugging themselves to keep warm. Manchester was in the middle of its regular early-morning hiatus. The diners, theatregoers and drinkers were long gone; the clubbers would emerge in an hour or two, when the streets would briefly come alive again. Meanwhile, I had the city almost to myself.

When I'd got back to the hotel, I'd gone straight to bed. I felt exhausted from the lack of sleep over the last two nights and anxious that I should be on top form when I eventually did the deal with Vinko Cuzak. But for all my tiredness, I couldn't sleep at all. My mind kept going back to Chow City and turning over Keane's less-than-helpful answers. When I pushed those thoughts away my mind switched to Lin again, wondering what she wasn't telling me – and why. Then it was Martha and her story about Charlie's problems with Barrie Peterson, Elaine Wilson's affair with the same man, and the still-unexplained phone call that I'd overheard in the lawyer's office. But, more than anything, every time I tried to shut my brain down, I kept on returning to Chow City, Barrie Peterson and Charlie's business dealings

By midnight, I'd had enough and decided that, if I was going to give Mr Lee any further information, then I had to start finding out a few of the things that other people weren't telling me. So I'd got out of bed and dressed in my old grey sweatshirt and black running bottoms and had gone to get my car.

Now, just minutes later I was standing in a dark backstreet, a block away from Chow City, shivering with cold as I rummaged in my car boot. I pulled the thin orange tow rope from under the flooring and wrapped it loosely around my waist and put on the lightweight running jacket to cover it. Finally I found a small torch, some leather gloves and my pick-locks, and stashed them all into the pockets. As an afterthought, I turned off my mobile before jogging through the deserted streets, keeping to the shadows, praying that I wouldn't be stopped and searched by some smartarse cop. I wasn't.

When I got there, Chow City was in complete darkness. There was a burglar alarm box on the front fascia, but there was no light on it and no evidence that it was live. Given that there were no movement detectors inside, and no plates on any of the doors, then it looked pretty certain that the place wasn't alarmed. Either they had a naïve belief in their own impregnability or they were really doing something illegal and preferred to handle their own security away from the prying eyes of Mr Plod.

Around the back, the yard behind the kitchens was empty except for the two big silver waste bins and a shallow pool of dirty black water. I jumped as a sudden scuffling broke out by my leg and a skinny cat shot from the shadows, backing away, body arched, spitting as it danced off into the street.

The yard itself was enclosed on the left and right by two single-storey outhouses with pitched roofs. Above me, Keane's office window was on my far left. The two toilets were to the right, directly above the kitchen door, with the unlatched window in the women's cubicle on the far right.

I suddenly felt scared and, for just a moment, wondered if the risk was really worth it. But I pushed the negative thoughts away and concentrated on pulling the leather gloves right up over my wrists and then laying a piece of old cardboard in the roadway directly opposite the toilet window.

When I set off, the waste bin was higher than I'd imagined and I struggled for a moment to pull my legs up the smooth sides. But once I was on top it was an easy climb onto the slates of the outhouse roof and then just a few short steps up to the ridge tiles. I stopped there for just a moment, taking stock. Around me the night was still. A police siren sounded somewhere in the distance. A bird flapped its wings nearby in protest at the sudden disturbance. My heart was noisier than anything else – thumping in my chest and pounding in my ears.

To my left, and on my level, was the toilet window.

I took careful note of the distance and checked that I could see the old cardboard marker that I'd left in the alley, then I put one foot on each side of the ridge and half-crawled, half-walked along the roof until I came to the wall of the main building.

The metal guttering below the main roof was level with my chest. It looked strong and firm, and it didn't give with pressure when I hung from it for a few moments. When I was satisfied that it would be strong enough, I scanned the length over the yard area, checking for any signs of rust or damage, reassured that it looked sound.

I stood there for a few moments, unwinding the thin rope from around my waist and rehearsing the next stage. Then I took a firm hold of the gutter and pulled myself up and onto the main roof. I lay for a moment, spread-eagled with the coil of rope in my right hand, my face pressed against the slates, breathing in the smell of ancient soot and lichen while searching with my fingers for whatever hold I could find. I pressed my body hard against the cold, green slates and inched myself painstakingly along the edge. After what seemed like an age, I was halfway along, level with the marker that I'd left in the alley, thirty or forty feet below me.

I lay there for a while, closing my eyes and preparing myself, trying to distract my mind from the drop below and the cold hard concrete of the yard, manoeuvring my body towards the edge of the roof until I was lying, half on, half off the slates. Now, with some effort, I could just reach the guttering.

I twisted my head to check the marker again, then, swallowing hard, I leaned out and found one of the gutter supports and threaded rope over it, pulling the ends back up towards me and then tying them round my arm. If the gutter broke, then there was no way that I wanted to fall the thirty or so feet onto the concrete below.

I breathed deeply again, twisting my shoulders and arms until I was grasping the inside of the gutter. Holding there for a just a second, praying that years of weight training would be enough to get me through, I ignored the surge of blood in my ears and the smell of my own fear. Then, finally and very slowly, I slid first my feet, then my legs, then my whole body, over the edge and out into space.

My shoulders and arms jolted painfully as my body dropped over the side. My left hand slipped off the gutter with the sudden force of the fall and I swung in the air, clutching the rope and pulling my body back up to the guttering, which was groaning and creaking above me. Somewhere in my head, a voice reminded me that cast iron always snapped rather than bent and, for a moment, my heart missed a beat. But the guttering was still holding – for the moment, anyway.

I hung motionless for a second or two, gathering my forces, hardly daring to breathe, focusing on the pain in my fingers rather than the tiredness in my arms and searching blindly with my legs for the window frame below me.

After what seemed like an age, I got both my feet onto the top of the frame and pushed, relieving the pressure on my hands and arms, before I dropped one foot down again, feeling carefully for the corner of the open window.

On the fifth or sixth attempt I managed to find the tiny gap and pushed the toe of my trainer just inside the edge, tugging and twisting until the window opened far enough for me to push my whole foot underneath and force it open.

My arms felt solid by now and my fingers numb. I closed my eyes and gripped harder again, catching the half-open window with my ankle and pulling it right up under the eaves with my calf. Then I let my arms take the strain for one last time, dropped both feet and squeezed down through the opening until my thighs were resting on the frame. I waited a moment, catching my breath, relief washing over me; then I grabbed the inside of the window with one hand, untied the rope from one arm with the other and pulled it free. Finally I pushed myself down, through the window, onto the washbasin, and into the cubicle.

I sat on the toilet feeling like a zombie. My arms were like lead, my heart was beating rapidly and the adrenalin was making me woozy and light-headed. I leaned back against the cistern, breathing hard, and stripped off my gloves, examining the bloody, lacerated fingers beneath and wondering vaguely why they didn't hurt any more. When I eventually stumbled to my feet and held them under the cold water tap the stabs of pain came sharp and hard.

Once I'd cleaned the wounds, I dabbed them dry with toilet paper and, with some difficulty, pulled on a pair of latex gloves. Then I wiped the wet from the floor, cleaned the basin, and closed the window. My leather gloves went in my pocket and the soiled paper down the toilet.

When I opened the door and stepped into the corridor, I was met by absolute darkness. When no movement detectors winked at me, I turned on my torch and stumbled along the passage to Keane's office door. As I had expected, it was locked.

I hoped I could remember what Beano had taught me. She'd spent days with me at home last year, while she was convalescing. We'd bought several kinds of locks and dismantled them in turn. She made me practice, first with one lever, then two, then three. We'd done mortise, barrel and padlocks over and over again. She'd taught me to feel and to listen, to use my fingers as eyes and, little by little, I'd learned which pick to use and on which kind of lock.

But now, doing it on my own, it seemed much harder. This lock was a mortise and, from the feel, it had to be a three-lever. Not the hardest lock to open, but for me demanding enough – especially when my fingers hurt like hell, and my arms still ached.

I knelt down on the floor and tried to relax. There was no reason to rush. I had hours to spare. Which was fortunate. Beano would have taken two minutes max to open this door. It took me the best part of ten just to locate the spring-mounted levers and to work out how to move them back. I kept hearing her voice. Swearing at me. *Use your fucking imagination, for Chrissake! Use the picks like they're extensions of your fingers.*

She'd gone on to compare picking locks to sex, telling me to caress each lever as if it were clitoral. To tickle, tantalise and tease, until it gave itself up. Yeah, well, it never seemed very erotic to me. Mind you, I'll never have the feel for it she has. Beano remains a genius in my eyes. The Lothario of the Lock.

The thought made me stop and think about her again – and, by association, about Cuzak.

When the third lever clicked back, I reached up, turned the handle and pushed the door open, crouching in the opening, shining the penlight beam around in the darkness, before going inside.

I didn't know what I was looking for. I just hoped there might be something that would move me a step nearer to finding out why Charlie had been killed. A document maybe, a set of minutes, a report. Something that might explain Keane's hostility, or tell me why a restaurant that had been so lavishly refurbished could be so poorly run.

I tried the computer first, hoping that it would tell me all I needed on Chow City and, in particular, on the business affairs of Charles Wilson, Peterson and Keane. But, as the screen bathed the office with soft blue light, a password box appeared. I turned the damn thing off in disgust. I can just about pick a lock, but bypassing computer security? Hell, give me a break.

A lined pad lay by the side of the computer. I flicked through it but every page was blank. When I found a pencil and tried the old trick of lightly rubbing the page with the lead to reveal any impressions, all I found were a few doodles, a lot of scribble and a telephone number. I wrote that down just in case and put the sheet in my pocket.

The desk drawers were empty, save for a few pens and some paperclips, so I tried the four-drawer filing cabinet next. Thankfully, it was unlocked but the bottom two drawers yielded nothing more exciting than a supply of waiters' pads, menus and other bits of stationery. The third drawer up was empty and I began to get a sinking feeling about my whole, stupid plan. Had I really taken such massive risks only to find that I was heading up a very blind alley?

The top drawer was full of suspension files neatly labelled. I shone the torch on the contents one by one. Twenty of them were alphabetical, containing various bits of correspondence. Everything from disputes with suppliers to architects' drawings and appeals over business rates. Again, nothing remotely informative. Nothing remotely worth the effort. I was despondent by the time I got to the XYZ folder, but the next file, towards the back of the drawer, contained a whole sheaf of legal-looking papers held together by a rubber band, which I removed from the drawer and spread out on the table.

The first document was a routine solicitor's letter from a firm I'd never heard of, advising Keane on Land Registry matters and confirming the safe storage of the deeds to the building. According to the letter, the restaurant property was now owned by a company called Chow City Millennium Ltd.

There were various other legal-looking papers as well, including incorporation documents, which confirmed that the ownership was split between Three Seas Business Group with 52 per cent, Barrie Peterson with 24 per cent and Charles Wilson with 24 per cent. I sat at the table and leafed through all the documents in the torchlight but there was nothing much else, beyond dated and convoluted Articles of Association, which at least confirmed that the only trading address was this one.

I put the documents back, feeling slightly better. From the papers it was clear that both the original partners still owned a significant chunk of what was now – on paper anyway – a very valuable piece of real estate.

Two files further back, another folder was headed VAT, and inside was a single copy of a statutory return. I shone the torch on it for a moment, then took it over to the table and studied the figures a little closer. Taxable sales for the quarter ending 30 September were stated as £661,328. I pulled a face and did a quick mental calculation. That was something like £220,000 per month. Divided by four, it was £55,000 per week. If every customer spent £30 on average, then that would be around 1,800 customers a week – 300 every day.

Jesus. That didn't make any sense at all.

I looked again, in case I'd got it wrong. But the figures were right and the document *was* printed with the name of Chow City Millennium Ltd. It had to be the turnover for this restaurant. Puzzled, I pulled the remaining files forward and discovered a wad of bank paying-in books right at the back of the drawer. A used one lay on top, devoid of pages but full of stubs that had been stamped by the bank.

When I flicked through and counted twelve of them, they added up to somewhere around £112,000. But what was even more staggering was that most of it was in cash. Not unusual for a thriving catering business, maybe, but how the hell did Keane and his staff squeeze that much money from such an empty restaurant?

I put the stubs back in the drawer and took out my tiny digital camera, photographing the VAT return before I put everything back. Then I ran the flashlight across the box files on the shelves. They looked just as boring and inconsequential as on my first visit here earlier. I couldn't imagine that they would tell me anything. But I started to check them anyway, just in case, photographing around fifteen of the documents in the first box. They were mostly invoices from suppliers: meat, vegetables, fish, bread – all the usual things that a restaurant would buy. Nothing strange at all. Except – just like the money – there was more than I expected.

I stopped for a moment to think. Rita, the waitress, had implied that all the meals were prepacked. She'd said something sarcastic about not employing chefs – yeah, and she'd had to cook a simple meal like an omelette herself. Yet most of the invoices were for raw ingredients: vegetables, fish, meat – the kinds of ingredients real chefs would use.

I thought again about the VAT return. The high volume of supplies could be some kind of a tax dodge, I supposed. But what I couldn't work out was why anyone would inflate both supply costs *and* sales. And, in any case, where the hell was all that cash coming from? Not from a busy restaurant, that was for sure.

I put everything back in its place and scanned the room to make sure that I hadn't left anything, then I closed the door behind me and locked it again with the picks – as if no one had ever called. Within a couple of minutes, I was on my way downstairs, clasping the little camera in my pocket.

I stopped at the foot of the stairs and looked around the restaurant in the dark. The chairs were all standing on tables so that the place seemed bigger and stranger than earlier in the evening. Over by the bar, the projection clock had gone but an espresso coffee machine winked a small green eye at me instead. Fire exits cast a green glow over the carpet by the kitchen door and round the main entrance, and, up above, a small red light winked steadily to the gentle whirr of a motor.

Shit!

I shone my torch up beyond the stationary fans, right into the racks of theatre lights. A small motorised video camera was swinging towards me, dipping down as it recorded the section of the restaurant closest to me. I swore quietly to myself and kept the flashlight steady until it turned away, then I fell through the door into the kitchen and shut it quickly behind me, breathing with relief.

But not for long. At the far end of the room, on the wall above a big steel cupboard, was another camera – and this one was pointing right at me. I swung the flashlight round at once and hurried over to the back door. It was a fire exit, but, when I pushed the bar, it stayed firmly shut. I stopped and closed my eyes, trying to stem the sudden panic in my head, forcing myself to think. If it was an escape route, then there had to be a key somewhere.

I kept the torch on the camera and ran my hand down the doorframe and across the wall by the side until I located the small glass-fronted box. Then, dizzy with relief, I smashed the glass with my elbow and pulled out the key. It took me a while, holding the torch on the camera with one hand, and fumbling with the key with the other, but I managed to find the lock and insert the key. To my relief it turned easily and I fell through the door as the fire alarm cut in with an ear-splitting howl.

Twenty-eight

When I woke, my fingers were so stiff that I could hardly pick up the alarm clock, let alone turn it off. My hands were sore and crisscrossed with lines of dark red lesions. When I hobbled to the window, opening the catch to let in some fresh air was a major challenge. I wanted to go back to bed and sleep for ever.

Then I remembered the CCTV cameras in the restaurant and a shiver ran down my spine. I should have known. A man like Keane might avoid conventional security, but he'd want to know what was going on. And, if there was a break-in, he'd want to deal with it himself.

Jesus!

I sat down on the bed again, rubbing cream onto my fingers, trying to get the circulation going and reasoning with myself.

The camera in the kitchen had probably recorded me – but it was dark, it would show nothing more than a shape with a torch.

Yeah, unless it was a night-imaging camera. Then what?

Nah, even one of those wouldn't be enough to positively identify you.

Maybe not, but Keane might well have a damn good idea who it could be.

Yeah, OK, so stay low. He can't prove anything – what's the big deal?

I ran the shower, playing scalding hot water over my hands until they stung, then over my arms, shoulders and down the middle of my back until the skin lost all feeling and the muscles underneath began to lose their stiffness. I towelled down and stretched my limbs for a good fifteen minutes, getting the blood flowing, clearing the toxins away. Little by little, I began to improve and, by the time I'd brushed my teeth and dried my hair, I felt almost human.

Yeah, almost.

Afterwards I sat on the bed and turned the camera over in my hands, thinking about the VAT return again. Keane was up to something, I knew it. Trouble was, I hadn't a clue what it might be, and, even if I had, what – if anything – it had to do with the sudden death of one of the partners.

But Lin might know. She'd said something about her accountancy degree – something about specialising in fraud. Maybe it was time to try to talk to her; maybe I really should go and have dinner with her tonight, as she wanted. Then I could ask all the questions about Chow City that were flying around in my head. And, just as important, I could resolve my suspicions about her.

But when I picked up my mobile and turned it on, I found I had something else to worry about. There were three text messages, all of them from Becky, spread out over several hours from late last night to eight o'clock this morning:

'Concert great. Where r u?'

'Cam, plse ring, worried about u.'

'Where the fuck r u?! Scared 4 u. RING plse NOW!'

I fell back on the bed and groaned. Shit! Yesterday was Wednesday – the night I was supposed to go to the concert with her! Becky would be beside herself, convinced that something terrible had happened to me. That I was lying dead in some derelict building or tied to the fucking tramlines in some old railway cutting. I kept telling her she should write a bloody thriller – with *her* imagination she'd outsell even Val McDermid.

She answered the phone almost before it rang. I was right. She sounded perilously close to hysteria.

'Becks, just calm down, will you? Something came up, that's all. I'm fine.'

As I expected, tearful concern evaporated into icy, embarrassed resentment. I was the child who causes alarm and then gets scolded for it. Subtext was suddenly everywhere.

'You could have rung!' *You don't care about me any more.*

'I know – I'm sorry – I forgot.' *Yeah, you're right, I don't.*

'You're always doing this to me, Cameron.' *Why don't you damn well do as I ask?*

'I told you, something came up. Another job.' *Because I want to live my own life!*

She was sighing theatrically at the other end. 'You've no sense of responsibility, Cameron – I mean... with that murder in the village and everything...'

I gritted my teeth. 'Becky, you've got to stop hounding me like this; it's driving me insane.'

'Well, you should ring if you're not going to turn up. What am I to think? Eh?'

I sighed heavily, but said nothing.

'Why are you still there, anyway?' she grunted, 'something to do with Beano, I suppose.'

'No, nothing at all to do with Beano. I'm on a new case. It's um, sort of matrimonial.' I chose my words carefully so that, technically at least, I wasn't lying, 'Look, I'm sorry that I missed the concert, but I had to take this job – the money's good and it's a new client. I couldn't afford to turn it down.'

'Yes, well, just ring me next time, will you? Really, Cam, I don't ask much.'

'Yeah, OK.' I bit my tongue and changed the subject. I was going to have to sort this out once and for all, but maybe not just now.

'Look, I need some advice. Can I run something past you?'

She breathed heavily into the phone. I could almost hear her stamping her feet in exasperation. 'Yes, all right. Go on!' *You're using me. You do it all the time.*

I took a deep breath and ploughed on. 'Well, this guy dies, OK.

The house that he and his wife lived in is an old family residence but it was owned jointly by him and his sister. The wife doesn't have a share. On his death, the husband's half is willed to the wife. OK so far?'

'Yes, Cameron, I'm with you.'

'The thing is, the wife is hard up. The sister has agreed to buy the wife's share of the house after the will is published but the wife doesn't want to wait that long. She needs money now – or at least some of it. Just tell me – can it be done?'

There was a short, critical silence. 'Cam, *where* on God's earth do you find these people?'

I took a deep breath. 'Can it be done or not?'

'Yes, it can. But it's highly unusual. Her solicitor would draw up what's called a *conditional contract* for the sale – the condition being the granting of probate.'

'Pardon?'

'The publishing of the will, Cameron. The contract couldn't take effect until the will was published – but contracts could be exchanged prior to that, and everything could be finalised in advance. Then, as soon as probate was granted, the money could be paid over immediately.'

'So there's no way she could get any money now – before, er, probate.'

'Well, yes, she could get some of it, if she was that desperate. If the sister wanted to buy the widow's inheritance badly enough, then she might be persuaded to put down a larger deposit, then pay the smaller balance when matters were finalised.'

'How large?'

'That would be up to the parties, but, whatever it was, the deposit would normally be retained by the solicitor.'

'So she still couldn't get her hands on the money until after the will was read?'

'That depends.'

'On what?'

'On her solicitor. It's not at all advisable but, if the widow was in great need, then I suppose that the solicitor may be persuaded to pay some of the deposit over straightaway.'

Jesus, as easy as that.

'And if there were business shares involved? Would the same thing apply?'

'Cameron. What on earth are you getting involved in?'

'Just tell me, Becks. Would the same thing apply?'

'Well... yes, I suppose it might. It could be a little more complicated. It really depends on the nature of the business – whether there were shares or just a partnership agreement, for instance, whether it was a public or private company. But it ought to be do-able, if the need existed. Very unusual, though. I wouldn't recommend any client of mine to take things at such a rush. A small bank loan would be far safer.'

'Thanks, Becky, that really helps.'

'Hang on, Cam. When are you coming back to York?'

I hesitated, reluctant to give any ground. 'I don't know. This job will take a day or two more I guess. Maybe the weekend, but I can't promise.'

'And your poor cat? You want me to keep on feeding him?' *You don't care about him either, do you? You're so selfish, Cameron!*

'Look, Becks, I'm really sorry that I forgot about last night. Just bear with me on this – please?' *Just fucking leave it, will you?*

'You're quite insufferable, Cameron, you know that, don't you?'

Silence.

'Yes, all right.' She smouldered, quietly. 'I'll look after Tibby – I always do, don't I? Just promise me that you'll take care. And *ring me*, Cameron, *ring me!*'

Twenty-nine

By the time I'd got dressed, it was nearly eight thirty. My hands were smarting, my body hurt and I felt totally demoralised after the conversation with Becky.

In lieu of breakfast, I took a brisk walk around the city centre, breathing in the cold morning air and clearing my head. I ended up at the Easy Internet Café in Exchange Street, where I bought an hour's web time from the vending machine in the lobby and then got myself an egg sandwich and a big mug of coffee from the café on the ground floor, before climbing the stairs to the computer room.

The IT revolution still amazes me. When I was a kid, PCs hadn't been invented and computers were used only by mega-businesses. Now, however depressed I felt, I couldn't help but be impressed by the hundreds of computer screens that packed the huge room. Even this early, more than half of the 360 terminals were in use and the air chattered with the relentless tapping of thousands of fingers.

I wound my way through the banks of screens until I found a reasonable space at the back of the room. Then I sat down with a vacant screen on either side and took out my phone.

They say that good investigation is a mixture of positive action and painstaking research. The former I like. The latter? Well, however tedious it might be, sometimes it can reveal a gem – something that you would never have found out in any other way. Maybe it's my background of debt-collection jobs and matrimonials, but credit checks usually seem like a good place to start. They're cheap, they're easy to get to and you can sometimes find out a lot about someone from the money they owe and the bills they can't pay.

But, before I did anything, I needed to make a call. I flicked through my notes until I found the name of the Jaguar dealer – the one I'd read off Peterson's number plate the night before last – and keyed in the number. When they answered, I got transferred to a man in the service department.

'Good morning,' I began, assuming the voice of an ever-efficient secretary. 'I'd like to book a car in for some minor repairs please. It's my boss's car. It's still on warranty... Mr Peterson, Mr Barrie Peterson... from Chow City Millennium?... Yes, he's got a problem with the heating system, it's running cold... Can you fix it soon?'

I gave the guy the registration number and I waited while he tapped a few keys.

'We can't manage it until Monday next week – is that all right?'

'Yes, that's very fine,' I confirmed. 'But can you collect? He's so busy at present, it would be a big help.'

I waited, holding my breath.

'Yes, of course, miss, that's no trouble. We'll bring a courtesy car. Do you want us to collect from his business or his home?'

'Home, please. Are you sure that you have his current address? Can you check?'

'Aye, OK, miss...' There was a short pause while computer keys were tapped. 'Yeah, I've got it here, Apartment 6b, Adelaide House, Brinton Street? Is that still the right one?'

'Yes,' I answered, quietly triumphant, 'that's the one.'

When I ended the call, I turned back to the screen, and keyed in my ticket number, wincing every time my sore, stiff fingers punched the keys. I washed down a couple of painkillers with a mouthful of coffee, while the machine booted up. When the EasyEverything screen appeared, I keyed in the address of the credit bureau that I use, then my password and account number. When the search screen popped up, I entered Peterson's name and address, pressed 'go' and then sat back and took a bite on the sandwich while I waited for the result.

I thought I must have made a mistake when the details appeared. That maybe I'd keyed in the wrong address or something. But the Barrie Peterson on the credit rating was undoubtedly the man who was at Elaine's two nights earlier. The age was right, the address was right – there was even a cross-reference to Chow City. But this man was far from prosperous. His credit score was very low, somewhere around the 'avoid at all costs' mark. He had a string of unpaid, uncollected loans, a long list of credit cards that had been withdrawn, at least half a dozen County Court judgements against him – as well as a whole series of outstanding settlements that he was paying off through court orders. My mind flipped back to the conversation with Martha – her comments about his 'borrowing' the restaurant's takings and how that had nearly spelled the end of the two men's original business.

When I clicked on the link to Chow City Millennium Ltd, I found a very different story. The rating was excellent and the record for the last year as clean as a whistle. No long-term creditors, no loans, no legal judgements and the directors were listed. John William Keane (managing), Barrie Edward Peterson (nonexecutive), Charles Baxter Wilson (nonexecutive), plus three other nonexecutive directors whose names meant nothing to me but who, I assumed, were placemen from the Three Seas Business Group, the outfit that had invested so heavily in the restaurant.

The report went on to say that Three Seas held a charge against the restaurant property and the assets of the business. That seemed reasonable: anyone who invested money of that order would expect some security.

Three Seas had the highest credit rating of all. Cash reserves were high, their long-term record reliable and consistent, and cash generation excellent. This business was a private one with a capitalisation of around £15 million. No loans, no mortgages. Richard Keane was the chief executive and chairman – an ex-banker, it said, with lots of letters after his name. So the office at Chow City was just somewhere he used when he was on the premises. His main base would be at Three Seas. When I clicked his personal rating, it was excellent too. An exceptionally high income. No outstanding debts. The credit agency was thrilled with his liquidity.

I took another bite on the sandwich and tried to pull everything I knew into the same space. Martha had told me of her brother's relief over the success of the refurbished restaurant. But she'd said that the new partners wouldn't advance profit share to him, or to Barrie Peterson, until the costs were paid off. OK, so maybe that was understandable. Charles had reacted sensibly, driving a modest car and reining in his wife's profligate spending. But what of Peterson? I flipped back onto his record and scanned the dates. His history of debt extended back over six years and continued remorselessly – up until six months earlier. Since then there had been no entries. No debts, no new finance. He'd either hit rock bottom or he'd changed his ways.

No, I didn't believe either. Thinking back to the night at Elaine's house, I recalled that he acted like a man who was in the money. Someone who knew how to spend it.

On impulse, I checked out Charles Wilson's record. It had already been withdrawn and the file was simply marked as 'deceased'. Pity, but at least that confirmed the files were right up to date.

I returned to Peterson's file and checked again in case I'd missed the finance arrangement on the Jaguar, but there was nothing. It was only a few weeks old. The tax disc was dated last month. On the information given here he would never have got clearance for a loan anyway. So, what? He'd won a fortune (unlikely, I thought); he was being bailed out by someone he knew and/or somebody had just given him an expensive new car? Of the three options, I preferred the last two.

I sat back and picked up the mug, thinking about the two original partners and the hurried part-takeover of the Cheshire Grill. They'd had equal shares in the old business, and – according to Martha – the sale had been forced by Peterson's dishonesty. Strange, then, that

Peterson seemed to be getting a better deal than his long-term partner. But why?

Martha had said that it was Peterson who found Three Seas in an effort to keep the business going. But what if Peterson's approach to Three Seas – or their approach to him – had more to do with his debt than with his concerns over the business?

It was a theory, but so far I'd come across nothing to back it up. And, even if Peterson *was* getting favours from Keane, it didn't prove anything – except, maybe, that Peterson had still been taking his old partner for a ride. And even *that* didn't mean he'd want to kill him.

I logged on again. This time I checked the credit ratings of everyone I'd come across in the last three days – Horace Pritchard, Mr Lee, the Golden Snapper, Martha Wilson and Elaine Wilson. No problems – all were classed as moderate to good risks. Mr Lee had the highest rating possible.

But I was missing something. I had to be.

I logged out of the credit agency again and searched for the archives of the *Evening Post* on the same names. There were several articles about Mr Lee. His award by local restaurateurs for services to the trade two years earlier, a fundraising dinner in his honour for a children's charity last December, a feature about Mr Lee's retirement from the police authority and an article in which the old man spoke out against the protection money that several city-centre restaurants were apparently paying to organised crime.

Pritchard turned out to be the uninteresting person I expected and there was nothing at all, not even a report on the statement that he had just given to the police. Martha Wilson and her sister-in-law were similarly missing from the newssheets. Charlie had a brief mention, five years earlier, when he had become the new chair of the City Centre Restaurateurs' Association. Barrie Peterson yielded nothing.

I downed the last of the coffee and started to log off when it dawned on me that I'd left one person out of the equation. However much I wanted to believe in her, it was an inescapable fact that Lin had made me feel slightly uneasy since I had first met her. I'd come to assume that her problem – whatever it was – had nothing at all to do with the case. Maybe I ought to make sure.

Feeling somewhat disloyal, I logged back onto the credit agency for the third time and keyed in Lin's name and address.

Nothing.

The fact that there was no record of her wasn't in itself suspicious. Some people don't use credit cards or take out loans – and if you don't borrow, you don't get a rating. But I did begin to worry when I tried a tracing agency site that I subscribe to and found no sign of anyone called Lin Lee in Greater Manchester. Hoping that it was a simple omission from the records, I logged onto their electoral roll search service and requested a reverse search – that's a search on an address, to reveal the name of the person living there. But, when I keyed in Lin's address and pressed 'submit', a completely different name came up.

There was no mention of Lin Lee.

The name of the person who lived at her address was *David Mackintosh.*

Thirty

When I left the internet café, the sky was an ominous grey, and a cold, gusty wind was scattering grit and old leaves around the streets. I'd planned on going straight to Bootle Street Police Station, but instead I began to wander aimlessly, staring idly in shop windows, wrapping myself up in my own private bubble. Trying to get my head round what I'd just found out.

David Mackintosh.

I felt miserable. Lin had lied to me. I'd seen all the signs and I'd pushed them away – even when it was obvious that she was holding something back. I don't know what I'd expected her secret to be – but I'd never thought it would be a man.

David Mackintosh

Sometimes I despair. A few days ago I was criticising Beano for letting her heart rule her head, but was I any better? Do I ever learn? It was Angel all over again. But this time I wasn't going to let it happen. This time I was ahead of the game.

I stopped at the window of a small jewellery shop and stared through the polished glass. My reflection stared back, mocking me. I was thirty-eight, for God's sake. I should have learned by now that it wasn't a good idea to put my trust in someone just because I liked them. I pressed my head against the cold glass and shut my eyes. The name rang around my head.

David Mackintosh. David Mackintosh.

Whoever he was, she'd deliberately kept his name from me, and I knew, I just knew, that he was part of her secret.

I stood up straight, pulled out my phone.

'Oh, hi, Cameron.' Her voice was ripe with pleasure. I could picture her standing there, eyes alight, her black hair tumbling down over her shoulders. Bile rose in my throat as I listened to her deceit. 'Hi, I was hoping you'd ring me.'

My belly began a series of slow somersaults as I fumbled for the words.

She noticed at once. 'What is it? What's the matter?'

That didn't make it any easier. I stared at the pads of gold rings and diamond brooches in front of me, suddenly breathless.

'You haven't been honest with me, Lin,' I said, unable to keep the bitterness from my voice.

I heard the sharp intake of breath, but she said nothing.

'You've lied to me.'

'I... Oh, shit! Cameron... I'm sorry, I didn't mean to mislead you, honest!'

'Oh, well, that's all right, then!'

'Yeah, I mean no – it *isn't* OK.'

'David Mackintosh – who *is* he, Lin? Your *lover?* Your *husband?'*

There was a short, stunned silence before she spoke again.

'Please don't talk like that. It's not what you think, I...' She faltered and stopped. It was a few seconds before she spoke again, and then her voice was trembling with dismay. 'It's not like that, Cameron. If anything, it's far worse.'

'So what is it?' I was still angry, but now I was confused as well.

She sniffed hard and her voice picked up. 'I can't tell you on the phone, Cameron. Please... come round tonight. I'll tell you everything, I promise.'

The hairs were prickling on the back of my neck. Suddenly I felt icy cold. Jesus, I'd been right when I didn't *want* to be right. I leaned hard against the window, trying to stop her getting to me. 'No, not tonight,' I insisted, trying to keep my voice steady. 'I'm busy. I want you to tell me now or not at all!'

Her voice caught in her throat. 'Cam, you know I can't do that. This is *really* difficult for me – please try to understand. There is a lot to tell you – but you must let me do it my way.'

I breathed out against the window and the jewellery faded away behind the misted glass. I couldn't just leave it like that. But tonight? Jesus, not tonight. Cuzak was going to ring me tonight and I had to be ready.

'This afternoon, then.'

'I'm sorry, I can't! I've got an interview at the Singapore High Commission in half an hour.' She sounded lost and hopeless, and my damned heart still skipped a beat for her. 'Can't you make it tonight – for just a little while?' she pleaded. 'An hour will do. It doesn't have to be dinner – just give me some time to explain everything properly. You probably won't want to stay, anyway – once you know.'

I bit my lip and kicked the shop fascia so hard that the window rattled and a man's face appeared at the back of the display. I stepped back a little and stared defiantly until the face disappeared. She knew damn well that I couldn't just end it like this.

'Yeah, OK,' I agreed, hating myself for yielding so easily. 'About seven, then. But I'm expecting an urgent call sometime tonight – I might have to leave in a hurry, OK?'

I put the phone away and looked at my reflection again, trying to calm my racing heart, trying to convince myself that I wanted to see her only because I needed to end it. I just needed to find out what the fuck had been going on, then I could let her go. I'd be OK after that. I'd known the woman for only three days. She meant nothing to me. Less than nothing.

It was then, as I started to move away, that I caught another reflection in the glass. Behind me. Across the street. A scruffy guy, in his mid-twenties, wearing an old green jacket, torn blue jeans and a faded khaki baseball hat.

Suddenly alert again, I turned and set off up the street, swinging left into a small square and stopping to browse in the window of a large bookshop at the corner, watching his reflection. He walked up casually behind me, hands in pockets, whistling, and sauntered past, as if he were just any guy on his way across town.

As soon as he'd got ahead of me I went into the shop and up the stairs to the first floor. I found the lift somewhere near the back, and pushed the call button, then returned to the front window and looked out onto the square.

He was still there, hanging about opposite the entrance, waiting for me to come out. One of Cuzak's gang, checking me out, making sure I was clean. Or maybe Keane had recognised me from the security video after all. It could be one of his.

I leaned against a bookcase and watched him for a while, marvelling at the narrow escape I'd just had. I'd been on my way to the cop shop to see Dyson. If he really was one of Cuzak's men – Jesus, it didn't even bear thinking about.

I waited for a full five minutes. As the minutes passed his casual, cocky manner began to change. Another ten and he began to look concerned, walking up and down, glancing uncertainly across at the bookshop. I could almost see his brain working. Five minutes later, he made his mind up and set off half running, half walking towards the bookshop doors. As soon as he moved I ran to the back of the store and pushed the call button again.

I was down on the ground floor a few seconds later – just in time to see his back disappearing up the stairs.

Thirty-one

I don't like police stations. I've been in several over the years and they've never had pleasant connotations. Claustrophobic interview rooms, cells that stink of disinfectant and urine, cynical coppers who never seem to take to me.

Bootle Street was the first one to break the mould and, as I walked under the blue lamp and through the doors, I hoped that Dyson would be as helpful to me now as I'd been to her last night. I'd left it until the last minute, so that it would be a simple take-it-or-leave-it. I just hoped she'd take it. Actually, I didn't think she had much choice.

She met me with a curious expression on her face. When I insisted on somewhere private to talk, she took me to one of the interview rooms at the back.

As we sat down on either side of the table, she eyed me testily out of the corner of her eye. 'I suppose this is about the Wilson case again.'

I shook my head, trying to think of an easy way to tell her and deciding that there wasn't one.

'I've arranged to buy a large quantity of drugs off a man called Vinko Cuzak – probably tonight.'

Her body stiffened and her eyes turned white before the words had even left my mouth. 'You've done what?' she exclaimed, open-mouthed. 'For God's sake, McGill! I thought you were an intelligent woman.'

I continued unabashed. 'I've set up a deal. He's going to ring me before midnight today to arrange a meet. He's promised me a fair amount of crack and some dope. I'm supposed to take five grand in used notes with me to pay him.'

She stared at me dumbfounded. Then, still without speaking, she got up and paced the floor, rubbing her forehead. By the time she stopped and leaned against the door, her face was set and any friendliness had turned to anger.

'Why are you telling me this?'

I shrugged and played the innocent. 'I've had second thoughts. I don't want to go to jail for drug dealing. I thought that, if I tipped you off, you might like to intervene.'

She gave me a sideways look. 'You expect me to believe that?'

'What's to believe?' I pulled a face. 'In a moment of stupidity, I agreed to buy some drugs. Now I've decided that I don't want to break the law, so I'm admitting what I've done, before I commit an offence.'

I saw the light dawning as she walked back and sat down again. 'This couldn't have anything to do with your friend Bernice Nolan, by any chance, could it?'

I looked back in all innocence. 'I don't know what you mean.'

'McGill, if you've been interfering in this case...'

I shook my head at her. 'I haven't done anything to cause you problems. But I can tell you this: when I talked to Cuzak he boasted openly that *he* beat up Mark Taylor, not Beano. He said it was for defaulting on drug debts.'

She breathed out sharply and a small muscle twitched on her cheek. 'Fine! All right, we'll get him to come along and make a statement, then we can clear everything up, can't we?'

I fixed her with my eyes. 'You see! I just knew that's what you'd say.'

She looked away for a moment, clearly both irritated and angry. 'Well, what do you expect? And how exactly is shopping Cuzak going to help the situation?'

I shrugged. 'If Cuzak is out of circulation, then Mark Taylor has no need to lie, has he?'

She looked at me in disbelief. 'God! I can't believe that you're so bloody impetuous! That you'd just jump in and risk your life on the back of a totally facile judgement like that!' She paused for a moment, staring at the ceiling, pushing her hair back, before she turned on me again. 'And what the hell makes you think that Cuzak won't have people on the outside? What the hell makes you think that he'd take the pressure off Taylor anyway?'

I stared her in the face. 'Trust me, Superintendent, I know what I'm doing.'

She glared back, 'Yeah, like hell you do!'

I shrugged as if it didn't matter. I couldn't tell her that I'd been to see Mazza, and that, just by visiting him, I'd involved him in what I was doing. If Cuzak got busted, then the finger would point at Taylor just as much as at me, I'd make sure of it. Mazza would save his skin only by cutting out fast. And no Mark Taylor, no case.

She stared at me hard. 'You realise what you've got yourself into, I suppose? Do you know just how dangerous Vinko Cuzak is?'

'I'm not stupid, Superintendent.'

She stared at me a moment as if she wasn't so sure. 'You understand that, if Cuzak finds out you've fingered him, he'll send people after you. You realise he'll probably put a price on your head?'

'I know. I'm going into this without any misconceptions.'

She turned and looked away for a moment, when she turned back her face was set. 'I won't let you do it.'

'Oh, come on, Superintendent, it's too late. If I back out now, I'm sunk anyway – and you know it.'

'It could be seen as entrapment.'

I shook my head at her. I'd already covered that angle. 'It can only be entrapment if you lot set it up. I've made the deal. Now I'm throwing myself on your mercy. Are you *really* going to just let him walk away?'

Dyson leaned back in her chair and sighed resentfully. 'You're using us.'

I couldn't help but smile a little. 'I'm offering you a big prize.'

She bit her lip and looked away. We both knew that the decision to go ahead or not wasn't hers. Now that she'd got over the initial shock, she'd have to take advice.

'All right, assuming I take the bait, what do you want from us?'

'The usual. A wire, body armour, a bag of what looks like money and a truckload of big blokes with truncheons, just round the corner.'

She pulled a face. 'How long have we got?'

'A few hours at most. He said he would ring before midnight. I think we can assume that he'll want to meet straightaway. I can stall him for a while, but I'd rather not. He's jumpy as it is.'

She glared at me for a moment and then picked up the phone, keeping her eyes firmly on mine as she pressed the buttons. 'Jack, it's Angela. Can you spare a few minutes? Yes, it's important: I've got something that you need to hear. I'm in Interview Two.'

She put the phone down and leaned back in her chair. 'Why are you doing this?'

'Off the record?'

She glared at me. 'Yes, all right. Off the record.'

'Beano's a friend.'

'So you said the other night. Even so...'

'I'm repaying a favour. I was arrested eighteen months ago in Hull – on suspicion of murder. She helped prove my innocence, and she nearly got herself killed in the process.'

'Well, that's all very honourable, McGill, but don't you think you're perhaps taking gratitude a little far?'

I tipped my head and looked her full in the face. 'No, I don't, actually. I think it would be lousy if she was locked away for ten years for something she didn't do. She's in a state already. It would finish her.'

The superintendent looked away. I slumped back in the chair, feeling pleased and scared all at the same time.

There was a tap on the door and it opened to reveal a rough-looking guy in jeans and a faded T-shirt, about forty, with a face that looked as if it might have been worked over more than a few times. Dyson waved him in and did the introductions. Superintendent Jack Greenwood was his name. She didn't say it in so many words, but he was clearly the officer in charge of the drug squad, the guy who would provide the backup – if there was any.

He smiled amicably enough and pulled up another chair. Dyson went through the basics with him, conveniently leaving out any reference to Beano. I watched him as she spoke. This time there was none of the outrage at what I was proposing, no advice to call it off, not even a glimmer of disapproval. But his brain turned on every word she spoke.

At the end, he sat quietly for a moment. When he lifted his head to look at me, I could see the disclaimer forming in his eyes before he even spoke. 'You understand that you're putting yourself at extreme risk with this, Cameron – even if we arrest Cuzak? He's not just another small-time dealer, there could be serious repercussions for you – you know that?'

'Of course. I know what goes on. I was a drugs counsellor for years. I know what Cuzak and his type are like. I know what they do to people.'

'So what are your plans? For afterwards, I mean.'

I looked him straight in the eyes, I'd been thinking about this for two days and still hadn't decided. But I knew full well what he wanted to hear.

'I'll leave the country for a while. I have friends in Amsterdam. When I come back – if I come back – I'll stay clear of Manchester.'

Greenwood nodded with satisfaction. I'd given the right answer. Dyson looked on disapprovingly. I guess that she preferred the steady drip of investigation to the heavy undertow of street crime. I guess that, given a choice, so did I. Even matrimonials seemed attractive right then.

Greenwood clearly preferred the rough stuff. If he was working the drug squad, he'd have to. There'd be no room for sensitivities there.

The guy chewed on his fingers for a while, weighing up the pros and the cons. But I could see from the gleam in his eye that there weren't many cons. After only a few moments, he let go of his hand and turned to me again.

'You're sure about this?'

'Yeah, absolutely.'

He raised his eyebrows and smiled at both of us. 'OK, then, guys, let's go for it, shall we?'

Thirty-two

When I left Bootle Street with the big blue holdall, I cut through the side streets to Piccadilly, keeping my wits about me in case I was followed again. But the streets were quiet and the short walk to the bus station passed without incident. Even so, I felt uneasy. Greenwood's health warning had pulled me up short. I'd been so tied up with setting up Cuzak that I'd forgotten just how little time I might have left to complete my investigation for Mr Lee. And the guy was right – if Cuzak was arrested tonight, then I really should get out of the city by the morning. If I was ever going to get to the bottom of Charlie's murder, then I had to do it fast.

When I pushed through the door into the Willows Café, Rita was already there, sitting behind one of the faded blue Formica tables next to the steamed-up window, finishing off a bacon sandwich. She waved and smiled at me like a long-lost friend as I came in. I smiled back and made my way to the counter to get myself a coffee.

When I joined her, I leaned back in the chair, trying to forget Cuzak, pushing away the gruesome images that had followed me all the way from Bootle Street. Rita clearly sensed my unease and tried to make friendly conversation. I went along with that and we chatted easily for a while about the weather, the buses, the lack of money – the usual kinds of meaningless drivel that we all use to open up our important conversations. After a few minutes, I took out two twenties and a ten, folded them up neatly and stuck them under her coffee mug. She looked up at me unsmiling, then put the money away in her purse.

We fell into an awkward silence for a few moments, then Rita perked up and began asking me the questions first. 'So come on, then, Cameron, spill the damn beans.' She leaned forward and flashed her eyes at me. 'You say you're a detective, and you're working for some big-nob insurance company. That must mean they suspect that someone wanted Charlie out of the way so they could pick up the dough.'

I shook my head. 'No, it just means they're making sure.'

'You mean, like making sure that he wasn't knocked off by the beneficiary?'

I smiled wryly at her. 'Yeah, you're pretty astute, Rita.'

She took a sip from the mug and waved her sandwich in the air at me. 'Yeah, well, I'm no one's fool, I can tell you that for nothin'.'

'So, come on, tell me about Chow City.'

She hesitated for a moment and pulled a face at me. 'What's to tell? You met laughing-boy Keane, so you'll already know what a bundle of friggin' fun he is. I used to like it better when it was the Cheshire Grill. It was a dump, yeah, but it was a happy dump. Jeez, these days even Mr Peterson's been goin' around like his cock's just dropped off.'

I smiled and shook my head. 'I must say, Keane and the others don't seem very upset by Charlie's death. I thought they might close as a sign of respect.'

'You *are* joking, Cameron, aren't you?' Rita tossed her head and grimaced. 'They don't give a damn. There's only, well, me and Sophie – that's the other waitress on my shift – and she hardly knew the poor fella. The rest of 'em – *even* Mr Peterson – don't seem to give a damn. Peterson's sort of sad, I suppose, but, hell, you'd imagine he'd be *really* cut up, seein' as it was him and Mr Wilson started the business.

'Actually, if you want my opinion' – she patted her handbag – 'and I suppose you do, considering the *ex gratia*, the whole damn setup's weird. They took me on again when they opened the new place – 'bout four months ago now. Mr Wilson was in charge of the hirin' and firin' then. Nice man. Seemed to pick good people. When we opened we were servin' really nice food – not the garbage I serve now. Then, as time went on, we saw less and less of him and other people started to take over instead. Jack Smelton for one – the guy in the monkey suit – and Joe Palliachelli, the misery behind the bar.' She shook her head. 'Hell, you'd imagine that people who invested so much money in a project would take care with the people they employ.'

'Yeah, I know exactly what you mean. Keane told me that Mr Wilson and Mr Peterson weren't involved much any more. How true is that?'

She grunted scornfully. 'He's lying. Peterson's in nearly every day – but only in the afternoons. Him and Keane have these meetings. Hell, I don't know what they talk about. Nothing to do with running the restaurant properly, anyway.'

'What about Mr Wilson?'

She looked sad. 'Yeah, poor guy. He used to insist on coming to work as per normal, but you could tell they didn't want him there. He still kept at it, though – I'll give him that. Every damn morning of the week, right up to the day he was killed.'

'You got on well with him?'

'Oh, yeah!' Her voice softened and she smiled affectionately. 'Yeah. He was a true gentleman, God rest his soul. He was always... well, a tad too nice to be boss, if you know what I mean. The others... ah, they're always on at you, treating you like dirt. But Mr Wilson – he used to chat to us, like he was a regular person.'

'What about?'

'Oh, nothing much, this and that. He used to tell me I looked nice sometimes or just came by to say thanks for workin' hard. That kinda thing.' She looked across at me and grimaced, her eyes wet with sorrow. 'He'd even have a laugh with us sometimes. Then, as time went on, we hardly saw him. Now this.' She sighed despondently.

'Jeez, what a way to go, eh? Anyways' – she clicked her tongue – 'that's one of the reasons I'm checkin' out. To be honest, I just can't take it any more.'

'What about Mr Peterson?'

'Peterson?' She pulled a face. 'Well, I'll tell you, Cameron, the guy's a schmuck. When I first started he used to try to bum money off me – can you believe that? A boss scrounging off his staff?'

'Maybe he just couldn't get to the bank.'

She looked at me as if I'd been born yesterday. 'Oh, yeah? And maybe his doggie lost the rabbit the night before.'

'He bets?' I prompted her.

She snorted. 'Oh, yeah, he *bets*, all right. I guess he tries to keep it quiet, but Mr Wilson was always making sarky comments to us. He said Peterson would bet on two flies crawling up a wall if he could get a taker. Seemed to be some kind of a sore point between them, if you ask me.'

'You don't seem to like Peterson much.'

She shrugged. 'Why would I?'

'And the restaurant, it doesn't seem to be very busy.'

She grunted scornfully. 'Well, that's got to be the understatement of the century. Believe me, Cameron, for a city-centre restaurant, it's piss poor. We're lucky to get twenty-five covers at midday, maybe forty on a night.'

I thought back to the VAT return and started to do a quick calculation in my head. 'So, at maybe thirty pounds a head that's…'

'Save your brain, sweetheart. They took three grand last week. I know 'cos I added up the bills when I was bored. I get maybe a hundred and fifty quid of it – plus tips, if I'm lucky. And there's another five like me, plus Monkey-Man and Joe behind the bar – so they're hardly making a fortune, are they? Certainly not enough to pay for the sharp suits and swanky cars, anyway.' She stopped suddenly. 'Poor Mr Wilson, he was a nice man, y'know? He deserved better than that.'

'Yeah, I guess. And Keane's in charge now, I understand.'

'Yeah. The guy's some big cheese with the outfit that put the money in. He's setting the place up properly, he says. Long-term investment, he says, and other such shit, though it beats me why a high flyer like him should waste his time in such a crappy restaurant. Seems like they must be made of money, if you ask me! Anyway, they want it all their way, that's for sure – that's why they sidelined Mr Wilson.' She stopped and made a face. 'Still, I dunno. Seems kinda weird. He was the one who really got a buzz out of running a restaurant, and yet it's Peterson that Keane seems to deal with. Almost like they've got something going – if y'know what I mean. Hell, I could understand Peterson selling out, but Charlie Wilson – he'd be the last person to go by choice.'

'He's there a lot, this Keane?'

She shook her head. 'Not so much. And, to give the guy his due, he generally stays off the floor. He's more interested in the money, I guess. Not such a big job as things stand, eh? Comes in some afternoons to see Peterson and most evenings to tally up the takings. Drops in and out other times.'

'And Charlie, what did he do, before Keane and his bunch came along?'

She hesitated, smiling affectionately, 'Well, years ago, the poor guy used to run the old restaurant. He'd look after the customers and let Peterson take care of the cash. Funny thing is, the Cheshire Grill – that's what they called it – was doing well, right up to the very last week. The damn place was always full. Then one day they got us together and told us they were broke. That they were merging with this conglomerate, who were going sink a fortune into the business and relaunch it. That was mebbe a year ago. It was just before then that things really fell apart between the two of 'em. Stress, I guess. Anyways, when they rehired me, I got the impression that poor old Charlie was being given the big E – 'cept he sure as hell didn't intend to go.

'You know, it was like he'd become irrelevant or something. Damn, he even told me that himself. Said it was like the new partners wanted him out.' She stopped and looked at me. 'They didn't seem to feel that way about Peterson, though. Funny thing, that. Keane was all chummy with the guy who wanted out, but couldn't wait to get rid of the guy that wanted in.'

She shook her head in bewilderment and gazed down into her empty coffee cup, stirring the froth around with the end of her spoon.

'You said that things "fell apart" between them.'

'Yeah, like I say, they seemed to go off each other just before Keane and his boys stepped in. And, just lately, the two of 'em were always having these damn fights. They used to get on fine. Hah! Last week they had a real bust-up – right there in the restaurant before we opened. A real slanging match. In the end Monkey-Man went up and separated them.'

'Any idea what it was about?'

'Oh, yeah. Well, kind of, anyway. Peterson was on his high horse. He wanted to sell the rest of their holding to Keane – huh, like I told you, he couldn't wait to get out. Mr Charles wanted the opposite – buy the damn place back. Course, he couldn't, 'cos Peterson had no damn money. Peterson got quite nasty, bawling something about not being able to sell the rest of his shares because his partner wouldn't. He even threatened Mr Charles, right there in the restaurant. Said if he didn't agree to sell, he'd regret it. Jeez, he sounded like he meant it, too.'

'How much of this did you tell the police, Rita?'

She coloured up a little and shook her head. 'Uh, precious little. Keane leaned on us beforehand and said it would be in everyone's interests not to discuss gossip with them. He said it like it was almost a threat, you know.' She looked down. 'This might seem cowardly, Cameron, but I hadn't got the other job then, and I can't afford to be out of work.'

She looked up, suddenly wide-eyed. 'Jesus, you think those arguments between the two guys... You think that Peterson could have... y'know...?'

I shook my head. 'I don't know, Rita. That's why I'm on the case.'

She nodded and smiled a little. 'Yeah, I can see that now. And frankly, Cameron, I'm not surprised. There's been a weird feeling about the business these last few weeks. Nothin' you can finger, y'know, but kind of, well, kind of uncomfortable.'

She leaned back in her chair and looked at her watch. 'Hell, I gotta go. You want to know anything else?'

'No, it's OK, thanks – you've been very helpful.'

She grinned broadly and stood up. 'That's OK, Cameron. It's not every day a girl gets to talk to a detective – if I think of anything else I'll give you a ring, OK? Meanwhile, I better get off to that rat hole. It's my last day, best not be late or Monkey-Man will dock my damn pay.'

I thanked her again and walked with her to the door, then I got myself another coffee, took out my notebook and began to write down everything I knew:

> Charles Wilson and Barrie Peterson used to get on well then fell out. They nearly went bust. Peterson had been 'borrowing' the takings to subsidise his gambling? Three Seas stepped in to save the day.

I sat back in the chair, absent-mindedly cupping the hot mug in both hands, then changing to the handle as the heat stung the sore skin on my fingers. Every time I thought about Peterson this morning, I kept coming back to the same question.

I started writing again:

> *Where was Peterson getting his money?* How could he afford such a lavish lifestyle when all the evidence said that he was flat broke?
>
> *How come Peterson was so close to Keane? Why wasn't it Charlie?* He was the only one of the two who seemed to care about the restaurant business.

I thought about the Chow City VAT return, and wrote down,

Inflated sales, inflated costs – why?

Elaine Wilson – Sale of Charlie's half-share in the house +
life insurance?

Barrie Peterson – Sale of Charlie's shares in Chow City =
Peterson getting what he wanted – an exit from the business.

Elaine knew about Charlie's cross-dressing night when she
hired me – why lie?

Where does Aunt Emily/Pritchard fit into all this? Who was
threatening him on the phone that night?

Then I started a new heading:

Motives for killing Charlie:

1. Skinheads

2. Elaine Wilson's greed.

3. Peterson's need to sell shares vs. Charlie's refusal. Easy way out.

4. Elaine Wilson + Barrie Peterson = greed and sex.

I stopped there, unsure of what else to write down. It seemed to me
that there was a fifth option and it involved Chow City but, somehow,
I still couldn't work it out what it was. I put the empty mug back on
the table and flicked through my notes for the hundredth time.

It was when I put my pen back in my pocket that I found the note
from the night before – the telephone number that I'd found on the
pad in Keane's office. I took out my phone and rang the number. A
guy answered – a man with a rich, deep voice. A man who answered

as if he was truly tired of people bothering him. A man who answered with the words, 'Lavender Taxis, where you wanna go?'

I told him I'd got the wrong number and sat back in shock.

Why would Keane, the ultra-straight boss of a restaurant group, have the number of a gay taxi firm on his notepad?

Thirty-three

Being followed earlier in the day had fuelled my paranoia. Cuzak didn't trust me. Keane could have recognised me on the video. Even the cops might want to keep their eyes on me now.

And the bag didn't help much either.

Jack Greenwood's canvas holdall was inconspicuous enough. Dirty blue and stained in places with something that I'd rather not think about. The kind of bag everyone uses and no one ever gives a second look. It was the contents that bothered me. The body armour, the earphone and the wire all neatly tucked inside, along with the £5,000 of fake notes that looked for all the world like the real thing.

So, as I left the Willows Café with the bag slung over my shoulder, everyone was suspect. Ordinary people, assuming their daily tasks, took on a threat that was not their own. The man loitering by the bus stop, watching me casually as I passed. The kid with the skateboard who was walking behind me. The woman across the road, in the raincoat, who suddenly stopped, looked briefly in the windows of Debenham's, then crossed over and walked behind me...

I turned just before the Arndale Centre and took to the quieter backstreets, stopping briefly around blind corners to wait – just in case I had a tail. But there was no one. I relaxed a little then: if he was going to reappear, then it would be most likely around the hotel.

But there didn't seem any likely candidates there, either. No one watching the entrance, or loitering across the road. Still, I walked down the car park ramp, just in case, checking every level as I went, walking each floor, scanning the neat rows of cars for any sign of life. A few people came and went: a middle-aged businessman, women returning from shopping, a young couple kissing in the back of a car. But there was no one who looked as if they might be working for either Keane or Cuzak.

I put the bag in the boot of my Clio and covered it with the emergency blanket that I always carry, then drove out, across the bridge and left down a side street soon after, pulling onto the pavement on the blind side of another junction and waiting again to see if I was being followed.

Jesus, I couldn't go on like this.

I sat there for a few minutes rubbing the muscles in my arms and flexing my fingers, trying to get some kind of perspective. Keane would know about the break-in all right, but why should he suspect me? The office was locked when I left. Nothing was disturbed. And, even if the cameras *had* picked me up as I walked into the kitchen, the image was likely to be fuzzy and unrecognisable.

It was far more likely that it was Cuzak's man who'd been tailing me earlier. That was his style – he'd proved it the other night. And as long as I was careful, just so long as they didn't know about the bugs and the body armour – or my visit to Bootle Street – it meant nothing.

I started the car again and drove through the streets that run parallel with Deansgate, working my way towards the Granada Studios end, and Brinton Street. When I got there I pulled into a meter and locked the car, checking the boot carefully to make sure it was secure, checking the car a second time just to make sure.

Adelaide House was about halfway along. A modern, purpose-built apartment block, built in mellow brick, with pastel blue windows and a stylishly simple metal portico. The double glass doors led into a small lobby, which was clad from top to bottom in white marble with terracotta highlights. There was a lift with a security card slot next to it, and a locked door with another card reader, leading to a flight of stairs. Above me a CCTV camera winked silently. I stayed cool and pushed the button for Peterson's flat. No reply.

I pushed it again – longer and harder – and held my breath. Nothing.

Damn, I really needed to talk to the guy before I saw Elaine again.

I thought for a moment, then backed off and leaned against the wall on the other side of the lobby. I should be patient. I should take my time. Every cloud has a silver lining, and maybe, just maybe, this one could be shinier than most.

I called Charlie's sister while I waited. She still sounded weary when she answered the phone, but there was a new resolve to her voice that hadn't been there the day before.

'Oh, hello, Cameron, it's nice to hear from you. How are you getting on with your investigation?'

'I'm making progress, Martha. Our chat yesterday was very helpful, thanks. I've found Aunt Emily and he's made a statement to the police.' She sounded genuinely pleased at the news but I moved on before she asked for more details. 'And how are you?'

'I'm much better, dear. Of course I'm still reeling, but I've made my mind up to get on with my life.' She sighed in resignation. 'It's all very upsetting, but what's done is done. No amount of crying is going to bring Charlie back.'

I thought about my sister. She was right, but it didn't mean the pain ever really went away. 'You're very sensible, Martha. It's bound to get easier once the funeral's over. Have you heard yet when the police are going to release him?'

'No, they're still quite vague, dear. They said it would be a day or two, maybe the weekend. I've spoken to the undertaker and he says that they'll collect him for me and make all the arrangements just as soon as the police give the go-ahead. You're quite right, though: it will be a relief when he's been laid to rest. Then I can begin to let go properly. You will come, won't you, Cameron? To the funeral, I mean.'

'Yes, yes, of course I will. It'll be an honour.'

We both fell silent for a moment. I guess that she was upset again. Me, well, I was touched by the invitation. For someone whom I'd never really known, Charlie Wilson was becoming rather special.

Then I thought of Cuzak and the sting that I'd arranged; my promise to Greenwood that I'd disappear for a while. 'You've got my phone number, Martha. Just let me know and... well, I'll definitely come over – if I can.'

'Thank you, dear. That means a lot.'

I hesitated for a moment, rummaging around for the right words before I came to the point of the call. 'Martha, I hope you don't mind me asking: I wondered how you were doing with the purchase of the half-share of the house from Elaine.'

'No, of course I don't mind. Actually, I'm just about through it all. Well, I think I am.' She sounded almost relaxed about it all now. 'In fact, my solicitor's only just left. I've just signed all the papers, and given him the banker's draft. So it's done. She's got what she wanted. And – I suppose – so have I. She's promised to move out tomorrow. After that, I need never see the woman ever again.'

'Tomorrow?' I repeated, surprised that it was so soon.

'That's what she said, Cameron, and I'm not going to argue with her, believe me.'

As she spoke, a well-dressed man with thinning grey hair came in through the glass entrance doors and eyed me suspiciously. I smiled broadly at him and he relaxed, inserting his security card in the slot, then walking into the newly opened lift.

'I'm sorry to be so nosy, Martha...' I faltered for a moment, concerned that I was being too intrusive. 'The deposit – do you mind telling me how much it was?'

'Cameron, if it helps, then I'm pleased to tell you *anything*, dear. It was eighty per cent of the agreed purchase price. I gave my solicitor a banker's cheque for four hundred thousand pounds.'

Jesus!

'So when will it be paid to Elaine's solicitor? Do you know?'

'Straightaway, I think. My solicitor mentioned a transfer or something. He was very disapproving. Said it was most irregular and strongly advised me to wait. But I told him. "I want her out," I said. "I want that evil woman off my back!" You understand, Cameron, don't you?'

'Yes, of course I do.'

'Anyway, he said it would be in her lawyer's account this afternoon. I asked him specifically because I wanted to make sure. I really don't want any more phone calls from the woman. I've had just about as much as I can stand.'

I could see her, standing in the hall burning with indignation. 'Yeah, well, I don't expect that you'll hear from her again.'

The display above the lift flashed and an arrow pointed insistently downwards.

'Well, thanks for your help, Martha. I'll have to go now. Thanks for being so helpful. And please let me know about the funeral arrangements.'

'Yes, I will. You'll tell me how things turn out with your investigation, won't you?'

'Yes, of course, but I still have some way to go. I've got to see Elaine next.'

She grunted scornfully. 'Well, rather you than me, dear!'

There was a whirr and a clunk as the lift stopped.

I laughed gently. 'Yeah, well, wish me luck.'

I walked forward to the lift as the doors opened and an elderly woman with neatly permed grey hair walked out pulling a shopping trolley behind her.

I smiled warmly as I walked into the lift. 'Forgot my card again!' I breathed, shaking my head at my own foolishness. 'What *am* I like?'

She smiled back at me as she left. 'Oh, it gets worse as you get older dear, I can tell you. I do it all the time.'

When she'd gone I pushed the button for the fifth floor and emerged a few moments later in the middle of a short, deeply carpeted corridor with four light-oak doors leading off. Apartment 5b was at one end.

I knocked first just to make sure, then pulled out my pick-locks and knelt down by the keyhole, listening for the lift, or for any sound from behind the other doors. A vacuum cleaner droned somewhere behind me as I located the first lever. A minute later, the lift whirred into action and took off – up or down, I couldn't tell which. I kept on working the picks, trying not to lose concentration. A moment later it set off again and I waited, concerned in case it stopped at this floor. It didn't. I found the second and third levers almost at once. By the time the vacuum cleaner had breathed its last breath, I was nearly there. Maybe it was the imminent danger of discovery, or the soreness in my fingers that made me more sensitive. Perhaps the lock was just well oiled but, whatever it was, this time it took me less than five minutes before the last lever clicked back and I pushed the door open, slid inside and slipped my hands into a pair of latex gloves.

Peterson's apartment was much as I expected. A small lobby led off into a light and spacious lounge, furnished in Scandinavian style and carpeted in a deep cream. Various pieces of modern art decorated the room, from the small clay sculptures on the sideboard to the woman's copperplate torso that stood, life-size, between the two big windows by the balcony.

But there was something sterile about the place. It was too tidy, too unlived in. There were no magazines on the table, no photographs or personal effects. The door to the left of the windows revealed a small galley kitchen with a well-used cooker and an impressive array of cooking utensils. But, when I opened the fridge, it was empty. The food cupboards were bare as well. Even the plastic waste bin had been emptied and washed.

I understood why, when I went into the bedroom.

A large Samsonite suitcase lay on the bed and, around it, several piles of neatly folded shirts, ties, slacks and jumpers. The chest of drawers and the wardrobe were empty. On the floor stood several black plastic bags, each of them filled with clothes.

The *en suite* bathroom was clean and scrubbed. No soap or

toothpaste sullied the clean white porcelain of the sink, and no dirty washing lurked in the laundry basket.

I walked back into the bedroom and took a closer look around. A passport and various papers lay on the bedside table and, next to them, a small red airline folder containing two tickets for the Friday service to Brazil. One was in the name of B A Peterson, the other E J Wilson.

Today was Thursday. They were flying tomorrow, Friday. On the noon flight.

Thirty-four

When she opened the door to me, Elaine Wilson was wearing what I supposed passed for casual wear: loose beige slacks in some kind of shiny manmade fabric and a fitted Western-style shirt with pink buttons and bows on the pockets. She looked surprised.

'I'd like a word.' I said, putting a boot into the doorway before she could slam it shut. She scowled through the gap, pushing ineffectually against my me, then prodding at my Doc Martens with one delicate sandalled foot.

'Horace Pritchard made a full statement to the police last night.'

She stopped pushing and stared belligerently. 'Yes, I know – they told me. So what?'

'So don't you think it might worry them: the fact that your solicitor was also your husband's best friend and – maybe even more significant – the last person to see him alive?'

She looked down her nose at me and pushed the door again. 'I think they were satisfied with my explanation. How was I to know that they knew each other?'

I forced the door open just a little more and shook my head at her. 'Not good enough, Elaine.'

She gasped in annoyance. 'I don't know what you mean.'

'Yes, you do. You knew all along about Pritchard's alter ego and his friendship with your husband.'

She coloured up and looked everywhere but at me.

'I don't think that the doorstep is the right place to discuss this – do you?'

She hesitated for a moment, then reluctantly let me push the door open. 'You'd better come in,' she conceded, tight-lipped and ungracious.

I walked past her into the half-light of the hall and stood by the old pew, wondering if it was as uncomfortable as it looked. She closed the door and waited, her blue eyes flashing anger.

Mine weren't exactly friendly, either.

'You played me for a fool, Elaine. Why didn't you tell me about Charlie's Monday nights? Or his friendship with the preacher's wife? Or his running battle with her husband? You also knew damn well that Horace Pritchard and Charlie were friends *and* that they were both transvestites. *You knew* all this because you'd had him followed – weeks ago.'

I watched all the colour drain from Elaine's heavily made-up face. Only the blusher remained, isolated in a sea of deathly white. She sat down on the pew and looked down into her lap. I sat down on the stairs opposite.

'I... wanted a divorce, that's all. You *know* that I wanted a divorce,' she said, quiet as a mouse.

'I know that you wanted *rid* of your husband Elaine – and on your terms. Is that the same thing?'

She shook her head and looked up at me. 'No, it wasn't like that,' she whimpered, lost and vulnerable all of a sudden. 'I know that I wasn't always very nice to him. I was just desperate to be free again.'

'So that you could go off with Barrie, I suppose?'

She gawped at me open-mouthed and forgot all about her little-girl-lost routine. 'How do you know about Barrie?'

I ignored the question. 'Why did you hire me, when you already knew the truth about your husband?'

She leaned forward, playing with her hair. 'I – I just needed more evidence. The other two private detectives were OK, but they didn't get any visual evidence. My solicitor said—' she grunted in displeasure, remembering that I knew who her solicitor was '— *Horace* told me that, with the right evidence, I could sue for divorce, citing the cross-dressing as unreasonable behaviour. That's why I needed the video.'

'You still should have levelled with me.'

'I know, but I thought you wouldn't take the case on.' She was playing with one of her earrings now, a delicate filigree teardrop. 'Don't you remember how much trouble I had persuading you to work for me?'

'All right – but you could have hired someone local. There are hundreds of private investigators in Manchester.'

'Yeah, I know, and they'd all stand out like a sore thumb in the village, wouldn't they? That's why I wanted Bernice to do it – then, when she couldn't, it had to be you.'

She blinked and rubbed the back of her neck. I watched her silently for a moment and then stood up and leaned against the banister rail, looking down on her.

'I don't believe you, Elaine.'

Her lips twitched and she began to fidget. 'Well, I can't help that, can I?'

'You've already admitted that you knew everything there was to know about Charlie's Monday nights. You were desperate for a divorce – and the best possible settlement. So, what could be easier? You blackmail Horace Pritchard into luring Charlie into the alley. Your boyfriend appears with a stolen car and runs him over. Aunt Emily escapes. I give the police a statement. And everyone conveniently puts it down to a dispute with the old preacher, or a hate killing.'

Elaine Wilson shook her head repeatedly as I spoke. She kept on doing it long after I'd finished, repeating 'no, you're wrong' over and over, like some kind of a mantra. Strands of hair were breaking loose from her neatly pinned hairstyle, and the fine lines of mascara below her eyes were beginning to spread like ink on a blotter. If I hadn't known what the woman was like, I might have been taken in completely.

I stood quietly for a moment watching her squirm. After a while she stopped the chanting and dabbed her eyes with a tissue. 'I know what you must think of me, Cameron. But it wasn't like that. I swear it wasn't.'

'Oh, wasn't it? So why are you in such a hurry to sell your husband's share of the house, then? And why are you and Barrie so desperate to leave the country?'

She looked up, blinking through her tears. 'How do you know all these things?'

Stupid question. 'I'm a detective, remember?'

She looked down at her hands and sniffed. 'Well, whatever it looks like, Cameron, we didn't kill him, I swear. I can't say that I'm exactly devastated by his death, but I promise you that I wouldn't have had anything to do with killing him – you've got to believe that.'

I was about to ask her whether she thought her boyfriend might be involved when the doorbell rang. She stood up and checked her face in the hall mirror, dabbing at the dishevelled makeup and quickly tidying her hair. Then she answered the door.

'You ready, sweetheart? We're late.' Barrie Peterson was standing on the doorstep looking positively cheerful. His good humour turned to concern when he saw Elaine's face. And to a caution when he noticed me.

'What's... going on?' He asked.

As Elaine fell sobbing into the shoulder of his immaculate navy-blue suit, Peterson stared daggers at me. 'She's the detective, Barrie – the one I hired on Monday.' She sobbed. 'She's accusing us of killing Charlie.'

He didn't take his eyes off me for a moment but, very gently, he eased Elaine away and then closed the door behind him. 'You're doing what?'

'Maybe we should sit down and talk about this like sensible people.' I suggested.

He looked at me sourly. 'Maybe I should just throw you out on your ear.'

I shook my head. 'Yeah, well, you could, but that would leave me no option but to go straight to the police.'

He stared back defiantly. 'So what? We don't have anything to fear from you. You're talking through your arse!'

'Maybe I am, but, if I tell the police what I know, then – innocent or not – you're most certainly going to miss your flight.'

However composed the rest of him may have looked, Peterson's eyes were witness to his anxiety. He stared at me for a moment and then checked his watch. 'All right. Five minutes. But that's all!'

We sat down in the lounge like three civilised people. Peterson sat on the settee with his arm draped protectively around Elaine. I perched on the edge of the big soft armchair and repeated everything I'd told Elaine, right up to the suggestion that they'd killed Charles Wilson themselves and tried to make it look like a hate killing. When I'd finished, Peterson tossed his head and snorted.

'And that's your case, is it? Well, if I may say so, *Miss* Detective, your accusations are quite ridiculous – as well as groundless. Charlie and I may have had our disagreements, but we go back a long way. He was a good friend. I would never have done anything to hurt him.'

I looked askance at his hypocrisy. 'Forgive my directness, Mr Peterson, but do you really expect me to believe that, when you've been having an affair with his wife?'

He shrugged. 'I'm perfectly aware of what it looks like. Elaine and I just happened to fall for each other. One can't cater for these things. It doesn't mean that I ever had anything against Charlie.'

'Except maybe that he wouldn't sell the rest of his shares in Chow City, like you asked him to?'

Peterson blanched momentarily and then quickly turned the sudden stiffening into a shrug. 'Merely a business disagreement.' He smiled. 'Nothing to do with our personal relationship.'

'No, but enough of a disagreement for you to threaten him at least once.'

He let go of Elaine and leaned forward menacingly. 'I don't know where you've got your information from, Miss Detective, but you're wrong. In any case, even if Charlie and I did disagree about the sale of the business, it was hardly grounds for killing him.'

I leaned back in the chair. 'Oh, I don't know. If you add it all up: the half-share of the house, the life insurance, the shares in Chow City... It must add up to well over a million pounds. People have killed for a lot less. You certainly had motive. And, as we've already discussed, you definitely had the means. And now – you're flying off to Brazil tomorrow.'

Elaine glanced quickly at Peterson and took hold of his hand. Peterson scowled at me. 'So, if you're so damn sure of yourself, why haven't you been to the police already?'

'Because I wanted to hear your side of the story first.'

'And Elaine's given you it.'

'Yes, she has. But I don't believe her.'

Neither of them said a word. I stood up. 'OK, then. Since, you won't give me a better explanation, I'll see if Superintendent Dyson is interested in what I have to say.'

Elaine wriggled on the settee and pulled at Peterson's arm. He shrugged her off and tried to rubbish the threat.

'OK. Go on, then! It's all supposition, anyway. Your accusations won't hold water with the police and you know it!'

He was right: I had no real evidence. But what I did have was one hell of a lever. Whether they had killed Charlie or not, Elaine Wilson and Barry Peterson were clearly in a desperate hurry to catch that flight.

'You could be right. But I have enough to warrant further investigation – and quite enough for the police to stop you leaving for now at least.'

There was a protracted silence accompanied by a number of meaningful looks and hand squeezes. In the end Peterson slumped back into the settee. I had him.

'All right, I'll do a deal with you. We haven't done anything wrong – but we *have* to leave tomorrow. I'll explain everything – as long as you promise not to go to the police. OK?'

I shrugged. 'Yeah. If you haven't done anything illegal, I won't have any *reason* to go to the police, will I?'

He studied me for a second, then grunted irritably. 'All right. You're right, we did want Charlie to sell his shares. The deal with Keane was that we both sold or neither of us could. I needed to get away for... well, all sorts of reasons. Elaine wanted to come with me. Neither of us had any money. I needed the share sale to go through. I tried for months to persuade Charlie but he had this ridiculous dream of buying the whole business back. He left me little choice in the end. I decided that if I couldn't persuade the pig-headed fool I would have to blackmail him instead.'

Peterson sat staring at his hands, looking wretched. I waited in silence, praying that he wasn't about to lose his bottle. Elaine closed her eyes and squeezed his hand in reassurance.

'Pritchard was easy prey. When I told him that I knew his secret he agreed to help without a murmur. The plan was to confront Charlie when he was cross-dressing. Pritchard was to get him out of the bar at a prearranged time and then disappear on some pretext. I was then going to "discover" Charlie and threaten to expose him if he didn't sell. Elaine hired you so that we had video tape as backup. If he hadn't agreed she was going to threaten a very public divorce with the video footage as evidence. One way or the other, we guessed that he'd be so ashamed and embarrassed that he'd agree to sell the remaining shares – which in turn meant that I would be able to sell mine. That would have given Elaine and I enough money to start over.' He stopped and looked me directly in the face. 'I'm not proud of all this, but I swear to you that we never intended him to be killed.'

I nodded and tried to keep the contempt out of my voice. 'So what went wrong?'

Peterson scratched his ear and shrugged. He looked genuinely upset. 'Your guess is as good as mine. I was at the Sackville Street end of the alley, walking up the street to confront Charlie. Without any warning this bloody Range Rover appeared at the far end and came tearing down the road straight for the poor sod. It crushed him against the fucking wall. I heard the scream. Christ, I can't describe how it...' He swallowed hard. 'Anyway, I jumped back into a doorway. The car flew past me and careered out into the village. I threw up, then got the hell out of there.'

'Yeah, very noble of you.'

'Oh, come on! What else could I do? It was just bad luck. Some maniac with a chip on his shoulder was looking for a victim. Poor Charlie just happened to be in the wrong place at the wrong time. That wasn't my fault!'

'Did you see who was in the Range Rover?'

He shook his head. 'No. Don't you think I'd have come forward if I had? All the windows were black. I didn't see anyone.'

Peterson sat back in the settee looking anything but unburdened. Elaine wrapped herself around his arm. I watched them for a moment wondering whether I believed them.

'Did you tell anyone what your plan was that night?'

Peterson shook his head wearily. 'No, of course not. That would have been stupid.'

I didn't argue the point. Whether he was telling the truth or not, the man was clearly scared. And I wasn't sure why. He might still be the killer – or he might have other reasons for wanting to get away in such a damned hurry.

'OK. So what happens with Charlie's shares now?'

Elaine looked up. Her eyes were clearer now and some of the old defiance was returning. 'I'm selling them. Barry is as well. The people who invested in Chow City have agreed, under the circumstances, to do a deal. All above board, all legal.'

'You mean another *conditional contract*.'

She looked at me abruptly. 'Yes, I think that's what they call it. They retain a small part of the funds until the legalities are completed.'

Peterson looked at his watch again, then at me. 'We need to leave. Are you going to go to the police?'

I thought about it but, apart from sheer vindictiveness, I didn't see much point in shopping them just yet. They may be guilty, they may be innocent. But, either way, I had no hard facts to go on. I decided that I wasn't going to make any move until I'd spoken to the lawyer again.

'Probably not,' I said.

Elaine got up and reached for her bag, her relief manifest. 'If you wait just a moment, Cameron, I'll pay you your fee now.'

I shook my head at her and got up to leave. 'No, you're too late, Elaine – I don't want your money.'

She stared at me, surprised. 'Why not?'

I looked back from the doorway and held her cold blue eyes. 'Because *you* broke the contract with *me*. If I take your money now, then that might put me under some sort of obligation to you again.'

She frowned.

'And frankly, Elaine, I'd rather not be in that position.'

Thirty-five

When I got to my car I started the engine, reversed into the gateway of the house next door and waited quietly in the failing light. I didn't like Elaine or her boyfriend, and I wasn't sure whether I believed their story, either. What I believed even less now was that Charlie had been killed by some crazy skinhead. Somehow, there were just too many other factors creeping into the frame.

When the Jaguar pulled out of the drive, I followed their tail lights onto Bury New Road, dropping a few cars behind as they crossed the motorway and headed towards the city. When they reached Strangeways, they took a right at the lights and headed for Salford, turning off the main road by the old bank to pick up Pritchard. Then they were on the move again, back into Manchester and heading over the big railway bridge next to Victoria Station, and into a network of narrower, darker streets a mile or so to the north of the city centre.

I turned off my headlights and held back as far as I dare as they twisted and turned through the maze of old streets. I nearly lost them at one point but I backtracked in time and caught sight of their headlights sweeping right into some kind of a yard a few hundred yards ahead. Large iron gates were closing behind them by the time I cruised past, and Elaine, Peterson and Pritchard were walking through the rear door into an old Victorian merchant building.

I pulled into a side street just down the road and walked back to take a closer look. Under the impressive, carved-stone portico, with its long-defunct coat of arms, stood a shiny black door. When I shone my penlight around, a polished brass plate flashed back at me, revealing the owners of the building. 'Three Seas Business Group Ltd, Registered Office', it said. So this was Keane's real office. This was the business that owned 52 per cent of Chow City and was probably, at this very moment, doing the deal that would give it full ownership.

As I walked back to my car I thought about the significance of Horace Pritchard's presence at the transaction. I already knew that he was working for Elaine and, by proxy at least, for Peterson. Clearly he would be needed there by them for such a hasty transaction.

I thought back to that night in his office and the phone call that he made as I listened at the door. I thought about the irate voice on the other end of the phone and Pritchard's bare-faced lie that he'd been phoning his wife. I already knew that the second-rate lawyer was a first-rate liar. Bur what if he was an even better liar than any of us – Elaine, Peterson, me or the police – had ever imagined?

Thirty-six

It was a good half-hour before the lights went out and I heard the sound of voices echoing from the car park. I kept my lights off and coasted to the junction, waiting for the Jaguar to leave.

I wondered how Elaine Wilson and Barrie Peterson felt right now. Elated, perhaps, or relieved. There was something very odd about the way they had so easily caved in when I threatened to go to the police. That could have meant that they were guilty of Charlie's murder after all. But I didn't think so. It seemed to me that it was much more an indication of how desperate they were to get away. I thought about their unseemly haste. Elaine's determination to sell the house and move out straightaway. Peterson's need to do a deal on the shares and get the hell out of the country.

For the first time, it occurred to me that they were frightened, just as Pritchard had been on the night he made that phone call. There was someone pulling all their strings – and it didn't take a genius to work out who that might be.

A flash of white light hit the street and the blue Jaguar swung out of the gate and off up the road away from me. I started the engine and pulled out very slowly, keeping my lights off so that they didn't see me following. Inside, my heart was beating harder now and my mind was racing. If I could corner Pritchard when they dropped him off, then maybe I could force him to tell me the truth. I hoped so, anyway. I was running out of time. Once Cuzak was arrested, I needed to get out of the city fast. With just a little luck, I could still wind up most of the investigation tonight and leave Mr Lee and the cops to sort out the detail.

I was so wrapped up in my own thoughts that I'd forgotten the most basic precautions. Before I even reached the gates, Keane's BMW swung out into the narrow road, heading straight at me. I stood on the brakes, blinded by his headlights. The big saloon came to a dignified halt just a foot away from my front bumper, flooding the Clio with incandescent light. I swore a string of obscenities.

My first instinct was to ram the car into reverse, and get the hell out of there. But there was no chance in such a narrow, winding street. Better to play cool. Bluff it out. And pray to God that Keane hadn't recognised me on his CCTV security.

Two of them got out of the car and walked out of the light towards me. Keane was on my side of the car, and his driver, a big bonehead of a man, on the other. Both looked as mean as hell.

Keane opened my door and courteously waved me out, fixing me with his disturbingly vacant eyes. I took my time, trying to look cool while my heart beat six bells out of my ribcage. He stood directly in front of me, staring into my face, his breath fogging the tiny space between us. Bonehead walked round the back of the Clio and stood on my right. They were both wearing smart black overcoats and leather gloves, like extras from some *Godfather* movie. I wondered fleetingly if they'd left the Homburgs in the car.

Keane's voice was soft and sarcastic. 'This is Cameron McGill, William,' he sneered. 'We met last night – she's playing at being a detective. She *claims* that she's working for an insurance company.' He smiled humourlessly. 'Now, don't you think that you're taking your work just a *tad* too seriously, girlie?'

I stared straight back at him. 'I'm just doing my job, Mr Keane. Now, if you'll move of my way, we can both go home.'

He shoved me back against the car, then looked me up and down. He was checking on my size, my shape, I knew it – comparing me to the image on the video.

I eyed him coolly. 'Didn't your mother ever tell you that it's rude to stare.'

'You lied to me, girlie,' he sneered, as if the very thought pained him.

I shrugged. 'I told you the truth. I'm retained by Commercial and Collateral, just like I said.'

He snorted with derision. 'Good try, but *I know who you are.*' He smiled and his eyes cut into me like ice picks. It was a game he was good at, a game he liked. 'You're from York. And you came here to do a job for Mrs Wilson. She's just been telling me about you.'

I raised my eyebrows. 'You're well informed. I suppose she also told you that she fired me the night Mr Wilson was killed. The insurers hired me the day after. They normally use my friend Bernice Nolan, but she's away. We cover for each other. If you want confirmation of that, ask Mrs Wilson. That's how she found me.'

He paused for a moment and I could almost see his brain turning. 'The letter that you showed me yesterday. Give!'

I was going to protest but before I could say another word Bonehead was pinning me to the car and Keane was rifling inside my jerkin. He found the letter in the inside pocket and unfolded it, studying the wording and the bogus heading in the light of the headlights.

'So, you're working on behalf of Mr Johnstone at Commercial and Collateral.' Keane took out his phone and smirked. 'Presumably you'll have no objection if I ring him.'

I shrugged. 'Please yourself, but I don't see what business it is of yours.'

He keyed in the number on the letterhead and waited while it rang out. I waited too, relieved that I'd had the foresight to put the BT test line number on the letterhead.

'They only work nine to five,' I observed helpfully. 'They'll all be at home by now.'

He gave me a curious look as he put the phone away. 'So why no telephone message?'

I shook my head in amazement. 'You've got a very suspicious

mind, Mr Keane. That's the private number for the claims administrator. I wouldn't expect a message.'

He nodded sceptically, holding my eyes as he put the letter away in his coat, promising me that he'd ring them again in the morning. Then he took a step closer, bringing his face right up to mine and enunciating every word. *'You – were – spying – on – us*. Why?'

Bonehead peered down at me and licked his lips in anticipation.

'I'm simply completing my investigation, Mr Keane. I know that you're sensitive about your business interests, but I have to submit a detailed report to the insurers tomorrow on Mrs Wilson and her movements. Strictly between you and me, they have serious concerns about her. She's the beneficiary, so you can see why they're being so careful.'

He took his time, watching me carefully, weighing up my story against his own feelings of intrusion, trying to decide whether I really was the person who broke into his restaurant the night before, calculating my honesty – or lack of it. Perhaps even assessing how dangerous I might be to him and his organisation.

After a while he tipped his head to one side. 'Very well, but you stay away from my restaurant and my staff from now on – you understand?'

I stared him down, suddenly angered by his arrogance. It was a mistake.

He stepped out of the way. Bonehead took his place and, without any warning, punched me full in the belly. I doubled over in pain and shock, wheezing desperately, fighting for breath as my lungs collapsed.

Keane grabbed my collar, pulling my face up to his. 'Do you understand, *Miss McGill*?'

I sucked in great gulps of air, forcing my lungs open, desperately trying to breathe again. Keane waited. Bonehead flexed his fingers in anticipation.

'Yeah... yeah, I... understand.'

Keane smiled and let go. Bonehead looked disappointed. 'Now why didn't you say that the first time?' he asked.

Yeah, why the fuck hadn't I?

I swallowed more air, expanding my lungs again. Keane took hold of my hair and pulled me roughly towards him.

'You're a nuisance, McGill, and I don't want to see or hear from you again. If I find that you have lied to me...' He patted my face and smiled nastily. 'You should be careful. You might get hurt.'

I tried to look scared. This wasn't difficult. Whatever was going on in my head, my body was shaking like hell, and my bowels felt as if they were taking a hike.

Keane liked that so much that he stroked my face again and smiled. 'Be a good girl, now, eh? File your report about Mrs Wilson tomorrow, then go home to York and mind somebody else's business.'

I nodded eagerly, as if he'd won. He gave me one last meaningful look, then turned and walked back into the headlights. The doors clunked shut, the engine roared to life and the car reversed at speed, then drove wildly towards me, mounting the pavement at the very last moment, accelerating past and scorching off into the night.

Thirty-seven

I stood there rubbing my belly and cursing my incompetence, wasting precious seconds before I set off after the Jag. I didn't have a hope in hell of catching it but, if I was lucky, Pritchard might call in at his office and I'd catch him there.

But all the lights were off in the old bank building when I cruised past. I hit the steering wheel in frustration and reversed into a side street, ready to head back into the city. But, before I could pull out, a large grey four-by-four emerged from behind the office and turned my way. Horace Pritchard, was hunched over the wheel of a Toyota Station Wagon, heading out of Salford.

I said a gracious thank-you to any deity that may have been listening and pulled out a good hundred yards behind, following him onto the motorway at the big gyratory system. The Toyota was easy to see under the lights, so I hung well back as we left the city. When he filtered onto the Southbound lane of the M60 I drew a little closer and stayed two or three cars back as he motored over the big flyover that straddles the Manchester Ship Canal.

Pritchard took the sliproad at Junction 7 and dipped under the motorway heading for Sale. He turned left into another busy road and then again into smaller suburban streets. I doused my headlights and followed, waiting until he'd turned at the end of the first road, then accelerating after him, reaching the junction in time to see him taking a right just up the road. When I reached the next turning the road was empty. I gave him enough time to get into the house, then drove slowly up the street of neat, lookalike boxes.

The big car was parked on the drive outside one of the more ostentatious detached houses with its own separate double garage and a tidy tarmac drive flecked with white chippings. I pulled into the kerb and got out.

Warm light shone through the drawn curtains, casting a faint glow across a neatly trimmed lawn and immaculately tended borders. Inside I could hear boys' voices. I could see the flicker of a television, and smell the garlicky-richness of their evening meal. A lovely, homely setting. It would be a pity if I had to spoil it for ever.

The boy who came to the door was around sixteen, no longer quite as pretty as the picture on his father's desk, his looks already declining into post-pubescence. He glowered at me self-consciously from the hall, trying to look cool but achieving nothing more than sulkiness.

'I'd like a word with your father, please.'

'Erm, yeah, OK. Who is it?'

'Cameron – Cameron McGill.'

The boy grunted and shut the door on me. Less than a minute later it opened again and Horace Pritchard's big white eyes stared out at me from the hall. His face was flushed and his eyeballs were chasing around in their sockets.

'What in God's name do you mean coming here?' he whispered, teeth clenched. 'For pity's sake, woman. I did what you wanted! Now leave me alone, will you?'

I've never seen so many emotions in a man's face. He was anxious, indignant and turgid – all at the same time. And embarrassed as well. He didn't like what I knew about him. Especially when I was standing on his doorstep knowing it.

He began to shut the door.

'We need to talk,' I said quietly. He opened it a little again.

A woman's voice sang out from the kitchen. 'Who is it, dear?'

He looked over his shoulder and replied offhandedly, 'Oh, nothing love, just business.' Then he turned back to me and dropped his voice. 'Ring me, tomorrow, I'll talk to you then.'

I held the door open this time. 'No, Horace. We talk *now*.' I made a show of glancing over his shoulder towards the kitchen 'Or maybe you'd rather I spoke to your wife instead?'

He stepped out instantly, pulling the door behind him and hissing aggressively into my face. 'How *dare* you come round here making threats? I've told the police everything I know! Now leave me alone, will you?'

I stood my ground. However convincing he might sound, I was more certain than ever that he'd lied to Dyson. 'Don't give me all that. You haven't told them the half of it.'

Pritchard shifted his feet and wiped his brow. Inside the house there was the clink of plates being arranged and cutlery being sorted. The smell of pasta sauce and cooked meat drifted through the half-open door. Pritchard swallowed, then asked me to wait a moment. I didn't tell him I was veggie: I thought it unlikely that he was asking his wife to set another place.

When he reappeared he was wearing a warm jacket and the same distraught expression. 'Come with me,' he snapped, walking round the side of the house and through a side door into the big garage. There was a red Corsa parked to one side, a work bench against the back wall and a few items of garden furniture. He shut the door firmly behind me. I don't think I've ever seen a man look so pink before.

'This is outrageous,' he blustered 'I risk my whole reputation to help and you still come round here making your disgusting threats.'

Yeah, sure.

I walked across to the car and leaned against the bonnet, ready to let rip. I was tired of his games and tired of being run round in circles. 'It's no good protesting your innocence with me, Horace. I know that you're being blackmailed. I know that you lied to the police.'

He stepped forward uncertainly. 'I... What are you talking about?'

'Barrie Peterson and Elaine Wilson have told me about your involvement the night Charlie was killed. I know that you're still helping them – I saw you all at the offices of Three Seas.'

He blinked at me and held out his hands in supplication. 'I was – I was acting for them. They were selling their shares. It's all perfectly legal.'

I shook my head at him. 'Yes, very good, Horace. I *had* gathered that much. But why did you lie to the police?'

Pritchard shook his head, swearing that he hadn't. Bleating that he was just a small-time solicitor trying to earn a living. But, as the seconds passed in silence, the sweat began to stand out in droplets on his balding head. Within a minute he was shuffling his feet.

It was time to push him a little harder.

'All right. If you won't tell me what's been happening, I'll tell you.' I walked over to within a few inches of his face, well inside his comfort zone. 'We've already established that you're helping Elaine Wilson to get her grubby little hands on Charlie's share of the house. Now you've just been doing the same with Charlie's share of Chow City and Peterson's share of the business.' I moved even closer. 'You may be doing nothing illegal, but *conditional contracts* like those are hardly conventional, are they?'

Pritchard stepped back.

'Tell me, why are Elaine Wilson and Barrie Peterson in such a hurry to leave the country, Horace? And why have you thrown your professional caution out of the window to help them?'

'I just do what my clients ask, that's all,' he said, weakly.

'And that included luring your friend into the alley last Monday – so they could kill him?'

His face crumpled and he began to shuffle away from me, shaking his head in denial. When I followed him and prodded him hard in the chest, he shook his head and began to wail.

'They told me that they just wanted to talk to him! They said that they had to persuade him to sell his shares! For God's sake, McGill, I'd no idea that they were going to kill him!'

I eyed him cynically. 'Accessory to murder, Horace. You could get fifteen years for that.'

'I didn't know!' he whined. 'He was my best friend! I wouldn't have helped anyone do that! Penny and I *were* really... close.' He swallowed miserably. Tears welled up in his eyes. 'We went to places that neither... of us would have managed on... our own. I needed her...' He looked away and closed his eyes. 'My life is very difficult sometimes.'

Yeah, especially just this moment.

He was backed up against the wall now, his face sagging and a teardrop dribbling down his face. I was hitting the mark, but now I needed him to tell me a few things, so I drew back a little and spoke more kindly.

'Yeah, I know. But why did you do it?' *I'm your pal now, Horace, you can tell me.* 'Why would you help those two morons blackmail such a good friend?'

'I – I'd no choice,' he sniffed. 'Barrie Peterson threatened to expose me, just like you did tonight. He said he'd mail every member of the local Law Society with a photograph of me dressed as Aunt Emily.'

'So you agreed to get Charlie out into the alley at an agreed time.'

'I'd no option,' he whined. 'I would have been a laughing stock!'

'So you *did* help Peterson kill him.'

'No! No I didn't. Peterson said that he was just going to blackmail him. He wanted to make him sell the shares, that's all.'

He watched me with big fish eyes. Tears were running down his face and mucus was dripping from his nose. His lips were wet with fear, and, although he was sweating profusely, the man was shivering with cold. He'd confirmed most of what Peterson had said – except for the added twist of murder. One of them was lying and, for the life of me, I couldn't decide which.

'All right. So who were you speaking to on the phone – that night in your office?'

He wiped his nose with the back of his sleeve and sniffed. 'It was Peterson. I rang him. He said that you'd been put there as a witness. If I kept to my story, you'd back me up and no one would suspect that it was anything other than a hate killing.'

I stared at him with contempt. 'And afterwards, Peterson pressured you to draw up conditional contracts for both the house and the shares?'

He hung his head. 'Yes, it was very irregular.'

'And, presumably, you passed all the monies over at once, rather than retain them, as would be normal.'

'I had no choice.'

'And how did Keane pay?'

He staggered past me and sat down heavily on an old plastic garden chair, his face flushed and drawn, his breathing laboured.

'How did he pay, Horace?'

He looked up at me with glazed eyes and opened his mouth to speak. I thought that for a moment he was going to give me some shit about professional confidences. Maybe he was. Maybe he decided that it was not the place or the time.

'Cash – it was cash.' He paused, then answered my next question before I'd even asked. 'In twenty-pound notes. A half-million pounds.'

He looked for all the world like a man who had no room left for lies. I felt sorry for him. A pathetic man whose life was falling apart. Not because he was different, but because he'd been too weak to stand up to the bullies around him. Too weak to put his friend or his own integrity first.

Pritchard gazed at me and sniffed again. 'I suppose you'll be taking me to the police again, will you?"

He looked like a wreck, a beaten man with no prospects at all. But I wasn't so sure. Pritchard and Peterson had both given me different versions of the same story. One of them was lying. One of them knew more than he was letting on. But which one was it? Before I went to Dyson I needed to be certain of my ground.

I squatted down in front of him and shook my head as if my heart were going out to him. 'I'm sorry, Horace. I don't have a choice – I'm going to have to go to the police.'

Pritchard flinched visibly and another tear trickled down over his lips.

'But, I know how difficult this is for you, so I'm prepared leave it until the morning. At least that will give you time to talk with your wife and family.'

A kind of relief flitted across his eyes.

'In the meantime, for your own safety, you mustn't tell anyone that you've talked to me – especially Peterson. Do you understand that?'

He swallowed hard. I gave him the hard look and repeated the warning again.

He looked up at me with big white eyes, wiped his face with a handkerchief and nodded in absolute agreement.

Then I left the garage and got back into my car.

Peterson or Pritchard? I still didn't know who to believe. But whichever one it was, I was certain that everything would be clearer by the morning.

Thirty-eight

I'd taken the 'Salford' in Lin's address as proof that Grandfather had set her up in the Quays – in some smart canal-side apartment with gold taps and spectacular views.

I couldn't have been more wrong. Lin's flat was one of many, situated above a row of seedy, almost derelict, suburban shops lining a long stretch of Langworth Road. It must have been a pleasant enough shopping street once, right in the middle of a working-class district. But the buildings had been badly neglected and now well over half the shops were shuttered and boarded as the area waited for demolition – and the inevitable redevelopment that was already transforming the rest of the city.

It was nearly a quarter to eight when I pulled into a vacant parking space by the kerb and retrieved the holdall from the boot. Anywhere else, I might have taken a chance and left it securely locked in the car, but not round here, not now. The lights from a Turkish takeaway and a small supermarket shone out across the pavement as I crossed over the road, but most of the other shops on either side had been closed a long time ago, their dirty shutters stained with graffiti and their doors boarded. My belly was jumping through hoops. I cursed myself for agreeing to this meeting. Tonight of all nights. When I should be keeping my mind clear and my wits sharp.

Lin's front door was sandwiched between a boarded-up newsagent's and a launderette that looked as if it was on its last legs.

I heard her feet on the bare wooden stairs soon after I knocked.

When the door opened, she hesitated, then greeted me with a simple, nervous 'Hi', standing awkwardly, biting her lip, trying to smile.

I shifted my feet, not quite knowing what to say. Since this morning's phone call, our easy friendship seemed to have turned into a clumsy liability.

All the same, the sight of her made my heart miss a beat. She was wearing faded-blue jeans with an oversized khaki shirt that perfectly complemented the deep colour of her eyes. She would have looked stunning, except that her face was drawn and anxious. I felt no better. My stomach was churning. Part of me was scared as hell over the meet with Cuzak, the other part on tenterhooks at what she might tell me. I saw her look at the bag. Jesus, I hoped she didn't think I'd come for the night.

To be honest, everything was beginning to feel surreal, as if I were an actor in some movie, reading from a script that didn't quite make sense. Peterson and Elaine with their getaway plans. Keane with his none-too-subtle threats. Pritchard with his cowardice. Lin with her secret. In my imagination, somewhere beyond the broken-down shops of Langworth Road, Cuzak was reaching for his phone, again and again, as he picked the time and the place where we would meet.

'You look anxious,' I said, for want of anything better to say.

She opened her eyes wide and then blinked. 'Yeah, well, that's 'cause I am. You don't look so good yourself.'

'No, I have a lot on. It's a difficult day.'

She led me up a flight of stairs and through a door into a small sitting room, taking my jacket and hanging it behind the door without saying a word. I put the bag down on the floor by the settee. She looked at it again.

'Just some equipment,' I explained, trying to pass it off. 'Didn't want to risk leaving it in the car.'

She nodded and tried to force a smile. 'You want a coffee?'

I shrugged. 'Why not? Black please, no sugar.'

She hesitated and threw me and my bag another anxious look, as if she was going to say something, but instead she turned and went into the adjoining kitchen. I felt that I ought to leave. This wasn't a good idea.

But I sat down on the plain two-seater settee anyway, and looked around the room, trying to take my mind off Vinko Cuzak and whatever might happen in the next few hours; wondering what I was going to tell Mr Lee tomorrow and whether I could get anywhere near to solving his case; trying to chill out over what Lin might say; and, if I'm honest, trying to work out why the hell it mattered. I hardly knew the woman. She was leaving for Singapore soon. Why should I care?

David Mackintosh.

I looked around me. There was no sign of any man and, sure as hell, the room wasn't decorated or furnished in anything like a male way. It was cosy and comfortable – a world away from the dereliction outside. The walls were a pale, dusky pink, the doors and woodwork a smoky green. Furniture was limited but tasteful. A birchwood dresser and coffee table, standing on a plain burgundy carpet. A computer with a modern slimline screen sat unobtrusively on a small desk in the corner. Two small table lamps added a warm glow, and a coal-effect gas fire completed the feeling of homeliness. Over in the corner there were some black bin liners, overflowing with clothes, just as in Peterson's flat.

For a moment I felt like crying.

I wished that Beano hadn't been so fucking stupid. I wished that Lin hadn't been so damn secretive. And I wished like hell that I didn't care so much about both of them.

Lin returned after a few minutes with two mugs of coffee and a plate of biscuits. She put them down on the occasional table and then sat cross-legged on the floor opposite me. I waited, but she said nothing. Just chewed on a biscuit and looked at her feet.

'I like your flat,' I began, lamely. We had to start somewhere. She didn't look as though she wanted to talk much. And I wasn't too sure I wanted to listen. 'I thought Grandpa would have set you up in some posh development.'

She gave me a sharp look, her voice edgy. 'I don't take handouts, Cameron. I get by on my loan, and on the part-time work that I do.'

I sighed and turned away in irritation.

She shook her head and flashed her big eyes in genuine regret. 'I'm sorry. I'm just... well, a little wound up.'

I breathed down my nose. 'Yeah, me too.'

She looked up again and frowned. 'So what's wrong?'

I shrugged. 'Oh, just work.'

She looked at the bag again and narrowed her eyes. 'You in trouble, Cameron?'

I tried to pass it off, but the carefree smile I'd intended froze on my face before it was formed. 'Just another job.' I smiled woodenly and took a swig of hot coffee. She carried on staring at the bag.

I glanced down, wondering if she was going to level with me soon, as she'd said she would. If not, there were other places that I'd rather be. Like Australia, maybe.

She got up and sat down next to me, laying a sympathetic hand on my arm.

'This is about this Cuzak man, Cameron, isn't it?'

I nearly choked. 'What? Where the fuck did you get that name?'

She looked at me nervously. 'Grandpa told me that he saw you talking to him. A drug dealer, he said.' She touched my arm again. 'He's worried about you, Cameron, and so am I. He's worried that you're dealing or something – he asked me to talk to you about it.'

I closed my eyes and groaned. Jesus, this was all I needed. I was furious with both of them. Him for betraying a confidence, her for having the gall to suggest something like that. I got up and retrieved the bag, grabbing for my coat.

Lin ran after me, her face crumbling. 'He likes you, Cameron! He's concerned about you, that's all!'

I took hold of the door handle. 'Yeah, well, he's *your* grandfather, not mine. Since *when* was I accountable to *him*?'

'Oh, come on, Cam,' she pleaded. 'He knows how fond I am of you!'

I knew that I was overreacting. I could feel myself being drawn into a row, spinning helplessly towards a vortex of insults and recriminations. That was the last thing I needed right now. I gripped the door handle harder and tried to calm down a little.

'I came here because you wanted to talk to me. I *thought* it was about something else, like you promised. I *thought* it was going to be about David Mackintosh.'

She rounded on me now, moving very close and spitting fire into my face. 'OK, McGill. I'll make you a deal. I'll tell you everything you need to know about me. Right from the beginning, without leaving a single thing out.'

She stopped and looked me straight in the eyes. 'But first I want an explanation from you – Grandpa thinks you're running drugs, and on the surface that's exactly what it looks like.' She stepped back and looked me straight in the eyes. 'Tell me he's wrong, Cameron. Tell me what all this is about!'

I didn't know what to say. However much I liked the woman, I couldn't risk compromising myself. So I tried to avoid the question instead.

'Look, Lin, I'm tired of all this – I'm not telling you a thing until I know who David Mackintosh is.'

She stopped in her tracks and stared at me angrily. Whatever my fears were, they seemed well founded.

'Will you please stop saying that name!' She shuddered and wrapped her arms around herself.

'Well just fucking *tell* me, can't you? Who the hell is he?'

She glared back at me angrily, tears forming in her eyes. 'No, Cameron, I damn well won't! Who the hell do you think you are, coming into my flat and ordering me around like this? I've already said that I want to tell you everything. But I won't be bullied – by you or anyone else. You're the one who keeps going on about respect. Well, for God's sake, show some to me, will you?'

I blanched at the criticism. I deserved it. My own anxiety was making me act like a idiot.

'Yeah, I'm sorry.' I put the bag down and let go of the door.

She dropped her arms down by her sides and wiped the tears from her eyes. 'That's better. Now, if I'm going to be honest with you, then you've got to start by being honest with me.'

I drew breath and closed my eyes for a second. *Jesus.*

'I'm not dealing.' I sighed, quieter, more reasonable now. But every nerve end in my body was bristling and my insides had turned to jelly. 'I'm helping the police. Actually, I'm trying to help a friend. Bernice Nolan – Beano. The one I told you about. You remember? She's been framed by Cuzak. I've set him up. Tonight's meet is a sting; the police will be waiting for us – it's the only way I know to get her off the hook.' I shrugged, trying to pass it off. 'That's all it is. Now, please, can we let it go?'

Her expression switched from resentment to concern. When she reached out her hand to me I noticed that it was trembling.

I steeled myself. 'Now *you* tell me what's going on. This David Mackintosh – is he your lover, or what?'

She shook her head slowly, sadly. 'No, Cameron, you've got it all wrong. David Mackintosh... uh... he... he doesn't exist any more.'

She breathed in deeply as if preparing herself, then opened her mouth to continue. Just at that moment my mobile rang and Vinko Cuzak revealed that I had just fifteen minutes to get to the meeting place by the canal.

Thirty-nine

My earphone crackled as I pulled the car off the motorway intersection and onto the rough track that led down to the canal.

'You read me, Cameron?' It was Greenwood, talking to me from who-knows-where.

I looked around trying to make out a movement, a car, a shadow – anything. But I appeared to be totally alone. 'Yeah, you're clear as a bell.'

'OK, we've got you now. Don't worry about anything. You can't see us but we *are* here and in position. Just keep cool. There's an officer with an infrared camera across on the other side of the canal. As soon as Cuzak arrives, get him to speak and identify himself. Ask him if he's got the gear. As soon as he starts to hand it over, we'll move in. Don't do anything to endanger yourself. Don't try to tackle him. As long as we get him on video and in possession then we're home and dry. You read?'

'Yeah, I understand.'

'Good woman.'

I parked the car and grabbed the bag of 'money' off the back seat, then started to make my way down the track to the canal.

The night was dry and clear. A sharp breeze was blowing into my face, stinging my eyes and catching my breath; the lapels of my jacket flapped noisily. Cuzak had been terse when he gave me the instructions. 'No light from torches,' he'd grunted. 'Use eyes. we meet under motorway. Bring money. You come alone, all right? No tricks, or you in big trouble – yes?'

As Lin looked on, watching my every move, I'd lied. I told him that I was a good hour away from that point on the Bridgewater Canal. He wasn't impressed, but he conceded forty minutes and I agreed. We were due to meet at nine thirty.

Lin had pleaded for me to tell her where I was going and, when I left without replying, she slammed the door behind me. I felt my belly tighten at the suddenness of the parting, but I pushed the thought of her away. It was a ten-minute drive, so I had a little under thirty minutes to spare. Just enough time enough to alert Jack Greenwood and to rig myself up.

Now, as I parked the car and began to walk down the hillside, disquiet was gnawing at my heart. The gravel crunched under my feet as I picked my way over the ruts and the ridges of the track. Across the water, shadows danced in and out of the fields. Clouds scudded across the face of the moon. The traffic drummed above me on the motorway. All around, the sodium lights cast eerie shadows over the hillside. But down by the canal it looked as black as pitch.

A small part of me whispered that it would have been better if Beano and I had never met, that she'd been stupid and that I was being equally stupid sticking my neck out for her. But the rest of me still vividly remembered that night in Hull, the time she got me in and out of the research laboratories, the bullet in her shoulder, and the bleeding that had almost killed her.

When I reached the towpath I stopped until the moon came out again, and looked up and down the canal. There was nothing significant to see – no boats on the water, no people; no sounds, no movement. Just the gentle lapping of the windblown water and the breeze murmuring in my one free ear.

To my left, about fifty yards away, the path disappeared into inky blackness under the motorway. The meeting place. I took a deep breath and walked on.

Ten yards on, the soft earth of the towpath turned to concrete and I walked into the pitch-black of the underpass, feeling my way in the darkness, a concrete wall on my left, deep water to my right. I spun round as something moved by my foot. A sudden noise. Struggling. Panic.

I drew back, reaching out for the comfort of the wall, gasping for air as two ducks flew off, flapping their wings, squawking noisily out of the underpass and into the clear night sky beyond. I stopped there for a moment, swallowing hard, letting my heartbeat slow. Trying to relax again.

The breeze stilled as I walked deeper into the blackness. The heavy scent of urine, dust and stagnation hung in the air. Ahead of me, on the other side of the motorway, the blackness gave way to a small rectangle of moonlight. But still no sound, no movement.

Somewhere, out of sight, over the other side of the canal, was a cop with a video camera. I kept telling myself that he could see me. That I was safe. That backup was only seconds away. All I had to do was talk to Cuzak. All they needed was to catch him with the drugs.

I knelt down by the wall, looking along the path, watching for a silhouette, straining for a sound. All the while, the wind outside played games with my ears, and my eyes sculpted shadows and shapes from the phantoms in my mind.

My watch glowed in the darkness of the tunnel. Nine forty-three. They were thirteen minutes late. What the fuck was Cuzak playing at?

Nine forty-five. 'Still no sign,' I murmured for the sake of the wire.

'OK, we read.'

Nine fifty-five. 'Nobody. Not a damn soul.'

'Yeah, OK.'

Ten oh one. 'I'll wait another five, then I'm coming up.'

'Yeah, agreed. Sorry – looks like you've been stood up.'

Jesus.

A few minutes later I started making my way back along the path and up the hill feeling despondent. Adrenalin was still coursing around my body with nowhere to go. I felt light-headed with the disappointment of failure.

'Sorry, everyone,' I croaked into the wire. 'I was sure the bastard would show.'

'It's OK, love.' Jack Greenwood sounded pragmatic in the earpiece. 'That's the way it goes. You did your best. Get back in your car. I'll join you there.'

He came within a few seconds, slipping out of the shrubs and sliding quietly into the passenger seat, then talking into his radio. 'I'm with her now. Stay primed, will you? They may still come.' Then he turned to me. 'You OK?'

'Oh, yeah,' I replied, wiping the cold sweat off my forehead. 'I'm just fucking delirious.'

He grinned. 'Don't take it personally, love. You did what you could, we all did.'

'Yeah, I know, but I don't understand why he didn't show. I was certain he would. The guy believed me. I know he did.' I frowned. 'You think he heard us talking?'

He shook his head. 'Doubtful. This new technology is pretty sophisticated.'

I still couldn't understand it. 'Well, maybe he saw you arrive. I thought a car was following me earlier, through Eccles. I assumed it was one of yours.'

'No, not us, love, we came off the motorway. Besides, we've been very careful. Traffic has CCTV on the roundabout. They were watching for him. He never even came near.'

I grunted. It still seemed odd.

'This car, the one you thought was following you – what did it look like?'

I shook my head. 'I don't know. All I saw was a pair of headlights. They just seemed to stay with me a little too long. I'm probably wrong. Jesus, I'm beginning to wonder about my judgement.'

'Well, keep your eyes skinned just in case. You've got a phone? Good, keep it handy and ring for us at the first sign of any contact. Maybe he's just winding you up. He could ring later with another meeting place.'

I yanked out the earpiece and pulled the transmitter off my belt.

Greenwood shook his head. 'Keep it for now. You might still need it.'

I grunted. 'Yeah, sure.'

Greenwood smiled patiently. He'd probably seen it all before. 'I'll have a car join you up on the main road and follow you back to the hotel. We'll stay here a while in case he's watching. If he doesn't make contact again, I'll still need a statement. You can ring me tomorrow and drop the stuff off at the same time.'

I thanked him again and arranged to see him the next day, late morning, then he disappeared back into the bushes.

I took off the vest and stashed it back in the bag, started the car and drove back up the track onto the big roundabout, turning onto the city road. Way behind me the comforting flash of headlights marked out my police escort.

Sorry, Beano. I don't know how, but for some reason I fucked up.

Suddenly I felt exhausted and demoralised. I'd been high on adrenalin for nearly an hour. Now I was coming down fast, bumming along on the bottom like a regular user. I'd given Beano my best shot. I'd no idea what to do next.

I thought about Lin as I drove. The way we'd parted. The way she'd shot back inside and slammed the door. I ought to go back and see her. After all the arguing, she'd still not had the chance to talk. But, no, it was too late. The moment had passed.

I still felt like shit when I turned onto the ramp by the hotel and made my way down to the riverside car park. In my heart I knew that I shouldn't have even contemplated seeing her tonight. Jesus, I was supposed to be a professional.

The first two floors of the car park were full but there was one empty bay left at the bottom level, by the low wall at the river end. As I manoeuvred into the small space I reflected that it didn't matter that Lin and I had been interrupted. We'd never exactly hit it off, had we? I wasn't even sure whose fault that was. Her with the mystery past or me with the hang-ups. Maybe it was both of us. Anyway, what did it matter?

I sat there for a while, thinking about Beano and the hopeless look in her eyes. I thought about Hannah too, and little Susie. I was the only chance they had, and I'd let them down. I seemed to be getting nowhere, whichever direction I went in.

I thought about Charlie as well. The broken bleeding body in the backstreet. How well was I doing there? Sure, all the evidence pointed at Elaine Wilson and her lover. They were the ones with the most to gain. They were the ones who were about to make a quick exit. But, hell, in my heart of hearts I knew it wasn't them – whatever Pritchard had said. Now he seemed my only hope. I just hoped that he'd use the opportunity I'd given him.

If my hunch was right, I should know by the morning.

I got out of the car and leaned over into the rear passenger seat to retrieve the bag and froze as a hand grabbed my throat and the cold steel of a gun barrel pressed into the back of my head.

Suddenly everything dropped into slow motion and a lousy evening turned quickly into the baddest of bad dreams.

Forty

'Get out, bitch!'

The voice was deep and slow and guttural. His hand was so big that it seemed to reach round the whole of my neck, squeezing my windpipe, making me fight for each precious breath. He shouted something at me – loud and menacing – but I couldn't hear for the blood that was pounding through my ears. I felt nauseous, light-headed, weak. For one hideous, unbearable moment, I really believed that I was going to die.

Once he'd dragged me out of the car he loosened his grip, and I devoured great lungfuls of air, relieved, even grateful, for the precious gift of my life. He crooked his left arm round my neck and pulled me backwards up against his own body, all the time, pressing the cold hard barrel of the gun into my skull.

'Let – me – go!' I croaked, pushing back the nausea, scared that I might choke on my own vomit.

He wrenched at my neck, leaving me gasping for air again. Images of Keane and his sidekick swept through my mind. I should have known – I should have been ready for him.

The gorilla lifted me bodily and pushed me through the low wall at the edge of the car park. I could feel his dick pressing into my thigh. His greedy, rapacious breath rasped in my ear. He turned onto a small path running by the river, hauling me out into the shadows.

Once beyond the lights of the car park, the thug dropped me onto my feet. I froze, trying to stay rational, trying to work it out. He slid the gun down onto my neck and pressed so hard that I could feel the vein beneath it throbbing.

'You don't try nothin' or I kill you,' he growled. I felt sick.

Then I smelled him, the man who'd been following behind us. And instantly I knew for certain what this was about.

Vinko Cuzak walked around in front of me, a big revolver dangling carelessly from his hand. A nasty mocking smile lit his greasy face. But his eyes were as hostile as ever. A vein on his neck twitched with pent-up anger.

He dropped the body armour and the transmitter at my feet and came up close, breathing all over me. 'So you try fuck with Vinko, uh?'

I stared back at him, bewildered. My brain was struggling to sort through all the events of the last few days. I'd been so fucking careful. I'd taken every care to make sure that he'd never suspect. Greenwood was sure his team hadn't been seen. Someone had betrayed me, they must have.

But the only people who knew were the cops.

'Who told you?' I croaked, defiantly.

The big guy pressed the gun deeper into my neck. Cuzak pushed his face into mine. 'It was little *bird*, McGill.'

I froze as he said it.

Lin knew as well – I'd told her just before I left.

Cuzak picked up the transmitter and threw it into the river with the body armour. 'Now, what we do with you, uh?' He set his head back and looked at me, breathing deeply through his nose, as if he was getting off on his own fucking importance.

'How come you know my real name?'

He spat at the ground, then waved the handgun in my face. 'I know very much about you, lady. You think Cuzak is thick foreign man, eh? Because my English no good, you think you go take me for ride, yes?' He stared at me, an unpleasant smile on his face. 'But you wrong, McGill. You see, I *investigate* also. I know you friend of this Beano. I know you try get me lock up, so your fat friend walk free. I am right, yes?'

I ignored him. Apart from the police, Lin was the only person who had all that information. But I didn't believe it. She'd never betray me...

Cuzak took a step back and jerked his head. 'Time you meet my friend Johnny, I think.'

The young boy from the estate walked round. He stood next to Cuzak, his legs spread wide, his head at an angle, smirking at me, cocky as hell. I stared back, unimpressed.

When Cuzak nodded, the guy behind me let go and stepped back. Cuzak twirled his finger at me and I turned round to look at the thug who'd very nearly strangled me. He was as ugly as I expected, and even bigger than I thought.

'We call my friend Teach, McGill. You want I tell you why?'

I stared back coldly at the hulk, still trying to work out what had happened.

'You call it nickname, I think,' Cuzak continued. 'Teach is short for Teacher – he teach lessons, yes?' He moved in behind me and rested his chin on my shoulder, breathing onto my face, so that his warm stinking breath filled my nostrils. Then he whispered, loudly, 'Now, he teach *you* big lesson, McGill.'

I looked to my right – the path was narrow; there was nowhere to run even if I got the chance. I looked left. A steep scrub-covered bank dropped away for about twenty feet, down to the black swirling waters of the Irlam. If Cuzak dropped his guard for a moment, I could drop over the edge. If I could make the first few yards, then I might survive. Handguns weren't so accurate, especially at night.

'If you're going to kill me just fucking get on with it, will you?' The voice I heard was my own. Careless and unfazed – yet, inside, my guts were churning.

Cuzak smiled joylessly and moved closer until the muzzle of his gun was pressing into my forehead. His voice trembled with emotion. 'You must be patient. My friend, he teach you lesson first. Make you sorry you lie to Vinko. When he finish, I kill you. I kill you fast maybe

– mmm – or I kill you very slow. Depend how I feel.'

I looked around me again for some way out. Cuzak looked faintly amused and dropped the gun down to his side. 'The water look good, yes?' He gestured towards the steep bank. 'Please, be guest of ours, have swim.'

I would have taken a chance and made a run for it but the gorilla grabbed my arm with one hand and punched me hard under the ribs with the other. Pain rocketed through my chest. As I fought for breath, he grabbed me by the hair and held me at arm's length, raising his other hand, ready to strike my face.

Cuzak suddenly panicked. 'No, not on face!' he shouted.

The man dropped his hand and let go. I took my chance and dived for his groin, grabbing his balls and twisting hard. He screamed out in rage and pulled me off, punching me in the guts again. When I folded over he jabbed my kidneys and I fell, screaming inside. Curling up in pain. Rolling on the ground. Trying to protect myself.

I lay there helpless. He circled around, sizing me up, choosing the best angle. Time slowed frame by frame. The big steel-capped boot drew slowly back, then it sliced through the air, gathering momentum, heading straight for my ribs. I reached out for it with my hands. But it smashed my feeble defences away and slammed into me, driving wave upon wave of pain through every fibre of my body.

I don't remember much more. He kicked me again, I know. But he was no more than a blur. My head began to swim and the voices of Cuzak and the others seemed to fade away, as if I was losing my grip on life.

Somewhere in the distance I could hear a car horn blaring. My body had lost all feeling. My brain was screaming in confusion. The horn went on and on and on like the sound of Hell itself.

I pulled my hands up to cover my ears and my body convulsed with pain.

Forty-one

Suddenly, it was quiet, deathly quiet. I forced my eyes open. Everything was black. Maybe, I really was dead.

No. I hurt too much.

I tried to stay in touch with something that I knew was real. The pain in my ribs. The sick in my throat. The damp ground beneath me. Then I remembered the river. If I could only reach the river, I could get away. Before they killed me. I had to get away – now, before they came back.

A hand gripped my shoulder and held me.

Sweet Jesus, they're still here.

'Cameron, It's all right, it's me. They've gone.' A familiar voice. A woman. A woman who was crying. 'You're OK. You're safe.'

I tried to turn and focus. A hand stroked my face. A voice pleaded with me for an answer. 'Cameron. Cameron, are you all right? For God's sake, say something. Talk to me – please!'

My eyes came into focus and reconnected with my brain. It was Lin. Jesus, it was Lin!

I groaned and tried to turn over onto my knees so that I could stand, but my legs were jelly and the pain ripped through my ribs like a thousand red-hot needles.

She took off her coat and laid it around my shoulders. 'Don't move, Cam. I'll get help. Just hang on.' She sniffed.

'No, no, don't!' I lifted myself up onto my knees and then stopped, waiting until the pain subsided. 'What... where are... they?'

'They've gone,' she breathed, holding onto me as if I might pass out again. 'I kept sounding the car horn. I think I scared them off.'

Slowly, gingerly, I straightened my back so that I could see her properly, wondering what the fuck she was doing there. Her face was scarred with the tracks of tears. Her eyes were big and frightened. I tried to take her in, remembering that someone had given me away. And that it could only have been her.

She watched me tearfully, and held onto my arm. 'I'm sorry, Cam, I should have come down straightaway. I thought you were safe. I didn't know.'

I breathed in short, shallow breaths. 'Are *you*... all right? Did they... hurt *you*?'

She stroked my face. 'I'm OK. They ran off down the path. It's you I'm worried about.' She took out her mobile and started to punch in a number.

Something snapped in my brain and I panicked. 'No. No, don't. I'm... OK. Stop. Please.' The effort drew all the air from my lungs. I waved my hand instead.

She looked at me in confusion. 'For God's sake! You need help, you need an ambulance. We need the police!' she shrieked. 'Cameron, they nearly *killed* you!'

'No... Please...' I shook my head firmly so that she could see that I meant it. 'No ambulance. No police.'

She put the phone down and I knelt there on the riverbank for a moment, trying to concentrate. Trying to recall something. Something important. But all I could think of was how lucky I'd been. How relieved I was that the violence had stopped.

Lin shook her head at me in desperation. 'You need a doctor.'

'No... No, I'm OK...' I held out my hand, bracing myself. 'Just help me up.'

She didn't respond.

'Lin, please!'

When she saw that I really meant it, she sighed in exasperation, put the phone away and grasped my hand. Little by little. Inch by hellish inch, she pulled and pushed until I was on my feet. I stood for a while, getting my breath back and letting the waves of pain ebb away a little. Along the path, the car park lights shone out as if everything were safe and sound. But it wasn't, was it? Cuzak had known that the cops were at the canal. That's why he'd never shown. I looked at Lin. She stared back at me – scared and helpless and supportive, all at the same time.

Jesus, no, I didn't want to believe that it could be her.

'Cameron, I really think we should get help.'

I shook my head and breathed a little deeper, carefully testing the boundaries of the pain. My throat felt like sandpaper; my belly and stomach were bruised and sore; but it was my ribs that hurt the most – sharp, white-hot jabs pierced me, every time I moved. Yeah, but my breathing was OK. No wheezing – and no taste of blood in my mouth, either. No coughing. I'd be OK. A tight bandage round my ribcage and I'd survive.

'I'm OK,' I assured her. 'I'm gonna be... OK. Just... get me out of here, will you?'

I put my arm around her neck and she took my weight, half-dragging me, half-pushing me along the path. Technicolor pain exploded through me with every step.

Who else had I told? There had to be someone else.

I gritted my teeth and held on tighter. Swearing at myself, trying to keep my mind focused.

Only the cops and Lin. I didn't tell anyone else.

We reached the car park wall and she started to manoeuvre me through the narrow gap, struggling to keep her balance, exhausted with the effort of carrying my weight. I stopped her and let go, leaning heavily against the wall, until we could both get our breath back.

I closed my eyes and tried to think. 'Lin... listen to me,' I gasped, swallowing heavily and regretting it at once. 'Listen, it's very important... that we keep this to ourselves.'

She stared at me, confused and appalled. I shook my head, trying to clear my brain, wishing that I could give her a nice logical explanation. I didn't believe that it was her who'd given me away. Why would she? And, if she had, why would she save me?

'Look... I can't explain. I can't even... work it out myself. But I don't want the police to know – not yet, not until... I've had time to think.'

She looked at me with her big eyes and sighed with resignation. When I started to move, she held out her arm to support me again. I waved her away, and shuffled the last few yards to my car, without any help at all.

As I leaned against the Clio, I thought about Greenwood again and wondered fleetingly what he'd say about the missing equipment. I didn't really care. My only priority now was to get back to my hotel room, take off those filthy clothes and sink into a scalding hot bath. Lin found the keys lying on the back seat where I had dropped them and locked the car for me while I leaned against the boot recovering.

'Can you give me... a lift to the hotel entrance?' I asked, holding my ribs. 'I don't think I... can cope with three flights of... steps.'

She shook her head at me and almost smiled. 'Jesus, Cameron, you just don't give up, do you?'

I blinked. 'What?'

She cocked her head at me and stuck her hands on her hips. 'You really think that I'm just going to dump you in the hotel and go home? Hell, what kind of friend do you think I am?'

I held my ribs and breathed a little easier. I guess the answer was pretty clear.

She pointed a finger at me. 'Stay right where you are and I'll bring my car as close as I can get it. You're coming home with me, McGill. You need some looking after.'

It took some careful manoeuvring to get me into the passenger side of the old Escort and we had to recline the seat so that I could lie out flat. But once I was in, except for the speed bumps on the ramp, it wasn't so bad. The immediate pain was easing a little as the endorphins kicked in.

As she drove, I felt well enough to ask her how the hell she'd found me. She glanced across and grimaced. 'I followed you,' she said, as if it were just a fact of life. 'I went back for my car keys, then I ran out after you.'

She saw the sudden look of concern in my eyes.

'And don't look at me like that. I was careful. Very careful. I drove around the roundabout over the canal, and parked up about a quarter-mile away, back on the main road, outside a chippy. I knew that I mustn't be seen.' She changed down and stopped at some lights, pulling the handbrake on, then forcing the gear stick into first. 'When you reappeared, I followed you back to the hotel.'

'Why? Why do that?'

She eyed me testily as the lights changed and the car moved forward again. 'Hell, why do you think? I was worried about you, Cameron. I wanted to know that you were OK.' She hesitated and eyed me ruefully. 'Anyway, I wanted you to come back afterwards – I wanted to keep my side of our bargain. You remember that?'

Yeah, I remembered all right.

'But when I got back here, it took me a few minutes to summon up the courage to come down and tackle you. I thought I'd let you get to your room first.' She sighed. 'I didn't want to end up confessing everything in some dirty multistorey.'

'Well, thanks. You saved my bacon.'

She looked across at me. 'Are vegetarians allowed to say that?'

I gave her a withering look. 'Yeah. OK, then, you saved my Quorn.'

She grinned at me now, 'Nah, you're right, doesn't have the same ring.'

She dropped a gear and pulled out to pass a lone cyclist. The old car stuttered in protest, and Lin floored the accelerator. 'So did you do the deal? And those men, who were they?'

I looked back at her, pleased that she was returning to normal. Relieved that she seemed ignorant about what had really happened down by the canal.

I related the whole story. I told her all about my crazy plan to get Beano off the hook. I told her about my trip to see Jack Greenwood, and I told her that Cuzak had never shown – well, not until I parked the car anyway. She was stunned.

'My God, Cameron.' She shook her head at me as she drove. 'I just can't believe that you would try something as stupid as that!'

I shrugged and then winced at the sudden pain. 'Well, I can't believe it went so wrong. Someone tipped Cuzak off. They must have done.' I hiked the seat up a little and looked across at her. 'You didn't tell anyone what I was doing, did you?'

She stared back at me, pained. 'You really think I would give you away like that?' she asked incredulously.

I shook my head. 'No, I don't. I just need to know if you told anyone, that's all.'

She breathed out indignantly. 'I rang Grandpa to reassure him – but only because he was so damn worried about you.'

I stared at her for a moment, considering the possibilities.

She pulled a face at me, her voice heavy with sarcasm. 'You think it was him? You think my grandfather mixes with people like Cuzak?'

I closed my eyes and sighed. 'No, of course not. Don't be so ridiculous. Just calm down, will you?'

She stared ahead into the night. 'Yeah, well, I'm sorry, Cameron. I'm still a little emotional. You almost got yourself killed, remember?'

'I know – and all for nothing. I really thought that I could help Beano. I really thought that it would work. Jesus, what a mess!'

Lin pulled to a stop outside her flat. '*What a mess?*' Her jaw dropped in disbelief. 'For Christ's sake, Cameron! You tried to set up one of the meanest dealers in the city. The sick bastard could have killed you!'

I turned back to her and frowned.

'Yeah, I know,' I replied. 'And you know something? I can't for the life of me work out why he didn't.'

Forty-two

When I struggled out of the car my body felt old and useless. Spikes of pain shot through my ribcage with every step. The stairs were the worst of all, demanding a suppleness that I couldn't give. Once we were inside the flat, Lin took over, leading me straight into the bathroom, and cutting the sweaty T-shirt off my back. She dumped it in the bin and then helped me out of my mud-caked jeans, leaving me standing at the washbasin in pants and bra, while I rinsed the dirt off my face and neck. By the time I'd finished, she was running a hot bath and handing me a glass of water and some painkillers.

'You sure you can cope with this?' She eyed me dubiously, nodding at the bath. 'You might get in OK, but getting out again could be a nightmare.'

'I'll be OK,' I assured her, leaning back breathlessly against the cold tiles. 'I need to soak. If I can get my circulation moving, then the bruising won't be so bad – and I might not be as stiff tomorrow.'

'What about your ribs?'

I shook my head and smiled as best I could. 'Stop worrying, will you? If you can get me a bandage, I'll be fine.'

She came and stood in front of me and stroked my arm, pulling a sad kind of face. 'I'm sorry if I'm nagging – it's only 'cause I'm worried about you.'

I stretched out my arm very carefully and slowly, then pulled her head towards me. She leaned forward and willingly held her cheek against mine. I felt comforted by her touch and, despite all the trauma and pain, I could still feel myself getting wet.

She drew back after a while and we gazed into each other's eyes. I could see all sorts of emotions in hers. Relief, concern, affection. And more than a little longing. When she realised that I wanted her as well, she moved away, smiled in embarrassment and then bent over and turned the taps off.

She tested the water with her hand and then looked over her shoulder at me, making a silly face and talking posh. 'I think madam will find the water to her liking.'

I stared back, unamused. 'Lin, you've got to tell me – we can't go on like this.'

She stood up straight and turned around. Her face was suddenly drawn again. I held out my hand to her and she came over and took hold of it, standing crestfallen before me, but resisting any intimacy.

'It's no good, Cameron. You and me – it can never work.'

'Why not?' I asked, more confused than ever. 'You want me, I want you. What else do we need?'

She shook her head. 'You're hurt. We can't—'

'Yeah, I know am. But that's not the reason you're holding back, is it?'

She looked down and shook her head.

'So, what's the problem? Tell me now – let's get it over with.'

She looked into my eyes and blinked. Hopelessness and longing chased each other across her face. She swallowed hard. 'If I tell you, you probably won't want to see me again.'

I squeezed her hand. 'Be brave. If you don't tell me, then we'll never know.'

She pulled her hand away and rubbed the back of her neck. 'You're going to be shocked.'

'Try me.'

She kept her eyes on mine and took a deep, deep breath.

'I'm transsexual.'

There was a moment's silence that seemed to last forever. The thought *had* crossed my mind, but I'd dismissed the idea as ridiculous. It *still* seemed ridiculous. My brain was struggling to process the information. 'You mean...?'

'I was born a boy, Cameron.' She shook her head. I could see the tears forming in her eyes, but her voice was firmer now. 'I'm not like you. I can never be like you. But I *am* proud of who I am. And I do consider myself a woman all the same.'

I shook my head. 'So David Mackintosh was *you*?'

She nodded glumly, taking in my shock. 'Yeah. I never got round to changing my name on the voters' list.' Her eyes opened wide and her face became set as she watched my reaction. 'You see? I told you that you wouldn't like it.'

'No. No, it's not that,' I protested, still trying to gather my thoughts. 'I – I'm just really *surprised*, that's all. The way you've been acting, I thought it must be something *really* bad.'

She pulled off a piece of toilet paper and dabbed her eyes. I breathed out heavily, feeling the pain cut across my ribcage. I was struggling to find an emotional reaction of some kind. If someone had asked me ten minutes before how I *might* feel, I couldn't have told them. Now, though, I began to laugh – partly out of relief, partly at my own surprising lack of response. She looked at me a little uncertainly and I shook my head at her. 'I don't care, Lin. We all have a past. I really, really like you – that's all that matters.'

I pulled her head towards me again and, this time, I kissed her full on the lips. She moved instinctively into me, then stepped back in sudden concern.

'Be careful, don't let me hurt you.'

'You're not hurting me.'

She bit her lip and looked at me in amazement. I smiled broadly at her and then she too began to laugh.

'You don't mind?' she asked, incredulously.

I shook my head. 'You're still the same woman to me. Not just the way you look, but the way you are. I've been attracted to you since we first met.'

'But... I thought... I mean you seemed to have such a down on people like Penny.'

I pulled her closer again, wincing a little as her body pressed on mine, but no longer caring. 'That's different, we both know that. And, anyway, I've learned a thing or two in these last few days.'

She buried her head into my neck, her voice faltering a little. 'Do you want to know about it?'

'If you want to tell me, I do.'

She drew back and smiled broadly. Suddenly she was happy. 'I think it'll make it easier for me if I can explain. Get into the water first. I'll tell you while you soak.'

She took my hand and helped me strip off my underwear, smiling up at me mischievously as she pulled my knickers down over my ankles. Then she helped me into the water and supported me as I lay on my back with my knees bent, letting the heat soak into my bruised and battered flesh.

When she sat on the edge of the bath, I studied her again. She was still the same person. Still the same unpretentious, straightforward and very attractive Chinese woman. OK, so maybe I could find pointers if I tried, but so what? We're all a mixture, anyway. You can pick out the masculine in most women. So why should it matter?

Lin saw me looking and smiled. Then she pushed her long hair back behind her shoulders, took a deep breath and began her story.

Forty-three

'I was born in Singapore, like I told you. But I was a boy baby.' She looked down at me and smiled. 'They called me David – David Mackintosh. My father was English.'

'My mum and dad loved me and I was well cared for. Actually I was spoilt. Grandfather Lee came to see me often and brought me little gifts. My father encouraged me to play with soldiers and guns, but grandpa was more sensitive than that. He let me do exactly what I wanted and together we would fly kites and ride bicycles. He taught me to cook in his first restaurant. He even bought me a doll once, because I asked him to. My father strongly disapproved. He was – he still is – a man's sort of man. Relations between them were always strained, anyway – and, as I got older, the situation got worse.

'I was eight years old when we moved over here – more than anything, I suspect because they wanted to get me away from Mr Lee. We were too close. I guess that they thought he was usurping them in some way.

'I think it was then that the truth began to hurt. I missed Grandpa terribly. I missed the way he always let me be myself. Somehow I felt all right when I was with him. Somehow he never really treated me like a boy.' She frowned. 'This is just my theory – I've never discussed it with Grandpa – but he had a daughter of his own once. She died young, I know that. Nobody would ever say why; no one in the family even talked about her. But Grandpa always said that I looked just like her – even though I was a boy. Anyway, I think that probably had something to do with the way he treated me, and I guess that I didn't mind at all.'

She smiled broadly at the memory. 'Actually, I liked it – I liked being compared so favourably to Soo May.

'Anyway, without him, life became bleak and I felt very unhappy with who I was. It wasn't just the way I was treated, that wasn't too bad. It's just that... everything just felt wrong – like I was being forced to be someone I wasn't. Like nobody recognised the real me. It was something that I couldn't explain, and that made it worse. I used to have friends of both sexes and I think that I was quite popular at school. But I was always closer to the girls. I liked the way they talked about things. They could be hurtful sometimes, but there was a companionship that I never found with other boys. They were always too concerned with competing against each other. Being stronger, braver, tougher, better. I never wanted to do that – I couldn't see the point. I suppose it was inevitable that eventually they would start picking on me.'

She stopped, looking a little concerned. 'I'm not boring you, am I?'

I shook my head and sponged hot water over my neck and shoulders. 'No, not at all.'

She took in my naked body for a moment and smiled with pleasure. Maybe I should have felt embarrassed, but I didn't. She was revealing more than I ever could. And she was doing it with an honesty that I found quite moving.

'Go on – please.'

She stood up, leaning back against the washbasin. 'Well, this sounds stupid now, but at the time, I was still convinced that everything would turn out all right when I grew up. I suppose I'd persuaded myself that, somehow, my male bits would shrink away and that I would grow breasts and be able to have a baby like the other girls. When one of my friends started her first period, I asked Mum when I would get mine.'

She looked at me wistfully, her voice quivering a little as she remembered. 'She… treated it as a joke. I cried all night. It was then I realised that I really was going to grow into a man. I didn't understand. I couldn't work out why I should feel like that. I thought I must be weird, or sick – or something. I tried to talk to my mum about it, but she just kept saying that it was a phase that I was going through. She must have told my father, because he suddenly started a campaign to toughen me up.' She stopped and looked at me, shaking her head. 'Can you believe it? He made me go for boxing lessons!'

'That's awful.'

Her eyes sparkled. 'Yeah, it was, except I managed to knock the shit out of one of the kids who'd been bullying me.'

I smiled, impressed as ever by her courage. She paused, more thoughtful now. 'My parents aren't bad people, but they didn't understand and they couldn't cope with it. Every time I tried to broach the subject, I got brushed off.' She paused, biting her lip and shaking her head. 'I was frightened, Cameron – so frightened, and so unhappy. I was only eleven, but I swallowed a whole bottle of aspirin.

'They found me, of course, or I wouldn't be here. And everyone, including the nurses in the hospital, was so angry with me for doing such a thing. They even made me see a psychiatrist. Huh, that didn't help, either. By then, I'd stopped trying to explain it to anyone.

'Grandfather flew over from Singapore the minute he heard the news. He was the only person who I still trusted and eventually he got it out of me. I told him because I had to tell someone. I suppose that I expected that even he would react just like the others. But, bless him, he did no such thing. Instead he gave my parents a good talking to, then he arranged for me to attend a new children's clinic just out of London – a place where they specialise in gender problems.'

She looked down at me and, for the first time, her eyes lit up.

'All at once I found myself talking to people who understood. I couldn't believe it! They told me that there were other boys and girls who felt that something was wrong with their gender. The doctors even explained why! They said that all foetuses are female and that gender isn't decided until twelve weeks after conception. It's to do with a hormone rush – either testosterone or oestrogen – and it gives the baby either a male-pattern or a female-pattern brain. Sometimes, they said – very rarely – something will go wrong and a foetus that is destined to become a boy baby will receive a big dose of oestrogen – so it develops a female-pattern brain. And vice-versa. The thing is, though, whatever happens to the brain, the body carries on developing as it originally intended. So that's why – even though I felt like a girl – I was growing up as a boy.'

For a moment I was lost for words. I've always believed that there was absolutely no difference between men and women and that all the inequality and male–female behaviour stuff was a product of society. But then, if I was right, why would anyone feel the need to change their sex? Why couldn't they just behave in a less gender-specific way?

She stared at me intently. 'Can you imagine what it felt like to be told that I had a recognised medical condition? Suddenly I realised that I wasn't such a freak. Suddenly I understood why I'd felt so different for so long.'

I didn't want to sound like a sceptic. Still, I had to ask. 'But what if you'd been allowed to just grow up the way you felt? If society was less divided into "boys do this" and "girls do that", do you think you would have been OK?'

She gave me *the look*. The one that says, *Jesus, I am so tired of answering this question*. But her voice was steady and her eyes held onto mine as she spoke.

'Cameron, I know this may be hard for you, but really you need to let some of that feminist dogma go. Take my word for it. Unless you've been in this position, it's hard to understand the deep-down differences between men and women. I didn't fit. I never would have fitted. I didn't have the outlook of a man, the instincts of a man or the identity of a man.' She paused and held my eyes. 'But I did have a man's body – and, believe me, it felt like shit.'

I nodded to show that I understood and poured some warm water over my hair. This wasn't the time or place for an ideological debate. Besides, I didn't really know what the hell I was arguing about – she looked and felt every bit a woman to me. So where was the problem? And why was I even asking the question?

'Yeah, well I guess you prove the point just by being you. I could never see you as a man, that's for sure.' She smiled back at me and I slid down into the water a little, relaxing again. 'So how old were you when you went to the clinic? Twelve, thirteen?'

She nodded. 'Yeah, twelve. They won't operate until you are at least eighteen and, in any case my parents were very hostile to the idea – and, well, to me too, I suppose. I think my father felt that I was some kind of slur against his own masculinity.'

'But your grandfather was different?'

She nodded, her face bathed in affection. 'Yes, he was quite rich by this time and he was spending a lot of his time on business interests in this country. He insisted on paying for my treatment. My parents were beside themselves with embarrassment over it all and jumped at the chance when he offered to take on responsibility for me.' She smiled and shrugged her shoulders. 'So I moved to Manchester and started a whole new life with him. I was given tablets which held off male puberty. I grew my hair and took on a girl's name. My new school treated me well. My schoolmates were weird at first, but after a while they were great – even the boys. Some of them were very protective of me.'

She came back and sat on the edge of the bath again, pulling her sleeves up, soaping the sponge, then washing me carefully on my arms, over and around my breasts and right down to my belly, where she drew back, blushing slightly. I looked up, smiling at her sudden modesty. She stuck her nose in the air and turned away, jokily bashful.

'OK, I'll take over,' I laughed, reaching out for the sponge. She smiled back comfortably and squeezed bathwater all over my head before handing it over.

'You better keep talking,' I suggested, somewhat ruefully, 'or I might just pull you in here with me.'

She grinned and pulled back in mock fear, then sat down on the toilet and continued with her story.

'Yeah, well, to cut a very long story short, I had the operation when I was twenty-one. Grandpa was happy to pay for it, but he wanted me to wait until then, to be absolutely sure.' She shook her head reflectively. 'Not that *I* ever had any doubts. But it stopped him being anxious.

'Afterwards I went through a sort of girl's puberty. My body changed its shape, I grew breasts and I finally became the real *me*. The only thing missing was...' – she blew through her nose – 'well, still is, periods.'

I looked up and pulled a face at her in disbelief. 'Hell, you are missing *absolutely nothing*, let me tell you.'

She nodded sadly. 'Yeah, I know, I've heard it all before, Cameron. All the same, it makes me different. If all other women have to suffer, then I'd rather suffer along with them. It's unfair. I feel excluded.'

I shook my head. 'Jesus, sometimes I really wish *I* could be excluded – 'specially this week.'

She shrugged and looked down, her brightness disintegrating.

I changed the subject. 'So you took Mr Lee's family name, not your father's?'

She brightened up instantly 'Yes. He said that it did him great honour. There is no way that I can ever repay him for the way he helped me. But it was a token at least, and, besides, I wanted to do it for myself as well.'

I suddenly remembered the night in Napoleon's and Natalie's sly comments. I'd been worried sick at the time; now it was all sliding into place.

'And Natalie?'

She pulled a sour face. 'Uh, *that* was a *big* mistake. It was, um, before the operation. I guess that I was quite needy, but Natalie only wanted me for one thing.' She hesitated, clearly embarrassed. 'Well, you know, my, um, equipment. But I was no good to her. I've – well, I've never actually been through male puberty, I never functioned, you know, as... a... um, a man.'

She stopped and looked down at me, seeking reassurance. I smiled back, amused at the thought of nasty Natalie getting her comeuppance. 'And since then?'

She pushed the hair away from her eyes and shrugged. 'There hasn't been anyone else. I've been a bit paranoid ever since then. Frightened that I'd never fit in. I knew that I identified as lesbian, but I've heard all sorts of stories from other transsexuals about how difficult it can be.'

I nodded. 'Yeah, I expect you have. Sometimes that's more to do with personalities, though, than politics. In any case, it's not like it used to be, thank God. Most dykes are more enlightened these days. It's how you behave that matters. There's no reason why you shouldn't be accepted. You're a nice person – even if you *are* an accountant!' She stuck her tongue out at me, but I just stared back at her, breathing her in, savouring the moment. 'And, Jesus, you are beautiful.'

She dropped her eyes, blushing a little. 'Well, anyway, that's why I was so arsey when I met you – I expected you to disapprove. I'm sorry if I was, um, difficult.'

I reached out for her hand and she came across to me. 'You haven't been so bad.'

'You sure you don't mind?'

I shook my head. Truly, it meant nothing to me. 'The only thing I'll mind is if I have to sleep alone tonight.'

Her eyes opened wide, part disbelief, mostly panic. 'But... I mean... I might hurt you.'

I shook my head and smiled. 'No, you won't.'

We stopped and stared at each other for a long time. Lin's face began to glow and, somewhere, below the water, I could feel myself responding.

I reached up, ignoring the pain, and pulled her down to me. We kissed, then she sponged my back and supported me while I washed my nether regions. When I'd done, she helped me out of the bath, dried me gently all over and wrapped the bandage tightly around my ribs.

After she'd finished, I took her hand and pulled her behind me, walking slowly, carefully, through into the bedroom and then lowering myself down and sitting on the bed. She stood between my legs and kissed me again. I closed my eyes, trying to calm my racing emotions. My ribs still hurt, my belly still felt bruised, but the painkillers, the bath and my own endorphins were doing their stuff.

Lin stood back and stepped out of her own jeans, removing each item of clothing until she too was naked. Her body was beautiful, her skin soft and slightly tanned, her belly full, her bottom small and rounded. She walked over to me again, this time pressing her small breasts against my face. I buried myself between them for a moment and then kissed each of her small nipples in turn; then her lips, her eyes, her hair.

She ran the palm of her hand over my breasts and then gently down over the bandages to my belly and my cunt, stroking the wetness, gently rubbing my clit. And smiling all the time. When I groaned in pleasure, she helped me onto the bed, laying me down, sliding a pillow beneath my head, then stepping back, peering carefully at me.

'Are you all right?'

'Yeah, more than you can ever know.'

I lay there on my back for a moment, watching her, breathing her in. Wanting her. She looked back, her eyes dancing with mischief.

'You look good enough to eat,' I said, flirting.

She bit her lip, then knelt between my legs, raising her eyebrows.

'That's funny,' she said, 'I was just thinking the same thing about you.'

Forty-four

I'm following Charlie down the backstreet. He's wearing a pink floral dress and five-inch heels. They don't suit him, and I want to catch him up, tell him to wear something more befitting his age and size, but he walks even faster and I can hardly keep up. When he reaches Chloë's Bar, he stops suddenly and glances anxiously back down the street towards me. His eyes are big and white and scared. His hair turns a much brighter shade of red under the sign and then it starts to disintegrate, trickling down his shoulders, and his back, collecting in a dirty pool on the ground.

The buildings evaporate and we're standing on a huge runway shrouded in mist. Charlie spins round and stares in my direction, opening his mouth in a silent scream. I wonder why he's so frightened of me. Then I hear footsteps, and I realise that it isn't me he's scared of at all. There's someone behind me, following us both. A black shape coming up the tarmac towards us. It's Cuzak. Sneering at me, laughing, waving to the gorilla standing behind him. It's Teach, and I turn to run but – I can't. Jesus, my feet won't move. My legs won't work.

Teach is above me now, swatting me like a fly so that I tumble helplessly onto the wet, bloody ground. I groan with the knowledge of what is to come and brace myself as the thug raises his hand to me.

Cuzak has been smiling, as if he's getting off on it all, but, suddenly, he looks anxious. '*Not on face! Not on face!*' He repeats it over and over in a singsong voice. The gorilla mimics him. '*Not on face! Not on face!*' He wipes my face tenderly with a handkerchief until it is clean and whole again. Then he swings his boot at me instead.

The pain exploded through my ribcage. I winced, catching my breath as I opened my eyes, expecting to be lying on some dirty tarmac. But it was quiet. And dark. And warm. And clean. I was OK – I was safe. Lin's bed. I was in Lin's bed.

The pain faded as I turned over onto my back, brushing Lin's arm. She stirred and mewed pleasurably, shifting her naked body so that it touched mine all the way down, then breathed steadily again.

I lay there for a while adjusting to reality, thinking about the images and the words. *'Not on face! Not on face!'* That's what Cuzak said last night. He hadn't wanted the violence to show. He'd made me *think* he was going to kill me, yet all the time he didn't want me marked. Why? Why the fuck should he care?

Lin nuzzled into me, touching my hand. I took hers and squeezed it gently, then turned and kissed her on the forehead. She made more sleepy noises and turned over, sighing with contentment.

But the voice still echoed through my head. *'Not – on – face!'*

I thought about the dream again. Charlie running away from Cuzak. Cuzak? How the hell could he be connected? He'd beaten the shit out of Mazza and he'd framed Beano. How could there possibly be a link with Charlie? My mind was playing games.

By now I was wide awake and my brain was going into hyperdrive, so I worked my way over to the edge of the bed and lowered my legs over the side, wincing as I contacted the floor and pushed myself upright. My whole body felt like lead. My neck ached and my head was throbbing. I pulled Lin's robe off the chair and crept around the bed and out into the bathroom.

When I put the light on and looked in the mirror, the bruises were already coming out on my upper arms and shoulders. My ribs still ached with every breath. Under the bandages, they too must be black and blue. And at least one of them was cracked, maybe even broken.

I looked closer and ran my hand over my head and neck, searching for damage. But I was completely unmarked. If Cuzak had really wanted to make an example of me, he'd have made the damage as visible as possible, as he had with Mazza: bloody nose, black eyes, mangled face and broken limbs.

Why had I been spared that?

I made a face at myself and hobbled my way through into the kitchen. Without turning on the light, I pulled back the curtains and scanned the road. Outside, it was still dark, quiet and peaceful, the only sound the whirr of an electric milk float and the gentle clink of bottles every time it stopped. I was about to let the curtain fall when a small light flared briefly in one of the parked cars, just a little way up. Then a red glow as someone drew on a cigarette.

The car was less than impressive: an old VW Golf that, even under the street lamps, looked as if it had seen better days. For just a moment my belly did a somersault. then I remembered that this was a working-class area. It was 6.25, some people started work early. The smoker was probably picking up a workmate.

I relaxed again and switched the light on, made myself a strong black coffee, found the painkillers and then lumbered back through into the sitting room and sat down on the most practical chair for my condition – the upright one in front of the computer.

But I'd hardly touched the seat when I remembered my camera and the shots I took in Chow City the night before last. So I got up and retrieved my jacket from the back of the door, rummaging in the pockets for the little camera and the USB connector that I always carried with it.

When I sat down again I pressed the start button on the computer and knocked back two painkillers with a mouthful of coffee. Then, as an afterthought, I took another. It was going to be a busy day.

The computer box had two USB ports, which, I hoped, meant that the operating system would be a recent one. It was. When it booted up, the Windows XP icon appeared on the screen. Opinion might be generally against Bill Gates's near-monopoly of computer systems, but right now I was just pleased to see software that would automatically display all the pictures I'd taken.

When the desktop appeared, I plugged the camera cable into the USB socket and waited. Various boxes and choices came up, and I clicked through them until I had a whole file containing thumbnail pictures of the various invoices and forms belonging to the restaurant. Then I scrolled through them over and over.

There was no way that they could ever use even a fraction of the food they seemed to be buying. But it was the VAT return that I kept coming back to. Tax fiddles usually involved depressing income and increasing bills. I still couldn't work out why anyone would want to overstate their sales. If they were working such a lucrative fiddle, then why didn't they just pocket the extra cash?

'You should be in bed, Miss McGill, resting your poor body.'

Lin's sudden mock-severity made me start and, when I turned my head to say hello, a bolt of pain shot down my right side.

'Hi. I couldn't sleep. Hope you don't mind me using your computer.'

She nuzzled into my neck from behind and ran her hand tantalisingly across my thigh. 'No, course not, but if you'd told me earlier, I might have been able to help.'

I smiled, remembering the night before, breathing in her warm smell again.

'Yeah, I thought of it, but I didn't want to wake you.'

She pulled another dining chair up next to me and leaned her head on my arm, looking up at me seductively with those big dark eyes. 'You can wake me any time you want, McGill.'

'Yeah.' I took a long look at her and then kissed her on the forehead. 'Nice thought, but this morning I have things to do.'

'Yeah, you detectives, you're all the same – work, work, work.' She laughed. Then, more seriously, 'How are you feeling, anyway?'

I shrugged. 'Oh, y'know.'

She studied me ruefully. 'Yeah, I know. It hurts like hell, but there's no way you're gonna give in to it.'

I looked back at her and kept my mouth shut.

She shook her head, then leaned across and took a swig of my coffee. 'OK, then,' she said brightly, 'what can I do to help?'

I scrolled through the pictures. 'I don't know really.' I sighed. 'I took these the other night in Chow City. They're just boring-looking invoices from their files, but there's something about them that...'

She frowned as she studied the screen and then squinted suspiciously at me. 'Cameron, how – in – God's – name – did – you – get – these?' she asked, very slowly, very carefully.

I raised my eyebrows and made a face. 'I, er, broke in.'

She stared back at me. 'You actually broke into Chow City?'

I shrugged. 'Yeah, well, it was late at night; no one was there.'

She nodded sarcastically. 'Oh, well, that's OK, then!' Then she shook her head and touched my arm. 'Cam, you worry me, you know that? You set up a drugs sting and you break into a restaurant. What else have you been doing while I've not been around?'

I bit my lip. 'Well, I broke into Barrie Peterson's flat as well.' She looked sideways at me. 'I think that maybe I should bring you up to speed, before we go any further, don't you?'

She pulled a face at me. 'Yeah, I think you better had.'

I went through everything. My conversation with Dorry, my interview with Keane, the subsequent break-in, my meeting with Rita, the search of Peterson's apartment, the visit to Elaine's and Peterson's 'confession', my second, more violent, confrontation with Keane outside Three Seas, and Pritchard's account of how Peterson killed Charlie.

Lin whistled through her teeth when I finished. 'My God, you've certainly been busy. And Peterson and Elaine are doing a runner, you say? You believe the lawyer? You really think it's them who killed poor Penny?'

'No.'

'But you said—'

'I said that it *looks* that way. Peterson wanted to force Charlie to sell his shares and Elaine wanted a share. They're both nasty characters but, somehow, I just don't see them as cold-blooded killers. '

'But what about Pritchard's account of what happened? I thought you said—'

'Yeah, I know, and I almost believed him last night.'

'But they're leaving in such a hurry, Cam.'

'Yeah, but I don't think it's because they killed Charlie.'

She frowned at me. 'So why?'

'I think someone's spooking them.'

'Who?'

'Keane maybe? He tried to scare me last night. He doesn't like me snooping around and I want to know why. The answer could be in these documents, but I'm damned if I can find it.'

She moved in closer. 'Mind if I take a look?'

'Nope, be my guest, Miss First-Class Honours – right now I could use an accountant's touch.'

She cuffed me playfully round the head and took over at the computer, starting with the invoices, listing the date of supply, the supplier and the amount on a pad by the keyboard. All fifteen were for goods supplied in one week during the current month. Six of them were for meat from three different catering suppliers in Greater Manchester. Five were for vegetables from firms in Liverpool and Preston. Four for fish from Fleetwood. What was remarkable was that the combined value totalled more than £9,000. Now, why didn't I think of adding them up?

When she'd done she eyed at me meaningfully. 'My God, Cam, that's one hell of a lot of food for a restaurant that's never even half full! If you work on normal catering margins that would mean that they would need to turn over something like fifty-three thousand pounds a week to use all that.'

I threw her a sideways look. 'Funny you should mention that – take a look at this.' I leaned over and clicked on another picture. 'According to the VAT return, that's pretty much what they're doing.'

I zoomed right in on the document, starting at the top and scrolling down. The return was for the quarter ending in September – the first three months' trading for the new restaurant. When I got to the quarter's taxable sales figure, I stopped and leaned back in the chair.

Lin peered at the screen and whistled through her teeth.

'Yeah, I know. Rita – the waitress – told me they were taking around three thousand quid a week. You think Rita got it *that* wrong? You think that they were really busy until we went in? Before Charlie got killed?'

Lin shrugged and pulled a face. 'You tell me, Cam – you've been in there twice now. And we've both tasted the food. Do *you* think business could have dropped off that much in a few weeks?' She pushed the buttons of her calculator. 'Cam, these figures mean that they have to be serving something like two hundred and fifty to three hundred people a day!'

I shook my head. 'With two waitresses and food like theirs? No way.'

Lin raised her eyebrows. 'So, what *do* you think?'

'What I've thought all along: they're doctoring the figures, they have to be.'

'Yeah, I agree. It's very easy to do, and provided that Customs and Excise are getting their payments, provided the proportions of costs to income look about right – which they do – and provided they are filing up-to-date company accounts and paying their tax on time, then no one's likely to ask any questions.'

'What about their accountants?'

'Same thing, really. Why should they question the sales figures? If all the paperwork checks out, if the audit trail looks clean, then why should they worry?' She paused and looked at me as if I were a little naïve. 'In any case, who's to say that their accountants aren't bent as well?'

Lin seemed excited. Me, I was merely confused.

'Hang on a minute. Look, I can understand businesses fiddling accounts and returns, but why aren't they taking a loss on the business and pocketing the cash? Upping their sales like this just means they pay more tax – and more VAT. What kind of a fiddle is that?'

She smiled. 'If they inflate their supplies as well – like they seem to be doing – it could be a damn good fiddle.'

I squinted at her. 'What?'

She paused for a moment, her eyes sparkling. 'Just forget that for now. Did you get a chance to see their bank statements?'

'No, but I saw the paying-in book.'

She smiled. 'Even better. What did it show?'

'They pay in daily and it's mostly cash, which I guess is to be expected for a restaurant. The amounts roughly tally with the VAT return.'

'And Pritchard told you that Keane paid cash for the shares?'

Lin had lost me somewhere. She was sitting back in the chair looking triumphant. I stopped and stared hard at her. 'I still don't get it.'

She ran her tongue around her lips and grinned at me. 'It's so perfect, it's almost beautiful.'

I stared at her. 'Lin?'

'Yes, Cam?'

'What the fuck are you on about?'

She shook her head at me but the smile faded quickly. 'You'd better tread carefully love – I think you've uncovered something really big.'

'Go on.'

'They're paying in lots of money – so the "sales" must exist, right?"

'Yeah, but—'

She held up her hand. 'I know, but they're not coming from the restaurant.'

I nodded. The thought had actually crossed my mind as well – I just couldn't make it fit until now. 'You're saying that the money's coming from other – illegal – operations.'

She nodded. 'Yep! Extortion, loan-sharking, illegal gambling, prostitution, drugs…' She paused. 'Do I need to go on?'

'They're money-laundering.'

'That's what it looks like to me. And it's more common than most people think. Illegal income, wherever it's from, is useless in large quantities. These days financial controls are so tight that, the minute you try to buy something big with cash, then somebody, somewhere will get suspicious. You can't just bank it, either. Every financial institution is paranoid about dirty money. You try to change large amounts of cash – or even pay them into an ordinary account – and the cops will be round before the ink's dry on the cashier's stamp.'

I leaned back in the chair. 'So the money has to be made legitimate, channelled through a respectable source – so that they can draw an income, write cheques and use the cash – like regular people.'

'Yeah, you got it, Cameron. Launderers use all sorts of sophisticated ways to clean up their money. But the most popular is still the simplest – use a business that everyone knows has a high cash turnover.' She smiled with satisfaction and downed the last of my coffee. 'Like wine bars, or supermarkets, or swanky, high-priced restaurants.'

Forty-five

I moved away from the computer and let Lin take over. She looked as if she was on familiar ground now, logging onto the Web and navigating the Companies House site with ease, as if she did it every day.

I was still trying to get my head round the implications of it all. 'You think Keane runs the illegal rackets as well as the money-laundering, then?'

She clicked on a heading and punched 'return'. 'I doubt it. They're more likely to specialise. Other people – other organisations – will run the crime syndicates, and then use Keane and his buddies for laundering the ill-gotten gains. Of course, they'll know each other. There'll be a customer–supplier relationship, just like in any business.'

'So the syndicates pay Keane the dirty cash, Three Seas makes it legal again through one of its restaurants, and then pays it back in some way?'

'Yeah – less a generous commission, of course. They can do that in any number of ways: through bogus pay, shareholder dividends, supply invoices – all that sort of stuff.'

'So you think that's where the high supply costs come in at Chow City? The big invoices for meat, fish and vegetables that we've just been looking at?'

She looked up at me and clicked her tongue. 'You got it, Cameron. Knowing what we do about Chow City, those invoices are almost certainly bogus. The goods are never delivered. They're just a simple method of getting the cash back out.'

I sat back in my chair. I was impressed, but still frustrated. Speculation was all very well, but hard evidence was what was needed. I said as much.

Lin glanced up at me with the whites of her eyes and threw me her professional smile. 'Well, let's see what else we can find out, shall we?'

I moved closer again and peered over her shoulder as she typed 'Chow City Millennium Ltd' into a text box.

'This is one of the most useful sites on the web for an accountant,' she explained. 'Every company registered in Britain is here, together with details of their legal returns and various other information.'

When she clicked 'go', a long list of names beginning with 'Ch' came up. The restaurant was a third of the way down the page and, when she clicked on the registration number next to it, the screen changed. She studied the new information that appeared and grunted with satisfaction.

'Good, everything's here. It'll cost you a fiver for a copy of their annual return and accounts for this year – you want to see them? You want me to go ahead?'

I gave her my credit card and, after she keyed the details in, an acknowledgement came on screen. After that she went back to the search screen again at my request and did the same thing again for Three Seas Business Group.

'That's it?' I asked, when she got up from the chair. It looked too easy.

She smiled, pleased that I was impressed. 'Yep, that's all there is to it! They'll email the reports within the next few minutes, then maybe we can see what's really going on.' She gave me the once over and pulled a face. 'In the meantime, Cameron McGill, I think I should find you something to wear. You probably won't want to be seen in public in my old robe.'

She bent down and kissed me on the lips and then disappeared back into the bedroom, emerging moments later with a white T-shirt and a pair of khaki combats over her arm. She was holding a pair of briefs in the air with the other hand.

'I hope you don't mind wearing my knickers.'

'After last night?' I laughed in disbelief. 'You've *got* to be kidding!'

She pushed the clothes into my hands and grinned, then she turned straight back to the screen. I stood there for a while, watching her as she opened her email inbox and downloaded the reports.

Hell, I still couldn't see how she could ever have been a man.

Little by little my mobility was improving and, though it took me a while to get into the trousers, I did manage it by myself. It was fortunate that we were close in size. The clothes could have almost been mine – maybe not what I would have chosen, exactly, but they were clean and fresh, and they smelled of her.

Nice.

By the time I returned, she'd printed both reports and she was sitting at the desk, poring over them. I looked over her shoulder for a while, but the long rows of figures and strange language were way out of my league. Lin, though, seemed to read them as if they were picture books – pointing at the figures on the screen and then tapping the calculator excitedly.

Maybe she was right: maybe accountancy was a life of adventure after all.

It was a good ten minutes before she emerged from her deep concentration and turned to speak to me again. She sounded bright enough, but her summary wasn't exactly what I wanted to hear.

'Well, it's all here, Cam,' she said, a little deflated now, 'but it doesn't exactly move us forward. They're squeaky clean. Both the restaurant and the holding company are up to date with everything and they're both solvent – well, actually, they're both rolling in money. Current assets are nearly three times current liabilities at Three Seas and around double at Chow City – that's unusually good for any business.

'The Chow City accounts were produced on the thirtieth of June this year – presumably the date when the restructured business opened for trading. As you can see here, it made a big loss, but that's because of the poor trading from the Cheshire Grill, and the subsequent closure for refurbishment. Capital-wise, it's sound. Keane wasn't lying to you about the investment, either – Three Seas have pumped in close to a million, so, even with a trading deficit of nearly two hundred thousand last year, they're well into the black.'

'What about Three Seas itself?'

She leaned forward and opened another screen. 'By normal business standards, it's still a relatively small outfit. They have a capitalisation of just under ten million. The company owns three restaurants apart from Chow City, all of them in Manchester. I'd need to see the accounts from the year before last to be sure, but they look like they're growing fast. The comparative figures for last year on this report indicate a growth of around two hundred per cent. That's amazing by any standards. And the profits are at the top of the scale for the sector.'

I leaned back against the settee. No major clues there, then.

She printed off the company returns and passed them across one by one. The figures meant nothing to me at all, but I read the director's report at the front of each one – *that* was in English at least. It said that 52 per cent of the shares in Chow City had been purchased by Three Seas for a peppercorn. Yeah, so the business as it stood then was worthless – that at least I could understand. But Peterson's and Wilson's new, smaller, holdings weren't. Lin said that they would each have had a 24 per cent share of the new capitalisation – close to £250,000 each. That confirmed what Pritchard had already told me. Elaine and her lover were doing very nicely out of Charlie's death. But what about Keane – was he doing even better?

I put the papers down with a sigh. 'No tax problems – nothing like that?'

Lin shook her head. 'Uh uh, Three Seas is even paying tax. It's all perfect – they're just about textbook accounts.'

A thought occurred to me. 'Could they be too perfect?'

She raised her eyebrows and grimaced. 'Mmm, it's a thought. If I obtained details of any other companies, I'd bet you that nearly all of them would have been filed in the last half of the permissible period – probably most of them close to the end. Company directors are usually busy people. Their accountants are busy. Company audits take time. Tax computations take time. And what does it matter? You go through the process and file the return within the due dates.'

Lin shifted in her seat, warming to her subject. 'These accounts were filed within three months of the year end. That's really early. I mean, to fit all that work in so fast, either their accountants have no other clients, or – just maybe – they're trying to make an impression.'

'Trying to *look* squeaky clean, so that none of the regulators or the Revenue give them a second look?'

'It's a possibility.' She tipped her head, hesitating slightly. 'However, there is something else that looks even more interesting. It might even give us a lead.'

'Go on.'

'Well, we already know that Three Seas owns the majority share of Chow City, plus other restaurants in the area. What I find really interesting is that Three Seas itself is owned by two other companies. One is called Welton Investment Businesses, the other Mandragon Retail Consortium. Mandragon owns a number of small supermarkets around Manchester; Welton seems to specialise in taxi firms based all over the northwest. There's a list of them here.'

I leaned forward and took a good look at the list of minicab firms and airport service businesses. Lin stopped and looked up at me in surprise. I stared back at her. We'd both seen the name at once. Lavender Taxis.

'Good God, Cameron, no wonder the guy was so unhelpful!'

'So they're part of the operation as well?'

'Yeah, of course. Taxis are another high-cash business. Hell, just how big is this?' She looked at me, her fingers poised over the keyboard. 'You want me to go on? Dig a little deeper. This could be the bit that tells us the most. But it'll cost.'

'Yeah – go ahead. Grandpa's paying.'

She turned back to the screen and hit the keys, spending a small fortune on my credit card, writing down copious information as she went. The two businesses that owned Three Seas were each owned by another three and each of them were in turn owned by several others. Lin followed the trail of each one, printing out the reports, listing the directors as she went and drawing what looked like an ever-burgeoning family tree. As the search went on, each new company got bigger and each set of accounts more complicated. Sometime after dawn, she downloaded the last one and sat back in triumph.

'Look, Cam, this company here – the thirty-fourth, by my reckoning – it's the end of the line.'

I frowned at her. The interminable trail of ownerships meant nothing. 'You've lost me.'

She shook her head, humouring me. 'All those other businesses, they all lead back to this one here. So the guy who owns this effectively owns the whole shebang.'

My eyes lit up. That I could understand. 'Well, come on, then. Who is he?'

'Ah.' She gave me a rueful look. 'Well, I can't actually tell you. There are no details. The business is based in Dominica. It's an offshore trust – a tax haven.'

'That's bad?'

'Mmm, it means we'll never be able to identify the ultimate owner of all these businesses. Dominica has passed some of the newest offshore legislation and companies can operate from there with total discretion.'

'You mean with total secrecy.'

She laughed. 'Yeah, that's probably more accurate. But it's also interesting. A complicated ownership structure like this is suspicious in itself, but, when it ends in one of the most secure tax havens in the world, well, let's say it raises some very interesting questions. It's more than likely that the owner of a chain like this – whoever he is – has something to hide, even if it's only tax evasion.'

'So hang on.' I ran my fingers through my hair and tried to put everything together. 'What you're saying is that this guy in Dominica runs a massive money-laundering network in the UK.

Lin looked pleased as punch. 'Yep, something like that – 'cept he doesn't have to live in Dominica: he could live anywhere.'

'And what about the suppliers? You said that the invoices I got from Chow City are probably bogus. They're just a way of getting the cash out.'

'Yeah.' Her eyes lit up again. 'If I'm right, the people who originate those bills are very likely to be the real customers at Chow City – and all the other businesses.'

'You mean the racketeers. The people who run the prostitution, gambling and loan-shark rings. They invoice Chow City for vegetables and the like, when, in reality, the invoice is there to cover the cash that they've sent for laundering.'

'Yeah, it's one way. There'll also be money going out in the form of dividends and fees, marketing and advertising and the like as well. The cash that you found in the paying-in books is their gross income. The gross profits generated at Three Seas have little to do with the restaurant – they're the difference between the dirty money paid in and the payments going out. It's *that* simple.'

She went through the same routine with the businesses who had sent the invoices. This time they were mostly small, independent firms, each of them making good money, each with a generous wages allocation, each paying generous dividends to shareholders and directors.

We both went quiet, absorbing the scenario, thinking it through again. After a while Lin turned round and put her hand on my knee, her voice laced with apprehension.

'This is big, Cam. I did all sorts of case histories for my dissertation, but I never saw anything like this. You've got to hand it over to the police straightaway. It's organised crime and, the size it is, it's very well established and likely to be very powerful. It must have been going for decades and it's likely to be very powerful.'

'Any chance you could be wrong?'

She shook her head. 'There's always a chance, but I don't think so. The ownership chain is too complicated for a reputable business. If you look at all the accounts we've downloaded, you'll see that they're all immensely complicated. There are all sorts of intercompany transfers, ownership and sales. Masses of complicated accountancy that must be designed to confuse anyone who gets too close.

'We also know that Chow City is not doing well as a restaurant, yet it seems to be buying a large volume of food and taking in lots of cash.' She shook her head again. 'I could be wrong, but I don't think I am – it's all just too coincidental.'

'OK, then, assuming you're right, if *we've* got this close, why didn't the authorities?'

She shook her head. 'It doesn't work like that. There are just too many limited companies out there. As long as everyone involved is careful. As long as all the businesses appear genuine, the cost-to-sales ratios are right, and they pay their taxes like respectable people, then no one is going to take a second look.'

'But what if someone does get too close? I mean, what happens when we tell the cops?'

She shrugged. 'If the Fraud Squad does its job properly, then there'll be mayhem. Most of the businesses will be raided and closed down. Lots of people will be arrested. The illegal rackets will be forced underground for a while. There'll be long expensive trials and – if the cops get *very* lucky – some of the directors will go to jail. But Mr Big will probably be OK – he's protected by his offshore trust. In fact, it's likely that very few people in the organisation even know who he is – come to that, he probably doesn't know them either. There must be a whole chain of command for something as complicated as this. If this really is laundering, Cameron, then, judging by the size of the organisation, it's got to be massive and very tightly run.'

'So Mr Big can sit back and enjoy his dirty money without fear of discovery?'

She pulled a face. 'Yep. He just pulls the strings and collects the nice clean dosh at the end of the production line. He probably never even gets his hands dirty. His chain of command will take care of all the work – and they'll be judged and paid purely on results, just like any legitimate business.'

'So someone like Keane might go to any lengths to extend his own power base, or his own earnings?'

'Or to protect himself and the organisation from discovery.'

I drew breath. 'You mean, if someone found out what he was doing – like Charlie?'

She nodded. 'Yeah – or Peterson.'

My brain began to spin as I added up all the new information and pooled it with the old. Filing everything in sequence and filling in the gaps. It all fitted now. It all fitted perfectly.

'You want to know how I think it all happened?' I asked her.

She moved closer and took hold of my hand. 'Yeah, you bet, Cameron. You bet I do!'

Forty-six

'I'll have to take this slowly – it's still coming together in my head and some of it's guesswork, but I'm pretty sure that I'm right.' I stopped for a moment and took a deep breath, sorting my thoughts into chronological order. 'OK, let's start about two years back. I think it goes something like this.

'Peterson is a gambler. His habit is under control for the first few years of his partnership with Charlie. They build a good business, they earn good money. Enough to pay for his hobby. Except, at some point, it stops being a hobby and becomes an obsession. He's in charge of the money so, when his salary from the Cheshire Grill is too small to cover his losses, he begins to "borrow" a little of the cash flow from the business without telling his partner. Then a little more – until he's bleeding it dry. Charlie finds out, but only when the business is on the verge of bankruptcy. That's when they fall out.

'Peterson is remorseful and promises Charlie that he'll pay all the money back. His partner – being a nice guy – believes him. But there's no way. That would mean Peterson giving up both his lavish lifestyle and his gambling – unthinkable for someone like him. The alternative is to borrow more money until the big, elusive, bankable win finally comes along. However, there's a problem – since his credit rating is lousy, he can't borrow from a legitimate source.'

'So he uses a loan shark?' Lin was already one step ahead.

'Yeah. And he takes on massive interest charges that multiply the original loan within months. He probably kids himself that it doesn't matter. He's had such a lousy run that the big win has to be just around the corner. So he keeps on borrowing, digging himself in deeper all the time. Meantime, he repays nothing and the business situation turns critical.

'But it gets worse. The loan sharks don't actually want the loan paid off because, that way, they lose the lucrative income. So they encourage Peterson to keep on borrowing, creating a vicious circle from which he has no escape. When that gets too much, the same people probably extend his gambling credit as well and allow him to run up even more massive debts.'

Lin smiled knowingly. 'Ah, yes. I see where all this is leading.'

'Yeah, they're setting the guy up. At some point – maybe even right at the beginning – Keane is tipped off about all this by the syndicate that's lending Peterson the money. He's interested, of course. The deeper the debt, the easier it is for him to take over the Cheshire Grill on the cheap. And, since Peterson hasn't the remotest hope of paying off the loans, he has no choice but to go along with Keane's "generous" offer to "invest" in the business.

'But it's a lifeline for Peterson, because it gets him out of the cycle of debt. It suits Keane, as well, because he can pay Peterson's debts off with his associates and acquire a prime freehold restaurant site at a knockdown price.'

Lin shifted on her chair. 'But hang on, Cam, if they wanted to get it for virtually nothing, then why would they put so much money into refurbishing the place?'

'They had to make the front convincing, so that nobody would suspect that it was just a laundering operation. Just like the accounts, everything had to look right – and in this case that meant respectable and prosperous.'

'But what about the lousy food? That wasn't much of a front, was it?'

'True, but they probably don't consider that important. Remember, they don't actually want many customers. They're not there to run a restaurant, so they keep real staff numbers and overheads as low as possible.'

'Yeah, that figures. They probably have a much larger make-believe payroll, which is a good way of distributing the cleaned-up money. But what if Peterson hadn't gone along with all this?'

I shook my head. 'He had no choice. He knew what kind of people he was dealing with. Keane would be the knight on the white horse. He probably promised Peterson lots of good things if he pitched in with them. A nice new Jaguar for instance, lots of cash to fund his gambling and his lifestyle, the promise that he could leave once they had a hundred per cent ownership – and, of course, the writing off of his debts. Given the choice, what would you do?'

She shook her head. 'Hell, Cam, I wouldn't even get to that point. The man's a fool.'

'Yeah. A fool with a *big* problem – his partner. Charlie loves the restaurant trade. In particular, he loves the Cheshire Grill. He cares passionately about keeping the business going. But, because of Peterson's gambling, they're heavily in debt to the bank. He knows that, if they don't do something, then the suits will pull the plug – and they'll both be made bankrupt.'

'So he agrees to the sale.'

'Yes, but he only agrees to a partial sale. Peterson persuades Keane that this is all hunky-dory. Once Charlie had been sidelined, he'll easily persuade him to sell the rest, and everything will be fine. Except his reasoning is built on faulty information.'

Lin snorted contemptuously. 'A kind of dead reckoning.'

I frowned at her.

'It's an old, unreliable form of navigation that relied heavily on faulty information. Sailors thought they knew where they were, but often they were miles off course. I've heard it used about business forecasts. About people who kid themselves that they're heading for good times, when in fact disaster is lurking around the next corner.'

'Yeah well, it's apt because this turns out to be dead reckoning in every sense. Peterson is wrong about Charlie being compliant. His partner refuses to give up his remaining quarter-share under any circumstances – in fact, he harbours a dream of buying the restaurant back one day.'

Lin screwed her face up. 'You think Charlie found out about the money-laundering?'

I shook my head. 'I doubt it. By the time the restaurant was really under way, he'd been sidelined. I doubt that they'd even let him see the figures.'

'No, I guess he'd have gone public straightaway. Even if it was only to get it back.'

'Yeah. Anyway, as time went on, Charlie digs his heels in and Keane puts more pressure on Peterson. The restaurant has been open for three months and Keane still owns just over half. Peterson had promised him a hundred per cent – and that's what he wants. If he lets matters lie, then it's likely that either Peterson or Charlie might find out what's going on. Keane realises that the easiest way forward is to get rid of Charlie, then buy the shares off his widow, and off Peterson. Keane obviously doesn't want any suspicion falling on him, so he devises a plan to make it look like someone else did it.'

'And, since Peterson was over the proverbial barrel, it was easy to rope him in.'

'Exactly. But Keane's clever. He doesn't tell Peterson what he's planning. He also knows about Charlie's Monday nights by now – thanks to Elaine's private investigators – so Keane suggests that Peterson and Elaine should catch him in the act and then blackmail him into selling the shares. Keane has already blackmailed Pritchard into spying for him, so he suggests that Elaine could use him – in his guise of Aunt Emily – to lure Charlie into the alley at prearranged time.'

'Then Emily disappears back into the bar to retrieve her handbag, leaving Penny to them. Hell, Cameron, you were right – some friend!'

'Yeah, I know, but Pritchard is so scared of being discovered that he'll do almost anything under pressure.'

'Including leading his friend to certain death?'

I shook my head. 'I don't think he knew that. He thought they were working on Peterson's blackmail plan – just like Elaine and Peterson himself did. None of them expected Keane to take over, or for one of his thugs to appear in the alley with the Range Rover.'

'So it was Keane who had Charlie killed, and he used all the others to set it up for him.'

'Yeah. And now they're all scared shitless. Peterson and his girlfriend can't wait to get out of the country, and Pritchard is filling his pants in case he gives the game away.'

'Hell, Cameron. How come you guessed it was Keane?'

'All sorts of reasons, but it was the phone call in Pritchard's office that clinched it. Last night Pritchard swore it was Peterson who he rang. But Peterson is soft-spoken with a strong northern accent. I couldn't hear any words, but the voice on the phone was powerful and the vowel sounds weren't anything like flat. Keane is from east London. There's a totally different rhythm to the sound of his voice.'

She tipped her head at me. 'Very observant, Miss McGill, if I may say so. but where do you fit into all this? Why would Elaine – or Keane – want you there?'

'Ah, yes. Well, I believe her when she says that she wanted a video for evidence – blackmail evidence. That's what she and Peterson believed as well. But Keane wanted me there so that an independent witness was available. He knew that all the trannies would make a run for it. He needed someone who would testify that it was a simple hit-and-run – a hate killing. And who better than an ineffectual woman PI?'

Lin laughed. 'Yeah, well, they screwed up good there, eh?'

'Mmm.'

'But all this – just so Keane could get his hands on the remaining shares. Seems a bit drastic when he already had control, doesn't it?'

'Not really. You've got to remember that Keane had spent a million pounds refurbishing Chow City. He'd probably only got authority for spending that sort of money on the condition that Three Seas owned it all. So when Charlie kept on refusing to sell, he was in a spot. He'd made a big misjudgement. So either he sorted it – or he would have to answer to someone further up the chain. He was probably too scared to let that happen.' I hesitated a moment. 'But there's something else. Keane had the Lavender Taxi number written on his pad. We know now that they're part of the bigger organisation – but Keane worked for Three Seas, so why would he be in touch with a small subsidiary of one of the other businesses in the organisation?'

Lin inclined her head. 'Search me, Cam – but who cares? We've got enough to nail them all here. Mind you, we still can't prove that it was Keane who killed Charlie.'

I nodded. 'You're right. I need Peterson and Pritchard to testify against Keane.'

'But Peterson's and Elaine are leaving this—'

'Not if I can help it, they aren't.' I pulled out my phone and checked my watch. 'It's nearly nine o'clock. They fly at twelve. They'll need to check in by ten, so that means they'll have to set off for the airport within the next half-hour. Provided Dyson can get to them in time, and make Peterson talk, then – with the financial evidence you've got there – she's home and dry.'

I walked over to the window and peered carefully through the curtains as Dyson's office phone rang out. The car I'd seen in the early hours – the one with the smoker in – had gone. But there was another one, a blue saloon, parked just outside. A well-muscled black guy was in the driving seat and he was staring at Lin's front door.

Lin was behind me. 'What is it?'

Dyson's phone continued to ring out without an answer so I ended the call. 'Does Pritchard – *Aunt Emily* – know where you live?'

She stared at me in confusion. 'No, I don't think so, but – I don't know. One or two other friends of mine have been back here; they could have told him.'

I glanced out onto the street again and my belly did a cartwheel. 'I was right about Pritchard. He must have talked to Keane last night. He knows I'm getting close. His buddy from Lavender Taxis is out there watching your flat.'

Lin peered through the slit in the curtains and let out a gasp.

I picked up my phone again and scrolled the directory until I found Dyson's mobile number. This time she answered.

Her voice was unexpectedly sharp – angry even.

'It's Cameron, I need to talk to you.'

She rounded on me at once, shouting down the phone. 'McGill! I damn well need to talk to you as well! Where the hell are you?'

Jesus, I knew she wouldn't be pleased after the mess-up last night – but I hadn't expected her to be *this* angry.

'I'm sorry about, Cuzak,' I said, rubbing my bandages. 'I still don't know what went wrong.'

'Yes, well I'm nicely covered in egg thanks to you. I don't know what the hell you've been up to, but I'm sure as hell going to find out!'

'What are you talking about?' I asked, staying cool. 'Someone tipped Cuzak off, that's all! I'm sorry, it wasn't my fault.'

'Yeah, I bet!' Suddenly she sounded very sarcastic. 'Then, just *by coincidence* I suppose, Mark Taylor's complaint against your friend is dropped – and she walks free?'

'What? You mean Beano?'

'Yeah, yeah, yeah. Beano.' Her voice was deeply sarcastic. 'After your little jaunt last night, Mazza suddenly got his memory back. Now he's saying that he was *mistaken*, that he's suddenly realised that your friend went to help him. He's certain now that some unknown thugs beat up the both of them. So your friend walks free.' I could feel the tension through the phone. 'Am I the only one that smells a very strong coincidence here?'

I dropped the mobile down to my side. *Jesus, how did that happen?*

'McGill? You still there?'

'Yeah. I'm sorry. I mean, I'm pleased she's... but I've no idea why...'

'Yeah, I bet!' She paused a moment and then became even more hostile. 'Anyway, that's not the reason I want to see you.'

I waited. Something in her tone made my belly turn again.

'You were at Horace Pritchard's house last night, I understand. His son's description matches yours.'

I screwed up my eyes and looked at Lin. She came and held my arm, concerned by the expression on my face.

'Yeah, I was there. Around teatime.'

'His wife says that she heard you arguing with him in the garage.'

'No! Well, yes, in a way. He lied to you. That's why I was ringing.'

She sounded hostile, bitter. 'Well maybe it would have been better if you'd rung me last night. Or, better still, if you hadn't interfered in the first place.'

'Look Superintendent, I'm sorry. I'm probably way out of order. But why are you getting so upset all of a sudden?'

There was a heavy silence. I could hear other voices in the background, men's voices. Further away I could hear a woman sobbing. When Dyson spoke again, she sounded grimmer than ever.

'Horace Pritchard hung himself in the early hours, McGill. And, other than his family, you appear to be the last person who saw him alive.'

Forty-seven

'Where are you?' she barked. 'I'll get you picked up.'

'It's OK, I'll come to the station,' I replied, trying to clear the sudden confusion in my mind. I mouthed the grim news to Lin. She caught her breath and took hold of my hand.

Dyson's voice was sharp and cold. 'No. I'd rather pick you up – tell me where you are.'

I hesitated for a moment. Dyson shouted down the phone. 'Tell me, damn it!'

'I'll have to get back to you.'

'Not good enough, McGill,' she answered, her voice more menacing by the second. 'This is serious, if you don't—'

I turned her off and slumped down on the settee, completely forgetting about my injuries and wincing as soon as I landed.

Lin stared at me wide-eyed. 'They've killed him? They've killed Pritchard?'

I squeezed her hand and pulled her down beside me. 'Dyson says he hung himself – but I find that hard to believe. I think this proves we're right, Lin. Keane's covering his tracks. He must have known that I'd talked to Pritchard last night and that the man was close to cracking. He's getting desperate. I think he's on a killing spree – he's getting rid of anyone who knows too much.'

Lin swallowed hard and all the colour drained from her face. 'That means...' She brought her hand up to her mouth. 'That man outside, Cam – he's waiting for you.'

I nodded. 'Yeah, maybe, maybe not. But there's someone else on his list who's way ahead of me.' I let go of her and picked up the phone again. 'Peterson knows enough to put Keane away for life. They'll go for him before me, you can count on it.'

I tried his apartment first but the phone rang out unanswered. So I tried Elaine's. She answered at once, sounding happier than I'd ever heard her.

'Elaine, it's Cameron McGill,' I began, urgently.

Her good mood seemed to evaporate instantly. 'Oh, yeah, and what do you want now?'

I took a deep breath and tried to sound as genuine as I knew how. 'Elaine, for your own safety, you mustn't go to the airport. When Barrie arrives, stay there with him. I'll come and explain.'

'Huh, you must be joking!' she retorted. 'Yesterday you were accusing us of murder. Today you want us to miss our flight. Just so we can have a chat? You think I'm stupid or what?'

'Yeah, I'm sorry, I was wrong. I believe you now – I know you weren't involved – but all the same you're both in great danger. You mustn't go to the airport, do you hear me?'

She heard me OK, but she still wasn't listening.

'Yeah, OK, little Miss Detective, but I think I can safely leave that decision to Barrie.'

'No, Elaine listen. Horace Pritchard's been—'

There was a click and the line went dead. I punched the settee angrily and tried again. It was engaged. She'd left the damn phone off the cradle.

I got up and hobbled to the door pulling my jacket off the hook. 'If I'm quick, maybe I can stop them.' Then I remembered that my car was still in the multistorey by the river. 'Can I borrow your car?'

She came across to me, open-mouthed. 'Cam, you can't. It's too dangerous! Call Dyson, let the police sort it out!'

I pushed my arms into my jacket and winced. 'Oh, come on, Lin, get real! There's no way that Dyson's going to listen to me right now.

I've embarrassed her once – she's not going to let me do it again.'

'But...' she spluttered, 'what about the man out there?'

I took hold of her shoulders and held her eyes. 'Don't worry, Keane's not going to risk anything round here in broad daylight. Besides, they don't know how much we know, and that must give me a little time. I'll lead him away from here and then lose him. As soon as I've gone, I want you to lock both doors and ring your grandfather. It's not safe here. Get him to pick you up straightaway. Tell him what's happened and what we suspect Keane is doing. Get him to ring his police contact – they'll listen to him. I'll ring him as soon as I can.'

She swallowed hard and gulped for air. 'Well – I'll come with you, then. You're not fit to drive.'

I picked the keys up from the coffee table. 'I'll cope. Just do as I say. I need you to warn Mr Lee. I need you to get him to ring the cops.'

She followed me to the top of the stairs and put her arms around my neck, pulling my face to hers and holding me there. I drew back and stroked her cheek with my hand. 'Don't worry. All I'm going to do is stop those two before they set off for the airport. After that, I'll come and join you and Grandfather and leave the rest to the police.'

She sniffed and squeezed my hand tightly. 'You promise?'

I nodded and pulled my hand away. 'Yeah, I promise. I'm not going to take any risks.'

The words were still echoing through my brain as I ran down the stairs. When I got to the bottom, I turned and smiled at her. She waved back, her face white and strained. My belly did another somersault and suddenly I felt sick. We'd been at loggerheads with each other all week. Now, the minute we'd resolved everything, I was leaving. At least she'd be safe. Whatever I might have said, I wasn't too sure about myself.

When I got outside, Lavender was watching me from the blue saloon. He sank down in the seat as I sauntered up the street past him. But I sensed him turning his head as I passed. And when I got into Lin's car, I heard his engine start.

I did a U-turn in the main road and drove back past him, then turned into the maze of condemned terraces behind the shops. When I looked in my mirror, he was coming off the main road as well, about twenty yards behind.

I took a left, down a short street of boarded-up back-to-backs, then right at the end, rumbling over the cobbles and up a longer street, picking up speed as I swept between the empty terraces, crashing the gears. I slewed left at a small junction, jerking the handbrake and sliding across the cobbles, past a row of half-demolished houses. The guy turned after me, some fifty yards back, accelerating suddenly as he realised what I was doing.

I skidded to the left at the end of a terrace, then floored the brake, swinging the wheel hard, accelerating down a narrow, weedy back alley. And stopped.

My tail was seconds behind and shot past the end at speed, pursuing me – he thought – around the next corner. I reversed out crazily, careering back the opposite way. Gunning the old Escort again. Cutting through a couple of streets, across the main road, and away. Breathing relief.

Surprised, but pleased that I'd dropped him so easily.

I cut through the backstreets watching my mirror closely, then headed northeast until I reached the Bury Road. The rush hour had eased by now and the midmorning traffic was yet to get under way, so I made good time and reached the big roundabout above the M63 at 9.12 with no one following.

I spotted the Jaguar on the opposite side, just half a mile down the road. Peterson was waiting at the traffic lights, looking distinctly stressed. Elaine was sitting next to him. I flashed my headlights and waved, but if they saw me they made no sign of it. When the lights changed, I watched helplessly as they drove off, heading back towards the motorway that I'd just crossed.

Swearing loudly, I stuck my arm out of the window and wrenched the wheel. A white van in the outside lane slammed its brakes full on and slewed to a halt just inches from my bumper. I ignored the angry swearing face at the wheel and swung out across it to a cacophony of hooting, cutting straight into the line of oncoming traffic, reversing, then swinging the wheel and accelerating after the Jaguar.

By the next set of traffic lights they were six cars in front. They just made the amber light, leaving the car behind them waiting at red. I hit the steering wheel and cursed. I needed to get to them before they hit the motorway. If Keane was going to get them, it would have to be there.

Jesus, hurry up!

I tapped impatiently on the wheel; then, just before the lights changed to green, I swung out into the middle of the road and put my foot down, leaning on my horn as I drove through the all-too-narrow gap between the oncoming traffic. Cars and vans swerved away into the kerb. Headlights flashed. Horns blared.

Even so, I didn't catch them before the motorway.

I took the westbound sliproad and gunned Lin's tired old car as hard as I could. The engine howled in protest as we hit the higher sixties and, by the mid-seventies, the whole car was shaking as if it was about to fall apart.

I gritted my teeth as the vibrations jolted my ribs, and floored the pedal. If I could catch them, then maybe I could still stop them in time. Maybe they'd let me explain. Maybe Peterson would listen to me, even if Elaine wouldn't. However arrogant the man was, he must have some idea what was going on. He certainly looked stressed, back there at the lights. He certainly looked like a man on the run.

I spotted the Jaguar a mile up the road, cruising easily at around seventy, maybe three hundred yards ahead. By the time it passed the split with the M61, I was within a hundred yards and gaining. I overtook the two cars behind them at the junction with the M62 and flashed my lights repeatedly.

I saw Peterson look in his mirror but, far from slowing, the Jaguar speeded up, moved out to overtake a van, then pulled back into the middle lane. I followed, past the white Transit, and drew alongside in the outside lane, waving at them to pull over. Peterson looked back sniffily and waved me away. I shook my head and pointed to the hard shoulder, urgently, desperately, begging him to stop.

I heard the juggernaut before I saw it. A loud thundering beast devouring the road. When I glanced in my mirror, it was nearly on me. A massive articulated wagon, fully laden, sweeping up behind the little Escort at over eighty miles an hour, as we mounted the big flyover straddling the Ship Canal. I dropped down a gear and floored the accelerator. But I was too late. The juggernaut hit the bumper with an explosive thump and the car shot forward, engine roaring, slewing and swerving across the road.

The lorry accelerated and rammed me again. I ignored the pain in my ribs and gripped the wheel, swinging the car left, skidding and wobbling across the road in front of the Jaguar, certain that the lorry would follow.

But the driver wasn't interested in me. When I looked back a second time, both the Jaguar and the lorry were climbing the flyover in deadly tandem. Elaine was waving her hands hysterically and screaming. Peterson was glancing up at the lorry, then back at the road, pumping his horn, swerving erratically back and forth.

He braked and the car fell back. But so too did the juggernaut, its rear end swinging out, slamming the saloon against the safety rails of the flyover, like a scorpion stinging its prey. Peterson accelerated wildly again. But the lorry was ready for the kill. I saw the driver swing the wheel, squeezing the car towards the edge. The juggernaut shuddered as it sliced into the Jaguar, dragging it screaming and crashing along the rails. Torn metal flew in all directions. The windscreen shattered into tiny white crystals, spattered first with pink and then red.

In less than the blink of an eye, Peterson's once-proud possession rose up onto its back wheels, performed a graceful half-turn, and tumbled through the railings, headlong into space.

Forty-eight

As the car fell away towards the canal, the killer in the juggernaut took off, screaming down the hill behind me, flashing his lights and leaning on his horn. I stood on the accelerator, desperately trying to coax something extra from the old heap of a car. In desperation, I swung the Escort onto the hard shoulder, hurtling along just inches from the crash barrier, still believing that I must be the next victim.

But the lorry shot past me, its back end careering across the road, cutting off to the left, flying down the sliproad as if every demon in Hell were on its tail.

I slammed all on and swerved to a stop, beads of cold sweat standing on my brow. Behind me, the screech of brakes and the smash of metal on metal rent the air. Small pieces of debris cascaded down the carriageway. On the brow, three cars lay slewed across the road and palls of black smoke spiralled up into the sky. At the edge of the flyover, jagged shards of metal pointed out into space. And, a hundred feet below them, the cold grey waters of the canal reached out for the wrecked car. It floated for a moment, glinting in the sunshine and then sank quickly into the depths.

I gritted my teeth, rammed the gear stick into first and gunned the old car down the sliproad. With Peterson gone, I had only one option left. If I could catch the lorry, get some photos of the driver, then maybe I could still prove Keane's guilt.

I stood up as I drove, so that I could scan the open land down to my left. The monster was there, in the near distance, passing in front of the green domes of the Trafford Centre, just a few hundred yards away, signalling left and driving now for all the world like just any other lorry driver on any other delivery run.

I cut out across a box van at the roundabout and swung recklessly round the corner onto the dual carriageway, pushing the old car mercilessly, heading for some traffic lights, checking all around me. I caught sight of the lorry's tail end to my left, passing down a new road that ran off into acres of undeveloped industrial land.

I jumped the red light and lurched around the corner, down the clean black tarmac to a small roundabout standing in the middle of nowhere. The lorry had turned to the right, so I followed, preparing to accelerate hard as I turned off. But I pumped the brake instead as the tarmac ran out and the smooth road gave way to an empty, weed-infested track. No lorry. Just a cloud of dust hanging in the air ahead.

I pulled onto the verge and got out, leaving the car unlocked, listening carefully for the sound of the juggernaut's engine. I thought I heard the hiss of air breaks somewhere up ahead, to the left. Otherwise, the only sound was the chattering of sparrows in the nearby hawthorn and the distant wail of the sirens somewhere up on the motorway.

The track seemed to run out a short distance ahead, disappearing into scrubland and trees. To my left, a bindweed-covered fence ran for fifteen or twenty yards, terminating in an open gateway, flanked by a pair of rusting, decrepit metal gates.

I set off and jogged along the boundary, ignoring the pain that was stabbing into my ribs and the stiffness in my back, letting the adrenalin wash over me, focusing my mind on what I had to do.

When I reached the gates, I stopped, wincing with pain, trying to breathe quietly while I took a recce. The yard in front of me looked like the remains of an old transit or warehousing depot: a vast cobbled area, now littered with piles of bricks and earth, and mountains of disintegrating wooden crates. And, in an open space just ahead, no more than ten paces away, with its tail to me, stood the killer lorry.

I sneaked through the gates into the cover of a pile of old crates, listening for any sound, any movement from the yard. Then, catching the faint murmur of male voices on the breeze, I scrambled across to the line of pallets on the lorry's left-hand side and worked my way behind them, pushing through the thistles and chest-high nettles by the fence until I was level with the front of the lorry, then sliding through a gap to take a closer look.

This side of the juggernaut was originally a shiny brown. The tarpaulin and the cab door proudly bore the gold and green livery of a major haulage business, but the sides of the vehicle were stained with blue and cut with deep shiny scars. I took my camera out and recorded the damage, listening to the voices all the while. There were two men, talking quietly, on the other side of the cab.

When I crouched down and peered under the chassis to the other side, I could see by their feet and legs that one of the men was in a suit, the other in overalls. Just beyond them were the wheels of a shiny black saloon. I smiled grimly to myself. Now I had exactly what I wanted. Keane and his sidekick with the lorry, only minutes after the killing. I could catch the time, the location and the evidence on the film. Whether Keane was found guilty of Charlie's murder no longer mattered. I would have more than enough to send Keane down for the murder of Barrie Peterson and Elaine Wilson.

I slid around the side of the cab until I could see the two men properly. Keane was on the left with his back to the cab and his arm around the shoulders of Bonehead, who had thumped me outside Three Seas. They were walking away, towards the BMW, obviously congratulating themselves on a job well done.

I took three shots of them walking away but, really, I needed to make them turn round for a full-on picture. There was only one way. I picked up a piece of wood and threw it in a slow arc over to the cab. It hit the ground on the other side with a dull thud and the two men turned as one, looking slightly away from me, but revealing their faces for my camera.

Click.

'What was that?' Keane's voice was sharp, edgy.

Click

Bonehead shrugged. He was still high on his dirty adrenalin. 'Uh, just a rat. A bird, mebbe.'

Click.

'It's OK, I tell ya, boss, no bastard saw me. It went like a fuckin' dream.'

Keane stared in the direction of the noise and then over at the cab, looking less certain. I dropped back and watched his feet from under the wheels. He took a step forward but then stopped and turned back again.

'C'mon boss, it's nuthin' let's just get the fuck outta here.'

He hesitated for just a moment, then turned back towards the waiting car.

I was just about to backtrack as well when my damn phone rang and the tune of 'Ride of the Valkyries' sang out loudly through the autumn sunshine.

I cancelled the call at once, cursing my own stupidity – but it was too late. Keane was glaring in my direction and screaming loudly. 'I told you; I fucking told you!' Then he was running towards me, pulling a mean-looking handgun out of his jacket.

Jesus, Cameron!

I took a deep breath and slid back among the pallets, gulping air, holding my ribs, skidding and stumbling over the debris and weeds as I pushed my way back along the fence. Keane followed noisily about twenty feet behind, shouting as he barged through the undergrowth, knocking the stacks of pallets aside.

I felt a rush of air near my head and heard the report a split second later. Splinters flew in all directions as wood from a pallet disintegrated near my left shoulder, showering me and filling the air with the scent of dusty old wood. I bent lower, holding my ribs and almost crawling, under the cover of the nettles and thistles. Another shot whined over my head as I reached halfway; a third smashed into a concrete fence post ahead of me, spraying dust and sparks all around.

Up ahead, pallets were tumbling over into the path, shutting off my only means of escape. I squeezed myself into a gap and stopped for a moment, shaking with fear, wondering how the fuck I could get away now. Trying to think above the noise of crashing wood on one side and the whine of bullets on the other.

When I edged forward and peered out into the yard, I could see Bonehead on my right – only yards away – walking slowly along the row, toppling each pile in turn.

I smiled grimly to myself and backed off a little, crouching low in the cover between the two piles of pallets and angling myself so that I could grasp the corner of the bottom pallet nearest to him with both hands.

The noise got louder as he worked his way along. The shouting behind me got closer as Keane pushed towards me from the other direction, screaming threats and firing into the scrub. But fate was on my side. Keane wasn't dressed for thistles and nettles. And Bonehead was almost hysterical, screaming with rage as he pushed his way mindlessly along the line, upending one pile of pallets after another.

I waited breathlessly as they both drew close. Hoping and praying. Breathing as deeply as I was able and preparing myself for the surge of pain that I knew would come when I lifted up the bottom pallet. When the last but one pile went crashing down, I started to lift. Bracing my legs and gritting my teeth as I pulled the dirty pile upwards off the ground, lifting the whole stack with a strength I never knew I had. Pain screamed through me as my body took the strain. Tears filled my eyes so that I could hardly see. My head began to spin. But the pile of old pallets rose higher, gathering momentum and tippled upwards, upwards and over.

Bonehead fell backwards, floundering under the falling wood. I took off, running as I've never run before, pumping my arms and pushing my legs, forcing away the pain as I flung myself across the yard. I felt light-headed by the time I reached the gates. By now I was stumbling...

breathless... and spent as I... hit the track. Too weak... to keep... moving...

When I stopped to draw breath, I glanced back. Bonehead was on his feet again, lurching across the yard after me. I took deeper breaths and ignored the pain, forcing myself on up the road, staggering onto the verge as he closed in. He yelled for me to stop. I lunged for the car door and hauled myself into the seat. He slammed into the car as I pulled the door shut.

I pushed the lock down as his face appeared in the side window: big and red and unshaven. He screamed at me to get out. I turned the key in the ignition, praying that Lin's car would hold out for just a little longer. The engine spluttered and died. The thug yelled an obscenity and put his fist through the glass, grabbing for me as crystals of glass sprayed everywhere. I ducked away and turned the key again. The engine coughed uncertainly, juddered a little, coughed again. The hand grabbed my jacket and yanked me towards the open window.

The engine burst into life. I rammed my foot down on the pedal and spun the wheel, taking off across the verge. The hand fell back, still grasping my jacket, pulling me backwards against the door. The wheels skidded on the wet ground, kicking turf and mud into the air. The man hung on, grabbing me harder, yanking me backwards against the door. I pumped the pedal. The wheels bit into the earth. The car catapulted forward, out onto the dry hard track.

My head hit the door frame and the hand fell away. I tore off down the track towards a dead end. I could see Bonehead in the mirror, still standing behind me, his arm dripping blood. Keane was up in front, walking out of the gates, lifting both hands, aiming the revolver straight at my head.

I swung the wheel and pulled hard on the handbrake, spinning the car round in a cloud of dust and grit, then floored the accelerator, and ducked. The rear window shattered and three holes appeared in the windscreen where my head would have been. Dust filled the car. Splinters of glass cascaded over my head. And my heart almost gave out.

Forty-nine

I floored the accelerator pedal again and ducked below the dashboard, flying blindly up the track. Bullets thumped and whistled around me. A hole appeared in the front passenger seat and a bullet punctured the dashboard. Bits of foam rubber flew all around me. More glass splintered from the windscreen as another slug whined through. The car thumped into the verge and I pulled it away again, bumping and pitching blindly over the rough ground.

I took a chance and lifted my head up. Just in time. The roundabout was nearly on me. I hit the brake and swung the car hard left, the back wheels slewing across the tarmac, bouncing off the hard kerb of the roundabout. Then I accelerated, wheels squealing, and took off up the road, swerving left through a red light at the main road, screaming out in front of a van and off into the traffic.

I kept my foot down, pushing and cajoling the old Escort along the carriageway, overtaking wildly and hoping for once that the traffic cops would pull me over. Naturally, they didn't. When I reached the big roundabout at Trafford Park, there was no sign of anyone following so I slowed down and turned off into a quiet side road.

I leaned back in my seat and closed my eyes. My ears were ringing and my mouth was dry with dust and fear. I rummaged in the glove compartment and threw a double dose of painkillers into my mouth, swilling the capsules down with the last of the flat Coke. Then I cleaned the cold sweat and dust from my face, and combed the crystals of broken glass out of my hair.

I sat quietly for a while, letting my racing heart slow. I was relieved – of course I was. But I was baffled as well. I'd seen everything. I even had photos. Yet Keane had made no real attempt to follow me.

I shrugged. It didn't matter one way or the other. Together with Lin's company information, I had more than enough to wrap everything up. I just had to report to Mr Lee first, as I'd promised, then I could see Dyson. Maybe the old man would come with me. Sure as hell, I didn't fancy seeing her on my own.

When I took out my phone to ring him, I remembered the call in the transit yard and wondered who the hell had phoned me at such an inopportune time. I guess I expected a message from Lin, telling me she was safe. But it was a number I didn't recognise. A land line. And there was a message on my voicemail.

The voice was deep and throaty. Happy. Familiar. And hearing it at just that moment melted my insides to butter.

'Hi, Cam, it's Beano. Just to say… I'm out! Yeah, I'm home, babe, and I'm so fucking grateful to you! Don't know how you did it, sweetheart, but thanks a million, you're a star! Anyhow, gimme a ring, will you? I want to buy you a million glasses of that lousy cough medicine you drink. Ring real soon, eh?'

I put the phone away and looked around me at the half-dozen cars parked in the quiet residential street, still not quite believing that I was safe. Jesus, I was pleased that Mazza had dropped the charges against Beano, but I couldn't imagine why. Whatever else may have happened, my plan with Cuzak had been a complete failure.

I leaned back in the seat and cradled my aching ribs, wondering again why Cuzak had spared my life. Back in the borderlands of my brain, something was bothering me – but every time I grasped out, it faded away.

I tried to call up the vivid dream again. The detail was fading, but

I could still see Charlie's face as he turned and looked past me towards Cuzak. And I could still hear Cuzak's words – the words he'd used when Teach was laying into me: 'Not on face! Not on face!' Looking back – in both the dream and the reality – Cuzak had sounded almost panicky, as if he was scared of someone, as if maybe he didn't want my injuries to show.

Somewhere deep in my subconscious, there was an answer – I knew there was – and it was tantalisingly close. I hit the wheel angrily and slumped back in the seat, running through the same script again and again.

Charlie Wilson, Cuzak and me. Why in God's name should I dream that Charlie and Cuzak were connected? They never even knew each other. Yet a small part of my brain kept insisting.

Vinko Cuzak, Mazza Taylor, Beano.

Charlie Wilson, Elaine Wilson, Barrie Peterson, John Keane.

There was a connection somewhere. A common denominator. Something blindingly obvious that pulled everything together. This wasn't just about Keane. This wasn't just about Beano.

I drove back onto the main road with the cold wind whistling through the car. Every few seconds, a few more crystals of glass would dislodge from the edges of the windscreen, stinging as they peppered my face. I blinked hard and zipped up my leather jacket, pulled up the collar against the cold and cursed with frustration. I wanted, more than anything, to end all this. But I didn't want to go to Dyson with less than a complete story. I couldn't face her sarcasm if I screwed up again. And, whatever was gnawing at my brain, I knew that it was important. Like the very last piece of the jigsaw. The part that made the picture whole.

I'd go to Mr Lee's first. Lin would be there with him by now. If I talked it over with them, everything might become clearer.

The wind cut into my eyes as I drove, making my eyes water. I grabbed an old tissue from my pocket and wiped them dry, thinking about Peterson and his debts, about Elaine and her greed. About

Charlie, the good guy who just wanted to be happy – someone who had found innocent solace in his cross-dressing. I thought about the fussy Aunt Emily and Pritchard, her pompous, cowardly alter-ego. At least four people had died this week because of Keane – maybe others on the motorway. And why? Was it just about Chow City and Keane – or was there something else? Something that I was still missing?

When I stopped at some traffic lights, I brushed a few more crystals of glass off my hair, and thought about Lin. I wondered what she'd say about her poor old car, the smashed windows, the bullet holes, the dents. I hoped it didn't matter. She'd be leaving for Singapore in a few weeks anyway. I closed my eyes, suddenly realising how much I wanted her to stay now. Jesus, I was going to miss her so much. She'd turned out to be a good friend – especially last night by the car park.

I rubbed my aching ribs again and his voice came echoing back at me. *'Not on face! Not on face!'*

How did Cuzak find out about the sting? And why hadn't he killed me when he realised that I'd set him up? I sighed and shook my head. It didn't make any sense. Even Mr Lee had said the man was a cold-blooded killer.

Yeah, hadn't he just?

I hit the brake and pulled into the kerb. A box van swerved round me blowing its horn at the sudden manoeuvre. All at once my heart was thumping and my belly was jumping through hoops.

The answer was so obvious, so extreme, so fucking unlikely, that it had never even occurred to me.

I turned the engine off and screwed up my eyes, trying to think it through. There could be only one reason why Cuzak knew about the sting. Only one reason why he wouldn't want me marked. Only one reason why he would have let me go. And only one reason why he'd tell Mazza to pull the evidence against Beano.

I pulled out my phone and rang the Golden Snapper. Mr Lee wasn't there – and neither was Lin. I rang Lin's flat, in case they still hadn't left. Nothing. I tried Lin's mobile. It transferred me straight to her voicemail. I left a short message asking her to ring me, trying not to sound too desperate. Trying hard not to do a Becky.

But I *was* panicking. I closed my eyes and tried to think logically. Maybe they were still driving back. Maybe Grandpa had just taken Lin somewhere safe. Yeah, that would be it. I tried the old man's mobile, and breathed a sigh of relief when he answered.

'Mr Lee, it's Cameron. Where are you?' I asked with more than a hint of urgency in my voice.

He replied in his usual measured way. 'Good morning, Cameron. I'm on my way to an appointment – I thought you were going to come and see me this morning.'

'I... was, I am...' I stuttered. 'Where's Lin? She *is* there with you, isn't she?'

He sounded confused. 'Why, no. I haven't heard from her since last night.'

Sweet Jesus, where was she?

I ran my fingers through my hair and pushed back the sudden nausea in my guts. What the hell was happening? Why the fuck hadn't she rung him as I'd told her to?

I shook my head and tried to concentrate again. 'You haven't heard from Lin this morning?'

He hesitated, suddenly cautious. 'No, not a word. Should I have?'

'Um... no... yes.' Jesus, I didn't want to worry him just yet. 'It's just that she said she'd ring you, that's all.'

The old man picked up on my anxiety and his voice turned suddenly darker. 'What is it, Cameron? What's wrong?'

Nothing, not as far as I know.' A half-lie. 'I just expected her to be with you, that's all.'

He hesitated a little, clearly concerned. 'Well, ring me back in half an hour and let's arrange that meeting. And Cameron, let me know when you've contacted Lin, will you? I want to know that everything is all right with her.'

I put the phone away in dismay and started the car. The blood was beating in my ears and my chest ached as if I could be having a seizure. *Lin had never got through to him this morning. She wasn't answering the phone.*

Jesus, no. I didn't even want to think about it.

When I got to the flat, I left the car on the pavement by the shops and ran to the outside door with my heart beating wildly. It opened with just a push and my stomach lurched as I walked up the stairs. At the top, the door to her flat was hanging on one hinge, a jagged hole in the top panel.

Inside, the lounge was a complete mess. Furniture was overturned. Broken crockery and sheets of paper were strewn everywhere. The computer was smashed to pieces and the company records that Lin had traced for me were gone.

I cleared a space on the settee, feeling lost and desperate.

They'd got her. One of Keane's men must have taken her soon after I left.

Now I understood why the guy in the blue car had let me get away so easily.

Now I understood why Keane had let me get away just now.

Fifty

By the time my phone rang, I was ready for him.

Keane sounded like a cheap cardsharp, intoxicated with his own luck, jubilant over his winning hand and the power it held for him.

'Ah, the little girlie detective,' he taunted.

But, if the game we were playing was poker, then I had a few good cards as well. What was more, I knew that – used well – they were even better than his.

'Where is she, Keane?' I demanded. 'What the fuck have done with her?'

He sniggered lightly at my discomfort. 'She's safe enough for now, McGill. Whether she stays that way is up to you.'

'OK, go on.' It hardly took a genius to work out what was coming.

'A simple deal, girlie. You profess to know all about *insurance*. Well, you are her... mm, shall we say, life policy?' He sniggered again at his own joke. 'You come and join me now – and your little girlfriend can walk free.'

'You're lying. You'll kill us both.'

'Oh, please,' he objected, greasily, sickeningly indignant, 'you've got me wrong. I don't want to kill *either* of you. I just want to negotiate. I can give you a good deal. Enough money to salve your conscience and allow me to get on with my business.'

Bullshit.

'How do I know I can trust you?'

'You'll have to take my word for it.' He grunted cynically and his voice turned to ice. 'You know very well that, if you don't co-operate, I'll kill you both anyway.'

I hesitated, thinking it through again, checking out what I needed to do.

But Keane was no pushover. 'Don't kid yourself, sweetheart: you make one wrong move, and we kill your girlfriend without hesitation – then we kill you. Is that quite clear?'

'Yeah, I guess.'

'OK. Good girl. Take a look outside.'

I walked to the window and pulled back the curtain. Across the street, Joe Palliachelli – the barman from Chow City – was watching me from the front of an old VW Golf.

'He's waiting for you, McGill. You don't even have to drive. Joe will be delighted to chauffeur you all the way here.

'Where are you?'

'Uh, please don't patronise me. You'll find out when you get here.'

I paused, playing for time. 'Just let me think for a moment.'

I had to do it, I had no choice. But I wanted to make sure that the card up my sleeve really was the trump. I went over the events of the last twenty-four hours again. I checked the facts; I put all the pieces together again. They still fitted. They still fitted perfectly.

'You could be lying. Let me talk to her.'

He thought about it for a moment and then passed the phone over. Lin screamed at me to stay away, just as I expected she would. I opened my mouth to try to reassure her, to tell her that it would be all right, but Keane took the phone back before I got a chance.

'So, are we going to kill her now – or what?' he demanded.

I sighed heavily and let my voice falter, as if I were scared out of my wits. This wasn't difficult. 'Yeah, OK... you win... but give me a minute, will you, Keane? I... I er... need the toilet... bad.'

Now he was angry. 'Don't you try to fuck around with me, girlie. You leave straightaway or your friend gets it.'

'Look Keane, I'm not kidding. I'm scared. I *need* to go!' I insisted.

'You think Joe wants his car to stink of shit for evermore?'

He hesitated a moment. I prayed that even a thug like him would have his sensibilities.

'Yeah, OK.' he agreed, reluctantly. 'But make it quick. I'm holding a gun to your little girlfriend's head. If you're not out in five, Joe'll be up there after you – and the girl's brains will be decorating the wall, OK?'

'Yeah, OK. Keep your hair on, will you? I just need a shit, that's all.'

He grunted contemptuously. 'So you said. But while you're doing it, just remember: you do a runner, or we see the merest sign of the law, and the girlie dies. OK?'

I ended the call and, without waiting, rang Mr Lee.

He was still in his car, somewhere in the city, on the way back to Chinatown. I had neither the time nor the inclination for niceties, so I gave it to him straight, without frills or preamble. I told him who'd killed Charlie and why. I told him that he'd also killed three others – and that he was now holding Lin. I left him in no doubt that he would kill her too, just as soon as he got hold of me.

I heard the sharp, shocked intake of breath but I carried on, indifferent now to his feelings.

'There's a man outside, waiting to take me to her. Keane says he'll do a deal and let us both go.'

Mr Lee's voice trembled as he spoke. 'He's lying, Cameron, he's lying. He'll kill both of you. You know too much.'

I paused a second for maximum effect. 'I know more than you think, Mr Lee,' I said, loading the words with meaning.

There was a sudden, awkward silence.

'Cameron, I...' The old man's voice faltered. 'I don't know...'

'Don't deny it, Mr Lee, there isn't time! You know exactly what I mean. It's not important. All that matters is that we stop them killing Lin.'

There was a moment's silence. When he spoke again, his voice was stronger and there was an edge of resolution. 'You're right, young lady. You're absolutely right. Are you prepared to go with this man?'

I swallowed hard. 'I don't think I have much choice. But I'm very scared, and so is Lin. We can't get through this by ourselves. You've got to get some help.'

'You can count on it, Cameron.' His voice was hard now, icy with anger. At last he sounded like the man I knew he had to be. 'Where are they holding her? Tell me now and I'll see to it.'

'I don't know – they won't say. But listen: I'm going to hide my phone and leave it turned on when I get in the car. I'll talk as we drive. I'll try to give you landmarks, street names – anything that may help. But please, don't reply or I'm dead.'

'Thank you Cameron. I'm exceedingly grateful. You can rely on me.' He said it with real humility and I was sure he meant it.

Without ending the call, I bent down and stuck the phone in my left sock so that just the flap with the microphone poked out of the top, then I walked out of the flat and down the stairs.

Across the road, Palliachelli was leaning against the Golf, smiling nastily in my direction, like some weird caricature of himself. 'You want some peanuts?' he asked, smirking. I gave him a stupid smile and the bonhomie slipped off his face like so much slime. 'Get in, *dyke*. Front seat. Where I can see you.'

I strapped myself in, trying to keep my cool, praying that the phone connection would hold as we drove through the city, wondering if I could pull it off. Knowing that it meant certain death for both of us if I didn't.

Palliachelli rammed the car into gear and took off. I breathed as evenly as I could, willing myself to keep calm, trying to keep my hands steady. As he crossed the motorway I lifted my left foot onto my right knee and held my ankle, hiding the phone with my hand, trying to act really cool.

'Gimme a clue, Joe,' I said. 'I feel better if I know where I'm being taken.'

He turned to me and sneered. 'You'll find out.'

'Yeah,' I said, enunciating clearly but trying not to be too obvious. 'Well we've just gone *over the motorway...* and *turned left...* so I guess that means *we're heading towards the city centre*, so that's a clue, isn't it?'

He turned and eyed me curiously.

'Just my little game, Joe,' I grinned pleasantly at him. 'I'm a detective – I like mysteries; I like solving them. Why don't you indulge me a little, eh?'

He threw me a withering look and drove on silently, heading towards the big gyratory system at the bottom of the M602. When he left on the Salford road, I made a big deal of it.

'See Joe, you took the *second exit* – now, that tells me that *we're heading to the west or north of the city*.'

He ignored me and I fingered the phone. Jesus, I hoped Mr Lee was getting this.

We turned right at the next roundabout and down Chapel Street, past the late Horace Pritchard's office. I didn't miss the chance to mention it as we passed. And this time Palliachelli responded with a smile so unpleasant that his yellow teeth positively shone.

'You killed him, didn't you? It wasn't suicide, was it?'

He smiled again, but never said a word.

A few minutes later, he turned left and drove round the back of Victoria Station. As we drove under the railway I closed my eyes and prayed that the signal would hold. When we reached the lights near the Brewery, he turned right.

'You like *Boddington's* beer, Joe?' I asked.

He grunted, 'It's OK.'

'Yeah, me too, always makes me thirsty *when I pass their brewery*. Great beer *Boddington's*. I drink it whenever I can.'

When he stopped at the next set of lights I glanced out of the window at the traffic and the people coming and going from the city. My belly was melting by now and, soon, I really might need that toilet. For all I knew I could be talking to myself. When he set off again, over the big railway bridge north of Victoria, I clenched my belly and resumed my cocky air. 'So we're going somewhere just to the *north of the city centre*, then?'

The big guy gave me an ugly look and drove straight ahead at the next set of lights, down Swan Street.

'See that?' I chirped – 'the big *CIS building on the right.* Used to work for them. Big, big outfit.'

He squinted at me, then sneered irritably. 'Just shut the fuck up, will you?'

I smiled back sourly, but I kept quiet while he waited at the traffic lights. I was really pushing it. Anyone with a little more brain would have sussed me already. I didn't speak again until he'd worked his way round the one-way system, and was back on the main road again.

'Mmm, *Great Ancoats Street,* eh? Jesus, this brings back memories as well. I used to work all around here, y'know. *CIS Building, Great Ancoats Street.* I even went into this big black *Express building* once or twice.'

He blew out impatiently through his hairy nose.

'How much further?' I asked.

'Next on the left.' he replied with complete uninterest.

On the inside I was a wreck by now. If Mr Lee was still connected, then we had a chance. If he wasn't, then, without a shade of doubt, it was the end. I pushed the thought away and continued the commentary. *'Next on the left,* eh? That soon!'

He looked at me as if he thought I'd lost it, then signalled and pulled round into Thread Street. I read the sign on the wall and repeated the name out loud, several times, using some reference or other to the glorious days of King Cotton.

Palliachelli wasn't impressed. He parked the car by the kerb, then released the safety on his gun. When he rammed it in my face, something inside me curled up and died.

'Out!'

I stayed where I was and looked through the windscreen at the ugly concrete Lego-like building just across the road. 'You mean we're going in there – *that old boarded-up car park?*'

He wrinkled his nose and smiled lopsidedly, as if suddenly I were bringing some joy into his life. 'Yeah, that's the place, *dyke.*' He leaned across and bared his nicotine-stained teeth, speaking nice and slowly, grinning with anticipation. '*On the roof*. Nice and high. So you better stay away from the fucking edge.'

Sometimes I just love it when people speak their minds.

I just prayed that someone was listening.

Fifty-one

Palliachelli jabbed me in the back with one hand as we walked across the road towards the derelict car park. He held his gun out of sight in the other. Just in case I lost my nerve, he said, grinning as if that would make him very happy.

Even in its heyday, this multistorey car park – like so many others – could never have been described as beautiful. Now the utilitarian 1960s building was an offence to the eyes as it crumbled into premature senility. Rust wept out of nearly every panel, staining the cracked, disintegrating concrete with rivers of brown. Small shrubs were already growing from the upper levels; multicoloured graffiti decorated the whole of the ground floor wall and empty tins and other rubbish lay strewn around its approaches.

The entrance/exit was closed off with large plywood boards, wrapped all around with razor wire. A big red sign was fixed in the middle: KEEP OUT – DANGEROUS BUILDING.

Yeah, right.

Palliachelli opened a small door at the side and pushed me through, clattering and stumbling, into a lobby at the foot of some stairs. I stopped and blinked in the near-darkness, holding my aching ribs, while he secured the door. It was the smell that assailed me first. Unpleasant and overwhelming – the sort of stink that burrows into every pore. A fetid cocktail of urine, excrement, vomit – and something else, equally unpleasant. Decay, maybe. Mould, something like that.

As my eyes adjusted, I saw that the debris around my feet was not just human waste. There was a sea of cut-up soft-drink cans, old needles and various items of wet, rotting clothing, mouldy food and plastic bottles. A shooting gallery, and a well-used one at that.

Palliachelli jabbed me hard in the back again and grunted. I stumbled forward, aluminium and plastic scrunching under my boots, then, as I reached out for the wall and steadied myself, I trod on something softer. Instantly the smell got worse, and I winced, thinking of all the diseases I could catch with just one simple fall.

Then I remembered that it might not matter anyway.

By the time we reached the first floor, the light improved, and he pushed me harder. My heart was beating three times to every step by the time we approached the second floor. I stopped, feigning exhaustion, leaning against the wall and catching my breath. Trying to give Mr Lee as much time as I could. Still praying that he knew where to find us.

But the barman was in a hurry, and he pressed the gun into the small of my back and pushed me roughly on the shoulder, barking at me to keep going.

I held my hand out and swallowed, my knees buckling. 'Just a minute... please... my shoelace...' I bent down and pulled the phone out of my sock, laying it down quietly in the dark. He grunted something obscene and smashed the back of my head with the flat of his hand, knocking me forward onto the hard steps. I scrambled to my feet again and pushed on, reflecting on just how much I'd like to kick the bastard head first down the stairs, onto all those needles.

He let me stop for a couple of seconds at the third floor, breathing heavily himself by now. But the respite didn't last long. Soon he was pushing me up the final flight to the roof of the building – and whatever fate awaited.

When I walked out of the stairs door, Keane was standing in the afternoon sunlight, halfway across the top level of the rubbish-strewn car park, legs akimbo, like some latter-day godfather. His smart black overcoat was unbuttoned and flapped gently in the breeze. He held a handgun, which he rested casually across one arm. To the left was the big guy from Lavender Taxis – the one who'd followed me earlier when I'd left Lin's flat. He leaned against the outside wall, flexing his muscles and hugging a small automatic to his chest as if it were some kind of a comfort blanket. Bonehead stood on the other side, still wearing his boiler suit and staring impassively towards me, a rifle pointing from his hip.

But no Lin.

Palliachelli kept shoving me every few paces so that I half-stumbled, half-walked towards them, past the entrance and exit ramps, and over into the wide open space where the welcoming committee was standing. Keane wrinkled his nose and stared hard as I approached. Bonehead bared shiny white teeth and Lavender pushed himself lazily off the wall and pointed his automatic my way.

I stopped a few feet away and eyeballed Keane, letting my anger show.

'Where is she?' I asked coldly.

He stared back and smiled, then turned and nodded. Bonehead jerked his head at Palliachelli and the two of them disappeared down the first ramp.

When I turned back, Keane was waving Lavender forward. The guy slung the automatic over his shoulder and ambled across, a sickly smile on his face.

'Get your fuckin' hands in the air, darlin,' he growled, chewing gum and eyeing me as if I were some piece of fresh meat. So the guy wasn't gay after all.

I did as he said, standing with my arms up and my legs apart so that he could frisk me all over. I held my breath while he ran his hands down my body and over my legs, but when he lingered on my crotch I lashed out with my boot, catching him on the shin.

He howled at the sudden pain and nearly swallowed the gum but, when he raised his hand to strike me, Keane barked at him to back off.

The guy glared at me for a moment, curling his lip. I stared back, burning with rage. No one did that to me, whatever the circumstances.

He walked back to his boss's side and made a show of fingering his gun and glaring resentfully in my direction. I ignored him and stuck my hands in my jerkin pocket, taking a casual look around. The roof was like the top floor of any car park, except that this one was even dirtier. It was surrounded by a four-foot-high, moss-encrusted concrete wall, decorated here and there with small saplings and weeds. The stairs were at one end and, in the middle behind us, there was a separate entrance and exit ramp.

Lin was being brought up the nearest one, a man holding each arm, part-lifting her, part-dragging her up the steep incline. Her hands were bound behind her, her mouth covered with grey tape, but she was kicking wildly and hanging back as much as she was able. When she saw me she stopped, and started pulling forward, trying to get to me. But the two men held her even harder and yanked her back.

I turned angrily on Keane. 'You've made your point,' I hissed. 'I'm here now. Let her go!'

He looked beyond me and nodded to his men. Bonehead ripped the tape off her mouth and Palliachelli shoved her roughly forward. She ran forward, stumbling and gasping, then stopped just a few feet away and took me in. Her beautiful dark eyes were red and stained with tears, her face white and drawn. She must have been certain that she was going to die but, incredibly, she walked the last few feet and smiled at me through her tears.

I put my arms around her and drew her into me.

'I'm sorry,' she sobbed. Pushing her head into mine. 'I'm sorry, Cam, I'm so sorry.'

'It's OK,' I whispered. 'It's going to be all right. Don't give up.'

She pulled away from me a little and frowned.

'Trust me,' I mouthed, stroking her face, trying to reassure her with my eyes, hoping all the time that I was right. She bit her lip and smiled weakly. She clearly wasn't convinced.

Hell, if I'm honest, neither was I.

'How very touching.' Keane walked across to us, a sick smile on his face. 'A pity to break up your little welcome, girls, but we must get on.'

Bonehead grabbed Lin from behind and pulled her away from me. Palliachelli twisted my arm behind my back, making me gasp in pain as he frogmarched me across the parking bays.

'What... about this... generous deal that you were... offering?' I yelled, breathlessly. 'You *said* you'd let us go!'

Keane walked across and breathed right into my face. His eyes were staring hard, but as always the focus was somewhere else. Somewhere in his own brain, somewhere in his own power-crazed ego.

'I was lying,' he said coldly. 'There is no deal. You know too much. I have to kill you both.'

What little colour there was in Lin's face drained away and her mouth fell open. I wanted to grab her, shake her. Tell her not to give up. The barman shoved me forward again and slammed me up against the outside wall, jabbing his gun into my neck and yanking my head forward so that I had no option but to look at the drop below. Bonehead dragged Lin across next to me and did the same with her.

Keane walked up behind and shoved his face between us, draping his arms around our shoulders, as if he were an old friend. 'Long way down, eh?' he remarked overpleasantly, his voice tinged with something like excitement.

Lin flinched and looked as if she was going to cry. I pushed Palliachelli back, just enough so that I could turn and look at Keane.

'You promised to let her go, remember? She doesn't know a thing. She can't harm you.'

He stared back impassively and pinched my nose. 'You think I'm naïve, uh? Come on, girlie! We saw the papers in her flat – she knows as much as you do. Besides, if I kill you, I *have* to kill her as well.' He shook his head in contempt. 'Hadn't you worked that one out?'

'Yeah,' I replied. 'I worked it out all right. That's why I made a contingency arrangement.'

He stopped and eyed me suspiciously for a moment, and looked across sharply at Palliachelli. The barman grunted and shook his head firmly. Keane's face relaxed into a smirk. 'Uh, very funny. You've got *a contingency arrangement.*' He looked round at all three men and grinned. 'You hear that boys, the little detective has made *a contingency arrangement.*'

Oh, how they all laughed.

I looked at Lin and tried to smile. She sniffed, the tiniest hope returning to her eyes. My stomach lurched again. Who was I kidding? If Mr Lee had heard my directions, help would have been there by now.

'I know things, Keane.' I looked him confidently in the eyes, telling myself that there was still a chance. 'For all your wheeling and dealing, I know things that you don't. Important things. Like how little time you and your men have left.'

He shook his head in derision. 'Oh, yeah, very good.'

I kept on staring at him. 'I'm not trying to scare you – just warn you, that's all. If you leave now and let us live, you might just escape with your lives.'

Palliachelli shook his head and laughed in disbelief. Lin blinked at me in confusion.

For a moment no one moved, then Keane's smile slipped quickly away. 'OK, that's enough. Get up on the wall, McGill!'

Suddenly I wanted to be sick. I looked at him open-mouthed. 'You're joking. You really think I'm going to get up there – just so you can push me off.'

He grabbed my hair, pulling my face so close that I could see every pore in his skin. 'You have a choice. Either you get up there nice and easy, or my boys throw you over.'

I blinked and drew breath, feeling more helpless, more despondent with every second that passed. I was running out of ideas fast. If help didn't arrive in the next two minutes, then we were sunk.

I nodded at Keane, as it were all over. 'Yeah, OK, you win. But before I go just tell me one thing.'

He let go of me and put his head on one side. 'What?' he asked, impatiently.

'What's this all about?'

He screwed up his face, as though I were asking a really difficult question.

'You've killed four people and you're about to kill two more,' I said. 'It can't just be because you wanted to buy another lousy restaurant for the money-laundering organisation. Jesus, Keane, you don't even own the business. What the fuck's in it for you?'

He raised his eyebrows. 'All right, little Miss Detective, since you're going to die anyway, I'll tell you. Let's just say we had a problem to solve. A very *old* problem.' He looked at each of his gang in turn. 'Some of us get tired of taking orders, of being held back, so me and my friends are taking over. And, if you know so much, McGill, you'll also know that the present "management" is too washed out to stop us. All the guys are doing it – that's what happens when the top dog gets old and toothless.'

He stepped closer and prodded me in the chest, staring resentfully into my face. 'Your interference has been a nuisance, girlie, but don't kid yourself. It's not going to change a thing.' He stared at me for a moment longer, then his eyes flared with anger, 'Now, stop wasting time – get up on the fucking wall!'

I looked all around me. To my right, Palliachelli was eyeing me eagerly. Lin was shaking, staring at me in desperation. By her side, Bonehead was looking at Keane, waiting for the order to grab me. Lavender stood just behind to his right, fingering his automatic.

I could make a run for it. A bullet might be quicker and at least it would look like murder, not suicide. On the other hand, if I got up on the wall, I could spin it out a little longer. I had to try, if only for Lin's sake.

'OK.' I put my hands in the air and swallowed hard, finding it harder than ever to hide my fear. 'I'm going to make this real easy for you, Keane. Just back off though – if I'm going to jump, I want to do it on my own.'

I looked at Lin and tried to smile. Tears were running down her cheeks. Keane sneered at me and waved his men back. Bonehead took hold of Lin and started to pull her away.

'Leave her!' I shouted. 'The same goes for her. If we do it, we both do it on our own.'

Keane nodded again and the thug released her, turning her round, stripping the tape off her wrists, then backing off. I waited until they were all a few feet away then I looked at Lin one last time, my voice catching in my throat. 'I'm sorry. I truly thought everything was going to work out.'

She stood there quite silent, her body rigid, her arms hanging by her side, her eyes frozen with distress.

Keane barked at me again and I backed off until I was level with the wall. They'd chosen well. Fifty feet below, the road and pavements were empty. There would be no last-minute entreaties from passers-by, no sudden cavalry charge by the cops. Mr Lee hadn't got my directions. I really was going to die.

My ribs screamed with pain as I pulled myself up onto the top and crouched for a moment. Then, slowly, deliberately, I stood up and spread my arms out wide, balancing precariously on the narrow coping.

I looked across at Lin and tried to smile some kind of sad apology, thinking that she didn't deserve to end up like this. Then I looked beyond her – at the four thugs all standing together in a nice neat row. Bonehead took a step forward, eager to see me go. Keane put a hand out and held him back.

'You have five seconds, McGill. Either jump or we push you.'

I looked back at him and nodded as he started to count.

Five. They were all looking my way. Bonehead was flexing his fists.

Four. Lavender was smiling nastily, chewing on his gum.

Three. Palliachelli was nodding in satisfaction.

Two. Keane was scowling at me with thunder in his eyes, waiting for the moment when I fell to my death.

One. But they should have been paying more attention. They should have been looking over by the ramp.

There was hardly any noise. A muffled thumping sound, that was all. And each of Keane's men shuddered very slightly, as if they'd all been stung simultaneously by a trio of troublesome wasps. Three sets of eyes opened wide in disbelief. Three jaws dropped in shared astonishment. And a deep, perfectly rounded hole appeared out of each forehead. The three of them leaned backwards in perfect time, falling away together in a graceful arc, like a well-rehearsed troupe performing a favourite routine.

As they hit the ground, three other men in black jerkins and balaclavas stood up and began walking the rest of the way up the ramp, smoke curling from the long silencers on their rifles. They aimed at Keane as they walked.

'Drop your gun!' one of them barked. 'Now!'

Keane looked back in astonishment and let the weapon fall to the ground.

Fifty-two

Two of the gunmen stopped a few feet away, their rifles trained on Keane's head. The third dropped his weapon to his side and walked towards Lin and me, signalling for me to get down from my precarious position. I swallowed hard and held out my hand. Lin took it and steadied me as I jumped back onto the right side of the wall.

She stared at me as I landed. White and shaking. Relief mixing with a new kind of alarm. I pulled her to me. 'It's OK, it's over. You're safe. I promise.'

She resisted, blinking in confusion, turning and staring open-mouthed around her. At the three dead bodies, each lying in a small pool of deep-red blood. At the assassins with their powerful automatics. At Keane, standing with his hands behind his head, shaking with the sure knowledge that his time had run out.

When the third gunman held out a hand, beckoning Lin to join him, she shrank back in alarm.

'Cameron... what...? Who are these men?' she gasped, clinging to my arm.

I hesitated, suddenly unsure of what to say. Everything had happened so fast. I wasn't prepared. All that I knew was that, for once, I mustn't tell her the truth.

I took hold of her shoulders and tried to calm her down. 'I... I can't explain, Lin. Not just yet anyway. They work for the launderers. They're employed by the man from Dominica. He must have found out what Keane was planning.'

The gunman took a step towards us and she shrank back, holding on tighter. I tried to ease her away, towards him. He stopped and looked at me, then waved her on, more urgently this time.

I knew that it was vital she leave the scene, so I turned and looked directly into her eyes. 'You've got to trust me, Lin. Go with him. Please. Go now. He won't hurt you, I promise.'

She looked up at me and swallowed. 'But... what about you?'

I squeezed her reassuringly and tried to smile. 'It's OK. I have to stay a while. They need to talk to me. Trust me – I'll follow very soon.'

I said it for all the world as if it were true, but the reality was that I didn't know what their intentions were. I knew for certain that, whatever happened, she'd be safe.

But me? I knew far too much now. I was no longer just a threat to Keane.

Lin nodded in resignation and let the gunman lead her away. She glanced back uncertainly with every step. Then, when she finally reached the stairs door, he shepherded her through. Quite suddenly, she was gone.

Keane glared across at me, breathing heavily now, a mixture of hate and anger, despair and disbelief etched across his face. I stared back at him coldly – at the arrogant, aggressive monster who was finally reduced to helpless captive.

But when Keane's eyes swung away from mine, I followed them.

Over in the middle of the floor, another figure was walking slowly up the steep ramp. A small, proud man, leaning on his walking stick at every step, but otherwise unaided. He stopped as he reached the top and glared across at Keane. Then he turned and studied me.

'Good afternoon, Mr Lee,' I said, meeting his eyes. 'I'm very relieved your men could make it.'

The old man said nothing in response, merely nodding in satisfaction, as he made his way slowly across the roof. Keane regarded me with disbelief.

'I warned you, Keane,' I chided. 'You shouldn't have dismissed this *little girlie's* warning quite so easily.'

Keane wrinkled his nose in distaste. Mr Lee stopped alongside the two gunmen. He looked across at me, then at the three bodies, nodding with grim satisfaction. Finally he lifted his eyes and stared at Keane with a cold unremitting gaze.

Keane blanched and took a small step back into Palliachelli's blood. One of the gunmen barked at him to stand still. He swallowed hard and opened his mouth to speak, but no sound came out.

The old man stepped forward another two paces, so that he was within a few feet of the man, to one side of the line of fire. His voice was harder now and his English no longer accentless. 'So, Mr Keane, what was it you were saying?' he snapped. 'Something about "too washed out"? Something to do with "old and toothless"? I ask you – does this look "old and toothless" to you?'

Keane blinked but said nothing.

Mr Lee walked right up to him and spat up into his face. 'Answer me!'

Keane shook his head wildly, scared out of his wits. 'No, no... no, you've got it wrong... I just said it to... I... really, I never...'

The old man held his eyes for a moment and then lifted his hand and struck him hard across the face. Keane recoiled and took a hand from his head. One of the gunmen barked at him again and he put it back. His eyes were everywhere and a dark stain was working its way down between his legs.

'Mr Keane, you disappoint me.' Mr Lee was quite calm now. 'I trusted you with my affairs. I trusted you with my money. You may never have met me, but you know my policy. You are aware that the slightest scandal or misdemeanour in one unit can destroy the whole enterprise. Yet, against my specific directions, you have indulged in blackmail and murder.

'Even that I could have forgiven. But when you plot against me, when you join with others to take over my organisation, then I cannot turn a blind eye.'

Keane backed off again, stumbling against Palliachelli's arm, floundering for a moment as he regained his balance, shaking his head, gasping. 'No... No, you've got it wrong... I would never...'

Mr Lee jabbed Keane hard in the chest, finally losing his composure and trembling with rage. 'And, on top of all this, you almost kill my own granddaughter.'

Keane's mouth fell open. 'Your... granddaughter?' He swallowed hard and shook his head. His voice rose an octave or two. 'I'd... I'd no idea... How could I possibly...?'

'Well, perhaps you should have taken a little more care.' Mr Lee wrinkled his nose in disgust, then walked back to his men.

He waited for a moment, clearly relishing Keane's dismay, then – very quietly – he issued the final order.

'Kill him.'

There was a muffled thump and the two automatics kicked upwards. Simultaneously, two small holes appeared in Keane's forehead. Fragments of bone, blood and brain sprayed out from the back of his head like the fizz from a ghastly ring-pull can. The already-dead man raised his eyes to heaven and staggered backwards – a marionette hanging in midair, arms outstretched, head lolling, eyes rolling.

Then he fell, crumpling into a heap in the spreading lake of blood and brain. A treasonous puppet whose strings had finally been cut.

Fifty-three

Mr Lee smiled grimly as he walked over to me. 'How did you know?'

I studied him calmly for a moment, wondering how I could have been so easily fooled by his veneer of respectability. Lin's *ever-loving grandfather* was no more than a ruthless killer. Someone who lived off the death and hardship of others.

'How did you know?' he asked again, more sharply this time.

'You made the mistake of trying to help me.'

He blanched, disconcerted at the unfriendly tone of my voice.

'You mean Cuzak, I suppose – and your friend Beano.'

I nodded. 'However unlikely it seemed, the only person who *could* have told Cuzak what I was doing was you. After you'd seen me talking to him that night in town, you rang Lin and asked her what was going on.' I stopped for a moment, finding it impossible to keep the contempt out of my voice. 'She thought you were concerned for my welfare. So, last night, when I told her what was happening, she rang you to let you know that it was all right – that I was working with the police.'

Mr Lee stood silently, unfazed by what I was saying.

'Once I realised that, it followed that Cuzak had to be one of your associates. Someone who you launder money for, maybe. When you warned him off, he came after me. He wanted to kill me, but you'd told him not to. You'd *told* him to leave me alone. So he just beat me up instead, taking care not to mark me anywhere where it might show.'

The old man nodded. The two gunmen stood and waited for their orders.

'But the biggest giveaway was Beano's release. The only person powerful enough to persuade Cuzak to change Mazza Taylor's story was you. Besides, other than the police, Lin and yourself, nobody else knew about my plan to get Beano out.'

Mr Lee raised his eyebrows at me. 'So, you should be grateful to me, Cameron. I've saved your friend from jail. I've also saved your life – twice. Cuzak would have killed you if I hadn't intervened, so would Keane.' He looked perplexed. 'So why are you treating me with such scorn?'

I stared at him with undisguised contempt. 'If you hadn't lied to me, I wouldn't have been in danger in the first place. And, more to the point, neither would Lin.'

He drew breath and swallowed hard. 'She is all right?'

I stared back at him, unimpressed by his concern. 'She thought she was going to die. She's just seen three men get killed. Now she's hiding on the stairs with a masked gunman. How all right do you expect her to be?'

Mr Lee gave me a penetrating look. Killer or not, he wasn't easy with my hostility. But, for now at any rate, he tried to ignore it. 'How come you connected me with Keane?'

I sighed. 'That was Lin.'

His face fell. 'She knows?' he asked, despair flooding his face, as if suddenly he might burst into tears at any moment. 'Lin knows?'

I stared back at him coldly. 'She knows all about your organisation, Mr Lee.' I waited, fixing him with my eyes, enjoying his obvious discomfort. I had the power to shatter his world if I wanted to. For all his money and power, I could still break his heart with just a few words. 'But she has no idea that you're involved in it.'

He breathed again, relieved beyond measure.

'Lin traced the ownership of Three Seas back to Dominica for me. Knowing what we did about the cash flow of Chow City, it was soon clear to both of us that it was a money-laundering operation. Once I'd realised about Cuzak, it was a short step to working out why you'd hired me.'

I paused for a moment, breathing heavily, spitting venom. 'You've used me. Just like Elaine Wilson and Peterson used me. Just like Keane used them. You didn't even know Charles Wilson, did you?'

He shook his head and sighed, clearly dismayed by my animosity. 'Cameron, I knew that something strange was going on and that it could concern my organisation. You're in business. I hired you to do a job. I paid you well. Does it really matter?'

I rounded on him angrily. 'Yes, it fucking does, actually! It matters a lot!'

He shook his head wearily. 'Believe me, I had no idea that you would take it so badly, or that it would become so dangerous for you.' He waved at the four bodies. 'I never believed for one moment that it would come to this. At my age, the loyalty of my people can be such a capricious quality. I simply didn't know who to trust. There are many who wait in the shadows ready to take over – and I suspected from the start that Keane might be one of them.'

I blew through my nose. 'Oh, so that's all right, then! I suppose it doesn't matter that you nearly got both me *and* your granddaughter thrown off the top of this building?'

He put his head on one side and studied me for a moment. His eyes hardened, his face lost any attempt at warmth and he stepped to within inches of my face.

'Maybe it doesn't matter whether you like it or not.' He spat the words into my face. 'If I am the ruthless gangster you obviously assume I am, then no doubt I should kill you as well.'

He stepped back again, holding me firmly with his penetrating eyes. 'Nobody would be any the wiser. The police will assume that it's just another war between rival gangs with you caught in the crossfire.'

I stared back, unblinking. 'You're right. But what about Lin? Are you going to kill her as well? She knows almost as much as I do – certainly enough to break up your empire. And, as long as she's unaware of your involvement, she's going to talk to the police and tell them what she knows.'

We stared belligerently at each other for what seemed like an age. It was classic catch-22. If he killed me, his granddaughter would know who and what he was. If he didn't kill me, then she would tell the police everything she knew.

I waited, realising that I was about to find out what his real values were.

Mr Lee shook his head and looked down, sighing audibly, then he turned to his two gunmen and waved them away. When he turned back to me, I saw the other old man again, the one I'd met in the restaurant, Lin's grandpa, the father who'd lost his daughter but found her again in Lin, the man I'd once liked and respected.

'I'm not going to harm you, Cameron.' He looked away momentarily in a show of genuine humility. 'Whatever the cost to me, you were prepared to die to save my granddaughter. I owe you my eternal gratitude and respect for that. How could I kill you? Without your intervention, Lin would already be dead.'

I wasn't so easily convinced. 'How can you know that I won't tell the police?'

The old man smiled weakly and looked at me with the whites of his eyes. 'If you decide to do so, then that is your prerogative. But consider this. Firstly, I just saved your life. You are in debt to me and – whether you approve of me or not you are an honourable woman. In the second place, it would break Lin's heart if she found out about me. And, thirdly, it would be futile. I have a cast-iron alibi. No one has seen me here, except you and my men. And who is going to believe that a frail old man is involved in a shooting like this?'

'I might tell Lin.'

Mr Lee shook his head sagely. 'You care for Lin like I do. You care enough to risk your life to protect her. Why should you want to hurt her now by revealing that the grandfather she loves and respects is no more than a ruthless gangster?'

I nodded. He was right. Whatever I thought about him and his dirty money, I'd no intention of giving him away to Lin.

'Yeah, all right,' I conceded. 'I won't say anything about you to your granddaughter or anyone else. But I can't stop Lin from talking to the police. They *are* going to find out about Three Seas and the rest of your empire.'

Mr Lee stepped forward and took hold of my hand. Reluctantly, I let him. His eyes were softer now and quite suddenly, as he stood there, the late-evening sun reflecting off his grey hair, he looked very weary.

'I'm an old man, Cameron, and I have very little time left. Probably less than you think. I am weary of the constant need to protect myself from unscrupulous men like Keane. When I was young... well, it was... thrilling, dangerous. Now...' He looked at me, his eyes red and strained. 'Now, I've had enough. This seems a suitable moment to retire. My empire will be brought neatly to a close by the authorities and none of the spoils will fall to those who seek to undermine me. I will not grieve, Cameron, I assure you.'

He looked across at the four bodies lying amid the blood, and grimaced. 'I do not enjoy killing. Sometimes it is necessary, but I have never got used to it.'

I let him put his arm around my shoulders and lead me away towards the stairs. Suddenly I felt sick.

With him. With all the killings. With myself.

'So what about you?' I asked. 'What will you do?'

He shook his head and smiled weakly. 'The Golden Snapper is a legitimate business and, after all these years, it is far more of a passion for me than the unpleasant politics of my organisation. It is clean and wholesome. When I die, it will pass to Lin. As for the rest, well, as I say, it is of no consequence.'

I nodded and turned to take one last look at the carnage. The two gunmen still hovered discreetly halfway down the ramp, waiting for him, watching over him.

Mr Lee embraced me briefly, then held me at arm's length. 'Now, you must go to Lin. Wait with her in the stairwell until we have gone, and then ring the police. I would be obliged if you would tell them – and my granddaughter too – that you don't know who it was that intervened. They will simply assume that it has been one of the regular turf wars that occur in any big city. You and Lin have enough information to prove that to them.'

We stood and looked at each other for a moment. It occurred to me that I should feel relief. But all I had was a sense of deep disappointment.

Mr Lee pressed my hand one last time. 'You've done well, Cameron. Better than I ever anticipated. But, in future, please take more care when you're in this city – I can't guarantee that I will be here to save your life a third time.'

I watched him go and thought back to the day I'd first walked into his restaurant. He'd seemed so urbane then. So gentle. Now I knew better. But for all his wealth and power, for all his past, the man still had his dignity. And, against all the odds, a certain weird integrity as well.

That, at least, was something.

Fifty-four

I watched the funeral service from the shelter of an old yew tree, about fifteen feet away from the ceremony. It didn't stop me from getting wet, but it did keep the cold northeasterly wind from my back. Martha had invited me to join her as an honoured guest at the graveside but, since I'd never even known the man, that didn't seem right. Besides, I felt more comfortable watching from a distance. I never did take to family groups.

This particular group was bigger than I expected. Aside from Martha, there were seven other women and five men standing around the grave, some with black umbrellas, others wearing hats, a few of them bare-headed. She'd made a big show of introducing me to them all – cousins, uncles, aunts and their spouses, from both sides of their parents' family. There was a scattering of family friends as well. Mostly older people who, I supposed, had seen Charlie grow up and were now mourning a death that was all out of sequence to the natural order.

Further back, among the headstones, other unofficial mourners were paying their last respects. Rita was there with the other waitress from Chow City. Dorry and Ernest Winterton looked on silently from the shadow of a large marble angel. Round the other side, well away from the preacher, three transvestites stood in a dignified line, pointing their umbrellas into the breeze, their faces pale even under the makeup. On either side of them stood other men of various ages in overcoats and rain jackets, two of them with other women. From time to time, one of the group would glance around the others with a sad smile. They all seemed to know each other.

I looked back towards the burial party, thinking about Charles Wilson again, wishing perhaps that I'd been a little more understanding. A little less critical of his cross-dressing. That made me think of Horace Pritchard as well. I could never have taken to the man, but he certainly didn't deserve to die. But then neither did Elaine Wilson or Barry Peterson. Four people, each less than perfect, maybe, but none of them actually bad – all dead because they got in the way of a money-making racket. I pulled my collar up against the wet and shuddered. I felt sick to the core.

Lin stood at the fringes under her umbrella. She was wearing a dark-navy fitted coat with a deep magenta scarf around her neck. Her head was bare save for a black velvet bow, which held her long hair back in a simple ponytail. She still looked numb. She still looked as if she hadn't quite recovered from the ordeal.

Mr Lee stood next to her dressed in a neat black gabardine and trilby, his collar turned up against the weather. It was only five days since the shooting, but somehow he appeared smaller and much older now – as if his physical condition had somehow been diminished when his power was stripped away.

Yeah. Well, the last five days had been difficult for all of us.

After Mr Lee had left me on the car park roof, I'd taken the stairs down to the third level. Lin was sitting glumly on the bottom step, by the lobby. The gunman was still standing awkwardly by her side, as if he didn't quite know what he should be doing. She turned her head and looked up at me as I came down, but then turned away again without uttering a word. The man nodded at me when I reached her, then disappeared down the stairs.

When I sat down next to her, I guess I expected – or at least hoped – that she'd lean into me for comfort and reassurance. It wasn't that I wanted to play the hero, or act like the big protector. To be honest, I needed the affection myself. I'd spent the last few hours coping with the unendurable. Right then I was falling apart. I needed the warmth of her body, the closeness of her skin. I wanted her to hold me and tell me that everything was fine.

I put my arm round her shoulder and asked her if she was all right. A stupid question in the circumstances, but it was all I could manage. She nodded her head slightly. A stupid answer as well. Maybe neither of us would ever be 'all right' again.

When I leaned into her and reached for her hand, she didn't react. She just sat there, her eyes glazed, her body rigid. I stroked her hair and rubbed her back. I kissed her cheek and held her, but none of it seemed to make any difference. She was numb, insensible and in a world of her own.

After a few minutes I led her down the stairs to the next level and rummaged around in the dark until I found my discarded phone. I dialled 999 rather than Dyson's number and led Lin out of the stairwell and down the ramps to the ground floor, avoiding most of the unpleasant detritus on the lower stairs.

The first siren came howling up Great Ancoats Street as we reached ground level. By the time we'd picked our way through the debris and out into the bright light of day, there were three squad cars outside and six uniformed cops, all of them in body armour, cautiously approaching the building.

I felt cold and tired now. Empty inside. Lin still hadn't said a word and, whatever was wrong with her, I blamed myself.

She was being checked over by a paramedic when Dyson arrived. I was talking to a cop, making the first of a seemingly infinite number of statements. Dyson screeched into the kerb and threw her car door open almost before the engine died.

'Just what the fuck is going on, McGill?' she yelled, hurtling across the road with a face like thunder.

I glared back at her and jerked my head at the car park. 'Your killer's in there – and he's dead, along with three of his men.' She could go fuck herself. I didn't care any more.

Dyson stared at me, speechless, her eyes flashing all around her, breathing heavily through her nose and rubbing the back of her neck. After a few moments, she turned to the cop, her voice only marginally calmer. 'I want her bringing in, OK!' Then, pointing her finger at me, 'I'll talk to you later!'

Lin went to hospital. I went to Bootle Street.

Dyson's mood had moderated by the time she sat down opposite me in the interview room. Even so, she wasn't exactly friendly.

'You put the phone down on me – I don't appreciate that.'

I glared back. 'If I hadn't, then I'd never have found the killer for you.'

'Really! And maybe six more people would still be alive!'

I leaned back in the chair and swore quietly to myself. It's always the same. They never like it when you do their job for them. They never show the slightest fucking gratitude.

'Keane was on a killing spree,' I snapped. 'When you rang from Pritchard's house, I realised that Peterson had to be next.'

She slammed the table. 'You should have told me: I could have stopped them long before the flyover.'

I leaned towards her and raised my voice as well. 'Yeah – and you'd have listened to me, I suppose?'

She looked away, breathing deeply, her chest heaving with emotion. When she looked back, she spoke more quietly, but edgily.

'All right, take me through everything.'

I told her the whole story. Almost everything I knew. How Mr Lee had hired me to find Aunt Emily and then to investigate Charlie Wilson's murder. My conversations with Dorry, Martha, Rita, Natalie, Elaine Wilson, Peterson, Pritchard and Keane. I told her about the money-laundering operation and the trail of businesses that led back to Dominica. I no longer had the printouts and I couldn't remember the names, but it didn't matter: they could fill in the details themselves when they searched Three Seas. In any case, I was sure that Lin would remember, when she recovered.

If she recovered.

Of course, I omitted to mention the break-in at Chow City, and the connection between Mr Lee and Vinko Cuzak. As far as she could tell, I knew nothing about the case against Beano falling apart. Nothing that I would admit, anyway.

She gave me the hard stare when I finished. 'So who killed Keane and his men? And how come they didn't harm you, or your friend?'

I shrugged. 'They had no argument with us. We weren't a threat – why should they kill us?'

She nodded cynically. 'Yeah, sure. So who were they?'

I shrugged. 'Search me. I told you, I never saw their faces and they hardly spoke. They were hoods, that's for sure. Part of the same mob, I would think. Keane said something about a takeover bid. I presume he was found out. You know the way it goes. In any case, I'm not complaining. I'm just relieved they acted when they did.'

She kept her eyes on mine. I blinked and looked away for a second. Nobody holds a stare for that long, even if – especially if – they're telling the truth.

'Come on, McGill, you know more than you're saying. Who runs this organisation?'

I slumped back in my chair and sighed at the irony of it all. They resent it when you get one over on them, then they get shirty when you don't give the answers they need. 'I don't know, Superintendent,' I replied irritably. 'But I do know that I've just handed you one of the biggest crime networks in the country – on a plate. I think that maybe, just maybe, you're gonna have to work the rest out for yourself.'

I thought it was a classic performance. So, clearly, did Dyson. She made me go over it all again – several times, in fact, during the Saturday and the Sunday. I got so used to being in the Bootle Street nick that it began to feel as if I might spend the rest of my life there. I don't know whether I ever convinced her totally, but in the end she gave up anyway. The turf-war angle wasn't likely to make her any friends on the Police Authority or in the media. But the busting of the crime syndicates was another matter entirely. On balance, she should have been more than pleased. And secretly, beneath that belligerent exterior, I guess she was. When I finally made my goodbyes on the Monday, she almost smiled.

The interminable interviews would have been bad enough on their own but I was worried sick about Lin all weekend as well. Because of my involvement in the case, they wouldn't let me see her in hospital. The cops had taken a statement from her on the Saturday and again on the Sunday, so I knew she was speaking again, but Dyson said that she was badly traumatised and that her account was sketchier than they would have liked. Still, in the end, it was enough to corroborate mine. And that seemed to satisfy them.

They let Lin leave hospital on the Monday. Mr Lee rang to tell me that she was staying with him for the moment and would I like to visit? I said yes, of course. I wanted to see her, wherever she was – even if it *was* in his apartment above the Golden Snapper.

In the event, the grandfather made himself scarce for the duration of my visit. Maybe he was showing what I'd once viewed as his unusual sensitivity. More likely he was too embarrassed to look me in the face. I can't say that I was sorry – I had no idea how I might react, either.

They'd prescribed her some kind of sedative and, although she recognised me and held me close when I first walked in, she didn't mention the shooting. She didn't talk much at all in fact – and nor did I. We just sat quietly together on the settee, my arm around her shoulder, her head on my breast. I guess we both needed space. I guess that we both needed some time to process our feelings.

I left after half an hour, feeling lost and inadequate.

I had lunch with Beano, Hannah and Susie at one of the 'normal' (i.e. inexpensive) restaurants in Chinatown. That made me feel better. Beano was on top form, back to her old self, plus some. Hannah kept looking across at me and smiling. Susie insisted on entertaining us all.

I don't think I convinced them when I said that her release owed nothing to me. I tried to avoid the subject and refused to say much about the shooting or Charles Wilson's murder either. Publicly, Beano put it down to my uncharacteristic modesty and turned it into a joke.

But when I caught her eye I could see that, in reality, she was doing her best to protect me. I smiled to let her know that I was onto her. I'd tell her everything someday soon, but right then I'd had as much as I could take. The nice thing was that she knew that already.

I went back home to York after that and spent two days in the house with just Tibby, my cat, for company. I turned on the answering machine and left the key in the lock. Becky tried her key a couple of times before giving up. Then she pushed a number of messages through the letterbox instead. She was worried sick, of course, imagining that I might be hanging from some beam or laid out in the bath with my wrists slashed.

But I didn't care. I was tired of it all. Tired of her. Tired of people. Becky knew me well enough to know that sometimes, when I needed space, no amount of knocking on doors or phoning would rouse me. My cat knew too and spent the entire time curled up next to me, as if to give me moral support.

I guess that Martha's call was what I needed. She rang on the Wednesday and left a message inviting me to the Friday funeral. I'd rung her back straightaway and accepted. I think it was then, maybe, that the clouds had begun to lift.

Now, as the rain eased off and the mourners drifted away, I felt like crying again. More from relief than sadness. More from a feeling that it was over at last. I could get back to my life again. Though what that life was, I still couldn't say. It certainly wouldn't involve following erring spouses any more. And at this particular moment, I wasn't even sure whether I still wanted to be a PI.

Martha came across to me, folding her umbrella, and held me in a long warm hug, not seeming to mind that I was dripping all over her. Then she drew back and gave me a smile so genuine that it made my heart miss a beat.

'Thank you for coming today, Cameron. That was nice of you.' She tipped her head at me. 'You look very pensive – are you all right?'

I smiled back and stroked her arm. 'I was just thinking what a relief it is that he's finally at rest. You must feel that more than anyone.'

She nodded and pulled a face. 'Yes. It's time to move on. We have to cope in the end, don't we?' She observed me again for a moment then patted my arm. 'You will come to the reception, won't you? It's in the hotel just down the road.'

I shook my head. 'If you don't mind, I'd rather not. No disrespect to anyone, Martha, but it's not my kind of thing.'

She smiled and took my hand. 'I understand. Thank you again. Just knowing that some kind of justice has been done makes Charlie's death a little easier to bear. I'm very grateful.' She leaned forward and kissed me on the cheek. 'Stay in touch, won't you?'

I said I would and she nodded pleasantly, but we both knew that it was a lie, and that this was just another in life's long line of goodbyes.

Lin and her grandfather were standing alone by the graveside now, paying their last respects. The old man had kept glancing across and, as soon as Martha left, he said something to his granddaughter, then turned and walked over to me.

I can't quite describe how I felt just then. Something akin to loathing rose in my throat as he approached, but sadness and disappointment and anger were there as well. And the knowledge that things between us – and maybe even between Lin and me – could never be the same again.

He proffered his hand. When I didn't take it, he looked crestfallen.

'How's Lin?' I asked, trying hard to stay civil.

He glanced back at his granddaughter, standing quietly, head bowed by the open grave. 'She's doing very well,' he answered in a voice tinged with dismay. 'She's a little quieter than normal, but she's improving. The doctor believes that she'll make a full recovery, given time. She asked to have a word with you before we leave.'

I nodded. I had nothing else to say to him. Clearly he had, so I waited.

'Cameron... I... understand that the police now regard the case as closed. I suppose I just wanted to thank you.'

'That's OK, Mr Lee. I guess I should thank you for not killing me along with the others.'

The sarcasm came out before I even thought about it, and I regretted it at once. The old man blanched visibly and steadied himself with his stick. I waited, feeling embarrassed now, but still less than benevolent.

'Cameron, please, that is not worthy of you.' He closed his eyes and shook his head from side to side. 'Please, for Lin's sake. I don't expect you to approve of my past and I cannot change it for you.'

I stared back at him unmoved. Then I noticed how much his hands were trembling and I guess I began to listen a little more carefully.

'Last week I was forced to reassess my values. My granddaughter was almost killed because of me. Can you understand how I feel about that?' He stopped and looked straight into my eyes. 'I told you the story of my daughter, Soo May. I told you that she... died.' He looked down at his feet and took a deep breath. 'But I didn't tell you how, did I?'

I shook my head, suddenly aware that the old man was on the verge of tears.

'It was a road traffic accident – but it wasn't an accident. It was one of my rivals in Singapore, in the early days. He resented my power and he tried to kill me.' He pulled out a white linen handkerchief and wiped his eyes. Then he breathed in deeply. 'He failed, but he killed my beautiful baby instead.'

He paused, looking straight at me, a single tear rolling down his cheek.

'And, last week, I nearly lost Lin.'

I sighed and nodded in sympathy.

'I understand how difficult this must be for you, young lady. But – please – do not let anger come between us. Whatever my failings in the past, I am trying to do the right thing now. I would value your support.'

He drew back a little and held out his hand again. This time I took it and he held on tight, grasping my hand with both of his, staring deep into my eyes with an intensity I hadn't seen before.

'After you've spoken to Lin, you must leave,' he said.

I frowned. 'I am. I'm going back to York tonight.'

He shook his head at me but his gaze never faltered.

'No, Cameron. I mean that you should leave the country for a while. Maybe for a long time. Cuzak is not a man to be crossed. I have protected you until now. I regret that I won't be able to do it for much longer.'

I nodded. I guess I already knew that. The dealer wasn't likely to forgive what I tried to do to him. And Mr Lee had just lost all his power.

The old man looked over at Lin, who was still standing by the graveside, and dropped my hand. 'I'll wait in the car – there's no hurry.' He looked back for just a moment, then smiled sorrowfully and left.

Lin was deep in thought when I came up behind her. I cleared my throat so as not to make her jump. She turned her head and smiled at me, then looked back into the grave. I walked closer and hesitantly slipped my arms around her waist. She leaned back into me and took my hands, holding them to her belly.

'I was talking to Martha earlier,' she said, leaning back and rubbing her cheek against mine. 'She told me that she dressed him for his funeral in his favourite frock and wig.' She looked back at me and smiled. 'That's really nice, don't you think?'

'Yeah. She's a nice woman; I like her a lot. I guess he was a nice guy as well.'

'Yeah, I'm sure he was. Penny as well.' She squeezed my hands and pulled me in closer. 'Y'know, I was just thinking, Cam, I owe Charlie a lot. I mean... I'm really sad over what's happened but, in spite of everything, I think that I've kind of grown up in the last two weeks. It's like... if none of this had happened, then nothing would have changed for me – I'd still be the same scared trans-woman. I'd still be trying to find my way through.'

She turned round to face me and ran her hand over my wet hair. 'You might think this sounds stupid, but meeting you, Cameron, and going through all that stuff last week – hell, I know it got to me, but now… it's kind of hard to explain, but… somehow I don't feel I need to apologise any more.'

She looked back over her shoulder and into the grave. 'All the same, I'm sad it had to happen this way.'

I put my hand on her cheek and turned her gently back to me. 'Well, at least some good came out of it all. Charlie would have liked that.'

'Yeah, I guess he would.'

She looked at me and pulled a face that summed it all up, then she held out her hand and led me away from the graveside and out onto one of the paths. We walked through the cemetery for some minutes before she spoke again.

'I'm sorry if I was a bit strange – after the shooting, I mean – and the other day in Grandpa's apartment.'

I shrugged. 'I was just worried about you. You feeling OK now?'

She nodded. 'Yeah. Still a bit overwhelmed.'

'Yeah, well it was a violent day. I'm not surprised if—'

Suddenly she shook her head. 'It wasn't just the violence, Cam.' She glanced over towards her grandfather's car in the far distance. 'I hope you weren't unkind to him.'

I stared back at her in astonishment. She knew.

'Why… why should I be unkind?' I asked carefully.

She smiled kind of sadly. 'You know very well why.'

I screwed my eyes up and she gave me that sideways look that she did so well.

'Relax, Cam, you don't have to keep up the pretence with me. I've suspected something was going on for years. I just never thought it would be anything like this. You can't be *that* close to someone and not know when things don't quite add up.'

'You *know.*'

She sighed. 'I do now. I've always avoided thinking about it before. It was mostly little things. The way he was always travelling, the businesses that he owned but never talked about. All the people and affairs that he kept me away from. It was always easy to find reasons, to convince myself that it was just my suspicious nature. Then, last Friday, when I was sitting on the steps with that gunman, it all started filling my mind. That's why I was so odd when you found me. I could hardly think any more, let alone speak.' She smiled sadly and walked on again, pulling me along behind her.

'But it was when I was started telling the police about the money-laundering that I really started to understand. It came to me all at once that it had to be *him* who owned the company in Dominica – and that it had to be *his* men who saved our lives.'

'I was hoping that you wouldn't realise – so was he.'

'Yeah, well, that was kind, Cameron.' She squeezed my hand and smiled properly now. 'Anyway, that's why I went so peculiar. But it's over and I'm adjusting now. The worse part was lying to the police.'

I raised my eyebrows. 'How do you feel about him now?' I asked.

She shrugged. 'I think I've decided it doesn't matter. Whatever he is, or has been – whatever he's done – I still believe that on balance he's a decent man. He's been wonderful to me – and I still love him.'

'Does he know that you know?'

She gave me a sharp look. 'No, he doesn't – and I don't want him to. It would break his heart. He would feel that he'd let me down terribly.'

'That's exactly what he said about you.'

'Yeah, and I'm sure he believes it. But, like I've told you before, Cam, I'm stronger than he thinks. It's been tough, but I'm through it.'

'He's lost nearly everything, you know that?'

She shook her head. 'Well, I can't say that I'm sorry about that. We uncovered a lot of stuff, Cameron. Still, all the same, I can't help but feel sorry for him.'

Suddenly she looked distraught.

'Well, you don't need to worry,' I said. 'He's cool about it. In fact, he told me he was relieved. And his identity is safe as long as we keep quiet. He's going to be able to live out his last days as an honest man. I think he's actually quite pleased about that.'

'Yeah, well, that's just as well.' She stopped walking and pulled me round so that I was facing her. 'He doesn't have much time left, Cam.'

'Oh, come on, Lin, you know how fit he is.' I reached out and held her shoulders, holding her beautiful eyes in mine. 'He'll be good for years yet!'

Her eyes filled up before the words had even left my mouth. She fell into me, sobbing inconsolably. I held her close for what seemed like an age. She was overwrought. She was bound to be emotional.

When she calmed down again, she pulled away from me, shaking her head and wiping her eyes with the back of her hand. 'He's dying, Cam. He told me last night. Cancer of the prostate. It's eating him alive.'

Jesus.

She shook her head very slowly, as if she couldn't believe what she was telling me. Then she laid her head on my shoulder and nuzzled into the warmth of my neck.

'All week – every day since that shooting – I've been hanging onto the way it was between you and me. Every hour of every day, I've been looking forward to seeing you again, to spending time with you.'

My spine tingled and my heart missed a beat. Suddenly I knew exactly what she was going to say, and I didn't want to hear it.

'I'm sorry, Cam.' She took out a hankie and blew her nose, then she swallowed hard and gathered herself together.

'I was hoping that you were going to stay,' I said. I felt lost.

'I want to, Cam.' She bit her lip to keep the tears at bay. 'I really want to, but I can't.' She stroked my face and sighed heavily. 'He wants to die in Singapore. He's been so kind to me in my life. I have to go with him. I have to be there to help him at the end. I'm so sorry.'

I put my finger to her lips and stopped her. 'You don't have to apologise. You love him. He loves you. I wouldn't expect you to do anything else.'

When she held me close, the pain in my head cut through me like a knife. The rain was falling again and all around us the light was fading. I felt like giving up. I'd always known that she'd be leaving.

But not like this. For the first time in my entire life, I'd found someone I didn't want to run away from. Someone I could learn to love and be loved by. Now she was being taken away by a man who'd nearly got us both killed.

After a few minutes I took a deep breath and pulled back, smiling at her as if it were just one of those things.

'When do you go?' I asked.

She pressed her lips together and looked as if she might cry again. 'Tonight, on the midnight flight.'

I shook the rain off my hair and stuck a smile on my face. 'OK, then, that means that we have at least five hours together. Time at least for a decent meal, in a decent restaurant.'

She glanced over towards Mr Lee's car and chewed on her lip. The beginnings of a smile crept over her face. 'I know just the place, Cam. In Chinatown. The food is perfect, the service is exceptional and – if I'm not mistaken – they are already airing one of the very last bottles of 1978 Châteauneuf-du-Pape in the whole world.'

'You mean the Golden Snapper?'

'Yeah, but this time, my dear, we'll be dining alone. Just you and me... one last time.' She tipped her head and studied me, judging my mood. 'Is that OK?'

I nodded, smiling genuinely now. A rain-soaked graveyard was hardly the best place to say goodbye. And it would be good to have a few more hours together. The Bentley was still waiting over on the roadway. 'You think that Mr Lee would give me a lift?' I asked.

'Are you kidding?' She laughed. 'He would be absolutely delighted.'

'OK, then.' I leant forward and kissed her lightly on the lips. 'In that case, mine's a black bean tofu.'

which is upon the sea coast, in the borders of Zeb'u-lun and Naph'ta-li.

14 That it might be fulfilled which was spoken by I-sa'iah the prophet, saying,

15 The land of Zeb'u-lun, and the land of Naph'ta-li, *by* the way of the sea, beyond Jor'dan, Gal'i-lee of the Gen'tiles;

16 The people which sat in darkness saw great light; and to them which sat in the region and shadow of death light is sprung up.

17 ¶ From that time Je'sus began to preach, and to say, Repent: for the kingdom of heaven is at hand.

18 ¶ And Je'sus, walking by the sea of Gal'i-lee, saw two brethren, Si'mon called Pe'ter, and Andrew his brother, casting a net into the sea: for they were fishers.

19 And he saith unto them, Follow me, and I will make you fishers of men.

20 And they straightway left *their* nets, and followed him.

21 And going on from thence, he saw other two brethren, James *the son* of Zeb'e-dee, and John his brother, in a ship with Zeb'e-dee their father, mending their nets; and he called them.

22 And they immediately left the ship and their father, and followed him.

23 ¶ And Je'sus went about all Gal'i-lee, teaching in their synagogues, and preaching the gospel of the kingdom, and healing all manner of sickness and all manner of disease among the people.

24 And his fame went throughout all Syr'i-a: and they brought unto him all sick people that were taken with divers diseases and torments, and those which were possessed with devils, and those which were lunatic, and those that had the palsy; and he healed them.

25 And there followed him great multitudes of people from Gal'i-lee, and *from* De-cap'o-lis, and *from* Je-ru'sa-lem, and *from* Ju-dæ'a, and *from* beyond Jor'dan.

5 And seeing the multitudes, he went up into a mountain: and when he was set, his disciples came unto him:

2 And he opened his mouth, and taught them, saying,

3 Blessed *are* the poor in spirit: for theirs is the kingdom of heaven.

4 Blessed *are* they that mourn: for they shall be comforted.

5 Blessed *are* the meek: for they shall inherit the earth.

6 Blessed *are* they which do hunger and thirst after righteousness: for they shall be filled.

7 Blessed *are* the merciful: for they shall obtain mercy.

8 Blessed *are* the pure in heart: for they shall see God.

9 Blessed *are* the peacemakers: for they shall be called the children of God.

10 Blessed *are* they which are persecuted for righteousness' sake: for theirs is the kingdom of heaven.

11 Blessed are ye, when *men*

shall revile you, and persecute *you*, and shall say all manner of evil against you falsely, for my sake.

12 Rejoice, and be exceeding glad: for great *is* your reward in heaven: for so persecuted they the prophets which were before you.

13 ¶ Ye are the salt of the earth: but if the salt have lost his savor, wherewith shall it be salted? it is thenceforth good for nothing, but to be cast out, and to be trodden under foot of men.

14 Ye are the light of the world. A city that is set on an hill cannot be hid.

15 Neither do men light a candle, and put it under a bushel, but on a candlestick; and it giveth light unto all that are in the house.

16 Let your light so shine before men, that they may see your good works, and glorify your Father which is in heaven.

17 ¶ Think not that I am come to destroy the law, or the prophets: I am not come to destroy, but to fulfill.

18 For verily I say unto you, Till heaven and earth pass, one jot or one tittle shall in no wise pass from the law, till all be fulfilled.

19 Whosoever therefore shall break one of these least commandments, and shall teach men so, he shall be called the least in the kingdom of heaven: but whosoever shall do and teach *them*, the same shall be

called great in the kingdom of heaven.

20 For I say unto you, That except your righteousness shall exceed *the righteousness* of the scribes and Phar'i-sees, ye shall in no case enter into the kingdom of heaven.

21 ¶ Ye have heard that it was said by them of old time, Thou shalt not kill; and whosoever shall kill shall be in danger of the judgment:

22 But I say unto you, That whosoever is angry with his brother without a cause shall be in danger of the judgment: and whosoever shall say to his brother, Raca, shall be in danger of the council: but whosoever shall say, Thou fool, shall be in danger of hell fire.

23 Therefore if thou bring thy gift to the altar, and there rememberest that thy brother hath aught against thee;

24 Leave there thy gift before the altar, and go thy way; first be reconciled to thy brother, and then come and offer thy gift.

25 Agree with thine adversary quickly, whiles thou art in the way with him; lest at any time the adversary deliver thee to the judge, and the judge deliver thee to the officer, and thou be cast into prison.

26 Verily I say unto thee, Thou shalt by no means come out thence, till thou hast paid the uttermost farthing.

27 ¶ Ye have heard that it was said by them of old time, Thou shalt not commit adultery:

28 But I say unto you, That whosoever looketh on a woman to lust after her hath committed adultery with her already in his heart.

29 And if thy right eye offend thee, pluck it out, and cast *it* from thee: for it is profitable for thee that one of thy members should perish, and not *that* thy whole body should be cast into hell.

30 And if thy right hand offend thee, cut it off, and cast *it* from thee: for it is profitable for thee that one of thy members should perish, and not *that* thy whole body should be cast into hell.

31 It hath been said, Whosoever shall put away his wife, let him give her a writing of divorcement:

32 But I say unto you, That whosoever shall put away his wife, saving for the cause of fornication, causeth her to commit adultery: and whosoever shall marry her that is divorced committeth adultery.

33 ¶ Again, ye have heard that it hath been said by them of old time, Thou shalt not forswear thyself, but shalt perform unto the Lord thine oaths:

34 But I say unto you, Swear not at all; neither by heaven; for it is God's throne:

35 Nor by the earth; for it is his footstool: neither by Je-ru'sa-lem; for it is the city of the great King.

36 Neither shalt thou swear by thy head, because thou canst not make one hair white or black.

37 But let your communication be, Yea, yea; Nay, nay: for whatsoever is more than these cometh of evil.

38 ¶ Ye have heard that it hath been said, An eye for an eye, and a tooth for a tooth:

39 But I say unto you, That ye resist not evil: but whosoever shall smite thee on thy right cheek, turn to him the other also.

40 And if any man will sue thee at the law, and take away thy coat, let him have *thy* cloak also.

41 And whosoever shall compel thee to go a mile, go with him twain.

42 Give to him that asketh thee, and from him that would borrow of thee turn not thou away.

43 ¶ Ye have heard that it hath been said, Thou shalt love thy neighbor, and hate thine enemy.

44 But I say unto you, Love your enemies, bless them that curse you, do good to them that hate you, and pray for them which despitefully use you, and persecute you;

45 That ye may be the children of your Father which is in heaven: for he maketh his sun to rise on the evil and on the good, and sendeth rain on the just and on the unjust.

46 For if ye love them which love you, what reward have ye? do not even the publicans the same?

47 And if ye salute your brethren only, what do ye more *than*

others? do not even the publicans so?

48 Be ye therefore perfect, even as your Father which is in heaven is perfect.

6 Take heed that ye do not your alms before men, to be seen of them: otherwise ye have no reward of your Father which is in heaven.

2 Therefore when thou doest *thine* alms, do not sound a trumpet before thee, as the hypocrites do in the synagogues and in the streets, that they may have glory of men. Verily I say unto you, They have their reward.

3 But when thou doest alms, let not thy left hand know what thy right hand doeth:

4 That thine alms may be in secret: and thy Father which seeth in secret himself shall reward thee openly.

5 ¶ And when thou prayest, thou shalt not be as the hypocrites *are:* for they love to pray standing in the synagogues and in the corners of the streets, that they may be seen of men. Verily I say unto you, They have their reward.

6 But thou, when thou prayest, enter into thy closet, and when thou hast shut thy door, pray to thy Father which is in secret; and thy Father which seeth in secret shall reward thee openly.

7 But when ye pray, use not vain repetitions, as the heathen *do:* for they think that they shall be heard for their much speaking.

8 Be not ye therefore like unto them: for your Father knoweth what things ye have need of, before ye ask him.

9 After this manner therefore pray ye: Our Father which art in heaven, Hallowed be thy name.

10 Thy kingdom come. Thy will be done in earth, as *it is* in heaven.

11 Give us this day our daily bread.

12 And forgive us our debts, as we forgive our debtors.

13 And lead us not into temptation, but deliver us from evil: For thine is the kingdom, and the power, and the glory, for ever. Amen.

14 For if ye forgive men their trespasses, your heavenly Father will also forgive you:

15 But if ye forgive not men their trespasses, neither will your Father forgive your trespasses.

16 ¶ Moreover when ye fast, be not, as the hypocrites, of a sad countenance: for they disfigure their faces, that they may appear unto men to fast. Verily I say unto you, They have their reward.

17 But thou, when thou fastest, anoint thine head, and wash thy face;

18 That thou appear not unto men to fast, but unto thy Father which is in secret: and thy Father, which seeth in secret, shall reward thee openly.

19 ¶ Lay not up for yourselves treasures upon earth, where moth and rust doth corrupt, and where thieves break through and steal:

20 But lay up for yourselves treasures in heaven, where neither moth nor rust doth corrupt, and where thieves do not break through nor steal:

21 For where your treasure is, there will your heart be also.

22 The light of the body is the eye: if therefore thine eye be single, thy whole body shall be full of light.

23 But if thine eye be evil, thy whole body shall be full of darkness. If therefore the light that is in thee be darkness, how great *is* that darkness!

24 ¶ No man can serve two masters: for either he will hate the one, and love the other; or else he will hold to the one, and despise the other. Ye cannot serve God and mammon.

25 Therefore I say unto you, Take no thought for your life, what ye shall eat, or what ye shall drink; nor yet for your body, what ye shall put on. Is not the life more than meat, and the body than raiment?

26 Behold the fowls of the air: for they sow not, neither do they reap, nor gather into barns; yet your heavenly Father feedeth them. Are ye not much better than they?

27 Which of you by taking thought can add one cubit unto his stature?

28 And why take ye thought for raiment? Consider the lilies of the field, how they grow; they toil not, neither do they spin:

29 And yet I say unto you, That even Sol'o-mon in all his glory was not arrayed like one of these.

30 Wherefore, if God so clothe the grass of the field, which today is, and tomorrow is cast into the oven, *shall he* not much more *clothe* you, O ye of little faith?

31 Therefore take no thought, saying, What shall we eat? or, What shall we drink? or, Wherewithal shall we be clothed?

32 (For after all these things do the Gen'tiles seek:) for your heavenly Father knoweth that ye have need of all these things.

33 But seek ye first the kingdom of God, and his righteousness; and all these things shall be added unto you.

34 Take therefore no thought for the morrow: for the morrow shall take thought for the things of itself. Sufficient unto the day *is* the evil thereof.

7 Judge not, that ye be not judged.

2 For with what judgment ye judge, ye shall be judged: and with what measure ye mete, it shall be measured to you again.

3 And why beholdest thou the mote that is in thy brother's eye, but considerest not the beam that is in thine own eye?

4 Or how wilt thou say to thy brother, Let me pull out the mote out of thine eye; and, behold, a beam *is* in thine own eye?

5 Thou hypocrite, first cast out the beam out of thine own eye; and then shalt thou see clearly to cast out the mote out of thy brother's eye.

6 ¶ Give not that which is holy unto the dogs, neither cast ye your pearls before swine, lest they trample them under their feet, and turn again and rend you.

7 ¶ Ask, and it shall be given you; seek, and ye shall find; knock, and it shall be opened unto you:

8 For everyone that asketh receiveth; and he that seeketh findeth; and to him that knocketh it shall be opened.

9 Or what man is there of you, whom if his son ask bread, will he give him a stone?

10 Or if he ask a fish, will he give him a serpent?

11 If ye then, being evil, know how to give good gifts unto your children, how much more shall your Father which is in heaven give good things to them that ask him?

12 Therefore all things whatsoever ye would that men should do to you, do ye even so to them: for this is the law and the prophets.

13 ¶ Enter ye in at the strait gate: for wide *is* the gate, and broad *is* the way, that leadeth to destruction, and many there be which go in thereat:

14 Because strait *is* the gate, and narrow *is* the way, which leadeth unto life, and few there be that find it.

15 ¶ Beware of false prophets, which come to you in sheep's clothing, but inwardly they are ravening wolves.

16 Ye shall know them by their fruits. Do men gather grapes of thorns, or figs of thistles?

17 Even so every good tree bringeth forth good fruit; but a corrupt tree bringeth forth evil fruit.

18 A good tree cannot bring forth evil fruit, neither *can* a corrupt tree bring forth good fruit.

19 Every tree that bringeth not forth good fruit is hewn down, and cast into the fire.

20 Wherefore by their fruits ye shall know them.

21 ¶ Not everyone that saith unto me, Lord, Lord, shall enter into the kingdom of heaven; but he that doeth the will of my Father which is in heaven.

22 Many will say to me in that day, Lord, Lord, have we not prophesied in thy name? and in thy name have cast out devils? and in thy name done many wonderful works?

23 And then will I profess unto them, I never knew you: depart from me, ye that work iniquity.

24 ¶ Therefore whosoever heareth these sayings of mine, and doeth them, I will liken him unto a wise man, which built his house upon a rock:

25 And the rain descended, and the floods came, and the winds blew, and beat upon that house; and it fell not: for it was founded upon a rock.

26 And everyone that heareth these sayings of mine, and doeth them not, shall be likened unto a foolish man, which built his house upon the sand:

27 And the rain descended,

and the floods came, and the winds blew, and beat upon that house; and it fell: and great was the fall of it.

28 And it came to pass, when Je'sus had ended these sayings, the people were astonished at his doctrine:

29 For he taught them as *one* having authority, and not as the scribes.

8 When he was come down from the mountain, great multitudes followed him.

2 And, behold, there came a leper and worshipped him, saying, Lord, if thou wilt, thou canst make me clean.

3 And Je'sus put forth *his* hand, and touched him, saying I will; be thou clean. And immediately his leprosy was cleansed.

4 And Je'sus saith unto him, See thou tell no man; but go thy way, show thyself to the priest, and offer the gift that Mo'ses commanded, for a testimony unto them.

5 ¶ And when Je'sus was entered into Ca-per'na-um, there came unto him a centurion, beseeching him,

6 And saying, Lord, my servant lieth at home sick of the palsy, grievously tormented.

7 And Je'sus saith unto him, I will come and heal him.

8 The centurion answered and said, Lord, I am not worthy that thou shouldest come under my roof: but speak the word only, and my servant shall be healed.

9 For I am a man under authority, having soldiers under me: and I say to this *man*, Go, and he goeth; and to another, Come, and he cometh; and to my servant, Do this, and he doeth *it*.

10 When Je'sus heard *it*, he marveled, and said to them that followed, Verily I say unto you, I have not found so great faith, no, not in Is'ra-el.

11 And I say unto you, That many shall come from the east and west, and shall sit down with A'bra-ham, and I'saac, and Ja'cob, in the kingdom of heaven.

12 But the children of the kingdom shall be cast into outer darkness: there shall be weeping and gnashing of teeth.

13 And Je'sus said unto the centurion, Go thy way; and as thou hast believed, *so* be it done unto thee. And his servant was healed in the selfsame hour.

14 ¶ And when Je'sus was come into Pe'ter's house, he saw his wife's mother laid, and sick of a fever.

15 And he touched her hand, and the fever left her: and she arose, and ministered unto them.

16 ¶ When the even was come, they brought unto him many that were possessed with devils: and he cast out the spirits with *his* word, and healed all that were sick:

17 That it might be fulfilled which was spoken by I-sa'iah the prophet, saying, Himself took our infirmities, and bare *our* sicknesses.

18 ¶ Now when Je'sus saw great multitudes about him, he

gave commandment to depart unto the other side.

19 And a certain scribe came, and said unto him, Master, I will follow thee whithersoever thou goest.

20 And Je'sus saith unto him, The foxes have holes, and the birds of the air *have* nests; but the Son of man hath not where to lay *his* head.

21 And another of his disciples said unto him, Lord, suffer me first to go and bury my father.

22 But Je'sus said unto him, Follow me; and let the dead bury their dead.

23 ¶ And when he was entered into a ship, his disciples followed him.

24 And, behold, there arose a great tempest in the sea, insomuch that the ship was covered with the waves: but he was asleep.

25 And his disciples came to *him,* and awoke him, saying, Lord, save us: we perish.

26 And he saith unto them, Why are ye fearful, O ye of little faith? Then he arose, and rebuked the winds and the sea; and there was a great calm.

27 But the men marveled, saying, What manner of man is this, that even the winds and the sea obey him!

28 ¶ And when he was come to the other side into the country of the Ger'ge-senes, there met him two possessed with devils, coming out of the tombs, exceeding fierce, so that no man might pass by that way.

29 And, behold, they cried out,

saying, What have we to do with thee, Je'sus, thou Son of God? art thou come hither to torment us before the time?

30 And there was a good way off from them an herd of many swine feeding.

31 So the devils besought him, saying, If thou cast us out, suffer us to go away into the herd of swine.

32 And he said unto them, Go. And when they were come out, they went into the herd of swine: and, behold, the whole herd of swine ran violently down a steep place into the sea, and perished in the waters.

33 And they that kept them fled, and went their ways into the city, and told everything, and what was befallen to the possessed of the devils.

34 And, behold, the whole city came out to meet Je'sus: and when they saw him, they besought *him* that he would depart out of their coasts.

9 And he entered into a ship, and passed over, and came into his own city.

2 And, behold, they brought to him a man sick of the palsy, lying on a bed: and Je'sus seeing their faith said unto the sick of the palsy; Son, be of good cheer; thy sins be forgiven thee.

3 And, behold, certain of the scribes said within themselves, This *man* blasphemeth.

4 And Je'sus knowing their thoughts said, Wherefore think ye evil in your hearts?

5 For whether is easier, to say,

Thy sins be forgiven thee; or to say, Arise, and walk?

6 But that ye may know that the Son of man hath power on earth to forgive sins, (then saith he to the sick of the palsy,) Arise, take up thy bed, and go unto thine house.

7 And he arose, and departed to his house.

8 But when the multitudes saw *it*, they marveled, and glorified God, which had given such power unto men.

9 ¶ And as Je'sus passed forth from thence, he saw a man, named Mat'thew, sitting at the receipt of custom: and he saith unto him, Follow me. And he arose, and followed him.

10 ¶ And it came to pass, as Je'sus sat at meat in the house, behold, many publicans and sinners came and sat down with him and his disciples.

11 And when the Phar'i-sees saw *it*, they said unto his disciples, Why eateth your Master with publicans and sinners?

12 But when Je'sus heard *that*, he said unto them, They that be whole need not a physician, but they that are sick.

13 But go ye and learn what *that* meaneth, I will have mercy, and not sacrifice: for I am not come to call the righteous, but sinners to repentance.

14 ¶ Then came to him the disciples of John, saying, Why do we and the Phar'i-sees fast oft, but thy disciples fast not?

15 And Je'sus said unto them, Can the children of the bride-chamber mourn, as long as the bridegroom is with them? but the days will come, when the bridegroom shall be taken from them, and then shall they fast.

16 No man putteth a piece of new cloth unto an old garment, for that which is put in to fill it up taketh from the garment, and the rent is made worse.

17 Neither do men put new wine into old bottles: else the bottles break, and the wine runneth out, and the bottles perish: but they put new wine into new bottles, and both are preserved.

18 ¶ While he spake these things unto them, behold, there came a certain ruler, and worshiped him, saying, My daughter is even now dead: but come and lay thy hand upon her, and she shall live.

19 And Je'sus arose, and followed him, and *so did* his disciples.

20 ¶ And, behold, a woman, which was diseased with an issue of blood twelve years, came behind *him*, and touched the hem of his garment:

21 For she said within herself, If I may but touch his garment, I shall be whole.

22 But Je'sus turned him about, and when he saw her, he said, Daughter, be of good comfort, thy faith hath made thee whole. And the woman was made whole from that hour.

23 And when Je'sus came into the ruler's house, and saw the minstrels and the people making a noise,

24 He said unto them, Give place: for the maid is not dead, but sleepeth. And they laughed him to scorn.

25 But when the people were put forth, he went in, and took her by the hand, and the maid arose.

26 And the fame hereof went abroad into all that land.

27 ¶ And when Je'sus departed thence, two blind men followed him, crying, and saying, Thou Son of Da'vid, have mercy on us.

28 And when he was come into the house, the blind men came to him: and Je'sus saith unto them, Believe ye that I am able to do this? They said unto him, Yea, Lord.

29 Then touched he their eyes, saying, According to your faith be it unto you.

30 And their eyes were opened; and Je'sus straitly charged them, saying, See that no man know it.

31 But they, when they were departed, spread abroad his fame in all that country.

32 ¶ As they went out, behold, they brought to him a dumb man possessed with a devil.

33 And when the devil was cast out, the dumb spake: and the multitudes marveled, saying, It was never so seen in Is'ra-el.

34 But the Phar'i-sees said, He casteth out devils through the prince of the devils.

35 And Je'sus went about all the cities and villages, teaching in their synagogues, and preaching the gospel of the kingdom, and healing every sickness and every disease among the people.

36 ¶ But when he saw the multitudes, he was moved with compassion on them, because they fainted, and were scattered abroad, as sheep having no shepherd.

37 Then saith he unto his disciples, The harvest truly is plenteous, but the laborers are few;

38 Pray ye therefore the Lord of the harvest, that he will send forth laborers into his harvest.

10 And when he had called unto him his twelve disciples, he gave them power against unclean spirits, to cast them out, and to heal all manner of sickness and all manner of disease.

2 Now the names of the twelve apostles are these; The first, Si'mon, who is called Pe'ter, and Andrew his brother; James the son of Zeb'e-dee, and John his brother;

3 Phil'ip, and Bar-thol'o-mew; Thom'as, and Mat'thew the publican; James the son of Al-phæ'us, and Leb-bæ'us, whose surname was Thad-dæ'us;

4 Si'mon the Ca'naan-ite, and Ju'das Is-car'i-ot, who also betrayed him.

5 These twelve Je'sus sent forth, and commanded them, saying, Go not into the way of the Gen'tiles, and into any city of the Sa-mar'i-tans enter ye not:

6 But go rather to the lost sheep of the house of Is'ra-el.

7 And as ye go, preach, saying,

The kingdom of heaven is at hand.

8 Heal the sick, cleanse the lepers, raise the dead, cast out devils: freely ye have received, freely give.

9 Provide neither gold, nor silver, nor brass in your purses,

10 Nor scrip for *your* journey, neither two coats, neither shoes, nor yet staves: for the workman is worthy of his meat.

11 And into whatsoever city or town ye shall enter, inquire who in it is worthy; and there abide till ye go thence.

12 And when ye come into an house, salute it.

13 And if the house be worthy, let your peace come upon it: but if it be not worthy, let your peace return to you.

14 And whosoever shall not receive you, nor hear your words, when ye depart out of that house or city, shake off the dust of your feet.

15 Verily I say unto you, It shall be more tolerable for the land of Sod'om and Gomor'rah in the day of judgment, than for that city.

16 ¶ Behold, I send you forth as sheep in the midst of wolves: be ye therefore wise as serpents, and harmless as doves.

17 But beware of men: for they will deliver you up to the councils, and they will scourge you in their synagogues;

18 And ye shall be brought before governors and kings for my sake for a testimony against them and the Gen'tiles.

19 But when they deliver you up, take no thought how or what ye shall speak: for it shall be given you in that same hour what ye shall speak.

20 For it is not ye that speak, but the Spirit of your Father which speaketh in you.

21 And the brother shall deliver up the brother to death, and the father the child: and the children shall rise up against *their* parents, and cause them to be put to death.

22 And ye shall be hated of all *men* for my name's sake: but he that endureth to the end shall be saved.

23 But when they persecute you in this city, flee ye into another: for verily I say unto you, Ye shall not have gone over the cities of Is'ra-el, till the Son of man be come.

24 The disciple is not above *his* master, nor the servant above his lord.

25 It is enough for the disciple that he be as his master, and the servant as his lord. If they have called the master of the house Be-el'ze-bub, how much more *shall they call* them of his household?

26 Fear them not therefore: for there is nothing covered, that shall not be revealed; and hid, that shall not be known.

27 What I tell you in darkness, *that* speak ye in light: and what ye hear in the ear, *that* preach ye upon the housetops.

28 And fear not them which kill the body, but are not able to kill the soul: but rather fear him

which is able to destroy both soul and body in hell.

29 Are not two sparrows sold for a farthing? and one of them shall not fall on the ground without your Father.

30 But the very hairs of your head are all numbered.

31 Fear ye not therefore, ye are of more value than many sparrows.

32 Whosoever therefore shall confess me before men, him will I confess also before my Father which is in heaven.

33 But whosoever shall deny me before men, him will I also deny before my Father which is in heaven.

34 Think not that I am come to send peace on earth: I came not to send peace, but a sword.

35 For I am come to set a man at variance against his father, and the daughter against her mother, and the daughter-in-law against her mother-in-law.

36 And a man's foes *shall be* they of his own household.

37 He that loveth father or mother more than me is not worthy of me: and he that loveth son or daughter more than me is not worthy of me.

38 And he that taketh not his cross, and followeth after me, is not worthy of me.

39 He that findeth his life shall lose it: and he that loseth his life for my sake shall find it.

40 ¶He that receiveth you receiveth me, and he that receiveth me receiveth him that sent me.

41 He that receiveth a prophet in the name of a prophet shall receive a prophet's reward; and he that receiveth a righteous man in the name of a righteous man shall receive a righteous man's reward.

42 And whosoever shall give to drink unto one of these little ones a cup of cold *water* only in the name of a disciple, verily I say unto you, he shall in no wise lose his reward.

11 And it came to pass, when Je′sus had made an end of commanding his twelve disciples, he departed thence to teach and to preach in their cities.

2 Now when John had heard in the prison the works of Christ, he sent two of his disciples,

3 And said unto him, Art thou he that should come, or do we look for another?

4 Je′sus answered and said unto them, Go and show John again those things which ye do hear and see:

5 The blind receive their sight, and the lame walk, the lepers are cleansed, and the deaf hear, the dead are raised up, and the poor have the gospel preached to them.

6 And blessed is *he*, whosoever shall not be offended in me.

7 ¶ And as they departed, Je′sus began to say unto the multitudes concerning John, What went ye out into the wilderness to see? A reed shaken with the wind?

8 But what went ye out for to see? A man clothed in soft raiment? behold, they that wear

MATTHEW

1 The book of the generation of Je'sus Christ, the son of Da'vid, the son of A'bra-ham.

2 A'bra-ham begat I'saac; and I'saac begat Ja'cob; and Ja'cob begat Ju'das and his brethren;

3 And Ju'das begat Pha'res and Za'ra of Tha'mar; and Pha'res begat Es'rom; and Es'rom begat A'ram;

4 And A'ram begat A-min'a-dab; and A-min'a-dab begat Na-as'son; and Na-as'son begat Sal'mon;

5 And Sal'mon begat Bo'oz of Ra'chab; and Bo'oz begat O'bed of Ruth; and O'bed begat Jes'se;

6 And Jes'se begat Da'vid the king; and Da'vid the king begat Sol'o-mon of her that had been the wife of U-ri'as;

7 And Sol'o-mon begat Ro-bo'am; and Ro-bo'am begat A-bi'a; and A-bi'a begat A'sa;

8 And A'sa begat Jos'a-phat; and Jos'a-phat begat Jo'ram; and Jo'ram begat O-zi'as;

9 And O-zi'as begat Jo'a-tham; and Jo'a-tham begat A'chaz; and A'chaz begat Ez-e-ki'as;

10 And Ez-e-ki'as begat Ma-nas'ses; and Ma-nas'ses begat A'mon; and A'mon begat Jo-si'as;

11 And Jo-si'as begat Jech-o-ni'as and his brethren, about the time they were carried away to Bab'y-lon:

12 And after they were brought to Bab'y-lon, Jech-o-ni'as begat Sa-la'thi-el; and Sa-la'thi-el begat Zo-rob'a-bel;

13 And Zo-rob'a-bel begat A-bi'ud; and A-bi'ud begat E-li'a-kim; and E-li'a-kim begat A'zor;

14 And A'zor begat Sa'doc; and Sa'doc begat A'chim; and A'chim begat E-li'ud;

15 And E-li'ud begat El-e-a'zar; and El-e-a'zar begat Mat'than; and Mat'than begat Ja'cob;

16 And Ja'cob begat Jo'seph the husband of Ma'ry, of whom was born Je'sus, who is called Christ.

17 So all the generations from A'bra-ham to Da'vid are fourteen generations; and from Da'vid until the carrying away into Bab'y-lon are fourteen generations; and from the carrying away into Bab'y-lon unto Christ are fourteen generations.

18 Now the birth of Jesus Christ was on this wise: When as his mother Ma'ry was espoused to Jo'seph, before they came together, she was found with child of the Ho'ly Ghost.

19 Then Jo'seph her husband, being a just man, and not willing to make her a public example, was minded to put her away privily.

20 But while he thought on these things, behold, the angel of the Lord appeared unto him in a dream, saying, Jo'seph, thou son of Da'vid, fear not to take unto thee Ma'ry thy wife: for

that which is conceived in her is of the Holy Ghost.

21 And she shall bring forth a son, and thou shalt call his name JESUS: for he shall save his people from their sins.

22 Now all this was done, that it might be fulfilled which was spoken of the Lord by the prophet, saying,

23 Behold, a virgin shall be with child, and shall bring forth a son, and they shall call his name Em-man'u-el, which being interpreted is, God with us.

24 Then Jo'seph being raised from sleep did as the angel of the Lord had bidden him, and took unto him his wife:

25 And knew her not till she had brought forth her firstborn son: and he called his name JESUS.

2 Now when Je'sus was born in Beth'le-hem of Ju-dæ'a in the days of Her'od the king, behold, there came wise men from the east to Je-ru'sa-lem,

2 Saying, Where is he that is born King of the Jews? for we have seen his star in the east, and are come to worship him.

3 When Her'od the king had heard these things, he was troubled, and all Je-ru'sa-lem with him.

4 And when he had gathered all the chief priests and scribes of the people together, he demanded of them where Christ should be born.

5 And they said unto him, In Beth'le-hem of Ju-dæ'a: for thus it is written by the prophet,

6 And thou Beth'le-hem, in the land of Ju'dah, art not the least among the princes of Ju'dah: for out of thee shall come a Governor, that shall rule my people Is'-ra-el.

7 Then Her'od, when he had privily called the wise men, inquired of them diligently what time the star appeared.

8 And he sent them to Beth'le-hem, and said, Go and search diligently for the young child; and when ye have found him, bring me word again, that I may come and worship him also.

9 When they had heard the king, they departed; and, lo, the star, which they saw in the east, went before them, till it came and stood over where the young child was.

10 When they saw the star, they rejoiced with exceeding great joy.

11 ¶ And when they were come into the house, they saw the young child with Ma'ry his mother, and fell down, and worshiped him: and when they had opened their treasures, they presented unto him gifts; gold, and frankincense, and myrrh.

12 And being warned of God in a dream that they should not return to Her'od, they departed into their own country another way.

13 And when they were departed, behold, the angel of the Lord appeareth to Jo'seph in a dream, saying, Arise, and take the young child and his mother, and flee into E'gypt, and be thou there until I bring thee word:

for Her'od will seek the young child to destroy him.

14 When he arose, he took the young child and his mother by night, and departed into E'gypt:

15 And was there until the death of Her'od: that it might be fulfilled which was spoken of the Lord by the prophet, saying, Out of E'gypt have I called my son.

16 ¶ Then Her'od, when he saw that he was mocked of the wise men, was exceeding wroth, and sent forth, and slew all the children that were in Beth'le-hem, and in all the coasts thereof, from two years old and under, according to the time which he had diligently inquired of the wise men.

17 Then was fulfilled that which was spoken by Jer-e-mi'ah the prophet, saying,

18 In Ra'ma was there a voice heard, lamentation, and weeping, and great mourning, Ra'-chel weeping for her children, and would not be comforted, because they are not.

19 ¶ But when Her'od was dead, behold, an angel of the Lord appeareth in a dream to Jo'seph in E'gypt,

20 Saying, Arise, and take the young child and his mother, and go into the land of Is'ra-el: for they are dead which sought the young child's life.

21 And he arose, and took the young child and his mother, and came into the land of Is'ra-el.

22 But when he heard that Ar-che-la'us did reign in Ju-dae'a in the room of his father Her'od,

he was afraid to go thither: notwithstanding, being warned of God in a dream, he turned aside into the parts of Gal'i-lee:

23 And he came and dwelt in a city called Naz'a-reth: that it might be fulfilled which was spoken by the prophets, He shall be called a Naz'a-rene.

3 In those days came John the Bap'tist, preaching in the wilderness of Ju-dae'a,

2 And saying, Repent ye: for the kingdom of heaven is at hand.

3 For this is he that was spoken of by the prophet E-sa'ias, saying, The voice of one crying in the wilderness, Prepare ye the way of the Lord, make his paths straight.

4 And the same John had his raiment of camel's hair, and a leathern girdle about his loins; and his meat was locusts and wild honey.

5 Then went out to him Je-ru'-sa-lem, and all Ju-dae'a, and all the region round about Jor'dan,

6 And were baptized of him in Jor'dan, confessing their sins.

7 ¶ But when he saw many of the Phar'i-sees and Sad'du-cees come to his baptism, he said unto them, O generation of vipers, who hath warned you to flee from the wrath to come?

8 Bring forth therefore fruits meet for repentance:

9 And think not to say within yourselves, We have A'bra-ham to our father: for I say unto you, that God is able of these stones to raise up children unto A'bra-ham.

10 And now also the axe is laid unto the root of the trees: therefore every tree which bringeth not forth good fruit is hewn down, and cast into the fire.

11 I indeed baptize you with water unto repentance: but he that cometh after me is mightier than I, whose shoes I am not worthy to bear: he shall baptize you with the Holy Ghost, and with fire:

12 Whose fan is in his hand, and he will thoroughly purge his floor, and gather his wheat into the garner; but he will burn up the chaff with unquenchable fire.

13 ¶ Then cometh Jesus from Galilee to Jordan unto John, to be baptized of him.

14 But John forbad him, saying, I have need to be baptized of thee, and comest thou to me?

15 And Jesus answering said unto him, Suffer it to be so now: for thus it becometh us to fulfil all righteousness. Then he suffered him.

16 And Jesus, when he was baptized, went up straightway out of the water: and, lo, the heavens were opened unto him, and he saw the Spirit of God descending like a dove, and lighting upon him:

17 And lo a voice from heaven, saying, This is my beloved Son, in whom I am well pleased.

Then was Jesus led up of the Spirit into the wilderness to be tempted of the devil.

2 And when he had fasted forty days and forty nights, he was afterward an hungered.

3 And when the tempter came to him, he said, If thou be the Son of God, command that these stones be made bread.

4 But he answered and said, It is written, Man shall not live by bread alone, but by every word that proceedeth out of the mouth of God.

5 Then the devil taketh him up into the holy city, and setteth him on a pinnacle of the temple,

6 And saith unto him, If thou be the Son of God, cast thyself down: for it is written, He shall give his angels charge concerning thee: and in their hands they shall bear thee up, lest at any time thou dash thy foot against a stone.

7 Jesus said unto him, It is written again, Thou shalt not tempt the Lord thy God.

8 Again, the devil taketh him up into an exceeding high mountain, and showeth him all the kingdoms of the world, and the glory of them;

9 And saith unto him, All these things will I give thee, if thou wilt fall down and worship me.

10 Then saith Jesus unto him, Get thee hence, Satan: for it is written, Thou shalt worship the Lord thy God, and him only shalt thou serve.

11 Then the devil leaveth him, and, behold, angels came and ministered unto him.

12 ¶ Now when Jesus had heard that John was cast into prison, he departed into Galilee;

13 And leaving Nazareth, he came and dwelt in Capernaum:

THE
NEW TESTAMENT
WITH PSALMS

Authorized King James Version

HOLMAN
BIBLE PUBLISHERS

Nashville, Tennessee

Printed in Belgium

14 06 05 04

soft *clothing* are in kings' houses.

9 But what went ye out for to see? A prophet? yea, I say unto you, and more than a prophet.

10 For this is *he*, of whom it is written, Behold, I send my messenger before thy face, which shall prepare thy way before thee.

11 Verily I say unto you, Among them that are born of women there hath not risen a greater than John the Bap'tist: notwithstanding he that is least in the kingdom of heaven is greater than he.

12 And from the days of John the Bap'tist until now the kingdom of heaven suffereth violence, and the violent take it by force.

13 For all the prophets and the law prophesied until John.

14 And if ye will receive *it*, this is E-li'jah, which was for to come.

15 He that hath ears to hear, let him hear.

16 ¶ But whereunto shall I liken this generation? It is like unto children sitting in the markets, and calling unto their fellows,

17 And saying, We have piped unto you, and ye have not danced; we have mourned unto you, and ye have not lamented.

18 For John came neither eating nor drinking, and they say, He hath a devil.

19 The Son of man came eating and drinking, and they say, Behold a man gluttonous, and a winebibber, a friend of publi-

cans and sinners. But wisdom is justified of her children.

20 ¶ Then began he to upbraid the cities wherein most of his mighty works were done, because they repented not:

21 Woe unto thee, Cho-ra'zin! woe unto thee, Beth-sa'i-da! for if the mighty works, which were done in you, had been done in Tyre and Si'don, they would have repented long ago in sackcloth and ashes.

22 But I say unto you, It shall be more tolerable for Tyre and Si'don at the day of judgment, than for you.

23 And thou, Ca-per'na-um, which art exalted unto heaven, shalt be brought down to hell: for if the mighty works, which have been done in thee, had been done in Sod'om, it would have remained until this day.

24 But I say unto you, That it shall be more tolerable for the land of Sod'om in the day of judgment, than for thee.

25 ¶ At that time Je'sus answered and said, I thank thee, O Father, Lord of heaven and earth, because thou hast hid these things from the wise and prudent, and hast revealed them unto babes.

26 Even so, Father: for so it seemed good in thy sight.

27 All things are delivered unto me of my Father: and no man knoweth the Son, but the Father; neither knoweth any man the Father, save the Son, and *he* to whomsoever the Son will reveal *him*.

28 ¶ Come unto me, all *ye* that

labor and are heavy laden, and I will give you rest.

29 Take my yoke upon you, and learn of me; for I am meek and lowly in heart: and ye shall find rest unto your souls.

30 For my yoke *is* easy, and my burden is light.

12 At that time Je′sus went on the sabbath day through the corn; and his disciples were an hungered, and began to pluck the ears of corn, and to eat.

2 But when the Phar′i-sees saw *it*, they said unto him, Behold, thy disciples do that which is not lawful to do upon the sabbath day.

3 But he said unto them, Have ye not read what Da′vid did, when he was an hungered, and they that were with him;

4 How he entered into the house of God, and did eat the showbread, which was not lawful for him to eat, neither for them which were with him, but only for the priests?

5 Or have ye not read in the law, how that on the sabbath days the priests in the temple profane the sabbath, and are blameless?

6 But I say unto you, That in this place is *one* greater than the temple.

7 But if ye had known what *this* meaneth, I will have mercy, and not sacrifice, ye would not have condemned the guiltless.

8 For the Son of man is Lord even of the sabbath day.

9 And when he was departed thence, he went into their synagogue:

10 ¶ And, behold, there was a man which had *his* hand withered. And they asked him, saying, Is it lawful to heal on the sabbath days? that they might accuse him.

11 And he said unto them, What man shall there be among you, that shall have one sheep, and if it fall into a pit on the sabbath day, will he not lay hold on it, and lift *it* out?

12 How much then is a man better than a sheep? Wherefore it is lawful to do well on the sabbath days.

13 Then saith he to the man, Stretch forth thine hand. And he stretched *it* forth; and it was restored whole, like as the other.

14 ¶ Then the Phar′i-sees went out, and held a council against him, how they might destroy him.

15 But when Je′sus knew *it*, he withdrew himself from thence: and great multitudes followed him, and he healed them all;

16 And charged them that they should not make him known:

17 That it might be fulfilled which was spoken by I-sa′iah the prophet, saying,

18 Behold my servant, whom I have chosen; my beloved, in whom my soul is well-pleased: I will put my spirit upon him, and he shall show judgment to the Gen′tiles.

19 He shall not strive, nor cry; neither shall any man hear his voice in the streets.

20 A bruised reed shall he not break, and smoking flax shall he

not quench, till he send forth judgment unto victory.

21 And in his name shall the Gen′tiles trust.

22 ¶ Then was brought unto him one possessed with a devil, blind, and dumb: and he healed him, insomuch that the blind and dumb both spake and saw.

23 And all the people were amazed, and said, Is not this the son of Da′vid?

24 But when the Phar′i-sees heard it, they said, This fellow doth not cast out devils, but by Be-el′ze-bub the prince of the devils.

25 And Je′sus knew their thoughts, and said unto them, Every kingdom divided against itself is brought to desolation; and every city or house divided against itself shall not stand.

26 And if Sa′tan cast out Sa′tan, he is divided against himself; how shall then his kingdom stand?

27 And if I by Be-el′ze-bub cast out devils, by whom do your children cast them out? therefore they shall be your judges.

28 But if I cast out devils by the Spirit of God, then the kingdom of God is come unto you.

29 Or else how can one enter into a strong man's house, and spoil his goods, except he first bind the strong man? and then he will spoil his house.

30 He that is not with me is against me; and he that gathereth not with me scattereth abroad.

31 ¶ Wherefore I say unto you, All manner of sin and blas-phemy shall be forgiven unto men: but the blasphemy against the Ho′ly Ghost shall not be forgiven unto men.

32 And whosoever speaketh a word against the Son of man, it shall be forgiven him: but whosoever speaketh against the Ho′ly Ghost, it shall not be forgiven him, neither in this world, neither in the world to come.

33 Either make the tree good, and his fruit good; or else make the tree corrupt, and his fruit corrupt: for the tree is known by his fruit.

34 O generation of vipers, how can ye, being evil, speak good things? for out of the abundance of the heart the mouth speaketh.

35 A good man out of the good treasure of the heart bringeth forth good things: and an evil man out of the evil treasure bringeth forth evil things.

36 But I say unto you, That every idle word that men shall speak, they shall give account thereof in the day of judgment.

37 For by thy words thou shalt be justified, and by thy words thou shalt be condemned.

38 ¶ Then certain of the scribes and of the Phar′i-sees answered, saying, Master, we would see a sign from thee.

39 But he answered and said unto them, An evil and adulterous generation seeketh after a sign; and there shall no sign be given to it, but the sign of the prophet Jo′nah:

40 For as Jo′nah was three days and three nights in the whale's belly; so shall the Son of man be

three days and three nights in the heart of the earth.

41 The men of Nin´e-veh shall rise in judgment with this generation, and shall condemn it: because they repented at the preaching of Jo´nah; and, behold, a greater than Jo´nah *is* here.

42 The queen of the south shall rise up in the judgment with this generation, and shall condemn it: for she came from the uttermost parts of the earth to hear the wisdom of Sol´o-mon; and, behold, a greater than Sol´o-mon *is* here.

43 When the unclean spirit is gone out of a man, he walketh through dry places, seeking rest, and findeth none.

44 Then he saith, I will return into my house from whence I came out; and when he is come, he findeth *it* empty, swept, and garnished.

45 Then goeth he, and taketh with himself seven other spirits more wicked than himself, and they enter in and dwell there: and the last *state* of that man is worse than the first. Even so shall it be also unto this wicked generation.

46 ¶ While he yet talked to the people, behold, *his* mother and his brethren stood without, desiring to speak with him.

47 Then one said unto him, Behold, thy mother and thy brethren stand without, desiring to speak with thee.

48 But he answered and said unto him that told him, Who is

my mother? and who are my brethren?

49 And he stretched forth his hand toward his disciples, and said, Behold my mother and my brethren!

50 For whosoever shall do the will of my Father which is in heaven, the same is my brother, and sister, and mother.

13 The same day went Je´sus out of the house, and sat by the seaside.

2 And great multitudes were gathered together unto him, so that he went into a ship, and sat; and the whole multitude stood on the shore.

3 And he spake many things unto them in parables, saying, Behold, a sower went forth to sow;

4 And when he sowed, some *seeds* fell by the wayside, and the fowls came and devoured them up:

5 Some fell upon stony places, where they had not much earth: and forthwith they sprung up, because they had no deepness of earth:

6 And when the sun was up, they were scorched; and because they had no root, they withered away.

7 And some fell among thorns; and the thorns sprung up, and choked them:

8 But other fell into good ground, and brought forth fruit, some an hundredfold, some sixtyfold, some thirtyfold.

9 Who hath ears to hear, let him hear.

10 And the disciples came, and

said unto him, Why speakest thou unto them in parables?

11 He answered and said unto them, Because it is given unto you to know the mysteries of the kingdom of heaven, but to them it is not given.

12 For whosoever hath, to him shall be given, and he shall have more abundance: but whosoever hath not, from him shall be taken away even that he hath.

13 Therefore speak I to them in parables: because they seeing see not, and hearing they hear not, neither do they understand.

14 And in them is fulfilled the prophecy of I-sa'iah, which saith, By hearing ye shall hear, and shall not understand; and seeing ye shall see, and shall not perceive:

15 For this people's heart is waxed gross, and *their* ears are dull of hearing, and their eyes they have closed; lest at anytime they should see with *their* eyes, and hear with *their* ears, and should understand with *their* heart, and should be converted, and I should heal them.

16 But blessed *are* your eyes, for they see: and your ears, for they hear.

17 For verily I say unto you, That many prophets and righteous *men* have desired to see *those things* which ye see, and have not seen *them;* and to hear *those things* which ye hear, and have not heard *them.*

18 ¶ Hear ye therefore the parable of the sower.

19 When anyone heareth the word of the kingdom, and under

standeth *it* not, then cometh the wicked *one,* and catcheth away that which was sown in his heart. This is he which received seed by the wayside.

20 But he that received the seed into stony places, the same is he that heareth the word, and anon with joy receiveth it;

21 Yet hath he not root in himself, but endureth for a while: for when tribulation or persecution ariseth because of the word, by and by he is offended.

22 He also that received seed among the thorns is he that heareth the word; and the care of this world, and the deceitfulness of riches, choke the word, and he becometh unfruitful.

23 But he that received seed into the good ground is he that heareth the word, and understandeth *it;* which also beareth fruit, and bringeth forth, some an hundredfold, some sixty, some thirty.

24 ¶ Another parable put he forth unto them, saying, The kingdom of heaven is likened unto a man which sowed good seed in his field:

25 But while men slept, his enemy came and sowed tares among the wheat, and went his way.

26 But when the blade was sprung up, and brought forth fruit, then appeared the tares also.

27 So the servants of the householder came and said unto him, Sir, didst not thou sow good seed in thy field? from whence then hath it tares?

28 He said unto them, An enemy hath done this. The servants said unto him, Wilt thou then that we go and gather them up?

29 But he said, Nay; lest while ye gather up the tares, ye root up also the wheat with them.

30 Let both grow together until the harvest: and in the time of harvest I will say to the reapers, Gather ye together first the tares, and bind them in bundles to burn them: but gather the wheat into my barn.

31 ¶ Another parable put he forth unto them, saying, The kingdom of heaven is like to a grain of mustard seed, which a man took, and sowed in his field:

32 Which indeed is the least of all seeds: but when it is grown, it is the greatest among herbs, and becometh a tree, so that the birds of the air come and lodge in the branches thereof.

33 ¶ Another parable spake he unto them; The kingdom of heaven is like unto leaven, which a woman took, and hid in three measures of meal, till the whole was leavened.

34 All these things spake Je´sus unto the multitude in parables; and without a parable spake he not unto them:

35 That it might be fulfilled which was spoken by the prophet, saying, I will open my mouth in parables; I will utter things which have been kept secret from the foundation of the world.

36 Then Je´sus sent the multitude away, and went into the house: and his disciples came unto him, saying, Declare unto us the parable of the tares of the field.

37 He answered and said unto them, He that soweth the good seed is the Son of man;

38 The field is the world; the good seed are the children of the kingdom; but the tares are the children of the wicked one;

39 The enemy that sowed them is the devil; the harvest is the end of the world; and the reapers are the angels.

40 As therefore the tares are gathered and burned in the fire; so shall it be in the end of this world.

41 The Son of man shall send forth his angels, and they shall gather out of his kingdom all things that offend, and them which do iniquity;

42 And shall cast them into a furnace of fire: there shall be wailing and gnashing of teeth.

43 Then shall the righteous shine forth as the sun in the kingdom of their Father. Who hath ears to hear, let him hear.

44 ¶ Again, the kingdom of heaven is like unto treasure hid in a field; the which when a man hath found, he hideth, and for joy thereof goeth and selleth all that he hath, and buyeth that field.

45 ¶ Again, the kingdom of heaven is like unto a merchant man, seeking goodly pearls:

46 Who, when he had found one pearl of great price, went

and sold all that he had, and bought it.

47 ¶ Again, the kingdom of heaven is like unto a net, that was cast into the sea, and gathered of every kind:

48 Which, when it was full, they drew to shore, and sat down, and gathered the good into vessels, but cast the bad away.

49 So shall it be at the end of the world: the angels shall come forth, and sever the wicked from among the just,

50 And shall cast them into the furnace of fire: there shall be wailing and gnashing of teeth.

51 Je'sus saith unto them, Have ye understood all these things? They say unto him, Yea, Lord.

52 Then said he unto them, Therefore every scribe which is instructed unto the kingdom of heaven is like unto a man that is an householder, which bringeth forth out of his treasure things new and old.

53 ¶ And it came to pass, that when Je'sus had finished these parables, he departed thence.

54 And when he was come into his own country, he taught them in their synagogue, insomuch that they were astonished, and said, Whence hath this man this wisdom, and these mighty works?

55 Is not this the carpenter's son? is not his mother called Ma'ry? and his brethren, James, and Jo'ses, and Si'mon, and Ju'das?

56 And his sisters, are they not all with us? Whence then hath this man all these things?

57 And they were offended in him. But Je'sus said unto them, A prophet is not without honor, save in his own country, and in his own house.

58 And he did not many mighty works there because of their unbelief.

14 At that time Her'od the tetrarch heard of the fame of Je'sus,

2 And said unto his servants, This is John the Bap'tist; he is risen from the dead; and therefore mighty works do show forth themselves in him.

3 ¶ For Her'od had laid hold on John, and bound him, and put him in prison for He-ro'di-as' sake, his brother Phil'ip's wife.

4 For John said unto him, It is not lawful for thee to have her.

5 And when he would have put him to death, he feared the multitude, because they counted him as a prophet.

6 But when Her'od's birthday was kept, the daughter of He-ro'di-as danced before them, and pleased Her'od.

7 Whereupon he promised with an oath to give her whatsoever she would ask.

8 And she, being before instructed of her mother, said, Give me here John Bap'tist's head in a charger.

9 And the king was sorry: nevertheless for the oath's sake, and them which sat with him at meat, he commanded it to be given her.

10 And he sent, and beheaded John in the prison.

11 And his head was brought in a charger, and given to the damsel: and she brought *it* to her mother.

12 And his disciples came, and took up the body, and buried it, and went and told Je'sus.

13 ¶ When Je'sus heard *of it*, he departed thence by ship into a desert place apart: and when the people had heard *thereof*, they followed him on foot out of the cities.

14 And Je'sus went forth, and saw a great multitude, and was moved with compassion toward them, and he healed their sick.

15 ¶ And when it was evening, his disciples came to him, saying, This is a desert place, and the time is now past; send the multitude away, that they may go into the villages, and buy themselves victuals.

16 But Je'sus said unto them, They need not depart; give ye them to eat.

17 And they say unto him, We have here but five loaves, and two fishes.

18 He said, Bring them hither to me.

19 And he commanded the multitude to sit down on the grass, and took the five loaves, and the two fishes, and looking up to heaven, he blessed, and brake, and gave the loaves to *his* disciples, and the disciples to the multitude.

20 And they did all eat, and were filled: and they took up of the fragments that remained twelve baskets full.

21 And they that had eaten were about five thousand men, beside women and children.

22 ¶ And straightway Je'sus constrained his disciples to get into a ship, and to go before him unto the other side, while he sent the multitudes away.

23 And when he had sent the multitudes away, he went up into a mountain apart to pray: and when the evening was come, he was there alone.

24 But the ship was now in the midst of the sea, tossed with waves: for the wind was contrary.

25 And in the fourth watch of the night Je'sus went unto them, walking on the sea.

26 And when the disciples saw him walking on the sea, they were troubled, saying, It is a spirit; and they cried out for fear.

27 But straightway Je'sus spake unto them, saying, Be of good cheer; it is I; be not afraid.

28 And Pe'ter answered him and said, Lord, if it be thou, bid me come unto thee on the water.

29 And he said, Come. And when Pe'ter was come down out of the ship, he walked on the water, to go to Je'sus.

30 But when he saw the wind boisterous, he was afraid; and beginning to sink, he cried, saying, Lord, save me.

31 And immediately Je'sus stretched forth *his* hand, and caught him, and said unto him,

O thou of little faith, wherefore didst thou doubt?

32 And when they were come into the ship, the wind ceased.

33 Then they that were in the ship came and worshipped him, saying, Of a truth thou art the Son of God.

34 ¶ And when they were gone over, they came into the land of Gen-nes'a-ret.

35 And when the men of that place had knowledge of him, they sent out into all that country round about, and brought unto him all that were diseased;

36 And besought him that they might only touch the hem of his garment: and as many as touched were made perfectly whole.

15 Then came to Je'sus scribes and Phar'i-sees, which were of Je-ru'sa-lem, saying,

2 Why do thy disciples transgress the tradition of the elders? for they wash not their hands when they eat bread.

3 But he answered and said unto them, Why do ye also transgress the commandment of God by your tradition?

4 For God commanded, saying, Honor thy father and mother: and, He that curseth father or mother, let him die the death.

5 But ye say, Whosoever shall say to his father or his mother, It is a gift, by whatsoever thou mightest be profited by me;

6 And honor not his father or his mother, he shall be free. Thus have ye made the com mandment of God of none effect by your tradition.

7 Ye hypocrites, well did I-sa'-iah prophesy of you, saying,

8 This people draweth nigh unto me with their mouth, and honoreth me with their lips; but their heart is far from me.

9 But in vain they do worship me, teaching for doctrines the commandments of men.

10 ¶ And he called the multitude, and said unto them, Hear, and understand:

11 Not that which goeth into the mouth defileth a man; but that which cometh out of the mouth, this defileth a man.

12 Then came his disciples, and said unto him, Knowest thou that the Phar'i-sees were offended, after they heard this saying?

13 But he answered and said, Every plant, which my heavenly Father hath not planted, shall be rooted up.

14 Let them alone: they be blind leaders of the blind. And if the blind lead the blind, both shall fall into the ditch.

15 Then answered Pe'ter and said unto him, Declare unto us this parable.

16 And Je'sus said, Are ye also yet without understanding?

17 Do not ye yet understand, that whatsoever entereth in at the mouth goeth into the belly, and is cast out into the draught?

18 But those things which proceed out of the mouth come forth from the heart; and they defile the man.

19 For out of the heart proceed

evil thoughts, murders, adulteries, fornications, thefts, false witness, blasphemies:

20 These are the things which defile a man: but to eat with unwashen hands defileth not a man.

21 ¶ Then Je′sus went thence, and departed into the coasts of Tyre and Si′don.

22 And, behold, a woman of Ca′naan came out of the same coasts, and cried unto him, saying, Have mercy on me, O Lord, thou son of Da′vid; my daughter is grievously vexed with a devil.

23 But he answered her not a word. And his disciples came and besought him, saying, Send her away; for she crieth after us.

24 But he answered and said, I am not sent but unto the lost sheep of the house of Is′ra-el.

25 Then came she and worshiped him, saying, Lord, help me.

26 But he answered and said, It is not meet to take the children's bread, and to cast it to dogs.

27 And she said, Truth, Lord: yet the dogs eat of the crumbs which fall from their masters' table.

28 Then Je′sus answered and said unto her, O woman, great is thy faith: be it unto thee even as thou wilt. And her daughter was made whole from that very hour.

29 And Je′sus departed from thence, and came nigh unto the sea of Gal′i-lee; and went up into a mountain, and sat down there.

30 And great multitudes came unto him, having with them those that were lame, blind, dumb, maimed, and many others, and cast them down at Je′sus' feet; and he healed them:

31 Insomuch that the multitude wondered, when they saw the dumb to speak, the maimed to be whole, the lame to walk, and the blind to see: and they glorified the God of Is′ra-el.

32 ¶ Then Je′sus called his disciples unto him, and said, I have compassion on the multitude, because they continue with me now three days, and have nothing to eat: and I will not send them away fasting, lest they faint in the way.

33 And his disciples say unto him, Whence should we have so much bread in the wilderness, as to fill so great a multitude?

34 And Je′sus saith unto them, How many loaves have ye? And they said, Seven, and a few little fishes.

35 And he commanded the multitude to sit down on the ground.

36 And he took the seven loaves and the fishes, and gave thanks, and brake them, and gave to his disciples, and the disciples to the multitude.

37 And they did all eat, and were filled: and they took up of the broken meat that was left seven baskets full.

38 And they that did eat were four thousand men, beside women and children.

39 And he sent away the multitude, and took ship, and came into the coasts of Mag'da-la.

16 The Phar'i-sees also with the Sad'du-cees came, and tempting desired him that he would show them a sign from heaven.

2 He answered and said unto them, When it is evening, *ye* say, *It will be* fair weather: for the sky is red.

3 And in the morning, *It will be* foul weather today: for the sky is red and lowering. O *ye* hypocrites, ye can discern the face of the sky; but can ye not *discern* the signs of the times?

4 A wicked and adulterous generation seeketh after a sign; and there shall no sign be given unto it, but the sign of the prophet Jo'nah. And he left them, and departed.

5 And when his disciples were come to the other side, they had forgotten to take bread.

6 ¶ Then Je'sus said unto them, Take heed and beware of the leaven of the Phar'i-sees and the Sad'du-cees.

7 And they reasoned among themselves, saying, It is because we have taken no bread.

8 *Which* when Je'sus perceived, he said unto them, O *ye* of little faith, why reason ye among yourselves, because ye have brought no bread?

9 Do ye not yet understand, neither remember the five loaves of the five thousand, and how many baskets ye took up?

10 Neither the seven loaves of the four thousand, and how many baskets ye took up?

11 How is it that ye do not understand that I spake *it* not to you concerning bread, that ye should beware of the leaven of the Phar'i-sees and of the Sad'du-cees?

12 Then understood they how that he bade *them* not beware of the leaven of bread, but of the doctrine of the Phar'i-sees and of the Sad'du-cees.

13 ¶ When Je'sus came into the coasts of Cæs-a-re'a Phi-lip'pi, he asked his disciples, saying, Whom do men say that I the Son of man am?

14 And they said, Some *say that thou art* John the Bap'tist: some, E-li'jah; and others, Jer-e-mi'ah, or one of the prophets.

15 He saith unto them, But whom say ye that I am?

16 And Si'mon Pe'ter answered and said, Thou art the Christ, the Son of the living God.

17 And Je'sus answered and said unto him, Blessed art thou, Si'mon Bar-jo'na: for flesh and blood hath not revealed *it* unto thee, but my Father which is in heaven.

18 And I say also unto thee, That thou art Pe'ter, and upon this rock I will build my church; and the gates of hell shall not prevail against it.

19 And I will give unto thee the keys of the kingdom of heaven: and whatsoever thou shalt bind on earth shall be bound in heaven: and whatsoever thou shalt loose on earth shall be loosed in heaven.

20 Then charged he his disciples that they should tell no man that he was Je'sus the Christ.

21 ¶ From that time forth began Je'sus to show unto his disciples, how that he must go unto Je-ru'sa-lem, and suffer many things of the elders and chief priests and scribes, and be killed, and be raised again the third day.

22 Then Pe'ter took him, and began to rebuke him, saying, Be it far from thee, Lord: this shall not be unto thee.

23 But he turned, and said unto Pe'ter, Get thee behind me, Sa'tan: thou art an offense unto me: for thou savorest not the things that be of God, but those that be of men.

24 ¶ Then said Je'sus unto his disciples, If any *man* will come after me, let him deny himself, and take up his cross, and follow me.

25 For whosoever will save his life shall lose it: and whosoever will lose his life for my sake shall find it.

26 For what is a man profited, if he shall gain the whole world, and lose his own soul? or what shall a man give in exchange for his soul?

27 For the Son of man shall come in the glory of his Father with his angels; and then he shall reward every man according to his works.

28 Verily I say unto you, There be some standing here, which shall not taste of death, till they see the Son of man coming in his kingdom.

17 And after six days Je'sus taketh Pe'ter, James, and John his brother, and bringeth them up into an high mountain apart,

2 And was transfigured before them: and his face did shine as the sun, and his raiment was white as the light.

3 And, behold, there appeared unto them Mo'ses and E-li'jah talking with him.

4 Then answered Pe'ter, and said unto Je'sus, Lord, it is good for us to be here: if thou wilt, let us make here three tabernacles; one for thee, and one for Mo'ses, and one for E-li'jah.

5 While he yet spake, behold, a bright cloud overshadowed them: and behold a voice out of the cloud, which said, This is my beloved Son, in whom I am well pleased; hear ye him.

6 And when the disciples heard *it,* they fell on their face, and were sore afraid.

7 And Je'sus came and touched them, and said, Arise, be not afraid.

8 And when they had lifted up their eyes, they saw no man, save Je'sus only.

9 And as they came down from the mountain, Je'sus charged them, saying, Tell the vision to no man, until the Son of man be risen again from the dead.

10 And his disciples asked him, saying, Why then say the scribes that E-li'jah must first come?

11 And Je'sus answered and said unto them, E-li'jah truly shall first come, and restore all things.

12 But I say unto you, That E-li'jah is come already, and they knew him not, but have done unto him whatsoever they listed. Likewise shall also the Son of man suffer of them.

13 Then the disciples understood that he spake unto them of John the Bap'tist.

14 ¶ And when they were come to the multitude, there came to him a certain man, kneeling down to him, and saying,

15 Lord, have mercy on my son: for he is lunatic, and sore vexed: for ofttimes he falleth into the fire, and oft into the water.

16 And I brought him to thy disciples, and they could not cure him.

17 Then Je'sus answered and said, O faithless and perverse generation, how long shall I be with you? how long shall I suffer you? bring him hither to me.

18 And Je'sus rebuked the devil; and he departed out of him: and the child was cured from that very hour.

19 Then came the disciples to Je'sus apart, and said, Why could not we cast him out?

20 And Je'sus said unto them, Because of your unbelief. for verily I say unto you, If ye have faith as a grain of mustard seed, ye shall say unto this mountain, Remove hence to yonder place; and it shall remove; and nothing shall be impossible unto you.

21 Howbeit this kind goeth not out but by prayer and fasting.

22 ¶ And while they abode in Gal'i-lee, Je'sus said unto them,

The Son of man shall be betrayed into the hands of men:

23 And they shall kill him, and the third day he shall be raised again. And they were exceeding sorry.

24 ¶ And when they were come to Ca-per'na-um, they that received tribute money came to Pe'ter, and said, Doth not your master pay tribute?

25 He saith, Yes. And when he was come into the house, Je'sus prevented him, saying, What thinkest thou, Si'mon? of whom do the kings of the earth take custom or tribute? of their own children, or of strangers?

26 Pe'ter saith unto him, Of strangers. Je'sus saith unto him, Then are the children free.

27 Notwithstanding, lest we should offend them, go thou to the sea, and cast an hook, and take up the fish that first cometh up; and when thou hast opened his mouth, thou shalt find a piece of money: that take, and give unto them for me and thee.

18 At the same time came the disciples unto Je'sus, saying, Who is the greatest in the kingdom of heaven?

2 And Je'sus called a little child unto him, and set him in the midst of them,

3 And said, Verily I say unto you, Except ye be converted, and become as little children, ye shall not enter into the kingdom of heaven.

4 Whosoever therefore shall humble himself as this little child, the same is greatest in the kingdom of heaven.

5 And whoso shall receive one such little child in my name receiveth me.

6 But whoso shall offend one of these little ones which believe in me, it were better for him that a millstone were hanged about his neck, and *that* he were drowned in the depth of the sea.

7 ¶ Woe unto the world because of offenses! for it must needs be that offenses come; but woe to that man by whom the offense cometh!

8 Wherefore if thy hand or thy foot offend thee, cut them off, and cast *them* from thee: it is better for thee to enter into life halt or maimed, rather than having two hands or two feet to be cast into everlasting fire.

9 And if thine eye offend thee, pluck it out, and cast *it* from thee: it is better for thee to enter into life with one eye, rather than having two eyes to be cast into hell fire.

10 Take heed that ye despise not one of these little ones; for I say unto you, That in heaven their angels do always behold the face of my Father which is in heaven.

11 For the Son of man is come to save that which was lost.

12 How think ye? if a man have an hundred sheep, and one of them be gone astray, doth he not leave the ninety and nine, and goeth into the mountains, and seeketh that which is gone astray?

13 And if so be that he find it, verily I say unto you, he re-joiceth more of that *sheep*, than of the ninety and nine which went not astray.

14 Even so it is not the will of your Father which is in heaven, that one of these little ones should perish.

15 ¶ Moreover if thy brother shall trespass against thee, go and tell him his fault between thee and him alone: if he shall hear thee, thou hast gained thy brother.

16 But if he will not hear *thee, then* take with thee one or two more, that in the mouth of two or three witnesses every word may be established.

17 And if he shall neglect to hear them, tell *it* unto the church: but if he neglect to hear the church, let him be unto thee as an heathen man and a publican.

18 Verily I say unto you, Whatsoever ye shall bind on earth shall be bound in heaven: and whatsoever ye shall loose on earth shall be loosed in heaven.

19 Again I say unto you, That if two of you shall agree on earth as touching anything that they shall ask, it shall be done for them of my Father which is in heaven.

20 For where two or three are gathered together in my name, there am I in the midst of them.

21 ¶ Then came Pe'ter to him, and said, Lord, how oft shall my brother sin against me, and I forgive him? till seven times?

22 Je'sus saith unto him, I say not unto thee, Until seven

times: but, Until seventy times seven.

23 ¶ Therefore is the kingdom of heaven likened unto a certain king, which would take account of his servants.

24 And when he had begun to reckon, one was brought unto him, which owed him ten thousand talents.

25 But forasmuch as he had not to pay, his lord commanded him to be sold, and his wife, and children, and all that he had, and payment to be made.

26 The servant therefore fell down, and worshipped him, saying, Lord, have patience with me, and I will pay thee all.

27 Then the lord of that servant was moved with compassion, and loosed him, and forgave him the debt.

28 But the same servant went out, and found one of his fellow servants, which owed him an hundred pence: and he laid hands on him, and took him by the throat, saying, Pay me that thou owest.

29 And his fellow servant fell down at his feet, and besought him, saying, Have patience with me, and I will pay thee all.

30 And he would not: but went and cast him into prison, till he should pay the debt.

31 So when his fellow servants saw what was done, they were very sorry, and came and told unto their lord all that was done.

32 Then his lord, after that he had called him, said unto him, O thou wicked servant, I forgave thee all that debt, because thou desiredst me:

33 Shouldest not thou also have had compassion on thy fellow servant, even as I had pity on thee?

34 And his lord was wroth, and delivered him to the tormentors, till he should pay all that was due unto him.

35 So likewise shall my heavenly Father do also unto you, if ye from your hearts forgive not everyone his brother their trespasses.

19 And it came to pass, that when Jesus had finished these sayings, he departed from Gal'i·lee, and came into the coasts of Ju·dæ'a beyond Jor'-dan;

2 And great multitudes followed him; and he healed them there.

3 ¶ The Phar'i·sees also came unto him, tempting him, and saying unto him, Is it lawful for a man to put away his wife for every cause?

4 And he answered and said unto them, Have ye not read, that he which made them at the beginning made them male and female,

5 And said, For this cause shall a man leave father and mother, and shall cleave to his wife: and they twain shall be one flesh?

6 Wherefore they are no more twain, but one flesh. What therefore God hath joined together, let not man put asunder.

7 They say unto him, Why did Mo'ses then command to give a

writing of divorcement, and to put her away?

8 He saith unto them, Mo'ses because of the hardness of your hearts suffered you to put away your wives: but from the beginning it was not so.

9 And I say unto you, Whosoever shall put away his wife, except it be for fornication, and shall marry another, committeth adultery: and whoso marrieth her which is put away doth commit adultery.

10 ¶ His disciples say unto him, If the case of the man be so with his wife, it is not good to marry.

11 But he said unto them, All men cannot receive this saying, save they to whom it is given.

12 For there are some eunuchs, which were so born from their mother's womb: and there are some eunuchs, which were made eunuchs of men: and there be eunuchs, which have made themselves eunuchs for the kingdom of heaven's sake. He that is able to receive it, let him receive it.

13 ¶ Then were there brought unto him little children, that he should put his hands on them, and pray: and the disciples rebuked them.

14 But Je'sus said, Suffer little children, and forbid them not, to come unto me: for of such is the kingdom of heaven.

15 And he laid his hands on them, and departed thence.

16 ¶ And, behold, one came and said unto him, Good Master, what good thing shall I do, that I may have eternal life?

17 And he said unto him, Why callest thou me good? there is none good but one, that is, God: but if thou wilt enter into life, keep the commandments.

18 He saith unto him, Which? Je'sus said, Thou shalt do no murder, Thou shalt not commit adultery, Thou shalt not steal, Thou shalt not bear false witness,

19 Honor thy father and thy mother: and, Thou shalt love thy neighbor as thyself.

20 The young man saith unto him, All these things have I kept from my youth up: what lack I yet?

21 Je'sus said unto him, If thou wilt be perfect, go and sell that thou hast, and give to the poor, and thou shalt have treasure in heaven: and come and follow me.

22 But when the young man heard that saying, he went away sorrowful: for he had great possessions.

23 ¶ Then said Je'sus unto his disciples, Verily I say unto you, That a rich man shall hardly enter into the kingdom of heaven.

24 And again I say unto you, It is easier for a camel to go through the eye of a needle, than for a rich man to enter into the kingdom of God.

25 When his disciples heard it, they were exceedingly amazed, saying, Who then can be saved?

26 But Je'sus beheld them, and said unto them, With men this is impossible; but with God all things are possible.

27 ¶ Then answered Pe'ter and said unto him, Behold, we have forsaken all, and followed thee; what shall we have therefore?

28 And Je'sus said unto them, Verily I say unto you, That ye which have followed me, in the regeneration when the Son of man shall sit in the throne of his glory, ye also shall sit upon twelve thrones, judging the twelve tribes of Is'ra-el.

29 And everyone that hath forsaken houses, or brethren, or sisters, or father, or mother, or wife, or children, or lands, for my name's sake, shall receive an hundredfold, and shall inherit everlasting life.

30 But many that are first shall be last; and the last shall be first.

20 For the kingdom of heaven is like unto a man that is an householder, which went out early in the morning to hire laborers into his vineyard.

2 And when he had agreed with the laborers for a penny a day, he sent them into his vineyard.

3 And he went out about the third hour, and saw others standing idle in the market place,

4 And said unto them; Go ye also into the vineyard, and whatsoever is right I will give you. And they went their way.

5 Again he went out about the sixth and ninth hour, and did likewise.

6 And about the eleventh hour he went out, and found others standing idle, and saith unto them, Why stand ye here all the day idle?

7 They say unto him, Because no man hath hired us. He saith unto them, Go ye also into the vineyard; and whatsoever is right, that shall ye receive.

8 So when even was come, the lord of the vineyard saith unto his steward, Call the laborers, and give them their hire, beginning from the last unto the first.

9 And when they came that were hired about the eleventh hour, they received every man a penny.

10 But when the first came, they supposed that they should have received more; and they likewise received every man a penny.

11 And when they had received it, they murmured against the goodman of the house,

12 Saying, These last have wrought but one hour, and thou hast made them equal unto us, which have borne the burden and heat of the day.

13 But he answered one of them, and said, Friend, I do thee no wrong: didst not thou agree with me for a penny?

14 Take that thine is, and go thy way: I will give unto this last, even as unto thee.

15 Is it not lawful for me to do what I will with mine own? Is thine eye evil, because I am good?

16 So the last shall be first, and the first last: for many be called, but few chosen.

17 ¶ And Je'sus going up to Je-ru'sa-lem took the twelve

disciples apart in the way, and said unto them,

18 Behold, we go up to Je·ru'sa·lem; and the Son of man shall be betrayed unto the chief priests and unto the scribes, and they shall condemn him to death,

19 And shall deliver him to the Gen'tiles to mock, and to scourge, and to crucify *him*: and the third day he shall rise again.

20 ¶ Then came to him the mother of Zeb'e·dee's children with her sons, worshipping *him*, and desiring a certain thing of him.

21 And he said unto her, What wilt thou? She saith unto him, Grant that these my two sons may sit, the one on my right hand, and the other on the left, in thy kingdom.

22 But Je'sus answered and said, Ye know not what ye ask. Are ye able to drink of the cup that I shall drink of, and to be baptized with the baptism that I am baptized with? They say unto him, We are able.

23 And he saith unto them, Ye shall drink indeed of my cup, and be baptized with the baptism that I am baptized with: but to sit on my right hand, and on my left, is not mine to give, but *it shall be given to them* for whom *it* is prepared of my Father.

24 And when the ten heard *it*, they were moved with indignation against the two brethren.

25 But Je'sus called them *unto him*, and said, Ye know that the princes of the Gen'tiles exercise dominion over them, and they that are great exercise authority upon them.

26 But it shall not be so among you: but whosoever will be great among you, let him be your minister;

27 And whosoever will be chief among you, let him be your servant:

28 Even as the Son of man came not to be ministered unto, but to minister, and to give his life a ransom for many.

29 And as they departed from Jer'i·cho, a great multitude followed him.

30 ¶ And, behold, two blind men sitting by the wayside, when they heard that Je'sus passed by, cried out, saying, Have mercy on us, O Lord, *thou* son of Da'vid.

31 And the multitude rebuked them, because they should hold their peace: but they cried the more, saying, Have mercy on us, O Lord, *thou* son of Da'vid.

32 And Je'sus stood still, and called them, and said, What will ye that I shall do unto you?

33 They say unto him, Lord, that our eyes may be opened.

34 So Je'sus had compassion *on them*, and touched their eyes: and immediately their eyes received sight, and they followed him.

21 And when they drew nigh unto Je·ru'sa·lem, and were come to Beth'pha·ge, unto the mount of Ol'ives, then sent Je'sus two disciples,

2 Saying unto them, Go into the village over against you, and

straightway ye shall find an ass tied, and a colt with her: loose *them*, and bring *them* unto me.

3 And if any *man* say aught unto you, ye shall say, The Lord hath need of them; and straightway he will send them.

4 All this was done, that it might be fulfilled which was spoken by the prophet, saying,

5 Tell ye the daughter of Zi'on, Behold, thy King cometh unto thee, meek, and sitting upon an ass, and a colt the foal of an ass.

6 And the disciples went, and did as Je'sus commanded them,

7 And brought the ass, and the colt, and put on them their clothes, and they set *him* thereon.

8 And a very great multitude spread their garments in the way; others cut down branches from the trees, and strewed *them* in the way.

9 And the multitudes that went before, and that followed, cried, saying, Ho-san'na to the son of Da'vid: Blessed *is* he that cometh in the name of the Lord; Ho-san'na in the highest.

10 And when he was come into Je-ru'sa-lem, all the city was moved, saying, Who is this?

11 And the multitude said, This is Je'sus the prophet of Naz'a-reth of Gal'i-lee.

12 ¶ And Je'sus went into the temple of God, and cast out all them that sold and bought in the temple, and overthrew the tables of the money changers, and the seats of them that sold doves,

13 And said unto them, It is written, My house shall be called the house of prayer; but ye have made it a den of thieves.

14 And the blind and the lame came to him in the temple; and he healed them.

15 And when the chief priests and scribes saw the wonderful things that he did, and the children crying in the temple, and saying, Ho-san'na to the son of Da'vid; they were sore displeased,

16 And said unto him, Hearest thou what these say? And Je'sus saith unto them, Yea; have ye never read, Out of the mouth of babes and sucklings thou hast perfected praise?

17 ¶ And he left them, and went out of the city into Beth'a-ny; and he lodged there.

18 Now in the morning as he returned into the city, he hungered.

19 And when he saw a fig tree in the way, he came to it, and found nothing thereon, but leaves only, and said unto it, Let no fruit grow on thee henceforward forever. And presently the fig tree withered away.

20 And when the disciples saw *it*, they marveled, saying, How soon is the fig tree withered away!

21 Je'sus answered and said unto them, Verily I say unto you, If ye have faith, and doubt not, ye shall not only do this which *is done* to the fig tree, but also if ye shall say unto this mountain, Be thou removed,

and be thou cast into the sea; it shall be done.

22 And all things, whatsoever ye shall ask in prayer, believing, ye shall receive.

23 ¶ And when he was come into the temple, the chief priests and the elders of the people came unto him as he was teaching, and said, By what authority doest thou these things? and who gave thee this authority?

24 And Je′sus answered and said unto them, I also will ask you one thing, which if ye tell me, I in likewise will tell you by what authority I do these things.

25 The baptism of John, whence was it? from heaven, or of men? And they reasoned with themselves, saying, If we shall say, From heaven; he will say unto us, Why did ye not then believe him?

26 But if we shall say, Of men; we fear the people; for all hold John as a prophet.

27 And they answered Je′sus, and said, We cannot tell. And he said unto them, Neither tell I you by what authority I do these things.

28 ¶ But what think ye? A *certain* man had two sons; and he came to the first, and said, Son, go work today in my vineyard.

29 He answered and said, I will not: but afterward he repented, and went.

30 And he came to the second, and said likewise. And he answered and said, I *go*, sir: and went not.

31 Whether of them twain did the will of *his* father? They say unto him, The first. Je′sus saith unto them, Verily I say unto you, That the publicans and the harlots go into the kingdom of God before you.

32 For John came unto you in the way of righteousness, and ye believed him not: but the publicans and the harlots believed him: and ye, when ye had seen *it*, repented not afterward, that ye might believe him.

33 ¶ Hear another parable: There was a certain householder, which planted a vineyard, and hedged it round about, and digged a winepress in it, and built a tower, and let it out to husbandmen, and went into a far country:

34 And when the time of the fruit drew near, he sent his servants to the husbandmen, that they might receive the fruits of it.

35 And the husbandmen took his servants, and beat one, and killed another, and stoned another.

36 Again, he sent other servants more than the first: and they did unto them likewise.

37 But last of all he sent unto them his son, saying, They will reverence my son.

38 But when the husbandmen saw the son, they said among themselves, This is the heir; come, let us kill him, and let us seize on his inheritance.

39 And they caught him, and cast *him* out of the vineyard, and slew *him*.

40 When the lord therefore of

the vineyard cometh, what will he do unto those husbandmen?

41 They say unto him, He will miserably destroy those wicked men, and will let out *his* vineyard unto other husbandmen, which shall render him the fruits in their seasons.

42 Je′sus saith unto them, Did ye never read in the scriptures, The stone which the builders rejected, the same is become the head of the corner: this is the Lord's doing, and it is marvellous in our eyes?

43 Therefore say I unto you, The kingdom of God shall be taken from you, and given to a nation bringing forth the fruits thereof.

44 And whosoever shall fall on this stone shall be broken: but on whomsoever it shall fall, it will grind him to powder.

45 And when the chief priests and Phar′i-sees had heard his parables, they perceived that he spake of them.

46 But when they sought to lay hands on him, they feared the multitude, because they took him for a prophet.

22 And Je′sus answered and spake unto them again by parables, and said,

2 The kingdom of heaven is like unto a certain king, which made a marriage for his son,

3 And sent forth his servants to call them that were bidden to the wedding: and they would not come.

4 Again, he sent forth other servants, saying, Tell them which are bidden, Behold, I have prepared my dinner: my oxen and *my* fatlings *are* killed, and all things *are* ready: come unto the marriage.

5 But they made light of *it*, and went their ways, one to his farm, another to his merchandise:

6 And the remnant took his servants, and entreated *them* spitefully, and slew *them*.

7 But when the king heard *thereof*, he was wroth: and he sent forth his armies, and destroyed those murderers, and burned up their city.

8 Then saith he to his servants, The wedding is ready, but they which were bidden were not worthy.

9 Go ye therefore into the highways, and as many as ye shall find, bid to the marriage.

10 So those servants went out into the highways, and gathered together all as many as they found, both bad and good: and the wedding was furnished with guests.

11 ¶ And when the king came in to see the guests, he saw there a man which had not on a wedding garment:

12 And he saith unto him, Friend, how camest thou in hither not having a wedding garment? And he was speechless.

13 Then said the king to the servants, Bind him hand and foot, and take him away, and cast *him* into outer darkness; there shall be weeping and gnashing of teeth.

14 For many are called, but few *are* chosen.

15 ¶ Then went the Phar'i-sees, and took counsel how they might entangle him in *his* talk.

16 And they sent out unto him their disciples with the He-ro'di-ans, saying, Master, we know that thou art true, and teachest the way of God in truth, neither carest thou for any *man:* for thou regardest not the person of men.

17 Tell us therefore, What thinkest thou? Is it lawful to give tribute unto Cæ'sar, or not?

18 But Je'sus perceived their wickedness, and said, Why tempt ye me, *ye* hypocrites?

19 Show me the tribute money. And they brought unto him a penny.

20 And he saith unto them, Whose *is* this image and superscription?

21 They say unto him, Cæ'sar's. Then saith he unto them, Render therefore unto Cæ'sar the things which are Cæ'sar's; and unto God the things that are God's.

22 When they had heard *these words,* they marveled, and left him, and went their way.

23 ¶ The same day came to him the Sad'du-cees, which say that there is no resurrection, and asked him,

24 Saying, Master, Mo'ses said, If a man die, having no children, his brother shall marry his wife, and raise up seed unto his brother.

25 Now there were with us seven brethren: and the first, when he had married a wife, deceased, and, having no issue, left his wife unto his brother:

26 Likewise the second also, and the third, unto the seventh.

27 And last of all the woman died also.

28 Therefore in the resurrection whose wife shall she be of the seven? for they all had her.

29 Je'sus answered and said unto them, Ye do err, not knowing the scriptures, nor the power of God.

30 For in the resurrection they neither marry, nor are given in marriage, but are as the angels of God in heaven.

31 But as touching the resurrection of the dead, have ye not read that which was spoken unto you by God, saying,

32 I am the God of A'bra-ham, and the God of I'saac, and the God of Ja'cob? God is not the God of the dead, but of the living.

33 And when the multitude heard *this,* they were astonished at his doctrine.

34 ¶ But when the Phar'i-sees had heard that he had put the Sad'du-cees to silence, they were gathered together.

35 Then one of them, *which was* a lawyer, asked *him a question,* tempting him, and saying,

36 Master, which *is* the great commandment in the law?

37 Je'sus said unto him, Thou shalt love the Lord thy God with all thy heart, and with all thy soul, and with all thy mind.

38 This is the first and great commandment.

39 And the second *is* like unto it, Thou shalt love thy neighbor as thyself.

40 On these two commandments hang all the law and the prophets.

41 ¶ While the Phar'i·sees were gathered together, Je'sus asked them,

42 Saying, What think ye of Christ? whose son is he? They say unto him, *The son* of Da'vid.

43 He saith unto them, How then doth Da'vid in spirit call him Lord, saying,

44 The LORD said unto my Lord, Sit thou on my right hand, till I make thine enemies thy footstool?

45 If Da'vid then call him Lord, how is he his son?

46 And no man was able to answer him a word, neither durst any *man* from that day forth ask him any more *questions.*

23 Then spake Je'sus to the multitude, and to his disciples,

2 Saying, The scribes and the Phar'i·sees sit in Mo'ses' seat:

3 All therefore whatsoever they bid you observe, *that* observe and do; but do not ye after their works: for they say, and do not.

4 For they bind heavy burdens and grievous to be borne, and lay *them* on men's shoulders; but they *themselves* will not move them with one of their fingers.

5 But all their works they do for to be seen of men: they make broad their phylacteries, and en-

large the borders of their garments,

6 And love the uppermost rooms at feasts, and the chief seats in the synagogues,

7 And greetings in the markets, and to be called of men, Rab'bi, Rab'bi.

8 But be not ye called Rab'bi: for one is your Master, *even* Christ; and all ye are brethren.

9 And call no *man* your father upon the earth: for one is your Father, which is in heaven.

10 Neither be ye called masters: for one is your Master, *even* Christ.

11 But he that is greatest among you shall be your servant.

12 And whosoever shall exalt himself shall be abased; and he that shall humble himself shall be exalted.

13 ¶ But woe unto you, scribes and Phar'i·sees, hypocrites! for ye shut up the kingdom of heaven against men: for ye neither go in *yourselves,* neither suffer ye them that are entering to go in.

14 Woe unto you, scribes and Phar'i·sees, hypocrites! for ye devour widows' houses, and for a pretense make long prayer: therefore ye shall receive the greater damnation.

15 Woe unto you, scribes and Phar'i·sees, hypocrites! for ye compass sea and land to make one proselyte, and when he is made, ye make him twofold more the child of hell than yourselves.

16 Woe unto you, *ye* blind

guides, which say, Whosoever shall swear by the temple, it is nothing; but whosoever shall swear by the gold of the temple, he is a debtor!

17 *Ye* fools and blind: for whether is greater, the gold, or the temple that sanctifieth the gold?

18 And, Whosoever shall swear by the altar, it is nothing; but whosoever sweareth by the gift that is upon it, he is guilty.

19 *Ye* fools and blind: for whether *is* greater, the gift, or the altar that sanctifieth the gift?

20 Whoso therefore shall swear by the altar, sweareth by it, and by all things thereon.

21 And whoso shall swear by the temple, sweareth by it, and by him that dwelleth therein.

22 And he that shall swear by heaven, sweareth by the throne of God, and by him that sitteth thereon.

23 Woe unto you, scribes and Phar'i-sees, hypocrites! for ye pay tithe of mint and anise and cummin, and have omitted the weightier *matters* of the law, judgment, mercy, and faith: these ought ye to have done, and not to leave the other undone.

24 *Ye* blind guides, which strain at a gnat, and swallow a camel.

25 Woe unto you, scribes and Phar'i-sees, hypocrites! for ye make clean the outside of the cup and of the platter, but within they are full of extortion and excess.

26 *Thou* blind Phar'i-see, cleanse first that *which is* within the cup and platter, that the outside of them may be clean also.

27 Woe unto you, scribes and Phar'i-sees, hypocrites! for ye are like unto whited sepulchers, which indeed appear beautiful outward, but are within full of dead *men's* bones, and of all uncleanness.

28 Even so ye also outwardly appear righteous unto men, but within ye are full of hypocrisy and iniquity.

29 Woe unto you, scribes and Phar'i-sees, hypocrites! because ye build the tombs of the prophets, and garnish the sepulchers of the righteous,

30 And say, If we had been in the days of our fathers, we would not have been partakers with them in the blood of the prophets.

31 Wherefore ye be witnesses unto yourselves, that ye are the children of them which killed the prophets.

32 Fill ye up then the measure of your fathers.

33 *Ye* serpents, *ye* generation of vipers, how can ye escape the damnation of hell?

34 ¶ Wherefore, behold, I send unto you prophets, and wise men, and scribes: and *some* of them ye shall kill and crucify; and *some* of them shall ye scourge in your synagogues, and persecute *them* from city to city:

35 That upon you may come all the righteous blood shed upon the earth, from the blood of

righteous A'bel unto the blood of Zech·a·ri'as son of Bar·a·chi'as, whom ye slew between the temple and the altar.

36 Verily I say unto you, All these things shall come upon this generation.

37 O Je·ru'sa·lem, Je·ru'sa·lem, *thou* that killest the prophets, and stonest them which are sent unto thee, how often would I have gathered thy children together, even as a hen gathereth her chickens under *her* wings, and ye would not!

38 Behold, your house is left unto you desolate.

39 For I say unto you, Ye shall not see me henceforth, till ye shall say, Blessed *is* he that cometh in the name of the Lord.

24 And Je'sus went out, and departed from the temple: and his disciples came to *him* for to show him the buildings of the temple.

2 And Je'sus said unto them, See ye not all these things? verily I say unto you, There shall not be left here one stone upon another, that shall not be thrown down.

3 ¶ And as he sat upon the mount of Ol'ives, the disciples came unto him privately, saying, Tell us, when shall these things be? and what *shall* be the sign of thy coming, and of the end of the world?

4 And Je'sus answered and said unto them, Take heed that no man deceive you.

5 For many shall come in my name, saying, I am Christ; and shall deceive many.

6 And ye shall hear of wars and rumors of wars: see that ye be not troubled: for all *these things* must come to pass, but the end is not yet.

7 For nation shall rise against nation, and kingdom against kingdom: and there shall be famines, and pestilences, and earthquakes, in divers places.

8 All these *are* the beginning of sorrows.

9 Then shall they deliver you up to be afflicted, and shall kill you: and ye shall be hated of all nations for my name's sake.

10 And then shall many be offended, and shall betray one another, and shall hate one another.

11 And many false prophets shall rise, and shall deceive many.

12 And because iniquity shall abound, the love of many shall wax cold.

13 But he that shall endure unto the end, the same shall be saved.

14 And this gospel of the kingdom shall be preached in all the world for a witness unto all nations; and then shall the end come.

15 When ye therefore shall see the abomination of desolation, spoken of by Dan'iel the prophet, stand in the holy place, (whoso readeth, let him understand:)

16 Then let them which be in Ju·dæ'a flee into the mountains:

17 Let him which is on the housetop not come down to take anything out of his house:

18 Neither let him which is in the field return back to take his clothes.

19 And woe unto them that are with child, and to them that give suck in those days!

20 But pray ye that your flight be not in the winter, neither on the sabbath day:

21 For then shall be great tribulation, such as was not since the beginning of the world to this time, no, nor ever shall be.

22 And except those days should be shortened, there should no flesh be saved: but for the elect's sake those days shall be shortened.

23 Then if any man shall say unto you, Lo, here *is* Christ, or there; believe *it* not.

24 For there shall arise false Christs, and false prophets, and shall show great signs and wonders; insomuch that, if *it were* possible, they shall deceive the very elect.

25 Behold, I have told you before.

26 Wherefore if they shall say unto you, Behold, he is in the desert; go not forth: behold, *he is* in the secret chambers; believe *it* not.

27 For as the lightning cometh out of the east, and shineth even unto the west; so shall also the coming of the Son of man be.

28 For wheresoever the carcass is, there will the eagles be gathered together.

29 ¶ Immediately after the tribulation of those days shall the sun be darkened, and the moon shall not give her light, and the stars shall fall from heaven, and the powers of the heavens shall be shaken:

30 And then shall appear the sign of the Son of man in heaven: and then shall all the tribes of the earth mourn, and they shall see the Son of man coming in the clouds of heaven with power and great glory.

31 And he shall send his angels with a great sound of a trumpet, and they shall gather together his elect from the four winds, from one end of heaven to the other.

32 Now learn a parable of the fig tree; When his branch is yet tender, and putteth forth leaves, ye know that summer *is* nigh:

33 So likewise ye, when ye shall see all these things, know that it is near, *even* at the doors.

34 Verily I say unto you, This generation shall not pass, till all these things be fulfilled.

35 Heaven and earth shall pass away, but my words shall not pass away.

36 ¶ But of that day and hour knoweth no *man*, no, not the angels of heaven, but my Father only.

37 But as the days of No'ah *were*, so shall also the coming of the Son of man be.

38 For as in the days that were before the flood they were eating and drinking, marrying and giving in marriage, until the day that No'ah entered into the ark,

39 And knew not until the flood came, and took them all away; so shall also the coming of the Son of man be.

40 Then shall two be in the field; the one shall be taken, and the other left.

41 Two *women shall be* grinding at the mill; the one shall be taken, and the other left.

42 ¶ Watch therefore: for ye know not what hour your Lord doth come.

43 But know this, that if the goodman of the house had known in what watch the thief would come, he would have watched, and would not have suffered his house to be broken up.

44 Therefore be ye also ready: for in such an hour as ye think not the Son of man cometh.

45 Who then is a faithful and wise servant, whom his lord hath made ruler over his household, to give them meat in due season?

46 Blessed *is* that servant, whom his lord when he cometh shall find so doing.

47 Verily I say unto you, That he shall make him ruler over all his goods.

48 But and if that evil servant shall say in his heart, My lord delayeth his coming;

49 And shall begin to smite *his* fellow servants, and to eat and drink with the drunken;

50 The lord of that servant shall come in a day when he looketh not for him, and in an hour that he is not aware of,

51 And shall cut him asunder, and appoint *him* his portion with the hypocrites: there shall be weeping and gnashing of teeth.

25 Then shall the kingdom of heaven be likened unto ten virgins, which took their lamps, and went forth to meet the bridegroom.

2 And five of them were wise, and five *were* foolish.

3 They that *were* foolish took their lamps, and took no oil with them:

4 But the wise took oil in their vessels with their lamps.

5 While the bridegroom tarried, they all slumbered and slept.

6 And at midnight there was a cry made, Behold, the bridegroom cometh; go ye out to meet him.

7 Then all those virgins arose, and trimmed their lamps.

8 And the foolish said unto the wise, Give us of your oil; for our lamps are gone out.

9 But the wise answered, saying, *Not so;* lest there be not enough for us and you: but go ye rather to them that sell, and buy for yourselves.

10 And while they went to buy, the bridegroom came; and they that were ready went in with him to the marriage: and the door was shut.

11 Afterward came also the other virgins, saying, Lord, Lord, open to us.

12 But he answered and said, Verily I say unto you, I know you not.

13 Watch therefore, for ye know neither the day nor the hour wherein the Son of man cometh.

14 ¶ For *the kingdom of heaven*

is as a man traveling into a far country, *who* called his own servants, and delivered unto them his goods.

15 And unto one he gave five talents, to another two, and to another one; to every man according to his several ability; and straightway took his journey.

16 Then he that had received the five talents went and traded with the same, and made *them* other five talents.

17 And likewise he that *had received* two, he also gained other two.

18 But he that had received one talent went and digged in the earth, and hid his lord's money.

19 After a long time the lord of those servants cometh, and reckoneth with them.

20 And so he that had received five talents came and brought other five talents, saying, Lord, thou deliveredst unto me five talents: behold, I have gained beside them five talents more.

21 His lord said unto him, Well done, *thou* good and faithful servant: thou hast been faithful over a few things, I will make thee ruler over many things: enter thou into the joy of thy lord.

22 He also that had received two talents came and said, Lord, thou deliveredst unto me two talents: behold, I have gained two other talents beside them.

23 His lord said unto him, Well done, good and faithful servant; thou hast been faithful over a few things, I will make thee ruler over many things: enter thou into the joy of thy lord.

24 Then he which had received the one talent came and said, Lord, I knew thee that thou art an hard man, reaping where thou hast not sown, and gathering where thou hast not strewed:

25 And I was afraid, and went and hid thy talent in the earth: lo, *there* thou hast *that is* thine.

26 His lord answered and said unto him, Thou wicked and slothful servant, thou knewest that I reap where I sowed not, and gather where I have not strewed:

27 Thou oughtest therefore to have put my money to the exchangers, and *then* at my coming I should have received mine own with usury.

28 Take therefore the talent from him, and give *it* unto him which hath ten talents.

29 For unto everyone that hath shall be given, and he shall have abundance: but from him that hath not shall be taken away even that which he hath.

30 And cast ye the unprofitable servant into outer darkness: there shall be weeping and gnashing of teeth.

31 ¶ When the Son of man shall come in his glory, and all the holy angels with him, then shall he sit upon the throne of his glory:

32 And before him shall be gathered all nations: and he shall separate them one from another, as a shepherd divideth *his* sheep from the goats:

33 And he shall set the sheep on his right hand, but the goats on the left.

34 Then shall the King say unto them on his right hand, Come, ye blessed of my Father, inherit the kingdom prepared for you from the foundation of the world:

35 For I was an hungered, and ye gave me meat: I was thirsty, and ye gave me drink: I was a stranger, and ye took me in:

36 Naked, and ye clothed me: I was sick, and ye visited me: I was in prison, and ye came unto me.

37 Then shall the righteous answer him, saying, Lord, when saw we thee an hungered, and fed *thee?* or thirsty, and gave *thee* drink?

38 When saw we thee a stranger, and took *thee* in? or naked, and clothed *thee?*

39 Or when saw we thee sick, or in prison, and came unto thee?

40 And the King shall answer and say unto them, Verily I say unto you, Inasmuch as ye have done *it* unto one of the least of these my brethren, ye have done *it* unto me.

41 Then shall he say also unto them on the left hand, Depart from me, ye cursed, into everlasting fire, prepared for the devil and his angels:

42 For I was an hungered, and ye gave me no meat: I was thirsty, and ye gave me no drink:

43 I was a stranger, and ye took me not in: naked, and ye

clothed me not: sick, and in prison, and ye visited me not.

44 Then shall they also answer him, saying, Lord, when saw we thee an hungered, or athirst, or a stranger, or naked, or sick, or in prison, and did not minister unto thee?

45 Then shall he answer them, saying, Verily I say unto you, Inasmuch as ye did *it* not to one of the least of these, ye did *it* not to me.

46 And these shall go away into everlasting punishment: but the righteous into life eternal.

26 And it came to pass, when Je'sus had finished all these sayings, he said unto his disciples,

2 Ye know that after two days is *the feast of* the passover, and the Son of man is betrayed to be crucified.

3 Then assembled together the chief priests, and the scribes, and the elders of the people, unto the palace of the high priest, who was called Ca'ia-phas,

4 And consulted that they might take Je'sus by subtlety, and kill *him*.

5 But they said, Not on the feast *day*, lest there be an uproar among the people.

6 ¶ Now when Je'sus was in Beth'a-ny, in the house of Si'mon the leper,

7 There came unto him a woman having an alabaster box of very precious ointment, and poured it on his head, as he sat *at meat.*

8 But when his disciples saw *it*,

they had indignation, saying, To what purpose is this waste?

9 For this ointment might have been sold for much, and given to the poor.

10 When Je´sus understood it, he said unto them, Why trouble ye the woman? for she hath wrought a good work upon me.

11 For ye have the poor always with you; but me ye have not always.

12 For in that she hath poured this ointment on my body, she did it for my burial.

13 Verily I say unto you, Wheresoever this gospel shall be preached in the whole world, there shall also this, that this woman hath done, be told for a memorial of her.

14 ¶ Then one of the twelve, called Ju´das Is-car´i-ot, went unto the chief priests,

15 And said unto them, What will ye give me, and I will deliver him unto you? And they covenanted with him for thirty pieces of silver.

16 And from that time he sought opportunity to betray him.

17 ¶ Now the first day of the feast of unleavened bread the disciples came to Je´sus, saying unto him, Where wilt thou that we prepare for thee to eat the passover?

18 And he said, Go into the city to such a man, and say unto him, The Master saith, My time is at hand; I will keep the passover at thy house with my disciples.

19 And the disciples did as Je´-sus had appointed them; and they made ready the passover.

20 Now when the even was come, he sat down with the twelve.

21 And as they did eat, he said, Verily I say unto you, that one of you shall betray me.

22 And they were exceeding sorrowful, and began everyone of them to say unto him, Lord, is it I?

23 And he answered and said, He that dippeth his hand with me in the dish, the same shall betray me.

24 The Son of man goeth as it is written of him: but woe unto that man by whom the Son of man is betrayed! it had been good for that man if he had not been born.

25 Then Ju´das, which betrayed him, answered and said, Master, is it I? He said unto him, Thou hast said.

26 ¶ And as they were eating, Je´sus took bread, and blessed it, and brake it, and gave it to the disciples, and said, Take, eat; this is my body.

27 And he took the cup, and gave thanks, and gave it to them, saying, Drink ye all of it;

28 For this is my blood of the new testament, which is shed for many for the remission of sins.

29 But I say unto you, I will not drink henceforth of this fruit of the vine, until that day when I drink it new with you in my Father's kingdom.

30 And when they had sung an

hymn, they went out into the mount of Ol'ives.

31 Then saith Je'sus unto them, All ye shall be offended because of me this night: for it is written, I will smite the shepherd, and the sheep of the flock shall be scattered abroad.

32 But after I am risen again, I will go before you into Gal'i-lee.

33 Pe'ter answered and said unto him, Though all *men* shall be offended because of thee, *yet* will I never be offended.

34 Je'sus said unto him, Verily I say unto thee, That this night, before the cock crow, thou shalt deny me thrice.

35 Pe'ter said unto him, Though I should die with thee, yet will I not deny thee. Likewise also said all the disciples.

36 ¶ Then cometh Je'sus with them unto a place called Gethsem'a-ne, and saith unto the disciples, Sit ye here, while I go and pray yonder.

37 And he took with him Pe'ter and the two sons of Zeb'e-dee, and began to be sorrowful and very heavy.

38 Then saith he unto them, My soul is exceeding sorrowful, even unto death: tarry ye here, and watch with me.

39 And he went a little farther, and fell on his face, and prayed, saying, O my Father, if it be possible, let this cup pass from me: nevertheless not as I will, but as thou wilt

40 And he cometh unto the disciples, and findeth them asleep, and saith unto Pe'ter, What, could ye not watch with me one hour?

41 Watch and pray, that ye enter not into temptation: the spirit indeed *is* willing, but the flesh is weak.

42 He went away again the second time, and prayed, saying, O my Father, if this cup may not pass away from me, except I drink it, thy will be done.

43 And he came and found them asleep again: for their eyes were heavy.

44 And he left them, and went away again, and prayed the third time, saying the same words.

45 Then cometh he to his disciples, and saith unto them, Sleep on now, and take *your* rest: behold, the hour is at hand, and the Son of man is betrayed into the hands of sinners.

46 Rise, let us be going: behold, he is at hand that doth betray me.

47 ¶ And while he yet spake, lo, Judas, one of the twelve, came, and with him a great multitude with swords and staves, from the chief priests and elders of the people.

48 Now he that betrayed him gave them a sign, saying, Whomsoever I shall kiss, that same is he: hold him fast.

49 And forthwith he came to Je'sus, and said, Hail, master; and kissed him.

50 And Je'sus said unto him, Friend, wherefore art thou come? Then came they, and laid hands on Je'sus, and took him.

51 And, behold, one of them

which were with Je'sus stretched out *his* hand, and drew his sword, and struck a servant of the high priest's, and smote off his ear.

52 Then said Je'sus unto him, Put up again thy sword into his place: for all they that take the sword shall perish with the sword.

53 Thinkest thou that I cannot now pray to my Father, and he shall presently give me more than twelve legions of angels?

54 But how then shall the scriptures be fulfilled, that thus it must be?

55 In that same hour said Je'sus to the multitudes, Are ye come out as against a thief with swords and staves for to take me? I sat daily with you teaching in the temple, and ye laid no hold on me.

56 But all this was done, that the scriptures of the prophets might be fulfilled. Then all the disciples forsook him, and fled.

57 ¶ And they that had laid hold on Je'sus led *him* away to Ca'iaphas the high priest, where the scribes and the elders were assembled.

58 But Pe'ter followed him afar off unto the high priest's palace, and went in, and sat with the servants, to see the end.

59 Now the chief priests, and elders, and all the council, sought false witness against Je'sus, to put him to death;

60 But found none: yea, though many false witnesses came, *yet* found they none. At the last came two false witnesses,

61 And said, This *fellow* said, I am able to destroy the temple of God, and to build it in three days.

62 And the high priest arose, and said unto him, Answerest thou nothing? what *is it which* these witness against thee?

63 But Je'sus held his peace. And the high priest answered and said unto him, I adjure thee by the living God, that thou tell us whether thou be the Christ, the Son of God.

64 Je'sus saith unto him, Thou hast said: nevertheless I say unto you, Hereafter shall ye see the Son of man sitting on the right hand of power, and coming in the clouds of heaven.

65 Then the high priest rent his clothes, saying, He hath spoken blasphemy; what further need have we of witnesses? behold, now ye have heard his blasphemy.

66 What think ye? They answered and said, He is guilty of death.

67 Then did they spit in his face, and buffeted him; and others smote *him* with the palms of their hands,

68 Saying, Prophesy unto us, thou Christ, Who is he that smote thee?

69 ¶ Now Pe'ter sat without in the palace: and a damsel came unto him, saying, Thou also wast with Je'sus of Gal'i-lee.

70 But he denied before *them* all, saying, I know not what thou sayest.

71 And when he was gone out into the porch, another *maid*

saw him, and said unto them that were there, This *fellow* was also with Je'sus of Naz'a-reth.

72 And again he denied with an oath, I do not know the man.

73 And after a while came unto *him* they that stood by, and said to Pe'ter, Surely thou also art *one* of them; for thy speech betrayeth thee.

74 Then began he to curse and to swear, *saying*, I know not the man. And immediately the cock crew.

75 And Pe'ter remembered the word of Je'sus, which said unto him, Before the cock crow, thou shalt deny me thrice. And he went out, and wept bitterly.

27 When the morning was come, all the chief priests and elders of the people took counsel against Je'sus to put him to death:

2 And when they had bound him, they led *him* away, and delivered him to Pon'ti-us Pi'-late the governor.

3 ¶ Then Ju'das, which had betrayed him, when he saw that he was condemned, repented himself, and brought again the thirty pieces of silver to the chief priests and elders,

4 Saying, I have sinned in that I have betrayed the innocent blood. And they said, What *is that* to us? see thou *to that*.

5 And he cast down the pieces of silver in the temple, and departed, and went and hanged himself.

6 And the chief priests took the silver pieces, and said, It is not lawful for to put them into the treasury, because it is the price of blood.

7 And they took counsel, and bought with them the potter's field, to bury strangers in.

8 Wherefore that field was called, The field of blood, unto this day.

9 Then was fulfilled that which was spoken by Jer-e-mi'ah the prophet, saying, And they took the thirty pieces of silver, the price of him that was valued, whom they of the children of Is'-ra-el did value;

10 And gave them for the potter's field, as the Lord appointed me.

11 And Je'sus stood before the governor: and the governor asked him, saying, Art thou the King of the Jews? And Je'sus said unto him, Thou sayest.

12 And when he was accused of the chief priests and elders, he answered nothing.

13 Then said Pi'late unto him, Hearest thou not how many things they witness against thee?

14 And he answered him to never a word; insomuch that the governor marveled greatly.

15 Now at *that* feast the governor was wont to release unto the people a prisoner, whom they would.

16 And they had then a notable prisoner, called Ba-rab'bas.

17 Therefore when they were gathered together, Pi'late said unto them, Whom will ye that I release unto you? Ba-rab'bas, or Je'sus which is called Christ?

18 For he knew that for envy they had delivered him.

19 ¶ When he was set down on the judgment seat, his wife sent unto him, saying, Have thou nothing to do with that just man: for I have suffered many things this day in a dream because of him.

20 But the chief priests and elders persuaded the multitude that they should ask Ba-rab'bas, and destroy Je'sus.

21 The governor answered and said unto them, Whether of the twain will ye that I release unto you? They said, Ba-rab'bas.

22 Pi'late saith unto them, What shall I do then with Je'sus which is called Christ? *They* all say unto them, Let him be crucified.

23 And the governor said, Why, what evil hath he done? But they cried out the more, saying, Let him be crucified.

24 ¶ When Pi'late saw that he could prevail nothing, but *that* rather a tumult was made, he took water, and washed *his* hands before the multitude, saying, I am innocent of the blood of this just person: see ye *to it*.

25 Then answered all the people, and said, His blood *be* on us, and on our children.

26 ¶ Then released he Ba-rab'-bas unto them: and when he had scourged Je'sus, he delivered *him* to be crucified.

27 Then the soldiers of the governor took Je'sus into the common hall, and gathered unto him the whole band *of soldiers*.

28 And they stripped him, and put on him a scarlet robe.

29 ¶ And when they had platted a crown of thorns, they put *it* upon his head, and a reed in his right hand: and they bowed the knee before him, and mocked him, saying, Hail, King of the Jews!

30 And they spit upon him, and took the reed, and smote him on the head.

31 And after that they had mocked him, they took the robe off from him, and put his own raiment on him, and led him away to crucify *him*.

32 And as they came out, they found a man of Cy-re'ne, Si'mon by name: him they compelled to bear his cross.

33 And when they were come unto a place called Gol'go-tha, that is to say, a place of a skull,

34 ¶ They gave him vinegar to drink mingled with gall: and when he had tasted *thereof*, he would not drink.

35 And they crucified him, and parted his garments, casting lots: that it might be fulfilled which was spoken by the prophet, They parted my garments among them, and upon my vesture did they cast lots.

36 And sitting down they watched him there;

37 And set up over his head his accusation written, THIS IS JE'SUS THE KING OF THE JEWS.

38 Then were there two thieves crucified with him, one on the right hand, and another on the left.

39 ¶ And they that passed by reviled him, wagging their heads,

40 And saying, Thou that destroyest the temple, and buildest *it* in three days, save thyself. If thou be the Son of God, come down from the cross.

41 Likewise also the chief priests mocking *him*, with the scribes and elders, said,

42 He saved others; himself he cannot save. If he be the King of Is-ra-el, let him now come down from the cross, and we will believe him.

43 He trusted in God; let him deliver him now, if he will have him: for he said, I am the Son of God.

44 The thieves also, which were crucified with him, cast the same in his teeth.

45 Now from the sixth hour there was darkness over all the land unto the ninth hour.

46 And about the ninth hour Je'sus cried with a loud voice, saying, E'li, E'li, la'ma sa-bach-tha'ni? that is to say, My God, my God, why hast thou forsaken me?

47 Some of them that stood there, when they heard *that*, said, This *man* calleth for E-li'jah.

48 And straightway one of them ran, and took a sponge, and filled *it* with vinegar, and put *it* on a reed, and gave him to drink.

49 The rest said, Let be, let us see whether E-li'jah will come to save him.

50 ¶ Je'sus, when he had cried again with a loud voice, yielded up the ghost.

51 And, behold, the veil of the temple was rent in twain from the top to the bottom; and the earth did quake, and the rocks rent;

52 And the graves were opened; and many bodies of the saints which slept arose,

53 And came out of the graves after his resurrection, and went into the holy city, and appeared unto many.

54 Now when the centurion, and they that were with him, watching Je'sus, saw the earthquake, and those things that were done, they feared greatly, saying, Truly this was the Son of God.

55 And many women were there beholding afar off, which followed Je'sus from Gal'i-lee, ministering unto him:

56 Among which was Ma'ry Mag-da-le'ne, and Ma'ry the mother of James and Jo'ses, and the mother of Zeb'e-dee's children.

57 When the even was come, there came a rich man of Ar-i-ma-thæ'a, named Jo'seph, who also himself was Je'sus' disciple:

58 He went to Pi'late, and begged the body of Je'sus. Then Pi'late commanded the body to be delivered.

59 And when Jo'seph had taken the body, he wrapped it in a clean linen cloth,

60 And laid it in his own new tomb, which he had hewn out in the rock: and he rolled a great

stone to the door of the sepulcher, and departed.

61 And there was Ma'ry Magda-le'ne, and the other Ma'ry, sitting over against the sepulcher.

62 ¶ Now the next day, that followed the day of the preparation, the chief priests and Phar'i-sees came together unto Pi'late,

63 Saying, Sir, we remember that that deceiver said, while he was yet alive, After three days I will rise again.

64 Command therefore that the sepulcher be made sure until the third day, lest his disciples come by night, and steal him away, and say unto the people, He is risen from the dead: so the last error shall be worse than the first.

65 Pi'late said unto them, Ye have a watch: go your way, make *it* as sure as ye can.

66 So they went, and made the sepulcher sure, sealing the stone, and setting a watch.

28 In the end of the sabbath, as it began to dawn toward the first *day* of the week, came Ma'ry Mag-da-le'ne and the other Ma'ry to see the sepulcher.

2 And, behold, there was a great earthquake: for the angel of the Lord descended from heaven, and came and rolled back the stone from the door, and sat upon it.

3 His countenance was like lightning, and his raiment white as snow:

4 And for fear of him the keepers did shake, and became as dead *men.*

5 And the angel answered and said unto the women, Fear not ye: for I know that ye seek Je'sus, which was crucified.

6 He is not here: for he is risen, as he said. Come, see the place where the Lord lay.

7 And go quickly, and tell his disciples that he is risen from the dead; and, behold, he goeth before you into Gal'i-lee; there shall ye see him: lo, I have told you.

8 And they departed quickly from the sepulcher with fear and great joy; and did run to bring his disciples word.

9 ¶ And as they went to tell his disciples, behold, Je'sus met them, saying, All hail. And they came and held him by the feet, and worshiped him.

10 Then said Je'sus unto them, Be not afraid: go tell my brethren that they go into Gal'i-lee, and there shall they see me.

11 ¶ Now when they were going, behold, some of the watch came into the city, and showed unto the chief priests all the things that were done.

12 And when they were assembled with the elders, and had taken counsel, they gave large money unto the soldiers,

13 Saying, Say ye, His disciples came by night, and stole him *away* while we slept.

14 And if this come to the governor's ears, we will persuade him, and secure you.

15 So they took the money, and did as they were taught: and

this saying is commonly reported among the Jews until this day.

16 ¶ Then the eleven disciples went away into Gal'i-lee, into a mountain where Je'sus had appointed them.

17 And when they saw him, they worshipped him: but some doubted.

18 And Je'sus came and spake unto them, saying, All power is given unto me in heaven and in earth.

19 ¶ Go ye therefore, and teach all nations, baptizing them in the name of the Father, and of the Son, and of the Ho'ly Ghost:

20 Teaching them to observe all things whatsoever I have commanded you: and, lo, I am with you always, *even* unto the end of the world. Amen.

MARK

1 The beginning of the gospel of Je'sus Christ, the Son of God;

2 As it is written in the prophets, Behold, I send my messenger before thy face, which shall prepare thy way before thee.

3 The voice of one crying in the wilderness, Prepare ye the way of the Lord, make his paths straight.

4 John did baptize in the wilderness, and preach the baptism of repentance for the remission of sins.

5 And there went out unto him all the land of Ju-dæ'a, and they of Je-ru'sa-lem, and were all baptized of him in the river of Jor'-dan, confessing their sins.

6 And John was clothed with camel's hair, and with a girdle of a skin about his loins; and he did eat locusts and wild honey;

7 And preached, saying, There cometh one mightier than I after me, the latchet of whose shoes I am not worthy to stoop down and unloose.

8 I indeed have baptized you with water: but he shall baptize you with the Ho'ly Ghost.

9 And it came to pass in those days, that Je'sus came from Naz'-a-reth of Gal'i-lee, and was baptized of John in Jor'dan.

10 And straightway coming up out of the water, he saw the heavens opened, and the Spirit like a dove descending upon him:

11 And there came a voice from heaven, *saying*, Thou art my beloved Son, in whom I am well pleased.

12 And immediately the Spirit driveth him into the wilderness.

13 And he was there in the wilderness forty days, tempted of Sa'tan; and was with the wild beasts; and the angels ministered unto him.

14 Now after that John was put in prison, Je'sus came into

Gal'i-lee, preaching the gospel of the kingdom of God,

15 And saying, The time is fulfilled, and the kingdom of God is at hand: repent ye, and believe the gospel.

16 Now as he walked by the sea of Gal'i-lee, he saw Si'mon and Andrew his brother casting a net into the sea: for they were fishers.

17 And Je'sus said unto them, Come ye after me, and I will make you to become fishers of men.

18 And straightway they forsook their nets, and followed him.

19 And when he had gone a little farther thence, he saw James the *son* of Zeb'e-dee, and John his brother, who also were in the ship mending their nets.

20 And straightway he called them: and they left their father Zeb'e-dee in the ship with the hired servants, and went after him.

21 And they went into Ca-per'-na-um; and straightway on the sabbath day he entered into the synagogue, and taught.

22 And they were astonished at his doctrine: for he taught them as one that had authority, and not as the scribes.

23 And there was in their synagogue a man with an unclean spirit; and he cried out,

24 Saying, Let *us* alone; what have we to do with thee, thou Je'sus of Naz'a-reth? art thou come to destroy us? I know thee who thou art, the Holy One of God.

25 And Je'sus rebuked him, saying, Hold thy peace, and come out of him.

26 And when the unclean spirit had torn him, and cried with a loud voice, he came out of him.

27 And they were all amazed, insomuch that they questioned among themselves, saying, What thing is this? what new doctrine *is* this? for with authority commandeth he even the unclean spirits, and they do obey him.

28 And immediately his fame spread abroad throughout all the region round about Gal'i-lee.

29 And forthwith, when they were come out of the synagogue, they entered into the house of Si'mon and Andrew, with James and John.

30 But Si'mon's wife's mother lay sick of a fever, and anon they tell him of her.

31 And he came and took her by the hand, and lifted her up; and immediately the fever left her, and she ministered unto them.

32 And at even, when the sun did set, they brought unto him all that were diseased, and them that were possessed with devils.

33 And all the city was gathered together at the door.

34 And he healed many that were sick of divers diseases, and cast out many devils; and suffered not the devils to speak, because they knew him.

35 And in the morning, rising up a great while before day, he went out, and departed into a solitary place, and there prayed.

36 And Si'mon and they that were with him followed after him.

37 And when they had found him, they said unto him, All men seek for thee.

38 And he said unto them, Let us go into the next towns, that I may preach there also: for therefore came I forth.

39 And he preached in their synagogues throughout all Gal'i-lee, and cast out devils.

40 And there came a leper to him, beseeching him, and kneeling down to him, and saying unto him, If thou wilt, thou canst make me clean.

41 And Je'sus, moved with compassion, put forth his hand, and touched him, and saith unto him, I will; be thou clean.

42 And as soon as he had spoken, immediately the leprosy departed from him, and he was cleansed.

43 And he straitly charged him, and forthwith sent him away;

44 And saith unto him, See thou say nothing to any man: but go thy way, show thyself to the priest, and offer for thy cleansing those things which Mo'ses commanded, for a testimony unto them.

45 But he went out, and began to publish it much, and to blaze abroad the matter, insomuch that Je'sus could no more openly enter into the city, but was without in desert places: and they came to him from every quarter.

2 And again he entered into Ca-per'na-um after some days; and it was noised that he was in the house.

2 And straightway many were gathered together, insomuch that there was no room to receive them, no, not so much as about the door: and he preached the word unto them.

3 And they come unto him, bringing one sick of the palsy, which was borne of four.

4 And when they could not come nigh unto him for the press, they uncovered the roof where he was: and when they had broken it up, they let down the bed wherein the sick of the palsy lay.

5 When Je'sus saw their faith, he said unto the sick of the palsy, Son, thy sins be forgiven thee.

6 But there were certain of the scribes sitting there, and reasoning in their hearts,

7 Why doth this man thus speak blasphemies? who can forgive sins but God only?

8 And immediately when Je'sus perceived in his spirit that they so reasoned within themselves, he said unto them, Why reason ye these things in your hearts?

9 Whether is it easier to say to the sick of the palsy, Thy sins be forgiven thee; or to say, Arise, and take up thy bed, and walk?

10 But that ye may know that the Son of man hath power on earth to forgive sins, (he saith to the sick of the palsy,)

11 I say unto thee, Arise, and

take up thy bed, and go thy way into thine house.

12 And immediately he arose, took up the bed, and went forth before them all; insomuch that they were all amazed, and glorified God, saying, We never saw it on this fashion.

13 And he went forth again by the seaside; and all the multitude resorted unto him, and he taught them.

14 And as he passed by, he saw Le'vi the *son* of Al-phæ'us sitting at the receipt of custom, and said unto him, Follow me. And he arose and followed him.

15 And it came to pass, that, as Je'sus sat at meat in his house, many publicans and sinners sat also together with Je'sus and his disciples: for there were many, and they followed him.

16 And when the scribes and Phar'i-sees saw him eat with publicans and sinners, they said unto his disciples, How is it that he eateth and drinketh with publicans and sinners?

17 When Je'sus heard *it*, he saith unto them, They that are whole have no need of the physician, but they that are sick: I came not to call the righteous, but sinners to repentance.

18 And the disciples of John and of the Phar'i-sees used to fast: and they come and say unto him, Why do the disciples of John and of the Phar'i-sees fast, but thy disciples fast not?

19 And Je'sus said unto them, Can the children of the bride-chamber fast, while the bridegroom is with them? as long as they have the bridegroom with them, they cannot fast.

20 But the days will come, when the bridegroom shall be taken away from them, and then shall they fast in those days.

21 No man also seweth a piece of new cloth on an old garment: else the new piece that filled it up taketh away from the old, and the rent is made worse.

22 And no man putteth new wine into old bottles: else the new wine doth burst the bottles, and the wine is spilled, and the bottles will be marred: but new wine must be put into new bottles.

23 And it came to pass, that he went through the corn fields on the sabbath day; and his disciples began, as they went, to pluck the ears of corn.

24 And the Phar'i-sees said unto him, Behold, why do they on the sabbath day that which is not lawful?

25 And he said unto them, Have ye never read what Da'vid did, when he had need, and was an hungered, he, and they that were with him?

26 How he went into the house of God in the days of A-bi'a-thar the high priest, and did eat the showbread, which is not lawful to eat but for the priests, and gave also to them which were with him?

27 And he said unto them, The sabbath was made for man, and not man for the sabbath:

28 Therefore the Son of man is Lord also of the sabbath.

3 And he entered again into the synagogue; and there was a man there which had a withered hand.

2 And they watched him, whether he would heal him on the sabbath day; that they might accuse him.

3 And he saith unto the man which had the withered hand, Stand forth.

4 And he saith unto them, Is it lawful to do good on the sabbath days, or to do evil? to save life, or to kill? But they held their peace.

5 And when he had looked round about on them with anger, being grieved for the hardness of their hearts, he saith unto the man, Stretch forth thine hand. And he stretched *it* out: and his hand was restored whole as the other.

6 And the Phar'i-sees went forth, and straightway took counsel with the He-ro'di-ans against him, how they might destroy him.

7 But Je'sus withdrew himself with his disciples to the sea: and a great multitude from Gal'i-lee followed him, and from Ju-dæ'a,

8 And from Je-ru'sa-lem, and from I-du-mæ'a, and *from* beyond Jor'dan; and they about Tyre and Si'don, a great multitude, when they had heard what great things he did, came unto him.

9 And he spake to his disciples, that a small ship should wait on him because of the multitude, lest they should throng him.

10 For he had healed many; insomuch that they pressed upon him for to touch him, as many as had plagues.

11 And unclean spirits, when they saw him, fell down before him, and cried, saying, Thou art the Son of God.

12 And he straitly charged them that they should not make him known.

13 And he goeth up into a mountain, and calleth *unto him* whom he would: and they came unto him.

14 And he ordained twelve, that they should be with him, and that he might send them forth to preach,

15 And to have power to heal sicknesses, and to cast out devils:

16 And Si'mon he surnamed Pe'ter;

17 And James the *son* of Zeb'e-dee, and John the brother of James; and he surnamed them Bo-an-er'ges, which is, The sons of thunder:

18 And Andrew, and Phil'ip, and Bar-thol'o-mew, and Mat'-thew, and Thom'as, and James the *son* of Al-phæ'us, and Thad-dæ'us, and Si'mon the Ca'naan-ite,

19 And Ju'das Is-car'i-ot, which also betrayed him: and they went into an house.

20 And the multitude cometh together again, so that they could not so much as eat bread.

21 And when his friends heard *of it*, they went out to lay hold on him: for they said, He is beside himself.

22 ¶ And the scribes which

came down from Je·ru'sa·lem said, He hath Beel'ze·bub, and by the prince of the devils casteth he out devils.

23 And he called them *unto him*, and said unto them in parables, How can Sa'tan cast out Sa'tan?

24 And if a kingdom be divided against itself, that kingdom cannot stand.

25 And if a house be divided against itself, that house cannot stand.

26 And if Sa'tan rise up against himself, and be divided, he cannot stand, but hath an end.

27 No man can enter into a strong man's house, and spoil his goods, except he will first bind the strong man; and then he will spoil his house.

28 Verily I say unto you, All sins shall be forgiven unto the sons of men, and blasphemies wherewith soever they shall blaspheme:

29 But he that shall blaspheme against the Ho'ly Ghost hath never forgiveness, but is in danger of eternal damnation:

30 Because they said, He hath an unclean spirit.

31 ¶ There came then his brethren and his mother, and, standing without, sent unto him, calling him.

32 And the multitude sat about him, and they said unto him, Behold, thy mother and thy brethren without seek for thee.

33 And he answered them, saying, Who is my mother, or my brethren?

34 And he looked round about on them which sat about him, and said, Behold my mother and my brethren!

35 For whosoever shall do the will of God, the same is my brother, and my sister, and mother.

4 And he began again to teach by the seaside: and there was gathered unto him a great multitude, so that he entered into a ship, and sat in the sea; and the whole multitude was by the sea on the land.

2 And he taught them many things by parables, and said unto them in his doctrine,

3 Hearken; Behold, there went out a sower to sow:

4 And it came to pass, as he sowed, some fell by the wayside, and the fowls of the air came and devoured it up.

5 And some fell on stony ground, where it had not much earth; and immediately it sprang up, because it had no depth of earth:

6 But when the sun was up, it was scorched; and because it had no root, it withered away.

7 And some fell among thorns, and the thorns grew up, and choked it, and it yielded no fruit.

8 And other fell on good ground, and did yield fruit that sprang up and increased; and brought forth, some thirty, and some sixty, and some an hundred.

9 And he said unto them, He that hath ears to hear, let him hear.

10 And when he was alone,

they that were about him with the twelve asked of him the parable.

11 And he said unto them, Unto you it is given to know the mystery of the kingdom of God: but unto them that are without, all *these* things are done in parables:

12 That seeing they may see, and not perceive; and hearing they may hear, and not understand; lest at anytime they should be converted, and *their* sins should be forgiven them.

13 And he said unto them, Know ye not this parable? and how then will ye know all parables?

14 ¶ The sower soweth the word.

15 And these are they by the wayside, where the word is sown; but when they have heard, Sa'tan cometh immediately, and taketh away the word that was sown in their hearts.

16 And these are they likewise which are sown on stony ground; who, when they have heard the word, immediately receive it with gladness;

17 And have no root in themselves, and so endure but for a time: afterward, when affliction or persecution ariseth for the word's sake, immediately they are offended:

18 And these are they which are sown among thorns; such as hear the word,

19 And the cares of this world, and the deceitfulness of riches, and the lusts of other things

entering in, choke the word, and it becometh unfruitful.

20 And these are they which are sown on good ground; such as hear the word, and receive *it*, and bring forth fruit, some thirtyfold, some sixty, and some an hundred.

21 ¶ And he said unto them, Is a candle brought to be put under a bushel, or under a bed? and not to be set on a candlestick?

22 For there is nothing hid, which shall not be manifested; neither was anything kept secret, but that it should come abroad.

23 If any man have ears to hear, let him hear.

24 And he said unto them, Take heed what ye hear: with what measure ye mete, it shall be measured to you: and unto you that hear shall more be given.

25 For he that hath, to him shall be given: and he that hath not, from him shall be taken even that which he hath.

26 ¶ And he said, So is the kingdom of God, as if a man should cast seed into the ground;

27 And should sleep, and rise night and day, and the seed should spring and grow up, he knoweth not how.

28 For the earth bringeth forth fruit of herself; first the blade, then the ear, after that the full corn in the ear.

29 But when the fruit is brought forth, immediately he putteth in the sickle, because the harvest is come.

30 ¶ And he said, Whereunto shall we liken the kingdom of God? or with what comparison shall we compare it?

31 *It is* like a grain of mustard seed, which, when it is sown in the earth, is less than all the seeds that be in the earth:

32 But when it is sown, it groweth up, and becometh greater than all herbs, and shooteth out great branches; so that the fowls of the air may lodge under the shadow of it.

33 And with many such parables spake he the word unto them, as they were able to hear *it*.

34 But without a parable spake he not unto them: and when they were alone, he expounded all things to his disciples.

35 And the same day, when the even was come, he saith unto them, Let us pass over unto the other side.

36 And when they had sent away the multitude, they took him even as he was in the ship. And there were also with him other little ships.

37 And there arose a great storm of wind, and the waves beat into the ship, so that it was now full.

38 And he was in the hinder part of the ship, asleep on a pillow: and they awake him, and say unto him, Master, carest thou not that we perish?

39 And he arose, and rebuked the wind, and said unto the sea, Peace, be still. And the wind ceased, and there was a great calm.

40 And he said unto them, Why are ye so fearful? how is it that ye have no faith?

41 And they feared exceedingly, and said one to another, What manner of man is this, that even the wind and the sea obey him?

5 And they came over unto the other side of the sea, into the country of the Gad′a-renes.

2 And when he was come out of the ship, immediately there met him out of the tombs a man with an unclean spirit,

3 Who had *his* dwelling among the tombs; and no man could bind him, no, not with chains:

4 Because that he had been often bound with fetters and chains, and the chains had been plucked asunder by him, and the fetters broken in pieces: neither could any *man* tame him.

5 And always, night and day, he was in the mountains, and in the tombs, crying, and cutting himself with stones.

6 But when he saw Je′sus afar off, he ran and worshipped him,

7 And cried with a loud voice, and said, What have I to do with thee, Je′sus, *thou* Son of the most high God? I adjure thee by God, that thou torment me not.

8 For he said unto him, Come out of the man, *thou* unclean spirit.

9 And he asked him, What *is* thy name? And he answered, saying, My name *is* Legion: for we are many.

10 And he besought him much

that he would not send them away out of the country.

11 Now there was there nigh unto the mountains a great herd of swine feeding.

12 And all the devils besought him, saying, Send us into the swine, that we may enter into them.

13 And forthwith Je'sus gave them leave. And the unclean spirits went out, and entered into the swine: and the herd ran violently down a steep place into the sea, (they were about two thousand;) and were choked in the sea.

14 And they that fed the swine fled, and told it in the city, and in the country. And they went out to see what it was that was done.

15 And they come to Je'sus, and see him that was possessed with the devil, and had the legion, sitting, and clothed, and in his right mind: and they were afraid.

16 And they that saw it told them how it befell to him that was possessed with the devil, and also concerning the swine.

17 And they began to pray him to depart out of their coasts.

18 And when he was come into the ship, he that had been possessed with the devil prayed him that he might be with him.

19 Howbeit Je'sus suffered him not, but saith unto him, Go home to thy friends, and tell them how great things the Lord hath done for thee, and hath had compassion on thee.

20 And he departed, and began to publish in De-cap'o-lis how great things Je'sus had done for him: and all men did marvel.

21 And when Je'sus was passed over again by ship unto the other side, much people gathered unto him: and he was nigh unto the sea.

22 And, behold, there cometh one of the rulers of the synagogue, Ja-i'rus by name; and when he saw him, he fell at his feet,

23 And besought him greatly, saying, My little daughter lieth at the point of death: I pray thee, come and lay thy hands on her, that she may be healed; and she shall live.

24 And Jesus went with him; and much people followed him, and thronged him.

25 And a certain woman, which had an issue of blood twelve years,

26 And had suffered many things of many physicians, and had spent all that she had, and was nothing bettered, but rather grew worse,

27 When she had heard of Je'sus, came in the press behind, and touched his garment.

28 For she said, If I may touch but his clothes, I shall be whole.

29 And straightway the fountain of her blood was dried up; and she felt in her body that she was healed of that plague.

30 And Je'sus, immediately knowing in himself that virtue had gone out of him, turned him about in the press, and said, Who touched my clothes?

31 And his disciples said unto

him, Thou seest the multitude thronging thee, and sayest thou, Who touched me?

32 And he looked round about to see her that had done this thing.

33 But the woman fearing and trembling, knowing what was done in her, came and fell down before him, and told him all the truth.

34 And he said unto her, Daughter, thy faith hath made thee whole; go in peace, and be whole of thy plague.

35 While he yet spake, there came from the ruler of the synagogue's *house certain* which said, Thy daughter is dead: why troublest thou the Master any further?

36 As soon as Je'sus heard the word that was spoken, he saith unto the ruler of the synagogue, Be not afraid, only believe.

37 And he suffered no man to follow him, save Pe'ter, and James, and John the brother of James.

38 And he cometh to the house of the ruler of the synagogue, and seeth the tumult, and them that wept and wailed greatly.

39 And when he was come in, he saith unto them, Why make ye this ado, and weep? the damsel is not dead, but sleepeth.

40 And they laughed him to scorn. But when he had put them all out, he taketh the father and the mother of the damsel, and them that were with him, and entereth in where the damsel was lying.

41 And he took the damsel by the hand, and said unto her, Tal'-i-tha cu'mi; which is, being interpreted, Damsel, I say unto thee, arise.

42 And straightway the damsel arose, and walked; for she was *of the age of* twelve years. And they were astonished with a great astonishment.

43 And he charged them straitly that no man should know it; and commanded that something should be given her to eat.

6 And he went out from thence, and came into his own country; and his disciples follow him.

2 And when the sabbath day was come, he began to teach in the synagogue: and many hearing *him* were astonished, saying, From whence hath this *man* these things? and what wisdom *is* this which is given unto him, that even such mighty works are wrought by his hands?

3 Is not this the carpenter, the son of Ma'ry, the brother of James, and Jo'ses, and of Ju'dah, and Si'mon? and are not his sisters here with us? And they were offended at him.

4 But Je'sus said unto them, A prophet is not without honor, but in his own country, and among his own kin, and in his own house.

5 And he could there do no mighty work, save that he laid his hands upon a few sick folk, and healed them.

6 And he marveled because of their unbelief. And he went

round about the villages, teaching.

7 ¶ And he called *unto him* the twelve, and began to send them forth by two and two; and gave them power over unclean spirits;

8 And commanded them that they should take nothing for *their* journey, save a staff only; no scrip, no bread, no money in *their* purse:

9 But *be* shod with sandals; and not put on two coats.

10 And he said unto them, In what place soever ye enter into an house, there abide till ye depart from that place.

11 And whosoever shall not receive you, nor hear you, when ye depart thence, shake off the dust under your feet for a testimony against them. Verily I say unto you, It shall be more tolerable for Sod'om and Go mor'rah in the day of judgment, than for that city.

12 And they went out, and preached that men should repent.

13 And they cast out many devils, and anointed with oil many that were sick, and healed *them*.

14 And king Her'od heard of *him*; (for his name was spread abroad:) and he said, That John the Bap'tist was risen from the dead, and therefore mighty works do show forth themselves in him.

15 Others said, That it is E-li'jah. And others said, That it is a prophet, or as one of the prophets.

16 But when Her'od heard *thereof*, he said, It is John, whom I beheaded: he is risen from the dead.

17 For Her'od himself had sent forth and laid hold upon John, and bound him in prison for He-ro'di-as' sake, his brother Phil'ip's wife: for he had married her.

18 For John had said unto Her'od, It is not lawful for thee to have thy brother's wife.

19 Therefore He-ro'di-as had a quarrel against him, and would have killed him; but she could not:

20 For Her'od feared John, knowing that he was a just man and an holy, and observed him; and when he heard him, he did many things, and heard him gladly.

21 And when a convenient day was come, that Her'od on his birthday made a supper to his lords, high captains, and chief *estates* of Gal'i-lee;

22 And when the daughter of the said He-ro'di-as came in, and danced, and pleased Her'od and them that sat with him, the king said unto the damsel, Ask of me whatsoever thou wilt, and I will give *it* thee.

23 And he sware unto her, Whatsoever thou shalt ask of me, I will give *it* thee, unto the half of my kingdom.

24 And she went forth, and said unto her mother, What shall I ask? And she said, The head of John the Bap'tist.

25 And she came in straightway with haste unto the king,

and asked, saying, I will that thou give me by and by in a charger the head of John the Bap'tist.

26 And the king was exceeding sorry; *yet* for his oath's sake, and for their sakes which sat with him, he would not reject her.

27 And immediately the king sent an executioner, and commanded his head to be brought: and he went and beheaded him in the prison,

28 And brought his head in a charger, and gave it to the damsel: and the damsel gave it to her mother.

29 And when his disciples heard *of it,* they came and took up his corpse, and laid it in a tomb.

30 And the apostles gathered themselves together unto Je'sus, and told him all things, both what they had done, and what they had taught.

31 And he said unto them, Come ye yourselves apart into a desert place, and rest a while: for there were many coming and going, and they had no leisure so much as to eat.

32 And they departed into a desert place by ship privately.

33 And the people saw them departing, and many knew him, and ran afoot thither out of all cities, and outwent them, and came together unto him.

34 And Je'sus, when he came out, saw much people, and was moved with compassion toward them, because they were as sheep not having a shepherd:

and he began to teach them many things.

35 And when the day was now far spent, his disciples came unto him, and said, This is a desert place, and now the time *is* far passed:

36 Send them away, that they may go into the country round about, and into the villages, and buy themselves bread: for they have nothing to eat.

37 He answered and said unto them, Give ye them to eat. And they say unto him, Shall we go and buy two hundred pennyworth of bread, and give them to eat?

38 He saith unto them, How many loaves have ye? go and see. And when they knew, they say, Five, and two fishes.

39 And he commanded them to make all sit down by companies upon the green grass.

40 And they sat down in ranks, by hundreds, and by fifties.

41 And when he had taken the five loaves and the two fishes, he looked up to heaven, and blessed, and brake the loaves, and gave *them* to his disciples to set before them; and the two fishes divided he among them all.

42 And they did all eat, and were filled.

43 And they took up twelve baskets full of the fragments, and of the fishes.

44 And they that did eat of the loaves were about five thousand men.

45 And straightway he constrained his disciples to get into

the ship, and to go to the other side before unto Beth-sa'i-da, while he sent away the people.

46 And when he had sent them away, he departed into a mountain to pray.

47 And when even was come, the ship was in the midst of the sea, and he alone on the land.

48 And he saw them toiling in rowing; for the wind was contrary unto them: and about the fourth watch of the night he cometh unto them, walking upon the sea, and would have passed by them.

49 But when they saw him walking upon the sea, they supposed it had been a spirit, and cried out:

50 For they all saw him, and were troubled. And immediately he talked with them, and saith unto them, Be of good cheer: it is I; be not afraid.

51 And he went up unto them into the ship; and the wind ceased: and they were sore amazed in themselves beyond measure, and wondered.

52 For they considered not the miracle of the loaves: for their heart was hardened.

53 And when they had passed over, they came into the land of Gen-nes'a-ret, and drew to the shore.

54 And when they were come out of the ship, straightway they knew him,

55 And ran through that whole region round about, and began to carry about in beds those that were sick, where they heard he was.

56 And whithersoever he entered, into villages, or cities, or country, they laid the sick in the streets, and besought him that they might touch if it were but the border of his garment: and as many as touched him were made whole.

7 Then came together unto him the Phar'i-sees, and certain of the scribes, which came from Je-ru'sa-lem.

2 And when they saw some of his disciples eat bread with defiled, that is to say, with unwashen, hands, they found fault.

3 For the Phar'i-sees, and all the Jews, except they wash their hands oft, eat not, holding the tradition of the elders.

4 And when they come from the market, except they wash, they eat not. And many other things there be, which they have received to hold, as the washing of cups, and pots, brazen vessels, and of tables.

5 Then the Phar'i-sees and scribes asked him, Why walk not thy disciples according to the tradition of the elders, but eat bread with unwashen hands?

6 He answered and said unto them, Well hath I-sa'iah prophesied of you hypocrites, as it is written, This people honoreth me with their lips, but their heart is far from me.

7 Howbeit in vain do they worship me, teaching for doctrines the commandments of men.

8 For laying aside the commandment of God, ye hold the tradition of men, as the washing of

pots and cups: and many other such like things ye do.

9 And he said unto them, Full well ye reject the commandment of God, that ye may keep your own tradition.

10 For Mo'ses said, Honor thy father and thy mother; and, Whoso curseth father or mother, let him die the death:

11 But ye say, If a man shall say to his father or mother, *It is* Corban, that is to say, a gift, by whatsoever thou mightest be profited by me; *he shall be free.*

12 And ye suffer him no more to do aught for his father or his mother;

13 Making the word of God of none effect through your tradition, which ye have delivered: and many such like things do ye.

14 ¶ And when he had called all the people *unto him,* he said unto them, Hearken unto me every one *of you,* and understand:

15 There is nothing from without a man, that entering into him can defile him: but the things which come out of him, those are they that defile the man.

16 If any man have ears to hear, let him hear.

17 And when he was entered into the house from the people, his disciples asked him concerning the parable.

18 And he saith unto them, Are ye so without understanding also? Do ye not perceive, that whatsoever thing from without entereth into the man, *it* cannot defile him;

19 Because it entereth not into his heart, but into the belly, and goeth out into the draught, purging all meats?

20 And he said, That which cometh out of the man, that defileth the man.

21 For from within, out of the heart of men, proceed evil thoughts, adulteries, fornications, murders,

22 Thefts, covetousness, wickedness, deceit, lasciviousness, an evil eye, blasphemy, pride, foolishness:

23 All these evil things come from within, and defile the man.

24 ¶ And from thence he arose, and went into the borders of Tyre and Si'don, and entered into an house, and would have no man know *it:* but he could not be hid.

25 For a *certain* woman, whose young daughter had an unclean spirit, heard of him, and came and fell at his feet:

26 The women was a Greek, a Sy-ro-phe-ni'cian by nation; and she besought him that he would cast forth the devil out of her daughter.

27 But Je'sus said unto her, Let the children first be filled: for it is not meet to take the children's bread, and to cast *it* unto the dogs.

28 And she answered and said unto him, Yes, Lord: yet the dogs under the table eat of the children's crumbs.

29 And he said unto her, For this saying go thy way; the devil is gone out of thy daughter.

30 And when she was come to

her house, she found the devil gone out, and her daughter laid upon the bed.

31 ¶ And again, departing from the coasts of Tyre and Si'don, he came unto the sea of Gal'i-lee, through the midst of the coasts of De-cap'o-lis.

32 And they bring unto him one that was deaf, and had an impediment in his speech; and they beseech him to put his hand upon him.

33 And he took him aside from the multitude, and put his fingers into his ears, and he spit, and touched his tongue;

34 And looking up to heaven, he sighed, and saith unto him, Eph'pha-tha, that is, Be opened.

35 And straightway his ears were opened, and the string of his tongue was loosed, and he spake plain.

36 And he charged them that they should tell no man: but the more he charged them, so much the more a great deal they published it;

37 And were beyond measure astonished, saying, He hath done all things well: he maketh both the deaf to hear, and the dumb to speak.

8 In those days the multitude being very great, and having nothing to eat, Je'sus called his disciples unto him, and saith unto them,

2 I have compassion on the multitude, because they have now been with me three days, and have nothing to eat:

3 And if I send them away fasting to their own houses, they will faint by the way: for divers of them came from far.

4 And his disciples answered him, From whence can a man satisfy these men with bread here in the wilderness?

5 And he asked them, How many loaves have ye? And they said, Seven.

6 And he commanded the people to sit down on the ground: and he took the seven loaves, and gave thanks, and brake, and gave to his disciples to set before them; and they did set them before the people.

7 And they had a few small fishes: and he blessed, and commanded to set them also before them.

8 So they did eat, and were filled: and they took up of the broken meat that was left seven baskets.

9 And they that had eaten were about four thousand: and he sent them away.

10 ¶ And straightway he entered into a ship with his disciples, and came into the parts of Dal-ma-nu'tha.

11 And the Phar'i-sees came forth, and began to question with him, seeking of him a sign from heaven, tempting him.

12 And he sighed deeply in his spirit, and saith, Why doth this generation seek after a sign? verily I say unto you, There shall no sign be given unto this generation.

13 And he left them, and entering into the ship again departed to the other side.

14 ¶ Now the disciples had

forgotten to take bread, neither had they in the ship with them more than one loaf.

15 And he charged them, saying, Take heed, beware of the leaven of the Phar'i-sees, and *of* the leaven of Her'od.

16 And they reasoned among themselves, saying, *It is* because we have no bread.

17 And when Je'sus knew *it,* he saith unto them, Why reason ye, because ye have no bread? perceive ye not yet, neither understand? have ye your heart yet hardened?

18 Having eyes, see ye not? and having ears, hear ye not? and do ye not remember?

19 When I brake the five loaves among five thousand, how many baskets full of fragments took ye up? They say unto him, Twelve.

20 And when the seven among four thousand, how many baskets full of fragments took ye up? And they said, Seven.

21 And he said unto them, How is it that ye do not understand?

22 ¶ And he cometh to Beth-sa'-i-da; and they bring a blind man unto him, and besought him to touch him.

23 And he took the blind man by the hand, and led him out of the town; and when he had spit on his eyes, and put his hands upon him, he asked him if he saw aught.

24 And he looked up, and said, I see men as trees, walking.

25 After that he put *his* hands again upon his eyes, and made him look up: and he was re-stored, and saw every man clearly.

26 And he sent him away to his house, saying, Neither go into the town, nor tell *it* to any in the town.

27 ¶ And Je'sus went out, and his disciples, into the towns of Cæs-a-re'a Phi-lip'pi: and by the way he asked his disciples, saying unto them, Whom do men say that I am?

28 And they answered, John the Bap'tist: but some *say,* E-li'-jah; and others, One of the prophets.

29 And he saith unto them, But whom say ye that I am? And Pe'-ter answereth and saith unto him, Thou art the Christ.

30 And he charged them that they should tell no man of him.

31 And he began to teach them, that the Son of man must suffer many things, and be rejected of the elders, and *of* the chief priests, and scribes, and be killed, and after three days rise again.

32 And he spake that saying openly. And Pe'ter took him, and began to rebuke him.

33 But when he had turned about and looked on his disciples, he rebuked Pe'ter, saying, Get thee behind me, Sa'tan: for thou savorest not the things that be of God, but the things that be of men.

34 ¶ And when he had called the people *unto him* with his disciples also, he said unto them, Whosoever will come after me, let him deny himself,

and take up his cross, and follow
me.

35 For whosoever will save his
life shall lose it; but whosoever
shall lose his life for my sake
and the gospel's, the same shall
save it.

36 For what shall it profit a
man, if he shall gain the whole
world, and lose his own soul?

37 Or what shall a man give in
exchange for his soul?

38 Whosoever therefore shall
be ashamed of me and of my
words in this adulterous and
sinful generation; of him also
shall the Son of man be
ashamed, when he cometh in
the glory of his Father with the
holy angels.

9 And he said unto them, Verily I say unto you, That there
be some of them that stand
here, which shall not taste of
death, till they have seen the
kingdom of God come with
power.

2 ¶ And after six days Je'sus
taketh *with him* Pe'ter, and
James, and John, and leadeth
them up Into an high mountain
apart by themselves: and he was
transfigured before them.

3 And his raiment became shining, exceeding white as snow;
so as no fuller on earth can
white them.

4 And there appeared unto
them E-li'jah with Mo'ses: and
they were talking with Je'sus.

5 And Pe'ter answered and said
to Je'sus, Master, it is good for
us to be here: and let us make
three tabernacles; one for thee,

and one for Mo'ses, and one for
E-li'jah.

6 For he wist not what to say;
for they were sore afraid.

7 And there was a cloud that
overshadowed them: and a
voice came out of the cloud,
saying, This is my beloved Son:
hear him.

8 And suddenly, when they
had looked round about, they
saw no man anymore, save Je'-
sus only with themselves.

9 And as they came down from
the mountain, he charged them
that they should tell no man
what things they had seen, till
the Son of man were risen from
the dead.

10 And they kept that saying
with themselves, questioning
one with another what the rising from the dead should mean.

11 ¶ And they asked him, saying, Why say the scribes that
E-li'jah must first come?

12 And he answered and told
them, E-li'jah verily cometh
first, and restoreth all things;
and how it is written of the Son
of man, that he must suffer
many things, and be set at
nought.

13 But I say unto you, That E-li'-
jah is indeed come, and they
have done unto him whatsoever
they listed, as it is written of
him.

14 ¶ And when he came to *his*
disciples, he saw a great multitude about them, and the
scribes questioning with them.

15 And straightway all the people, when they beheld him,

were greatly amazed, and running to *him* saluted him.

16 And he asked the scribes, What question ye with them?

17 And one of the multitude answered and said, Master, I have brought unto thee my son, which hath a dumb spirit;

18 And wheresoever he taketh him, he teareth him: and he foameth, and gnasheth with his teeth, and pineth away: and I spake to thy disciples that they should cast him out; and they could not.

19 He answereth him, and saith, O faithless generation, how long shall I be with you? how long shall I suffer you? bring him unto me.

20 And they brought him unto him: and when he saw him, straightway the spirit tore him; and he fell on the ground, and wallowed foaming.

21 And he asked his father, How long is it ago since this came unto him? And he said, Of a child.

22 And ofttimes it hath cast him into the fire, and into the waters, to destroy him: but if thou canst do any thing, have compassion on us, and help us.

23 Je'sus said unto him, If thou canst believe, all things *are* possible to him that believeth.

24 And straightway the father of the child cried out, and said with tears, Lord, I believe; help thou mine unbelief.

25 When Je'sus saw that the people came running together, he rebuked the foul spirit, saying unto him, Thou dumb and deaf spirit, I charge thee, come out of him, and enter no more into him.

26 And *the spirit* cried, and rent him sore, and came out of him: and he was as one dead; insomuch that many said, He is dead.

27 But Je'sus took him by the hand, and lifted him up; and he arose.

28 And when he was come into the house, his disciples asked him privately, Why could not we cast him out?

29 And he said unto them, This kind can come forth by nothing, but by prayer and fasting.

30 ¶ And they departed thence, and passed through Gal'i-lee; and he would not that any man should know *it*.

31 For he taught his disciples, and said unto them, The Son of man is delivered into the hands of men, and they shall kill him; and after that he is killed, he shall rise the third day.

32 But they understood not that saying, and were afraid to ask him.

33 ¶ And he came to Ca-per'-na-um: and being in the house he asked them, What was it that ye disputed among yourselves by the way?

34 But they held their peace: for by the way they had disputed among themselves, who *should be* the greatest.

35 And he sat down, and called the twelve, and saith unto them, If any man desire to be first, *the same* shall be last of all, and servant of all.

36 And he took a child, and set him in the midst of them: and when he had taken him in his arms, he said unto them,

37 Whosoever shall receive one of such children in my name, receiveth me: and whosoever shall receive me, receiveth not me, but him that sent me.

38 ¶ And John answered him, saying, Master, we saw one casting out devils in thy name, and he followeth not us: and we forbade him, because he followeth not us.

39 But Je'sus said, Forbid him not: for there is no man which shall do a miracle in my name, that can lightly speak evil of me.

40 For he that is not against us is on our part.

41 For whosoever shall give you a cup of water to drink in my name, because ye belong to Christ, verily I say unto you, he shall not lose his reward.

42 And whosoever shall offend one of these little ones that believe in me, it is better for him that a millstone were hanged about his neck, and he were cast into the sea.

43 And if thy hand offend thee, cut it off: it is better for thee to enter into life maimed, than having two hands to go into hell, into the fire that never shall be quenched:

44 Where their worm dieth not, and the fire is not quenched.

45 And if thy foot offend thee, cut it off: it is better for thee to enter halt into life, than having two feet to be cast into hell, into

the fire that never shall be quenched:

46 Where their worm dieth not, and the fire is not quenched.

47 And if thine eye offend thee, pluck it out: it is better for thee to enter into the kingdom of God with one eye, than having two eyes to be cast into hell fire:

48 Where their worm dieth not, and the fire is not quenched.

49 For everyone shall be salted with fire, and every sacrifice shall be salted with salt.

50 Salt is good: but if the salt have lost his saltness, wherewith will ye season it? Have salt in yourselves, and have peace one with another.

10 And he arose from thence, and cometh into the coasts of Ju-dæ'a by the farther side of Jor'dan: and the people resort unto him again; and, as he was wont, he taught them again.

2 ¶ And the Phar'i-sees came to him, and asked him, Is it lawful for a man to put away his wife? tempting him.

3 And he answered and said unto them, What did Mo'ses command you?

4 And they said, Mo'ses suffered to write a bill of divorcement, and to put her away.

5 And Je'sus answered and said unto them, For the hardness of your heart he wrote you this precept.

6 But from the beginning of the creation God made them male and female.

7 For this cause shall a man leave his father and mother, and cleave to his wife;

8 And they twain shall be one flesh: so then they are no more twain, but one flesh.

9 What therefore God hath joined together, let not man put asunder.

10 And in the house his disciples asked him again of the same *matter.*

11 And he saith unto them, Whosoever shall put away his wife, and marry another, committeth adultery against her.

12 And if a woman put away her husband, and be married to another, she committeth adultery.

13 ¶ And they brought young children to him, that he should touch them: and *his* disciples rebuked those that brought *them.*

14 But when Je´sus saw *it,* he was much displeased, and said unto them, Suffer the little children to come unto me, and forbid them not: for of such is the kingdom of God.

15 Verily I say unto you, Whosoever shall not receive the kingdom of God as a little child, he shall not enter therein.

16 And he took them up in his arms, put *his* hands upon them, and blessed them.

17 ¶ And when he was gone forth into the way, there came one running, and kneeled to him, and asked him, Good Master, what shall I do that I may inherit eternal life?

18 And Je´sus said unto him,

Why callest thou me good? *there is* none good but one, *that is,* God.

19 Thou knowest the commandments, Do not commit adultery, Do not kill, Do not steal, Do not bear false witness, Defraud not, Honor thy father and mother.

20 And he answered and said unto him, Master, all these have I observed from my youth.

21 Then Je´sus beholding him loved him, and said unto him, One thing thou lackest: go thy way, sell whatsoever thou hast, and give to the poor, and thou shalt have treasure in heaven: and come, take up the cross, and follow me.

22 And he was sad at that saying, and went away grieved: for he had great possessions.

23 ¶ And Je´sus looked round about, and saith unto his disciples, How hardly shall they that have riches enter into the kingdom of God!

24 And the disciples were astonished at his words. But Je´sus answereth again, and saith unto them, Children, how hard is it for them that trust in riches to enter into the kingdom of God!

25 It is easier for a camel to go through the eye of a needle, than for a rich man to enter into the kingdom of God.

26 And they were astonished out of measure, saying among themselves, Who then can be saved?

27 And Je´sus looking upon them saith, With men *it is*

impossible, but not with God: for with God all things are possible.

28 ¶ Then Pe'ter began to say unto him, Lo, we have left all, and have followed thee.

29 And Je'sus answered and said, Verily I say unto you, There is no man that hath left house, or brethren, or sisters, or father, or mother, or wife, or children, or lands, for my sake, and the gospel's,

30 But he shall receive an hundredfold now in this time, houses, and brethren, and sisters, and mothers, and children, and lands, with persecutions; and in the world to come eternal life.

31 But many that are first shall be last; and the last first.

32 ¶ And they were in the way going up to Je-ru'sa-lem; and Je'sus went before them: and they were amazed; and as they followed, they were afraid. And he took again the twelve, and began to tell them what things should happen unto him,

33 Saying, Behold, we go up to Je-ru'sa-lem; and the Son of man shall be delivered unto the chief priests, and unto the scribes; and they shall condemn him to death, and shall deliver him to the Gen'tiles:

34 And they shall mock him, and shall scourge him, and shall spit upon him, and shall kill him: and the third day he shall rise again.

35 ¶ And James and John, the sons of Zeb'e-dee, come unto him, saying, Master, we would

that thou shouldest do for us whatsoever we shall desire.

36 And he said unto them, What would ye that I should do for you?

37 They said unto him, Grant unto us that we may sit, one on thy right hand, and the other on thy left hand, in thy glory.

38 But Je'sus said unto them, Ye know not what ye ask: can ye drink of the cup that I drink of? and be baptized with the baptism that I am baptized with?

39 And they said unto him, We can. And Je'sus said unto them, Ye shall indeed drink of the cup that I drink of; and with the baptism that I am baptized withal shall ye be baptized:

40 But to sit on my right hand and on my left hand is not mine to give; but it shall be given to them for whom it is prepared.

41 And when the ten heard it, they began to be much displeased with James and John.

42 But Je'sus called them to him, and saith unto them, Ye know that they which are accounted to rule over the Gen'tiles exercise lordship over them; and their great ones exercise authority upon them.

43 But so shall it not be among you: but whosoever will be great among you, shall be your minister:

44 And whosoever of you will be the chiefest, shall be servant of all.

45 For even the Son of man came not to be ministered unto,

but to minister, and to give his life a ransom for many.

46 ¶ And they came to Jer'i-cho: and as he went out of Jer'i-cho with his disciples and a great number of people, blind Bar-ti-mæ'us, the son of Ti-mæ'us, sat by the highway side begging.

47 And when he heard that it was Je'sus of Naz'a-reth, he began to cry out, and say, Je'sus, thou son of Da'vid, have mercy on me.

48 And many charged him that he should hold his peace: but he cried the more a great deal, Thou son of Da'vid, have mercy on me.

49 And Je'sus stood still, and commanded him to be called. And they call the blind man, saying unto him, Be of good comfort, rise; he calleth thee.

50 And he, casting away his garment, rose, and came to Je'sus.

51 And Je'sus answered and said unto him, What wilt thou that I should do unto thee? The blind man said unto him, Lord, that I might receive my sight.

52 And Je'sus said unto him, Go thy way; thy faith hath made thee whole. And immediately he received his sight, and followed Je'sus in the way.

11 And when they came nigh to Je-ru'sa-lem, unto Beth'-pha-ge and Beth'a-ny, at the mount of Ol'ives, he sendeth forth two of his disciples,

2 And saith unto them, Go your way into the village over against you: and as soon as ye be entered into it, ye shall find a colt tied, whereon never man sat; loose him, and bring him.

3 And if any man say unto you, Why do ye this? say ye that the Lord hath need of him; and straightway he will send him hither.

4 And they went their way, and found the colt tied by the door without in a place where two ways met; and they loose him.

5 And certain of them that stood there said unto them, What do ye, loosing the colt?

6 And they said unto them even as Je'sus had commanded: and they let them go.

7 And they brought the colt to Je'sus, and cast their garments on him; and he sat upon him.

8 And many spread their garments in the way: and others cut down branches off the trees, and strewed them in the way.

9 And they that went before, and they that followed, cried, saying, Ho-san'na; Blessed is he that cometh in the name of the Lord:

10 Blessed be the kingdom of our father Da'vid, that cometh in the name of the Lord: Ho-san'na in the highest.

11 And Je'sus entered into Je-ru'sa-lem, and into the temple: and when he had looked round about upon all things, and now the eventide was come, he went out unto Beth'a-ny with the twelve.

12 ¶ And on the morrow, when they were come from Beth'a-ny, he was hungry:

13 And seeing a fig tree afar off having leaves, he came, if haply

he might find anything thereon: and when he came to it, he found nothing but leaves; for the time of figs was not *yet*.

14 And Je´sus answered and said unto it, No man eat fruit of thee hereafter forever. And his disciples heard *it*.

15 ¶ And they come to Je-ru´sa-lem: and Je´sus went into the temple, and began to cast out them that sold and bought in the temple, and overthrew the tables of the money changers, and the seats of them that sold doves;

16 And would not suffer that any man should carry *any* vessel through the temple.

17 And he taught, saying unto them, Is it not written, My house shall be called of all nations the house of prayer? but ye have made it a den of thieves.

18 And the scribes and chief priests heard *it*, and sought how they might destroy him: for they feared him, because all the people was astonished at his doctrine.

19 And when even was come, he went out of the city.

20 ¶ And in the morning, as they passed by, they saw the fig tree dried up from the roots.

21 And Pe´ter calling to remembrance saith unto him, Master, behold, the fig tree which thou cursedst is withered away.

22 And Je´sus answering saith unto them, Have faith in God.

23 For verily I say unto you, That whosoever shall say unto this mountain, Be thou removed, and be thou cast into

the sea; and shall not doubt in his heart, but shall believe that those things which he saith shall come to pass; he shall have whatsoever he saith.

24 Therefore I say unto you, What things soever ye desire, when ye pray, believe that ye receive *them*, and ye shall have *them*.

25 And when ye stand praying, forgive, if ye have aught against any: that your Father also which is in heaven may forgive your trespasses.

26 But if ye do not forgive, neither will your Father which is in heaven forgive your trespasses.

27 ¶ And they come again to Je-ru´sa-lem: and as he was walking in the temple, there come to him the chief priests, and the scribes, and the elders,

28 And say unto him, By what authority doest thou these things? and who gave thee this authority to do these things?

29 And Je´sus answered and said unto them, I will also ask of you one question, and answer me, and I will tell you by what authority I do these things.

30 The baptism of John, was *it* from heaven, or of men? answer me.

31 And they reasoned with themselves, saying, If we shall say, From heaven; he will say, Why then did ye not believe him?

32 But if we shall say, Of men; they feared the people: for all *men* counted John, that he was a prophet indeed.

33 And they answered and said unto Je'sus, We cannot tell. And Je'sus answering saith unto them, Neither do I tell you by what authority I do these things.

12 And he began to speak unto them by parables. A certain man planted a vineyard, and set an hedge about *it*, and digged *a place for* the wine vat, and built a tower, and let it out to husbandmen, and went into a far country.

2 And at the season he sent to the husbandmen a servant, that he might receive from the husbandmen of the fruit of the vineyard.

3 And they caught *him*, and beat him, and sent *him* away empty.

4 And again he sent unto them another servant; and at him they cast stones, and wounded *him* in the head, and sent *him* away shamefully handled.

5 And again he sent another; and him they killed, and many others; beating some, and killing some.

6 Having yet therefore one son, his well-beloved, he sent him also last unto them, saying, They will reverence my son.

7 But those husbandmen said among themselves, This is the heir; come, let us kill him, and the inheritance shall be ours.

8 And they took him, and killed *him*, and cast *him* out of the vineyard.

9 What shall therefore the lord of the vineyard do? he will come and destroy the husbandmen, and will give the vineyard unto others.

10 And have ye not read this scripture; The stone which the builders rejected is become the head of the corner:

11 This was the Lord's doing, and it is marvelous in our eyes?

12 And they sought to lay hold on him, but feared the people: for they knew that he had spoken the parable against them: and they left him, and went their way.

13 ¶ And they send unto him certain of the Phar'i-sees and of the He-ro'di-ans, to catch him in *his* words.

14 And when they were come, they say unto him, Master, we know that thou art true, and carest for no man: for thou regardest not the person of men, but teachest the way of God in truth: Is it lawful to give tribute to Cae'sar, or not?

15 Shall we give, or shall we not give? But he, knowing their hypocrisy, said unto them, Why tempt ye me? bring me a penny, that I may see *it*.

16 And they brought *it*. And he saith unto them, Whose *is* this image and superscription? And they said unto him, Cae'sar's.

17 And Je'sus answering said unto them, Render to Cae'sar the things that are Cae'sar's, and to God the things that are God's. And they marveled at him.

18 ¶ Then come unto him the Sad'du-cees, which say there is no resurrection; and they asked him, saying,

19 Master, Mo'ses wrote unto us, If a man's brother die, and leave his wife behind him, and leave no children, that his brother should take his wife, and raise up seed unto his brother.

20 Now there were seven brethren: and the first took a wife, and dying left no seed.

21 And the second took her, and died, neither left he any seed: and the third likewise.

22 And the seven had her, and left no seed: last of all the woman died also.

23 In the resurrection therefore, when they shall rise, whose wife shall she be of them? for the seven had her to wife.

24 And Je'sus answering said unto them, Do ye not therefore err, because ye know not the scriptures, neither the power of God?

25 For when they shall rise from the dead, they neither marry, nor are given in marriage; but are as the angels which are in heaven.

26 And as touching the dead, that they rise: have ye not read in the book of Mo'ses, how in the bush God spake unto him, saying, I am the God of A'bra-ham, and the God of I'saac, and the God of Ja'cob?

27 He is not the God of the dead, but the God of the living: ye therefore do greatly err.

28 ¶ And one of the scribes came, and having heard them reasoning together, and perceiving that he had answered them

well, asked him, Which is the first commandment of all?

29 And Je'sus answered him, The first of all the commandments is, Hear, O Is'ra-el; The Lord our God is one Lord:

30 And thou shalt love the Lord thy God with all thy heart, and with all thy soul, and with all thy mind, and with all thy strength: this is the first commandment.

31 And the second is like, namely this, Thou shalt love thy neighbor as thyself. There is none other commandment greater than these.

32 And the scribe said unto him, Well, Master, thou hast said the truth: for there is one God; and there is none other but he:

33 And to love him with all the heart, and with all the understanding, and with all the soul, and with all the strength, and to love his neighbor as himself, is more than all whole burnt offerings and sacrifices.

34 And when Je'sus saw that he answered discreetly, he said unto him, Thou art not far from the kingdom of God. And no man after that durst ask him any question.

35 ¶ And Je'sus answered and said, while he taught in the temple, How say the scribes that Christ is the son of Da'vid?

36 For Da'vid himself said by the Ho'ly Ghost, The Lord said to my Lord, Sit thou on my right hand, till I make thine enemies thy footstool.

37 Da'vid therefore himself

calleth him Lord; and whence is he *then* his son? And the common people heard him gladly.

38 ¶ And he said unto them in his doctrine, Beware of the scribes, which love to go in long clothing, and *love* salutations in the market places,

39 And the chief seats in the synagogues, and the uppermost rooms at feasts:

40 Which devour widows' houses, and for a pretense make long prayers: these shall receive greater damnation.

41 ¶ And Je'sus sat over against the treasury, and beheld how the people cast money into the treasury: and many that were rich cast in much.

42 And there came a certain poor widow, and she threw in two mites, which make a farthing.

43 And he called *unto him* his disciples, and saith unto them, Verily I say unto you, That this poor widow hath cast more in, than all they which have cast into the treasury:

44 For all *they* did cast in of their abundance; but she of her want did cast in all that she had, *even* all her living.

13 And as he went out of the temple, one of his disciples saith unto him, Master, see what manner of stones and what buildings *are here!*

2 And Je'sus answering said unto him, Seest thou these great buildings? there shall not be left one stone upon another, that shall not be thrown down.

3 And as he sat upon the mount of Ol'ives over against the temple, Pe'ter and James and John and An'drew asked him privately,

4 Tell us, when shall these things be? and what *shall* be the sign when all these things shall be fulfilled?

5 And Je'sus answering them began to say, Take heed lest any *man* deceive you:

6 For many shall come in my name, saying, I am *Christ*; and shall deceive many.

7 And when ye shall hear of wars and rumors of wars, be ye not troubled: for *such things* must needs be; but the end *shall* not *be* yet.

8 For nation shall rise against nation, and kingdom against kingdom: and there shall be earthquakes in divers places, and there shall be famines and troubles: these *are* the beginnings of sorrows.

9 ¶ But take heed to yourselves: for they shall deliver you up to councils; and in the synagogues ye shall be beaten: and ye shall be brought before rulers and kings for my sake, for a testimony against them.

10 And the gospel must first be published among all nations.

11 But when they shall lead *you*, and deliver you up, take no thought beforehand what ye shall speak, neither do ye premeditate: but whatsoever shall be given you in that hour, that speak ye: for it is not ye that speak, but the Ho'ly Ghost.

12 Now the brother shall betray the brother to death, and

the father the son; and children shall rise up against *their* parents, and shall cause them to be put to death.

13 And ye shall be hated of all *men* for my name's sake: but he that shall endure unto the end, the same shall be saved.

14 ¶ But when ye shall see the abomination of desolation, spoken of by Dan′iel the prophet, standing where it ought not, (let him that readeth understand,) then let them that be in Ju-dæ′a flee to the mountains:

15 And let him that is on the housetop not go down into the house, neither enter *therein*, to take anything out of his house:

16 And let him that is in the field not turn back again for to take up his garment.

17 But woe to them that are with child, and to them that give suck in those days!

18 And pray ye that your flight be not in the winter.

19 For *in* those days shall be affliction, such as was not from the beginning of the creation which God created unto this time, neither shall be.

20 And except that the Lord had shortened those days, no flesh should be saved: but for the elect's sake, whom he hath chosen, he hath shortened the days.

21 And then if any man shall say to you, Lo, here *is* Christ; or, lo, *he is* there; believe *him* not:

22 For false Christs and false prophets shall rise, and shall show signs and wonders, to seduce, if *it were* possible, even the elect.

23 But take ye heed: behold, I have foretold you all things.

24 ¶ But in those days, after that tribulation, the sun shall be darkened, and the moon shall not give her light,

25 And the stars of heaven shall fall, and the powers that are in heaven shall be shaken.

26 And then shall they see the Son of man coming in the clouds with great power and glory.

27 And then shall he send his angels, and shall gather together his elect from the four winds, from the uttermost part of the earth to the uttermost part of heaven.

28 Now learn a parable of the fig tree; When her branch is yet tender, and putteth forth leaves, ye know that summer is near:

29 So ye in like manner, when ye shall see these things come to pass, know that it is nigh, *even* at the doors.

30 Verily I say unto you, that this generation shall not pass, till all these things be done.

31 Heaven and earth shall pass away: but my words shall not pass away.

32 ¶ But of that day and *that* hour knoweth no man, no, not the angels which are in heaven, neither the Son, but the Father.

33 Take ye heed, watch and pray: for ye know not when the time is.

34 *For the Son of man is* as a man taking a far journey, who left his house, and gave authority

to his servants, and to every man his work, and commanded the porter to watch.

35 Watch ye therefore: for ye know not when the master of the house cometh, at even, or at midnight, or at the cock-crowing, or in the morning:

36 Lest coming suddenly he find you sleeping.

37 And what I say unto you I say unto all, Watch.

14 After two days was *the* feast of the passover, and of unleavened bread: and the chief priests and the scribes sought how they might take him by craft, and put *him* to death.

2 But they said, Not on the feast *day*, lest there be an uproar of the people.

3 ¶ And being in Beth'a-ny in the house of Si'mon the leper, as he sat at meat, there came a woman having an alabaster box of ointment of spikenard very precious; and she brake the box, and poured *it* on his head.

4 And there were some that had indignation within themselves, and said, Why was this waste of the ointment made?

5 For it might have been sold for more than three hundred pence, and have been given to the poor. And they murmured against her.

6 And Je'sus said, Let her alone; why trouble ye her? she hath wrought a good work on me.

7 For ye have the poor with you always, and whensoever ye will ye may do them good: but me ye have not always.

8 She hath done what she could: she is come aforehand to anoint my body to the burying.

9 Verily I say unto you, Wheresoever this gospel shall be preached throughout the whole world, *this* also that she hath done shall be spoken of for a memorial of her.

10 ¶ And Ju'das Is-car'i-ot, one of the twelve, went unto the chief priests, to betray him unto them.

11 And when they heard *it*, they were glad, and promised to give him money. And he sought how he might conveniently betray him.

12 ¶ And the first day of unleavened bread, when they killed the passover, his disciples said unto him, Where wilt thou that we go and prepare that thou mayest eat the passover?

13 And he sendeth forth two of his disciples, and saith unto them, Go ye into the city, and there shall meet you a man bearing a pitcher of water: follow him.

14 And wheresoever he shall go in, say ye to the goodman of the house, The Master saith, Where is the guestchamber, where I shall eat the passover with my disciples?

15 And he will show you a large upper room furnished *and* prepared: there make ready for us.

16 And his disciples went forth, and came into the city, and found as he had said unto them: and they made ready the passover.

17 And in the evening he cometh with the twelve.

18 And as they sat and did eat, Je'sus said, Verily I say unto you, One of you which eateth with me shall betray me.

19 And they began to be sorrowful, and to say unto him one by one, Is it I? and another said, Is it I?

20 And he answered and said unto them, It is one of the twelve, that dippeth with me in the dish.

21 The Son of man indeed goeth, as it is written of him: but woe to that man by whom the Son of man is betrayed! good were it for that man if he had never been born.

22 ¶ And as they did eat, Je'sus took bread, and blessed, and brake it, and gave to them, and said, Take, eat: this is my body.

23 And he took the cup, and when he had given thanks, he gave it to them: and they all drank of it.

24 And he said unto them, This is my blood of the new testament, which is shed for many.

25 Verily I say unto you, I will drink no more of the fruit of the vine, until that day that I drink it new in the kingdom of God.

26 ¶ And when they had sung an hymn, they went out into the mount of Ol'ives.

27 And Je'sus saith unto them, All ye shall be offended because of me this night: for it is written, I will smite the shepherd, and the sheep shall be scattered.

28 But after that I am risen, I will go before you into Gal'i-lee.

29 But Pe'ter said unto him, Although all shall be offended, yet will not I.

30 And Je'sus saith unto him, Verily I say unto thee, That this day, even in this night, before the cock crow twice, thou shalt deny me thrice.

31 But he spake the more vehemently, If I should die with thee, I will not deny thee in any wise. Likewise also said they all.

32 And they came to a place which was named Geth-sem'a-ne: and he saith to his disciples, Sit ye here, while I shall pray.

33 And he taketh with him Pe'ter and James and John, and began to be sore amazed, and to be very heavy;

34 And saith unto them, My soul is exceeding sorrowful unto death: tarry ye here, and watch.

35 And he went forward a little, and fell on the ground, and prayed that, if it were possible, the hour might pass from him.

36 And he said, Ab'ba, Father, all things are possible unto thee; take away this cup from me: nevertheless not what I will, but what thou wilt.

37 And he cometh, and findeth them sleeping, and saith to Pe'ter, Si'mon, sleepest thou? couldest not thou watch one hour?

38 Watch ye and pray, lest ye enter into temptation. The spirit truly is ready, but the flesh is weak.

39 And again he went away, and prayed, and spake the same words.

40 And when he returned, he found them asleep again, (for their eyes were heavy,) neither wist they what to answer him.

41 And he cometh the third time, and saith unto them, Sleep on now, and take *your* rest: it is enough, the hour is come; behold, the Son of man is betrayed into the hands of sinners.

42 Rise up, let us go; lo, he that betrayeth me is at hand.

43 ¶ And immediately, while he yet spake, cometh Ju'das, one of the twelve, and with him a great multitude with swords and staves, from the chief priests and the scribes and the elders.

44 And he that betrayed him had given them a token, saying, Whomsoever I shall kiss, that same is he; take him, and lead *him* away safely.

45 And as soon as he was come, he goeth straightway to him, and saith, Master, master; and kissed him.

46 ¶ And they laid their hands on him, and took him.

47 And one of them that stood by drew a sword, and smote a servant of the high priest, and cut off his ear.

48 And Je'sus answered and said unto them, Are ye come out, as against a thief, with swords and *with* staves to take me?

49 I was daily with you in the temple teaching, and ye took me not: but the scriptures must be fulfilled.

50 And they all forsook him, and fled.

51 And there followed him a certain young man, having a linen cloth cast about *his* naked *body;* and the young men laid hold on him:

52 And he left the linen cloth, and fled from them naked.

53 ¶ And they led Je'sus away to the high priest: and with him were assembled all the chief priests and the elders and the scribes.

54 And Pe'ter followed him afar off, even into the palace of the high priest: and he sat with the servants, and warmed himself at the fire.

55 And the chief priests and all the council sought for witness against Je'sus to put him to death; and found none.

56 For many bare false witness against him, but their witness agreed not together.

57 And there arose certain, and bare false witness against him, saying,

58 We heard him say, I will destroy this temple that is made with hands, and within three days I will build another made without hands.

59 But neither so did their witness agree together.

60 And the high priest stood up in the midst, and asked Je'sus, saying, Answerest thou nothing? what *is it which* these witness against thee?

61 But he held his peace, and answered nothing. Again the high priest asked him, and said unto him, Art thou the Christ, the Son of the Blessed?

62 And Je'sus said, I am: and ye shall see the Son of man sitting

on the right hand of power, and coming in the clouds of heaven.
63 Then the high priest rent his clothes, and saith, What need we any further witnesses?
64 Ye have heard the blasphemy: what think ye? And they all condemned him to be guilty of death.
65 And some began to spit on him, and to cover his face, and to buffet him, and to say unto him, Prophesy: and the servants did strike him with the palms of their hands.
66 ¶ And as Pe'ter was beneath in the palace, there cometh one of the maids of the high priest:
67 And when she saw Pe'ter warming himself, she looked upon him, and said, And thou also wast with Je'sus of Naz'a-reth.
68 But he denied, saying, I know not, neither understand I what thou sayest. And he went out into the porch; and the cock crew.
69 And a maid saw him again, and began to say to them that stood by, This is one of them.
70 And he denied it again. And a little after, they that stood by said again to Pe'ter, Surely thou art one of them: for thou art a Gal'i-læ'an, and thy speech agreeth thereto.
71 But he began to curse and to swear, saying, I know not this man of whom ye speak.
72 And the second time the cock crew And Pe'ter called to mind the word that Je'sus said unto him, Before the cock crow twice, thou shalt deny me

thrice. And when he thought thereon, he wept.

15 And straightway in the morning the chief priests held a consultation with the elders and scribes and the whole council, and bound Je'sus, and carried him away, and delivered him to Pi'late.
2 And Pi'late asked him, Art thou the King of the Jews? And he answering said unto him, Thou sayest it.
3 And the chief priests accused him of many things: but he answered nothing.
4 And Pi'late asked him again, saying, Answerest thou nothing? behold how many things they witness against thee.
5 But Je'sus yet answered nothing; so that Pi'late marveled.
6 Now at that feast he released unto them one prisoner, whomsoever they desired.
7 And there was one named Bar-ab'bas, which lay bound with them that had made insurrection with him, who had committed murder in the insurrection.
8 And the multitude crying aloud began to desire him to do as he had ever done unto them.
9 And Pi'late answered them, saying, Will ye that I release unto you the King of the Jews?
10 For he knew that the chief priests had delivered him for envy.
11 But the chief priests moved the people, that he should rather release Ba-rab'bas unto them.
12 And Pi'late answered and

said again unto them, What will ye then that I shall do *unto him* whom ye call the King of the Jews?

13 And they cried out again, Crucify him.

14 Then Pi'late said unto them, Why, what evil hath he done? And they cried out the more exceedingly, Crucify him.

15 ¶ And *so* Pi'late, willing to content the people, released Ba-rab'bas unto them, and delivered Je'sus, when he had scourged *him*, to be crucified.

16 And the soldiers led him away into the hall, called Præ-to'ri-um; and they call together the whole band.

17 And they clothed him with purple, and platted a crown of thorns, and put it about his *head*,

18 And began to salute him, Hail, King of the Jews!

19 And they smote him on the head with a reed, and did spit upon him, and bowing *their* knees worshiped him.

20 And when they had mocked him, they took off the purple from him, and put his own clothes on him, and led him out to crucify him.

21 And they compel one Si'-mon a Cy-re'ni-an, who passed by, coming out of the country, the father of Al-ex-an'der and Ru'fus, to bear his cross.

22 And they bring him unto the place Gol'go-tha, which is, being interpreted, The place of a skull.

23 And they gave him to drink

wine mingled with myrrh: but he received *it* not.

24 And when they had crucified him, they parted his garments, casting lots upon them, what every man should take.

25 And it was the third hour, and they crucified him.

26 And the superscription of his accusation was written over, THE KING OF THE JEWS.

27 And with him they crucify two thieves; the one on his right hand, and the other on his left.

28 And the scripture was fulfilled, which saith, And he was numbered with the transgressors.

29 And they that passed by railed on him, wagging their heads, and saying, Ah, thou that destroyest the temple, and buildest *it* in three days,

30 Save thyself, and come down from the cross.

31 Likewise also the chief priests mocking said among themselves with the scribes, He saved others; himself he cannot save.

32 Let Christ the King of Is'ra-el descend now from the cross, that we may see and believe. And they that were crucified with him reviled him.

33 And when the sixth hour was come, there was darkness over the whole land until the ninth hour.

34 And at the ninth hour Je'-sus cried with a loud voice, saying, E-lo'i, E-lo'i, la'ma sa-bach-tha'ni? which is, being

interpreted, My God, my God, why hast thou forsaken me?

35 And some of them that stood by, when they heard *it*, said, Behold, he calleth E·li'jah.

36 And one ran and filled a sponge full of vinegar, and put *it* on a reed, and gave him to drink, saying, Let alone; let us see whether E·li'jah will come to take him down.

37 And Je'sus cried with a loud voice, and gave up the ghost.

38 And the vail of the temple was rent in twain from the top to the bottom.

39 ¶ And when the centurion, which stood over against him, saw that he so cried out, and gave up the ghost, he said, Truly this man was the Son of God.

40 There were also women looking on afar off: among whom was Ma'ry Mag·da·le'ne, and Ma'ry the mother of James the less and of Jo'ses, and Sa·lo'me;

41 (Who also, when he was in Gal'i·lee, followed him, and ministered unto him;) and many other women which came up with him unto Je·ru'sa·lem.

42 ¶ And now when the even was come, because it was the preparation, that is, the day before the sabbath,

43 Jo'seph of Ar·i·ma·thæ'a, an honorable counselor, which also waited for the kingdom of God, came, and went in boldly unto Pi'late, and craved the body of Je'sus.

44 And Pi'late marveled if he were already dead: and calling *unto him* the centurion, he asked him whether he had been any while dead.

45 And when he knew *it* of the centurion, he gave the body to Jo'seph.

46 And he bought fine linen, and took him down, and wrapped him in the linen, and laid him in a sepulcher which was hewn out of a rock, and rolled a stone unto the door of the sepulcher.

47 And Ma'ry Mag·da·le'ne and Ma'ry *the mother* of Jo'ses beheld where he was laid.

16 And when the sabbath was past, Ma'ry Mag·da·le'ne, and Ma'ry *the mother* of James, and Sa·lo'me, had bought sweet spices, that they might come and anoint him.

2 And very early in the morning the first *day* of the week, they came unto the sepulcher at the rising of the sun.

3 And they said among themselves, Who shall roll away the stone from the door of the sepulcher?

4 And when they looked, they saw that the stone was rolled away: for it was very great.

5 And entering into the sepulcher, they saw a young man sitting on the right side, clothed in a long white garment; and they were affrighted.

6 And he saith unto them, Be not affrighted: Ye seek Je'sus of Naz'a·reth, which was crucified: he is risen; he is not here: behold the place where they laid him.

7 But go your way, tell his disciples and Pe'ter that he goeth

before you into Gal'i·lee: there shall ye see him, as he said unto you.

8 And they went out quickly, and fled from the sepulcher; for they trembled and were amazed: neither said they anything to any *man;* for they were afraid.

9 ¶ Now when *Jesus* was risen early the first *day* of the week, he appeared first to Ma'ry Mag·da·le'ne, out of whom he had cast seven devils.

10 *And* she went and told them that had been with him, as they mourned and wept.

11 And they, when they had heard that he was alive, and had been seen of her, believed not.

12 ¶ After that he appeared in another form unto two of them, as they walked, and went into the country.

13 And they went and told *it* unto the residue: neither believed they them.

14 ¶ Afterward he appeared unto the eleven as they sat at meat, and upbraided them with their unbelief and hardness of heart, because they believed not them which had seen him after he was risen.

15 And he said unto them, Go ye into all the world, and preach the gospel to every creature.

16 He that believeth and is baptized shall be saved: but he that believeth not shall be damned.

17 And these signs shall follow them that believe; In my name shall they cast out devils; they shall speak with new tongues;

18 They shall take up serpents; and if they drink any deadly thing, it shall not hurt them; they shall lay hands on the sick, and they shall recover.

19 ¶ So then after the Lord had spoken unto them, he was received up into heaven, and sat on the right hand of God.

20 And they went forth, and preached everywhere, the Lord working with *them,* and confirming the word with signs following. Amen.

LUKE

1 Forasmuch as many have taken in hand to set forth in order a declaration of those things which are most surely believed among us,

2 Even as they delivered them unto us, which from the beginning were eyewitnesses, and ministers of the word;

3 It seemed good to me also, having had perfect understanding of all things from the very first, to write unto thee in order, most excellent The·oph'i·lus,

4 That thou mightest know the certainty of those things, wherein thou hast been instructed.

5 ¶ There was in the days of Her'od, the king of Ju·dæ'a,

a certain priest named Zech-a-ri'ah, of the course of A-bi'a: and his wife was of the daughters of Aar'on, and her name was E-liz'a-beth.

6 And they were both righteous before God, walking in all the commandments and ordinances of the Lord blameless.

7 And they had no child, because that E-liz'a-beth was barren, and they both were now well stricken in years.

8 And it came to pass, that while he executed the priest's office before God in the order of his course,

9 According to the custom of the priest's office, his lot was to burn incense when he went into the temple of the Lord.

10 And the whole multitude of the people were praying without at the time of incense.

11 And there appeared unto him an angel of the Lord standing on the right side of the altar of incense.

12 And when Zech-a-ri'ah saw him, he was troubled, and fear fell upon him.

13 But the angel said unto him, Fear not, Zech-a-ri'ah: for thy prayer is heard; and thy wife E-liz'a-beth shall bear thee a son, and thou shalt call his name John.

14 And thou shalt have joy and gladness; and many shall rejoice at his birth.

15 For he shall be great in the sight of the Lord, and shall drink neither wine nor strong drink; and he shall be filled with the Ho'ly Ghost, even from his mother's womb.

16 And many of the children of Is'ra-el shall he turn to the Lord their God.

17 And he shall go before him in the spirit and power of E-li'-jah, to turn the hearts of the fathers to the children, and the disobedient to the wisdom of the just; to make ready a people prepared for the Lord.

18 And Zech-a-ri'ah said unto the angel, Whereby shall I know this? for I am an old man, and my wife well stricken in years.

19 And the angel answering said unto him, I am Ga'bri-el, that stand in the presence of God; and am sent to speak unto thee, and to show thee these glad tidings.

20 And, behold, thou shalt be dumb, and not able to speak, until the day that these things shall be performed, because thou believest not my words, which shall be fulfilled in their season.

21 And the people waited for Zech-a-ri'ah, and marveled that he tarried so long in the temple.

22 And when he came out, he could not speak unto them: and they perceived that he had seen a vision in the temple: for he beckoned unto them, and remained speechless.

23 And it came to pass, that, as soon as the days of his ministration were accomplished, he departed to his own house.

24 And after those days his wife E-liz'a-beth conceived, and hid herself five months, saying,

25 Thus hath the LORD dealt with me in the days wherein he looked on *me*, to take away my reproach among men.

26 And in the sixth month the angel Ga'bri-el was sent from God unto a city of Gal'i-lee, named Naz'a-reth,

27 To a virgin espoused to a man whose name was Jo'seph, of the house of Da'vid; and the virgin's name *was* Mary.

28 And the angel came in unto her, and said, Hail, *thou that art* highly favored, the Lord *is* with thee: blessed *art* thou among women.

29 And when she saw *him*, she was troubled at his saying, and cast in her mind what manner of salutation this should be.

30 And the angel said unto her, Fear not, Ma'ry: for thou hast found favor with God.

31 And, behold, thou shalt conceive in thy womb, and bring forth a son, and shalt call his name JE'SUS.

32 He shall be great, and shall be called the Son of the Highest: and the Lord God shall give unto him the throne of his father Da'vid:

33 And he shall reign over the house of Ja'cob forever; and of his kingdom there shall be no end.

34 Then said Ma'ry unto the angel, How shall this be, seeing I know not a man?

35 And the angel answered and said unto her, The Ho'ly Ghost shall come upon thee, and the power of the Highest shall overshadow thee: therefore also that holy thing which shall be born of thee shall be called the Son of God.

36 And, behold, thy cousin E-liz'a-beth, she hath also conceived a son in her old age: and this is the sixth month with her, who was called barren.

37 For with God nothing shall be impossible.

38 And Ma'ry said, Behold, the handmaid of the Lord; be it unto me according to thy word. And the angel departed from her.

39 And Ma'ry arose in those days, and went into the hill country with haste, into a city of Ju'dah;

40 And entered into the house of Zech-a-ri'ah, and saluted E-liz'-a-beth.

41 And it came to pass, that, when E-liz'a-beth heard the salutation of Ma'ry, the babe leaped in her womb; and E-liz'a-beth was filled with the Ho'ly Ghost:

42 And she spake out with a loud voice, and said, Blessed *art* thou among women, and blessed *is* the fruit of thy womb.

43 And whence *is* this to me, that the mother of my Lord should come to me?

44 For, lo, as soon as the voice of thy salutation sounded in mine ears, the babe leaped in my womb for joy.

45 And blessed *is* she that believed: for there shall be a performance of those things which were told her from the Lord.

46 And Ma'ry said, My soul doth magnify the Lord,

47 And my spirit hath rejoiced in God my Savior.

48 For he hath regarded the low estate of his handmaiden: for, behold, from henceforth all generations shall call me blessed.

49 For he that is mighty hath done to me great things; and holy *is* his name.

50 And his mercy *is* on them that fear him from generation to generation.

51 He hath showed strength with his arm; he hath scattered the proud in the imagination of their hearts.

52 He hath put down the mighty from *their* seats, and exalted them of low degree.

53 He hath filled the hungry with good things; and the rich he hath sent empty away.

54 He hath helped his servant Is'ra-el, in remembrance of *his* mercy;

55 As he spake to our fathers, to A'bra-ham, and to his seed for ever.

56 And Ma'ry abode with her about three months, and returned to her own house.

57 Now E-liz'a-beth's full time came that she should be delivered; and she brought forth a son.

58 And her neighbors and her cousins heard how the Lord had showed great mercy upon her; and they rejoiced with her.

59 And it came to pass, that on the eighth day they came to circumcise the child; and they called him Zech-a-ri'ah, after the name of his father.

60 And his mother answered and said, Not *so*; but he shall be called John.

61 And they said unto her, There is none of thy kindred that is called by this name.

62 And they made signs to his father, how he would have him called.

63 And he asked for a writing table, and wrote, saying, His name is John. And they marveled all.

64 And his mouth was opened immediately, and his tongue *loosed*, and he spake, and praised God.

65 And fear came on all that dwelt round about them: and all these sayings were noised abroad throughout all the hill country of Ju-dæ'a.

66 And all they that heard *them* laid *them* up in their hearts, saying, What manner of child shall this be! And the hand of the Lord was with him.

67 And his father Zech-a-ri'ah was filled with the Ho'ly Ghost, and prophesied, saying,

68 Blessed *be* the Lord God of Is'ra-el; for he hath visited and redeemed his people,

69 And hath raised up an horn of salvation for us in the house of his servant Da'vid;

70 As he spake by the mouth of his holy prophets, which have been since the world began:

71 That we should be saved from our enemies, and from the hand of all that hate us;

72 To perform the mercy *promised* to our fathers, and to remember his holy covenant;

73 The oath which he sware to our father A'bra-ham,

74 That he would grant unto

us, that we being delivered out of the hand of our enemies might serve him without fear,

75 In holiness and righteousness before him, all the days of our life.

76 And thou, child, shalt be called the prophet of the Highest: for thou shalt go before the face of the Lord to prepare his ways;

77 To give knowledge of salvation unto his people by the remission of their sins,

78 Through the tender mercy of our God; whereby the dayspring from on high hath visited us,

79 To give light to them that sit in darkness and *in* the shadow of death, to guide our feet into the way of peace.

80 And the child grew, and waxed strong in spirit, and was in the deserts till the day of his showing unto Is'ra-el.

2 And it came to pass in those days, that there went out a decree from Cæ'sar Au-gus'tus, that all the world should be taxed.

2 (*And* this taxing was first made when Cy-re'ni-us was governor of Syr'i-a.)

3 And all went to be taxed, everyone into his own city.

4 And Jo'seph also went up from Gal'i-lee, out of the city of Naz'a-reth, into Ju-dæ'a, unto the city of Da'vid, which is called Beth'le-hem; (because he was of the house and lineage of Da'vid:)

5 To be taxed with Ma'ry his espoused wife, being great with child.

6 And so it was, that, while they were there, the days were accomplished that she should be delivered.

7 And she brought forth her firstborn son, and wrapped him in swaddling clothes, and laid him in a manger; because there was no room for them in the inn.

8 And there were in the same country shepherds abiding in the field, keeping watch over their flock by night.

9 And, lo, the angel of the Lord came upon them, and the glory of the Lord shone round about them: and they were sore afraid.

10 And the angel said unto them, Fear not: for, behold, I bring you good tidings of great joy, which shall be to all people.

11 For unto you is born this day in the city of Da'vid a Savior, which is Christ the Lord.

12 And this *shall be* a sign unto you; Ye shall find the babe wrapped in swaddling clothes, lying in a manger.

13 And suddenly there was with the angel a multitude of the heavenly host praising God, and saying,

14 Glory to God in the highest, and on earth peace, good will toward men.

15 And it came to pass, as the angels were gone away from them into heaven, the shepherds said one to another, Let us now go even unto Beth'le-hem, and see this thing which is

come to pass, which the Lord hath made known unto us.

16 And they came with haste, and found Ma'ry, and Jo'seph, and the babe lying in a manger.

17 And when they had seen *it*, they made known abroad the saying which was told them concerning this child.

18 And all they that heard *it* wondered at those things which were told them by the shepherds.

19 But Ma'ry kept all these things, and pondered *them* in her heart.

20 And the shepherds returned, glorifying and praising God for all the things that they had heard and seen, as it was told unto them.

21 And when eight days were accomplished for the circumcising of the child, his name was called JE'SUS, which was so named of the angel before he was conceived in the womb.

22 And when the days of her purification according to the law of Mo'ses were accomplished, they brought him to Je-ru'sa-lem, to present *him* to the Lord;

23 (As it is written in the law of the Lord, Every male that openeth the womb shall be called holy to the Lord;)

24 And to offer a sacrifice according to that which is said in the law of the Lord, A pair of turtledoves, or two young pigeons.

25 And, behold, there was a man in Je-ru'sa-lem, whose name *was* Sim'e-on; and the same man *was* just and devout,

waiting for the consolation of Is'ra-el: and the Ho'ly Ghost was upon him.

26 And it was revealed unto him by the Ho'ly Ghost, that he should not see death, before he had seen the Lord's Christ.

27 And he came by the Spirit into the temple: and when the parents brought in the child Je'sus, to do for him after the custom of the law,

28 Then took he him up in his arms, and blessed God, and said,

29 Lord, now lettest thou thy servant depart in peace, according to thy word.

30 For mine eyes have seen thy salvation,

31 Which thou hast prepared before the face of all people;

32 A light to lighten the Gen'tiles, and the glory of thy people Is'ra el.

33 And Jo'seph and his mother marveled at those things which were spoken of him.

34 And Sim'e-on blessed them, and said unto Ma'ry his mother, Behold, this *child* is set for the fall and rising again of many in Is'ra-el; and for a sign which shall be spoken against;

35 (Yea, a sword shall pierce through thy own soul also,) that the thoughts of many hearts may be revealed.

36 And there was one An'na, a prophetess, the daughter of Phan-u'el, of the tribe of A'sher: she was of a great age, and had lived with an husband seven years from her virginity;

37 And she *was* a widow of about fourscore and four years,

which departed not from the temple, but served *God* with fastings and prayers night and day.

38 And she coming in that instant gave thanks likewise unto the Lord, and spake of him to all them that looked for redemption in Je·ru′sa·lem.

39 And when they had performed all things according to the law of the Lord, they returned into Gal′i·lee, to their own city Naz′a·reth.

40 And the child grew, and waxed strong in spirit, filled with wisdom: and the grace of God was upon him.

41 Now his parents went to Je·ru′sa·lem every year at the feast of the passover.

42 And when he was twelve years old, they went up to Je·ru′sa·lem after the custom of the feast.

43 And when they had fulfilled the days, as they returned, the child Je′sus tarried behind in Je·ru′sa·lem; and Jo′seph and his mother knew not *of it.*

44 But they, supposing him to have been in the company, went a day's journey; and they sought him among *their* kinsfolk and acquaintance.

45 And when they found him not, they turned back again to Je·ru′sa·lem, seeking him.

46 And it came to pass, that after three days they found him in the temple, sitting in the midst of the doctors, both hearing them, and asking them questions.

47 And all that heard him were astonished at his understanding and answers.

48 And when they saw him, they were amazed: and his mother said unto him, Son, why hast thou thus dealt with us? behold, thy father and I have sought thee sorrowing.

49 And he said unto them, How is it that ye sought me? wist ye not that I must be about my Father's business?

50 And they understood not the saying which he spake unto them.

51 And he went down with them, and came to Naz′a·reth, and was subject unto them: but his mother kept all these sayings in her heart.

52 And Je′sus increased in wisdom and stature, and in favor with God and man.

3 Now in the fifteenth year of the reign of Ti·be′ri·us Cæ′sar, Pon′ti·us Pi′late being governor of Ju·dæ′a, and Her′od being tetrarch of Gal′i·lee, and his brother Phil′ip tetrarch of I·tu·ræ′a and of the region of Trach·o·ni′tis, and Ly·sa′ni·as the tetrarch of Ab·i·le′ne,

2 An′nas and Ca′ia·phas being the high priests, the word of God came unto John the son of Zech·a·ri′ah in the wilderness.

3 And he came into all the country about Jor′dan, preaching the baptism of repentance for the remission of sins;

4 As it is written in the book of the words of I·sa′iah the prophet, saying, The voice of one crying in the wilderness,

Prepare ye the way of the Lord, make his paths straight.

5 Every valley shall be filled, and every mountain and hill shall be brought low; and the crooked shall be made straight, and the rough ways *shall be* made smooth;

6 And all flesh shall see the salvation of God.

7 Then said he to the multitude that came forth to be baptized of him, O generation of vipers, who hath warned you to flee from the wrath to come?

8 Bring forth therefore fruits worthy of repentance, and begin not to say within yourselves, We have A'bra-ham to *our* father: for I say unto you, That God is able of these stones to raise up children unto A'bra-ham.

9 And now also the ax is laid unto the root of the trees: every tree therefore which bringeth not forth good fruit is hewn down, and cast into the fire.

10 And the people asked him, saying, What shall we do then?

11 He answereth and saith unto them, He that hath two coats, let him impart to him that hath none; and he that hath meat, let him do likewise.

12 Then came also publicans to be baptized, and said unto him, Master, what shall we do?

13 And he said unto them, Exact no more than that which is appointed you.

14 And the soldiers likewise demanded of him, saying, And what shall we do? And he said unto them, Do violence to no man, neither accuse *any* falsely; and be content with your wages.

15 And as the people were in expectation, and all men mused in their hearts of John, whether he were the Christ, or not;

16 John answered, saying unto *them* all, I indeed baptize you with water; but one mightier that I cometh, the latchet of whose shoes I am not worthy to unloose: he shall baptize you with the Ho'ly Ghost and with fire:

17 Whose fan *is* in his hand, and he will thoroughly purge his floor, and will gather the wheat into his garner; but the chaff he will burn with fire unquenchable.

18 And many other things in his exhortation preached he unto the people.

19 But Her'od the tetrarch, being reproved by him for He-ro'-di-as his brother Phil'ip's wife, and for all the evils which Her'od had done,

20 Added yet this above all, that he shut up John in prison.

21 Now when all the people were baptized, it came to pass, that Je'sus also being baptized, and praying, the heaven was opened,

22 And the Ho'ly Ghost descended in a bodily shape like a dove upon him, and a voice came from heaven, which said, Thou art my beloved Son; in thee I am well pleased.

23 And Je'sus himself began to be about thirty years of age, being (as was supposed) the son

of Jo'seph, which was *the son*
of He'li,

24 Which was *the son* of Mat'-
that, which was *the son* of
Le'vi, which was *the son* of
Mel'chi, which was *the son* of
Jan'na, which was *the son* of
Jo'seph,

25 Which was *the son* of Mat-
ta-thi'as, which was *the son* of
A'mos, which was *the son* of
Na'um, which was *the son* of
Es'li, which was *the son* of
Nag'ge,

26 Which was *the son* of Ma'-
ath, which was *the son* of Mat-
ta-thi'as, which was *the son* of
Sem'e-i, which was *the son* of
Jo'seph, which was *the son* of
Ju'dah,

27 Which was *the son* of Jo-
an'na, which was *the son* of
Rhe'sa, which was *the son* of
Zo-rob'a-bel, which was *the son*
of Sa-la'thi-el, which was *the son*
of Ne'ri,

28 Which was *the son* of Mel'-
chi, which was *the son* of Ad'di,
which was *the son* of Co'sam,
which was *the son* of El-mo'-
dam, which was *the son* of Er,

29 Which was *the son* of Jo'se,
which was *the son* of E-li-e'zer,
which was *the son* of Jo'rim,
which was *the son* of Mat'that,
which was *the son* of Le'vi,

30 Which was *the son* of Sim'-
e-on, which was *the son* of
Ju'dah, which was *the son* of
Jo'seph, which was *the son* of
Jo'nan, which was *the son* of
E-li'a-kim,

31 Which was *the son* of
Me'le-a, which was *the son* of

Me'nan, which was *the son* of
Mat'ta-tha, which was *the son*
of Na'than, which was *the son*
of Da'vid,

32 Which was *the son* of Jes'-
se, which was *the son* of O'bed,
which was *the son* of Bo'oz,
which was *the son* of Sal'mon,
which was *the son* of Na-as'son,

33 Which was *the son* of
A-min'a-dab, which was *the son*
of A'ram, which was *the son* of
Es'rom, which was *the son* of
Pha'res, which was *the son* of
Ju'dah,

34 Which was *the son* of
Ja'cob, which was *the son* of
I'saac, which was *the son* of
A'bra-ham, which was *the son*
of Tha'ra, which was *the son* of
Na'chor,

35 Which was *the son* of
Sa'ruch, which was *the son* of
Ra'gau, which was *the son* of
Pha'lec, which was *the son* of
He'ber, which was *the son* of
Sa'la,

36 Which was *the son* of Ca-i'-
nan, which was *the son* of Ar-
phax'ad, which was *the son* of
Shem, which was *the son* of
No'ah, which was *the son* of
La'mech,

37 Which was *the son* of Ma-
thu'sa-la, which was *the son* of
E'noch, which was *the son* of
Ja'red, which was *the son* of
Ma-le'le-el, which was *the son*
of Ca-i'nan,

38 Which was *the son* of E'nos,
which was *the son* of Seth,
which was *the son* of Ad'am,
which was *the son* of God.

4 And Je'sus being full of the Ho'ly Ghost returned from Jor'dan, and was led by the Spirit into the wilderness,

2 Being forty days tempted of the devil. And in those days he did eat nothing: and when they were ended, he afterward hungered.

3 And the devil said unto him, If thou be the Son of God, command this stone that it be made bread.

4 And Je'sus answered him, saying, It is written, That man shall not live by bread alone, but by every word of God.

5 And the devil taking him up into an high mountain, showed unto him all the kingdoms of the world in a moment of time.

6 And the devil said unto him, All this power will I give thee, and the glory of them: for that is delivered unto me; and to whomsoever I will I give it.

7 If thou therefore wilt worship me, all shall be thine.

8 And Je'sus answered and said unto him, Get thee behind me, Sa'tan: for it is written, Thou shalt worship the Lord thy God, and him only shalt thou serve.

9 And he brought him to Je-ru'sa-lem, and set him on a pinnacle of the temple, and said unto him, If thou be the Son of God, cast thyself down from hence:

10 For it is written, He shall give his angels charge over thee, to keep thee:

11 And in *their* hands they shall bear thee up, lest at anytime thou dash thy foot against a stone.

12 And Je'sus answering said unto him, It is said, Thou shalt not tempt the Lord thy God.

13 And when the devil had ended all the temptation, he departed from him for a season.

14 ¶ And Je'sus returned in the power of the Spirit into Gal'i-lee: and there went out a fame of him through all the region round about.

15 And he taught in their synagogues, being glorified of all.

16 ¶ And he came to Naz'a-reth, where he had been brought up: and, as his custom was, he went into the synagogue on the sabbath day, and stood up for to read.

17 And there was delivered unto him the book of the prophet I-sa'iah. And when he had opened the book, he found the place where it was written,

18 The Spirit of the Lord *is* upon me, because he hath anointed me to preach the gospel to the poor; he hath sent me to heal the brokenhearted, to preach deliverance to the captives, and recovering of sight to the blind, to set at liberty them that are bruised,

19 To preach the acceptable year of the Lord.

20 And he closed the book, and he gave *it* again to the minister, and sat down. And the eyes of all them that were in the synagogue were fastened on him.

21 And he began to say unto them, This day is this scripture fulfilled in your ears.

22 And all bare him witness, and wondered at the gracious

words which proceeded out of his mouth. And they said, Is not this Jo'seph's son?

23 And he said unto them, Ye will surely say unto me this proverb, Physician, heal thyself: whatsoever we have heard done in Ca·per'na·um, do also here in thy country.

24 And he said, Verily I say unto you, No prophet is accepted in his own country.

25 But I tell you of a truth, many widows were in Is'ra·el in the days of E·li'jah, when the heaven was shut up three years and six months, when great famine was throughout all the land;

26 But unto none of them was E·li'jah sent, save unto Sa·rep'ta, a city of Si'don, unto a woman that was a widow.

27 And many lepers were in Is'ra·el in the time of El·i·sha the prophet; and none of them was cleansed, saving Na'a·man the Syr'i·an.

28 And all they in the synagogue, when they heard these things, were filled with wrath,

29 And rose up, and thrust him out of the city, and led him unto the brow of the hill whereon their city was built, that they might cast him down headlong.

30 But he passing through the midst of them went his way,

31 And came down to Ca·per'na·um, a city of Gal'i·lee, and taught them on the sabbath days.

32 And they were astonished at his doctrine: for his word was with power.

33 ¶ And in the synagogue there was a man, which had a spirit of an unclean devil, and cried out with a loud voice,

34 Saying, Let us alone; what have we to do with thee, thou Je'sus of Naz'a·reth? art thou come to destroy us? I know thee who thou art; the Holy One of God.

35 And Je'sus rebuked him, saying, Hold thy peace, and come out of him. And when the devil had thrown him in the midst, he came out of him, and hurt him not.

36 And they were all amazed, and spake among themselves, saying, What a word is this! for with authority and power he commandeth the unclean spirits, and they come out.

37 And the fame of him went out into every place of the country round about.

38 ¶ And he arose out of the synagogue, and entered into Si'mon's house. And Si'mon's wife's mother was taken with a great fever; and they besought him for her.

39 And he stood over her, and rebuked the fever; and it left her: and immediately she arose and ministered unto them.

40 ¶ Now when the sun was setting, all they that had any sick with divers diseases brought them unto him; and he laid his hands on every one of them, and healed them.

41 And devils also came out of many, crying out, and saying, Thou art Christ the Son of God. And he rebuking them suffered

them not to speak: for they knew that he was Christ.

42 And when it was day, he departed and went into a desert place: and the people sought him, and came unto him, and stayed him, that he should not depart from them.

43 And he said unto them, I must preach the kingdom of God to other cities also: for therefore am I sent.

44 And he preached in the synagogues of Gal'i-lee.

5 And it came to pass, that, as the people pressed upon him to hear the word of God, he stood by the lake of Gen-nes'a-ret,

2 And saw two ships standing by the lake: but the fishermen were gone out of them, and were washing their nets.

3 And he entered into one of the ships, which was Si'mon's, and prayed him that he would thrust out a little from the land. And he sat down, and taught the people out of the ship.

4 Now when he had left speaking, he said unto Si'mon, Launch out into the deep, and let down your nets for a draught.

5 And Si'mon answering said unto him, Master, we have toiled all the night, and have taken nothing: nevertheless at thy word I will let down the net.

6 And when they had this done, they enclosed a great multitude of fishes: and their net brake.

7 And they beckoned unto their partners, which were in the other ship, that they should come and help them. And they came, and filled both the ships, so that they began to sink.

8 When Si'mon Pe'ter saw it, he fell down at Je'sus' knees, saying, Depart from me; for I am a sinful man, O Lord.

9 For he was astonished, and all that were with him, at the draught of the fishes which they had taken:

10 And so was also James, and John, the sons of Zeb'e-dee, which were partners with Si'mon. And Je'sus said unto Si'mon, Fear not; from henceforth thou shalt catch men.

11 And when they had brought their ships to land, they forsook all, and followed him.

12 ¶ And it came to pass, when he was in a certain city, behold a man full of leprosy: who seeing Je'sus fell on his face, and besought him, saying, Lord, if thou wilt, thou canst make me clean.

13 And he put forth his hand, and touched him, saying, I will: be thou clean. And immediately the leprosy departed from him.

14 And he charged him to tell no man: but go, and show thyself to the priest, and offer for thy cleansing, according as Mo'ses commanded, for a testimony unto them.

15 But so much the more went there a fame abroad of him: and great multitudes came together to hear, and to be healed by him of their infirmities.

16 ¶ And he withdrew himself into the wilderness, and prayed.

17 And it came to pass on a

certain day, as he was teaching, that there were Phar'i-sees and doctors of the law sitting by, which were come out of every town of Gal'i-lee, and Ju-dæ'a, and Je-ru'sa-lem: and the power of the Lord was *present* to heal them.

18 ¶ And, behold, men brought in a bed a man which was taken with a palsy: and they sought *means* to bring him in, and to lay him before him.

19 And when they could not find by what *way* they might bring him in because of the multitude, they went upon the housetop, and let him down through the tiling with *his* couch into the midst before Je'sus.

20 And when he saw their faith, he said unto him, Man, thy sins are forgiven thee.

21 And the scribes and the Phar'i-sees began to reason, saying, Who is this which speaketh blasphemies? Who can forgive sins, but God alone?

22 But when Je'sus perceived their thoughts, he answering said unto them, What reason ye in your hearts?

23 Whether is easier, to say, Thy sins be forgiven thee; or to say, Rise up and walk?

24 But that ye may know that the Son of man hath power upon earth to forgive sins, (he said unto the sick of the palsy,) I say unto thee, Arise, and take ˄ thy couch, and go into thine ˄ ˄

˄ d immediately he rose up ˄ hem, and took up that

whereon he lay, and departed to his own house, glorifying God.

26 And they were all amazed, and they glorified God, and were filled with fear, saying, We have seen strange things today.

27 ¶ And after these things he went forth, and saw a publican, named Le'vi, sitting at the receipt of custom: and he said unto him, Follow me.

28 And he left all, rose up, and followed him.

29 And Le'vi made him a great feast in his own house: and there was a great company of publicans and of others that sat down with them.

30 But their scribes and Phar'i-sees murmured against his disciples, saying, Why do ye eat and drink with publicans and sinners?

31 And Je'sus answering said unto them, They that are whole need not a physician; but they that are sick.

32 I came not to call the righteous, but sinners to repentance.

33 ¶ And they said unto him, Why do the disciples of John fast often, and make prayers, and likewise *the disciples* of the Phar'i-sees; but thine eat and drink?

34 And he said unto them, Can ye make the children of the bridechamber fast, while the bridegroom is with them?

35 But the days will come, when the bridegroom shall be taken away from them, and then shall they fast in those days.

36 ¶ And he spake also a parable

unto them; No man putteth a piece of a new garment upon an old; if otherwise, then both the new maketh a rent, and the piece that was *taken* out of the new agreeth not with the old.

37 And no man putteth new wine into old bottles; else the new wine will burst the bottles, and be spilled, and the bottles shall perish.

38 But new wine must be put into new bottles; and both are preserved.

39 No man also having drunk old *wine* straightway desireth new: for he saith, The old is better.

6 And it came to pass on the second sabbath after the first, that he went through the corn fields; and his disciples plucked the ears of corn, and did eat, rubbing *them* in *their* hands.

2 And certain of the Phar'i-sees said unto them, Why do ye that which is not lawful to do on the sabbath days?

3 And Je'sus answering them said, Have ye not read so much as this, what Da'vid did, when himself was an hungered, and they which were with him;

4 How he went into the house of God, and did take and eat the showbread, and gave also to them that were with him; which it is not lawful to eat but for the priests alone?

5 And he said unto them, That the Son of man is Lord also of the sabbath.

6 And it came to pass also on another sabbath, that he en-tered into the synagogue and taught: and there was a man whose right hand was withered.

7 And the scribes and Phar'i-sees watched him, whether he would heal on the sabbath day; that they might find an accusa-tion against him.

8 But he knew their thoughts, and said to the man which had the withered hand, Rise up, and stand forth in the midst. And he arose and stood forth.

9 Then said Je'sus unto them, I will ask you one thing; Is it lawful on the sabbath days to do good, or to do evil? to save life, or to destroy *it?*

10 And looking round about upon them all, he said unto the man, Stretch forth thy hand. And he did so: and his hand was restored whole as the other.

11 And they were filled with madness; and communed one with another what they might do to Je'sus.

12 And it came to pass in those days, that he went out into a mountain to pray, and contin-ued all night in prayer to God.

13 ¶ And when it was day, he called *unto him* his disciples: and of them he chose twelve, whom also he named apostles;

14 Si'mon, (whom he also named Pe'ter,) and Andrew his brother, James and John, Phil'ip and Bar-thol'o-mew,

15 Mat'thew and Thom'as, James the *son* of Al-phæ'us, and Si'mon called Ze-lo'tes,

16 And Ju'das *the brother* of James, and Ju'das Is-car'i-ot, which also was the traitor.

17 ¶ And he came down with them, and stood in the plain, and the company of his disciples, and a great multitude of people out of all Ju-dæ′a and Je-ru′sa-lem, and from the sea coast of Tyre and Si′don, which came to hear him, and to be healed of their diseases;

18 And they that were vexed with unclean spirits: and they were healed.

19 And the whole multitude sought to touch him: for there went virtue out of him, and healed them all.

20 ¶ And he lifted up his eyes on his disciples, and said, Blessed be ye poor: for yours is the kingdom of God.

21 Blessed are ye that hunger now: for ye shall be filled. Blessed are ye that weep now: for ye shall laugh.

22 Blessed are ye, when men shall hate you, and when they shall separate you from their company, and shall reproach you, and cast out your name as evil, for the Son of man's sake.

23 Rejoice ye in that day, and leap for joy: for, behold, your reward is great in heaven: for in the like manner did their fathers unto the prophets.

24 But woe unto you that are rich! for ye have received your consolation.

25 Woe unto you that are full! for ye shall hunger. Woe unto you that laugh now! for ye shall mourn and weep.

26 Woe unto you, when all men shall speak well of you! for

so did their fathers to the false prophets.

27 ¶ But I say unto you which hear, Love your enemies, do good to them which hate you.

28 Bless them that curse you, and pray for them which despitefully use you.

29 And unto him that smiteth thee on the one cheek offer also the other; and him that taketh away thy cloak forbid not to take thy coat also.

30 Give to every man that asketh of thee; and of him that taketh away thy goods ask them not again.

31 And as ye would that men should do to you, do ye also to them likewise.

32 For if ye love them which love you, what thank have ye? for sinners also love those that love them.

33 And if ye do good to them which do good to you, what thank have ye? for sinners also do even the same.

34 And if ye lend to them of whom ye hope to receive, what thank have ye? for sinners also lend to sinners, to receive as much again.

35 But love ye your enemies, and do good, and lend, hoping for nothing again; and your reward shall be great, and ye shall be the children of the Highest: for he is kind unto the unthankful and to the evil.

36 Be ye therefore merciful, as your Father also is merciful.

37 Judge not, and ye shall not be judged: condemn not, and ye

shall not be condemned: forgive, and ye shall be forgiven:

38 Give, and it shall be given unto you; good measure, pressed down, and shaken together, and running over, shall men give into your bosom. For with the same measure that ye mete withal it shall be measured to you again.

39 And he spake a parable unto them, Can the blind lead the blind? shall they not both fall into the ditch?

40 The disciple is not above his master: but everyone that is perfect shall be as his master.

41 And why beholdest thou the mote that is in thy brother's eye, but perceivest not the beam that is in thine own eye?

42 Either how canst thou say to thy brother, Brother, let me pull out the mote that is in thine eye, when thou thyself be holdest not the beam that is in thine own eye? Thou hypocrite, cast out first the beam out of thine own eye, and then shalt thou see clearly to pull out the mote that is in thy brother's eye.

43 For a good tree bringeth not forth corrupt fruit; neither doth a corrupt tree bring forth good fruit.

44 For every tree is known by his own fruit. For of thorns men do not gather figs, nor of a bramble bush gather they grapes.

45 A good man out of the good treasure of his heart bringeth forth that which is good; and an evil man out of the evil treasure of his heart bringeth forth that which is evil: for of the abundance of the heart his mouth speaketh.

46 ¶ And why call ye me, Lord, Lord, and do not the things which I say?

47 Whosoever cometh to me, and heareth my sayings, and doeth them, I will show you to whom he is like:

48 He is like a man which built an house, and digged deep, and laid the foundation on a rock: and when the flood arose, the stream beat vehemently upon that house, and could not shake it: for it was founded upon a rock.

49 But he that heareth, and doeth not, is like a man that without a foundation built an house upon the earth; against which the stream did beat vehemently, and immediately it fell, and the ruin of that house was great.

7 Now when he had ended all his sayings in the audience of the people, he entered into Ca-per'na-um.

2 And a certain centurion's servant, who was dear unto him, was sick, and ready to die.

3 And when he heard of Je'sus, he sent unto him the elders of the Jews, beseeching him that he would come and heal his servant.

4 And when they came to Je'sus, they besought him instantly, saying, That he was worthy for whom he should do this:

5 For he loveth our nation, and he hath built us a synagogue.

6 Then Je'sus went with them.

And when he was now not far from the house, the centurion sent friends to him, saying unto him, Lord, trouble not thyself: for I am not worthy that thou shouldest enter under my roof:

7 Wherefore neither thought I myself worthy to come unto thee: but say in a word, and my servant shall be healed.

8 For I also am a man set under authority, having under me soldiers, and I say unto one, Go, and he goeth; and to another, Come, and he cometh; and to my servant, Do this, and he doeth it.

9 When Je'sus heard these things, he marveled at him, and turned him about, and said unto the people that followed him, I say unto you, I have not found so great faith, no, not in Is'ra-el.

10 And they that were sent, returning to the house, found the servant whole that had been sick.

11 ¶ And it came to pass the day after, that he went into a city called Na'in; and many of his disciples went with him, and much people.

12 Now when he came nigh to the gate of the city, behold, there was a dead man carried out, the only son of his mother, and she was a widow: and much people of the city was with her.

13 And when the Lord saw her, he had compassion on her, and said unto her, Weep not.

14 And he came and touched the bier; and they that bare him stood still. And he said, Young man, I say unto thee, Arise.

15 And he that was dead sat up, and began to speak. And he delivered him to his mother.

16 And there came a fear on all: and they glorified God, saying, That a great prophet is risen up among us; and, That God hath visited his people.

17 And this rumor of him went forth throughout all Ju-dæ'a, and throughout all the region round about.

18 And the disciples of John showed him of all these things.

19 ¶ And John calling *unto him* two of his disciples sent *them* to Je'sus, saying, Art thou he that should come? or look we for another?

20 When the men were come unto him, they said, John Bap'tist hath sent us unto thee, saying, Art thou he that should come? or look we for another?

21 And in that same hour he cured many of *their* infirmities and plagues, and of evil spirits; and unto many *that were* blind he gave sight.

22 Then Je'sus answering said unto them, Go your way, and tell John what things ye have seen and heard; how that the blind see, the lame walk, the lepers are cleansed, the deaf hear, the dead are raised, to the poor the gospel is preached.

23 And blessed is *he,* whosoever shall not be offended in me.

24 ¶ And when the messengers of John were departed, he began to speak unto the people concerning John, What went ye out

into the wilderness for to see? A reed shaken with the wind?

25 But what went ye out for to see? A man clothed in soft raiment? Behold, they which are gorgeously apparelled, and live delicately, are in kings' courts.

26 But what went ye out for to see? A prophet? Yea, I say unto you, and much more than a prophet.

27 This is *he*, of whom it is written, Behold, I send my messenger before thy face, which shall prepare thy way before thee.

28 For I say unto you, Among those that are born of women there is not a greater prophet than John the Bap'tist: but he that is least in the kingdom of God is greater than he.

29 And all the people that heard *him*, and the publicans, justified God, being baptized with the baptism of John.

30 But the Phar'i-sees and lawyers rejected the counsel of God against themselves, being not baptized of him.

31 ¶ And the Lord said, Whereunto then shall I liken the men of this generation? and to what are they like?

32 They are like unto children sitting in the marketplace, and calling one to another, and saying, We have piped unto you, and ye have not danced; we have mourned to you, and ye have not wept.

33 For John the Bap'tist came neither eating bread nor drinking wine; and ye say, He hath a devil.

34 The Son of man is come eating and drinking; and ye say, Behold a gluttonous man, and a winebibber, a friend of publicans and sinners!

35 But wisdom is justified of all her children.

36 ¶ And one of the Phar'i-sees desired him that he would eat with him. And he went into the Phar'i-see's house, and sat down to meat.

37 And, behold, a woman in the city, which was a sinner, when she knew that Je'sus sat at meat in the Phar'i-see's house, brought an alabaster box of ointment,

38 And stood at his feet behind *him* weeping, and began to wash his feet with tears, and did wipe *them* with the hairs of her head, and kissed his feet, and anointed *them* with the ointment.

39 Now when the Phar'i-see which had bidden him saw *it*, he spake within himself, saying, This man, if he were a prophet, would have known who and what manner of woman *this is* that toucheth him: for she is a sinner.

40 And Je'sus answering said unto him, Si'mon, I have somewhat to say unto thee. And he saith, Master, say on.

41 There was a certain creditor which had two debtors: the one owed five hundred pence, and the other fifty.

42 And when they had nothing to pay, he frankly forgave them both. Tell me therefore, which of them will love him most?

43 Si'mon answered and said, I suppose that *he*, to whom he forgave most. And he said unto him, Thou hast rightly judged.

44 And he turned to the woman, and said unto Si'mon, Seest thou this woman? I entered into thine house, thou gavest me no water for my feet: but she hath washed my feet with tears, and wiped *them* with the hairs of her head.

45 Thou gavest me no kiss: but this woman since the time I came in hath not ceased to kiss my feet.

46 My head with oil thou didst not anoint: but this woman hath anointed my feet with ointment.

47 Wherefore I say unto thee, Her sins, which are many, are forgiven; for she loved much: but to whom little is forgiven, *the same* loveth little.

48 And he said unto her, Thy sins are forgiven.

49 And they that sat at meat with him began to say within themselves, Who is this that forgiveth sins also?

50 And he said to the woman, Thy faith hath saved thee; go in peace.

8 And it came to pass afterward, that he went throughout every city and village, preaching and showing the glad tidings of the kingdom of God: and the twelve *were* with him,

2 And certain women, which had been healed of evil spirits and infirmities, Ma'ry called Mag-da-le'ne, out of whom went seven devils,

3 And Jo-an'na the wife of Chu'za Her'od's steward, and Su-san'na, and many others, which ministered unto him of their substance.

4 ¶ And when much people were gathered together, and were come to him out of every city, he spake by a parable:

5 A sower went out to sow his seed: and as he sowed, some fell by the wayside; and it was trodden down, and the fowls of the air devoured it.

6 And some fell upon a rock; and as soon as it was sprung up, it withered away, because it lacked moisture.

7 And some fell among thorns; and the thorns sprang up with it, and choked it.

8 And other fell on good ground, and sprang up, and bare fruit a hundredfold. And when he had said these things, he cried, He that hath ears to hear, let him hear.

9 And his disciples asked him, saying, What might this parable be?

10 And he said, Unto you it is given to know the mysteries of the kingdom of God: but to others in parables; that seeing they might not see, and hearing they might not understand.

11 Now the parable is this: The seed is the word of God.

12 Those by the wayside are they that hear; then cometh the devil, and taketh away the word out of their hearts, lest they should believe and be saved.

13 They on the rock *are they*, which, when they hear, receive the word with joy; and these

have no root, which for a while believe, and in time of temptation fall away.

14 And that which fell among thorns are they, which, when they have heard, go forth, and are choked with cares and riches and pleasures of *this* life, and bring no fruit to perfection.

15 But that on the good ground are they, which in an honest and good heart, having heard the word, keep *it*, and bring forth fruit with patience.

16 ¶ No man, when he hath lighted a candle, covereth it with a vessel, or putteth *it* under a bed; but setteth *it* on a candlestick, that they which enter in may see the light.

17 For nothing is secret, that shall not be made manifest; neither *any*thing hid, that shall not be known and come abroad.

18 Take heed therefore how ye hear: for whosoever hath, to him shall be given; and whosoever hath not, from him shall be taken even that which he seemeth to have.

19 ¶ Then came to him *his* mother and his brethren, and could not come at him for the press.

20 And it was told him *by certain* which said, Thy mother and thy brethren stand without, desiring to see thee.

21 And he answered and said unto them, My mother and my brethren are these which hear the word of God, and do it.

22 ¶ Now it came to pass on a certain day, that he went into a ship with his disciples: and he said unto them, Let us go over unto the other side of the lake. And they launched forth.

23 But as they sailed he fell asleep: and there came down a storm of wind on the lake; and they were filled *with water*, and were in jeopardy.

24 And they came to him, and awoke him, saying, Master, master, we perish. Then he arose, and rebuked the wind and the raging of the water: and they ceased, and there was a calm.

25 And he said unto them, Where is your faith? And they being afraid wondered, saying one to another, What manner of man is this! for he commandeth even the winds and water, and they obey him.

26 ¶ And they arrived at the country of the Gad'a-renes, which is over against Gal'i-lee.

27 And when he went forth to land, there met him out of the city a certain man, which had devils long time, and wore no clothes, neither abode in *any* house, but in the tombs.

28 When he saw Je'sus, he cried out, and fell down before him, and with a loud voice said, What have I to do with thee, Je'sus, *thou* Son of God most high? I beseech thee, torment me not.

29 (For he had commanded the unclean spirit to come out of the man. For oftentimes it had caught him: and he was kept bound with chains and in fetters; and he brake the bands, and was driven of the devil into the wilderness.)

30 And Je'sus asked him, say-

ing, What is thy name? And he said, Legion: because many devils were entered into him.

31 And they besought him that he would not command them to go out into the deep.

32 And there was there an herd of many swine feeding on the mountain: and they besought him that he would suffer them to enter into them. And he suffered them.

33 Then went the devils out of the man, and entered into the swine: and the herd ran violently down a steep place into the lake, and were choked.

34 When they that fed *them* saw what was done, they fled, and went and told *it* in the city and in the country.

35 Then they went out to see what was done; and came to Je'sus, and found the man, out of whom the devils were departed, sitting at the feet of Je'sus, clothed, and in his right mind: and they were afraid.

36 They also which saw *it* told them by what means he that was possessed of the devils was healed.

37 ¶ Then the whole multitude of the country of the Gad'a-renes round about besought him to depart from them; for they were taken with great fear: and he went up into the ship, and returned back again.

38 Now the man out of whom the devils were departed besought him that he might be with him: but Je'sus sent him away, saying,

39 Return to thine own house, and show how great things God hath done unto thee. And he went his way, and published throughout the whole city how great things Je'sus had done unto him.

40 And it came to pass, that, when Je'sus was returned, the people *gladly* received him: for they were all waiting for him.

41 ¶ And, behold, there came a man named Ja-i'rus, and he was a ruler of the synagogue: and he fell down at Je'sus' feet, and besought him that he would come into his house:

42 For he had one only daughter, about twelve years of age, and she lay dying. But as he went the people thronged him.

43 ¶ And a woman having an issue of blood twelve years, which had spent all her living upon physicians, neither could be healed of any,

44 Came behind *him,* and touched the border of his garment: and immediately her issue of blood stanched.

45 And Je'sus said, Who touched me? When all denied, Pe'ter and they that were with him said, Master, the multitude throng thee and press *thee,* and sayest thou, Who touched me?

46 And Je'sus said, Somebody hath touched me: for I perceive that virtue is gone out of me.

47 And when the woman saw that she was not hid, she came trembling, and falling down before him, she declared unto him before all the people for what cause she had touched him, and

how she was healed immediately.

48 And he said unto her, Daughter, be of good comfort: thy faith hath made thee whole; go in peace.

49 ¶ While he yet spake, there cometh one from the ruler of the synagogue's *house*, saying to him, Thy daughter is dead; trouble not the Master.

50 But when Je'sus heard *it*, he answered him, saying, Fear not: believe only, and she shall be made whole.

51 And when he came into the house, he suffered no man to go in, save Pe'ter, and James, and John, and the father and the mother of the maiden.

52 And all wept, and bewailed her: but he said, Weep not; she is not dead, but sleepeth.

53 And they laughed him to scorn, knowing that she was dead.

54 And he put them all out, and took her by the hand, and called, saying, Maid, arise.

55 And her spirit came again, and she arose straightway: and he commanded to give her meat.

56 And her parents were astonished: but he charged them that they should tell no man what was done.

9 Then he called his twelve disciples together, and gave them power and authority over all devils, and to cure diseases.

2 And he sent them to preach the kingdom of God, and to heal the sick.

3 And he said unto them, Take nothing for *your* journey, neither staves, nor scrip, neither bread, neither money; neither have two coats apiece.

4 And whatsoever house ye enter into, there abide, and thence depart.

5 And whosoever will not receive you, when ye go out of that city, shake off the very dust from your feet for a testimony against them.

6 And they departed, and went through the towns, preaching the gospel, and healing every where.

7 ¶ Now Her'od the tetrarch heard of all that was done by him: and he was perplexed, because that it was said of some, that John was risen from the dead;

8 And of some, that E-li'jah had appeared; and of others, that one of the old prophets was risen again.

9 And Her'od said, John have I beheaded: but who is this, of whom I hear such things? And he desired to see him.

10 ¶ And the apostles, when they were returned, told him all that they had done. And he took them, and went aside privately into a desert place belonging to the city called Beth-sa'i-da.

11 And the people, when they knew *it*, followed him: and he received them, and spake unto them of the kingdom of God, and healed them that had need of healing.

12 And when the day began to wear away, then came the twelve, and said unto him, Send

the multitude away, that they may go into the towns and country round about, and lodge, and get victuals: for we are here in a desert place.

13 But he said unto them, Give ye them to eat. And they said, We have no more but five loaves and two fishes; except we should go and buy meat for all this people.

14 For they were about five thousand men. And he said to his disciples, Make them sit down by fifties in a company.

15 And they did so, and made them all sit down.

16 Then he took the five loaves and the two fishes, and looking up to heaven, he blessed them, and brake, and gave to the disciples to set before the multitude.

17 And they did eat, and were all filled: and there was taken up of fragments that remained to them twelve baskets.

18 ¶ And it came to pass, as he was alone praying, his disciples were with him: and he asked them, saying, Whom say the people that I am?

19 They answering said, John the Bap'tist; but some say, E-li'-jah; and others say, that one of the old prophets is risen again.

20 He said unto them, But whom say ye that I am? Pe'ter answering said, The Christ of God.

21 And he straitly charged them, and commanded them to tell no man that thing;

22 Saying, The Son of man must suffer many things, and be rejected of the elders and chief priests and scribes, and be slain, and be raised the third day.

23 ¶ And he said to them all, If any man will come after me, let him deny himself, and take up his cross daily, and follow me.

24 For whosoever will save his life shall lose it: but whosoever will lose his life for my sake, the same shall save it.

25 For what is a man advantaged, if he gain the whole world, and lose himself, or be cast away?

26 For whosoever shall be ashamed of me and of my words, of him shall the Son of man be ashamed, when he shall come in his own glory, and in his Father's, and of the holy angels.

27 But I tell you of a truth, there be some standing here, which shall not taste of death, till they see the kingdom of God.

28 ¶ And it came to pass about an eight days after these sayings, he took Pe'ter and John and James, and went up into a mountain to pray.

29 And as he prayed, the fashion of his countenance was altered, and his raiment was white and glistering.

30 And, behold, there talked with him two men, which were Mo'ses and E-li'jah:

31 Who appeared in glory, and spake of his decease which he should accomplish at Je-ru'-sa-lem.

32 But Pe'ter and they that were with him were heavy with sleep: and when they were awake, they saw his glory, and

the two men that stood with him.

33 And it came to pass, as they departed from him, Pe'ter said unto Je'sus, Master, it is good for us to be here: and let us make three tabernacles; one for thee, and one for Mo'ses, and one for E-li'jah: not knowing what he said.

34 While he thus spake, there came a cloud, and overshadowed them: and they feared as they entered into the cloud.

35 And there came a voice out of the cloud, saying, This is my beloved Son: hear him.

36 And when the voice was past, Je'sus was found alone. And they kept *it* close, and told no man in those days any of those things which they had seen.

37 ¶ And it came to pass, that on the next day, when they were come down from the hill, much people met him.

38 And, behold, a man of the company cried out, saying, Master, I beseech thee, look upon my son: for he is mine only child.

39 And, lo, a spirit taketh him, and he suddenly crieth out; and it teareth him that he foameth again, and bruising him hardly departeth from him.

40 And I besought thy disciples to cast him out; and they could not.

41 And Je'sus answering said, O faithless and perverse generation, how long shall I be with you, and suffer you? Bring thy son hither.

42 And as he was yet a coming, the devil threw him down, and tore *him*. And Je'sus rebuked the unclean spirit, and healed the child, and delivered him again to his father.

43 ¶ And they were all amazed at the mighty power of God. But while they wondered every one at all things which Je'sus did, he said unto his disciples,

44 Let these sayings sink down into your ears: for the Son of man shall be delivered into the hands of men.

45 But they understood not this saying, and it was hid from them, that they perceived it not: and they feared to ask him of that saying.

46 ¶ Then there arose a reasoning among them, which of them should be greatest.

47 And Je'sus, perceiving the thought of their heart, took a child, and set him by him,

48 And said unto them, Whosoever shall receive this child in my name receiveth me: and whosoever shall receive me receiveth him that sent me: for he that is least among you all, the same shall be great.

49 ¶ And John answered and said, Master, we saw one casting out devils in thy name; and we forbade him, because he followeth not with us.

50 And Je'sus said unto him, Forbid *him* not: for he that is not against us is for us.

51 ¶ And it came to pass, when the time was come that he should be received up, he stead-

fastly set his face to go to Je·ru'-
sa·lem,

52 And sent messengers before
his face: and they went, and
entered into a village of the Sa-
mar'i·tans, to make ready for
him.

53 And they did not receive
him, because his face was as
though he would go to Je·ru'sa-
lem.

54 And when his disciples
James and John saw *this*, they
said, Lord, wilt thou that we
command fire to come down
from heaven, and consume
them, even as E·li'jah did?

55 But he turned, and rebuked
them, and said, Ye know not
what manner of spirit ye are of.

56 For the Son of man is not
come to destroy men's lives, but
to save *them*. And they went to
another village.

57 ¶ And it came to pass, that,
as they went in the way, a
certain *man* said unto him,
Lord, I will follow thee whithersoever thou goest.

58 And Je'sus said unto him,
Foxes have holes, and birds of
the air *have* nests; but the Son
of man hath not where to lay *his*
head.

59 And he said unto another,
Follow me. But he said, Lord,
suffer me first to go and bury my
father.

60 Je'sus said unto him, Let the
dead bury their dead: but go
thou and preach the kingdom of
God.

61 And another also said, Lord,
I will follow thee; but let me

first go bid them farewell,
which are at home at my house.

62 And Je'sus said unto him,
No man, having put his hand to
the plow, and looking back, is fit
for the kingdom of God.

10 After these things the Lord
appointed other seventy
also, and sent them two and two
before his face into every city
and place, whither he himself
would come.

2 Therefore said he unto them,
The harvest truly *is* great, but
the laborers *are* few: pray ye
therefore the Lord of the harvest, that he would send forth
laborers into his harvest.

3 Go your ways: behold, I send
you forth as lambs among
wolves.

4 Carry neither purse, nor
scrip, nor shoes: and salute no
man by the way.

5 And into whatsoever house
ye enter, first say, Peace *be* to
this house.

6 And if the son of peace be
there, your peace shall rest
upon it: if not, it shall turn to
you again.

7 And in the same house remain, eating and drinking such
things as they give: for the laborer is worthy of his hire. Go
not from house to house.

8 And into whatsoever city ye
enter, and they receive you, eat
such things as are set before
you:

9 And heal the sick that are
therein, and say unto them, The
kingdom of God is come nigh
unto you.

10 But into whatsoever city ye

enter, and they receive you not, go your ways out into the streets of the same, and say,

11 Even the very dust of your city, which cleaveth on us, we do wipe off against you: notwithstanding be ye sure of this, that the kingdom of God is come nigh unto you.

12 But I say unto you, that it shall be more tolerable in that day for Sod'om, than for that city.

13 Woe unto thee, Cho-ra'zin! woe unto thee, Beth-sa'i-da! for if the mighty works had been done in Tyre and Si'don, which have been done in you, they had a great while ago repented, sitting in sackcloth and ashes.

14 But it shall be more tolerable for Tyre and Si'don at the judgment, than for you.

15 And thou, Ca-per'na-um, which art exalted to heaven, shalt be thrust down to hell.

16 He that heareth you heareth me; and he that despiseth you despiseth me; and he that despiseth me despiseth him that sent me.

17 ¶ And the seventy returned again with joy, saying, Lord, even the devils are subject unto us through thy name.

18 And he said unto them, I beheld Sa'tan as lightning fall from heaven.

19 Behold, I give unto you power to tread on serpents and scorpions, and over all the power of the enemy: and nothing shall by any means hurt you.

20 Notwithstanding in this rejoice not, that the spirits are subject unto you; but rather rejoice, because your names are written in heaven.

21 ¶ In that hour Je'sus rejoiced in spirit, and said, I thank thee, O Father, Lord of heaven and earth, that thou hast hid these things from the wise and prudent, and hast revealed them unto babes: even so, Father; for so it seemed good in thy sight.

22 All things are delivered to me of my Father: and no man knoweth who the Son is, but the Father; and who the Father is, but the Son, and he to whom the Son will reveal him.

23 And he turned him unto his disciples, and said privately, Blessed are the eyes which see the things that ye see:

24 For I tell you, that many prophets and kings have desired to see those things which ye see, and have not seen them; and to hear those things which ye hear, and have not heard them.

25 ¶ And, behold, a certain lawyer stood up, and tempted him, saying, Master, what shall I do to inherit eternal life?

26 He said unto him, What is written in the law? how readest thou?

27 And he answering said, Thou shalt love the Lord thy God with all thy heart, and with all thy soul, and with all thy strength, and with all thy mind; and thy neighbor as thyself.

28 And he said unto him, Thou hast answered right: this do, and thou shalt live.

29 But he, willing to justify

himself, said unto Je'sus, And who is my neighbor?

30 And Je'sus answering said, A certain *man* went down from Je-ru'sa-lem to Jer'i-cho, and fell among thieves, which stripped him of his raiment, and wounded *him*, and departed, leaving *him* half dead.

31 And by chance there came down a certain priest that way: and when he saw him, he passed by on the other side.

32 And likewise a Le'vite, when he was at the place, came and looked on *him*, and passed by on the other side.

33 But a certain Sa-mar'i-tan, as he journeyed, came where he was: and when he saw him, he had compassion *on him*,

34 And went to *him*, and bound up his wounds, pouring in oil and wine, and set him on his own beast, and brought him to an inn, and took care of him.

35 And on the morrow when he departed, he took out two pence, and gave *them* to the host, and said unto him, Take care of him; and whatsoever thou spendest more, when I come again, I will repay thee.

36 Which now of these three, thinkest thou, was neighbor unto him that fell among the thieves?

37 And he said, He that showed mercy on him. Then said Je'sus unto him, Go, and do thou likewise.

38 ¶ Now it came to pass, as they went, that he entered into a certain village: and a certain woman named Mar'tha received him into her house.

39 And she had a sister called Ma'ry, which also sat at Je'sus' feet, and heard his word.

40 But Mar'tha was cumbered about much serving, and came to him, and said, Lord, dost thou not care that my sister hath left me to serve alone? bid her therefore that she help me.

41 And Je'sus answered and said unto her, Mar'tha, Mar'tha, thou art careful and troubled about many things:

42 But one thing is needful: and Ma'ry hath chosen that good part, which shall not be taken away from her.

11 And it came to pass, that, as he was praying in a certain place, when he ceased, one of his disciples said unto him, Lord, teach us to pray, as John also taught his disciples.

2 And he said unto them, When ye pray, say, Our Father which art in heaven, Hallowed be thy name. Thy kingdom come. Thy will be done, as in heaven, so in earth.

3 Give us day by day our daily bread.

4 And forgive us our sins; for we also forgive everyone that is indebted to us. And lead us not into temptation; but deliver us from evil.

5 And he said unto them, Which of you shall have a friend, and shall go unto him at midnight, and say unto him, Friend, lend me three loaves;

6 For a friend of mine in his

journey is come to me, and I have nothing to set before him?

7 And he from within shall answer and say, Trouble me not: the door is now shut, and my children are with me in bed; I cannot rise and give thee.

8 I say unto you, Though he will not rise and give him, because he is his friend, yet because of his importunity he will rise and give him as many as he needeth.

9 And I say unto you, Ask, and it shall be given you; seek, and ye shall find; knock, and it shall be opened unto you.

10 For every one that asketh receiveth; and he that seeketh findeth; and to him that knocketh it shall be opened.

11 If a son shall ask bread of any of you that is a father, will he give him a stone? or if he ask a fish, will he for a fish give him a serpent?

12 Or if he shall ask an egg, will he offer him a scorpion?

13 If ye then, being evil, know how to give good gifts unto your children: how much more shall your heavenly Father give the Holy Spirit to them that ask him?

14 ¶ And he was casting out a devil, and it was dumb. And it came to pass, when the devil was gone out, the dumb spake; and the people wondered.

15 But some of them said, He casteth out devils through Be'el'-ze-bub the chief of the devils.

16 And others, tempting him, sought of him a sign from heaven.

17 But he, knowing their thoughts, said unto them, Every kingdom divided against itself is brought to desolation; and a house divided against a house falleth.

18 If Sa'tan also be divided against himself, how shall his kingdom stand? because ye say that I cast out devils through Be'-el'ze-bub.

19 And if I by Be'el'ze-bub cast out devils, by whom do your sons cast them out? therefore shall they be your judges.

20 But if I with the finger of God cast out devils, no doubt the kingdom of God is come upon you.

21 When a strong man armed keepeth his palace, his goods are in peace:

22 But when a stronger than he shall come upon him, and overcome him, he taketh from him all his armor wherein he trusted, and divideth his spoils.

23 He that is not with me is against me: and he that gathereth not with me scattereth.

24 When the unclean spirit is gone out of a man, he walketh through dry places, seeking rest; and finding none, he saith, I will return unto my house whence I came out.

25 And when he cometh, he findeth it swept and garnished.

26 Then goeth he, and taketh to him seven other spirits more wicked than himself; and they enter in, and dwell there: and the last state of that man is worse than the first.

27 ¶ And it came to pass, as he

spake these things, a certain woman of the company lifted up her voice, and said unto him, Blessed *is* the womb that bare thee, and the paps which thou hast sucked.

28 But he said, Yea rather, blessed *are* they that hear the word of God, and keep it.

29 ¶ And when the people were gathered thick together, he began to say, This is an evil generation: they seek a sign; and there shall no sign be given it, but the sign of Jo'nah the prophet.

30 For as Jo'nah was a sign unto the Nin'e-vites, so shall also the Son of man be to this generation.

31 The queen of the south shall rise up in the judgment with the men of this generation, and condemn them: for she came from the utmost parts of the earth to hear the wisdom of Sol'o-mon; and, behold, a greater than Sol'o-mon *is* here.

32 The men of Nin'e-veh shall rise up in the judgment with this generation, and shall condemn it: for they repented at the preaching of Jo'nah; and, behold, a greater than Jo'nah *is* here.

33 No man, when he hath lighted a candle, putteth *it* in a secret place, neither under a bushel, but on a candlestick, that they which come in may see the light.

34 The light of the body is the eye: therefore when thine eye is single, thy whole body also is full of light; but when *thine eye*

is evil, thy body also *is* full of darkness.

35 Take heed therefore that the light which is in thee be not darkness.

36 If thy whole body therefore *be* full of light, having no part dark, the whole shall be full of light, as when the bright shining of a candle doth give thee light.

37 ¶ And as he spake, a certain Phar'i-see besought him to dine with him: and he went in, and sat down to meat.

38 And when the Phar'i-see saw *it*, he marveled that he had not first washed before dinner.

39 And the Lord said unto him, Now do ye Phar'i-sees make clean the outside of the cup and the platter; but your inward part is full of ravening and wickedness.

40 *Ye* fools, did not he that made that which is without make that which is within also?

41 But rather give alms of such things as ye have; and, behold, all things are clean unto you.

42 But woe unto you, Phar'i-sees! for ye tithe mint and rue and all manner of herbs, and pass over judgment and the love of God: these ought ye to have done, and not to leave the other undone.

43 Woe unto you, Phar'i-sees! for ye love the uppermost seats in the synagogues, and greetings in the markets.

44 Woe unto you, scribes and Phar'i-sees, hypocrites! for ye are as graves which appear not, and the men that walk over *them* are not aware *of them.*

45 ¶ Then answered one of the lawyers, and said unto him, Master, thus saying thou reproachest us also.

46 And he said, Woe unto you also, ye lawyers! for ye lade men with burdens grievous to be borne, and ye yourselves touch not the burdens with one of your fingers.

47 Woe unto you! for ye build the sepulchers of the prophets, and your fathers killed them.

48 Truly ye bear witness that ye allow the deeds of your fathers: for they indeed killed them, and ye build their sepulchers.

49 Therefore also said the wisdom of God, I will send them prophets and apostles, and some of them they shall slay and persecute:

50 That the blood of all the prophets, which was shed from the foundation of the world, may be required of this generation;

51 From the blood of A'bel unto the blood of Zech-a-ri'ah, which perished between the altar and the temple: verily I say unto you, It shall be required of this generation.

52 Woe unto you, lawyers! for ye have taken away the key of knowledge: ye entered not in yourselves, and them that were entering in ye hindered.

53 And as he said these things unto them, the scribes and the Phar'i-sees began to urge him vehemently, and to provoke him to speak of many things:

54 Laying wait for him, and

seeking to catch something out of his mouth, that they might accuse him.

12 In the meantime, when there were gathered together an innumerable multitude of people, insomuch that they trode one upon another, he began to say unto his disciples first of all, Beware ye of the leaven of the Phar'i-sees, which is hypocrisy.

2 For there is nothing covered, that shall not be revealed; neither hid, that shall not be known.

3 Therefore whatsoever ye have spoken in darkness shall be heard in the light; and that which ye have spoken in the ear in closets shall be proclaimed upon the housetops.

4 And I say unto you my friends, Be not afraid of them that kill the body, and after that have no more that they can do.

5 But I will forewarn you whom ye shall fear: Fear him, which after he hath killed hath power to cast into hell; yea, I say unto you, Fear him.

6 Are not five sparrows sold for two farthings, and not one of them is forgotten before God?

7 But even the very hairs of your head are all numbered. Fear not therefore: ye are of more value than many sparrows.

8 Also I say unto you, Whosoever shall confess me before men, him shall the Son of man also confess before the angels of God:

9 But he that denieth me

before men shall be denied before the angels of God.

10 And whosoever shall speak a word against the Son of man, it shall be forgiven him: but unto him that blasphemeth against the Ho'ly Ghost it shall not be forgiven.

11 And when they bring you unto the synagogues, and *unto* magistrates, and powers, take ye no thought how or what thing ye shall answer, or what ye shall say:

12 For the Ho'ly Ghost shall teach you in the same hour what ye ought to say.

13 ¶ And one of the company said unto him, Master, speak to my brother, that he divide the inheritance with me.

14 And he said unto him, Man, who made me a judge or a divider over you?

15 And he said unto them, Take heed, and beware of covetousness: for a man's life consisteth not in the abundance of the things which he possesseth.

16 And he spake a parable unto them, saying, The ground of a certain rich man brought forth plentifully:

17 And he thought within himself, saying, What shall I do, because I have no room where to bestow my fruits?

18 And he said, This will I do: I will pull down my barns, and build greater; and there will I bestow all my fruits and my goods.

19 And I will say to my soul, Soul, thou hast much goods laid up for many years; take thine ease, eat, drink, *and* be merry.

20 But God said unto him, *Thou* fool, this night thy soul shall be required of thee: then whose shall those things be, which thou hast provided?

21 So *is* he that layeth up treasure for himself, and is not rich toward God.

22 ¶ And he said unto his disciples, Therefore I say unto you, Take no thought for your life, what ye shall eat; neither for the body, what ye shall put on.

23 The life is more than meat, and the body *is more* than raiment.

24 Consider the ravens: for they neither sow nor reap; which neither have storehouse nor barn; and God feedeth them: how much more are ye better than the fowls?

25 And which of you with taking thought can add to his stature one cubit?

26 If ye then be not able to do that thing which is least, why take ye thought for the rest?

27 Consider the lilies how they grow: they toil not, they spin not; and yet I say unto you, that Sol'o-mon in all his glory was not arrayed like one of these.

28 If then God so clothe the grass, which is today in the field, and tomorrow is cast into the oven; how much more *will he clothe* you, O ye of little faith?

29 And seek not ye what ye shall eat, or what ye shall drink, neither be ye of doubtful mind.

30 For all these things do the

nations of the world seek after: and your Father knoweth that ye have need of these things.

31 ¶ But rather seek ye the kingdom of God; and all these things shall be added unto you.

32 Fear not, little flock; for it is your Father's good pleasure to give you the kingdom.

33 Sell that ye have, and give alms; provide yourselves bags which wax not old, a treasure in the heavens that faileth not, where no thief approacheth, neither moth corrupteth.

34 For where your treasure is, there will your heart be also.

35 Let your loins be girded about, and your lights burning;

36 And ye yourselves like unto men that wait for their lord, when he will return from the wedding; that when he cometh and knocketh, they may open unto him immediately.

37 Blessed are those servants, whom the lord when he cometh shall find watching: verily I say unto you, that he shall gird himself, and make them to sit down to meat, and will come forth and serve them.

38 And if he shall come in the second watch, or come in the third watch, and find them so, blessed are those servants.

39 And this know, that if the goodman of the house had known what hour the thief would come, he would have watched, and not have suffered his house to be broken through.

40 Be ye therefore ready also: for the Son of man cometh at an hour when ye think not.

41 ¶ Then Pe'ter said unto him, Lord, speakest thou this parable unto us, or even to all?

42 And the Lord said, Who then is that faithful and wise steward, whom his lord shall make ruler over his household, to give them their portion of meat in due season?

43 Blessed is that servant, whom his lord when he cometh shall find so doing.

44 Of a truth I say unto you, that he will make him ruler over all that he hath.

45 But and if that servant say in his heart, My lord delayeth his coming; and shall begin to beat the menservants and maidens, and to eat and drink, and to be drunken;

46 The lord of that servant will come in a day when he looketh not for him, and at an hour when he is not aware, and will cut him in sunder, and will appoint him his portion with the unbelievers.

47 And that servant, which knew his lord's will, and prepared not himself, neither did according to his will, shall be beaten with many stripes.

48 But he that knew not, and did commit things worthy of stripes, shall be beaten with few stripes. For unto whomsoever much is given, of him shall be much required: and to whom men have committed much, of him they will ask the more.

49 ¶ I am come to send fire on the earth; and what will I, if it be already kindled?

50 But I have a baptism to be

baptized with; and how am I straitened till it be accomplished!

51 Suppose ye that I am come to give peace on earth? I tell you, Nay; but rather division:

52 For from henceforth there shall be five in one house divided, three against two, and two against three.

53 The father shall be divided against the son, and the son against the father; the mother against the daughter, and the daughter against the mother; the mother-in-law against her daughter-in-law, and the daughter-in-law against her mother-in-law.

54 ¶ And he said also to the people, When ye see a cloud rise out of the west, straightway ye say, There cometh a shower; and so it is.

55 And when *ye see* the south wind blow, ye say, There will be heat; and it cometh to pass.

56 *Ye* hypocrites, ye can discern the face of the sky and of the earth; but how is it that ye do not discern this time?

57 Yea, and why even of yourselves judge ye not what is right?

58 ¶ When thou goest with thine adversary to the magistrate, *as thou art* in the way, give diligence that thou mayest be delivered from him; lest he hale thee to the judge, and the judge deliver thee to the officer, and the officer cast thee into prison.

59 I tell thee, thou shalt not depart thence, till thou hast paid the very last mite.

13 There were present at that season some that told him of the Gal-i-læ'ans, whose blood Pi'late had mingled with their sacrifices.

2 And Je'sus answering said unto them, Suppose ye that these Gal-i-læ'ans were sinners above all the Gal-i-læ'ans, because they suffered such things?

3 I tell you, Nay: but, except ye repent, ye shall all likewise perish.

4 Or those eighteen, upon whom the tower in Si-lo'am fell, and slew them, think ye that they were sinners above all men that dwelt in Je-ru'sa-lem?

5 I tell you, Nay: but, except ye repent, ye shall all likewise perish.

6 ¶ He spake also this parable; A certain *man* had a fig tree planted in his vineyard; and he came and sought fruit thereon, and found none.

7 Then said he unto the dresser of his vineyard, Behold, these three years I come seeking fruit on this fig tree, and find none: cut it down; why cumbereth it the ground?

8 And he answering said unto him, Lord, let it alone this year also, till I shall dig about it, and dung *it*:

9 And if it bear fruit, *well*: and if not, *then* after that thou shalt cut it down.

10 And he was teaching in one of the synagogues on the sabbath.

11 ¶ And, behold, there was a

woman which had a spirit of infirmity eighteen years, and was bowed together, and could in no wise lift up *herself.*

12 And when Je'sus saw her, he called *her to him,* and said unto her, Woman, thou art loosed from thine infirmity.

13 And he laid *his* hands on her: and immediately she was made straight, and glorified God.

14 And the ruler of the synagogue answered with indignation, because that Je'sus had healed on the sabbath day, and said unto the people, There are six days in which men ought to work: in them therefore come and be healed, and not on the sabbath day.

15 The Lord then answered him, and said, Thou hypocrite, doth not each one of you on the sabbath loose his ox or *his* ass from the stall, and lead *him* away to watering?

16 And ought not this woman, being a daughter of A'bra-ham, whom Sa'tan hath bound, lo, these eighteen years, be loosed from this bond on the sabbath day?

17 And when he had said these things, all his adversaries were ashamed: and all the people re-joiced for all the glorious things that were done by him.

18 ¶ Then said he, Unto what is the kingdom of God like? and whereunto shall I resemble it?

19 It is like a grain of mustard seed, which a man took, and cast into his garden; and it grew, and waxed a great tree;

and the fowls of the air lodged in the branches of it.

20 And again he said, Whereunto shall I liken the kingdom of God?

21 It is like leaven, which a woman took and hid in three measures of meal, till the whole was leavened.

22 And he went through the cities and villages, teaching, and journeying toward Je-ru'sa-lem.

23 Then said one unto him, Lord, are there few that be saved? And he said unto them,

24 ¶ Strive to enter in at the strait gate: for many, I say unto you, will seek to enter in, and shall not be able.

25 When once the master of the house is risen up, and hath shut to the door, and ye begin to stand without, and to knock at the door, saying, Lord, Lord, open unto us; and he shall answer and say unto you, I know you not whence ye are:

26 Then shall ye begin to say, We have eaten and drunk in thy presence, and thou hast taught in our streets.

27 But he shall say, I tell you, I know you not whence ye are; depart from me, all *ye* workers of iniquity.

28 There shall be weeping and gnashing of teeth, when ye shall see A'bra-ham, and I'saac, and Ja'cob, and all the prophets, in the kingdom of God, and you *yourselves* thrust out.

29 And they shall come from the east, and *from* the west, and from the north, and *from* the

south, and shall sit down in the kingdom of God.

30 And, behold, there are last which shall be first, and there are first which shall be last.

31 ¶ The same day there came certain of the Phar'i-sees, saying unto him, Get thee out, and depart hence: for Her'od will kill thee.

32 And he said unto them, Go ye, and tell that fox, Behold, I cast out devils, and I do cures today and tomorrow, and the third *day* I shall be perfected.

33 Nevertheless I must walk today, and tomorrow, and the *day* following: for it cannot be that a prophet perish out of Je-ru'sa-lem.

34 O Je-ru'sa-lem, Je-ru'sa-lem, which killest the prophets, and stonest them that are sent unto thee; how often would I have gathered thy children together, as a hen *doth gather* her brood under *her* wings, and ye would not!

35 Behold, your house is left unto you desolate: and verily I say unto you, Ye shall not see me, until *the time* come when ye shall say, Blessed *is* he that cometh in the name of the Lord.

14 And it came to pass, as he went into the house of one of the chief Phar'i-sees to eat bread on the sabbath day, that they watched him.

2 And, behold, there was a certain man before him which had the dropsy.

3 And Je'sus answering spake unto the lawyers and Phar'i-sees, saying, Is it lawful to heal on the sabbath day?

4 And they held their peace. And he took *him,* and healed him, and let him go;

5 And answered them, saying, Which of you shall have an ass or an ox fallen into a pit, and will not straightway pull him out on the sabbath day?

6 And they could not answer him again to these things.

7 ¶ And he put forth a parable to those which were bidden, when he marked how they chose out the chief rooms; saying unto them,

8 When thou art bidden of any *man* to a wedding, sit not down in the highest room; lest a more honorable man than thou be bidden of him;

9 And he that bade thee and him come and say to thee, Give this man place; and thou begin with shame to take the lowest room.

10 But when thou art bidden, go and sit down in the lowest room; that when he that bade thee cometh, he may say unto thee, Friend, go up higher: then shalt thou have worship in the presence of them that sit at meat with thee.

11 For whosoever exalteth himself shall be abased; and he that humbleth himself shall be exalted.

12 ¶ Then said he also to him that bade him, When thou makest a dinner or a supper, call not thy friends, nor thy brethren, neither thy kinsmen, nor *thy* rich neighbors; lest they

also bid thee again, and a recompense be made thee.

13 But when thou makest a feast, call the poor, the maimed, the lame, the blind:

14 And thou shalt be blessed; for they cannot recompense thee: for thou shalt be recompensed at the resurrection of the just.

15 ¶ And when one of them that sat at meat with him heard these things, he said unto him, Blessed *is* he that shall eat bread in the kingdom of God.

16 Then said he unto him, A certain man made a great supper, and bade many:

17 And sent his servant at supper time to say to them that were bidden, Come; for all things are now ready.

18 And they all with one *consent* began to make excuse. The first said unto him, I have bought a piece of ground, and I must needs go and see it: I pray thee have me excused.

19 And another said, I have bought five yoke of oxen, and I go to prove them: I pray thee have me excused.

20 And another said, I have married a wife, and therefore I cannot come.

21 So that servant came, and showed his lord these things. Then the master of the house being angry said to his servant, Go out quickly into the streets and lanes of the city, and bring in hither the poor, and the maimed, and the halt, and the blind.

22 And the servant said, Lord,

it is done as thou hast commanded, and yet there is room.

23 And the lord said unto the servant, Go out into the highways and hedges, and compel *them* to come in, that my house may be filled.

24 For I say unto you, That none of those men which were bidden shall taste of my supper.

25 ¶ And there went great multitudes with him: and he turned, and said unto them,

26 If any *man* come to me, and hate not his father, and mother, and wife, and children, and brethren, and sisters, yea, and his own life also, he cannot be my disciple.

27 And whosoever doth not bear his cross, and come after me, cannot be my disciple.

28 For which of you, intending to build a tower, sitteth not down first, and counteth the cost, whether he have *sufficient* to finish *it?*

29 Lest haply, after he hath laid the foundation, and is not able to finish *it,* all that behold *it* begin to mock him,

30 Saying, This man began to build, and was not able to finish.

31 Or what king, going to make war against another king, sitteth not down first, and consulteth whether he be able with ten thousand to meet him that cometh against him with twenty thousand?

32 Or else, while the other is yet a great way off, he sendeth an ambassage, and desireth conditions of peace.

33 So likewise, whosoever he

be of you that forsaketh not all that he hath, he cannot be my disciple.

34 ¶ Salt *is* good: but if the salt have lost his savor, wherewith shall it be seasoned?

35 It is neither fit for the land, nor yet for the dunghill; *but* men cast it out. He that hath ears to hear, let him hear.

15 Then drew near unto him all the publicans and sinners for to hear him.

2 And the Phar'i-sees and scribes murmured, saying, This man receiveth sinners, and eateth with them.

3 ¶ And he spake this parable unto them, saying,

4 What man of you, having an hundred sheep, if he lose one of them, doth not leave the ninety and nine in the wilderness, and go after that which is lost, until he find it?

5 And when he hath found *it,* he layeth *it* on his shoulders, rejoicing.

6 And when he cometh home, he calleth together *his* friends and neighbors, saying unto them, Rejoice with me; for I have found my sheep which was lost.

7 I say unto you, that likewise joy shall be in heaven over one sinner that repenteth, more than over ninety and nine just persons, which need no repentance.

8 ¶ Either what woman having ten pieces of silver, if she lose one piece, doth not light a candle, and sweep the house, and seek diligently till she find *it?*

9 And when she hath found *it,* she calleth *her* friends and *her* neighbors together, saying, Rejoice with me; for I have found the piece which I had lost.

10 Likewise, I say unto you, there is joy in the presence of the angels of God over one sinner that repenteth.

11 ¶ And he said, A certain man had two sons:

12 And the younger of them said to *his* father, Father, give me the portion of goods that falleth *to me.* And he divided unto them *his* living.

13 And not many days after the younger son gathered all together, and took his journey into a far country, and there wasted his substance with riotous living.

14 And when he had spent all, there arose a mighty famine in that land; and he began to be in want.

15 And he went and joined himself to a citizen of that country; and he sent him into his fields to feed swine.

16 And he would fain have filled his belly with the husks that the swine did eat: and no man gave unto him.

17 And when he came to himself, he said, How many hired servants of my father's have bread enough and to spare, and I perish with hunger!

18 I will arise and go to my father, and will say unto him, Father, I have sinned against heaven, and before thee,

19 And am no more worthy to

be called thy son: make me as one of thy hired servants.

20 And he arose, and came to his father. But when he was yet a great way off, his father saw him, and had compassion, and ran, and fell on his neck, and kissed him.

21 And the son said unto him, Father, I have sinned against heaven, and in thy sight, and am no more worthy to be called thy son.

22 But the father said to his servants, Bring forth the best robe, and put it on him; and put a ring on his hand, and shoes on his feet:

23 And bring hither the fatted calf, and kill it; and let us eat, and be merry:

24 For this my son was dead, and is alive again; he was lost, and is found. And they began to be merry.

25 Now his elder son was in the field: and as he came and drew nigh to the house, he heard music and dancing.

26 And he called one of the servants, and asked what these things meant.

27 And he said unto him, Thy brother is come; and thy father hath killed the fatted calf, because he hath received him safe and sound.

28 And he was angry, and would not go in: therefore came his father out, and entreated him.

29 And he answering said to his father, Lo, these many years do I serve thee, neither transgressed I at anytime thy com-

mandment: and yet thou never gavest me a kid, that I might make merry with my friends:

30 But as soon as this thy son was come, which hath devoured thy living with harlots, thou hast killed for him the fatted calf.

31 And he said unto him, Son, thou art ever with me, and all that I have is thine.

32 It was meet that we should make merry, and be glad: for this thy brother was dead, and is alive again; and was lost, and is found.

16 And he said also unto his disciples, There was a certain rich man, which had a steward; and the same was accused unto him that he had wasted his goods.

2 And he called him, and said unto him, How is it that I hear this of thee? give an account of thy stewardship; for thou mayest be no longer steward.

3 Then the steward said within himself, What shall I do? for my lord taketh away from me the stewardship: I cannot dig; to beg I am ashamed.

4 I am resolved what to do, that, when I am put out of the stewardship, they may receive me into their houses.

5 So he called every one of his lord's debtors unto him, and said unto the first, How much owest thou unto my lord?

6 And he said, An hundred measures of oil. And he said unto him, Take thy bill, and sit down quickly, and write fifty.

7 Then said he to another, And how much owest thou? And he

said, An hundred measures of wheat. And he said unto him, Take thy bill, and write fourscore.

8 And the lord commended the unjust steward, because he had done wisely: for the children of this world are in their generation wiser than the children of light.

9 And I say unto you, Make to yourselves friends of the mammon of unrighteousness; that, when ye fail, they may receive you into everlasting habitations.

10 He that is faithful in that which is least is faithful also in much: and he that is unjust in the least is unjust also in much.

11 If therefore ye have not been faithful in the unrighteous mammon, who will commit to your trust the true *riches?*

12 And if ye have not been faithful in that which is another man's, who shall give you that which is your own?

13 ¶ No servant can serve two masters: for either he will hate the one, and love the other; or else he will hold to the one, and despise the other. Ye cannot serve God and mammon.

14 And the Phar'i-sees also, who were covetous, heard all these things: and they derided him.

15 And he said unto them, Ye are they which justify yourselves before men; but God knoweth your hearts: for that which is highly esteemed among men is abomination in the sight of God.

16 The law and the prophets *were* until John: since that time

the kingdom of God is preached, and every man presseth into it.

17 And it is easier for heaven and earth to pass, than one tittle of the law to fail.

18 Whosoever putteth away his wife, and marrieth another, committeth adultery: and whosoever marrieth her that is put away from *her* husband committeth adultery.

19 ¶ There was a certain rich man, which was clothed in purple and fine linen, and fared sumptuously every day:

20 And there was a certain beggar named Laz'a-rus, which was laid at his gate, full of sores,

21 And desiring to be fed with the crumbs which fell from the rich man's table: moreover the dogs came and licked his sores.

22 And it came to pass, that the beggar died, and was carried by the angels into A'bra-ham's bosom: the rich man also died, and was buried;

23 And in hell he lifted up his eyes, being in torments, and seeth A'bra-ham afar off, and Laz'a-rus in his bosom.

24 And he cried and said, Father A'bra-ham, have mercy on me, and send Laz'a-rus, that he may dip the tip of his finger in water, and cool my tongue; for I am tormented in this flame.

25 But A'bra-ham said, Son, remember that thou in thy lifetime receivedst thy good things, and likewise Laz'a-rus evil things: but now he is comforted, and thou art tormented.

26 And beside all this, between us and you there is a great gulf

fixed: so that they which would pass from hence to you cannot; neither can they pass to us, that *would come* from thence.

27 Then he said, I pray thee therefore, father, that thou wouldest send him to my father's house:

28 For I have five brethren; that he may testify unto them, lest they also come into this place of torment.

29 A'bra-ham saith unto him, They have Mo'ses and the prophets; let them hear them.

30 And he said, Nay, father A'bra-ham: but if one went unto them from the dead, they will repent.

31 And he said unto him, If they hear not Mo'ses and the prophets, neither will they be persuaded, though one rose from the dead.

17 Then said he unto the disciples, It is impossible but that offenses will come: but woe unto him, through whom they come!

2 It were better for him that a millstone were hanged about his neck, and he cast into the sea, than that he should offend one of these little ones.

3 ¶ Take heed to yourselves: If thy brother trespass against thee, rebuke him; and if he repent, forgive him.

4 And if he trespass against thee seven times in a day, and seven times in a day turn again to thee, saying, I repent; thou shalt forgive him.

5 And the apostles said unto the Lord, Increase our faith.

6 And the Lord said, If ye had faith as a grain of mustard seed, ye might say unto this sycamine tree, Be thou plucked up by the root, and be thou planted in the sea; and it should obey you.

7 But which of you, having a servant plowing or feeding cattle, will say unto him by and by, when he is come from the field, Go and sit down to meat?

8 And will not rather say unto him, Make ready wherewith I may sup, and gird thyself, and serve me, till I have eaten and drunken; and afterward thou shalt eat and drink?

9 Doth he thank that servant because he did the things that were commanded him? I trow not.

10 So likewise ye, when ye shall have done all those things which are commanded you, say, We are unprofitable servants: we have done that which was our duty to do.

11 ¶ And it came to pass, as he went to Je-ru'sa-lem, that he passed through the midst of Sa-ma'ri-a and Gal'i-lee.

12 And as he entered into a certain village, there met him ten men that were lepers, which stood afar off:

13 And they lifted up *their* voices, and said, Je'sus, Master, have mercy on us.

14 And when he saw *them*, he said unto them, Go show yourselves unto the priests. And it came to pass, that, as they went, they were cleansed.

15 And one of them, when he saw that he was healed, turned

back, and with a loud voice glorified God,

16 And fell down on *his* face at his feet, giving him thanks: and he was a Sa-mar'i-tan.

17 And Je'sus answering said, Were there not ten cleansed? but where *are* the nine?

18 There are not found that returned to give glory to God, save this stranger.

19 And he said unto him, Arise, go thy way: thy faith hath made thee whole.

20 ¶ And when he was demanded of the Phar'i-sees, when the kingdom of God should come, he answered them and said, The kingdom of God cometh not with observation:

21 Neither shall they say, Lo here! or, lo there! for, behold, the kingdom of God is within you.

22 And he said unto the disciples, The days will come, when ye shall desire to see one of the days of the Son of man, and ye shall not see *it*.

23 And they shall say to you, See here; or, see there: go not after *them*, nor follow *them*.

24 For as the lightning, that lighteneth out of the one *part* under heaven, shineth unto the other *part* under heaven; so shall also the Son of man be in his day.

25 But first must he suffer many things, and be rejected of this generation.

26 And as it was in the days of No'ah, so shall it be also in the days of the Son of man.

27 They did eat, they drank, they married wives, they were given in marriage, until the day that No'ah entered into the ark, and the flood came, and destroyed them all.

28 Likewise also as it was in the days of Lot; they did eat, they drank, they bought, they sold, they planted, they builded;

29 But the same day that Lot went out of Sod'om it rained fire and brimstone from heaven, and destroyed *them* all.

30 Even thus shall it be in the day when the Son of man is revealed.

31 In that day, he which shall be upon the housetop, and his stuff in the house, let him not come down to take it away: and he that is in the field, let him likewise not return back.

32 Remember Lot's wife.

33 Whosoever shall seek to save his life shall lose it; and whosoever shall lose his life shall preserve it.

34 I tell you, in that night there shall be two *men* in one bed; the one shall be taken, and the other shall be left.

35 Two *women* shall be grinding together; the one shall be taken, and the other left.

36 Two *men* shall be in the field; the one shall be taken, and the other left.

37 And they answered and said unto him, Where, Lord? And he said unto them, Wheresoever the body *is*, thither will the eagles be gathered together.

18 And he spake a parable unto them *to this end,* that men ought always to pray, and not to faint;

2 Saying, There was in a city a judge, which feared not God, neither regarded man:

3 And there was a widow in that city; and she came unto him, saying, Avenge me of mine adversary.

4 And he would not for a while: but afterward he said within himself, Though I fear not God, nor regard man:

5 Yet because this widow troubleth me, I will avenge her, lest by her continual coming she weary me.

6 And the Lord said, Hear what the unjust judge saith.

7 And shall not God avenge his own elect, which cry day and night unto him, though he bear long with them?

8 I tell you that he will avenge them speedily. Nevertheless when the Son of man cometh, shall he find faith on the earth?

9 **And he spake this parable** unto certain which trusted in themselves that they were righteous, and despised others:

10 Two men went up into the temple to pray; the one a Phar'i-see, and the other a publican

11 The Phar'i-see stood and prayed thus with himself, God, I thank thee, that I am not as other men *are,* extortioners, unjust, adulterers, or even as this publican

12 I fast twice in the week, I give tithes of all that I possess.

13 And the publican, standing afar off, would not lift up so much as *his* eyes unto heaven, but smote upon his breast, saying, God be merciful to me a sinner.

14 I tell you, this man went down to his house justified *rather* than the other: for everyone that exalteth himself shall be abased; and he that humbleth himself shall be exalted.

15 And they brought unto him also infants, that he would touch them: but when *his* disciples saw *it,* they rebuked them.

16 But Je'sus called them *unto him,* and said, Suffer little children to come unto me, and forbid them not: for of such is the kingdom of God.

17 Verily I say unto you, Whosoever shall not receive the kingdom of God as a little child shall in no wise enter therein.

18 And a certain ruler asked him, saying, Good Master, what shall I do to inherit eternal life?

19 And Je'sus said unto him, Why callest thou me good? none *is* good, save one, *that is,* God.

20 Thou knowest the commandments, Do not commit adultery, Do not kill, Do not steal, Do not bear false witness, Honor thy father and thy mother.

21 And he said, All these have I kept from my youth up.

22 Now when Je'sus heard these things, he said unto him, Yet lackest thou one thing: sell all that thou hast, and distribute unto the poor, and thou shalt have treasure in heaven: and come, follow me.

23 And when he heard this, he was very sorrowful: for he was very rich.

24 And when Je'sus saw that he was very sorrowful, he said, How hardly shall they that have riches enter into the kingdom of God!

25 For it is easier for a camel to go through a needle's eye, than for a rich man to enter into the kingdom of God.

26 And they that heard *it* said, Who then can be saved?

27 And he said, The things which are impossible with men are possible with God.

28 Then Pe'ter said, Lo, we have left all, and followed thee.

29 And he said unto them, Verily I say unto you, There is no man that hath left house, or parents, or brethren, or wife, or children, for the kingdom of God's sake,

30 Who shall not receive manifold more in this present time, and in the world to come life everlasting.

31 ¶ Then he took *unto him* the twelve, and said unto them, Behold, we go up to Je-ru'sa-lem, and all things that are written by the prophets concerning the Son of man shall be accomplished.

32 For he shall be delivered unto the Gen'tiles, and shall be mocked, and spitefully entreated, and spitted on:

33 And they shall scourge *him,* and put him to death: and the third day he shall rise again.

34 And they understood none of these things: and this saying was hid from them, neither knew they the things which were spoken.

35 ¶ And it came to pass, that as he was come nigh unto Jer'i-cho, a certain blind man sat by the wayside begging:

36 And hearing the multitude pass by, he asked what it meant.

37 And they told him, that Je'-sus of Naz'a-reth passeth by.

38 And he cried, saying, Je'sus, *thou* son of Da'vid, have mercy on me.

39 And they which went before rebuked him, that he should hold his peace: but he cried so much the more, Thou son of Da'vid, have mercy on me.

40 And Je'sus stood, and commanded him to be brought unto him: and when he was come near, he asked him,

41 Saying, What wilt thou that I shall do unto thee? And he said, Lord, that I may receive my sight.

42 And Je'sus said unto him, Receive thy sight: thy faith hath saved thee.

43 And immediately he received his sight, and followed him, glorifying God: and all the people, when they saw *it,* gave praise unto God.

19 And Je'sus entered and passed through Jer'i-cho.

2 And, behold, *there was* a man named Zac-chæ'us, which was the chief among the publicans, and he was rich.

3 And he sought to see Je'sus who he was; and could not for

the press, because he was little of stature

4 And he ran before, and climbed up into a sycamore tree to see him: for he was to pass that *way*.

5 And when Je'sus came to the place, he looked up, and saw him, and said unto him, Zac-chæ'us, make haste, and come down; for today I must abide at thy house.

6 And he made haste, and came down, and received him joyfully.

7 And when they saw *it*, they all murmured, That he was gone to be guest with a man that is a sinner.

8 And Zac-chæ'us stood, and said unto the Lord; Behold, Lord, the half of my goods I give to the poor; and if I have taken anything from any man by false accusation, I restore *him* fourfold.

9 And Je'sus said unto him, This day is salvation come to this house, forsomuch as he also is a son of A'bra-ham.

10 For the Son of man is come to seek and to save that which was lost.

11 And as they heard these things, he added and spake a parable, because he was nigh to Je-ru'sa-lem, and because they thought that the kingdom of God should immediately appear.

12 He said therefore, A certain nobleman went into a far country to receive for himself a kingdom, and to return.

13 And he called his ten servants, and delivered them ten

pounds, and said unto them, Occupy till I come.

14 But his citizens hated him, and sent a message after him, saying, We will not have this *man* to reign over us.

15 And it came to pass, that when he was returned, having received the kingdom, then he commanded these servants to be called unto him, to whom he had given the money, that he might know how much every man had gained by trading.

16 Then came the first, saying, Lord, thy pound hath gained ten pounds.

17 And he said unto him, Well, thou good servant: because thou hast been faithful in a very little, have thou authority over ten cities.

18 And the second came, saying, Lord, thy pound hath gained five pounds.

19 And he said likewise to him, Be thou also over five cities.

20 And another came, saying, Lord, behold, *here is* thy pound, which I have kept laid up in a napkin:

21 For I feared thee, because thou art an austere man: thou takest up that thou layedst not down, and reapest that thou didst not sow.

22 And he saith unto him, Out of thine own mouth will I judge thee, *thou* wicked servant. Thou knewest that I was an austere man, taking up that I laid not down, and reaping that I did not sow:

23 Wherefore then gavest not thou my money into the bank,

that at my coming I might have required mine own with usury?

24 And he said unto them that stood by, Take from him the pound, and give *it* to him that hath ten pounds.

25 (And they said unto him, Lord, he hath ten pounds.)

26 For I say unto you, That unto everyone which hath shall be given; and from him that hath not, even that he hath shall be taken away from him.

27 But those mine enemies, which would not that I should reign over them, bring hither, and slay *them* before me.

28 ¶ And when he had thus spoken, he went before, ascending up to Je·ru'sa·lem.

29 And it came to pass, when he was come nigh to Beth'pha·ge and Beth'a·ny, at the mount called *the mount* of Ol'ives, he sent two of his disciples,

30 Saying, Go ye into the village over against *you;* in the which at your entering ye shall find a colt tied, whereon yet never man sat: loose him, and bring *him* hither.

31 And if any man ask you, Why do ye loose *him?* thus shall ye say unto him, Because the Lord hath need of him.

32 And they that were sent went their way, and found even as he had said unto them.

33 And as they were loosing the colt, the owners thereof said unto them, Why loose ye the colt?

34 And they said, The Lord hath need of him.

35 And they brought him to Je'-sus: and they cast their garments upon the colt, and they set Je'sus thereon.

36 And as he went, they spread their clothes in the way.

37 And when he was come nigh, even now at the descent of the mount of Ol'ives, the whole multitude of the disciples began to rejoice and praise God with a loud voice for all the mighty works that they had seen;

38 Saying, Blessed *be* the King that cometh in the name of the Lord: peace in heaven, and glory in the highest.

39 And some of the Phar'i·sees from among the multitude said unto him, Master, rebuke thy disciples.

40 And he answered and said unto them, I tell you that, if these should hold their peace, the stones would immediately cry out.

41 ¶ And when he was come near, he beheld the city, and wept over it,

42 Saying, If thou hadst known, even thou, at least in this thy day, the things *which belong* unto thy peace! but now they are hid from thine eyes.

43 For the days shall come upon thee, that thine enemies shall cast a trench about thee, and compass thee round, and keep thee in on every side,

44 And shall lay thee even with the ground, and thy children within thee; and they shall not leave in thee one stone upon another; because thou knewest not the time of thy visitation.

45 And he went into the temple,

and began to cast out them that sold therein, and them that bought;

46 Saying unto them, It is written, My house is the house of prayer: but ye have made it a den of thieves.

47 And he taught daily in the temple. But the chief priests and the scribes and the chief of the people sought to destroy him,

48 And could not find what they might do: for all the people were very attentive to hear him.

20 And it came to pass, that on one of those days, as he taught the people in the temple, and preached the gospel, the chief priests and the scribes came upon him with the elders,

2 And spake unto him, saying, Tell us, by what authority doest thou these things? or who is he that gave thee this authority?

3 And he answered and said unto them, I will also ask you one thing; and answer me:

4 The baptism of John, was it from heaven, or of men?

5 And they reasoned with themselves, saying, If we shall say, From heaven; he will say, Why then believed ye him not?

6 But and if we say, Of men; all the people will stone us: for they be persuaded that John was a prophet.

7 And they answered, that they could not tell whence it was.

8 And Je'sus said unto them, Neither tell I you by what authority I do these things.

9 Then began he to speak to the people this parable; A certain man planted a vineyard, and let it forth to husbandmen, and went into a far country for a long time.

10 And at the season he sent a servant to the husbandmen, that they should give him of the fruit of the vineyard: but the husbandmen beat him, and sent him away empty.

11 And again he sent another servant: and they beat him also, and entreated him shamefully, and sent him away empty.

12 And again he sent a third: and they wounded him also, and cast him out.

13 Then said the lord of the vineyard, What shall I do? I will send my beloved son: it may be they will reverence him when they see him.

14 But when the husbandmen saw him, they reasoned among themselves, saying, This is the heir: come, let us kill him, that the inheritance may be ours.

15 So they cast him out of the vineyard, and killed him. What therefore shall the lord of the vineyard do unto them?

16 He shall come and destroy these husbandmen, and shall give the vineyard to others. And when they heard it, they said, God forbid.

17 And he beheld them, and said, What is this then that is written, The stone which the builders rejected, the same is become the head of the corner?

18 Whosoever shall fall upon that stone shall be broken; but on whomsoever it shall fall, it will grind him to powder.

19 ¶ And the chief priests and

the scribes the same hour sought to lay hands on him; and they feared the people: for they perceived that he had spoken this parable against them.

20 And they watched *him*, and sent forth spies, which should feign themselves just men, that they might take hold of his words, that so they might deliver him unto the power and authority of the governor.

21 And they asked him, saying, Master, we know that thou sayest and teachest rightly, neither acceptest thou the person *of any*, but teachest the way of God truly:

22 Is it lawful for us to give tribute unto Cæ'sar, or no?

23 But he perceived their craftiness, and said unto them, Why tempt ye me?

24 Show me a penny. Whose image and superscription hath it? They answered and said, Cæ'-sar's.

25 And he said unto them, Render therefore unto Cæ'sar's the things which be Cæ'sar's, and unto God the things which be God's.

26 And they could not take hold of his words before the people: and they marveled at his answer, and held their peace.

27 ¶ Then came to *him* certain of the Sad'du-cees, which deny that there is any resurrection; and they asked him,

28 Saying, Master, Mo'ses wrote unto us, If any man's brother die, having a wife, and he die without children, that his brother should take his wife,

and raise up seed unto his brother.

29 There were therefore seven brethren: and the first took a wife, and died without children.

30 And the second took her to wife, and he died childless.

31 And the third took her; and in like manner the seven also: and they left no children, and died.

32 Last of all the woman died also.

33 Therefore in the resurrection whose wife of them is she? for seven had her to wife.

34 And Je'sus answering said unto them, The children of this world marry, and are given in marriage:

35 But they which shall be accounted worthy to obtain that world, and the resurrection from the dead, neither marry, nor are given in marriage:

36 Neither can they die anymore: for they are equal unto the angels; and are the children of God, being the children of the resurrection.

37 Now that the dead are raised, even Mo'ses showed at the bush, when he calleth the Lord the God of A'bra-ham, and the God of I'saac, and the God of Ja'cob.

38 For he is not a God of the dead, but of the living: for all live unto him.

39 ¶ Then certain of the scribes answering said, Master, thou hast well said.

40 And after that they durst not ask him any *question at all*.

41 And he said unto them,

How say they that Christ is Da'-vid's son?

42 And Da'vid himself saith in the book of Psalms, The LORD said unto my Lord, Sit thou on my right hand,

43 Till I make thine enemies thy footstool.

44 Da'vid therefore calleth him Lord, how is he then his son?

45 ¶ Then in the audience of all the people he said unto his disciples,

46 Beware of the scribes, which desire to walk in long robes, and love greetings in the markets, and the highest seats in the synagogues, and the chief rooms at feasts;

47 Which devour widows' houses, and for a show make long prayers: the same shall receive greater damnation.

21 And he looked up, and saw the rich men casting their gifts into the treasury.

2 And he saw also a certain poor widow casting in thither two mites.

3 And he said, Of a truth I say unto you, that this poor widow hath cast in more than they all:

4 For all these have of their abundance cast in unto the offerings of God: but she of her penury hath cast in all the living that she had.

5 ¶ And as some spake of the temple, how it was adorned with goodly stones and gifts, he said,

6 As for these things which ye behold, the days will come, in the which there shall not be left

one stone upon another, that shall not be thrown down.

7 And they asked him, saying, Master, but when shall these things be? and what sign will there be when these things shall come to pass?

8 And he said, Take heed that ye be not deceived: for many shall come in my name, saying, I am Christ; and the time draweth near: go ye not therefore after them.

9 But when ye shall hear of wars and commotions, be not terrified: for these things must first come to pass; but the end is not by and by.

10 Then said he unto them, Nation shall rise against nation, and kingdom against kingdom:

11 And great earthquakes shall be in divers places, and famines, and pestilences; and fearful sights and great signs shall there be from heaven.

12 But before all these, they shall lay their hands on you, and persecute you, delivering you up to the synagogues, and into prisons, being brought before kings and rulers for my name's sake.

13 And it shall turn to you for a testimony.

14 Settle it therefore in your hearts, not to meditate before what ye shall answer:

15 For I will give you a mouth and wisdom, which all your adversaries shall not be able to gainsay nor resist.

16 And ye shall be betrayed both by parents, and brethren, and kinsfolks, and friends; and

some of you shall they cause to be put to death.

17 And ye shall be hated of all *men* for my name's sake.

18 But there shall not an hair of your head perish.

19 In your patience possess ye your souls.

20 And when ye shall see Je-ru'-sa-lem compassed with armies, then know that the desolation thereof is nigh.

21 Then let them which are in Ju-dæ'a flee to the mountains; and let them which are in the midst of it depart out; and let not them that are in the countries enter thereinto.

22 For these be the days of vengeance, that all things which are written may be fulfilled.

23 But woe unto them that are with child, and to them that give suck, in those days! for there shall be great distress in the land, and wrath upon this people.

24 And they shall fall by the edge of the sword, and shall be led away captive into all nations: and Je-ru'sa-lem shall be trodden down of the Gen'tiles, until the times of the Gen'tiles be fulfilled.

25 ¶ And there shall be signs in the sun, and in the moon, and in the stars; and upon the earth distress of nations, with perplexity; the sea and the waves roaring;

26 Men's hearts failing them for fear, and for looking after those things which are coming on the earth: for the powers of heaven shall be shaken.

27 And then shall they see the Son of man coming in a cloud with power and great glory.

28 And when these things begin to come to pass, then look up, and lift up your heads; for your redemption draweth nigh.

29 And he spake to them a **parable;** Behold the fig tree, and all the trees;

30 When they now shoot forth, ye see and know of your own selves that summer is now nigh at hand.

31 So likewise ye, when ye see these things come to pass, know ye that the kingdom of God is nigh at hand.

32 Verily I say unto you, This generation shall not pass away, till all be fulfilled.

33 Heaven and earth shall pass away: but my words shall not pass away.

34 ¶ And take heed to yourselves, lest at anytime your hearts be overcharged with surfeiting, and drunkenness, and cares of this life, and *so* that day come upon you unawares.

35 For as a snare shall it come on all them that dwell on the face of the whole earth.

36 Watch ye therefore, and pray always, that ye may be accounted worthy to escape all these things that shall come to pass, and to stand before the Son of man.

37 And in the day time he was teaching in the temple; and at night he went out, and abode in the mount that is called *the mount* of Ol'ives.

38 And all the people came

early in the morning to him in the temple, for to hear him

22 Now the feast of unleavened bread drew nigh, which is called the Passover.

2 And the chief priests and scribes sought how they might kill him; for they feared the people.

3 ¶ Then entered Sa'tan into Ju'das surnamed Is-car'i-ot, being of the number of the twelve.

4 And he went his way, and communed with the chief priests and captains, how he might betray him unto them.

5 And they were glad, and covenanted to give him money.

6 And he promised, and sought opportunity to betray him unto them in the absence of the multitude.

7 ¶ Then came the day of unleavened bread, when the passover must be killed.

8 And he sent Pe'ter and John, saying, Go and prepare us the passover, that we may eat.

9 And they said unto him, Where wilt thou that we prepare?

10 And he said unto them, Behold, when ye are entered into the city, there shall a man meet you, bearing a pitcher of water; follow him into the house where he entereth in.

11 And ye shall say unto the goodman of the house, The Master saith unto thee, Where is the guestchamber, where I shall eat the passover with my disciples?

12 And he shall show you a large upper room furnished: there make ready.

13 And they went, and found as he had said unto them: and they made ready the passover.

14 And when the hour was come, he sat down, and the twelve apostles with him.

15 And he said unto them, With desire I have desired to eat this passover with you before I suffer:

16 For I say unto you, I will not anymore eat thereof, until it be fulfilled in the kingdom of God.

17 And he took the cup, and gave thanks, and said, Take this, and divide it among yourselves:

18 For I say unto you, I will not drink of the fruit of the vine, until the kingdom of God shall come.

19 ¶ And he took bread, and gave thanks, and brake it, and gave unto them, saying, This is my body which is given for you: this do in remembrance of me.

20 Likewise also the cup after supper, saying, This cup is the new testament in my blood, which is shed for you.

21 ¶ But, behold, the hand of him that betrayeth me is with me on the table.

22 And truly the Son of man goeth, as it was determined: but woe unto that man by whom he is betrayed!

23 And they began to inquire among themselves, which of them it was that should do this thing.

24 ¶ And there was also a strife among them, which of them should be accounted the greatest.

25 And he said unto them, The

kings of the Gen′tiles exercise lordship over them; and they that exercise authority upon them are called benefactors.

26 But ye *shall* not *be* so: but he that is greatest among you, let him be as the younger; and he that is chief, as he that doth serve.

27 For whether *is* greater, he that sitteth at meat, or he that serveth? *is* not he that sitteth at meat? but I am among you as he that serveth.

28 Ye are they which have continued with me in my temptations.

29 And I appoint unto you a kingdom, as my Father hath appointed unto me;

30 That ye may eat and drink at my table in my kingdom, and sit on thrones judging the twelve tribes of Is′ra-el.

31 ¶ And the Lord said, Si′mon, Si′mon, behold, Sa′tan hath desired *to have* you, that he may sift *you* as wheat:

32 But I have prayed for thee, that thy faith fail not: and when thou art converted, strengthen thy brethren.

33 And he said unto him, Lord, I am ready to go with thee, both into prison, and to death.

34 And he said, I tell thee, Pe′-ter, the cock shall not crow this day, before thou shalt thrice deny that thou knowest me.

35 And he said unto them, When I sent you without purse, and scrip, and shoes, lacked ye any thing? And they said, Nothing.

36 Then said he unto them, But now, he that hath a purse, let him take *it,* and likewise *his* scrip: and he that hath no sword, let him sell his garment, and buy one.

37 For I say unto you, that this that is written must yet be accomplished in me, And he was reckoned among the transgressors: for the things concerning me have an end.

38 And they said, Lord, behold, here *are* two swords. And he said unto them, It is enough.

39 ¶ And he came out, and went, as he was wont, to the mount of Ol′ives; and his disciples also followed him.

40 And when he was at the place, he said unto them, Pray that ye enter not into temptation.

41 And he was withdrawn from them about a stone's cast, and kneeled down, and prayed,

42 Saying, Father, if thou be willing, remove this cup from me: nevertheless not my will, but thine, be done.

43 And there appeared an angel unto him from heaven, strengthening him.

44 And being in an agony he prayed more earnestly: and his sweat was as it were great drops of blood falling down to the ground.

45 And when he rose up from prayer, and was come to his disciples, he found them sleeping for sorrow,

46 And said unto them, Why sleep ye? rise and pray, lest ye enter into temptation.

47 ¶ And while he yet spake, behold a multitude, and he that was called Ju'das, one of the twelve, went before them, and drew near unto Je'sus to kiss him.

48 But Je'sus said unto him, Ju'das, betrayest thou the Son of man with a kiss?

49 When they which were about him saw what would follow, they said unto him, Lord, shall we smite with the sword?

50 ¶ And one of them smote the servant of the high priest, and cut off his right ear.

51 And Je'sus answered and said, Suffer ye thus far. And he touched his ear, and healed him.

52 Then Je'sus said unto the chief priests, and captains of the temple, and the elders, which were come to him, Be ye come out, as against a thief, with swords and staves?

53 When I was daily with you in the temple, ye stretched forth no hands against me: but this is your hour, and the power of darkness.

54 ¶ Then took they him, and led him, and brought him into the high priest's house. And Pe'ter followed afar off.

55 And when they had kindled a fire in the midst of the hall, and were set down together, Pe'ter sat down among them.

56 But a certain maid beheld him as he sat by the fire, and earnestly looked upon him, and said, This man was also with him.

57 And he denied him, saying, Woman, I know him not.

58 And after a little while another saw him, and said, Thou art also of them. And Pe'ter said, Man, I am not.

59 And about the space of one hour after another confidently affirmed, saying, Of a truth this *fellow* also was with him: for he is a Gal-i-læ'an.

60 And Pe'ter said, Man, I know not what thou sayest. And immediately, while he yet spake, the cock crew.

61 And the Lord turned, and looked upon Pe'ter. And Pe'ter remembered the word of the Lord, how he had said unto him, Before the cock crow, thou shalt deny me thrice.

62 And Pe'ter went out, and wept bitterly.

63 ¶ And the men that held Je'sus mocked him, and smote *him*.

64 And when they had blindfolded him, they struck him on the face, and asked him, saying, Prophesy, who is it that smote thee?

65 And many other things blasphemously spake they against him.

66 ¶ And as soon as it was day, the elders of the people and the chief priests and the scribes came together, and led him into their council, saying,

67 Art thou the Christ? tell us. And he said unto them, If I tell you, ye will not believe:

68 And if I also ask *you*, ye will not answer me, nor let *me* go.

69 Hereafter shall the Son of

man sit on the right hand of the power of God.

70 Then said they all, Art thou then the Son of God? And he said unto them, Ye say that I am.

71 And they said, What need we any further witness? for we ourselves have heard of his own mouth.

23 And the whole multitude of them arose, and led him unto Pi'late.

2 And they began to accuse him, saying, We found this *fellow* perverting the nation, and forbidding to give tribute to Cæ'sar, saying that he himself is Christ a King.

3 And Pi'late asked him, saying, Art thou the King of the Jews? And he answered him and said, Thou sayest *it*.

4 Then said Pi'late to the chief priests and *to* the people, I find no fault in this man.

5 And they were the more fierce, saying, He stirreth up the people, teaching throughout all Jew'ry, beginning from Gal'i-lee to this place.

6 When Pi'late heard of Gal'i-lee, he asked whether the man were a Gal-i-læ'an.

7 And as soon as he knew that he belonged unto Her'od's jurisdiction, he sent him to Her'od, who himself also was at Je-ru'sa-lem at that time.

8 ¶ And when Her'od saw Je'sus, he was exceeding glad: for he was desirous to see him of a long *season*, because he had heard many things of him; and he hoped to have seen some miracle done by him.

9 Then he questioned with him in many words; but he answered him nothing.

10 And the chief priests and scribes stood and vehemently accused him.

11 And Her'od with his men of war set him at nought, and mocked *him*, and arrayed him in a gorgeous robe, and sent him again to Pi'late.

12 ¶ And the same day Pi'late and Her'od were made friends together: for before they were at enmity between themselves.

13 ¶ And Pi'late, when he had called together the chief priests and the rulers and the people,

14 Said unto them, Ye have brought this man unto me, as one that perverteth the people: and, behold, I, having examined *him* before you, have found no fault in this man touching those things whereof ye accuse him:

15 No, nor yet Her'od: for I sent you to him; and, lo, nothing worthy of death is done unto him.

16 I will therefore chastise him, and release *him*.

17 (For of necessity he must release one unto them at the feast.)

18 And they cried out all at once, saying, Away with this *man*, and release unto us Ba-rab'bas:

19 (Who for a certain sedition made in the city, and for murder, was cast into prison.)

20 Pi'late therefore, willing to release Je'sus, spake again to them.

21 But they cried, saying, Crucify *him*, crucify him.

22 And he said unto them the third time, Why, what evil hath he done? I have found no cause of death in him: I will therefore chastise him, and let *him* go.

23 And they were instant with loud voices, requiring that he might be crucified. And the voices of them and of the chief priests prevailed.

24 And Pi′late gave sentence that it should be as they required.

25 And he released unto them him that for sedition and murder was cast into prison, whom they had desired; but he delivered Je′sus to their will.

26 And as they led him away, they laid hold upon one Si′mon, a Cy-re′ni-an, coming out of the country, and on him they laid the cross, that he might bear *it* after Je′sus.

27 ¶ And there followed him a great company of people, and of women, which also bewailed and lamented him.

28 But Je′sus turning unto them said, Daughters of Je-ru′salem, weep not for me, but weep for yourselves, and for your children.

29 For, behold, the days are coming, in the which they shall say, Blessed *are* the barren, and the wombs that never bare, and the paps which never gave suck.

30 Then shall they begin to say to the mountains, Fall on us; and to the hills, Cover us.

31 For if they do these things in a green tree, what shall be done in the dry?

32 And there were also two other, malefactors, led with him to be put to death.

33 And when they were come to the place, which is called Cal′va-ry, there they crucified him, and the malefactors, one on the right hand, and the other on the left.

34 ¶ Then said Je′sus, Father, forgive them; for they know not what they do. And they parted his raiment, and cast lots.

35 And the people stood beholding. And the rulers also with them derided him, saying, He saved others; let him save himself, if he be Christ, the chosen of God.

36 And the soldiers also mocked him, coming to him, and offering him vinegar,

37 And saying, If thou be the king of the Jews, save thyself.

38 And a superscription also was written over him in letters of Greek, and Lat′in, and He′brew, THIS IS THE KING OF THE JEWS.

39 ¶ And one of the malefactors which were hanged railed on him, saying, If thou be Christ, save thyself and us.

40 But the other answering rebuked him, saying, Dost not thou fear God, seeing thou art in the same condemnation?

41 And we indeed justly; for we receive the due reward of our deeds: but this man hath done nothing amiss.

42 And he said unto Je′sus,

Lord, remember me when thou comest into thy kingdom.

43 And Je'sus said unto him, Verily I say unto thee, Today shalt thou be with me in paradise.

44 And it was about the sixth hour, and there was a darkness over all the earth until the ninth hour.

45 And the sun was darkened, and the veil of the temple was rent in the midst.

46 ¶ And when Je'sus had cried with a loud voice, he said, Father, into thy hands I commend my spirit: and having said thus, he gave up the ghost.

47 Now when the centurion saw what was done, he glorified God, saying, Certainly this was a righteous man.

48 And all the people that came together to that sight, beholding the things which were done, smote their breasts, and returned.

49 And all his acquaintance, and the women that followed him from Gal'i-lee, stood afar off, beholding these things.

50 ¶ And, behold, there was a man named Jo'seph, a counselor; and he was a good man, and a just:

51 (The same had not consented to the counsel and deed of them;) he was of Ar-i-ma-thæ'a, a city of the Jews: who also himself waited for the kingdom of God.

52 This man went unto Pi'late, and begged the body of Je'sus.

53 And he took it down, and wrapped it in linen, and laid it in a sepulcher that was hewn in stone, wherein never man before was laid.

54 And that day was the preparation, and the sabbath drew on.

55 And the women also, which came with him from Gal'i-lee, followed after, and beheld the sepulcher, and how his body was laid.

56 And they returned, and prepared spices and ointments; and rested the sabbath day according to the commandment.

24 Now upon the first day of the week, very early in the morning, they came unto the sepulcher, bringing the spices which they had prepared, and certain others with them.

2 And they found the stone rolled away from the sepulcher.

3 And they entered in, and found not the body of the Lord Je'sus.

4 And it came to pass, as they were much perplexed thereabout, behold, two men stood by them in shining garments:

5 And as they were afraid, and bowed down their faces to the earth, they said unto them, Why seek ye the living among the dead?

6 He is not here, but is risen: remember how he spake unto you when he was yet in Gal'i-lee,

7 Saying, The Son of man must be delivered into the hands of sinful men, and be crucified, and the third day rise again.

8 And they remembered his words,

9 And returned from the sepulcher, and told all these things

unto the eleven, and to all the rest.

10 It was Ma'ry Mag-da-le'ne, and Jo-an'na, and Ma'ry *the mother* of James, and other *women that were* with them, which told these things unto the apostles.

11 And their words seemed to them as idle tales, and they believed them not.

12 Then arose Pe'ter, and ran unto the sepulchre; and stooping down, he beheld the linen clothes laid by themselves, and departed, wondering in himself at that which was come to pass.

13 ¶ And, behold, two of them went that same day to a village called Em'ma-us, which was from Je-ru'sa-lem *about* threescore furlongs.

14 And they talked together of all these things which had happened.

15 And it came to pass, that, while they communed *together* and reasoned, Je'sus himself drew near, and went with them.

16 But their eyes were held that they should not know him.

17 And he said unto them, What manner of communications *are* these that ye have one to another, as ye walk, and are sad?

18 And the one of them, whose name was Cle'o-pas, answering said unto him, Art thou only a stranger in Je-ru'sa-lem, and hast not known the things which are come to pass there in these days?

19 And he said unto them,

What things? And they said unto him, Concerning Je'sus of Naz'-a-reth, which was a prophet mighty in deed and word before God and all the people:

20 And how the chief priests and our rulers delivered him to be condemned to death, and have crucified him.

21 But we trusted that it had been he which should have re deemed Is'ra-el; and beside all this, today is the third day since these things were done.

22 Yea, and certain women also of our company made us astonished, which were early at the sepulchre;

23 And when they found not his body, they came, saying, that they had also seen a vision of angels, which said that he was alive.

24 And certain of them which were with us went to the sepulcher, and found *it* even so as the women had said: but him they saw not.

25 Then he said unto them, O fools, and slow of heart to believe all that the prophets have spoken:

26 Ought not Christ to have suffered these things, and to enter into his glory?

27 And beginning at Mo'ses and all the prophets, he expounded unto them in all the scriptures the things concerning himself.

28 And they drew nigh unto the village, whither they went: and he made as though he would have gone further.

29 But they constrained him,

saying, Abide with us: for it is toward evening, and the day is far spent. And he went in to tarry with them.

30 And it came to pass, as he sat at meat with them, he took bread, and blessed *it*, and brake, and gave to them.

31 And their eyes were opened, and they knew him; and he vanished out of their sight.

32 And they said one to another, Did not our heart burn within us, while he talked with us by the way, and while he opened to us the scriptures?

33 And they rose up the same hour, and returned to Je-ru'sa-lem, and found the eleven gathered together, and them that were with them,

34 Saying, The Lord is risen indeed, and hath appeared to Si'mon.

35 And they told what things *were done* in the way, and how he was known of them in breaking of bread.

36 ¶ And as they thus spake, Je'sus himself stood in the midst of them, and saith unto them, Peace *be* unto you.

37 But they were terrified and affrighted, and supposed that they had seen a spirit.

38 And he said unto them, Why are ye troubled? and why do thoughts arise in your hearts?

39 Behold my hands and my feet, that it is I myself: handle me, and see; for a spirit hath not flesh and bones, as ye see me have.

40 And when he had thus spoken, he showed them *his* hands and *his* feet.

41 And while they yet believed not for joy, and wondered, he said unto them, Have ye here any meat?

42 And they gave him a piece of a broiled fish, and of an honeycomb.

43 And he took *it*, and did eat before them.

44 And he said unto them, These *are* the words which I spake unto you, while I was yet with you, that all things must be fulfilled, which were written in the law of Mo'ses, and *in* the prophets, and *in* the psalms, concerning me.

45 Then opened he their understanding, that they might understand the scriptures,

46 And said unto them, Thus it is written, and thus it behooved Christ to suffer, and to rise from the dead the third day:

47 And that repentance and remission of sins should be preached in his name among all nations, beginning at Je-ru'sa-lem.

48 And ye are witnesses of these things.

49 ¶ And, behold, I send the promise of my Father upon you: but tarry ye in the city of Je-ru'sa-lem, until ye be endued with power from on high.

50 ¶ And he led them out as far as to Beth'a-ny, and he lifted up his hands, and blessed them.

51 And it came to pass, while he blessed them, he was parted from them, and carried up into heaven.

52 And they worshiped him, and returned to Je·ru'sa·lem with great joy:

53 And were continually in the temple, praising and blessing God. Amen.

JOHN

1 In the beginning was the Word, and the Word was with God, and the Word was God.

2 The same was in the beginning with God.

3 All things were made by him; and without him was not anything made that was made.

4 In him was life; and the life was the light of men.

5 And the light shineth in darkness; and the darkness comprehended it not.

6 ¶ There was a man sent from God, whose name was John.

7 The same came for a witness, to bear witness of the Light, that all men through him might believe.

8 He was not that Light, but was sent to bear witness of that Light.

9 That was the true Light, which lighteth every man that cometh into the world.

10 He was in the world, and the world was made by him, and the world knew him not.

11 He came unto his own, and his own received him not.

12 But as many as received him, to them gave he power to become the sons of GOD, even to them that believe on his name:

13 Which were born, not of blood, nor of the will of the flesh, nor of the will of man, but of God.

14 And the Word was made flesh, and dwelt among us, (and we beheld his glory, the glory as of the only begotten of the Father,) full of grace and truth.

15 ¶ John bare witness of him, and cried, saying, This was he of whom I spake, He that cometh after me is preferred before me: for he was before me.

16 And of his fullness have all we received, and grace for grace.

17 For the law was given by Mo'ses, but grace and truth came by Je'sus Christ.

18 No man hath seen God at any time; the only begotten Son, which is in the bosom of the Father, he hath declared him.

19 ¶ And this is the record of John, when the Jews sent priests and Le'vites from Je·ru'sa·lem to ask him, Who art thou?

20 And he confessed, and denied not; but confessed, I am not the Christ.

21 And they asked him, What then? Art thou E·li'jah? And he saith, I am not. Art thou that prophet? And he answered, No.

22 Then said they unto him, Who art thou? that we may give an answer to them that sent us. What sayest thou of thyself?

23 He said, I *am* the voice of one crying in the wilderness, Make straight the way of the Lord, as said the prophet I-sa'iah.

24 And they which were sent were of the Phar'i-sees.

25 And they asked him, and said unto him, Why baptizest thou then, if thou be not that Christ, nor E-li'jah, neither that prophet?

26 John answered them, saying, I baptize with water: but there standeth one among you, whom ye know not;

27 He it is, who coming after me is preferred before me, whose shoe's latchet I am not worthy to unloose.

28 These things were done in Beth-ab'a-ra beyond Jor'dan, where John was baptizing.

29 ¶ The next day John seeth Je'sus coming unto him, and saith, Behold the Lamb of God, which taketh away the sin of the world.

30 This is he of whom I said, After me cometh a man which is preferred before me: for he was before me.

31 And I knew him not: but that he should be made manifest to Is'ra-el, therefore am I come baptizing with water.

32 And John bare record, saying, I saw the Spirit descending from heaven like a dove, and it abode upon him.

33 And I knew him not: but he that sent me to baptize with water, the same said unto me, Upon whom thou shalt see the Spirit descending, and remaining on him, the same is he which baptizeth with the Ho'ly Ghost.

34 And I saw, and bare record that this is the Son of God.

35 ¶ Again the next day after John stood, and two of his disciples;

36 And looking upon Je'sus as he walked, he saith, Behold the Lamb of God!

37 And the two disciples heard him speak, and they followed Je'sus.

38 Then Je'sus turned, and saw them following, and saith unto them, What seek ye? They said unto him, Rab'bi, (which is to say, being interpreted, Master,) where dwellest thou?

39 He saith unto them, Come and see. They came and saw where he dwelt, and abode with him that day: for it was about the tenth hour.

40 One of the two which heard John *speak*, and followed him, was Andrew, Si'mon Pe'ter's brother.

41 He first findeth his own brother Si'mon, and saith unto him, We have found the Mes-si'as, which is, being interpreted, the Christ.

42 And he brought him to Je'sus. And when Je'sus beheld him, he said, Thou art Si'mon the son of Jo'na: thou shalt be called Ce'phas, which is by interpretation, A stone.

43 ¶ The day following Je'sus

would go forth into Gal'i-lee, and findeth Phil'ip, and saith unto him, Follow me.

44 Now Phil'ip was of Beth-sa'i-da, the city of Andrew and Pe'ter.

45 Phil'ip findeth Na-than'a-el, and saith unto him, We have found him, of whom Mo'ses in the law, and the prophets, did write, Je'sus of Naz'a-reth, the son of Jo'seph.

46 And Na-than'a-el said unto him, Can there any good thing come out of Naz'a-reth? Phil'ip saith unto him, Come and see.

47 Je'sus saw Na-than'a-el coming to him, and saith of him, Behold an Is'ra-el-ite indeed, in whom is no guile!

48 Na-than'a-el saith unto him, Whence knowest thou me? Je'sus answered and said unto him, Before that Phil'ip called thee, when thou wast under the fig tree, I saw thee.

49 Na-than'a-el answered and saith unto him, Rab'bi, thou art the Son of God; thou art the King of Is'ra-el.

50 Je'sus answered and said unto him, Because I said unto thee, I saw thee under the fig tree, believest thou? thou shalt see greater things than these.

51 And he saith unto him, Verily, verily, I say unto you, Hereafter ye shall see heaven open, and the angels of God ascending and descending upon the Son of man.

2 And the third day there was a marriage in Ca'na of Gal'i-lee; and the mother of Je'sus was there:

2 And both Je'sus was called, and his disciples, to the marriage.

3 And when they wanted wine, the mother of Je'sus saith unto him, They have no wine.

4 Je'sus saith unto her, Woman, what have I to do with thee? mine hour is not yet come.

5 His mother saith unto the servants, Whatsoever he saith unto you, do it.

6 And there were set there six waterpots of stone, after the manner of the purifying of the Jews, containing two or three firkins apiece.

7 Je'sus saith unto them, Fill the waterpots with water. And they filled them up to the brim.

8 And he saith unto them, Draw out now, and bear unto the governor of the feast. And they bare it.

9 When the ruler of the feast had tasted the water that was made wine, and knew not whence it was: (but the servants which drew the water knew;) the governor of the feast called the bridegroom,

10 And saith unto him, Every man at the beginning doth set forth good wine; and when men have well drunk, then that which is worse: but thou hast kept the good wine until now.

11 This beginning of miracles did Je'sus in Ca'na of Gal'i-lee, and manifested forth his glory; and his disciples believed on him.

12 ¶ After this he went down to Ca-per'na-um, he, and his mother, and his brethren, and

his disciples: and they continued there not many days.

13 ¶ And the Jews' passover was at hand, and Je'sus went up to Je-ru'sa-lem,

14 And found in the temple those that sold oxen and sheep and doves, and the changers of money sitting:

15 And when he had made a scourge of small cords, he drove them all out of the temple, and the sheep, and the oxen; and poured out the changers' money, and overthrew the tables;

16 And said unto them that sold doves, Take these things hence; make not my Father's house an house of merchandise.

17 And his disciples remembered that it was written, The zeal of thine house hath eaten me up.

18 ¶ Then answered the Jews and said unto him, What sign showest thou unto us, seeing that thou doest these things?

19 Je'sus answered and said unto them, Destroy this temple, and in three days I will raise it up.

20 Then said the Jews, Forty and six years was this temple in building, and wilt thou rear it up in three days?

21 But he spake of the temple of his body.

22 When therefore he was risen from the dead, his disciples remembered that he had said this unto them; and they believed the scripture, and the word which Je'sus had said.

23 ¶ Now when he was in Je-ru'-sa-lem at the passover, in the feast day, many believed in his name, when they saw the miracles which he did.

24 But Je'sus did not commit himself unto them, because he knew all men,

25 And needed not that any should testify of man: for he knew what was in man.

3 There was a man of the Phar'i-sees, named Nic-o-de'mus, a ruler of the Jews:

2 The same came to Je'sus by night, and said unto him, Rab'bi, we know that thou art a teacher come from God: for no man can do these miracles that thou doest, except God be with him.

3 Je'sus answered and said unto him, Verily, verily, I say unto thee, Except a man be born again, he cannot see the kingdom of God.

4 Nic-o-de'mus saith unto him, How can a man be born when he is old? can he enter the second time into his mother's womb, and be born?

5 Je'sus answered, Verily, verily, I say unto thee, Except a man be born of water and of the Spirit, he cannot enter into the kingdom of God.

6 That which is born of the flesh is flesh; and that which is born of the Spirit is spirit.

7 Marvel not that I said unto thee, Ye must be born again.

8 The wind bloweth where it listeth, and thou hearest the sound thereof, but canst not tell whence it cometh, and whither

it goeth: so is everyone that is
born of the Spirit.

9 Nic·o·de'mus answered and
said unto him, How can these
things be?

10 Je'sus answered and said
unto him, Art thou a master of
Is'ra·el, and knowest not these
things?

11 Verily, verily, I say unto
thee, We speak that we do
know, and testify that we have
seen; and ye receive not our
witness.

12 If I have told you earthly
things, and ye believe not, how
shall ye believe, if I tell you of
heavenly things?

13 And no man hath ascended
up to heaven, but he that came
down from heaven, even the
Son of man which is in heaven.

14 ¶ And as Mo'ses lifted up the
serpent in the wilderness, even
so must the Son of man be lifted
up:

15 That whosoever believeth
in him should not perish, but
have eternal life.

16 ¶ For God so loved the
world, that he gave his only
begotten Son, that whosoever
believeth in him should not perish, but have everlasting life.

17 For God sent not his Son
into the world to condemn the
world; but that the world
through him might be saved.

18 ¶ He that believeth on him is
not condemned: but he that believeth not is condemned already, because he hath not believed in the name of the only
begotten Son of God.

19 And this is the condemna-

tion, that light is come into the
world, and men loved darkness
rather than light, because their
deeds were evil.

20 For everyone that doeth evil
hateth the light, neither cometh
to the light, lest his deeds
should be reproved.

21 But he that doeth truth cometh to the light, that his deeds
may be made manifest, that they
are wrought in God.

22 ¶ After these things came Je'-
sus and his disciples into the
land of Ju·dæ'a; and there he
tarried with them, and baptized.

23 ¶ And John also was baptizing in Æ'non near to Sa'lim,
because there was much water
there: and they came, and were
baptized.

24 For John was not yet cast
into prison.

25 ¶ Then there arose a question between some of John's
disciples and the Jews about
purifying.

26 And they came unto John,
and said unto him, Rab'bi, he
that was with thee beyond Jor'-
dan, to whom thou barest witness, behold, the same baptizeth, and all men come to
him.

27 John answered and said, A
man can receive nothing, except it be given him from
heaven.

28 Ye yourselves bear me witness, that I said, I am not the
Christ, but that I am sent before
him.

29 He that hath the bride is the
bridegroom: but the friend of
the bridegroom, which standeth

and heareth him, rejoiceth greatly because of the bridegroom's voice: this my joy therefore is fulfilled.

30 He must increase, but I *must* decrease.

31 He that cometh from above is above all: he that is of the earth is earthly, and speaketh of the earth: he that cometh from heaven is above all.

32 And what he hath seen and heard, that he testifieth; and no man receiveth his testimony.

33 He that hath received his testimony hath set to his seal that God is true.

34 For he whom God hath sent speaketh the words of God: for God giveth not the Spirit by measure *unto him.*

35 The Father loveth the Son, and hath given all things into his hand.

36 He that believeth on the Son hath everlasting life: and he that believeth not the Son shall not see life; but the wrath of God abideth on him.

4 When therefore the Lord knew how the Phar'i-sees had heard that Je'sus made and baptized more disciples than John,

2 (Though Je'sus himself baptized not, but his disciples,)

3 He left Ju-dæ'a, and departed again into Gal'i-lee.

4 And he must needs go through Sa-ma'ri-a.

5 Then cometh he to a city of Sa-ma'ri-a, which is called Sy'char, near to the parcel of ground that Ja'cob gave to his son Jo'seph.

6 Now Ja'cob's well was there. Je'sus therefore, being wearied with *his* journey, sat thus on the well: *and* it was about the sixth hour.

7 There cometh a woman of Sa-ma'ri-a to draw water: Je'sus saith unto her, Give me to drink.

8 (For his disciples were gone away unto the city to buy meat.)

9 Then saith the woman of Sa-ma'ri-a unto him, How is it that thou, being a Jew, askest drink of me, which am a woman of Sa-ma'ri-a? for the Jews have no dealings with the Sa-mar'i-tans.

10 Je'sus answered and said unto her, If thou knewest the gift of God, and who it is that saith to thee, Give me to drink; thou wouldest have asked of him, and he would have given thee living water.

11 The woman saith unto him, Sir, thou hast nothing to draw with, and the well is deep: from whence then hast thou that living water?

12 Art thou greater than our father Ja'cob, which gave us the well, and drank thereof himself, and his children, and his cattle?

13 Je'sus answered and said unto her, Whosoever drinketh of this water shall thirst again:

14 But whosoever drinketh of the water that I shall give him shall never thirst; but the water that I shall give him shall be in him a well of water springing up into everlasting life.

15 The woman saith unto him, Sir, give me this water, that I

thirst not, neither come hither to draw.

16 Je'sus saith unto her, Go, call thy husband, and come hither.

17 The woman answered and said, I have no husband. Je'sus said unto her, Thou hast well said, I have no husband:

18 For thou hast had five husbands; and he whom thou now hast is not thy husband: in that saidst thou truly.

19 The woman saith unto him, Sir, I perceive that thou art a prophet.

20 Our fathers worshipped in this mountain; and ye say, that in Je-ru'sa-lem is the place where men ought to worship.

21 Je'sus saith unto her, Woman, believe me, the hour cometh, when ye shall neither in this mountain, nor yet at Je-ru'sa-lem, worship the Father.

22 Ye worship ye know not what: we know what we worship: for salvation is of the Jews.

23 But the hour cometh, and now is, when the true worshippers shall worship the Father in spirit and in truth: for the Father seeketh such to worship him.

24 God is a Spirit: and they that worship him must worship him in spirit and in truth.

25 The woman saith unto him, I know that Mes-si'as cometh, which is called Christ: when he is come, he will tell us all things.

26 Je'sus saith unto her, I that speak unto thee am he.

27 ¶ And upon this came his disciples, and marveled that he talked with the woman: yet no man said, What seekest thou? or, Why talkest thou with her?

28 The woman then left her waterpot, and went her way into the city, and saith to the men,

29 Come, see a man, which told me all things that ever I did: is not this the Christ?

30 Then they went out of the city, and came unto him.

31 ¶ In the meanwhile his disciples prayed him, saying, Master, eat.

32 But he said unto them, I have meat to eat that ye know not of.

33 Therefore said the disciples one to another, Hath any man brought him aught to eat?

34 Je'sus saith unto them, My meat is to do the will of him that sent me, and to finish his work.

35 Say not ye, There are yet four months, and then cometh harvest? behold, I say unto you, Lift up your eyes, and look on the fields; for they are white already to harvest.

36 And he that reapeth receiveth wages, and gathereth fruit unto life eternal: that both he that soweth and he that reapeth may rejoice together.

37 And herein is that saying true, One soweth, and another reapeth.

38 I sent you to reap that whereon ye bestowed no labor: other men labored, and ye are entered into their labors.

39 ¶ And many of the Sa-mar'i-tans of that city believed on him

for the saying of the woman, which testified, He told me all that ever I did.

40 So when the Sa·mar'i·tans were come unto him, they besought him that he would tarry with them: and he abode there two days.

41 And many more believed because of his own word;

42 And said unto the woman, Now we believe, not because of thy saying: for we have heard *him* ourselves, and know that this is indeed the Christ, the Savior of the world.

43 ¶ Now after two days he departed thence, and went into Gal'i·lee.

44 For Je'sus himself testified, that a prophet hath no honor in his own country.

45 Then when he was come into Gal'i·lee, the Gal·i·læ'ans received him, having seen all the things that he did at Je·ru'sa·lem at the feast: for they also went unto the feast.

46 So Je'sus came again into Ca'na of Gal'i·lee, where he made the water wine. And there was a certain nobleman, whose son was sick at Ca·per'na·um.

47 When he heard that Je'sus was come out of Ju·dæ'a into Gal'i·lee, he went unto him, and besought him that he would come down, and heal his son: for he was at the point of death.

48 Then said Je'sus unto him, Except ye see signs and wonders, ye will not believe.

49 The nobleman saith unto him, Sir, come down ere my child die.

50 Je'sus saith unto him, Go thy way; thy son liveth. And the man believed the word that Je'sus had spoken unto him, and he went his way.

51 And as he was now going down, his servants met him, and told *him*, saying, Thy son liveth.

52 Then inquired he of them the hour when he began to amend. And they said unto him, Yesterday at the seventh hour the fever left him.

53 So the father knew that *it was* at the same hour, in the which Je'sus said unto him, Thy son liveth: and himself believed, and his whole house.

54 This *is* again the second miracle *that* Je'sus did, when he was come out of Ju·dæ'a into Gal'i·lee.

5 After this there was a feast of the Jews; and Je'sus went up to Je·ru'sa·lem.

2 Now there is at Je·ru'sa·lem by the sheep *market* a pool, which is called in the He'brew tongue Be·thes'da, having five porches.

3 In these lay a great multitude of impotent folk, of blind, halt, withered, waiting for the moving of the water.

4 For an angel went down at a certain season into the pool, and troubled the water: whosoever then *first* after the troubling of the water stepped in was made whole of whatsoever disease he had.

5 And a certain man was there, which had an infirmity thirty and eight years.

6 When Je'sus saw him lie, and knew that he had been now a long time *in that case*, he saith unto him, Wilt thou be made whole?

7 The impotent man answered him, Sir, I have no man, when the water is troubled, to put me into the pool: but while I am coming, another stepped down before me.

8 Je'sus saith unto him, Rise, take up thy bed, and walk.

9 And immediately the man was made whole, and took up his bed, and walked: and on the same day was the sabbath.

10 ¶ The Jews therefore said unto him that was cured, It is the sabbath day: it is not lawful for thee to carry *thy* bed.

11 He answered them, He that made me whole, the same said unto me, Take up thy bed, and walk.

12 Then asked they him, What man is that which said unto thee, Take up thy bed, and walk?

13 And he that was healed wist not who it was: for Je'sus had conveyed himself away, a multitude being in *that* place.

14 Afterward Je'sus findeth him in the temple, and said unto him, Behold, thou art made whole: sin no more, lest a worse thing come unto thee.

15 The man departed, and told the Jews that it was Je'sus, which had made him whole.

16 And therefore did the Jews persecute Je'sus, and sought to slay him, because he had done these things on the sabbath day.

17 ¶ But Je'sus answered them, My Father worketh hitherto, and I work.

18 Therefore the Jews sought the more to kill him, because he not only had broken the sabbath, but said also that God was his Father, making himself equal with God.

19 Then answered Je'sus and said unto them, Verily, verily, I say unto you, The Son can do nothing of himself; but what he seeth the Father do: for what things soever he doeth, these also doeth the Son likewise.

20 For the Father loveth the Son, and sheweth him all things that himself doeth: and he will shew him greater works than these, that ye may marvel.

21 For as the Father raiseth up the dead, and quickeneth *them*; even so the Son quickeneth whom he will.

22 For the Father judgeth no man, but hath committed all judgment unto the Son:

23 That all men should honour the Son, even as they honour the Father. He that honoureth not the Son honoureth not the Father which hath sent him.

24 Verily, verily, I say unto you, He that heareth my word, and believeth on him that sent me, hath everlasting life, and shall not come into condemnation; but is passed from death unto life.

25 Verily, verily, I say unto you, The hour is coming, and now is, when the dead shall hear the voice of the Son of

God: and they that hear shall live.

26 For as the Father hath life in himself; so hath he given to the Son to have life in himself;

27 And hath given him authority to execute judgment also, because he is the Son of man.

28 Marvel not at this: for the hour is coming, in the which all that are in the graves shall hear his voice,

29 And shall come forth; they that have done good, unto the resurrection of life; and they that have done evil, unto the resurrection of damnation.

30 I can of mine own self do nothing: as I hear, I judge: and my judgment is just; because I seek not mine own will, but the will of the Father which hath sent me.

31 If I bear witness of myself, my witness is not true.

32 ¶ There is another that beareth witness of me; and I know that the witness which he witnesseth of me is true.

33 Ye sent unto John, and he bare witness unto the truth.

34 But I receive not testimony from man: but these things I say, that ye might be saved.

35 He was a burning and a shining light: and ye were willing for a season to rejoice in his light.

36 ¶ But I have greater witness than *that* of John: for the works which the Father hath given me to finish, the same works that I do, bear witness of me, that the Father hath sent me.

37 And the Father himself, which hath sent me, hath borne witness of me. Ye have neither heard his voice at any time, nor seen his shape.

38 And ye have not his word abiding in you: for whom he hath sent, him ye believe not.

39 ¶ Search the scriptures; for in them ye think ye have eternal life: and they are they which testify of me.

40 And ye will not come to me, that ye might have life.

41 I receive not honor from men.

42 But I know you, that ye have not the love of God in you.

43 I am come in my Father's name, and ye receive me not: if another shall come in his own name, him ye will receive.

44 How can ye believe, which receive honor one of another, and seek not the honor that *cometh* from God only?

45 Do not think that I will accuse you to the Father: there is *one* that accuseth you, *even* Mo'ses, in whom ye trust.

46 For had ye believed Mo'ses, ye would have believed me: for he wrote of me.

47 But if ye believe not his writings, how shall ye believe my words?

6 After these things Je'sus went over the sea of Gal'i-lee, which is *the* sea of Ti-be'ri-as.

2 And a great multitude followed him, because they saw his miracles which he did on them that were diseased.

3 And Je'sus went up into a mountain, and there he sat with his disciples.

4 And the passover, a feast of the Jews, was nigh.

5 ¶ When Je'sus then lifted up *his* eyes, and saw a great company come unto him, he saith unto Phil'ip, Whence shall we buy bread, that these may eat?

6 And this he said to prove him: for he himself knew what he would do.

7 Phil'ip answered him, Two hundred pennyworth of bread is not sufficient for them, that every one of them may take a little.

8 One of his disciples, Andrew, Si'mon Pe'ter's brother, saith unto him,

9 There is a lad here, which hath five barley loaves, and two small fishes: but what are they among so many?

10 And Je'sus said, Make the men sit down. Now there was much grass in the place. So the men sat down, in number about five thousand.

11 And Je'sus took the loaves; and when he had given thanks, he distributed to the disciples, and the disciples to them that were set down; and likewise of the fishes as much as they would.

12 When they were filled, he said unto his disciples, Gather up the fragments that remain, that nothing be lost.

13 Therefore they gathered *them* together, and filled twelve baskets with the fragments of the five barley loaves, which remained over and above unto them that had eaten.

14 Then those men, when they had seen the miracle that Je'sus did, said, This is of a truth that prophet that should come into the world.

15 ¶ When Je'sus therefore perceived that they would come and take him by force, to make him a king, he departed again into a mountain himself alone.

16 And when even was *now* come, his disciples went down unto the sea,

17 And entered into a ship, and went over the sea toward Ca-per'na-um. And it was now dark, and Je'sus was not come to them.

18 And the sea arose by reason of a great wind that blew.

19 So when they had rowed about five and twenty or thirty furlongs, they see Je'sus walking on the sea, and drawing nigh unto the ship: and they were afraid.

20 But he saith unto them, It is I, be not afraid.

21 Then they willingly received him into the ship: and immediately the ship was at the land whither they went.

22 ¶ The day following, when the people which stood on the other side of the sea saw that there was none other boat there, save that one whereinto his disciples were entered, and that Je'sus went not with his disciples into the boat, but *that* his disciples were gone away alone;

23 (Howbeit there came other boats from Ti-be'ri-as nigh unto the place where they did eat

bread, after that the Lord had given thanks:)

24 When the people therefore saw that Je'sus was not there, neither his disciples, they also took shipping, and came to Ca-per'na-um, seeking for Je'sus.

25 And when they had found him on the other side of the sea, they said unto him, Rab'bi, when camest thou hither?

26 Je'sus answered them and said, Verily, verily, I say unto you, Ye seek me, not because ye saw the miracles, but because ye did eat of the loaves, and were filled.

27 Labor not for the meat which perisheth, but for that meat which endureth unto everlasting life, which the Son of man shall give unto you: for him hath God the Father sealed.

28 Then said they unto him, What shall we do, that we might work the works of God?

29 Je'sus answered and said unto them, This is the work of God, that ye believe on him whom he hath sent.

30 They said therefore unto him, What sign showest thou then, that we may see, and believe thee? what dost thou work?

31 Our fathers did eat manna in the desert; as it is written, He gave them bread from heaven to eat.

32 Then Je'sus said unto them, Verily, verily, I say unto you, Mo'ses gave you not that bread from heaven; but my Father giveth you the true bread from heaven.

33 For the bread of God is he which cometh down from heaven, and giveth life unto the world.

34 Then said they unto him, Lord, evermore give us this bread.

35 And Je'sus said unto them, I am the bread of life: he that cometh to me shall never hunger; and he that believeth on me shall never thirst.

36 But I said unto you, That ye also have seen me, and believe not.

37 All that the Father giveth me shall come to me; and him that cometh to me I will in no wise cast out.

38 For I came down from heaven, not to do mine own will, but the will of him that sent me.

39 And this is the Father's will which hath sent me, that of all which he hath given me I should lose nothing, but should raise it up again at the last day.

40 And this is the will of him that sent me, that everyone which seeth the Son, and believeth on him, may have everlasting life: and I will raise him up at the last day.

41 The Jews then murmured at him, because he said, I am the bread which came down from heaven.

42 And they said, Is not this Je'-sus, the son of Jo'seph, whose father and mother we know? how is it then that he saith, I came down from heaven?

43 Je'sus therefore answered

and said unto them, Murmur not among yourselves.

44 No man can come to me, except the Father which hath sent me draw him: and I will raise him up at the last day.

45 It is written in the prophets, And they shall be all taught of God. Every man therefore that hath heard, and hath learned of the Father, cometh unto me.

46 Not that any man hath seen the Father, save he which is of God, he hath seen the Father.

47 Verily, verily, I say unto you, He that believeth on me hath everlasting life.

48 I am that bread of life.

49 Your fathers did eat manna in the wilderness, and are dead.

50 This is the bread which cometh down from heaven, that a man may eat thereof, and not die.

51 I am the living bread which came down from heaven: if any man eat of this bread, he shall live forever: and the bread that I will give is my flesh, which I will give for the life of the world.

52 The Jews therefore strove among themselves, saying, How can this man give us *his* flesh to eat?

53 Then Je'sus said unto them, Verily, verily, I say unto you, Except ye eat the flesh of the Son of man, and drink his blood, ye have no life in you.

54 Whoso eateth my flesh, and drinketh my blood, hath eternal life; and I will raise him up at the last day.

55 For my flesh is meat indeed, and my blood is drink indeed.

56 He that eateth my flesh, and drinketh my blood, dwelleth in me, and I in him.

57 As the living Father hath sent me, and I live by the Father: so he that eateth me, even he shall live by me.

58 This is that bread which came down from heaven: not as your fathers did eat manna, and are dead: he that eateth of this bread shall live forever.

59 These things said he in the synagogue, as he taught in Caper'na-um.

60 Many therefore of his disciples, when they had heard *this,* said, This is an hard saying; who can hear it?

61 When Je'sus knew in himself that his disciples murmured at it, he said unto them, Doth this offend you?

62 *What* and if ye shall see the Son of man ascend up where he was before?

63 It is the spirit that quickeneth; the flesh profiteth nothing: the words that I speak unto you, *they* are spirit, and *they* are life.

64 But there are some of you that believe not. For Je'sus knew from the beginning who they were that believed not, and who should betray him.

65 And he said, Therefore said I unto you, that no man can come unto me, except it were given unto him of my Father.

66 ¶ From that *time* many of his disciples went back, and walked no more with him.

67 Then said Je'sus unto the twelve, Will ye also go away?

68 Then Si'mon Pe'ter answered him, Lord, to whom shall we go? thou hast the words of eternal life.

69 And we believe and are sure that thou art that Christ, the Son of the living God.

70 Je'sus answered them, Have not I chosen you twelve, and one of you is a devil?

71 He spake of Ju'das Is·car'i·ot *the son* of Si'mon: for he it was that should betray him, being one of the twelve.

7 After these things Je'sus walked in Gal'i·lee: for he would not walk in Jew'ry, because the Jews sought to kill him.

2 Now the Jews' feast of tabernacles was at hand.

3 His brethren therefore said unto him, Depart hence, and go into Ju·dæ'a, that thy disciples also may see the works that thou doest.

4 For *there is* no man *that* doeth anything in secret, and he himself seeketh to be known openly. If thou do these things, show thyself to the world.

5 For neither did his brethren believe in him.

6 Then Je'sus said unto them, My time is not yet come: but your time is always ready.

7 The world cannot hate you; but me it hateth, because I testify of it, that the works thereof are evil.

8 Go ye up unto this feast: I go not up yet unto this feast; for my time is not yet full come.

9 When he had said these words unto them, he abode *still* in Gal'i·lee.

10 ¶ But when his brethren were gone up, then went he also up unto the feast, not openly, but as it were in secret.

11 Then the Jews sought him at the feast, and said, Where is he?

12 And there was much murmuring among the people concerning him: for some said, He is a good man: others said, Nay; but he deceiveth the people.

13 Howbeit no man spake openly of him for fear of the Jews.

14 ¶ Now about the midst of the feast Je'sus went up into the temple, and taught.

15 And the Jews marveled, saying, How knoweth this man letters, having never learned?

16 Je'sus answered them, and said, My doctrine is not mine, but his that sent me.

17 If any man will do his will, he shall know of the doctrine, whether it be of God, or *whether* I speak of myself.

18 He that speaketh of himself seeketh his own glory: but he that seeketh his glory that sent him, the same is true, and no unrighteousness is in him.

19 Did not Mo'ses give you the law, and *yet* none of you keepeth the law? Why go ye about to kill me?

20 The people answered and said, Thou hast a devil: who goeth about to kill thee?

21 Je'sus answered and said

unto them, I have done one work, and ye all marvel.

22 Mo'ses therefore gave unto you circumcision; (not because it is of Mo'ses, but of the fathers;) and ye on the sabbath day circumcise a man.

23 If a man on the sabbath day receive circumcision, that the law of Mo'ses should not be broken; are ye angry at me, because I have made a man every whit whole on the sabbath day?

24 Judge not according to the appearance, but judge righteous judgment.

25 Then said some of them of Je-ru'sa-lem, Is not this he, whom they seek to kill?

26 But, lo, he speaketh boldly, and they say nothing unto him. Do the rulers know indeed that this is the very Christ?

27 Howbeit we know this man whence he is: but when Christ cometh, no man knoweth whence he is.

28 Then cried Je'sus in the temple as he taught, saying, Ye both know me, and ye know whence I am: and I am not come of myself, but he that sent me is true, whom ye know not.

29 But I know him: for I am from him, and he hath sent me.

30 Then they sought to take him: but no man laid hands on him, because his hour was not yet come.

31 And many of the people believed on him, and said, When Christ cometh, will he do more miracles than these which this man hath done?

32 ¶ The Phar'i-sees heard that the people murmured such things concerning him; and the Phar'i-sees and the chief priests sent officers to take him.

33 Then said Je'sus unto them, Yet a little while am I with you, and then I go unto him that sent me.

34 Ye shall seek me, and shall not find me: and where I am, thither ye cannot come.

35 Then said the Jews among themselves, Whither will he go, that we shall not find him? will he go unto the dispersed among the Gen'tiles, and teach the Gen'tiles?

36 What manner of saying is this that he said, Ye shall seek me, and shall not find me: and where I am, thither ye cannot come?

37 In the last day, that great day of the feast, Je'sus stood and cried, saying, If any man thirst, let him come unto me, and drink.

38 He that believeth on me, as the scripture hath said, out of his belly shall flow rivers of living water.

39 (But this spake he of the Spirit, which they that believe on him should receive: for the Ho'ly Ghost was not yet given; because that Je'sus was not yet glorified.)

40 ¶ Many of the people therefore, when they heard this saying, said, Of a truth this is the Prophet.

41 Others said, This is the Christ. But some said, Shall Christ come out of Gal'i lee?

42 Hath not the scripture said, That Christ cometh of the seed of Da'vid, and out of the town of Beth'le-hem, where Da'vid was?

43 So there was a division among the people because of him.

44 And some of them would have taken him; but no man laid hands on him.

45 ¶ Then came the officers to the chief priests and Phar'i-sees; and they said unto them, Why have ye not brought him?

46 The officers answered, Never man spake like this man.

47 Then answered them the Phar'i-sees, Are ye also deceived?

48 Have any of the rulers or of the Phar'i-sees believed on him?

49 But this people who knoweth not the law are cursed.

50 Nic-o-de'mus saith unto them, (he that came to Je'sus by night, being one of them,)

51 Doth our law judge any man, before it hear him, and know what he doeth?

52 They answered and said unto him, Art thou also of Gal'i-lee? Search, and look: for out of Gal'i-lee ariseth no prophet.

53 And every man went unto his own house.

8 Jesus went unto the mount of Ol'ives.

2 And early in the morning he came again into the temple, and all the people came unto him; and he sat down, and taught them.

3 And the scribes and Phar'i-sees brought unto him a woman taken in adultery; and when they had set her in the midst,

4 They say unto him, Master, this woman was taken in adultery, in the very act.

5 Now Mo'ses in the law commanded us, that such should be stoned: but what sayest thou?

6 This they said, tempting him, that they might have to accuse him. But Je'sus stooped down, and with *his* finger wrote on the ground, *as though he heard them not.*

7 So when they continued asking him, he lifted up himself, and said unto them, He that is without sin among you, let him first cast a stone at her.

8 And again he stooped down, and wrote on the ground.

9 And they which heard *it,* being convicted by *their own* conscience, went out one by one, beginning at the eldest, *even* unto the last: and Je'sus was left alone, and the woman standing in the midst.

10 When Je'sus had lifted up himself, and saw none but the woman, he said unto her, Woman, where are those thine accusers? hath no man condemned thee?

11 She said, No man, Lord. And Je'sus said unto her, Neither do I condemn thee: go, and sin no more.

12 ¶ Then spake Je'sus again unto them, saying, I am the light of the world: he that followeth me shall not walk in darkness, but shall have the light of life.

13 The Phar'i-sees therefore said unto him, Thou bearest

record of thyself; thy record is not true.

14 Je'sus answered and said unto them, Though I bear record of myself, yet my record is true: for I know whence I came, and whither I go; but ye cannot tell whence I come, and whither I go.

15 Ye judge after the flesh; I judge no man.

16 And yet if I judge, my judgment is true: for I am not alone, but I and the Father that sent me.

17 It is also written in your law, that the testimony of two men is true.

18 I am one that bear witness of myself, and the Father that sent me beareth witness of me.

19 Then said they unto him, Where is thy Father? Je'sus answered, Ye neither know me, nor my Father: if ye had known me, ye should have known my Father also.

20 These words spake Je'sus in the treasury, as he taught in the temple: and no man laid hands on him; for his hour was not yet come.

21 Then said Je'sus again unto them, I go my way, and ye shall seek me, and shall die in your sins: whither I go, ye cannot come.

22 Then said the Jews, Will he kill himself? because he saith, Whither I go, ye cannot come.

23 And he said unto them, Ye are from beneath, I am from above: ye are of this world; I am not of this world.

24 I said therefore unto you,

that ye shall die in your sins: for if ye believe not that I am he, ye shall die in your sins.

25 Then said they unto him, Who art thou? And Je'sus saith unto them, Even the same that I said unto you from the beginning.

26 I have many things to say and to judge of you: but he that sent me is true; and I speak to the world those things which I have heard of him.

27 They understood not that he spake to them of the Father.

28 Then said Je'sus unto them, When ye have lifted up the Son of man, then shall ye know that I am he, and that I do nothing of myself; but as my Father hath taught me, I speak these things.

29 And he that sent me is with me: the Father hath not left me alone; for I do always those things that please him.

30 As he spake these words, many believed on him.

31 Then said Je'sus to those Jews which believed on him, If ye continue in my word, then are ye my disciples indeed;

32 And ye shall know the truth, and the truth shall make you free.

33 ¶ They answered him, We be A'bra-ham's seed, and were never in bondage to any man: how sayest thou, Ye shall be made free?

34 Je'sus answered them, Verily, verily, I say unto you, Whosoever committeth sin is the servant of sin.

35 And the servant abideth not

in the house forever: *but* the Son abideth ever.

36 If the Son therefore shall make you free, ye shall be free indeed.

37 I know that ye are A'bra-ham's seed; but ye seek to kill me, because my word hath no place in you.

38 I speak that which I have seen with my Father: and ye do that which ye have seen with your father.

39 They answered and said unto him, A'bra-ham is our father. Je'sus saith unto them, If ye were A'bra-ham's children, ye would do the works of A'bra-ham.

40 But now ye seek to kill me, a man that hath told you the truth, which I have heard of God: this did not A'bra-ham.

41 Ye do the deeds of *your* father. Then said they to him, We be not born of fornication; we have one Father, *even* God.

42 Je'sus said unto them, If God were your Father, ye would love me: for I proceeded forth and came from God; neither came I of myself, but he sent me.

43 Why do ye not understand my speech? *even* because ye cannot hear my word.

44 Ye are of *your* father the devil, and the lusts of your father ye will do. He was a murderer from the beginning, and abode not in the truth, because there is no truth in him. When he speaketh a lie, he speaketh of his own: for he is a liar, and the father of it.

45 And because I tell *you* the truth, ye believe me not.

46 Which of you convinceth me of sin? And if I say the truth, why do ye not believe me?

47 He that is of God heareth God's words: ye therefore hear *them* not, because ye are not of God.

48 Then answered the Jews, and said unto him, Say we not well that thou art a Sa-mar'i-tan, and hast a devil?

49 Je'sus answered, I have not a devil; but I honor my Father, and ye do dishonor me.

50 And I seek not mine own glory: there is one that seeketh and judgeth.

51 Verily, verily, I say unto you, If a man keep my saying, he shall never see death.

52 Then said the Jews unto him, Now we know that thou hast a devil. A'bra-ham is dead, and the prophets; and thou sayest, If a man keep my saying, he shall never taste of death.

53 Art thou greater than our father A'bra-ham, which is dead? and the prophets are dead: whom makest thou thyself?

54 Je'sus answered, If I honor myself, my honor is nothing: it is my Father that honoreth me; of whom ye say, that he is your God:

55 Yet ye have not known him; but I know him: and if I should say, I know him not, I shall be a liar like unto you: but I know him, and keep his saying.

56 Your father A'bra-ham re-

joiced to see my day: and he saw it, and was glad.

57 Then said the Jews unto him, Thou art not yet fifty years old, and hast thou seen A'bra-ham?

58 Je'sus said unto them, Verily, verily, I say unto you, Before A'bra-ham was, I am.

59 Then took they up stones to cast at him: but Je'sus hid himself, and went out of the temple, going through the midst of them, and so passed by.

9 And as Je'sus passed by, he saw a man which was blind from his birth.

2 And his disciples asked him, saying, Master, who did sin, this man, or his parents, that he was born blind?

3 Je'sus answered, Neither hath this man sinned, nor his parents: but that the works of God should be made manifest in him.

4 I must work the works of him that sent me, while it is day: the night cometh, when no man can work.

5 As long as I am in the world, I am the light of the world.

6 When he had thus spoken, he spat on the ground, and made clay of the spittle, and he anointed the eyes of the blind man with the clay,

7 And said unto him, Go wash in the pool of Si-lo'am, (which is by interpretation, Sent.) He went his way therefore, and washed, and came seeing.

8 ¶ The neighbors therefore, and they which before had seen him that he was blind, said, Is not this he that sat and begged?

9 Some said, This is he: others said, He is like him: but he said, I am he.

10 Therefore said they unto him, How were thine eyes opened?

11 He answered and said, A man that is called Je'sus made clay, and anointed mine eyes, and said unto me, Go to the pool of Si-lo'am, and wash: and I went and washed, and I received sight.

12 Then said they unto him, Where is he? He said, I know not.

13 ¶ They brought to the Phar'i-sees him that aforetime was blind.

14 And it was the sabbath day when Je'sus made the clay, and opened his eyes.

15 Then again the Phar'i-sees also asked him how he had received his sight. He said unto them, He put clay upon mine eyes, and I washed, and do see.

16 Therefore said some of the Phar'i-sees, This man is not of God, because he keepeth not the sabbath day. Others said, How can a man that is a sinner do such miracles? And there was a division among them.

17 They say unto the blind man again, What sayest thou of him, that he hath opened thine eyes? He said, He is a prophet.

18 But the Jews did not believe concerning him, that he had been blind, and received his sight, until they called the

parents of him that had received his sight.

19 And they asked them, saying, Is this your son, who ye say was born blind? how then doth he now see?

20 His parents answered them and said, We know that this is our son, and that he was born blind:

21 But by what means he now seeth, we know not; or who hath opened his eyes, we know not: he is of age; ask him: he shall speak for himself.

22 These *words* spake his parents, because they feared the Jews: for the Jews had agreed already, that if any man did confess that he was Christ, he should be put out of the synagogue.

23 Therefore said his parents, He is of age; ask him.

24 Then again called they the man that was blind, and said unto him, Give God the praise: we know that this man is a sinner.

25 He answered and said, Whether he be a sinner *or no*, I know not: one thing I know, that, whereas I was blind, now I see.

26 Then said they to him again, What did he to thee? how opened he thine eyes?

27 He answered them, I have told you already, and ye did not hear: wherefore would ye hear *it* again? will ye also be his disciples?

28 Then they reviled him, and said, Thou art his disciple; but we are Mo'ses' disciples.

29 We know that God spake unto Mo'ses: *as for* this *fellow*, we know not from whence he is.

30 The man answered and said unto them, Why herein is a marvelous thing, that ye know not from whence he is, and *yet* he hath opened mine eyes.

31 Now we know that God heareth not sinners: but if any man be a worshiper of God, and doeth his will, him he heareth.

32 Since the world began was it not heard that any man opened the eyes of one that was born blind.

33 If this man were not of God, he could do nothing.

34 They answered and said unto him, Thou wast altogether born in sins, and dost thou teach us? And they cast him out.

35 Je'sus heard that they had cast him out; and when he had found him, he said unto him, Dost thou believe on the Son of God?

36 He answered and said, Who is he, Lord, that I might believe on him?

37 And Je'sus said unto him, Thou hast both seen him, and it is he that talketh with thee.

38 And he said, Lord, I believe. And he worshiped him.

39 ¶ And Je'sus said, For judgment I am come into this world, that they which see not might see; and that they which see might be made blind.

40 And *some* of the Phar'i-sees which were with him heard these words, and said unto him, Are we blind also?

41 Je'sus said unto them, If ye were blind, ye should have no sin: but now ye say, We see; therefore your sin remaineth.

10 Verily, verily, I say unto you, He that entereth not by the door into the sheepfold, but climbeth up some other way, the same is a thief and a robber.

2 But he that entereth in by the door is the shepherd of the sheep.

3 To him the porter openeth; and the sheep hear his voice: and he calleth his own sheep by name, and leadeth them out.

4 And when he putteth forth his own sheep, he goeth before them, and the sheep follow him: for they know his voice.

5 And a stranger will they not follow, but will flee from him: for they know not the voice of strangers.

6 This parable spake Je'sus unto them: but they understood not what things they were which he spake unto them

7 Then said Je'sus unto them again, Verily, verily, I say unto you, I am the door of the sheep.

8 All that ever came before me are thieves and robbers: but the sheep did not hear them

9 I am the door: by me if any man enter in, he shall be saved, and shall go in and out, and find pasture.

10 The thief cometh not, but for to steal, and to kill, and to destroy: I am come that they might have life, and that they might have it more abundantly.

11 I am the good shepherd: the good shepherd giveth his life for the sheep.

12 But he that is an hireling, and not the shepherd, whose own the sheep are not, seeth the wolf coming, and leaveth the sheep, and fleeth: and the wolf catcheth them, and scattereth the sheep.

13 The hireling fleeth, because he is an hireling, and careth not for the sheep.

14 I am the good shepherd, and know my *sheep*, and am known of mine.

15 As the Father knoweth me, even so know I the Father: and I lay down my life for the sheep.

16 And other sheep I have, which are not of this fold: them also I must bring, and they shall hear my voice; and there shall be one fold, *and* one shepherd.

17 Therefore doth my Father love me, because I lay down my life, that I might take it again.

18 No man taketh it from me, but I lay it down of myself. I have power to lay it down, and I have power to take it again. This commandment have I received of my Father.

19 ¶ There was a division therefore again among the Jews for these sayings.

20 And many of them said, He hath a devil, and is mad; why hear ye him?

21 Others said, These are not the words of him that hath a devil. Can a devil open the eyes of the blind?

22 ¶ And it was at Je'ru'sa'lem the feast of the dedication, and it was winter.

23 And Je′sus walked in the temple in Sol′o·mon's porch.

24 Then came the Jews round about him, and said unto him, How long dost thou make us to doubt? If thou be the Christ, tell us plainly.

25 Je′sus answered them, I told you, and ye believed not: the works that I do in my Father's name, they bear witness of me.

26 But ye believe not, because ye are not of my sheep, as I said unto you.

27 My sheep hear my voice, and I know them, and they follow me:

28 And I give unto them eternal life; and they shall never perish, neither shall any *man* pluck them out of my hand.

29 My Father, which gave *them* me, is greater than all; and no *man* is able to pluck *them* out of my Father's hand.

30 I and *my* Father are one.

31 Then the Jews took up stones again to stone him.

32 Je′sus answered them, Many good works have I showed you from my Father; for which of those works do ye stone me?

33 The Jews answered him, saying, For a good work we stone thee not; but for blasphemy; and because that thou, being a man, makest thyself God.

34 Je′sus answered them, Is it not written in your law, I said, Ye are gods?

35 If he called them gods, unto whom the word of God came, and the scripture cannot be broken;

36 Say ye of him, whom the Father hath sanctified, and sent into the world, Thou blasphemest; because I said, I am the Son of God?

37 If I do not the works of my Father, believe me not.

38 But if I do, though ye believe not me, believe the works: that ye may know, and believe, that the Father *is* in me, and I in him.

39 Therefore they sought again to take him: but he escaped out of their hand,

40 And went away again beyond Jor′dan into the place where John at first baptized; and there he abode.

41 And many resorted unto him, and said, John did no miracle: but all things that John spake of this man were true.

42 And many believed on him there.

11 Now a certain *man* was sick, *named* Laz′a·rus, of Beth′a·ny, the town of Ma′ry and her sister Mar′tha.

2 (It was *that* Ma′ry which anointed the Lord with ointment, and wiped his feet with her hair, whose brother Laz′a·rus was sick.)

3 Therefore his sisters sent unto him, saying, Lord, behold, he whom thou lovest is sick.

4 When Je′sus heard *that*, he said, This sickness is not unto death, but for the glory of God, that the Son of God might be glorified thereby.

5 Now Je′sus loved Mar′tha, and her sister, and Laz′a·rus.

6 When he had heard therefore that he was sick, he abode two

days still in the same place where he was.

7 Then after that saith he to *his* disciples, Let us go into Ju·dæ'a again.

8 *His* disciples say unto him, Master, the Jews of late sought to stone thee; and goest thou thither again?

9 Je'sus answered, Are there not twelve hours in the day? If any man walk in the day, he stumbleth not, because he seeth the light of this world.

10 But if a man walk in the night, he stumbleth, because there is no light in him.

11 These things said he: and after that he saith unto them, Our friend Laz'a·rus sleepeth; but I go, that I may awake him out of sleep.

12 Then said his disciples, Lord, if he sleep, he shall do well.

13 Howbeit Je'sus spake of his death: but they thought that he had spoken of taking of rest in sleep.

14 Then said Je'sus unto them plainly, Laz'a·rus is dead.

15 And I am glad for your sakes that I was not there, to the intent ye may believe; nevertheless let us go unto him.

16 Then said Thom'as, which is called Did'y·mus, unto his fellow disciples, Let us also go, that we may die with him.

17 Then when Je'sus came, he found that he had *lain* in the grave four days already.

18 Now Beth'a·ny was nigh unto Je·ru'sa·lem, about fifteen furlongs off:

19 And many of the Jews came to Mar'tha and Ma'ry, to comfort them concerning their brother.

20 Then Mar'tha, as soon as she heard that Je'sus was coming, went and met him: but Ma'ry sat *still* in the house.

21 Then said Mar'tha unto Je'sus, Lord, if thou hadst been here, my brother had not died.

22 But I know, that even now, whatsoever thou wilt ask of God, God will give *it* thee.

23 Je'sus saith unto her, Thy brother shall rise again.

24 Mar'tha saith unto him, I know that he shall rise again in the resurrection at the last day.

25 Je'sus said unto her, I am the resurrection, and the life: he that believeth in me, though he were dead, yet shall he live:

26 And whosoever liveth and believeth in me shall never die. Believest thou this?

27 She saith unto him, Yea, Lord: I believe that thou art the Christ, the Son of God, which should come into the world.

28 And when she had so said, she went her way, and called Ma'ry her sister secretly, saying, The Master is come, and calleth for thee.

29 As soon as she heard *that,* she arose quickly, and came unto him.

30 Now Je'sus was not yet come into the town, but was in that place where Mar'tha met him.

31 The Jews then which were with her in the house, and comforted her, when they saw

Ma'ry, that she rose up hastily and went out, followed her, saying, She goeth unto the grave to weep there.

32 Then when Ma'ry was come where Je'sus was, and saw him, she fell down at his feet, saying unto him, Lord, if thou hadst been here, my brother had not died.

33 When Je'sus therefore saw her weeping, and the Jews also weeping which came with her, he groaned in the spirit, and was troubled,

34 And said, Where have ye laid him? They said unto him, Lord, come and see.

35 Je'sus wept.

36 Then said the Jews, Behold how he loved him!

37 And some of them said, Could not this man, which opened the eyes of the blind, have caused that even this man should not have died?

38 Je'sus therefore again groaning in himself cometh to the grave. It was a cave, and a stone lay upon it.

39 Je'sus said, Take ye away the stone. Mar'tha, the sister of him that was dead, saith unto him, Lord, by this time he stinketh: for he hath been *dead* four days.

40 Je'sus saith unto her, Said I not unto thee, that, if thou wouldest believe, thou shouldest see the glory of God?

41 Then they took away the stone *from the place* where the dead was laid. And Je'sus lifted up *his* eyes, and said, Father, I thank thee that thou hast heard me.

42 And I knew that thou hearest me always: but because of the people which stand by I said *it*, that they may believe that thou hast sent me.

43 And when he thus had spoken, he cried with a loud voice, Laz'a-rus, come forth.

44 And he that was dead came forth, bound hand and foot with graveclothes: and his face was bound about with a napkin. Je'sus saith unto them, Loose him, and let him go.

45 Then many of the Jews which came to Ma'ry, and had seen the things which Je'sus did, believed on him.

46 But some of them went their ways to the Phar'i-sees, and told them what things Je'sus had done.

47 ¶ Then gathered the chief priests and the Phar'i-sees a council, and said, What do we? for this man doeth many miracles.

48 If we let him thus alone, all *men* will believe on him: and the Ro'mans shall come and take away both our place and nation.

49 And one of them, *named* Ca'ia-phas, being the high priest that same year, said unto them, Ye know nothing at all,

50 Nor consider that it is expedient for us, that one man should die for the people, and that the whole nation perish not.

51 And this spake he not of himself: but being high priest

that year, he prophesied that Je'-sus should die for that nation;

52 And not for that nation only, but that also he should gather together in one the children of God that were scattered abroad.

53 Then from that day forth they took counsel together for to put him to death.

54 Je'sus therefore walked no more openly among the Jews; but went thence unto a country near to the wilderness, into a city called E'phra-im, and there continued with his disciples.

55 ¶ And the Jews' passover was nigh at hand: and many went out of the country up to Je-ru'sa-lem before the passover, to purify themselves.

56 Then sought they for Je'sus, and spake among themselves, as they stood in the temple, What think ye, that he will not come to the feast?

57 Now both the chief priests and the Phar'i-sees had given a commandment, that, if any man knew where he were, he should show it, that they might take him.

12 Then Je'sus six days before the passover came to Beth'a-ny, where Laz'a-rus was which had been dead, whom he raised from the dead.

2 There they made him a supper; and Mar'tha served: but Laz'a-rus was one of them that sat at the table with him.

3 Then took Ma'ry a pound of ointment of spikenard, very costly, and anointed the feet of Je'sus, and wiped his feet with her hair: and the house was filled with the odor of the ointment.

4 Then saith one of his disciples, Ju'das Is-car'i-ot, Si'mon's son, which should betray him,

5 Why was not this ointment sold for three hundred pence, and given to the poor?

6 This he said, not that he cared for the poor; but because he was a thief, and had the bag, and bare what was put therein.

7 Then said Je'sus, Let her alone: against the day of my burying hath she kept this.

8 For the poor always ye have with you; but me ye have not always.

9 Much people of the Jews therefore knew that he was there: and they came not for Je'sus' sake only, but that they might see Laz'a-rus also, whom he had raised from the dead.

10 ¶ But the chief priests consulted that they might put Laz'a-rus also to death;

11 Because that by reason of him many of the Jews went away, and believed on Je'sus.

12 ¶ On the next day much people that were come to the feast, when they heard that Je'sus was coming to Je-ru'sa-lem,

13 Took branches of palm trees, and went forth to meet him, and cried, Ho-san'na: Blessed is the King of Is'ra-el that cometh in the name of the Lord.

14 And Je'sus, when he had found a young ass, sat thereon; as it is written,

15 Fear not, daughter of Zi'on:

behold, thy King cometh, sitting on an ass's colt.

16 These things understood not his disciples at the first: but when Je'sus was glorified, then remembered they that these things were written of him, and *that* they had done these things unto him.

17 The people therefore that was with him when he called Laz'a-rus out of his grave, and raised him from the dead, bare record.

18 For this cause the people also met him, for that they heard that he had done this miracle.

19 The Phar'i-sees therefore said among themselves, Perceive ye how ye prevail nothing? behold, the world is gone after him.

20 ¶ And there were certain Greeks among them that came up to worship at the feast:

21 The same came therefore to Phil'ip, which was of Beth-sa'i-da of Gal'i-lee, and desired him, saying, Sir, we would see Je'sus.

22 Phil'ip cometh and telleth An'drew: and again An'drew and Phil'ip tell Je'sus.

23 ¶ And Je'sus answered them, saying, The hour is come, that the Son of man should be glorified.

24 Verily, verily, I say unto you, Except a corn of wheat fall into the ground and die, it abideth alone: but if it die, it bringeth forth much fruit.

25 He that loveth his life shall lose it; and he that hateth his life in this world shall keep it unto life eternal.

26 If any man serve me, let him follow me; and where I am, there shall also my servant be: if any man serve me, him will *my* Father honor.

27 Now is my soul troubled; and what shall I say? Father, save me from this hour: but for this cause came I unto this hour.

28 Father, glorify thy name. Then came there a voice from heaven, *saying,* I have both glorified *it,* and will glorify *it* again.

29 The people therefore, that stood by, and heard *it,* said that it thundered: others said, An angel spake to him.

30 Je'sus answered and said, This voice came not because of me, but for your sakes.

31 Now is the judgment of this world: now shall the prince of this world be cast out.

32 And I, if I be lifted up from the earth, will draw all *men* unto me.

33 This he said, signifying what death he should die.

34 The people answered him, We have heard out of the law that Christ abideth for ever: and how sayest thou, The Son of man must be lifted up? who is this Son of man?

35 Then Je'sus said unto them, Yet a little while is the light with you. Walk while ye have the light, lest darkness come upon you: for he that walketh in darkness knoweth not whither he goeth.

36 While ye have light, believe

in the light, that ye may be the children of light. These things spake Je'sus, and departed, and did hide himself from them.

37 ¶ But though he had done so many miracles before them, yet they believed not on him:

38 That the saying of I-sa'iah the prophet might be fulfilled, which he spake, Lord, who hath believed our report? and to whom hath the arm of the Lord been revealed?

39 Therefore they could not believe, because that I-sa'iah said again,

40 He hath blinded their eyes, and hardened their heart; that they should not see with *their* eyes, nor understand with *their* heart, and be converted, and I should heal them.

41 These things said I-sa'iah, when he saw his glory, and spake of him.

42 ¶ Nevertheless among the chief rulers also many believed on him; but because of the Phar'i-sees they did not confess *him*, lest they should be put out of the synagogue:

43 For they loved the praise of men more than the praise of God.

44 ¶ Je'sus cried and said, He that believeth on me, believeth not on me, but on him that sent me.

45 And he that seeth me seeth him that sent me.

46 I am come a light into the world, that whosoever believeth on me should not abide in darkness.

47 And if any man hear my words, and believe not, I judge him not: for I came not to judge the world, but to save the world.

48 He that rejecteth me, and receiveth not my words, hath one that judgeth him: the word that I have spoken, the same shall judge him in the last day.

49 For I have not spoken of myself; but the Father which sent me, he gave me a commandment, what I should say, and what I should speak.

50 And I know that his commandment is life everlasting: whatsoever I speak therefore, even as the Father said unto me, so I speak.

13 Now before the feast of the passover, when Je'sus knew that his hour was come that he should depart out of this world unto the Father, having loved his own which were in the world, he loved them unto the end.

2 And supper being ended, the devil having now put into the heart of Ju'das Is-car'i-ot, Si'mon's son, to betray him;

3 Je'sus knowing that the Father had given all things into his hands, and that he was come from God, and went to God;

4 He riseth from supper, and laid aside his garments; and took a towel, and girded himself.

5 After that he poureth water into a basin, and began to wash the disciples' feet, and to wipe *them* with the towel wherewith he was girded.

6 Then cometh he to Si'mon

Pe'ter: and Pe'ter saith unto him, Lord, dost thou wash my feet?

7 Je'sus answered and said unto him, What I do thou knowest not now; but thou shalt know hereafter.

8 Pe'ter saith unto him, Thou shalt never wash my feet. Je'sus answered him, If I wash thee not, thou hast no part with me.

9 Si'mon Pe'ter saith unto him, Lord, not my feet only, but also *my* hands and *my* head.

10 Je'sus saith to him, He that is washed needeth not save to wash *his* feet, but is clean every whit: and ye are clean, but not all.

11 For he knew who should betray him; therefore said he, Ye are not all clean.

12 So after he had washed their feet, and had taken his garments, and was set down again, he said unto them, Know ye what I have done to you?

13 Ye call me Master and Lord: and ye say well; for *so* I am.

14 If I then, *your* Lord and Master, have washed your feet; ye also ought to wash one another's feet.

15 For I have given you an example, that ye should do as I have done to you.

16 Verily, verily, I say unto you, The servant is not greater than his lord; neither he that is sent greater than he that sent him.

17 If ye know these things, happy are ye if ye do them.

18 ¶ I speak not of you all: I know whom I have chosen: but

that the scripture may be fulfilled, He that eateth bread with me hath lifted up his heel against me.

19 Now I tell you before it come, that, when it is come to pass, ye may believe that I am *he.*

20 Verily, verily, I say unto you, He that receiveth whomsoever I send receiveth me; and he that receiveth me receiveth him that sent me.

21 When Je'sus had thus said, he was troubled in spirit, and testified, and said, Verily, verily, I say unto you, that one of you shall betray me.

22 Then the disciples looked one on another, doubting of whom he spake.

23 Now there was leaning on Je'sus' bosom one of his disciples, whom Je'sus loved.

24 Si'mon Pe'ter therefore beckoned to him, that he should ask who it should be of whom he spake.

25 He then lying on Je'sus' breast saith unto him, Lord, who is it?

26 Je'sus answered, He it is, to whom I shall give a sop, when I have dipped *it.* And when he had dipped the sop, he gave *it* to Ju'das Is-car'i-ot, *the son* of Si'mon.

27 And after the sop Sa'tan entered into him. Then said Je'sus unto him, That thou doest, do quickly.

28 Now no man at the table knew for what intent he spake this unto him.

29 For some *of them* thought,

because Ju'das had the bag, that Je'sus had said unto him, Buy those things that we have need of against the feast; or, that he should give something to the poor.

30 He then having received the sop went immediately out: and it was night

31 ¶ Therefore, when he was gone out, Je'sus said, Now is the Son of man glorified, and God is glorified in him.

32 If God be glorified in him, God shall also glorify him in himself, and shall straightway glorify him.

33 Little children, yet a little while I am with you. Ye shall seek me: and as I said unto the Jews, Whither I go, ye cannot come; so now I say to you.

34 A new commandment I give unto you, That ye love one another; as I have loved you, that ye also love one another.

35 By this shall all men know that ye are my disciples, if ye have love one to another.

36 ¶ Si'mon Pe'ter said unto him, Lord, whither goest thou? Je'sus answered him, Whither I go, thou canst not follow me now; but thou shalt follow me afterwards.

37 Pe'ter said unto him, Lord, why cannot I follow thee now? I will lay down my life for thy sake.

38 Je'sus answered him, Wilt thou lay down thy life for my sake? Verily, verily, I say unto thee, The cock shall not crow, till thou hast denied me thrice.

14 Let not your heart be troubled: ye believe in God, believe also in me.

2 In my Father's house are many mansions: if it were not so, I would have told you. I go to prepare a place for you.

3 And if I go and prepare a place for you, I will come again, and receive you unto myself; that where I am, there ye may be also.

4 And whither I go ye know, and the way ye know.

5 Thom'as saith unto him, Lord, we know not whither thou goest; and how can we know the way?

6 Je'sus saith unto him, I am the way, the truth, and the life: no man cometh unto the Father, but by me.

7 If ye had known me, ye should have known my Father also: and from henceforth ye know him, and have seen him.

8 Phil'ip saith unto him, Lord, show us the Father, and it sufficeth us.

9 Je'sus saith unto him, Have I been so long time with you, and yet hast thou not known me, Phil'ip? he that hath seen me hath seen the Father; and how sayest thou then, Show us the Father?

10 Believest thou not that I am in the Father, and the Father in me? the words that I speak unto you I speak not of myself: but the Father that dwelleth in me, he doeth the works.

11 Believe me that I am in the Father, and the Father in me: or

else believe me for the very works' sake.

12 Verily, verily, I say unto you, He that believeth on me, the works that I do shall he do also; and greater *works* than these shall he do; because I go unto my Father.

13 And whatsoever ye shall ask in my name, that will I do, that the Father may be glorified in the Son.

14 If ye shall ask any thing in my name, I will do *it*.

15 ¶ If ye love me, keep my commandments.

16 And I will pray the Father, and he shall give you another Comforter, that he may abide with you for ever;

17 *Even* the Spirit of truth; whom the world cannot receive, because it seeth him not, neither knoweth him: but ye know him; for he dwelleth with you, and shall be in you.

18 I will not leave you comfortless: I will come to you.

19 Yet a little while, and the world seeth me no more; but ye see me: because I live, ye shall live also.

20 At that day ye shall know that I *am* in my Father, and ye in me, and I in you.

21 He that hath my commandments, and keepeth them, he it is that loveth me: and he that loveth me shall be loved of my Father, and I will love him, and will manifest myself to him.

22 Ju′das saith unto him, not Is-car′i-ot, Lord, how is it that thou wilt manifest thyself unto us, and not unto the world?

23 Je′sus answered and said unto him, If a man love me, he will keep my words: and my Father will love him, and we will come unto him, and make our abode with him.

24 He that loveth me not keepeth not my sayings: and the word which ye hear is not mine, but the Father's which sent me.

25 These things have I spoken unto you, being *yet* present with you.

26 But the Comforter, *which is* the Ho′ly Ghost, whom the Father will send in my name, he shall teach you all things, and bring all things to your remembrance, whatsoever I have said unto you.

27 Peace I leave with you, my peace I give unto you: not as the world giveth, give I unto you. Let not your heart be troubled, neither let it be afraid.

28 Ye have heard how I said unto you, I go away, and come *again* unto you. If ye loved me, ye would rejoice, because I said, I go unto the Father: for my Father is greater than I.

29 And now I have told you before it come to pass, that, when it is come to pass, ye might believe.

30 Hereafter I will not talk much with you: for the prince of this world cometh, and hath nothing in me.

31 But that the world may know that I love the Father; and as the Father gave me commandment, even so I do. Arise, let us go hence.

15 I am the true vine, and my Father is the husbandman.

2 Every branch in me that beareth not fruit he taketh away: and every *branch* that beareth fruit, he purgeth it, that it may bring forth more fruit.

3 Now ye are clean through the word which I have spoken unto you.

4 Abide in me, and I in you. As the branch cannot bear fruit of itself, except it abide in the vine; no more can ye, except ye abide in me.

5 I am the vine, ye *are* the branches: He that abideth in me, and I in him, the same bringeth forth much fruit: for without me ye can do nothing.

6 If a man abide not in me, he is cast forth as a branch, and is withered; and men gather them, and cast *them* into the fire, and they are burned.

7 If ye abide in me, and my words abide in you, ye shall ask what ye will, and it shall be done unto you.

8 Herein is my Father glorified, that ye bear much fruit; so shall ye be my disciples.

9 As the Father hath loved me, so have I loved you: continue ye in my love.

10 If ye keep my commandments, ye shall abide in my love; even as I have kept my Father's commandments, and abide in his love.

11 These things have I spoken unto you, that my joy might remain in you, and *that* your joy might be full.

12 This is my commandment, That ye love one another, as I have loved you.

13 Greater love hath no man than this, that a man lay down his life for his friends.

14 Ye are my friends, if ye do whatsoever I command you.

15 Henceforth I call you not servants; for the servant knoweth not what his lord doeth: but I have called you friends; for all things that I have heard of my Father I have made known unto you.

16 Ye have not chosen me, but I have chosen you, and ordained you, that ye should go and bring forth fruit, and *that* your fruit should remain: that whatsoever ye shall ask of the Father in my name, he may give it you.

17 These things I command you, that ye love one another.

18 If the world hate you, ye know that it hated me before *it hated* you.

19 If ye were of the world, the world would love his own: but because ye are not of the world, but I have chosen you out of the world, therefore the world hateth you.

20 Remember the word that I said unto you, The servant is not greater than his lord. If they have persecuted me, they will also persecute you; if they have kept my saying, they will keep yours also.

21 But all these things will they do unto you for my name's sake, because they know not him that sent me.

22 If I had not come and spoken unto them, they had not

had sin: but now they have no cloak for their sin.

23 He that hateth me hateth my Father also.

24 If I had not done among them the works which none other man did, they had not had sin: but now have they both seen and hated both me and my Father.

25 But *this cometh to pass,* that the word might be fulfilled that is written in their law, They hated me without a cause.

26 But when the Comforter is come, whom I will send unto you from the Father, *even* the Spirit of truth, which proceedeth from the Father, he shall testify of me:

27 And ye also shall bear witness, because ye have been with me from the beginning.

16 These things have I spoken unto you, that ye should not be offended.

2 They shall put you out of the synagogues: yea, the time cometh, that whosoever killeth you will think that he doeth God service.

3 And these things will they do unto you, because they have not known the Father, nor me.

4 But these things have I told you, that when the time shall come, ye may remember that I told you of them. And these things I said not unto you at the beginning, because I was with you.

5 But now I go my way to him that sent me; and none of you asketh me, Whither goest thou?

6 But because I have said these

things unto you, sorrow hath filled your heart.

7 Nevertheless I tell you the truth; It is expedient for you that I go away: for if I go not away, the Comforter will not come unto you; but if I depart, I will send him unto you.

8 And when he is come, he will reprove the world of sin, and of righteousness, and of judgment:

9 Of sin, because they believe not on me;

10 Of righteousness, because I go to my Father, and ye see me no more;

11 Of judgment, because the prince of this world is judged.

12 I have yet many things to say unto you, but ye cannot bear them now.

13 Howbeit when he, the Spirit of truth, is come, he will guide you into all truth: for he shall not speak of himself; but whatsoever he shall hear, *that* shall he speak: and he will show you things to come.

14 He shall glorify me: for he shall receive of mine, and shall show *it* unto you.

15 All things that the Father hath are mine: therefore said I, that he shall take of mine, and shall show *it* unto you.

16 A little while, and ye shall not see me: and again, a little while, and ye shall see me, because I go to the Father.

17 Then said *some* of his disciples among themselves, What is this that he saith unto us, A little while, and ye shall not see me: and again, a little while,

and ye shall see me: and, Because I go to the Father?

18 They said therefore, What is this that he saith, A little while? we cannot tell what he saith.

19 Now Je′sus knew that they were desirous to ask him, and said unto them, Do ye inquire among yourselves of that I said, A little while, and ye shall not see me: and again, a little while, and ye shall see me?

20 Verily, verily, I say unto you, That ye shall weep and lament, but the world shall rejoice: and ye shall be sorrowful, but your sorrow shall be turned into joy.

21 A woman when she is in travail hath sorrow, because her hour is come: but as soon as she is delivered of the child, she remembereth no more the anguish, for joy that a man is born into the world.

22 And ye now therefore have sorrow: but I will see you again, and your heart shall rejoice, and your joy no man taketh from you.

23 And in that day ye shall ask me nothing. Verily, verily, I say unto you, Whatsoever ye shall ask the Father in my name, he will give it you.

24 Hitherto have ye asked nothing in my name: ask, and ye shall receive, that your joy may be full.

25 These things have I spoken unto you in proverbs: but the time cometh, when I shall no more speak unto you in proverbs, but I shall shew you plainly of the Father.

26 At that day ye shall ask in my name: and I say not unto you, that I will pray the Father for you:

27 For the Father himself loveth you, because ye have loved me, and have believed that I came out from God.

28 I came forth from the Father, and am come into the world: again, I leave the world, and go to the Father.

29 His disciples said unto him, Lo, now speakest thou plainly, and speakest no proverb.

30 Now are we sure that thou knowest all things, and needest not that any man should ask thee: by this we believe that thou camest from God.

31 Je′sus answered them, Do ye now believe?

32 Behold, the hour cometh, yea, is now come, that ye shall be scattered, every man to his own, and shall leave me alone: and yet I am not alone, because the Father is with me.

33 These things I have spoken unto you, that in me ye might have peace. In the world ye shall have tribulation: but be of good cheer; I have overcome the world.

17 These words spake Je′sus, and lifted up his eyes to heaven, and said, Father, the hour is come; glorify thy Son, that thy Son also may glorify thee:

2 As thou hast given him power over all flesh, that he should give eternal life to as many as thou hast given him.

3 And this is life eternal, that

they might know thee the only true God, and Je′sus Christ, whom thou hast sent.

4 I have glorified thee on the earth: I have finished the work which thou gavest me to do.

5 And now, O Father, glorify thou me with thine own self with the glory which I had with thee before the world was.

6 I have manifested thy name unto the men which thou gavest me out of the world: thine they were, and thou gavest them me; and they have kept thy word.

7 Now they have known that all things whatsoever thou hast given me are of thee.

8 For I have given unto them the words which thou gavest me; and they have received *them*, and have known surely that I came out from thee, and they have believed that thou didst send me.

9 I pray for them: I pray not for the world, but for them which thou hast given me; for they are thine.

10 And all mine are thine, and thine are mine; and I am glorified in them.

11 And now I am no more in the world, but these are in the world, and I come to thee. Holy Father, keep through thine own name those whom thou hast given me, that they may be one, as we *are*.

12 While I was with them in the world, I kept them in thy name: those that thou gavest me I have kept, and none of them is lost, but the son of perdition; that the scripture might be fulfilled.

13 And now come I to thee; and these things I speak in the world, that they might have my joy fulfilled in themselves.

14 I have given them thy word; and the world hath hated them, because they are not of the world, even as I am not of the world.

15 I pray not that thou shouldest take them out of the world, but that thou shouldest keep them from the evil.

16 They are not of the world, even as I am not of the world.

17 Sanctify them through thy truth: thy word is truth.

18 As thou hast sent me into the world, even so have I also sent them into the world.

19 And for their sakes I sanctify myself, that they also might be sanctified through the truth.

20 Neither pray I for these alone, but for them also which shall believe on me through their word;

21 That they all may be one; as thou, Father, *art* in me, and I in thee, that they also may be one in us: that the world may believe that thou hast sent me.

22 And the glory which thou gavest me I have given them; that they may be one, even as we are one:

23 I in them, and thou in me, that they may be made perfect in one; and that the world may know that thou hast sent me, and hast loved them, as thou hast loved me.

24 Father, I will that they also,

whom thou hast given me, be with me where I am; that they may behold my glory, which thou hast given me: for thou lovedst me before the foundation of the world.

25 O righteous Father, the world hath not known thee: but I have known thee, and these have known that thou hast sent me.

26 And I have declared unto them thy name, and will declare it: that the love wherewith thou hast loved me may be in them, and I in them.

18 When Je'sus had spoken these words, he went forth with his disciples over the brook Ce'dron, where was a garden, into the which he entered, and his disciples.

2 And Ju'das also, which betrayed him, knew the place: for Je'sus ofttimes resorted thither with his disciples.

3 Ju'das then, having received a band of men and officers from the chief priests and Phar'i-sees, cometh thither with lanterns and torches and weapons.

4 Je'sus therefore, knowing all things that should come upon him, went forth, and said unto them, Whom seek ye?

5 They answered him, Je'sus of Naz'a-reth. Je'sus saith unto them, I am he. And Ju'das also, which betrayed him, stood with them.

6 As soon then as he had said unto them, I am he, they went backward, and fell to the ground

7 Then asked he them again, Whom seek ye? And they said, Je'sus of Naz'a-reth.

8 Je'sus answered, I have told you that I am he: if therefore ye seek me, let these go their way:

9 That the saying might be fulfilled, which he spake, Of them which thou gavest me have I lost none.

10 Then Si'mon Pe'ter having a sword drew it, and smote the high priest's servant, and cut off his right ear. The servant's name was Mal'chus.

11 Then said Je'sus unto Pe'ter, Put up thy sword into the sheath: the cup which my Father hath given me, shall I not drink it?

12 Then the band and the captain and officers of the Jews took Je'sus, and bound him,

13 And led him away to An'nas first; for he was father-in-law to Ca'ia-phas, which was the high priest that same year.

14 Now Ca'ia-phas was he, which gave counsel to the Jews, that it was expedient that one man should die for the people.

15 ¶ And Si'mon Pe'ter followed Je'sus, and so did another disciple: that disciple was known unto the high priest, and went in with Je'sus into the palace of the high priest.

16 But Pe'ter stood at the door without. Then went out that other disciple, which was known unto the high priest, and spake unto her that kept the door, and brought in Pe'ter.

17 Then saith the damsel that kept the door unto Pe'ter, Art

not thou also *one* of this man's disciples? He saith, I am not.

18 And the servants and officers stood there, who had made a fire of coals; for it was cold: and they warmed themselves: and Pe'ter stood with them, and warmed himself.

19 ¶ The high priest then asked Je'sus of his disciples, and of his doctrine.

20 Je'sus answered him, I spake openly to the world; I ever taught in the synagogue, and in the temple, whither the Jews always resort; and in secret have I said nothing.

21 Why askest thou me? ask them which heard me, what I have said unto them: behold, they know what I said.

22 And when he had thus spoken, one of the officers which stood by struck Je'sus with the palm of his hand, saying, Answerest thou the high priest so?

23 Je'sus answered him, If I have spoken evil, bear witness of the evil: but if well, why smitest thou me?

24 Now An'nas had sent him bound unto Ca'ia-phas the high priest.

25 And Si'mon Pe'ter stood and warmed himself. They said therefore unto him, Art not thou also *one* of his disciples? He denied *it*, and said, I am not.

26 One of the servants of the high priest, being *his* kinsman whose ear Pe'ter cut off, saith, Did not I see thee in the garden with him?

27 Pe'ter then denied again: and immediately the cock crew.

28 ¶ Then led they Je'sus from Ca'ia-phas unto the hall of judgment: and it was early; and they themselves went not into the judgment hall, lest they should be defiled; but that they might eat the passover.

29 Pi'late then went out unto them, and said, What accusation bring ye against this man?

30 They answered and said unto him, If he were not a malefactor, we would not have delivered him up unto thee.

31 Then said Pi'late unto them, Take ye him, and judge him according to your law. The Jews therefore said unto him, It is not lawful for us to put any man to death:

32 That the saying of Je'sus might be fulfilled, which he spake, signifying what death he should die.

33 Then Pi'late entered into the judgment hall again, and called Je'sus, and said unto him, Art thou the King of the Jews?

34 Je'sus answered him, Sayest thou this thing of thyself, or did others tell it thee of me?

35 Pi'late answered, Am I a Jew? Thine own nation and the chief priests have delivered thee unto me: what hast thou done?

36 Je'sus answered, My kingdom is not of this world: if my kingdom were of this world, then would my servants fight, that I should not be delivered to the Jews: but now is my kingdom not from hence.

37 Pi'late therefore said unto

him, Art thou a king then? Je'-
sus answered, Thou sayest that I
am a king. To this end was I
born, and for this cause came I
into the world, that I should
bear witness unto the truth.
Every one that is of the truth
heareth my voice.

38 Pi'late saith unto him, What
is truth? And when he had said
this, he went out again unto the
Jews, and saith unto them, I find
in him no fault *at all.*

39 But ye have a custom, that I
should release unto you one at
the passover: will ye therefore
that I release unto you the King
of the Jews?

40 Then cried they all again,
saying, Not this man, but Ba-
rab'bas. Now Ba-rab'bas was a
robber.

19 Then Pi'late therefore took
Je'sus, and scourged *him.*

2 And the soldiers platted a
crown of thorns, and put *it* on
his head, and they put on him a
purple robe,

3 And said, Hail, King of the
Jews! and they smote him with
their hands.

4 Pi'late therefore went forth
again, and saith unto them, Behold, I bring him forth to you,
that ye may know that I find no
fault in him.

5 Then came Je'sus forth, wearing the crown of thorns, and the
purple robe. And Pi'late saith
unto them, Behold the man!

6 When the chief priests therefore and officers saw him, they
cried out, saying, Crucify *him,*
crucify *him.* Pi'late saith unto

them, Take ye him, and crucify
him: for I find no fault in him.

7 The Jews answered him, We
have a law, and by our law he
ought to die, because he made
himself the Son of God.

8 ¶ When Pi'late therefore heard
that saying, he was the more
afraid;

9 And went again into the judgment hall, and saith unto Je'sus,
Whence art thou? But Je'sus
gave him no answer.

10 Then saith Pi'late unto him,
Speakest thou not unto me?
knowest thou not that I have
power to crucify thee, and have
power to release thee?

11 Je'sus answered, Thou couldest have no power *at all* against
me, except it were given thee
from above: therefore he that
delivered me unto thee hath the
greater sin.

12 And from thenceforth Pi'-
late sought to release him: but
the Jews cried out, saying, If
thou let this man go, thou art
not Cæ'sar's friend: whosoever
maketh himself a king speaketh
against Cæ'sar.

13 ¶ When Pi'late therefore
heard that saying, he brought Je'-
sus forth, and sat down in the
judgment seat in a place that is
called the Pavement, but in the
He'brew, Gab'ba-tha.

14 And it was the preparation
of the passover, and about the
sixth hour: and he saith unto
the Jews, Behold your King!

15 But they cried out, Away
with *him,* away with *him,* crucify him. Pi'late saith unto
them, Shall I crucify your King?

The chief priests answered, We have no king but Cæ'sar.

16 Then delivered he him therefore unto them to be crucified. And they took Je'sus, and led *him* away.

17 And he bearing his cross went forth into a place called *the place* of a skull, which is called in the He'brew Gol'go-tha:

18 Where they crucified him, and two other with him, on either side one, and Je'sus in the midst.

19 ¶ And Pi'late wrote a title, and put *it* on the cross. And the writing was, JE'SUS OF NAZ'A-RETH THE KING OF THE JEWS.

20 This title then read many of the Jews: for the place where Je'-sus was crucified was nigh to the city: and it was written in He'-brew, *and* Greek, *and* Lat'in.

21 Then said the chief priests of the Jews to Pi'late, Write not, The King of the Jews; but that he said, I am King of the Jews.

22 Pi'late answered, What I have written I have written.

23 ¶ Then the soldiers, when they had crucified Je'sus, took his garments, and made four parts, to every soldier a part; and also *his* coat: now the coat was without seam, woven from the top throughout.

24 They said therefore among themselves, Let us not rend it, but cast lots for it, whose it shall be: that the scripture might be fulfilled, which saith, They parted my raiment among them, and for my vesture they did cast lots. These things therefore the soldiers did.

25 ¶ Now there stood by the cross of Je'sus his mother, and his mother's sister, Ma'ry the *wife* of Cle'o-phas, and Ma'ry Mag-da-le'ne.

26 When Je'sus therefore saw his mother, and the disciple standing by, whom he loved, he saith unto his mother, Woman, behold thy son!

27 Then saith he to the disciple, Behold thy mother! And from that hour that disciple took her unto his own *home.*

28 ¶ After this, Je'sus knowing that all things were now accomplished, that the scripture might be fulfilled, saith, I thirst.

29 Now there was set a vessel full of vinegar: and they filled a sponge with vinegar, and put *it* upon hyssop, and put *it* to his mouth.

30 When Je'sus therefore had received the vinegar, he said, It is finished: and he bowed his head, and gave up the ghost.

31 The Jews therefore, because it was the preparation, that the bodies should not remain upon the cross on the sabbath day, (for that sabbath day was an high day,) besought Pi'late that their legs might be broken, and *that* they might be taken away.

32 Then came the soldiers, and brake the legs of the first, and of the other which was crucified with him.

33 But when they came to Je'-sus, and saw that he was dead already, they brake not his legs:

34 But one of the soldiers with a spear pierced his side, and

forthwith came there out blood and water

35 And he that saw it bare record, and his record is true, and he knoweth that he saith true, that ye might believe.

36 For these things were done, that the scripture should be fulfilled, A bone of him shall not be broken.

37 And again another scripture saith, They shall look on him whom they pierced.

38 ¶ And after this Jo'seph of Ar-i-ma-thæ'a, being a disciple of Je'sus, but secretly for fear of the Jews, besought Pi'late that he might take away the body of Je'sus: and Pi'late gave him leave. He came therefore, and took the body of Je'sus.

39 And there came also Nic-o-de'mus, which at the first came to Je'sus by night, and brought a mixture of myrrh and aloes, about an hundred pound weight.

40 Then took they the body of Je'sus, and wound it in linen clothes with the spices, as the manner of the Jews is to bury.

41 Now in the place where he was crucified there was a garden; and in the garden a new sepulcher, wherein was never man yet laid.

42 There laid they Je'sus therefore because of the Jews' preparation day; for the sepulcher was nigh at hand.

20 The first day of the week cometh Ma'ry Mag-da-le'ne early, when it was yet dark, unto the sepulcher, and seeth the stone taken away from the sepulcher.

2 Then she runneth, and cometh to Si'mon Pe'ter, and to the other disciple, whom Je'sus loved, and saith unto them, They have taken away the Lord out of the sepulcher, and we know not where they have laid him.

3 Pe'ter therefore went forth, and that other disciple, and came to the sepulcher.

4 So they ran both together: and the other disciple did outrun Pe'ter, and came first to the sepulcher.

5 And he stooping down, and looking in, saw the linen clothes lying; yet went he not in.

6 Then cometh Si'mon Pe'ter following him, and went into the sepulcher, and seeth the linen clothes lie,

7 And the napkin, that was about his head, not lying with the linen clothes, but wrapped together in a place by itself.

8 Then went in also that other disciple, which came first to the sepulcher, and he saw, and believed.

9 For as yet they knew not the scripture, that he must rise again from the dead.

10 Then the disciples went away again unto their own home.

11 ¶ But Ma'ry stood without at the sepulcher weeping: and as she wept, she stooped down, and looked into the sepulcher,

12 And seeth two angels in white sitting, the one at the head, and the other at the feet,

where the body of Je'sus had lain.

13 And they say unto her, Woman, why weepest thou? She saith unto them, Because they have taken away my Lord, and I know not where they have laid him.

14 And when she had thus said, she turned herself back, and saw Je'sus standing, and knew not that it was Je'sus.

15 Je'sus saith unto her, Woman, why weepest thou? whom seekest thou? She, supposing him to be the gardener, saith unto him, Sir, if thou have borne him hence, tell me where thou hast laid him, and I will take him away.

16 Je'sus saith unto her, Ma'ry. She turned herself, and saith unto him, Rab-bo'ni; which is to say, Master.

17 Je'sus saith unto her, Touch me not; for I am not yet ascended to my Father: but go to my brethren, and say unto them, I ascend unto my Father, and your Father; and to my God, and your God.

18 Ma'ry Mag-da-le'ne came and told the disciples that she had seen the Lord, and that he had spoken these things unto her.

19 ¶ Then the same day at evening, being the first day of the week, when the doors were shut where the disciples were assembled for fear of the Jews, came Je'sus and stood in the midst, and saith unto them, Peace be unto you.

20 And when he had so said, he showed unto them his hands and his side. Then were the disciples glad, when they saw the Lord.

21 Then said Je'sus to them again, Peace be unto you: as my Father hath sent me, even so send I you.

22 And when he had said this, he breathed on them, and saith unto them, Receive ye the Ho'ly Ghost:

23 Whose soever sins ye remit, they are remitted unto them; and whose soever sins ye retain, they are retained.

24 ¶ But Thom'as, one of the twelve, called Did'y-mus, was not with them when Je'sus came.

25 The other disciples therefore said unto them, We have seen the Lord. But he said unto them, Except I shall see in his hands the print of the nails, and put my finger into the print of the nails, and thrust my hand into his side, I will not believe.

26 ¶ And after eight days again his disciples were within, and Thom'as with them: then came Je'sus, the doors being shut, and stood in the midst, and said, Peace be unto you.

27 Then saith he to Thom'as, Reach hither thy finger, and behold my hands; and reach hither thy hand, and thrust it into my side: and be not faithless, but believing.

28 And Thom'as answered and said unto him, My Lord and my God.

29 Je'sus saith unto him, Thom'as, because thou hast seen me,

thou hast believed: blessed *are* they that have not seen, and *yet* have believed.

30 ¶ And many other signs truly did Je´sus in the presence of his disciples, which are not written in this book:

31 But these are written, that ye might believe that Je´sus is the Christ, the Son of God; and that believing ye might have life through his name.

21 After these things Je´sus showed himself again to the disciples at the sea of Ti-be´-ri-as: and on this wise showed he *himself.*

2 There were together Si´mon Pe´ter, and Thom´as called Did´y-mus, and Na-than´a-el of Ca´na in Gal´i-lee, and the *sons* of Zeb´e-dee, and two other of his disciples.

3 Si´mon Pe´ter saith unto them, I go a fishing. They say unto him, We also go with thee. They went forth, and entered into a ship immediately; and that night they caught nothing.

4 But when the morning was now come, Je´sus stood on the shore: but the disciples knew not that it was Je´sus.

5 Then Je´sus saith unto them, Children, have ye any meat? They answered him, No.

6 And he said unto them, Cast the net on the right side of the ship, and ye shall find. They cast therefore, and now they were not able to draw it for the multitude of fishes.

7 Therefore that disciple whom Je´sus loved saith unto Pe´ter, It is the Lord. Now when Si´mon

Pe´ter heard that it was the Lord, he girt *his* fisher's coat *unto him,* (for he was naked,) and did cast himself into the sea.

8 And the other disciples came in a little ship; (for they were not far from land, but as it were two hundred cubits,) dragging the net with fishes.

9 As soon then as they were come to land, they saw a fire of coals there, and fish laid thereon, and bread.

10 Je´sus saith unto them, Bring of the fish which ye have now caught.

11 Si´mon Pe´ter went up, and drew the net to land full of great fishes, an hundred and fifty and three: and for all there were so many, yet was not the net broken.

12 Je´sus saith unto them, Come *and* dine. And none of the disciples durst ask him, Who art thou? knowing that it was the Lord.

13 Je´sus then cometh, and taketh bread, and giveth them, and fish likewise.

14 This is now the third time that Je´sus showed himself to his disciples, after that he was risen from the dead.

15 ¶ So when they had dined, Je´sus saith to Si´mon Pe´ter, Si´mon, *son* of Jo´nah, lovest thou me more than these? He saith unto him, Yea, Lord; thou knowest that I love thee. He saith unto him, Feed my lambs.

16 He saith to him again the second time, Si´mon, *son* of Jo´nah, lovest thou me? He saith

unto him, Yea, Lord; thou knowest that I love thee. He saith unto him, Feed my sheep.

17 He saith unto him the third time, Si'mon, son of Jo'nah, lovest thou me? Pe'ter was grieved because he said unto him the third time, Lovest thou me? And he said unto him, Lord, thou knowest all things; thou knowest that I love thee. Je'sus saith unto him, Feed my sheep.

18 Verily, verily, I say unto thee, When thou wast young, thou girdedst thyself, and walkedst whither thou wouldest: but when thou shalt be old, thou shalt stretch forth thy hands, and another shall gird thee, and carry thee whither thou wouldest not.

19 This spake he, signifying by what death he should glorify God. And when he had spoken this, he saith unto him, Follow me.

20 Then Pe'ter, turning about, seeth the disciple whom Je'sus loved following; which also leaned on his breast at supper, and said, Lord, which is he that betrayeth thee?

21 Pe'ter seeing him saith to Je'sus, Lord, and what shall this man do?

22 Je'sus saith unto him, If I will that he tarry till I come, what is that to thee? follow thou me.

23 Then went this saying abroad among the brethren, that that disciple should not die: yet Je'sus said not unto him, He shall not die; but, If I will that he tarry till I come, what is that to thee?

24 This is the disciple which testifieth of these things, and wrote these things: and we know that his testimony is true.

25 And there are also many other things which Je'sus did, the which, if they should be written every one, I suppose that even the world itself could not contain the books that should be written. Amen.

ACTS

1 The former treatise have I made, O The-oph'i-lus, of all that Je'sus began both to do and teach,

2 Until the day in which he was taken up, after that he through the Ho'ly Ghost had given commandments unto the apostles whom he had chosen:

3 To whom also he showed himself alive after his passion by many infallible proofs, being seen of them forty days, and speaking of the things pertaining to the kingdom of God:

4 And, being assembled together with them, commanded them that they should not depart from Je-ru'sa-lem, but wait for the promise of the Father,

which, *saith he,* ye have heard of me.

5 For John truly baptized with water; but ye shall be baptized with the Ho'ly Ghost not many days hence.

6 When they therefore were come together, they asked of him, saying, Lord, wilt thou at this time restore again the kingdom to Is'ra-el?

7 And he said unto them, It is not for you to know the times or the seasons, which the Father hath put in his own power.

8 But ye shall receive power after that the Ho'ly Ghost is come upon you: and ye shall be witnesses unto me both in Je-ru'sa-lem, and in all Ju-dæ'a, and in Sa-ma'ri-a, and unto the uttermost part of the earth.

9 And when he had spoken these things, while they beheld, he was taken up; and a cloud received him out of their sight.

10 And while they looked stedfastly toward heaven as he went up, behold, two men stood by them in white apparel;

11 Which also said, Ye men of Gal'i-lee, why stand ye gazing up into heaven? this same Je'sus, which is taken up from you into heaven, shall so come in like manner as ye have seen him go into heaven.

12 Then returned they unto Je-ru'sa-lem from the mount called Ol'i-vet, which is from Je-ru'sa-lem a sabbath day's journey.

13 And when they were come in, they went up into an upper room, where abode both Pe'ter, and James, and John, and An-

drew, Phil'ip, and Thom'as, Bar-thol'o-mew, and Mat'thew, James *the son of* Al-phæ'us, and Si'mon Ze-lo'tes, and Ju'das *the brother of* James.

14 These all continued with one accord in prayer and supplication, with the women, and Ma'ry the mother of Je'sus, and with his brethren.

15 ¶ And in those days Pe'ter stood up in the midst of the disciples, and said, (the number of names together were about an hundred and twenty,)

16 Men *and* brethren, this scripture must needs have been fulfilled, which the Ho'ly Ghost by the mouth of Da'vid spake before concerning Ju'das, which was guide to them that took Je'sus.

17 For he was numbered with us, and had obtained part of this ministry.

18 Now this man purchased a field with the reward of iniquity; and falling headlong, he burst asunder in the midst, and all his bowels gushed out.

19 And it was known unto all the dwellers at Je-ru'sa-lem, insomuch as that field is called in their proper tongue, A-cel'da-ma, that is to say, The field of blood.

20 For it is written in the book of Psalms, Let his habitation be desolate, and let no man dwell therein: and his bishoprick let another take.

21 Wherefore of these men which have companied with us all the time that the Lord Je'sus went in and out among us,

22 Beginning from the baptism of John, unto that same day that he was taken up from us, must one be ordained to be a witness with us of his resurrection.

23 And they appointed two, Jo'seph called Bar'sa-bas, who was surnamed Jus'tus, and Mat-thi'as.

24 And they prayed, and said, Thou, Lord, which knowest the hearts of all men, show whether of these two thou hast chosen,

25 That he may take part of this ministry and apostleship, from which Ju'das by transgression fell, that he might go to his own place.

26 And they gave forth their lots; and the lot fell upon Mat-thi'as; and he was numbered with the eleven apostles.

2 And when the day of Pen'te-cost was fully come, they were all with one accord in one place.

2 And suddenly there came a sound from heaven as of a rushing mighty wind, and it filled all the house where they were sitting.

3 And there appeared unto them cloven tongues like as of fire, and it sat upon each of them.

4 And they were all filled with the Ho'ly Ghost, and began to speak with other tongues, as the Spirit gave them utterance.

5 And there were dwelling at Je-ru'sa-lem Jews, devout men, out of every nation under heaven.

6 Now when this was noised abroad, the multitude came together, and were confounded, because that every man heard them speak in his own language.

7 And they were all amazed and marveled, saying one to another, Behold, are not all these which speak Gal-i-læ'ans?

8 And how hear we every man in our own tongue, wherein we were born?

9 Par'thi-ans, and Medes, and E'lam-ites, and the dwellers in Mes-o-po-ta'mi-a, and in Ju-dæ'a, and Cap-pa-do'ci-a, in Pon'tus, and A'sia,

10 Phryg'i-a, and Pam-phyl'i-a, in E'gypt, and in the parts of Lib'y-a about Cy-re'ne, and strangers of Rome, Jews and proselytes,

11 Cretes and A-ra'bi-ans, we do hear them speak in our tongues the wonderful works of God.

12 And they were all amazed, and were in doubt, saying one to another, What meaneth this?

13 Others mocking said, These men are full of new wine.

14 ¶ But Pe'ter, standing up with the eleven, lifted up his voice, and said unto them, Ye men of Ju-dæ'a, and all ye that dwell at Je-ru'sa-lem, be this known unto you, and hearken to my words:

15 For these are not drunken, as ye suppose, seeing it is but the third hour of the day.

16 But this is that which was spoken by the prophet Jo'el;

17 And it shall come to pass in the last days, saith God, I will pour out of my Spirit upon all

flesh: and your sons and your daughters shall prophesy, and your young men shall see visions, and your old men shall dream dreams:

18 And on my servants and on my handmaidens I will pour out in those days of my Spirit; and they shall prophesy:

19 And I will show wonders in heaven above, and signs in the earth beneath; blood, and fire, and vapor of smoke:

20 The sun shall be turned into darkness, and the moon into blood, before that great and notable day of the Lord come:

21 And it shall come to pass, *that* whosoever shall call on the name of the Lord shall be saved.

22 Ye men of Is'ra-el, hear these words; Je'sus of Naz'areth, a man approved of God among you by miracles and wonders and signs, which God did by him in the midst of you, as ye yourselves also know:

23 Him, being delivered by the determinate counsel and foreknowledge of God, ye have taken, and by wicked hands have crucified and slain:

24 Whom God hath raised up, having loosed the pains of death: because it was not possible that he should be held of it.

25 For Da'vid speaketh concerning him, I foresaw the Lord always before my face, for he is on my right hand, that I should not be moved:

26 Therefore did my heart rejoice, and my tongue was glad; moreover also my flesh shall rest in hope:

27 Because thou wilt not leave my soul in hell, neither wilt thou suffer thine Holy One to see corruption.

28 Thou hast made known to me the ways of life; thou shalt make me full of joy with thy countenance.

29 Men *and* brethren, let me freely speak unto you of the patriarch Da'vid, that he is both dead and buried, and his sepulcher is with us unto this day.

30 Therefore being a prophet, and knowing that God had sworn with an oath to him, that of the fruit of his loins, according to the flesh, he would raise up Christ to sit on his throne;

31 He seeing this before spake of the resurrection of Christ, that his soul was not left in hell, neither his flesh did see corruption.

32 This Je'sus hath God raised up, whereof we all are witnesses.

33 Therefore being by the right hand of God exalted, and having received of the Father the promise of the Ho'ly Ghost, he hath shed forth this, which ye now see and hear.

34 For Da'vid is not ascended into the heavens: but he saith himself, The LORD said unto my Lord, Sit thou on my right hand,

35 Until I make thy foes thy footstool.

36 Therefore let all the house of Is'ra-el know assuredly, that God hath made that same Je'sus, whom ye have crucified, both Lord and Christ.

37 ¶ Now when they heard

this, they were pricked in their heart, and said unto Pe'ter and to the rest of the apostles, Men *and* brethren, what shall we do?

38 Then Pe'ter said unto them, Repent, and be baptized every-one of you in the name of Je'sus Christ for the remission of sins, and ye shall receive the gift of the Ho'ly Ghost.

39 For the promise is unto you, and to your children, and to all that are afar off, *even* as many as the Lord our God shall call.

40 And with many other words did he testify and exhort, say-ing, Save yourselves from this untoward generation.

41 ¶ Then they that gladly re-ceived his word were baptized: and the same day there were added *unto them* about three thousand souls.

42 And they continued stead-fastly in the apostles' doctrine and fellowship, and in breaking of bread, and in prayers.

43 And fear came upon every soul: and many wonders and signs were done by the apostles.

44 And all that believed were together, and had all things com-mon;

45 And sold their possessions and goods, and parted them to all *men,* as every man had need.

46 And they, continuing daily with one accord in the temple, and breaking bread from house to house, did eat their meat with gladness and singleness of heart,

47 Praising God, and having fa-vor with all the people. And the Lord added to the church daily such as should be saved.

3 Now Pe'ter and John went up together into the temple at the hour of prayer, *being* the ninth *hour.*

2 And a certain man lame from his mother's womb was carried, whom they laid daily at the gate of the temple which is called Beautiful, to ask alms of them that entered into the temple;

3 Who seeing Pe'ter and John about to go into the temple asked an alms.

4 And Pe'ter, fastening his eyes upon him with John, said, Look on us.

5 And he gave heed unto them, expecting to receive something of them.

6 Then Pe'ter said, Silver and gold have I none; but such as I have give I thee: In the name of Je'sus Christ of Naz'a-reth rise up and walk.

7 And he took him by the right hand, and lifted *him* up: and immediately his feet and ankle bones received strength.

8 And he leaping up stood, and walked, and entered with them into the temple, walking, and leaping, and praising God.

9 And all the people saw him walking and praising God:

10 And they knew that it was he which sat for alms at the Beautiful gate of the temple: and they were filled with wonder and amazement at that which had happened unto him.

11 And as the lame man which was healed held Pe'ter and John, all the people ran together

unto them in the porch that is called Sol'o-mon's, greatly wondering.

12 ¶ And when Pe'ter saw it, he answered unto the people, Ye men of Is'ra-el, why marvel ye at this? or why look ye so earnestly on us, as though by our own power or holiness we had made this man to walk?

13 The God of A'bra-ham, and of I'saac, and of Ja'cob, the God of our fathers, hath glorified his Son Je'sus; whom ye delivered up, and denied him in the presence of Pi'late, when he was determined to let him go.

14 But ye denied the Holy One and the Just, and desired a murderer to be granted unto you;

15 And killed the Prince of life, whom God hath raised from the dead; whereof we are witnesses.

16 And his name through faith in his name hath made this man strong, whom ye see and know: yea, the faith which is by him hath given him this perfect soundness in the presence of you all.

17 And now, brethren, I wot that through ignorance ye did it, as did also your rulers.

18 But those things, which God before had shewed by the mouth of all his prophets, that Christ should suffer, he hath so fulfilled.

19 ¶ Repent ye therefore, and be converted, that your sins may be blotted out, when the times of refreshing shall come from the presence of the Lord;

20 And he shall send Je'sus Christ, which before was preached unto you:

21 Whom the heaven must receive until the times of restitution of all things, which God hath spoken by the mouth of all his holy prophets since the world began.

22 For Mo'ses truly said unto the fathers, A prophet shall the Lord your God raise up unto you of your brethren, like unto me; him shall ye hear in all things whatsoever he shall say unto you.

23 And it shall come to pass, that every soul, which will not hear that prophet, shall be destroyed from among the people.

24 Yea, and all the prophets from Sam'u-el and those that follow after, as many as have spoken, have likewise foretold of these days.

25 Ye are the children of the prophets, and of the covenant which God made with our fathers, saying unto A'bra-ham, And in thy seed shall all the kindreds of the earth be blessed.

26 Unto you first God, having raised up his Son Je'sus, sent him to bless you, in turning away every one of you from his iniquities.

4 And as they spake unto the people, the priests, and the captain of the temple, and the Sad'du-cees, came upon them,

2 Being grieved that they taught the people, and preached through Je'sus the resurrection from the dead.

3 And they laid hands on them, and put them in hold unto the

next day: for it was now eventide.

4 Howbeit many of them which heard the word believed; and the number of the men was about five thousand.

5 ¶ And it came to pass on the morrow, that their rulers, and elders, and scribes,

6 And An'nas the high priest, and Ca'ia-phas, and John, and Al-ex-an'der, and as many as were of the kindred of the high priest, were gathered together at Je-ru'sa-lem.

7 And when they had set them in the midst, they asked, By what power, or by what name, have ye done this?

8 Then Pe'ter, filled with the Ho'ly Ghost, said unto them, Ye rulers of the people, and elders of Is'ra-el,

9 If we this day be examined of the good deed done to the impotent man, by what means he is made whole;

10 Be it known unto you all, and to all the people of Is'ra-el, that by the name of Je'sus Christ of Naz'a-reth, whom ye crucified, whom God raised from the dead, *even* by him doth this man stand here before you whole.

11 This is the stone which was set at nought of you builders, which is become the head of the corner.

12 Neither is there salvation in any other: for there is none other name under heaven given among men, whereby we must be saved.

13 ¶ Now when they saw the boldness of Pe'ter and John, and perceived that they were unlearned and ignorant men, they marveled; and they took knowledge of them, that they had been with Je'sus.

14 And beholding the man which was healed standing with them, they could say nothing against it.

15 But when they had commanded them to go aside out of the council, they conferred among themselves,

16 Saying, What shall we do to these men? for that indeed a notable miracle hath been done by them *is* manifest to all them that dwell in Je-ru'sa-lem; and we cannot deny *it*.

17 But that it spread no further among the people, let us straitly threaten them, that they speak henceforth to no man in this name.

18 And they called them, and commanded them not to speak at all nor teach in the name of Je'sus.

19 But Pe'ter and John answered and said unto them, Whether it be right in the sight of God to hearken unto you more than unto God, judge ye.

20 For we cannot but speak the things which we have seen and heard.

21 So when they had further threatened them, they let them go, finding nothing how they might punish them, because of the people: for all *men* glorified God for that which was done.

22 For the man was above forty

years old, on whom this miracle of healing was showed.

23 ¶ And being let go, they went to their own company, and reported all that the chief priests and elders had said unto them.

24 And when they heard that, they lifted up their voice to God with one accord, and said, Lord, thou art God, which hast made heaven, and earth, and the sea, and all that in them is:

25 Who by the mouth of thy servant Da'vid hast said, Why did the heathen rage, and the people imagine vain things?

26 The kings of the earth stood up, and the rulers were gathered together against the Lord, and against his Christ.

27 For of a truth against thy holy child Je'sus, whom thou hast anointed, both Her'od, and Pon'ti-us Pi'late, with the Gen'tiles, and the people of Is'ra-el, were gathered together,

28 For to do whatsoever thy hand and thy counsel determined before to be done.

29 And now, Lord, behold their threatenings: and grant unto thy servants, that with all boldness they may speak thy word,

30 By stretching forth thine hand to heal; and that signs and wonders may be done by the name of thy holy child Je'sus.

31 ¶ And when they had prayed, the place was shaken where they were assembled together; and they were all filled with the Ho'ly Ghost, and they spake the word of God with boldness.

32 And the multitude of them that believed were of one heart and of one soul: neither said any of them that ought of the things which he possessed was his own; but they had all things common.

33 And with great power gave the apostles witness of the resurrection of the Lord Je'sus: and great grace was upon them all.

34 Neither was there any among them that lacked: for as many as were possessors of lands or houses sold them, and brought the prices of the things that were sold,

35 And laid them down at the apostles' feet: and distribution was made unto every man according as he had need.

36 And Jo'ses, who by the apostles was surnamed Bar'na-bas, (which is, being interpreted, The son of consolation,) a Le'vite, and of the country of Cy'prus,

37 Having land, sold it, and brought the money, and laid it at the apostles' feet.

5 But a certain man named An-a-ni'as, with Sap-phi'ra his wife, sold a possession,

2 And kept back part of the price, his wife also being privy to it, and brought a certain part, and laid it at the apostles' feet.

3 But Pe'ter said, An-a-ni'as, why hath Sa'tan filled thine heart to lie to the Ho'ly Ghost, and to keep back part of the price of the land?

4 Whiles it remained, was it

not thine own? and after it was sold, was it not in thine own power? why hast thou conceived this thing in thine heart? thou hast not lied unto men, but unto God.

5 And An-a-ni'as hearing these words fell down, and gave up the ghost: and great fear came on all them that heard these things.

6 And the young men arose, wound him up, and carried him out, and buried him.

7 And it was about the space of three hours after, when his wife, not knowing what was done, came in.

8 And Pe'ter answered unto her, Tell me whether ye sold the land for so much? And she said, Yea, for so much.

9 Then Pe'ter said unto her, How is it that ye have agreed together to tempt the Spirit of the Lord? behold, the feet of them which have buried thy husband are at the door, and shall carry thee out.

10 Then fell she down straightway at his feet, and yielded up the ghost: and the young men came in, and found her dead, and, carrying her forth, buried her by her husband.

11 And great fear came upon all the church, and upon as many as heard these things.

12 ¶ And by the hands of the apostles were many signs and wonders wrought among the people; (and they were all with one accord in Sol'o-mon's porch.

13 And of the rest durst no man join himself to them: but the people magnified them.

14 And believers were the more added to the Lord, multitudes both of men and women.)

15 Insomuch that they brought forth the sick into the streets, and laid them on beds and couches, that at the least the shadow of Pe'ter passing by might overshadow some of them.

16 There came also a multitude out of the cities round about unto Je-ru'sa-lem, bringing sick folks, and them which were vexed with unclean spirits: and they were healed every one.

17 ¶ Then the high priest rose up, and all they that were with him, (which is the sect of the Sad'du-cees,) and were filled with indignation,

18 And laid their hands on the apostles, and put them in the common prison.

19 But the angel of the Lord by night opened the prison doors, and brought them forth, and said,

20 Go, stand and speak in the temple to the people all the words of this life.

21 And when they heard that, they entered into the temple early in the morning, and taught. But the high priest came, and they that were with him, and called the council together, and all the senate of the children of Is'ra-el, and sent to the prison to have them brought.

22 But when the officers came, and found them not in the prison, they returned, and told,

23 Saying, The prison truly found we shut with all safety, and the keepers standing without before the doors: but when we had opened, we found no man within.

24 Now when the high priest and the captain of the temple and the chief priests heard these things, they doubted of them whereunto this would grow.

25 Then came one and told them, saying, Behold, the men whom ye put in prison are standing in the temple, and teaching the people.

26 Then went the captain with the officers, and brought them without violence: for they feared the people, lest they should have been stoned.

27 And when they had brought them, they set them before the council: and the high priest asked them,

28 Saying, Did not we straitly command you that ye should not teach in this name? and, behold, ye have filled Jerusalem with your doctrine, and intend to bring this man's blood upon us.

29 ¶ Then Peter and the other apostles answered and said, We ought to obey God rather than men.

30 The God of our fathers raised up Jesus, whom ye slew and hanged on a tree.

31 Him hath God exalted with his right hand to be a Prince and a Savior, for to give repentance to Israel, and forgiveness of sins.

32 And we are his witnesses of these things; and so is also the Holy Ghost, whom God hath given to them that obey him.

33 ¶ When they heard that, they were cut to the heart, and took counsel to slay them.

34 Then stood there up one in the council, a Pharisee, named Gamaliel, a doctor of the law, had in reputation among all the people, and commanded to put the apostles forth a little space;

35 And said unto them, Ye men of Israel, take heed to yourselves what ye intend to do as touching these men.

36 For before these days rose up Theudas, boasting himself to be somebody; to whom a number of men, about four hundred, joined themselves: who was slain; and all, as many as obeyed him, were scattered, and brought to nought.

37 After this man rose up Judas of Galilee in the days of the taxing, and drew away much people after him: he also perished; and all, even as many as obeyed him, were dispersed.

38 And now I say unto you, Refrain from these men, and let them alone: for if this counsel or this work be of men, it will come to nought:

39 But if it be of God, ye cannot overthrow it; lest haply ye be found even to fight against God.

40 And to him they agreed: and when they had called the apostles, and beaten them, they commanded that they should not speak in the name of Jesus, and let them go.

41 ¶ And they departed from

the presence of the council, rejoicing that they were counted worthy to suffer shame for his name.

42 And daily in the temple, and in every house, they ceased not to teach and preach Je´sus Christ.

6 And in those days, when the number of the disciples was multiplied, there arose a murmuring of the Gre´cians against the He´brews, because their widows were neglected in the daily ministration.

2 Then the twelve called the multitude of the disciples *unto them,* and said, It is not reason that we should leave the word of God, and serve tables.

3 Wherefore, brethren, look ye out among you seven men of honest report, full of the Ho´ly Ghost and wisdom, whom we may appoint over this business.

4 But we will give ourselves continually to prayer, and to the ministry of the word.

5 ¶ And the saying pleased the whole multitude: and they chose Ste´phen, a man full of faith and of the Ho´ly Ghost, and Phil´ip, and Proch´o-rus, and Ni-ca´nor, and Ti´mon, and Par´me-nas, and Nic´o-las a proselyte of An´ti-och:

6 Whom they set before the apostles: and when they had prayed, they laid *their* hands on them.

7 And the word of God increased; and the number of the disciples multiplied in Je-ru´sa-lem greatly; and a great com-

pany of the priests were obedient to the faith.

8 And Ste´phen, full of faith and power, did great wonders and miracles among the people.

9 ¶ Then there arose certain of the synagogue, which is called *the synagogue* of the Lib´er-tines, and Cy-re´ni-ans, and Al-ex-an´dri-ans, and of them of Ci-li´cia and of A´sia, disputing with Ste´phen.

10 And they were not able to resist the wisdom and the spirit by which he spake.

11 Then they suborned men, which said, We have heard him speak blasphemous words against Mo´ses, and *against* God.

12 And they stirred up the people, and the elders, and the scribes, and came upon *him,* and caught him, and brought *him* to the council,

13 And set up false witnesses, which said, This man ceaseth not to speak blasphemous words against this holy place, and the law:

14 For we have heard him say, that this Je´sus of Naz´a-reth shall destroy this place, and shall change the customs which Mo´ses delivered us.

15 And all that sat in the council, looking steadfastly on him, saw his face as it had been the face of an angel.

7 Then said the high priest, Are these things so?

2 And he said, Men, brethren, and fathers, hearken; The God of glory appeared unto our father A´bra-ham, when he was

in Mes·o·po·ta'mi·a, before he dwelt in Ha'ran,

3 And said unto him, Get thee out of thy country, and from thy kindred, and come into the land which I shall show thee.

4 Then came he out of the land of the Chal·dæ'ans, and dwelt in Ha'ran: and from thence, when his father was dead, he removed him into this land, wherein ye now dwell.

5 And he gave him none inheritance in it, no, not so much as to set his foot on: yet he promised that he would give it to him for a possession, and to his seed after him, when as yet he had no child.

6 And God spake on this wise, That his seed should sojourn in a strange land; and that they should bring them into bondage, and entreat them evil four hundred years.

7 And the nation to whom they shall be in bondage will I judge, said God: and after that shall they come forth, and serve me in this place.

8 And he gave him the covenant of circumcision: and so A'bra·ham begat I'saac, and circumcised him the eighth day; and I'saac begat Ja'cob; and Ja'cob begat the twelve patriarchs.

9 And the patriarchs, moved with envy, sold Jo'seph into E'gypt: but God was with him,

10 And delivered him out of all his afflictions, and gave him favor and wisdom in the sight of Pha'raoh king of E'gypt; and he made him governor over E'gypt and all his house.

11 Now there came a dearth over all the land of E'gypt and Ca'naan, and great affliction: and our fathers found no sustenance.

12 But when Ja'cob heard that there was corn in E'gypt, he sent out our fathers first.

13 And at the second time Jo'seph was made known to his brethren; and Jo'seph's kindred was made known unto Pha'raoh.

14 Then sent Jo'seph, and called his father Ja'cob to him, and all his kindred, threescore and fifteen souls.

15 So Ja'cob went down into E'gypt, and died, he, and our fathers,

16 And were carried over into She'chem, and laid in the sepulcher that A'bra·ham bought for a sum of money of the sons of Em'mor the father of She'chem.

17 But when the time of the promise drew nigh, which God had sworn to A'bra·ham, the people grew and multiplied in E'gypt,

18 Till another king arose, which knew not Jo'seph.

19 The same dealt subtly with our kindred, and evil entreated our fathers, so that they cast out their young children, to the end they might not live.

20 In which time Mo'ses was born, and was exceeding fair, and nourished up in his father's house three months:

21 And when he was cast out, Pha'raoh's daughter took him up, and nourished him for her own son.

22 And Mo'ses was learned in all the wisdom of the E-gyp'-tians, and was mighty in words and in deeds.

23 And when he was full forty years old, it came into his heart to visit his brethren the children of Is'ra-el.

24 And seeing one *of them* suffer wrong, he defended *him*, and avenged him that was oppressed, and smote the E-gyp'-tian:

25 For he supposed his brethren would have understood how that God by his hand would deliver them: but they understood not.

26 And the next day he showed himself unto them as they strove, and would have set them at one again, saying, Sirs, ye are brethren; why do ye wrong one to another?

27 But he that did his neighbor wrong thrust him away, saying, Who made thee a ruler and a judge over us?

28 Wilt thou kill me, as thou didst the E-gyp'tian yesterday?

29 Then fled Mo'ses at this saying, and was a stranger in the land of Mid'i-an, where he begat two sons.

30 And when forty years were expired, there appeared to him in the wilderness of mount Si'-nai an angel of the Lord in a flame of fire in a bush.

31 When Mo'ses saw *it*, he wondered at the sight: and as he drew near to behold *it*, the voice of the Lord came unto him,

32 *Saying,* I *am* the God of thy fathers, the God of A'bra-ham, and the God of I'saac, and the God of Ja'cob. Then Mo'ses trembled, and durst not behold.

33 Then said the Lord to him, Put off thy shoes from thy feet: for the place where thou standest is holy ground.

34 I have seen, I have seen the affliction of my people which is in E'gypt, and I have heard their groaning, and am come down to deliver them. And now come, I will send thee into E'gypt.

35 This Mo'ses whom they refused, saying, Who made thee a ruler and a judge? the same did God send *to be* a ruler and a deliverer by the hand of the angel which appeared to him in the bush.

36 He brought them out, after that he had showed wonders and signs in the land of E'gypt, and in the Red sea, and in the wilderness forty years.

37 ¶ This is that Mo'ses, which said unto the children of Is'ra-el, A prophet shall the Lord your God raise up unto you of your brethren, like unto me; him shall ye hear.

38 This is he, that was in the church in the wilderness with the angel which spake to him in the mount Si'nai, and *with* our fathers: who received the lively oracles to give unto us:

39 To whom our fathers would not obey, but thrust *him* from them, and in their hearts turned back again into E'gypt,

40 Saying unto Aar'on, Make us gods to go before us: for *as for* this Mo'ses, which brought

us out of the land of E'gypt, we wot not what is become of him.

41 And they made a calf in those days, and offered sacrifice unto the idol, and rejoiced in the works of their own hands.

42 Then God turned, and gave them up to worship the host of heaven; as it is written in the book of the prophets, O ye house of Is'ra-el, have ye offered to me slain beasts and sacrifices *by the space of* forty years in the wilderness?

43 Yea, ye took up the tabernacle of Mo'loch, and the star of your god Rem'phan, figures which ye made to worship them: and I will carry you away beyond Bab'y-lon.

44 Our fathers had the tabernacle of witness in the wilderness, as he had appointed, speaking unto Mo'ses, that he should make it according to the fashion that he had seen.

45 Which also our fathers that came after brought in with Je'sus into the possession of the Gen'tiles, whom God drove out before the face of our fathers, unto the days of Da'vid;

46 Who found favor before God, and desired to find a tabernacle for the God of Ja'cob,

47 But Sol'o-mon built him an house.

48 Howbeit the most High dwelleth not in temples made with hands; as saith the prophet,

49 Heaven *is* my throne, and earth *is* my footstool; what house will ye build me? saith

the Lord: or what *is* the place of my rest?

50 Hath not my hand made all these things?

51 ¶ Ye stiffnecked and uncircumcised in heart and ears, ye do always resist the Ho'ly Ghost: as your fathers *did,* so do ye.

52 Which of the prophets have not your fathers persecuted? and they have slain them which showed before of the coming of the Just One; of whom ye have been now the betrayers and murderers:

53 Who have received the law by the disposition of angels, and have not kept *it.*

54 ¶ When they heard these things, they were cut to the heart, and they gnashed on him with *their* teeth.

55 But he, being full of the Ho'ly Ghost, looked up steadfastly into heaven, and saw the glory of God, and Je'sus standing on the right hand of God,

56 And said, Behold, I see the heavens opened, and the Son of man standing on the right hand of God.

57 Then they cried out with a loud voice, and stopped their ears, and ran upon him with one accord,

58 And cast *him* out of the city, and stoned *him:* and the witnesses laid down their clothes at a young man's feet, whose name was Saul.

59 And they stoned Ste'phen, calling upon *God,* and saying, Lord Je'sus, receive my spirit.

60 And he kneeled down, and

cried with a loud voice, Lord, lay not this sin to their charge. And when he had said this, he fell asleep.

8 And Saul was consenting unto his death. And at that time there was a great persecution against the church which was at Je-ru'sa-lem; and they were all scattered abroad throughout the regions of Ju-dæ'a and Sa-ma'ri-a, except the apostles.

2 And devout men carried Ste'phen *to his burial,* and made great lamentation over him.

3 As for Saul, he made havoc of the church, entering into every house, and haling men and women committed *them* to prison.

4 Therefore they that were scattered abroad went everywhere preaching the word.

5 Then Phil'ip went down to the city of Sa-ma'ri-a, and preached Christ unto them.

6 And the people with one accord gave heed unto those things which Phil'ip spake, hearing and seeing the miracles which he did.

7 For unclean spirits, crying with loud voice, came out of many that were possessed *with them:* and many taken with palsies, and that were lame, were healed.

8 And there was great joy in that city.

9 But there was a certain man, called Si'mon, which beforetime in the same city used sorcery, and bewitched the people of Sa-ma'ri-a, giving out that himself was some great one:

10 To whom they all gave heed, from the least to the greatest, saying, This man is the great power of God.

11 And to him they had regard, because that of long time he had bewitched them with sorceries.

12 But when they believed Phil'ip preaching the things concerning the kingdom of God, and the name of Je'sus Christ, they were baptized, both men and women.

13 Then Si'mon himself believed also: and when he was baptized, he continued with Phil'ip, and wondered, beholding the miracles and signs which were done.

14 Now when the apostles which were at Je-ru'sa-lem heard that Sa-ma'ri-a had received the word of God, they sent unto them Pe'ter and John:

15 Who, when they were come down, prayed for them, that they might receive the Ho'ly Ghost:

16 (For as yet he was fallen upon none of them: only they were baptized in the name of the Lord Je'sus.)

17 Then laid they *their* hands on them, and they received the Ho'ly Ghost.

18 And when Si'mon saw that through laying on of the apostles' hands the Ho'ly Ghost was given, he offered them money,

19 Saying, Give me also this power, that on whomsoever I lay hands, he may receive the Ho'ly Ghost.

20 But Pe'ter said unto him, Thy money perish with thee, because thou hast thought that the gift of God may be purchased with money.

21 Thou hast neither part nor lot in this matter: for thy heart is not right in the sight of God.

22 Repent therefore of this thy wickedness, and pray God, if perhaps the thought of thine heart may be forgiven thee.

23 For I perceive that thou art in the gall of bitterness, and *in* the bond of iniquity.

24 Then answered Si'mon, and said, Pray ye to the Lord for me, that none of these things which ye have spoken come upon me.

25 And they, when they had testified and preached the word of the Lord, returned to Je-ru'sa-lem, and preached the gospel in many villages of the Sa-mar'i-tans.

26 And the angel of the Lord spake unto Phil'ip, saying, Arise, and go toward the south unto the way that goeth down from Je-ru'sa-lem unto Ga'za, which is desert.

27 And he rose and went: and, behold, a man of E-thi-o'pi-a, an eunuch of great authority under Can'da-ce queen of the E-thi-o'-pi-ans, who had the charge of all her treasure, and had come to Je-ru'sa-lem for to worship,

28 Was returning, and sitting in his chariot read I-sa'iah the prophet.

29 Then the Spirit said unto Phil'ip, Go near, and join thyself to this chariot.

30 And Phil'ip ran thither to *him,* and heard him read the prophet I-sa'iah, and said, Understandest thou what thou readest?

31 And he said, How can I, except some man should guide me? And he desired Phil'ip that he would come up and sit with him.

32 The place of the scripture which he read was this, He was led as a sheep to the slaughter; and like a lamb dumb before his shearer, so opened he not his mouth:

33 In his humiliation his judgment was taken away: and who shall declare his generation? for his life is taken from the earth.

34 And the eunuch answered Phil'ip, and said, I pray thee, of whom speaketh the prophet this? of himself, or of some other man?

35 Then Phil'ip opened his mouth, and began at the same scripture, and preached unto him Je'sus.

36 And as they went on *their* way, they came unto a certain water: and the eunuch said, See, *here is* water; what doth hinder me to be baptized?

37 And Phil'ip said, If thou believest with all thine heart, thou mayest. And he answered and said, I believe that Je'sus Christ is the Son of God.

38 And he commanded the chariot to stand still: and they went down both into the water, both Phil'ip and the eunuch; and he baptized him.

39 And when they were come up out of the water, the Spirit of

the Lord caught away Phil'ip,
that the eunuch saw him no
more: and he went on his way
rejoicing.

40 But Phil'ip was found at
A·zo'tus: and passing through
he preached in all the cities, till
he came to Cæs·a·re'a.

9 And Saul, yet breathing out
threatenings and slaughter
against the disciples of the Lord,
went unto the high priest,

2 And desired of him letters to
Da·mas'cus to the synagogues,
that if he found any of this way,
whether they were men or
women, he might bring them
bound unto Je·ru'sa·lem.

3 And as he journeyed, he
came near Da·mas'cus: and suddenly there shined round about
him a light from heaven:

4 And he fell to the earth, and
heard a voice saying unto him,
Saul, Saul, why persecutest thou
me?

5 And he said, Who art thou,
Lord? And the Lord said, I am
Je'sus whom thou persecutest:
it is hard for thee to kick against
the pricks.

6 And he trembling and astonished said, Lord, what wilt thou
have me to do? And the Lord
said unto him, Arise, and go
into the city, and it shall be told
thee what thou must do. ·

7 And the men which jour-
neyed with him stood speechless, hearing a voice, but seeing
no man.

8 And Saul arose from the
earth; and when his eyes were
opened, he saw no man: but

they led him by the hand, and
brought him into Da·mas'cus.

9 And he was three days without sight, and neither did eat
nor drink.

10 ¶ And there was a certain
disciple at Da·mas'cus, named
An·a·ni'as; and to him said the
Lord in a vision, An·a·ni'as. And
he said, Behold, I am here,
Lord.

11 And the Lord said unto
him, Arise, and go into the
street which is called Straight,
and inquire in the house of Ju'-
das for one called Saul, of Tar'-
sus: for, behold, he prayeth,

12 And hath seen in a vision a
man named An·a·ni'as coming
in, and putting his hand on him,
that he might receive his sight.

13 Then An·a·ni'as answered,
Lord, I have heard by many of
this man, how much evil he
hath done to thy saints at Je·ru'-
sa·lem:

14 And here he hath authority
from the chief priests to bind all
that call on thy name.

15 But the Lord said unto him,
Go thy way: for he is a chosen
vessel unto me, to bear my name
before the Gen'tiles, and kings,
and the children of Is'ra·el:

16 For I will show him how
great things he must suffer for
my name's sake.

17 And An·a·ni'as went his
way, and entered into the
house; and putting his hands on
him said, Brother Saul, the Lord,
even Je'sus, that appeared unto
thee in the way as thou camest,
hath sent me, that thou

mightest receive thy sight, and be filled with the Ho'ly Ghost.

18 And immediately there fell from his eyes as it had been scales: and he received sight forthwith, and arose, and was baptized.

19 And when he had received meat, he was strengthened. Then was Saul certain days with the disciples which were at Da-mas'cus.

20 And straightway he preached Christ in the synagogues, that he is the Son of God.

21 But all that heard him were amazed, and said; Is not this he that destroyed them which called on this name in Je-ru'sa-lem, and came hither for that intent, that he might bring them bound unto the chief priests?

22 But Saul increased the more in strength, and confounded the Jews which dwelt at Da-mas'cus, proving that this is very Christ.

23 ¶ And after that many days were fulfilled, the Jews took counsel to kill him:

24 But their laying await was known of Saul. And they watched the gates day and night to kill him.

25 Then the disciples took him by night, and let *him* down by the wall in a basket.

26 And when Saul was come to Je-ru'sa-lem, he assayed to join himself to the disciples: but they were all afraid of him, and believed not that he was a disciple.

27 But Bar'na-bas took him, and brought *him* to the apostles, and declared unto them how he had seen the Lord in the way, and that he had spoken to him, and how he had preached boldly at Da-mas'cus in the name of Je'sus.

28 And he was with them coming in and going out at Je-ru'sa-lem.

29 And he spake boldly in the name of the Lord Je'sus, and disputed against the Gre'cians: but they went about to slay him.

30 *Which* when the brethren knew, they brought him down to Caes-a-re'a, and sent him forth to Tar'sus.

31 Then had the churches rest throughout all Ju-dæ'a and Gal'i-lee and Sa-ma'ri-a, and were edified; and walking in the fear of the Lord, and in the comfort of the Ho'ly Ghost, were multiplied.

32 ¶ And it came to pass, as Pe'ter passed throughout all *quarters*, he came down also to the saints which dwelt at Lyd'da.

33 And there he found a certain man named Æ'ne-as, which had kept his bed eight years, and was sick of the palsy.

34 And Pe'ter said unto him, Æ'ne-as, Je'sus Christ maketh thee whole: arise, and make thy bed. And he arose immediately.

35 And all that dwelt at Lyd'da and Sa'ron saw him, and turned to the Lord.

36 ¶ Now there was at Jop'pa a certain disciple named Tab'i-tha, which by interpretation is called Dor'cas: this woman was full of good works and alms-deeds which she did.

37 And it came to pass in those days, that she was sick, and died: whom when they had washed, they laid *her* in an upper chamber.

38 And forasmuch as Lyd'da was nigh to Jop'pa, and the disciples had heard that Pe'ter was there, they sent unto him two men, desiring *him* that he would not delay to come to them.

39 Then Pe'ter arose and went with them. When he was come, they brought him into the upper chamber: and all the widows stood by him weeping, and showing the coats and garments which Dor'cas made, while she was with them.

40 But Pe'ter put them all forth, and kneeled down, and prayed; and turning *him* to the body said, Tab'i-tha, arise. And she opened her eyes: and when she saw Pe'ter, she sat up.

41 And he gave her *his* hand, and lifted her up, and when he had called the saints and widows, presented her alive.

42 And it was known throughout all Jop'pa; and many believed in the Lord.

43 And it came to pass, that he tarried many days in Jop'pa with one Si'mon a tanner.

10 There was a certain man in Cæs-a-re'a called Cor-ne'lius, a centurion of the band called the Ital'ian *band*,

2 A devout *man*, and one that feared God with all his house, which gave much alms to the people, and prayed to God always.

3 He saw in a vision evidently about the ninth hour of the day an angel of God coming in to him, and saying unto him, Cor-ne'lius.

4 And when he looked on him, he was afraid, and said, What is it, Lord? And he said unto him, Thy prayers and thine alms are come up for a memorial before God.

5 And now send men to Jop'pa, and call for *one* Si'mon, whose surname is Pe'ter:

6 He lodgeth with one Si'mon a tanner, whose house is by the seaside: he shall tell thee what thou oughtest to do.

7 And when the angel which spake unto Cor-ne'lius was departed, he called two of his household servants, and a devout soldier of them that waited on him continually;

8 And when he had declared all *these* things unto them, he sent them to Jop'pa.

9 ¶ On the morrow, as they went on their journey, and drew nigh unto the city, Pe'ter went up upon the housetop to pray about the sixth hour:

10 And he became very hungry, and would have eaten: but while they made ready, he fell into a trance,

11 And saw heaven opened, and a certain vessel descending unto him, as it had been a great sheet knit at the four corners, and let down to the earth:

12 Wherein were all manner of fourfooted beasts of the earth, and wild beasts, and creeping things, and fowls of the air.

13 And there came a voice to him, Rise, Pe'ter; kill, and eat.

14 But Pe'ter said, Not so, Lord; for I have never eaten anything that is common or unclean.

15 And the voice spake unto him again the second time, What God hath cleansed, that call not thou common.

16 This was done thrice: and the vessel was received up again into heaven.

17 Now while Pe'ter doubted in himself what this vision which he had seen should mean, behold, the men which were sent from Cor-ne'lius had made inquiry for Si'mon's house, and stood before the gate,

18 And called, and asked whether Si'mon, which was surnamed Pe'ter, were lodged there.

19 ¶ While Pe'ter thought on the vision, the Spirit said unto him, Behold, three men seek thee.

20 Arise therefore, and get thee down, and go with them, doubting nothing: for I have sent them.

21 Then Pe'ter went down to the men which were sent unto him from Cor-ne'lius; and said, Behold, I am he whom ye seek: what is the cause wherefore ye are come?

22 And they said, Cor-ne'lius the centurion, a just man, and one that feareth God, and of good report among all the nation of the Jews, was warned from God by an holy angel to send for thee into his house, and to hear words of thee.

23 Then called he them in, and lodged them. And on the morrow Pe'ter went away with them, and certain brethren from Jop'pa accompanied him.

24 And the morrow after they entered into Caes-a-re'a. And Cor-ne'lius waited for them, and had called together his kinsmen and near friends.

25 And as Pe'ter was coming in, Cor-ne'lius met him, and fell down at his feet, and worshipped him.

26 But Pe'ter took him up, saying, Stand up; I myself also am a man.

27 And as he talked with him, he went in, and found many that were come together.

28 And he said unto them, Ye know how that it is an unlawful thing for a man that is a Jew to keep company, or come unto one of another nation; but God hath showed me that I should not call any man common or unclean.

29 Therefore came I unto you without gainsaying, as soon as I was sent for: I ask therefore for what intent ye have sent for me?

30 And Cor-ne'lius said, Four days ago I was fasting until this hour; and at the ninth hour I prayed in my house, and, behold, a man stood before me in bright clothing,

31 And said, Cor-ne'lius, thy prayer is heard, and thine alms are had in remembrance in the sight of God.

32 Send therefore to Jop'pa, and call hither Si'mon, whose surname is Pe'ter; he is lodged in the house of *one* Si'mon a tanner by the seaside: who, when he cometh, shall speak unto thee.

33 Immediately therefore I sent to thee; and thou hast well done that thou art come. Now therefore are we all here present before God, to hear all things that are commanded thee of God.

34 ¶ Then Pe'ter opened *his* mouth, and said, Of a truth I perceive that God is no respecter of persons:

35 But in every nation he that feareth him, and worketh righteousness, is accepted with him.

36 The word which *God* sent unto the children of Is'ra-el, preaching peace by Je'sus Christ: (he is Lord of all:)

37 That word, *I say*, ye know, which was published throughout all Ju-dæ'a, and began from Gal'i-lee, after the baptism which John preached;

38 How God anointed Je'sus of Naz'a-reth with the Ho'ly Ghost and with power: who went about doing good, and healing all that were oppressed of the devil; for God was with him.

39 And we are witnesses of all things which he did both in the land of the Jews, and in Je-ru'sa-lem; whom they slew and hanged on a tree:

40 Him God raised up the third day, and showed him openly;

41 Not to all the people, but unto witnesses chosen before of God, *even* to us, who did eat and drink with him after he rose from the dead.

42 And he commanded us to preach unto the people, and to testify that it is he which was ordained of God *to be* the Judge of quick and dead.

43 To him give all the prophets witness, that through his name whosoever believeth in him shall receive remission of sins.

44 ¶ While Pe'ter yet spake these words, the Ho'ly Ghost fell on all them which heard the word.

45 And they of the circumcision which believed were astonished, as many as came with Pe'ter, because that on the Gen'tiles also was poured out the gift of the Ho'ly Ghost.

46 For they heard them speak with tongues, and magnify God. Then answered Pe'ter,

47 Can any man forbid water, that these should not be baptized, which have received the Ho'ly Ghost as well as we?

48 And he commanded them to be baptized in the name of the Lord. Then prayed they him to tarry certain days.

11 And the apostles and brethren that were in Ju-dæ'a heard that the Gen'tiles had also received the word of God.

2 And when Pe'ter was come up to Je-ru'sa-lem, they that were of the circumcision contended with him,

3 Saying, Thou wentest in to men uncircumcised, and didst eat with them.

4 But Pe'ter rehearsed *the matter* from the beginning, and

expounded *it* by order unto them, saying,

5 I was in the city of Jop'pa praying: and in a trance I saw a vision, A certain vessel descend, as it had been a great sheet, let down from heaven by four corners; and it came even to me:

6 Upon the which when I had fastened mine eyes, I considered, and saw fourfooted beasts of the earth, and wild beasts, and creeping things, and fowls of the air.

7 And I heard a voice saying unto me, Arise, Pe'ter: slay and eat.

8 But I said, Not so, Lord: for nothing common or unclean hath at anytime entered into my mouth.

9 But the voice answered me again from heaven, What God hath cleansed, *that* call not thou common.

10 And this was done three times: and all were drawn up again into heaven.

11 And, behold, immediately there were three men already come unto the house where I was, sent from Cæs-a-re'a unto me.

12 And the spirit bade me go with them, nothing doubting. Moreover these six brethren accompanied me, and we entered into the man's house:

13 And he showed us how he had seen an angel in his house, which stood and said unto him, Send men to Jop'pa, and call for Si'mon, whose surname is Pe'ter;

14 Who shall tell thee words, whereby thou and all thy house shall be saved.

15 And as I began to speak, the Ho'ly Ghost fell on them, as on us at the beginning.

16 Then remembered I the word of the Lord, how that he said, John indeed baptized with water; but ye shall be baptized with the Ho'ly Ghost.

17 Forasmuch then as God gave them the like gift as *he did* unto us, who believed on the Lord Je'sus Christ; what was I, that I could withstand God?

18 When they heard these things, they held their peace, and glorified God, saying, Then hath God also to the Gen'tiles granted repentance unto life.

19 ¶ Now they which were scattered abroad upon the persecution that arose about Ste'phen travelled as far as Phœ-ni'ci-a, and Cy'prus, and An'ti-och, preaching the word to none but unto the Jews only.

20 And some of them were men of Cy'prus and Cy-re'ne, which, when they were come to An'ti-och, spake unto the Gre'cians, preaching the Lord Je'sus.

21 And the hand of the Lord was with them: and a great number believed, and turned unto the Lord.

22 ¶ Then tidings of these things came unto the ears of the church which was in Je-ru'salem: and they sent forth Bar'nabas, that he should go as far as An'ti-och.

23 Who, when he came, and had seen the grace of God, was glad, and exhorted them all, that

with purpose of heart they would cleave unto the Lord.

24 For he was a good man, and full of the Ho'ly Ghost and of faith: and much people was added unto the Lord.

25 Then departed Bar'na-bas to Tar'sus, for to seek Saul:

26 And when he had found him, he brought him unto An'ti-och. And it came to pass, that a whole year they assembled themselves with the church, and taught much people. And the disciples were called Chris'-tians first in An'ti-och.

27 ¶ And in these days came prophets from Je-ru'sa-lem unto An'ti-och.

28 And there stood up one of them named Ag'a-bus, and signified by the Spirit that there should be great dearth throughout all the world: which came to pass in the days of Clau'di-us Cæ'sar.

29 Then the disciples, every man according to his ability, determined to send relief unto the brethren which dwelt in Ju-dæ'a:

30 Which also they did, and sent it to the elders by the hands of Bar'na-bas and Saul.

12 Now about that time Her'od the king stretched forth *his* hands to vex certain of the church.

2 And he killed James the brother of John with the sword.

3 And because he saw it pleased the Jews, he proceeded further to take Pe'ter also. (Then were the days of unleavened bread.)

4 And when he had apprehended him, he put *him* in prison, and delivered *him* to four quaternions of soldiers to keep him; intending after Easter to bring him forth to the people.

5 Pe'ter therefore was kept in prison: but prayer was made without ceasing of the church unto God for him.

6 And when Her'od would have brought him forth, the same night Pe'ter was sleeping between two soldiers, bound with two chains: and the keepers before the door kept the prison.

7 And, behold, the angel of the Lord came upon *him*, and a light shined in the prison: and he smote Pe'ter on the side, and raised him up, saying, Arise up quickly. And his chains fell off from *his* hands.

8 And the angel said unto him, Gird thyself, and bind on *thy* sandals. And so he did. And he saith unto him, Cast *thy* garment about thee, and follow me.

9 And he went out, and followed him; and wist not that it was true which was done by the angel; but thought he saw a vision.

10 When they were past the first and the second ward, they came unto the iron gate that leadeth unto the city; which opened to them of his own accord: and they went out, and passed on through one street; and forthwith the angel departed from him.

11 And when Pe'ter was come to himself, he said, Now I know

of a surety, that the Lord hath sent his angel, and hath delivered me out of the hand of Her'od, and *from* all the expectation of the people of the Jews.

12 And when he had considered the thing, he came to the house of Ma'ry the mother of John, whose surname was Mark; where many were gathered together praying.

13 And as Pe'ter knocked at the door of the gate, a damsel came to hearken, named Rho'da.

14 And when she knew Pe'ter's voice, she opened not the gate for gladness, but ran in, and told how Pe'ter stood before the gate.

15 And they said unto her, Thou art mad. But she constantly affirmed that it was even so. Then said they, It is his angel.

16 But Pe'ter continued knocking: and when they had opened the door, and saw him, they were astonished.

17 But he, beckoning unto them with the hand to hold their peace, declared unto them how the Lord had brought him out of the prison. And he said, Go show these things unto James, and to the brethren. And he departed, and went into another place.

18 Now as soon as it was day, there was no small stir among the soldiers, what was become of Pe'ter.

19 And when Her'od had sought for him, and found him not, he examined the keepers, and commanded that *they* should be put to death. And he went down from Ju-dæ'a to Cæs-a-re'a, and *there* abode.

20 ¶ And Her'od was highly displeased with them of Tyre and Si'don: but they came with one accord to him, and, having made Blas'tus the king's chamberlain their friend, desired peace; because their country was nourished by the king's *country*.

21 And upon a set day Her'od, arrayed in royal apparel, sat upon his throne, and made an oration unto them.

22 And the people gave a shout, *saying*, It is the voice of a god, and not of a man.

23 And immediately the angel of the Lord smote him, because he gave not God the glory: and he was eaten of worms, and gave up the ghost.

24 ¶ But the word of God grew and multiplied.

25 And Bar'na-bas and Saul returned from Je-ru'sa-lem, when they had fulfilled *their* ministry, and took with them John, whose surname was Mark.

13 Now there were in the church that was at An'ti-och certain prophets and teachers; as Bar'na-bas, and Sim'e-on that was called Ni'ger, and Lu'cius of Cy-re'ne, and Man'a-en, which had been brought up with Her'od the tetrarch, and Saul.

2 As they ministered to the Lord, and fasted, the Ho'ly Ghost said, Separate me Bar'na-bas and Saul for the work whereunto I have called them.

3 And when they had fasted and prayed, and laid *their* hands on them, they sent *them* away.

4 ¶ So they, being sent forth by the Ho'ly Ghost, departed unto Se·leu'ci·a; and from thence they sailed to Cy'prus.

5 And when they were at Sal'a·mis, they preached the word of God in the synagogues of the Jews: and they had also John to *their* minister.

6 And when they had gone through the isle unto Pa'phos, they found a certain sorcerer, a false prophet, a Jew, whose name *was* Bar·je'sus:

7 Which was with the deputy of the country, Ser'gi·us Pau'lus, a prudent man; who called for Bar'na·bas and Saul, and desired to hear the word of God.

8 But El'y·mas the sorcerer (for so is his name by interpretation) withstood them, seeking to turn away the deputy from the faith.

9 Then Saul, (who also *is called* Paul,) filled with the Ho'ly Ghost, set his eyes on him,

10 And said, O full of all subtlety and all mischief, *thou* child of the devil, *thou* enemy of all righteousness, wilt thou not cease to pervert the right ways of the Lord?

11 And now, behold, the hand of the Lord *is* upon thee, and thou shalt be blind, not seeing the sun for a season. And immediately there fell on him a mist and a darkness; and he went about seeking some to lead him by the hand.

12 Then the deputy, when he saw what was done, believed, being astonished at the doctrine of the Lord.

13 Now when Paul and his company loosed from Pa'phos, they came to Per'ga in Pam·phyl'i·a: and John departing from them returned to Je·ru'sa·lem.

14 ¶ But when they departed from Per'ga, they came to An'ti·och in Pi·sid'i·a, and went into the synagogue on the sabbath day, and sat down.

15 And after the reading of the law and the prophets the rulers of the synagogue sent unto them, saying, *Ye* men *and* brethren, if ye have any word of exhortation for the people, say on.

16 Then Paul stood up, and beckoning with *his* hand said, Men of Is'ra·el, and ye that fear God, give audience.

17 The God of this people of Is'ra·el chose our fathers, and exalted the people when they dwelt as strangers in the land of E'gypt, and with an high arm brought he them out of it.

18 And about the time of forty years suffered he their manners in the wilderness.

19 And when he had destroyed seven nations in the land of Ca'naan, he divided their land to them by lot.

20 And after that he gave *unto them* judges about the space of four hundred and fifty years, until Sam'u·el the prophet.

21 And afterward they desired a king: and God gave unto them Saul the son of Kish, a man of the tribe of Ben'ja·min, by the space of forty years.

22 And when he had removed him, he raised up unto them Da'vid to be their king; to whom also he gave testimony, and said, I have found Da'vid the son of Jes'se, a man after mine own heart, which shall fulfill all my will.

23 Of this man's seed hath God according to his promise raised unto Is'ra-el a Savior, Je'sus:

24 When John had first preached before his coming the baptism of repentance to all the people of Is'ra-el.

25 And as John fulfilled his course, he said, Whom think ye that I am? I am not he. But, behold, there cometh one after me, whose shoes of his feet I am not worthy to loose.

26 Men and brethren, children of the stock of A'bra-ham, and whosoever among you feareth God, to you is the word of this salvation sent.

27 For they that dwell at Je-ru'sa-lem, and their rulers, because they knew him not, nor yet the voices of the prophets which are read every sabbath day, they have fulfilled them in condemning him.

28 And though they found no cause of death in him, yet desired they Pi'late that he should be slain.

29 And when they had fulfilled all that was written of him, they took him down from the tree, and laid him in a sepulcher.

30 But God raised him from the dead:

31 And he was seen many days of them which came up with him from Gal'i-lee to Je-ru'sa-lem, who are his witnesses unto the people.

32 And we declare unto you glad tidings, how that the promise which was made unto the fathers,

33 God hath fulfilled the same unto us their children, in that he hath raised up Je'sus again; as it is also written in the second psalm, Thou art my Son, this day have I begotten thee.

34 And as concerning that he raised him up from the dead, now no more to return to corruption, he said on this wise, I will give you the sure mercies of Da'vid.

35 Wherefore he saith also in another psalm, Thou shalt not suffer thine Holy One to see corruption.

36 For Da'vid, after he had served his own generation by the will of God, fell on sleep, and was laid unto his fathers, and saw corruption:

37 But he, whom God raised again, saw no corruption.

38 ¶ Be it known unto you therefore, men and brethren, that through this man is preached unto you the forgiveness of sins:

39 And by him all that believe are justified from all things, from which ye could not be justified by the law of Mo'ses.

40 Beware therefore, lest that come upon you, which is spoken of in the prophets;

41 Behold, ye despisers, and wonder, and perish: for I work a work in your days, a work

which ye shall in no wise believe, though a man declare it unto you.

42 And when the Jews were gone out of the synagogue, the Gentiles besought that these words might be preached to them the next sabbath.

43 Now when the congregation was broken up, many of the Jews and religious proselytes followed Paul and Bar'na-bas: who, speaking to them, persuaded them to continue in the grace of God.

44 ¶ And the next sabbath day came almost the whole city together to hear the word of God.

45 But when the Jews saw the multitudes, they were filled with envy, and spake against those things which were spoken by Paul, contradicting and blaspheming.

46 Then Paul and Bar'na-bas waxed bold, and said, It was necessary that the word of God should first have been spoken to you: but seeing ye put it from you, and judge yourselves unworthy of everlasting life, lo, we turn to the Gentiles.

47 For so hath the Lord commanded us, *saying*, I have set thee to be a light of the Gentiles, that thou shouldest be for salvation unto the ends of the earth.

48 And when the Gentiles heard this, they were glad, and glorified the word of the Lord: and as many as were ordained to eternal life believed.

49 And the word of the Lord was published throughout all the region.

50 But the Jews stirred up the devout and honorable women, and the chief men of the city, and raised persecution against Paul and Bar'na-bas, and expelled them out of their coasts.

51 But they shook off the dust of their feet against them, and came unto I-co'ni-um.

52 And the disciples were filled with joy, and with the Ho'ly Ghost.

14 And it came to pass in I-co'ni-um, that they went both together into the synagogue of the Jews, and so spake, that a great multitude both of the Jews and also of the Greeks believed.

2 But the unbelieving Jews stirred up the Gentiles, and made their minds evil affected against the brethren.

3 Long time therefore abode they speaking boldly in the Lord, which gave testimony unto the word of his grace, and granted signs and wonders to be done by their hands.

4 But the multitude of the city was divided: and part held with the Jews, and part with the apostles.

5 And when there was an assault made both of the Gentiles, and also of the Jews with their rulers, to use *them* despitefully, and to stone them,

6 They were aware of *it*, and fled unto Lys'tra and Der'be, cities of Lyc-a-o'ni-a, and unto the region that lieth round about:

7 And there they preached the gospel.

8 ¶ And there sat a certain man at Lys'tra, impotent in his feet, being a cripple from his mother's womb, who never had walked:

9 The same heard Paul speak: who steadfastly beholding him, and perceiving that he had faith to be healed,

10 Said with a loud voice, Stand upright on thy feet. And he leaped and walked.

11 And when the people saw what Paul had done, they lifted up their voices, saying in the speech of Lyc-a-o'ni-a, The gods are come down to us in the likeness of men.

12 And they called Bar'na-bas, Ju'pi-ter; and Paul, Mer-cu'ri-us, because he was the chief speaker.

13 Then the priest of Ju'pi-ter, which was before their city, brought oxen and garlands unto the gates, and would have done sacrifice with the people.

14 Which when the apostles, Bar'na-bas and Paul, heard of, they rent their clothes, and ran in among the people, crying out,

15 And saying, Sirs, why do ye these things? We also are men of like passions with you, and preach unto you that ye should turn from these vanities unto the living God, which made heaven, and earth, and the sea, and all things that are therein:

16 Who in times past suffered all nations to walk in their own ways.

17 Nevertheless he left not himself without witness, in that he did good, and gave us rain from heaven, and fruitful seasons, filling our hearts with food and gladness.

18 And with these sayings scarce restrained they the people, that they had not done sacrifice unto them.

19 ¶ And there came thither certain Jews from An'ti-och and I-co'ni-um, who persuaded the people, and, having stoned Paul, drew him out of the city, supposing he had been dead.

20 Howbeit, as the disciples stood round about him, he rose up, and came into the city: and the next day he departed with Bar'na-bas to Der'be.

21 And when they had preached the gospel to that city, and had taught many, they returned again to Lys'tra, and to I-co'ni-um, and An'ti-och,

22 Confirming the souls of the disciples, and exhorting them to continue in the faith, and that we must through much tribulation enter into the kingdom of God.

23 And when they had ordained them elders in every church, and had prayed with fasting, they commended them to the Lord, on whom they believed.

24 And after they had passed throughout Pi-sid'i-a, they came to Pam-phyl'i-a.

25 And when they had preached the word in Per'ga, they went down into At-ta'li-a:

26 And thence sailed to An'ti-och, from whence they had

been recommended to the grace of God for the work which they fulfilled.

27 And when they were come, and had gathered the church together, they rehearsed all that God had done with them, and how he had opened the door of faith unto the Gen´tiles.

28 And there they abode long time with the disciples.

15 And certain men which came down from Ju-dæ´a taught the brethren, *and said,* Except ye be circumcised after the manner of Mo´ses, ye cannot be saved.

2 When therefore Paul and Bar´na-bas had no small dissension and disputation with them, they determined that Paul and Bar´na-bas, and certain other of them, should go up to Je-ru´sa-lem unto the apostles and elders about this question.

3 And being brought on their way by the church, they passed through Phœ-ni´ci-a and Sa-ma´ri-a, declaring the conversion of the Gen´tiles: and they caused great joy unto all the brethren.

4 And when they were come to Je-ru´sa-lem, they were received of the church, and *of* the apostles and elders, and they declared all things that God had done with them.

5 But there rose up certain of the sect of the Phar´i-sees which believed, saying, That it was needful to circumcise them, and to command *them* to keep the law of Mo´ses.

6 ¶ And the apostles and elders came together for to consider of this matter.

7 And when there had been much disputing, Pe´ter rose up, and said unto them, Men *and* brethren, ye know how that a good while ago God made choice among us, that the Gen´tiles by my mouth should hear the word of the gospel, and believe.

8 And God, which knoweth the hearts, bare them witness, giving them the Ho´ly Ghost, even as *he did* unto us;

9 And put no difference between us and them, purifying their hearts by faith.

10 Now therefore why tempt ye God, to put a yoke upon the neck of the disciples, which neither our fathers nor we were able to bear?

11 But we believe that through the grace of the Lord Je´sus Christ we shall be saved, even as they.

12 ¶ Then all the multitude kept silence, and gave audience to Bar´na-bas and Paul, declaring what miracles and wonders God had wrought among the Gen´tiles by them.

13 ¶ And after they had held their peace, James answered, saying, Men *and* brethren, hearken unto me:

14 Sim´e-on hath declared how God at the first did visit the Gen´tiles, to take out of them a people for his name.

15 And to this agree the words of the prophets; as it is written,

16 After this I will return, and will build again the tabernacle

of Da'vid, which is fallen down; and I will build again the ruins thereof, and I will set it up:

17 That the residue of men might seek after the Lord, and all the Gen'tiles, upon whom my name is called, saith the Lord, who doeth all these things.

18 Known unto God are all his works from the beginning of the world.

19 Wherefore my sentence is, that we trouble not them, which from among the Gen'tiles are turned to God:

20 But that we write unto them, that they abstain from pollutions of idols, and *from* fornication, and *from* things strangled, and *from* blood.

21 For Mo'ses of old time hath in every city them that preach him, being read in the synagogues every sabbath day.

22 Then pleased it the apostles and elders, with the whole church, to send chosen men of their own company to An'ti-och with Paul and Bar'na-bas; *namely*, Ju'das surnamed Bar'sabas, and Si'las, chief men among the brethren:

23 And they wrote *letters* by them after this manner; The apostles and elders and brethren *send* greeting unto the brethren which are of the Gen'tiles in An'ti-och and Syr'i-a and Ci-li'ci-a:

24 Forasmuch as we have heard, that certain which went out from us have troubled you with words, subverting your souls, saying, Ye must be circumcised, and keep the law: to

whom we gave no *such* commandment:

25 It seemed good unto us, being assembled with one accord, to send chosen men unto you with our beloved Bar'na-bas and Paul,

26 Men that have hazarded their lives for the name of our Lord Je'sus Christ.

27 We have sent therefore Ju'das and Si'las, who shall also tell *you* the same things by mouth.

28 For it seemed good to the Ho'ly Ghost, and to us, to lay upon you no greater burden than these necessary things;

29 That ye abstain from meats offered to idols, and from blood, and from things strangled, and from fornication: from which if ye keep yourselves, ye shall do well. Fare ye well.

30 So when they were dismissed, they came to An'ti-och: and when they had gathered the multitude together, they delivered the epistle:

31 *Which* when they had read, they rejoiced for the consolation.

32 And Ju'das and Si'las, being prophets also themselves, exhorted the brethren with many words, and confirmed *them*.

33 And after they had tarried *there* a space, they were let go in peace from the brethren unto the apostles.

34 Notwithstanding it pleased Si'las to abide there still.

35 Paul also and Bar'na-bas continued in An'ti-och, teaching and preaching the word of the Lord, with many others also.

36 ¶ And some days after Paul said unto Bar'na-bas, Let us go again and visit our brethren in every city where we have preached the word of the Lord, *and see* how they do.

37 And Bar'na-bas determined to take with them John, whose surname was Mark.

38 But Paul thought not good to take with them, who departed from them from Pam-phyl'i-a, and went not with them to the work.

39 And the contention was so sharp between them, that they departed asunder the one from the other: and so Bar'na-bas took Mark, and sailed unto Cy'prus;

40 And Paul chose Si'las, and departed, being recommended by the brethren unto the grace of God.

41 And he went through Syr'i-a and Ci-li'ci-a, confirming the churches.

16 Then came he to Der'be and Lys'tra: and, behold, a certain disciple was there, named Ti-mo'the-us, the son of a certain woman, which was a Jew'ess, and believed; but his father *was* a Greek:

2 Which was well reported of by the brethren that were at Lys'tra and I-co'ni-um.

3 Him would Paul have to go forth with him; and took and circumcised him because of the Jews which were in those quarters: for they knew all that his father was a Greek.

4 And as they went through the cities, they delivered them the decrees for to keep, that were ordained of the apostles and elders which were at Je-ru'sa-lem.

5 And so were the churches established in the faith, and increased in number daily.

6 Now when they had gone throughout Phryg'i-a and the region of Ga-la'ti-a, and were forbidden of the Ho'ly Ghost to preach the word in A'sia,

7 After they were come to Mys'i-a, they assayed to go into Bi-thyn'i-a: but the Spirit suffered them not.

8 And they passing by Mys'i-a came down to Tro'as.

9 And a vision appeared to Paul in the night; There stood a man of Mac-e-do'ni-a, and prayed him, saying, Come over into Mac-e-do'ni-a, and help us.

10 And after he had seen the vision, immediately we endeavored to go into Mac-e-do'ni-a, assuredly gathering that the Lord had called us for to preach the gospel unto them.

11 Therefore loosing from Tro'-as, we came with a straight course to Sam-o-thra'cia, and the next *day* to Ne-ap'o-lis;

12 And from thence to Phi-lip'pi, which is the chief city of that part of Mac-e-do'ni-a, *and* a colony: and we were in that city abiding certain days.

13 And on the sabbath we went out of the city by a river side, where prayer was wont to be made; and we sat down, and spake unto the women which resorted *thither*.

14 ¶ And a certain woman named Lyd'i-a, a seller of purple, of the city of Thy-a-ti'ra, which

worshiped God, heard us: whose heart the Lord opened, that she attended unto the things which were spoken of Paul.

15 And when she was baptized, and her household, she besought us, saying, If ye have judged me to be faithful to the Lord, come into my house, and abide there. And she constrained us.

16 ¶ And it came to pass, as we went to prayer, a certain damsel possessed with a spirit of divination met us, which brought her masters much gain by soothsaying:

17 The same followed Paul and us, and cried, saying, These men are the servants of the most high God, which show unto us the way of salvation.

18 And this did she many days. But Paul, being grieved, turned and said to the spirit, I command thee in the name of Je'sus Christ to come out of her. And he came out the same hour.

19 ¶ And when her masters saw that the hope of their gains was gone, they caught Paul and Si'las, and drew them into the marketplace unto the rulers,

20 And brought them to the magistrates, saying, These men, being Jews, do exceedingly trouble our city,

21 And teach customs, which are not lawful for us to receive, neither to observe, being Ro'mans.

22 And the multitude rose up together against them: and the magistrates rent off their clothes, and commanded to beat them.

23 And when they had laid many stripes upon them, they cast them into prison, charging the jailor to keep them safely:

24 Who, having received such a charge, thrust them into the inner prison, and made their feet fast in the stocks.

25 ¶ And at midnight Paul and Si'las prayed, and sang praises unto God: and the prisoners heard them.

26 And suddenly there was a great earthquake, so that the foundations of the prison were shaken: and immediately all the doors were opened, and every-one's bands were loosed.

27 And the keeper of the prison awaking out of his sleep, and seeing the prison doors open, he drew out his sword, and would have killed himself, supposing that the prisoners had been fled.

28 But Paul cried with a loud voice, saying, Do thyself no harm: for we are all here.

29 Then he called for a light, and sprang in, and came trembling, and fell down before Paul and Si'las,

30 And brought them out, and said, Sirs, what must I do to be saved?

31 And they said, Believe on the Lord Je'sus Christ, and thou shalt be saved, and thy house.

32 And they spake unto him the word of the Lord, and to all that were in his house.

33 And he took them the same hour of the night, and washed

their stripes; and was baptized, he and all his, straightway.

34 And when he had brought them into his house, he set meat before them, and rejoiced, believing in God with all his house.

35 And when it was day, the magistrates sent the sergeants, saying, Let those men go.

36 And the keeper of the prison told this saying to Paul, The magistrates have sent to let you go: now therefore depart, and go in peace.

37 But Paul said unto them, They have beaten us openly uncondemned, being Ro′mans, and have cast *us* into prison; and now do they thrust us out privily? nay verily; but let them come themselves and fetch us out.

38 And the sergeants told these words unto the magistrates: and they feared, when they heard that they were Ro′mans.

39 And they came and besought them, and brought *them* out, and desired *them* to depart out of the city.

40 And they went out of the prison, and entered into *the house of* Lyd′i-a: and when they had seen the brethren, they comforted them, and departed.

17 Now when they had passed through Am-phip′o-lis and Ap-ol-lo′ni-a, they came to Thes-sa-lo-ni′ca, where was a synagogue of the Jews:

2 And Paul, as his manner was, went in unto them, and three sabbath days reasoned with them out of the scriptures,

3 Opening and alleging, that Christ must needs have suffered, and risen again from the dead; and that this Je′sus, whom I preach unto you, is Christ.

4 And some of them believed, and consorted with Paul and Si′las; and of the devout Greeks a great multitude, and of the chief women not a few.

5 ¶ But the Jews which believed not, moved with envy, took unto them certain lewd fellows of the baser sort, and gathered a company, and set all the city on an uproar, and assaulted the house of Ja′son, and sought to bring them out to the people.

6 And when they found them not, they drew Ja′son and certain brethren unto the rulers of the city, crying, These that have turned the world upside down are come hither also;

7 Whom Ja′son hath received: and these all do contrary to the decrees of Cæ′sar, saying that there is another king, *one* Je′sus.

8 And they troubled the people and the rulers of the city, when they heard these things.

9 And when they had taken security of Ja′son, and of the other, they let them go.

10 ¶ And the brethren immediately sent away Paul and Si′las by night unto Be-re′a: who coming *thither* went into the synagogue of the Jews.

11 These were more noble than those in Thes-sa-lo-ni′ca, in that they received the word with all readiness of mind, and

searched the scriptures daily, whether those things were so.

12 Therefore many of them believed; also of honorable women which were Greeks, and of men, not a few.

13 But when the Jews of Thes sa-lo-ni'ca had knowledge that the word of God was preached of Paul at Be re'a, they came thither also, and stirred up the people.

14 And then immediately the brethren sent away Paul to go as it were to the sea: but Si'las and Ti mo'the us abode there still.

15 And they that conducted Paul brought him unto Ath'ens: and receiving a commandment unto Si'las and Ti-mo'the-us for to come to him with all speed, they departed.

16 ¶ Now while Paul waited for them at Ath'ens, his spirit was stirred in him, when he saw the city wholly given to idolatry.

17 Therefore disputed he in the synagogue with the Jews, and with the devout persons, and in the market daily with them that met with him.

18 Then certain philosophers of the Ep-i-cu-re'ans, and of the Sto'icks, encountered him. And some said, What will this babbler say? other some, He seemeth to be a setter forth of strange gods: because he preached unto them Je'sus, and the resurrection.

19 And they took him, and brought him unto Ar-e-op'a-gus, saying, May we know what this new doctrine, whereof thou speakest, is?

20 For thou bringest certain strange things to our ears: we would know therefore what these things mean.

21 (For all the Ath-e'ni-ans and strangers which were there spent their time in nothing else, but either to tell, or to hear some new thing.)

22 ¶ Then Paul stood in the midst of Mars' hill, and said, Ye men of Ath'ens, I perceive that in all things ye are too superstitious.

23 For as I passed by, and beheld your devotions, I found an altar with this inscription, TO THE UNKNOWN GOD. Whom therefore ye ignorantly worship, him declare I unto you.

24 God that made the world and all things therein, seeing that he is Lord of heaven and earth, dwelleth not in temples made with hands;

25 Neither is worshipped with men's hands, as though he needed any thing, seeing he giveth to all life, and breath, and all things;

26 And hath made of one blood all nations of men for to dwell on all the face of the earth, and hath determined the times before appointed, and the bounds of their habitation;

27 That they should seek the Lord, if haply they might feel after him, and find him, though he be not far from every one of us:

28 For in him we live, and move, and have our being; as certain also of your own poets have said, For we are also his offspring.

29 Forasmuch then as we are the offspring of God, we ought not to think that the Godhead is like unto gold, or silver, or stone, graven by art and man's device.

30 And the times of this ignorance God winked at; but now commandeth all men everywhere to repent:

31 Because he hath appointed a day, in the which he will judge the world in righteousness by *that* man whom he hath ordained; *whereof* he hath given assurance unto all *men*, in that he hath raised him from the dead.

32 ¶ And when they heard of the resurrection of the dead, some mocked: and others said, We will hear thee again of this *matter*.

33 So Paul departed from among them.

34 Howbeit certain men clave unto him, and believed: among the which *was* Di-o-nys'ius the Ar-e-op'a-gite, and a woman named Dam'a-ris, and others with them.

18 After these things Paul departed from Ath'ens, and came to Cor'inth;

2 And found a certain Jew named A'qui-la, born in Pon'tus, lately come from It'a-ly, with his wife Pris-cil'la; (because that Clau'di-us had commanded all Jews to depart from Rome:) and came unto them.

3 And because he was of the same craft, he abode with them, and wrought: for by their occupation they were tentmakers.

4 And he reasoned in the synagogue every sabbath, and persuaded the Jews and the Greeks.

5 And when Si'las and Ti-mo'the-us were come from Mac-e-do'ni-a, Paul was pressed in the spirit, and testified to the Jews *that* Je'sus *was* Christ.

6 And when they opposed themselves, and blasphemed, he shook *his* raiment, and said unto them, Your blood *be* upon your own heads; I *am* clean: from henceforth I will go unto the Gen'tiles.

7 ¶ And he departed thence, and entered into a certain man's house, named Jus'tus, *one* that worshiped God, whose house joined hard to the synagogue.

8 And Cris'pus, the chief ruler of the synagogue, believed on the Lord with all his house; and many of the Co-rin'thi-ans hearing believed, and were baptized.

9 Then spake the Lord to Paul in the night by a vision, Be not afraid, but speak, and hold not thy peace:

10 For I am with thee, and no man shall set on thee to hurt thee: for I have much people in this city.

11 And he continued *there* a year and six months, teaching the word of God among them.

12 ¶ And when Gal'li-o was the deputy of A-cha'ia, the Jews made insurrection with one accord against Paul, and brought him to the judgment seat,

13 Saying, This *fellow* persuadeth men to worship God contrary to the law.

14 And when Paul was now about to open his mouth, Gal'li-o said unto the Jews, If it were a matter of wrong or wicked lewdness, O ye Jews, reason would that I should bear with you:

15 But if it be a question of words and names, and of your law, look ye to it; for I will be no judge of such matters.

16 And he drove them from the judgment seat.

17 Then all the Greeks took Sos'the-nes, the chief ruler of the synagogue, and beat him before the judgment seat. And Gal'li-o cared for none of those things.

18 ¶ And Paul after this tarried there yet a good while, and then took his leave of the brethren, and sailed thence into Syr'i-a, and with him Pris-cil'la and A'qui-la; having shorn his head in Cen'-chre-a: for he had a vow.

19 And he came to Eph'e-sus, and left them there: but he himself entered into the synagogue, and reasoned with the Jews.

20 When they desired him to tarry longer time with them, he consented not;

21 But bade them farewell, saying, I must by all means keep this feast that cometh in Je-ru'sa-lem: but I will return again unto you, if God will. And he sailed from Eph'e-sus.

22 And when he had landed at Cæs-a-re'a, and gone up, and saluted the church, he went down to An'ti-och.

23 And after he had spent some time there, he departed, and went over all the country of Ga-la'tia and Phryg'i-a in order, strengthening all the disciples.

24 ¶ And a certain Jew named A-pol'los, born at Al-ex-an dri-a, an eloquent man, and mighty in the scriptures, came to Eph'e-sus.

25 This man was instructed in the way of the Lord; and being fervent in the spirit, he spake and taught diligently the things of the Lord, knowing only the baptism of John.

26 And he began to speak boldly in the synagogue: whom when A'qui-la and Pris-cil'la had heard, they took him unto them, and expounded unto him the way of God more perfectly.

27 And when he was disposed to pass into A-cha'ia, the brethren wrote, exhorting the disciples to receive him: who, when he was come, helped them much which had believed through grace:

28 For he mightily convinced the Jews, and that publicly, showing by the scriptures that Je'sus was Christ.

19 And it came to pass, that, while A-pol'los was at Cor'inth, Paul having passed through the upper coasts came to Eph'e-sus: and finding certain disciples,

2 He said unto them, Have ye received the Ho'ly Ghost since ye believed? And they said unto him, We have not so much as heard whether there be any Ho'ly Ghost.

3 And he said unto them, Unto what were ye baptized? And they said, Unto John's baptism.

4 Then said Paul, John verily baptized with the baptism of repentance, saying unto the people, that they should believe on him which should come after him, that is, on Christ Je'sus.

5 When they heard this, they were baptized in the name of the Lord Je'sus.

6 And when Paul had laid his hands upon them, the Ho'ly Ghost came on them; and they spake with tongues, and prophesied.

7 And all the men were about twelve.

8 And he went into the synagogue, and spake boldly for the space of three months, disputing and persuading the things concerning the kingdom of God.

9 But when divers were hardened, and believed not, but spake evil of that way before the multitude, he departed from them, and separated the disciples, disputing daily in the school of one Ty-ran'nus.

10 And this continued by the space of two years; so that all they which dwelt in A'sia heard the word of the Lord Je'sus, both Jews and Greeks.

11 And God wrought special miracles by the hands of Paul:

12 So that from his body were brought unto the sick handkerchiefs or aprons, and the diseases departed from them, and the evil spirits went out of them.

13 ¶ Then certain of the vagabond Jews, exorcists, took upon them to call over them which had evil spirits the name of the Lord Je'sus, saying, We adjure you by Je'sus whom Paul preacheth.

14 And there were seven sons of one Sce'va, a Jew, and chief of the priests, which did so.

15 And the evil spirit answered and said, Je'sus I know, and Paul I know; but who are ye?

16 And the man in whom the evil spirit was leaped on them, and overcame them, and prevailed against them, so that they fled out of that house naked and wounded.

17 And this was known to all the Jews and Greeks also dwelling at Eph'e-sus; and fear fell on them all, and the name of the Lord Je'sus was magnified.

18 And many that believed came, and confessed, and showed their deeds.

19 Many of them also which used curious arts brought their books together, and burned them before all men: and they counted the price of them, and found it fifty thousand pieces of silver.

20 So mightily grew the word of God and prevailed.

21 ¶ After these things were ended, Paul purposed in the spirit, when he had passed through Mac-e-do'ni-a and A-cha'ia, to go to Je-ru'sa-lem, saying, After I have been there, I must also see Rome.

22 So he sent into Mac-e-do'ni-a two of them that ministered

unto him, Ti-mo'the-us and E-ras'tus; but he himself stayed in A'sia for a season.

23 And the same time there arose no small stir about that way.

24 For a certain *man* named De-me'tri-us, a silversmith, which made silver shrines for Di-an'a, brought no small gain unto the craftsmen;

25 Whom he called together with the workmen of like occupation, and said, Sirs, ye know that by this craft we have our wealth.

26 Moreover ye see and hear, that not alone at Eph'e-sus, but almost throughout all A'sia, this Paul hath persuaded and turned away much people, saying that they be no gods, which are made with hands.

27 So that not only this our craft is in danger to be set at nought; but also that the temple of the great goddess Di-an'a should be despised, and her magnificence should be destroyed, whom all A'sia and the world worshipeth.

28 And when they heard *these sayings,* they were full of wrath, and cried out, saying, Great *is* Di-an'a of the E-phe'sians.

29 And the whole city was filled with confusion: and having caught Ga'ius and Ar-is-tar'-chus, men of Mac-e-do'ni-a, Paul's companions in travel, they rushed with one accord into the theatre.

30 And when Paul would have entered in unto the people, the disciples suffered him not.

31 And certain of the chief of A'sia, which were his friends, sent unto him, desiring *him* that he would not adventure himself into the theatre.

32 Some therefore cried one thing, and some another: for the assembly was confused; and the more part knew not wherefore they were come together.

33 And they drew Al-ex-an'der out of the multitude, the Jews putting him forward. And Al-ex-an'der beckoned with the hand, and would have made his defense unto the people.

34 But when they knew that he was a Jew, all with one voice about the space of two hours cried out, Great *is* Di-an'a of the E-phe'sians.

35 And when the townclerk had appeased the people, he said, *Ye* men of Eph'e-sus, what man is there that knoweth not how that the city of the E-phe'-sians is a worshiper of the great goddess Di-an'a, and of the image which fell down from Ju'pi-ter?

36 Seeing then that these things cannot be spoken against, ye ought to be quiet, and to do nothing rashly.

37 For ye have brought hither these men, which are neither robbers of churches, nor yet blasphemers of your goddess.

38 Wherefore if De-me'tri-us, and the craftsmen which are with him, have a matter against any man, the law is open, and there are deputies. let them implead one another.

39 But if ye inquire anything

concerning other matters, it shall be determined in a lawful assembly.

40 For we are in danger to be called in question for this day's uproar, there being no cause whereby we may give an account of this concourse.

41 And when he had thus spoken, he dismissed the assembly.

20 And after the uproar was ceased, Paul called unto *him* the disciples, and embraced *them*, and departed for to go into Mac·e·do'ni·a.

2 And when he had gone over those parts, and had given them much exhortation, he came into Greece,

3 And *there* abode three months. And when the Jews laid wait for him, as he was about to sail into Syr'i·a, he purposed to return through Mac·e·do'ni·a.

4 And there accompanied him into A'sia Sop'a·ter of Be·re'a; and of the Thes·sa·lo'ni·ans, Ar·is·tar'chus and Se·cun'dus; and Ga'ius of Der'be, and Ti·mo'the·us; and of A'sia, Tych'i·cus and Troph'i·mus.

5 These going before tarried for us at Tro'as.

6 And we sailed away from Phi·lip'pi after the days of unleavened bread, and came unto them to Tro'as in five days; where we abode seven days.

7 And upon the first *day* of the week, when the disciples came together to break bread, Paul preached unto them, ready to depart on the morrow; and continued his speech until midnight.

8 And there were many lights in the upper chamber, where they were gathered together.

9 And there sat in a window a certain young man named Eu'ty·chus, being fallen into a deep sleep: and as Paul was long preaching, he sunk down with sleep, and fell down from the third loft, and was taken up dead.

10 And Paul went down, and fell on him, and embracing *him* said, Trouble not yourselves; for his life is in him.

11 When he therefore was come up again, and had broken bread, and eaten, and talked a long while, even till break of day, so he departed.

12 And they brought the young man alive, and were not a little comforted.

13 ¶ And we went before to ship, and sailed unto As'sos, there intending to take in Paul: for so had he appointed, minding himself to go afoot.

14 And when he met with us at As'sos, we took him in, and came to Mit·y·le'ne.

15 And we sailed thence, and came the next *day* over against Chi'os; and the next *day* we arrived at Sa'mos, and tarried at Tro·gyl'li·um; and the next *day* we came to Mi·le'tus.

16 For Paul had determined to sail by Eph'e·sus, because he would not spend the time in A'sia: for he hasted, if it were possible for him, to be at Je·ru'sa·lem the day of Pen'te·cost.

17 ¶ And from Mi-le'tus he sent to Eph'e-sus, and called the elders of the church.

18 And when they were come to him, he said unto them, Ye know, from the first day that I came into A'sia, after what manner I have been with you at all seasons,

19 Serving the Lord with all humility of mind, and with many tears, and temptations, which befell me by the lying in wait of the Jews:

20 And how I kept back nothing that was profitable unto you, but have showed you, and have taught you publicly, and from house to house,

21 Testifying both to the Jews, and also to the Greeks, repentance toward God, and faith toward our Lord Je'sus Christ.

22 And now, behold, I go bound in the spirit unto Je-ru'salem, not knowing the things that shall befall me there:

23 Save that the Ho'ly Ghost witnesseth in every city, saying that bonds and afflictions abide me.

24 But none of these things move me, neither count I my life dear unto myself, so that I might finish my course with joy, and the ministry, which I have received of the Lord Je'sus, to testify the gospel of the grace of God.

25 And now, behold, I know that ye all, among whom I have gone preaching the kingdom of God, shall see my face no more.

26 Wherefore I take you to record this day, that I am pure from the blood of all men

27 For I have not shunned to declare unto you all the counsel of God.

28 ¶ Take heed therefore unto yourselves, and to all the flock, over the which the Ho'ly Ghost hath made you overseers, to feed the church of God, which he hath purchased with his own blood.

29 For I know this, that after my departing shall grievous wolves enter in among you, not sparing the flock.

30 Also of your own selves shall men arise, speaking perverse things, to draw away disciples after them.

31 Therefore watch, and remember, that by the space of three years I ceased not to warn everyone night and day with tears.

32 And now, brethren, I commend you to God, and to the word of his grace, which is able to build you up, and to give you an inheritance among all them which are sanctified.

33 I have coveted no man's silver, or gold, or apparel.

34 Yea, ye yourselves know, that these hands have ministered unto my necessities, and to them that were with me.

35 I have showed you all things, how that so laboring ye ought to support the weak, and to remember the words of the Lord Je'sus, how he said, It is more blessed to give than to receive.

36 ¶ And when he had thus

spoken, he kneeled down, and prayed with them all.

37 And they all wept sore, and fell on Paul's neck, and kissed him,

38 Sorrowing most of all for the words which he spake, that they should see his face no more. And they accompanied him unto the ship.

21 And it came to pass, that after we were gotten from them, and had launched, we came with a straight course unto Co'os, and the day following unto Rhodes, and from thence unto Pat'a-ra:

2 And finding a ship sailing over unto Phœ-ni'cia, we went aboard, and set forth.

3 Now when we had discovered Cy'prus, we left it on the left hand, and sailed into Syr'i-a, and landed at Tyre: for there the ship was to unlade her burden.

4 And finding disciples, we tarried there seven days: who said to Paul through the Spirit, that he should not go up to Je-ru'sa-lem.

5 And when we had accomplished those days, we departed and went our way; and they all brought us on our way, with wives and children, till we were out of the city: and we kneeled down on the shore, and prayed.

6 And when we had taken our leave one of another, we took ship; and they returned home again.

7 And when we had finished our course from Tyre, we came to Ptol-e-ma'is, and saluted the brethren, and abode with them one day.

8 And the next day we that were of Paul's company departed, and came unto Cæs-a-re'a: and we entered into the house of Phil'ip the evangelist, which was one of the seven; and abode with him.

9 And the same man had four daughters, virgins, which did prophesy.

10 And as we tarried there many days, there came down from Ju-dæ'a a certain prophet, named Ag'a-bus.

11 And when he was come unto us, he took Paul's girdle, and bound his own hands and feet, and said, Thus saith the Ho'ly Ghost, So shall the Jews at Je-ru'sa-lem bind the man that owneth this girdle, and shall deliver him into the hands of the Gen'tiles.

12 And when we heard these things, both we, and they of that place, besought him not to go up to Je-ru'sa-lem.

13 Then Paul answered, What mean ye to weep and to break mine heart? for I am ready not to be bound only, but also to die at Je-ru'sa-lem for the name of the Lord Je'sus.

14 And when he would not be persuaded, we ceased, saying, The will of the Lord be done.

15 And after those days we took up our carriages, and went up to Je-ru'sa-lem.

16 There went with us also certain of the disciples of Cæs-a-re'a, and brought with them one Mna'son of Cy'prus, an old

disciple, with whom we should lodge

17 And when we were come to Je·ru'sa·lem, the brethren received us gladly.

18 And the *day* following Paul went in with us unto James; and all the elders were present.

19 And when he had saluted them, he declared particularly what things God had wrought among the Gen'tiles by his ministry.

20 And when they heard *it*, they glorified the Lord, and said unto him, Thou seest, brother, how many thousands of Jews there are which believe; and they are all zealous of the law:

21 And they are informed of thee, that thou teachest all the Jews which are among the Gen'tiles to forsake Mo'ses, saying that they ought not to circumcise *their* children, neither to walk after the customs.

22 What is it therefore? the multitude must needs come together: for they will hear that thou art come.

23 Do therefore this that we say to thee: We have four men which have a vow on them;

24 Them take, and purify thyself with them, and be at charges with them, that they may shave *their* heads: and all may know that those things, whereof they were informed concerning thee, are nothing; but *that* thou thyself also walkest orderly, and keepest the law.

25 As touching the Gen'tiles which believe, we have written *and* concluded that they ob-serve no such thing, save only that they keep themselves from *things* offered to idols, and from blood, and from strangled, and from fornication.

26 Then Paul took the men, and the next day purifying himself with them entered into the temple, to signify the accomplishment of the days of purification, until that an offering should be offered for every one of them.

27 And when the seven days were almost ended, the Jews which were of A'sia, when they saw him in the temple, stirred up all the people, and laid hands on him,

28 Crying out, Men of Is'ra·el, help: This is the man, that teacheth all *men* everywhere against the people, and the law, and this place: and further brought Greeks also into the temple, and hath polluted this holy place.

29 (For they had seen before with him in the city Troph'i·mus an E·phe'sian, whom they supposed that Paul had brought into the temple.)

30 And all the city was moved, and the people ran together: and they took Paul, and drew him out of the temple: and forthwith the doors were shut.

31 And as they went about to kill him, tidings came unto the chief captain of the band, that all Je·ru'sa·lem was in an uproar.

32 Who immediately took soldiers and centurions, and ran down unto them: and when

they saw the chief captain and the soldiers, they left beating of Paul.

33 Then the chief captain came near, and took him, and commanded *him* to be bound with two chains; and demanded who he was, and what he had done.

34 And some cried one thing, some another, among the multitude: and when he could not know the certainty for the tumult, he commanded him to be carried into the castle.

35 And when he came upon the stairs, so it was, that he was borne of the soldiers for the violence of the people.

36 For the multitude of the people followed after, crying, Away with him.

37 And as Paul was to be led into the castle, he said unto the chief captain, May I speak unto thee? Who said, Canst thou speak Greek?

38 Art not thou that E·gyp'tian, which before these days madest an uproar, and leddest out into the wilderness four thousand men that were murderers?

39 But Paul said, I am a man *which am* a Jew of Tar'sus, *a city* in Ci·li'cia, a citizen of no mean city: and, I beseech thee, suffer me to speak unto the people.

40 And when he had given him license, Paul stood on the stairs, and beckoned with the hand unto the people. And when there was made a great silence, he spake unto *them* in the He'-brew tongue, saying,

22 Men, brethren, and fathers, hear ye my defense *which I make* now unto you.

2 (And when they heard that he spake in the He'brew tongue to them, they kept the more silence: and he saith,)

3 I am verily a man *which am* a Jew, born in Tar'sus, *a city* in Ci·li'cia, yet brought up in this city at the feet of Ga·ma'li·el, *and* taught according to the perfect manner of the law of the fathers, and was zealous toward God, as ye all are this day.

4 And I persecuted this way unto the death, binding and delivering into prisons both men and women.

5 As also the high priest doth bear me witness, and all the estate of the elders: from whom also I received letters unto the brethren, and went to Da·mas'cus, to bring them which were there bound unto Je·ru'sa·lem, for to be punished.

6 And it came to pass, that, as I made my journey, and was come nigh unto Da·mas'cus about noon, suddenly there shone from heaven a great light round about me.

7 And I fell unto the ground, and heard a voice saying unto me, Saul, Saul, why persecutest thou me?

8 And I answered, Who art thou, Lord? And he said unto me, I am Je'sus of Naz'a·reth, whom thou persecutest.

9 And they that were with me saw indeed the light, and were afraid; but they heard not the voice of him that spake to me.

10 And I said, What shall I do, Lord? And the Lord said unto me, Arise, and go into Da-mas'-cus; and there it shall be told thee of all things which are appointed for thee to do.

11 And when I could not see for the glory of that light, being led by the hand of them that were with me, I came into Da-mas'-cus.

12 And one An-a-ni'-as, a devout man according to the law, having a good report of all the Jews which dwelt there,

13 Came unto me, and stood, and said unto me, Brother Saul, receive thy sight. And the same hour I looked up upon him.

14 And he said, The God of our fathers hath chosen thee, that thou shouldest know his will, and see that Just One, and shouldest hear the voice of his mouth.

15 For thou shalt be his witness unto all men of what thou hast seen and heard.

16 And now why tarriest thou? arise, and be baptized, and wash away thy sins, calling on the name of the Lord.

17 And it came to pass, that, when I was come again to Je-ru'-sa-lem, even while I prayed in the temple, I was in a trance;

18 And saw him saying unto me, Make haste, and get thee quickly out of Je-ru'-sa-lem: for they will not receive thy testimony concerning me.

19 And I said, Lord, they know that I imprisoned and beat in every synagogue them that believed on thee:

20 And when the blood of thy martyr Ste'-phen was shed, I also was standing by, and consenting unto his death, and kept the raiment of them that slew him.

21 And he said unto me, Depart: for I will send thee far hence unto the Gen'-tiles.

22 And they gave him audience unto this word, and then lifted up their voices, and said, Away with such a fellow from the earth: for it is not fit that he should live.

23 And as they cried out, and cast off their clothes, and threw dust into the air,

24 The chief captain commanded him to be brought into the castle, and bade that he should be examined by scourging; that he might know wherefore they cried so against him.

25 And as they bound him with thongs, Paul said unto the centurion that stood by, Is it lawful for you to scourge a man that is a Ro'-man, and uncondemned?

26 When the centurion heard that, he went and told the chief captain, saying, Take heed what thou doest: for this man is a Ro'-man.

27 Then the chief captain came, and said unto him, Tell me, art thou a Ro'-man? He said, Yea.

28 And the chief captain answered, With a great sum obtained I this freedom. And Paul said, But I was free born.

29 Then straightway they departed from him which should have examined him: and the chief captain also was afraid,

after he knew that he was a Ro'-man, and because he had bound him.

30 On the morrow, because he would have known the certainty wherefore he was accused of the Jews, he loosed him from *his* bands, and commanded the chief priests and all their council to appear, and brought Paul down, and set him before them.

23 And Paul, earnestly beholding the council, said, Men *and* brethren, I have lived in all good conscience before God until this day.

2 And the high priest An-a-ni'as commanded them that stood by him to smite him on the mouth.

3 Then said Paul unto him, God shall smite thee, *thou* whited wall: for sittest thou to judge me after the law, and commandest me to be smitten contrary to the law?

4 And they that stood by said, Revilest thou God's high priest?

5 Then said Paul, I wist not, brethren, that he was the high priest: for it is written, Thou shalt not speak evil of the ruler of thy people.

6 But when Paul perceived that the one part were Sad'du-cees, and the other Phar'i-sees, he cried out in the council, Men *and* brethren, I am a Phar'i-see, the son of a Phar'i-see: of the hope and resurrection of the dead I am called in question.

7 And when he had so said, there arose a dissension between the Phar'i-sees and the Sad'du-cees: and the multitude was divided.

8 For the Sad'du-cees say that there is no resurrection, neither angel, nor spirit: but the Phar'i-sees confess both.

9 And there arose a great cry: and the scribes *that were* of the Phar'i-sees' part arose, and strove, saying, We find no evil in this man: but if a spirit or an angel hath spoken to him, let us not fight against God.

10 And when there arose a great dissension, the chief captain, fearing lest Paul should have been pulled in pieces of them, commanded the soldiers to go down, and to take him by force from among them, and to bring *him* into the castle.

11 And the night following the Lord stood by him, and said, Be of good cheer, Paul: for as thou hast testified of me in Je-ru'sa-lem, so must thou bear witness also at Rome.

12 And when it was day, certain of the Jews banded together, and bound themselves under a curse, saying that they would neither eat nor drink till they had killed Paul.

13 And they were more than forty which had made this conspiracy.

14 And they came to the chief priests and elders, and said, We have bound ourselves under a great curse, that we will eat nothing until we have slain Paul.

15 Now therefore ye with the council signify to the chief captain that he bring him down unto you tomorrow, as though ye would inquire something

more perfectly concerning him: and we, or ever he come near, are ready to kill him.

16 And when Paul's sister's son heard of their lying in wait, he went and entered into the castle, and told Paul.

17 Then Paul called one of the centurions unto him, and said, Bring this young man unto the chief captain: for he hath a certain thing to tell him.

18 So he took him, and brought him to the chief captain, and said, Paul the prisoner called me unto him, and prayed me to bring this young man unto thee, who hath something to say unto thee.

19 Then the chief captain took him by the hand, and went with him aside privately, and asked him, What is that thou hast to tell me?

20 And he said, The Jews have agreed to desire thee that thou wouldest bring down Paul tomorrow into the council, as though they would inquire somewhat of him more perfectly.

21 But do not thou yield unto them: for there lie in wait for him of them more than forty men, which have bound themselves with an oath, that they will neither eat nor drink till they have killed him: and now are they ready, looking for a promise from thee.

22 So the chief captain then let the young man depart, and charged him, See thou tell no man that thou hast showed these things to me.

23 And he called unto him two centurions, saying, Make ready two hundred soldiers to go to Cæs-a-re'a, and horsemen threescore and ten, and spearmen two hundred, at the third hour of the night;

24 And provide them beasts, that they may set Paul on, and bring him safe unto Fe'lix the governor.

25 And he wrote a letter after this manner:

26 Clau'di-us Lys'i-as unto the most excellent governor Fe'lix sendeth greeting.

27 This man was taken of the Jews, and should have been killed of them: then came I with an army, and rescued him, having understood that he was a Ro'-man.

28 And when I would have known the cause wherefore they accused him, I brought him forth into their council:

29 Whom I perceived to be accused of questions of their law, but to have nothing laid to his charge worthy of death or of bonds.

30 And when it was told me how that the Jews laid wait for the man, I sent straightway to thee, and gave commandment to his accusers also to say before thee what they had against him. Farewell.

31 Then the soldiers, as it was commanded them, took Paul, and brought him by night to An-tip'a-tris.

32 On the morrow they left the horsemen to go with him, and returned to the castle:

33 Who, when they came to

Cæs·a·re′a, and delivered the epistle to the governor, presented Paul also before him.

34 And when the governor had read the letter, he asked of what province he was. And when he understood that he was of Ci·li′ci·a;

35 I will hear thee, said he, when thine accusers are also come. And he commanded him to be kept in Her′od's judgment hall.

24 And after five days An·a·ni′as the high priest descended with the elders, and with a certain orator named Ter·tul′lus, who informed the governor against Paul.

2 And when he was called forth, Ter·tul′lus began to accuse him, saying, Seeing that by thee we enjoy great quietness, and that very worthy deeds are done unto this nation by thy providence,

3 We accept it always, and in all places, most noble Fe′lix, with all thankfulness.

4 Notwithstanding, that I be not further tedious unto thee, I pray thee that thou wouldest hear us of thy clemency a few words.

5 For we have found this man a pestilent fellow, and a mover of sedition among all the Jews throughout the world, and a ringleader of the sect of the Naz′a·renes:

6 Who also hath gone about to profane the temple: whom we took, and would have judged according to our law.

7 But the chief captain Lys′ias came upon us, and with great violence took him away out of our hands,

8 Commanding his accusers to come unto thee: by examining of whom thyself mayest take knowledge of all these things, whereof we accuse him.

9 And the Jews also assented, saying that these things were so.

10 Then Paul, after that the governor had beckoned unto him to speak, answered, Forasmuch as I know that thou hast been of many years a judge unto this nation, I do the more cheerfully answer for myself:

11 Because that thou mayest understand, that there are yet but twelve days since I went up to Je·ru′sa·lem for to worship.

12 And they neither found me in the temple disputing with any man, neither raising up the people, neither in the synagogues, nor in the city:

13 Neither can they prove the things whereof they now accuse me.

14 But this I confess unto thee, that after the way which they call heresy, so worship I the God of my fathers, believing all things which are written in the law and in the prophets:

15 And have hope toward God, which they themselves also allow, that there shall be a resurrection of the dead, both of the just and unjust.

16 And herein do I exercise myself, to have always a conscience void of offense toward God, and toward men.

17 Now after many years I

came to bring alms to my nation, and offerings.

18 Whereupon certain Jews from A'sia found me purified in the temple, neither with multitude, nor with tumult.

19 Who ought to have been here before thee, and object, if they had aught against me.

20 Or else let these same *here* say, if they have found any evildoing in me, while I stood before the council,

21 Except it be for this one voice, that I cried standing among them, Touching the resurrection of the dead I am called in question by you this day.

22 And when Fe'lix heard these things, having more perfect knowledge of *that* way, he deferred them, and said, When Lys'i-as the chief captain shall come down, I will know the uttermost of your matter.

23 And he commanded a centurion to keep Paul, and to let *him* have liberty, and that he should forbid none of his acquaintance to minister or come unto him.

24 And after certain days, when Fe'lix came with his wife Dru-sil'la, which was a Jew'ess, he sent for Paul, and heard him concerning the faith in Christ.

25 And as he reasoned of righteousness, temperance, and judgment to come, Fe'lix trembled, and answered, Go thy way for this time; when I have a convenient season, I will call for thee.

26 He hoped also that money should have been given him of Paul, that he might loose him: wherefore he sent for him the

oftener, and communed with him

27 But after two years Por'ci-us Fes'tus came into Fe'lix' room: and Fe'lix, willing to show the Jews a pleasure, left Paul bound.

25

Now when Fes'tus was come into the province, after three days he ascended from Cæs-a-re'a to Je-ru'sa-lem.

2 Then the high priest and the chief of the Jews informed him against Paul, and besought him,

3 And desired favor against him, that he would send for him to Je-ru'sa-lem, laying wait in the way to kill him.

4 But Fes'tus answered, that Paul should be kept at Cæs-a-re'a, and that he himself would depart shortly *thither*.

5 Let them therefore, said he, which among you are able, go down with *me*, and accuse this man, if there be any wickedness in him.

6 And when he had tarried among them more than ten days, he went down unto Cæs-a-re'a; and the next day sitting on the judgment seat commanded Paul to be brought.

7 And when he was come, the Jews which came down from Je-ru'sa-lem stood round about, and laid many and grievous complaints against Paul, which they could not prove.

8 While he answered for himself, Neither against the law of the Jews, neither against the temple, nor yet against Cae'sar, have I offended anything at all.

9 But Fes'tus, willing to do the Jews a pleasure, answered Paul,

and said, Wilt thou go up to Je-ru'sa-lem, and there be judged of these things before me?

10 Then said Paul, I stand at Cæ'sar's judgment seat, where I ought to be judged: to the Jews have I done no wrong, as thou very well knowest.

11 For if I be an offender, or have committed anything worthy of death, I refuse not to die: but if there be none of these things whereof these accuse me, no man may deliver me unto them. I appeal unto Cæ'sar.

12 Then Fes'tus, when he had conferred with the council, answered, Hast thou appealed unto Cæ'sar? unto Cæ'sar shalt thou go.

13 And after certain days king A-grip'pa and Ber-ni'ce came unto Cæs-a-re'a to salute Fes'tus.

14 And when they had been there many days, Fes'tus declared Paul's cause unto the king, saying, There is a certain man left in bonds by Fe'lix:

15 About whom, when I was at Je-ru'sa-lem, the chief priests and the elders of the Jews informed me, desiring to have judgment against him.

16 To whom I answered, It is not the manner of the Ro'mans to deliver any man to die, before that he which is accused have the accusers face to face, and have license to answer for himself concerning the crime laid against him.

17 Therefore, when they were come thither, without any delay

on the morrow I sat on the judgment seat, and commanded the man to be brought forth.

18 Against whom when the accusers stood up, they brought none accusation of such things as I supposed:

19 But had certain questions against him of their own superstition, and of one Je'sus, which was dead, whom Paul affirmed to be alive.

20 And because I doubted of such manner of questions, I asked him whether he would go to Je-ru'sa-lem, and there be judged of these matters.

21 But when Paul had appealed to be reserved unto the hearing of Au-gus'tus, I commanded him to be kept till I might send him to Cæ'sar.

22 Then A-grip'pa said unto Fes'tus, I would also hear the man myself. Tomorrow, said he, thou shalt hear him.

23 And on the morrow, when A-grip'pa was come, and Ber-ni'ce, with great pomp, and was entered into the place of hearing, with the chief captains, and principal men of the city, at Fes'tus' commandment Paul was brought forth.

24 And Fes'tus said, King A-grip'pa, and all men which are here present with us, ye see this man, about whom all the multitude of the Jews have dealt with me, both at Je-ru'sa-lem, and also here, crying that he ought not to live any longer.

25 But when I found that he had committed nothing worthy of death, and that he himself

hath appealed to Au·gus'tus, I have determined to send him.

26 Of whom I have no certain thing to write unto my lord. Wherefore I have brought him forth before you, and specially before thee, O king A·grip'pa, that, after examination had, I might have somewhat to write.

27 For it seemeth to be unreasonable to send a prisoner, and not withal to signify the crimes *laid* against him.

26 Then A·grip'pa said unto Paul, Thou art permitted to speak for thyself. Then Paul stretched forth the hand, and answered for himself:

2 I think myself happy, king A·grip'pa, because I shall answer for myself this day before thee touching all the things whereof I am accused of the Jews:

3 Especially *because I know* thee to be expert in all customs and questions which are among the Jews: wherefore I beseech thee to hear me patiently.

4 My manner of life from my youth, which was at the first among mine own nation at Je·ru'sa·lem, know all the Jews;

5 Which knew me from the beginning, if they would testify, that after the most straitest sect of our religion I lived a Phar'i·see.

6 And now I stand and am judged for the hope of the promise made of God unto our fathers:

7 Unto which *promise* our twelve tribes, instantly serving God day and night, hope to come. For which hope's sake, king A·grip'pa, I am accused of the Jews.

8 Why should it be thought a thing incredible with you, that God should raise the dead?

9 I verily thought with myself, that I ought to do many things contrary to the name of Je'sus of Naz'a·reth.

10 Which thing I also did in Je·ru'sa·lem: and many of the saints did I shut up in prison, having received authority from the chief priests; and when they were put to death, I gave my voice against *them*.

11 And I punished them oft in every synagogue, and compelled *them* to blaspheme; and being exceedingly mad against them, I persecuted *them* even unto strange cities.

12 Whereupon as I went to Da·mas'cus with authority and commission from the chief priests,

13 At midday, O king, I saw in the way a light from heaven, above the brightness of the sun, shining round about me and them which journeyed with me.

14 And when we were all fallen to the earth, I heard a voice speaking unto me, and saying in the He'brew tongue, Saul, Saul, why persecutest thou me? *It is* hard for thee to kick against the pricks.

15 And I said, Who art thou, Lord? And he said, I am Je'sus whom thou persecutest.

16 But rise, and stand upon thy feet: for I have appeared unto thee for this purpose, to make thee a minister and a witness

both of these things which thou hast seen, and of those things in the which I will appear unto thee;

17 Delivering thee from the people, and *from* the Gen'tiles, unto whom now I send thee,

18 To open their eyes, *and* to turn *them* from darkness to light, and *from* the power of Sa'tan unto God, that they may receive forgiveness of sins, and inheritance among them which are sanctified by faith that is in me.

19 Whereupon, O king A-grip'pa, I was not disobedient unto the heavenly vision:

20 But showed first unto them of Da-mas'cus, and at Je-ru'sa-lem, and throughout all the coasts of Ju-dæ'a, and *then* to the Gen'tiles, that they should repent and turn to God, and do works meet for repentance.

21 For these causes the Jews caught me in the temple, and went about to kill *me*.

22 Having therefore obtained help of God, I continue unto this day, witnessing both to small and great, saying none other things than those which the prophets and Mo'ses did say should come:

23 That Christ should suffer, *and* that he should be the first that should rise from the dead, and should show light unto the people, and to the Gen'tiles.

24 And as he thus spake for himself, Fes'tus said with a loud voice, Paul, thou art beside thyself; much learning doth make thee mad.

25 But he said, I am not mad, most noble Fes'tus; but speak forth the words of truth and soberness.

26 For the king knoweth of these things, before whom also I speak freely: for I am persuaded that none of these things are hidden from him; for this thing was not done in a corner.

27 King A-grip'pa, believest thou the prophets? I know that thou believest.

28 Then A-grip'pa said unto Paul, Almost thou persuadest me to be a Chris'tian.

29 And Paul said, I would to God, that not only thou, but also all that hear me this day, were both almost, and altogether such as I am, except these bonds.

30 And when he had thus spoken, the king rose up, and the governor, and Ber-ni'ce, and they that sat with them:

31 And when they were gone aside, they talked between themselves, saying, This man doeth nothing worthy of death or of bonds.

32 Then said A-grip'pa unto Fes'tus, This man might have been set at liberty, if he had not appealed unto Cæ'sar.

27 And when it was determined that we should sail into It'a-ly, they delivered Paul and certain other prisoners unto *one* named Ju'lius, a centurion of Au-gus'tus' band.

2 And entering into a ship of Ad-ra-myt'ti-um, we launched, meaning to sail by the coasts of A'sia; *one* Ar-is-tar'chus, a

Mac-e-do'ni-an of Thes-sa-lo-
ni'ca, being with us.

3 And the next day we touched
at Si'don. And Ju'lius courteously entreated Paul, and gave
him liberty to go unto his
friends to refresh himself.

4 And when we had launched
from thence, we sailed under
Cy'prus, because the winds
were contrary.

5 And when we had sailed over
the sea of Ci li'cia and Pam-phyl'-
i-a, we came to My'ra, a city of
Ly'cia.

6 And there the centurion
found a ship of Al-ex-an'dri-a
sailing into It'a-ly; and he put us
therein.

7 And when we had sailed
slowly many days, and scarce
were come over against Cni'-
dus, the wind not suffering us,
we sailed under Crete, over
against Sal-mo'ne;

8 And, hardly passing it, came
unto a place which is called The
fair havens; nigh whereunto
was the city of La-se'a.

9 Now when much time was
spent, and when sailing was
now dangerous, because the fast
was now already past, Paul ad-
monished them,

10 And said unto them, Sirs, I
perceive that this voyage will be
with hurt and much damage,
not only of the lading and ship,
but also of our lives.

11 Nevertheless the centurion
believed the master and the
owner of the ship, more than
those things which were spoken
by Paul.

12 And because the haven was

not commodious to winter in,
the more part advised to depart
thence also, if by any means
they might attain to Phe-ni'ce,
and there to winter; which is
an haven of Crete, and lieth
toward the south west and
north west.

13 And when the south wind
blew softly, supposing that they
had obtained their purpose, loosing thence, they sailed close by
Crete.

14 But not long after there
arose against it a tempestuous
wind, called Eu-roc'ly-don.

15 And when the ship was
caught, and could not bear up
into the wind, we let her drive.

16 And running under a certain island which is called Clau'-
da, we had much work to come
by the boat:

17 Which when they had taken
up, they used helps, under-
girding the ship; and, fearing
lest they should fall into the
quicksands, struck sail, and so
were driven.

18 And we being exceedingly
tossed with a tempest, the next
day they lightened the ship;

19 And the third day we cast
out with our own hands the
tackling of the ship.

20 And when neither sun nor
stars in many days appeared,
and no small tempest lay on us,
all hope that we should be saved
was then taken away.

21 But after long abstinence
Paul stood forth in the midst of
them, and said, Sirs, ye should
have hearkened unto me, and
not have loosed from Crete, and

to have gained this harm and loss.

22 And now I exhort you to be of good cheer: for there shall be no loss of *any man's* life among you, but of the ship.

23 For there stood by me this night the angel of God, whose I am, and whom I serve,

24 Saying, Fear not, Paul; thou must be brought before Cæ'sar: and, lo, God hath given thee all them that sail with thee.

25 Wherefore, sirs, be of good cheer: for I believe God, that it shall be even as it was told me.

26 Howbeit we must be cast upon a certain island.

27 But when the fourteenth night was come, as we were driven up and down in A'dri-a, about midnight the shipmen deemed that they drew near to some country;

28 And sounded, and found *it* twenty fathoms: and when they had gone a little further, they sounded again, and found *it* fifteen fathoms.

29 Then fearing lest we should have fallen upon rocks, they cast four anchors out of the stern, and wished for the day.

30 And as the shipmen were about to flee out of the ship, when they had let down the boat into the sea, under color as though they would have cast anchors out of the foreship,

31 Paul said to the centurion and to the soldiers, Except these abide in the ship, ye cannot be saved.

32 Then the soldiers cut off the ropes of the boat, and let her fall off.

33 And while the day was coming on, Paul besought *them* all to take meat, saying, This day is the fourteenth day that ye have tarried and continued fasting, having taken nothing.

34 Wherefore I pray you to take *some* meat: for this is for your health: for there shall not an hair fall from the head of any of you.

35 And when he had thus spoken, he took bread, and gave thanks to God in presence of them all: and when he had broken *it*, he began to eat.

36 Then were they all of good cheer, and they also took *some* meat.

37 And we were in all in the ship two hundred threescore and sixteen souls.

38 And when they had eaten enough, they lightened the ship, and cast out the wheat into the sea.

39 And when it was day, they knew not the land: but they discovered a certain creek with a shore, into the which they were minded, if it were possible, to thrust in the ship.

40 And when they had taken up the anchors, they committed *themselves* unto the sea, and loosed the rudder bands, and hoisted up the mainsail to the wind, and made toward shore.

41 And falling into a place where two seas met, they ran the ship aground; and the forepart stuck fast, and remained unmovable, but the

hinder part was broken with the violence of the waves.

42 And the soldiers' counsel was to kill the prisoners, lest any of them should swim out, and escape.

43 But the centurion, willing to save Paul, kept them from *their* purpose; and commanded that they which could swim should cast *themselves* first *into the sea*, and get to land:

44 And the rest, some on boards, and some on *broken pieces* of the ship. And so it came to pass, that they escaped all safe to land.

28 And when they were escaped, then they knew that the island was called Mel'i-ta.

2 And the barbarous people showed us no little kindness: for they kindled a fire, and received us everyone, because of the present rain, and because of the cold.

3 And when Paul had gathered a bundle of sticks, and laid *them* on the fire, there came a viper out of the heat, and fastened on his hand.

4 And when the barbarians saw the *venomous* beast hang on his hand, they said among themselves, No doubt this man is a murderer, whom, though he hath escaped the sea, yet vengeance suffereth not to live.

5 And he shook off the beast into the fire, and felt no harm.

6 Howbeit they looked when he should have swollen, or fallen down dead suddenly: but after they had looked a great while, and saw no harm come to him, they changed their minds, and said that he was a god.

7 In the same quarters were possessions of the chief man of the island, whose name was Pub'li-us; who received us, and lodged us three days courteously.

8 And it came to pass, that the father of Pub'li-us lay sick of a fever and of a bloody flux: to whom Paul entered in, and prayed, and laid his hands on him, and healed him.

9 So when this was done, others also, which had diseases in the island, came, and were healed:

10 Who also honored us with many honors; and when we departed, they laded *us* with such things as were necessary.

11 And after three months we departed in a ship of Al-ex-an'dri-a, which had wintered in the isle, whose sign was Cas'tor and Pol'lux.

12 And landing at Syr'a-cuse, we tarried *there* three days.

13 And from thence we fetched a compass, and came to Rhe'gi-um: and after one day the south wind blew, and we came the next day to Pu-te'o-li:

14 Where we found brethren, and were desired to tarry with them seven days: and so we went toward Rome.

15 And from thence, when the brethren heard of us, they came to meet us as far as Ap'pi-i forum, and The three taverns: whom when Paul saw, he thanked God, and took courage.

16 And when we came to

Rome, the centurion delivered the prisoners to the captain of the guard: but Paul was suffered to dwell by himself with a soldier that kept him.

17 And it came to pass, that after three days Paul called the chief of the Jews together: and when they were come together, he said unto them, Men *and* brethren, though I have committed nothing against the people, or customs of our fathers, yet was I delivered prisoner from Je-ru'sa-lem into the hands of the Ro'mans.

18 Who, when they had examined me, would have let *me* go, because there was no cause of death in me.

19 But when the Jews spake against *it*, I was constrained to appeal unto Cæ'sar; not that I had aught to accuse my nation of.

20 For this cause therefore have I called for you, to see *you*, and to speak with *you*: because that for the hope of Is'ra-el I am bound with this chain.

21 And they said unto him, We neither received letters out of Ju-dæ'a concerning thee, neither any of the brethren that came showed or spake any harm of thee.

22 But we desire to hear of thee what thou thinkest: for as concerning this sect, we know that everywhere it is spoken against.

23 And when they had appointed him a day, there came many to him into *his* lodging; to whom he expounded and testi-fied the kingdom of God, persuading them concerning Je'sus, both out of the law of Mo'ses, and *out of* the prophets, from morning till evening.

24 And some believed the things which were spoken, and some believed not.

25 And when they agreed not among themselves, they departed, after that Paul had spoken one word, Well spake the Ho'ly Ghost by I-sa'iah the prophet unto our fathers,

26 Saying, Go unto this people, and say, Hearing ye shall hear, and shall not understand; and seeing ye shall see, and not perceive:

27 For the heart of this people is waxed gross, and their ears are dull of hearing, and their eyes have they closed; lest they should see with *their* eyes, and hear with *their* ears, and understand with *their* heart, and should be converted, and I should heal them.

28 Be it known therefore unto you, that the salvation of God is sent unto the Gen'tiles, and *that* they will hear it.

29 And when he had said these words, the Jews departed, and had great reasoning among themselves.

30 And Paul dwelt two whole years in his own hired house, and received all that came in unto him,

31 Preaching the kingdom of God, and teaching those things which concern the Lord Je'sus Christ, with all confidence, no man forbidding him.

ROMANS

1 Paul, a servant of Jesus Christ, called to be an apostle, separated unto the gospel of God,

2 (Which he had promised afore by his prophets in the holy scriptures,)

3 Concerning his Son Jesus Christ our Lord, which was made of the seed of David according to the flesh;

4 And declared to be the Son of God with power, according to the spirit of holiness, by the resurrection from the dead:

5 By whom we have received grace and apostleship, for obedience to the faith among all nations, for his name:

6 Among whom are ye also the called of Jesus Christ:

7 To all that be in Rome, beloved of God, called to be saints: Grace to you and peace from God our Father, and the Lord Jesus Christ.

8 First, I thank my God through Jesus Christ for you all, that your faith is spoken of throughout the whole world.

9 For God is my witness, whom I serve with my spirit in the gospel of his Son, that without ceasing I make mention of you always in my prayers;

10 Making request, if by any means now at length I might have a prosperous journey by the will of God to come unto you.

11 For I long to see you, that I may impart unto you some spiritual gift, to the end ye may be established;

12 That is, that I may be comforted together with you by the mutual faith both of you and me.

13 Now I would not have you ignorant, brethren, that oftentimes I purposed to come unto you, (but was let hitherto,) that I might have some fruit among you also, even as among other Gentiles.

14 I am debtor both to the Greeks, and to the Barbarians; both to the wise, and to the unwise.

15 So, as much as in me is, I am ready to preach the gospel to you that are at Rome also.

16 For I am not ashamed of the gospel of Christ: for it is the power of God unto salvation to everyone that believeth; to the Jew first, and also to the Greek.

17 For therein is the righteousness of God revealed from faith to faith: as it is written, The just shall live by faith.

18 For the wrath of God is revealed from heaven against all ungodliness and unrighteousness of men, who hold the truth in unrighteousness;

19 Because that which may be known of God is manifest in them; for God hath showed it unto them.

20 For the invisible things of him from the creation of the world are clearly seen, being

understood by the things that are made, *even* his eternal power and Godhead; so that they are without excuse:

21 Because that, when they knew God, they glorified *him* not as God, neither were thankful; but became vain in their imaginations, and their foolish heart was darkened.

22 Professing themselves to be wise, they became fools,

23 And changed the glory of the uncorruptible God into an image made like to corruptible man, and to birds, and fourfooted beasts, and creeping things.

24 Wherefore God also gave them up to uncleanness through the lusts of their own hearts, to dishonour their own bodies between themselves:

25 Who changed the truth of God into a lie, and worshipped and served the creature more than the Creator, who is blessed for ever. Amen.

26 For this cause God gave them up unto vile affections: for even their women did change the natural use into that which is against nature:

27 And likewise also the men, leaving the natural use of the woman, burned in their lust one toward another; men with men working that which is unseemly, and receiving in themselves that recompense of their error which was meet.

28 And even as they did not like to retain God in *their* knowledge, God gave them over to a reprobate mind, to do those things which are not convenient;

29 Being filled with all unrighteousness, fornication, wickedness, covetousness, maliciousness; full of envy, murder, debate, deceit, malignity; whisperers,

30 Backbiters, haters of God, despiteful, proud, boasters, inventors of evil things, disobedient to parents,

31 Without understanding, covenantbreakers, without natural affection, implacable, unmerciful:

32 Who knowing the judgment of God, that they which commit such things are worthy of death, not only do the same, but have pleasure in them that do them.

2 Therefore thou art inexcusable, O man, whosoever thou art that judgest: for wherein thou judgest another, thou condemnest thyself; for thou that judgest doest the same things.

2 But we are sure that the judgment of God is according to truth against them which commit such things.

3 And thinkest thou this, O man, that judgest them which do such things, and doest the same, that thou shalt escape the judgment of God?

4 Or despisest thou the riches of his goodness and forbearance and longsuffering; not knowing that the goodness of God leadeth thee to repentance?

5 But after thy hardness and impenitent heart treasurest up unto thyself wrath against the

day of wrath and revelation of the righteous judgment of God;

6 Who will render to every man according to his deeds:

7 To them who by patient continuance in well-doing seek for glory and honor and immortality, eternal life:

8 But unto them that are contentious, and do not obey the truth, but obey unrighteousness, indignation and wrath,

9 Tribulation and anguish, upon every soul of man that doeth evil, of the Jew first, and also of the Gen'tile;

10 But glory, honor, and peace, to every man that worketh good, to the Jew first, and also to the Gentile:

11 For there is no respect of persons with God.

12 For as many as have sinned without law shall also perish without law: and as many as have sinned in the law shall be judged by the law;

13 (For not the hearers of the law are just before God, but the doers of the law shall be justified.

14 For when the Gen'tiles, which have not the law, do by nature the things contained in the law, these, having not the law, are a law unto themselves:

15 Which show the work of the law written in their hearts, their conscience also bearing witness, and their thoughts the meanwhile accusing or else excusing one another;)

16 In the day when God shall judge the secrets of men by Je'sus Christ according to my gospel.

17 Behold, thou art called a Jew, and restest in the law, and makest thy boast of God,

18 And knowest his will, and approvest the things that are more excellent, being instructed out of the law;

19 And art confident that thou thyself art a guide of the blind, a light of them which are in darkness,

20 An instructor of the foolish, a teacher of babes, which hast the form of knowledge and of the truth in the law.

21 Thou therefore which teachest another, teachest thou not thyself? thou that preachest a man should not steal, dost thou steal?

22 Thou that sayest a man should not commit adultery, dost thou commit adultery? thou that abhorrest idols, dost thou commit sacrilege?

23 Thou that makest thy boast of the law, through breaking the law dishonourest thou God?

24 For the name of God is blasphemed among the Gen'tiles through you, as it is written.

25 For circumcision verily profiteth, if thou keep the law: but if thou be a breaker of the law, thy circumcision is made uncircumcision.

26 Therefore if the uncircumcision keep the righteousness of the law, shall not his uncircumcision be counted for circumcision?

27 And shall not uncircumcision which is by nature, if it

fulfill the law, judge thee, who by the letter and circumcision dost transgress the law?

28 For he is not a Jew, which is one outwardly; neither *is that* circumcision, which is outward in the flesh:

29 But he *is* a Jew, which is one inwardly; and circumcision *is that* of the heart, in the spirit, *and* not in the letter; whose praise *is* not of men, but of God.

3 What advantage then hath the Jew? or what profit *is there* of circumcision?

2 Much every way: chiefly, because that unto them were committed the oracles of God.

3 For what if some did not believe? shall their unbelief make the faith of God without effect?

4 God forbid: yea, let God be true, but every man a liar; as it is written, That thou mightest be justified in thy sayings, and mightest overcome when thou art judged.

5 But if our unrighteousness commend the righteousness of God, what shall we say? *Is* God unrighteous who taketh vengeance? (I speak as a man)

6 God forbid: for then how shall God judge the world?

7 For if the truth of God hath more abounded through my lie unto his glory; why yet am I also judged as a sinner?

8 And not *rather*, (as we be slanderously reported, and as some affirm that we say,) Let us do evil, that good may come? whose damnation is just.

9 What then? are we better than they? No, in no wise: for we have before proved both Jews and Gen'tiles, that they are all under sin;

10 As it is written, There is none righteous, no, not one:

11 There is none that understandeth, there is none that seeketh after God.

12 They are all gone out of the way, they are together become unprofitable: there is none that doeth good, no, not one.

13 Their throat *is* an open sepulcher; with their tongues they have used deceit; the poison of asps *is* under their lips:

14 Whose mouth *is* full of cursing and bitterness:

15 Their feet *are* swift to shed blood:

16 Destruction and misery *are* in their ways:

17 And the way of peace have they not known:

18 There is no fear of God before their eyes.

19 Now we know that what things soever the law saith, it saith to them who are under the law: that every mouth may be stopped, and all the world may become guilty before God.

20 Therefore by the deeds of the law there shall no flesh be justified in his sight: for by the law *is* the knowledge of sin.

21 But now the righteousness of God without the law is manifested, being witnessed by the law and the prophets;

22 Even the righteousness of God *which* is by faith of Je'sus Christ unto all and upon all

them that believe: for there is no difference:

23 For all have sinned, and come short of the glory of God;

24 Being justified freely by his grace through the redemption that is in Christ Je´sus:

25 Whom God hath set forth to be a propitiation through faith in his blood, to declare his righteousness for the remission of sins that are past, through the forbearance of God;

26 To declare, I say, at this time his righteousness: that he might be just, and the justifier of him which believeth in Je´sus.

27 Where is boasting then? It is excluded. By what law? of works? Nay: but by the law of faith.

28 Therefore we conclude that a man is justified by faith without the deeds of the law.

29 Is he the God of the Jews only? is he not also of the Gen´tiles? Yes, of the Gen´tiles also:

30 Seeing it is one God, which shall justify the circumcision by faith, and uncircumcision through faith.

31 Do we then make void the law through faith? God forbid: yea, we establish the law.

4 What shall we say then that A´bra-ham our father, as pertaining to the flesh, hath found?

2 For if A´bra-ham were justified by works, he hath whereof to glory; but not before God.

3 For what saith the scripture? A´bra-ham believed God, and it was counted unto him for righteousness.

4 Now to him that worketh is the reward not reckoned of grace, but of debt.

5 But to him that worketh not, but believeth on him that justifieth the ungodly, his faith is counted for righteousness.

6 Even as Da´vid also describeth the blessedness of the man, unto whom God imputeth righteousness without works,

7 Saying, Blessed are they whose iniquities are forgiven, and whose sins are covered.

8 Blessed is the man to whom the Lord will not impute sin.

9 Cometh this blessedness then upon the circumcision only, or upon the uncircumcision also? for we say that faith was reckoned to A´bra-ham for righteousness.

10 How was it then reckoned? when he was in circumcision, or in uncircumcision? Not in circumcision, but in uncircumcision.

11 And he received the sign of circumcision, a seal of the righteousness of faith which he had yet being uncircumcised: that he might be the father of all them that believe, though they be not circumcised; that righteousness might be imputed unto them also:

12 And the father of circumcision to them who are not of the circumcision only, but who also walk in the steps of that faith of our father A´bra-ham, which he had being yet uncircumcised.

13 For the promise, that he should be the heir of the world, was not to A´bra-ham, or to his seed, through the law, but

through the righteousness of faith.

14 For if they which are of the law be heirs, faith is made void, and the promise made of none effect:

15 Because the law worketh wrath: for where no law is, there is no transgression.

16 Therefore it is of faith, that it might be by grace; to the end the promise might be sure to all the seed; not to that only which is of the law, but to that also which is of the faith of A'bra-ham; who is the father of us all,

17 (As it is written, I have made thee a father of many nations,) before him whom he believed, even God, who quick-eneth the dead, and calleth those things which be not as though they were.

18 Who against hope believed in hope, that he might become the father of many nations, according to that which was spoken, So shall thy seed be.

19 And being not weak in faith, he considered not his own body now dead, when he was about an hundred years old, neither yet the deadness of Sa'-rah's womb:

20 He staggered not at the promise of God through unbe-lief; but was strong in faith, giving glory to God;

21 And being fully persuaded that, what he had promised, he was able also to perform.

22 And therefore it was im-puted to him for righteousness.

23 Now it was not written for his sake alone, that it was im-puted to him;

24 But for us also, to whom it shall be imputed, if we believe on him that raised up Je'sus our Lord from the dead;

25 Who was delivered for our offenses, and was raised again for our justification.

5 Therefore being justified by faith, we have peace with God through our Lord Je'sus Christ:

2 By whom also we have access by faith into this grace wherein we stand, and rejoice in hope of the glory of God.

3 And not only so, but we glory in tribulations also: knowing that tribulation worketh pa-tience;

4 And patience, experience; and experience, hope:

5 And hope maketh not ashamed; because the love of God is shed abroad in our hearts by the Ho'ly Ghost which is given unto us.

6 For when we were yet with-out strength, in due time Christ died for the ungodly.

7 For scarcely for a righteous man will one die: yet peradven-ture for a good man some would even dare to die.

8 But God commendeth his love toward us, in that, while we were yet sinners, Christ died for us.

9 Much more then, being now justified by his blood, we shall be saved from wrath through him.

10 For if, when we were ene-mies, we were reconciled to

God by the death of his Son, much more, being reconciled, we shall be saved by his life.

11 And not only so, but we also joy in God through our Lord Je'sus Christ, by whom we have now received the atonement.

12 Wherefore, as by one man sin entered into the world, and death by sin; and so death passed upon all men, for that all have sinned:

13 (For until the law sin was in the world: but sin is not imputed when there is no law.

14 Nevertheless death reigned from Ad'am to Mo'ses, even over them that had not sinned after the similitude of Ad'am's transgression, who is the figure of him that was to come.

15 But not as the offense, so also *is* the free gift. For if through the offense of one many be dead, much more the grace of God, and the gift by grace, which is by one man, Je'sus Christ, hath abounded unto many.

16 And not as *it was* by one that sinned, *so is* the gift: for the judgment *was* by one to condemnation, but the free gift *is* of many offenses unto justification.

17 For if by one man's offense death reigned by one; much more they which receive abundance of grace and of the gift of righteousness shall reign in life by one, Je'sus Christ.)

18 Therefore as by the offense of one *judgment came* upon all men to condemnation; even so by the righteousness of one *the free gift came* upon all men unto justification of life.

19 For as by one man's disobedience many were made sinners, so by the obedience of one shall many be made righteous.

20 Moreover the law entered, that the offense might abound. But where sin abounded, grace did much more abound:

21 That as sin hath reigned unto death, even so might grace reign through righteousness unto eternal life by Je'sus Christ our Lord.

6 What shall we say then? Shall we continue in sin, that grace may abound?

2 God forbid. How shall we, that are dead to sin, live any longer therein?

3 Know ye not, that so many of us as were baptized into Je'sus Christ were baptized into his death?

4 Therefore we are buried with him by baptism into death: that like as Christ was raised up from the dead by the glory of the Father, even so we also should walk in newness of life.

5 For if we have been planted together in the likeness of his death, we shall be also *in the likeness of his* resurrection:

6 Knowing this, that our old man is crucified with *him,* that the body of sin might be destroyed, that henceforth we should not serve sin.

7 For he that is dead is freed from sin.

8 Now if we be dead with Christ, we believe that we shall also live with him:

9 Knowing that Christ being raised from the dead dieth no more; death hath no more dominion over him.

10 For in that he died, he died unto sin once: but in that he liveth, he liveth unto God.

11 Likewise reckon ye also yourselves to be dead indeed unto sin, but alive unto God through Je'sus Christ our Lord.

12 Let not sin therefore reign in your mortal body, that ye should obey it in the lusts thereof.

13 Neither yield ye your members *as* instruments of unrighteousness unto sin: but yield yourselves unto God, as those that are alive from the dead, and your members *as* instruments of righteousness unto God.

14 For sin shall not have dominion over you: for ye are not under the law, but under grace.

15 What then? shall we sin, because we are not under the law, but under grace? God forbid.

16 Know ye not, that to whom ye yield yourselves servants to obey, his servants ye are to whom ye obey; whether of sin unto death, or of obedience unto righteousness?

17 But God be thanked, that ye were the servants of sin, but ye have obeyed from the heart that form of doctrine which was delivered you.

18 Being then made free from sin, ye became the servants of righteousness.

19 I speak after the manner of men because of the infirmity of your flesh: for as ye have yielded your members servants to uncleanness and to iniquity unto iniquity; even so now yield your members servants to righteousness unto holiness.

20 For when ye were the servants of sin, ye were free from righteousness.

21 What fruit had ye then in those things whereof ye are now ashamed? for the end of those things *is* death.

22 But now being made free from sin, and become servants to God, ye have your fruit unto holiness, and the end everlasting life.

23 For the wages of sin *is* death; but the gift of God *is* eternal life through Je'sus Christ our Lord.

7 Know ye not, brethren, (for I speak to them that know the law,) how that the law hath dominion over a man as long as he liveth?

2 For the woman which hath an husband is bound by the law to *her* husband so long as he liveth; but if the husband be dead, she is loosed from the law of *her* husband.

3 So then if, while *her* husband liveth, she be married to another man, she shall be called an adulteress: but if her husband be dead, she is free from that law; so that she is no adulteress, though she be married to another man.

4 Wherefore, my brethren, ye also are become dead to the law by the body of Christ; that ye should be married to another,

even to him who is raised from the dead, that we should bring forth fruit unto God.

5 For when we were in the flesh, the motions of sins, which were by the law, did work in our members to bring forth fruit unto death.

6 But now we are delivered from the law, that being dead wherein we were held; that we should serve in newness of spirit, and not *in* the oldness of the letter.

7 What shall we say then? *Is* the law sin? God forbid. Nay, I had not known sin, but by the law: for I had not known lust, except the law had said, Thou shalt not covet.

8 But sin, taking occasion by the commandment, wrought in me all manner of concupiscence. For without the law sin *was* dead.

9 For I was alive without the law once: but when the commandment came, sin revived, and I died.

10 And the commandment, which *was ordained* to life, I found *to be* unto death.

11 For sin, taking occasion by the commandment, deceived me, and by it slew me.

12 Wherefore the law *is* holy, and the commandment holy, and just, and good.

13 Was then that which is good made death unto me? God forbid. But sin, that it might appear sin, working death in me by that which is good; that sin by the commandment might become exceeding sinful.

14 For we know that the law is spiritual: but I am carnal, sold under sin.

15 For that which I do I allow not: for what I would, that do I not; but what I hate, that do I.

16 If then I do that which I would not, I consent unto the law that *it is* good.

17 Now then it is no more I that do it, but sin that dwelleth in me.

18 For I know that in me (that is, in my flesh,) dwelleth no good thing: for to will is present with me; but *how* to perform that which is good I find not.

19 For the good that I would I do not: but the evil which I would not, that I do.

20 Now if I do that I would not, it is no more I that do it, but sin that dwelleth in me.

21 I find then a law, that, when I would do good, evil is present with me.

22 For I delight in the law of God after the inward man:

23 But I see another law in my members, warring against the law of my mind, and bringing me into captivity to the law of sin which is in my members.

24 O wretched man that I am! who shall deliver me from the body of this death?

25 I thank God through Je'sus Christ our Lord. So then with the mind I myself serve the law of God; but with the flesh the law of sin.

8 There *is* therefore now no condemnation to them which are in Christ Je'sus, who walk not after the flesh, but after the Spirit.

2 For the law of the Spirit of life in Christ Je'sus hath made me free from the law of sin and death.

3 For what the law could not do, in that it was weak through the flesh, God sending his own Son in the likeness of sinful flesh, and for sin, condemned sin in the flesh:

4 That the righteousness of the law might be fulfilled in us, who walk not after the flesh, but after the Spirit.

5 For they that are after the flesh do mind the things of the flesh; but they that are after the Spirit the things of the Spirit.

6 For to be carnally minded *is* death; but to be spiritually minded *is* life and peace.

7 Because the carnal mind *is* enmity against God: for it is not subject to the law of God, neither indeed can be.

8 So then they that are in the flesh cannot please God.

9 But ye are not in the flesh, but in the Spirit, if so be that the Spirit of God dwell in you. Now if any man have not the Spirit of Christ, he is none of his.

10 And if Christ *be* in you, the body *is* dead because of sin; but the Spirit *is* life because of righteousness.

11 But if the Spirit of him that raised up Je'sus from the dead dwell in you, he that raised up Christ from the dead shall also quicken your mortal bodies by his Spirit that dwelleth in you.

12 Therefore, brethren, we are debtors, not to the flesh, to live after the flesh.

13 For if ye live after the flesh, ye shall die: but if ye through the Spirit do mortify the deeds of the body, ye shall live.

14 For as many as are led by the Spirit of God, they are the sons of God.

15 For ye have not received the spirit of bondage again to fear; but ye have received the Spirit of adoption, whereby we cry, Ab'ba, Father.

16 The Spirit itself beareth witness with our spirit, that we are the children of God:

17 And if children, then heirs; heirs of God, and joint-heirs with Christ; if so be that we suffer with *him,* that we may be also glorified together.

18 For I reckon that the sufferings of this present time *are* not worthy *to be compared* with the glory which shall be revealed in us.

19 For the earnest expectation of the creature waiteth for the manifestation of the sons of God.

20 For the creature was made subject to vanity, not willingly, but by reason of him who hath subjected *the same* in hope,

21 Because the creature itself also shall be delivered from the bondage of corruption into the glorious liberty of the children of God.

22 For we know that the whole creation groaneth and travaileth in pain together until now.

23 And not only *they,* but ourselves also, which have the

firstfruits of the Spirit, even we ourselves groan within ourselves, waiting for the adoption, to wit, the redemption of our body.

24 For we are saved by hope: but hope that is seen is not hope: for what a man seeth, why doth he yet hope for?

25 But if we hope for that we see not, then do we with patience wait for it.

26 Likewise the Spirit also helpeth our infirmities: for we know not what we should pray for as we ought: but the Spirit itself maketh intercession for us with groanings which cannot be uttered.

27 And he that searcheth the hearts knoweth what is the mind of the Spirit, because he maketh intercession for the saints according to the will of God.

28 And we know that all things work together for good to them that love God, to them who are the called according to his purpose.

29 For whom he did foreknow, he also did predestinate to be conformed to the image of his Son, that he might be the firstborn among many brethren.

30 Moreover whom he did predestinate, them he also called: and whom he called, them he also justified: and whom he justified, them he also glorified.

31 What shall we then say to these things? If God be for us, who can be against us?

32 He that spared not his own Son, but delivered him up for us all, how shall he not with him also freely give us all things?

33 Who shall lay any thing to the charge of God's elect? It is God that justifieth.

34 Who is he that condemneth? It is Christ that died, yea rather, that is risen again, who is even at the right hand of God, who also maketh intercession for us.

35 Who shall separate us from the love of Christ? shall tribulation, or distress, or persecution, or famine, or nakedness, or peril, or sword?

36 As it is written, For thy sake we are killed all the day long; we are accounted as sheep for the slaughter.

37 Nay, in all these things we are more than conquerors through him that loved us.

38 For I am persuaded, that neither death, nor life, nor angels, nor principalities, nor powers, nor things present, nor things to come,

39 Nor height, nor depth, nor any other creature, shall be able to separate us from the love of God, which is in Christ Jesus our Lord.

9 I say the truth in Christ, I lie not, my conscience also bearing me witness in the Holy Ghost,

2 That I have great heaviness and continual sorrow in my heart.

3 For I could wish that myself were accursed from Christ for my brethren, my kinsmen according to the flesh:

4 Who are Is-ra-el-ites; to

whom *pertaineth* the adoption, and the glory, and the covenants, and the giving of the law, and the service *of God*, and the promises;

5 Whose *are* the fathers, and of whom as concerning the flesh Christ *came*, who is over all, God blessed for ever. Amen.

6 Not as though the word of God hath taken none effect. For they are not all Is'ra-el, which are of Is'ra-el:

7 Neither, because they are the seed of A'bra-ham, *are they* all children: but, In I'saac shall thy seed be called.

8 That is, They which are the children of the flesh, these *are* not the children of God: but the children of the promise are counted for the seed.

9 For this *is* the word of promise, At this time will I come, and Sa'rah shall have a son.

10 And not only *this;* but when Re-bec'ca also had conceived by one, *even* by our father I'saac;

11 (For *the children* being not yet born, neither having done any good or evil, that the purpose of God according to election might stand, not of works, but of him that calleth;)

12 It was said unto her, The elder shall serve the younger.

13 As it is written, Ja'cob have I loved, but E'sau have I hated.

14 What shall we say then? *Is there* unrighteousness with God? God forbid.

15 For he saith to Mo'ses, I will have mercy on whom I will have mercy, and I will have

compassion on whom I will have compassion.

16 So then *it is* not of him that willeth, nor of him that runneth, but of God that showeth mercy.

17 For the scripture saith unto Pha'raoh, Even for this same purpose have I raised thee up, that I might show my power in thee, and that my name might be declared throughout all the earth.

18 Therefore hath he mercy on whom he will *have mercy*, and whom he will he hardeneth.

19 Thou wilt say then unto me, Why doth he yet find fault? For who hath resisted his will?

20 Nay but, O man, who art thou that repliest against God? Shall the thing formed say to him that formed *it*, Why hast thou made me thus?

21 Hath not the potter power over the clay, of the same lump to make one vessel unto honor, and another unto dishonor?

22 *What* if God, willing to show *his* wrath, and to make his power known, endured with much longsuffering the vessels of wrath fitted to destruction:

23 And that he might make known the riches of his glory on the vessels of mercy, which he had afore prepared unto glory,

24 Even us, whom he hath called, not of the Jews only, but also of the Gen'tiles?

25 As he saith also in O'see, I will call them my people, which were not my people; and her beloved, which was not beloved.

26 And it shall come to pass, *that* in the place where it was said unto them, Ye *are* not my people; there shall they be called the children of the living God.

27 Esa'ias also crieth concerning Is'ra-el, Though the number of the children of Is'ra-el be as the sand of the sea, a remnant shall be saved:

28 For he will finish the work, and cut *it* short in righteousness: because a short work will the Lord make upon the earth.

29 And as I-sa'iah said before, Except the Lord of Sab'a-oth had left us a seed, we had been as Sod'om, and been made like unto Go-mor'rah.

30 What shall we say then? That the Gen'tiles, which followed not after righteousness, have attained to righteousness, even the righteousness which is of faith.

31 But Is'ra-el, which followed after the law of righteousness, hath not attained to the law of righteousness.

32 Wherefore? Because *they sought it* not by faith, but as it were by the works of the law. For they stumbled at that stumbling stone;

33 As it is written, Behold, I lay in Zi'on a stumblingstone and rock of offense: and whosoever believeth on him shall not be ashamed.

10 Brethren, my heart's desire and prayer to God for Is'ra-el is, that they might be saved.

2 For I bear them record that they have a zeal of God, but not according to knowledge.

3 For they being ignorant of God's righteousness, and going about to establish their own righteousness, have not submitted themselves unto the righteousness of God.

4 For Christ *is* the end of the law for righteousness to every one that believeth.

5 For Mo'ses describeth the righteousness which is of the law, That the man which doeth those things shall live by them.

6 But the righteousness which is of faith speaketh on this wise, Say not in thine heart, Who shall ascend into heaven? (that is, to bring Christ down *from above*:)

7 Or, Who shall descend into the deep? (that is, to bring up Christ again from the dead.)

8 But what saith it? The word is nigh thee, *even* in thy mouth, and in thy heart: that is, the word of faith, which we preach;

9 That if thou shalt confess with thy mouth the Lord Je'sus, and shalt believe in thine heart that God hath raised him from the dead, thou shalt be saved.

10 For with the heart man believeth unto righteousness; and with the mouth confession is made unto salvation.

11 For the scripture saith, Whosoever believeth on him shall not be ashamed.

12 For there is no difference between the Jew and the Greek: for the same Lord over all is rich unto all that call upon him.

13 For whosoever shall call

upon the name of the Lord shall be saved.

14 How then shall they call on him in whom they have not believed? and how shall they believe in him of whom they have not heard? and how shall they hear without a preacher?

15 And how shall they preach, except they be sent? as it is written, How beautiful are the feet of them that preach the gospel of peace, and bring glad tidings of good things!

16 But they have not all obeyed the gospel. For I·sa'iah saith, Lord, who hath believed our report?

17 So then faith *cometh* by hearing, and hearing by the word of God.

18 But I say, Have they not heard? Yes verily, their sound went into all the earth, and their words unto the ends of the world.

19 But I say, Did not Is'ra-el know? First Mo'ses saith, I will provoke you to jealousy by *them that are* no people, *and* by a foolish nation I will anger you.

20 But I·sa'iah is very bold, and saith, I was found of them that sought me not; I was made manifest unto them that asked not after me.

21 But to Is'ra-el he saith, All day long I have stretched forth my hands unto a disobedient and gainsaying people.

11 I say then, Hath God cast away his people? God forbid. For I also am an Is'ra-el-ite, of the seed of A'bra-ham, *of* the tribe of Ben'ja-min.

2 God hath not cast away his people which he foreknew. Wot ye not what the scripture saith of E·li'jah? how he maketh intercession to God against Is'ra-el, saying,

3 Lord, they have killed thy prophets, and digged down thine altars; and I am left alone, and they seek my life.

4 But what saith the answer of God unto him? I have reserved to myself seven thousand men, who have not bowed the knee to *the image of* Ba'al.

5 Even so then at this present time also there is a remnant according to the election of grace.

6 And if by grace, then *is it* no more of works: otherwise grace is no more grace. But if *it be* of works, then is it no more grace: otherwise work is no more work.

7 What then? Is'ra-el hath not obtained that which he seeketh for; but the election hath obtained it, and the rest were blinded

8 (According as it is written, God hath given them the spirit of slumber, eyes that they should not see, and ears that they should not hear;) unto this day.

9 And Da'vid saith, Let their table be made a snare, and a trap, and a stumbling block, and a recompense unto them:

10 Let their eyes be darkened, that they may not see, and bow down their back always.

11 I say then, Have they stumbled that they should fall? God

forbid: but *rather* through their fall salvation *is come* unto the Gen'tiles, for to provoke them to jealousy.

12 Now if the fall of them *be* the riches of the world, and the diminishing of them the riches of the Gen'tiles; how much more their fullness?

13 For I speak to you Gen'tiles, inasmuch as I am the apostle of the Gen'tiles, I magnify mine office:

14 If by any means I may provoke to emulation *them which are* my flesh and might save some of them.

15 For if the casting away of them *be* the reconciling of the world, what *shall* the receiving *of them be,* but life from the dead?

16 For if the firstfruit *be* holy, the lump *is* also *holy:* and if the root *be* holy, so *are* the branches.

17 And if some of the branches be broken off, and thou, being a wild olive tree, wert grafted in among them, and with them partakest of the root and fatness of the olive tree;

18 Boast not against the branches. But if thou boast, thou bearest not the root, but the root thee.

19 Thou wilt say then, The branches were broken off, that I might be grafted in.

20 Well; because of unbelief they were broken off, and thou standest by faith. Be not highminded, but fear:

21 For if God spared not the natural branches, *take heed* lest he also spare not thee.

23 Behold therefore the goodness and severity of God: on them which fell, severity; but toward thee, goodness, if thou continue in *his* goodness: otherwise thou also shalt be cut off.

23 And they also, if they abide not still in unbelief, shall be grafted in: for God is able to graft them in again.

24 For if thou wert cut out of the olive tree which is wild by nature, and wert grafted contrary to nature into a good olive tree: how much more shall these, which be the natural *branches,* be grafted into their own olive tree?

25 For I would not, brethren, that ye should be ignorant of this mystery, lest ye should be wise in your own conceits; that blindness in part is happened to Is'ra-el, until the fullness of the Gen'tiles be come in.

26 And so all Is'ra-el shall be saved: as it is written, There shall come out of Zi'on the Deliverer, and shall turn away ungodliness from Ja'cob:

27 For this *is* my covenant unto them, when I shall take away their sins.

28 As concerning the gospel, *they are* enemies for your sakes: but as touching the election, *they are* beloved for the fathers' sakes.

29 For the gifts and calling of God *are* without repentance.

30 For as ye in times past have not believed God, yet have now

obtained mercy through their unbelief:

31 Even so have these also now not believed, that through your mercy they also may obtain mercy.

32 For God hath concluded them all in unbelief, that he might have mercy upon all.

33 O the depth of the riches both of the wisdom and knowledge of God! how unsearchable *are* his judgments, and his ways past finding out!

34 For who hath known the mind of the Lord? or who hath been his counselor?

35 Or who hath first given to him, and it shall be recompensed unto him again?

36 For of him, and through him, and to him, *are* all things: to whom *be* glory forever. Amen.

12 I beseech you therefore, brethren, by the mercies of God, that ye present your bodies a living sacrifice, holy, acceptable unto God, *which is* your reasonable service.

2 And be not conformed to this world: but be ye transformed by the renewing of your mind, that ye may prove what *is* that good, and acceptable, and perfect, will of God.

3 For I say, through the grace given unto me, to every man that is among you, not to think *of himself* more highly than he ought to think; but to think soberly, according as God hath dealt to every man the measure of faith.

4 For as we have many members in one body, and all members have not the same office:

5 So we, *being* many, are one body in Christ, and everyone members one of another.

6 Having then gifts differing according to the grace that is given to us, whether prophecy, *let us prophesy* according to the proportion of faith;

7 Or ministry, *let us wait on our* ministering: or he that teacheth, on teaching;

8 Or he that exhorteth, on exhortation: he that giveth, *let him do it* with simplicity; he that ruleth, with diligence; he that showeth mercy, with cheerfulness.

9 *Let* love be without dissimulation. Abhor that which is evil; cleave to that which is good.

10 *Be* kindly affectioned one to another with brotherly love; in honor preferring one another;

11 Not slothful in business; fervent in spirit; serving the Lord;

12 Rejoicing in hope; patient in tribulation; continuing instant in prayer;

13 Distributing to the necessity of saints; given to hospitality.

14 Bless them which persecute you: bless, and curse not.

15 Rejoice with them that do rejoice, and weep with them that weep.

16 *Be* of the same mind one toward another. Mind not high things, but condescend to men of low estate. Be not wise in your own conceits.

17 Recompense to no man evil for evil. Provide things honest in the sight of all men.

18 If it be possible, as much as lieth in you, live peaceably with all men.

19 Dearly beloved, avenge not yourselves, but *rather* give place unto wrath: for it is written, Vengeance *is* mine; I will repay, saith the Lord.

20 Therefore if thine enemy hunger, feed him; if he thirst, give him drink: for in so doing thou shalt heap coals of fire on his head.

21 Be not overcome of evil, but overcome evil with good.

13 Let every soul be subject unto the higher powers. For there is no power but of God: the powers that be are ordained of God.

2 Whosoever therefore resisteth the power, resisteth the ordinance of God: and they that resist shall receive to themselves damnation.

3 For rulers are not a terror to good works, but to the evil. Wilt thou then not be afraid of the power? do that which is good, and thou shalt have praise of the same:

4 For he is the minister of God to thee for good. But if thou do that which is evil, be afraid; for he beareth not the sword in vain: for he is the minister of God, a revenger to *execute* wrath upon him that doeth evil.

5 Wherefore ye must needs be subject, not only for wrath, but also for conscience sake.

6 For for this cause pay ye tribute also: for they are God's ministers, attending continually upon this very thing.

7 Render therefore to all their dues: tribute to whom tribute *is due*; custom to whom custom; fear to whom fear; honor to whom honor.

8 Owe no man anything, but to love one another: for he that loveth another hath fulfilled the law.

9 For this, Thou shalt not commit adultery, Thou shalt not kill, Thou shalt not steal, Thou shalt not bear false witness, Thou shalt not covet; and if *there be* any other commandment, it is briefly comprehended in this saying, namely, Thou shalt love thy neighbor as thyself.

10 Love worketh no ill to his neighbor: therefore love *is* the fulfilling of the law.

11 And that, knowing the time, that now *it is* high time to awake out of sleep: for now *is* our salvation nearer than when we believed.

12 The night is far spent, the day is at hand: let us therefore cast off the works of darkness, and let us put on the armor of light.

13 Let us walk honestly, as in the day; not in rioting and drunkenness, not in chambering and wantonness, not in strife and envying.

14 But put ye on the Lord Je'sus Christ, and make not provision for the flesh, to *fulfill* the lusts *thereof*.

14 Him that is weak in the faith receive ye, *but* not to doubtful disputations.

2 For one believeth that he may

eat all things: another, who is weak, eateth herbs.

3 Let not him that eateth despise him that eateth not; and let not him which eateth not judge him that eateth: for God hath received him.

4 Who art thou that judgest another man's servant? to his own master he standeth or falleth. Yea, he shall be held up: for God is able to make him stand.

5 One man esteemeth one day above another: another esteemeth every day alike. Let every man be fully persuaded in his own mind.

6 He that regardeth the day, regardeth it unto the Lord; and he that regardeth not the day, to the Lord he doth not regard it. He that eateth, eateth to the Lord, for he giveth God thanks; and he that eateth not, to the Lord he eateth not, and giveth God thanks.

7 For none of us liveth to himself, and no man dieth to himself.

8 For whether we live, we live unto the Lord; and whether we die, we die unto the Lord: whether we live therefore, or die, we are the Lord's.

9 For to this end Christ both died, and rose, and revived, that he might be Lord both of the dead and living.

10 But why dost thou judge thy brother? or why dost thou set at nought thy brother? for we shall all stand before the judgment seat of Christ.

11 For it is written, As I live, saith the Lord, every knee shall bow to me, and every tongue shall confess to God.

12 So then everyone of us shall give account of himself to God.

13 Let us not therefore judge one another anymore: but judge this rather, that no man put a stumbling block or an occasion to fall in his brother's way.

14 I know, and am persuaded by the Lord Je'sus, that there is nothing unclean of itself: but to him that esteemeth anything to be unclean, to him it is unclean.

15 But if thy brother be grieved with thy meat, now walkest thou not charitably. Destroy not him with thy meat, for whom Christ died.

16 Let not then your good be evil spoken of:

17 For the kingdom of God is not meat and drink; but righteousness, and peace, and joy in the Ho'ly Ghost.

18 For he that in these things serveth Christ is acceptable to God, and approved of men.

19 Let us therefore follow after the things which make for peace, and things wherewith one may edify another.

20 For meat destroy not the work of God. All things indeed are pure; but it is evil for that man who eateth with offense.

21 It is good neither to eat flesh, nor to drink wine, nor anything whereby thy brother stumbleth, or is offended, or is made weak.

22 Hast thou faith? have it to thyself before God. Happy is he

that condemneth not himself in that thing which he alloweth.

23 And he that doubteth is damned if he eat, because *he eateth* not of faith: for whatsoever *is* not of faith is sin.

15 We then that are strong ought to bear the infirmities of the weak, and not to please ourselves.

2 Let everyone of us please *his* neighbor for *his* good to edification.

3 For even Christ pleased not himself; but, as it is written, The reproaches of them that reproached thee fell on me.

4 For whatsoever things were written aforetime were written for our learning, that we through patience and comfort of the scriptures might have hope.

5 Now the God of patience and consolation grant you to be likeminded one toward another according to Christ Je'sus:

6 That ye may with one mind *and* one mouth glorify God, even the Father of our Lord Je'sus Christ.

7 Wherefore receive ye one another, as Christ also received us to the glory of God.

8 Now I say that Je'sus Christ was a minister of the circumcision for the truth of God, to confirm the promises *made* unto the fathers:

9 And that the Gen'tiles might glorify God for *his* mercy; as it is written, For this cause I will confess to thee among the Gen'tiles, and sing unto thy name.

10 And again he saith, Rejoice, ye Gen'tiles, with his people.

11 And again, Praise the Lord, all ye Gen'tiles; and laud him, all ye people.

12 And again, I-sa'iah saith, There shall be a root of Jes'se, and he that shall rise to reign over the Gen'tiles; in him shall the Gen'tiles trust.

13 Now the God of hope fill you with all joy and peace in believing, that ye may abound in hope, through the power of the Ho'ly Ghost.

14 And I myself also am persuaded of you, my brethren, that ye also are full of goodness, filled with all knowledge, able also to admonish one another.

15 Nevertheless, brethren, I have written the more boldly unto you in some sort, as putting you in mind, because of the grace that is given to me of God,

16 That I should be the minister of Je'sus Christ to the Gen'tiles, ministering the gospel of God, that the offering up of the Gen'tiles might be acceptable, being sanctified by the Ho'ly Ghost.

17 I have therefore whereof I may glory through Je'sus Christ in those things which pertain to God.

18 For I will not dare to speak of any of those things which Christ hath not wrought by me, to make the Gen'tiles obedient, by word and deed,

19 Through mighty signs and wonders, by the power of the Spirit of God; so that from Je-ru'-sa-lem, and round about unto Il-lyr'i-cum, I have fully preached the gospel of Christ.

20 Yea, so have I strived to preach the gospel, not where Christ was named, lest I should build upon another man's foundation:

21 But as it is written, To whom he was not spoken of, they shall see: and they that have not heard shall understand.

22 For which cause also I have been much hindered from coming to you.

23 But now having no more place in these parts, and having a great desire these many years to come unto you;

24 Whensoever I take my journey into Spain, I will come to you: for I trust to see you in my journey, and to be brought on my way thitherward by you, if first I be somewhat filled with your *company*.

25 But now I go unto Je-ru'sa-lem to minister unto the saints.

26 For it hath pleased them of Mac-e-do'ni-a and A-cha'ia to make a certain contribution for the poor saints which are at Je-ru'sa-lem.

27 It hath pleased them verily; and their debtors they are. For if the Gen'tiles have been made partakers of their spiritual things, their duty is also to minister unto them in carnal things.

28 When therefore I have performed this, and have sealed to them this fruit, I will come by you into Spain.

29 And I am sure that, when I come unto you, I shall come in the fullness of the blessing of the gospel of Christ.

30 Now I beseech you, brethren, for the Lord Je'sus Christ's sake, and for the love of the Spirit, that ye strive together with me in *your* prayers to God for me;

31 That I may be delivered from them that do not believe in Ju-dæ'a; and that my service which *I have* for Je-ru'sa-lem may be accepted of the saints;

32 That I may come unto you with joy by the will of God, and may with you be refreshed.

33 Now the God of peace *be* with you all. Amen.

16 I commend unto you Phe'-be our sister, which is a servant of the church which is at Cenchre-a:

2 That ye receive her in the Lord, as becometh saints, and that ye assist her in whatsoever business she hath need of you: for she hath been a succorer of many, and of myself also.

3 Greet Pris-cil'la and A'qui-la my helpers in Christ Je'sus:

4 Who have for my life laid down their own necks: unto whom not only I give thanks, but also all the churches of the Gen'tiles.

5 Likewise *greet* the church that is in their house. Salute my well-beloved E-pæn'e-tus, who is the firstfruits of A-cha'ia unto Christ.

6 Greet Ma'ry, who bestowed much labor on us.

7 Salute An-dro-ni'cus and Ju'nia, my kinsmen, and my fellow prisoners, who are of note among the apostles, who also were in Christ before me.

8 Greet Am'pli·as my beloved in the Lord.

9 Salute Ur'bane, our helper in Christ, and Sta'chys my beloved.

10 Salute A·pelles approved in Christ. Salute them which are of Ar·is·to·bu'lus' household.

11 Salute He·ro'di·on my kinsman. Greet them that be of the household of Nar·cis'sus, which are in the Lord.

12 Salute Try·phe'na and Try·pho'sa, who labor in the Lord. Salute the beloved Per'sis, which labored much in the Lord.

13 Salute Ru'fus chosen in the Lord, and his mother and mine.

14 Salute A·syn'cri·tus, Phle'gon, Her'mas, Pat'ro·bas, Her'mes, and the brethren which are with them.

15 Salute Phi·lol'o·gus, and Ju'lia, Ne're·us, and his sister, and O·lym'pas, and all the saints which are with them.

16 Salute one another with an holy kiss. The churches of Christ salute you.

17 Now I beseech you, brethren, mark them which cause divisions and offenses contrary to the doctrine which ye have learned; and avoid them.

18 For they that are such serve not our Lord Je'sus Christ, but their own belly; and by good words and fair speeches deceive the hearts of the simple.

19 For your obedience is come abroad unto all men. I am glad therefore on your behalf: but yet I would have you wise unto that which is good, and simple concerning evil.

20 And the God of peace shall bruise Sa'tan under your feet shortly. The grace of our Lord Je'sus Christ be with you. Amen.

21 Ti·mo'the·us my workfellow, and Lu'cius, and Ja'son, and So·sip'a·ter, my kinsmen, salute you.

22 I Ter'tius, who wrote this epistle, salute you in the Lord.

23 Ga'ius mine host, and of the whole church, saluteth you. E·ras'tus the chamberlain of the city saluteth you, and Quar'tus a brother.

24 The grace of our Lord Je'sus Christ be with you all. Amen.

25 Now to him that is of power to stablish you according to my gospel, and the preaching of Je'sus Christ, according to the revelation of the mystery, which was kept secret since the world began,

26 But now is made manifest, and by the scriptures of the prophets, according to the commandment of the everlasting God, made known to all nations for the obedience of faith:

27 To God only wise, be glory through Je'sus Christ forever. Amen.

1 CORINTHIANS

1 Paul, called *to be* an apostle of Je'sus Christ through the will of God, and Sos'the-nes *our* brother,

2 Unto the church of God which is at Cor'inth, to them that are sanctified in Christ Je'sus, called *to be* saints, with all that in every place call upon the name of Je'sus Christ our Lord, both theirs and ours:

3 Grace *be* unto you, and peace, from God our Father, and *from* the Lord Je'sus Christ.

4 I thank my God always on your behalf, for the grace of God which is given you by Je'sus Christ;

5 That in everything ye are enriched by him, in all utterance, and *in* all knowledge;

6 Even as the testimony of Christ was confirmed in you:

7 So that ye come behind in no gift; waiting for the coming of our Lord Je'sus Christ:

8 Who shall also confirm you unto the end, *that ye may be* blameless in the day of our Lord Je'sus Christ.

9 God *is* faithful, by whom ye were called unto the fellowship of his Son Je'sus Christ our Lord.

10 Now I beseech you, brethren, by the name of our Lord Je'sus Christ, that ye all speak the same thing, and *that* there be no divisions among you; but *that* ye be perfectly joined together in the same mind and in the same judgment.

11 For it hath been declared unto me of you, my brethren, by them *which are of the house* of Chlo'e, that there are contentions among you.

12 Now this I say, that every one of you saith, I am of Paul; and I of A-pol'los; and I of Ce'phas; and I of Christ.

13 Is Christ divided? was Paul crucified for you? or were ye baptized in the name of Paul?

14 I thank God that I baptized none of you, but Cris'pus and Ga'ius;

15 Lest any should say that I had baptized in mine own name.

16 And I baptized also the household of Steph'a-nas: besides, I know not whether I baptized any other.

17 For Christ sent me not to baptize, but to preach the gospel: not with wisdom of words, lest the cross of Christ should be made of none effect.

18 For the preaching of the cross is to them that perish foolishness; but unto us which are saved it is the power of God.

19 For it is written, I will destroy the wisdom of the wise, and will bring to nothing the understanding of the prudent.

20 Where *is* the wise? where *is* the scribe? where *is* the disputer of this world? hath not

God made foolish the wisdom of this world?

21 For after that in the wisdom of God the world by wisdom knew not God, it pleased God by the foolishness of preaching to save them that believe.

22 For the Jews require a sign, and the Greeks seek after wisdom:

23 But we preach Christ crucified, unto the Jews a stumbling block, and unto the Greeks foolishness;

24 But unto them which are called, both Jews and Greeks, Christ the power of God, and the wisdom of God.

25 Because the foolishness of God is wiser than men; and the weakness of God is stronger than men.

26 For ye see your calling, brethren, how that not many wise men after the flesh, not many mighty, not many noble, are called:

27 But God hath chosen the foolish things of the world to confound the wise; and God hath chosen the weak things of the world to confound the things which are mighty;

28 And base things of the world, and things which are despised, hath God chosen, yea, and things which are not, to bring to nought things that are:

29 That no flesh should glory in his presence.

30 But of him are ye in Christ Je′sus, who of God is made unto us wisdom, and righteousness, and sanctification, and redemption:

31 That, according as it is written, He that glorieth, let him glory in the Lord.

2 And I, brethren, when I came to you, came not with excellency of speech or of wisdom, declaring unto you the testimony of God.

2 For I determined not to know any thing among you, save Je′sus Christ, and him crucified.

3 And I was with you in weakness, and in fear, and in much trembling.

4 And my speech and my preaching was not with enticing words of man's wisdom, but in demonstration of the Spirit and of power:

5 That your faith should not stand in the wisdom of men, but in the power of God.

6 Howbeit we speak wisdom among them that are perfect: yet not the wisdom of this world, nor of the princes of this world, that come to nought:

7 But we speak the wisdom of God in a mystery, even the hidden wisdom, which God ordained before the world unto our glory:

8 Which none of the princes of this world knew: for had they known it, they would not have crucified the Lord of glory.

9 But as it is written, Eye hath not seen, nor ear heard, neither have entered into the heart of man, the things which God hath prepared for them that love him

10 But God hath revealed them unto us by his Spirit: for the

262

Spirit searcheth all things, yea, the deep things of God.

11 For what man knoweth the things of a man, save the spirit of man which is in him? even so the things of God knoweth no man, but the Spirit of God.

12 Now we have received, not the spirit of the world, but the spirit which is of God; that we might know the things that are freely given to us of God.

13 Which things also we speak, not in the words which man's wisdom teacheth, but which the Ho'ly Ghost teacheth; comparing spiritual things with spiritual.

14 But the natural man receiveth not the things of the Spirit of God: for they are foolishness unto him: neither can he know *them,* because they are spiritually discerned.

15 But he that is spiritual judgeth all things, yet he himself is judged of no man.

16 For who hath known the mind of the Lord, that he may instruct him? But we have the mind of Christ.

3 And I, brethren, could not speak unto you as unto spiritual, but as unto carnal, *even* as unto babes in Christ.

2 I have fed you with milk, and not with meat: for hitherto ye were not able *to bear it,* neither yet now are ye able.

3 For ye are yet carnal: for whereas *there is* among you envying, and strife, and divisions, are ye not carnal, and walk as men?

4 For while one saith, I am of

Paul; and another, I *am* of A-pol'los; are ye not carnal?

5 Who then is Paul, and who *is* A-pol'los, but ministers by whom ye believed, even as the Lord gave to every man?

6 I have planted, A-pol'los watered; but God gave the increase.

7 So then neither is he that planteth any thing, neither he that watereth; but God that giveth the increase.

8 Now he that planteth and he that watereth are one: and every man shall receive his own reward according to his own labor.

9 For we are laborers together with God: ye are God's husbandry, *ye are* God's building.

10 According to the grace of God which is given unto me, as a wise masterbuilder, I have laid the foundation, and another buildeth thereon. But let every man take heed how he buildeth thereupon.

11 For other foundation can no man lay than that is laid, which is Je'sus Christ.

12 Now if any man build upon this foundation gold, silver, precious stones, wood, hay, stubble;

13 Every man's work shall be made manifest: for the day shall declare it, because it shall be revealed by fire; and the fire shall try every man's work of what sort it is.

14 If any man's work abide which he hath built thereupon, he shall receive a reward.

15 If any man's work shall be

burned, he shall suffer loss: but he himself shall be saved; yet so as by fire.

16 Know ye not that ye are the temple of God, and *that* the Spirit of God dwelleth in you?

17 If any man defile the temple of God, him shall God destroy; for the temple of God is holy, which *temple* ye are.

18 Let no man deceive himself. If any man among you seemeth to be wise in this world, let him become a fool, that he may be wise.

19 For the wisdom of this world is foolishness with God. For it is written, He taketh the wise in their own craftiness.

20 And again, The Lord knoweth the thoughts of the wise, that they are vain.

21 Therefore let no man glory in men. For all things are yours;

22 Whether Paul or A·pol'los, or Ce'phas, or the world, or life, or death, or things present, or things to come; all are yours;

23 And ye are Christ's; and Christ *is* God's.

4 Let a man so account of us, as of the ministers of Christ, and stewards of the mysteries of God.

2 Moreover it is required in stewards, that a man be found faithful.

3 But with me it is a very small thing that I should be judged of you, or of man's judgment: yea, I judge not mine own self.

4 For I know nothing by myself; yet am I not hereby justified: but he that judgeth me is the Lord.

5 Therefore judge nothing before the time, until the Lord come, who both will bring to light the hidden things of darkness, and will make manifest the counsels of the hearts: and then shall every man have praise of God.

6 And these things, brethren, I have in a figure transferred to myself and *to* A·pol'los for your sakes; that ye might learn in us not to think *of men* above that which is written, that no one of you be puffed up for one against another.

7 For who maketh thee to differ *from another?* and what hast thou that thou didst not receive? now if thou didst receive *it,* why dost thou glory, as if thou hadst not received *it?*

8 Now ye are full, now ye are rich, ye have reigned as kings without us: and I would to God ye did reign, that we also might reign with you.

9 For I think that God hath set forth us the apostles last, as it were appointed to death: for we are made a spectacle unto the world, and to angels, and to men.

10 We *are* fools for Christ's sake, but ye *are* wise in Christ; we *are* weak, but ye *are* strong; ye *are* honorable, but we *are* despised.

11 Even unto this present hour we both hunger, and thirst, and are naked, and are buffeted, and have no certain dwelling place;

12 And labor, working with our own hands: being reviled, we

bless; being persecuted, we suffer it:

13 Being defamed, we entreat: we are made as the filth of the world, *and are* the offscouring of all things unto this day.

14 I write not these things to shame you, but as my beloved sons I warn *you.*

15 For though ye have ten thousand instructors in Christ, yet *have ye* not many fathers: for in Christ Je'sus I have begotten you through the gospel.

16 Wherefore I beseech you, be ye followers of me.

17 For this cause have I sent unto you Ti-mo'the-us, who is my beloved son, and faithful in the Lord, who shall bring you into remembrance of my ways which be in Christ, as I teach everywhere in every church.

18 Now some are puffed up, as though I would not come to you.

19 But I will come to you shortly, if the Lord will, and will know, not the speech of them which are puffed up, but the power.

20 For the kingdom of God *is* not in word, but in power.

21 What will ye? shall I come unto you with a rod, or in love, and *in* the spirit of meekness?

5 It is reported commonly *that there is* fornication among you, and such fornication as is not so much as named among the Gen'tiles, that one should have his father's wife.

2 And ye are puffed up, and have not rather mourned, that he that hath done this deed

might be taken away from among you.

3 For I verily, as absent in body, but present in spirit, have judged already, as though I were present, *concerning* him that hath so done this deed,

4 In the name of our Lord Je'-sus Christ, when ye are gathered together, and my spirit, with the power of our Lord Je'-sus Christ,

5 To deliver such an one unto Sa'tan for the destruction of the flesh, that the spirit may be saved in the day of the Lord Je'sus.

6 Your glorying *is* not good. Know ye not that a little leaven leaveneth the whole lump?

7 Purge out therefore the old leaven, that ye may be a new lump, as ye are unleavened. For even Christ our passover is sacrificed for us:

8 Therefore let us keep the feast, not with old leaven, neither with the leaven of malice and wickedness; but with the unleavened *bread* of sincerity and truth.

9 I wrote unto you in an epistle not to company with fornicators:

10 Yet not altogether with the fornicators of this world, or with the covetous, or extortioners, or with idolaters; for then must ye needs go out of the world.

11 But now I have written unto you not to keep company, if any man that is called a brother be a fornicator, or covetous, or an idolater, or a railer, or a

drunkard, or an extortioner; with such an one not to eat.

12 For what have I to do to judge them also that are without? do not ye judge them that are within?

13 But them that are without God judgeth. Therefore put away from among yourselves that wicked person.

6 Dare any of you, having a matter against another, go to law before the unjust, and not before the saints?

2 Do ye not know that the saints shall judge the world? and if the world shall be judged by you, are ye unworthy to judge the smallest matters?

3 Know ye not that we shall judge angels? how much more things that pertain to this life?

4 If then ye have judgments of things pertaining to this life, set them to judge who are least esteemed in the church.

5 I speak to your shame. Is it so, that there is not a wise man among you? no, not one that shall be able to judge between his brethren?

6 But brother goeth to law with brother, and that before the unbelievers.

7 Now therefore there is utterly a fault among you, because ye go to law one with another. Why do ye not rather take wrong? why do ye not rather *suffer yourselves to* be defrauded?

8 Nay, ye do wrong, and defraud, and that *your* brethren.

9 Know ye not that the unrighteous shall not inherit the king dom of God? Be not deceived: neither fornicators, nor idolaters, nor adulterers, nor effeminate, nor abusers of themselves with mankind,

10 Nor thieves, nor covetous, nor drunkards, nor revilers, nor extortioners, shall inherit the kingdom of God.

11 And such were some of you: but ye are washed, but ye are sanctified, but ye are justified in the name of the Lord Je´sus, and by the Spirit of our God.

12 All things are lawful unto me, but all things are not expedient: all things are lawful for me, but I will not be brought under the power of any.

13 Meats for the belly, and the belly for meats: but God shall destroy both it and them. Now the body is not for fornication, but for the Lord; and the Lord for the body.

14 And God hath both raised up the Lord, and will also raise up us by his own power.

15 Know ye not that your bodies are the members of Christ? shall I then take the members of Christ, and make *them* the members of an harlot? God forbid.

16 What? know ye not that he which is joined to an harlot is one body? for two, saith he, shall be one flesh.

17 But he that is joined unto the Lord is one spirit.

18 Flee fornication. Every sin that a man doeth is without the body; but he that committeth fornication sinneth against his own body.

19 What? know ye not that your body is the temple of the Ho'ly Ghost *which is* in you, which ye have of God, and ye are not your own?

20 For ye are bought with a price: therefore glorify God in your body, and in your spirit, which are God's.

7 Now concerning the things whereof ye wrote unto me: *It is* good for a man not to touch a woman.

2 Nevertheless, *to avoid* fornication, let every man have his own wife, and let every woman have her own husband.

3 Let the husband render unto the wife due benevolence: and likewise also the wife unto the husband.

4 The wife hath not power of her own body, but the husband: and likewise also the husband hath not power of his own body, but the wife.

5 Defraud ye not one the other, except *it be* with consent for a time, that ye may give yourselves to fasting and prayer; and come together again, that Sa'tan tempt you not for your incontinency.

6 But I speak this by permission, *and* not of commandment.

7 For I would that all men were even as I myself. But every man hath his proper gift of God, one after this manner, and another after that.

8 I say therefore to the unmarried and widows, It is good for them if they abide even as I.

9 But if they cannot contain, let them marry: for it is better to marry than to burn.

10 And unto the married I command, *yet* not I, but the Lord, Let not the wife depart from *her* husband:

11 But and if she depart, let her remain unmarried, or be reconciled to *her* husband: and let not the husband put away *his* wife.

12 But to the rest speak I, not the Lord: If any brother have a wife that believeth not, and she be pleased to dwell with him, let him not put her away.

13 And the woman which hath an husband that believeth not, and if he be pleased to dwell with her, let her not leave him.

14 For the unbelieving husband is sanctified by the wife, and the unbelieving wife is sanctified by the husband: else were your children unclean; but now are they holy.

15 But if the unbelieving depart, let him depart. A brother or a sister is not under bondage in such *cases:* but God hath called us to peace.

16 For what knowest thou, O wife, whether thou shalt save *thy* husband? or how knowest thou, O man, whether thou shalt save *thy* wife?

17 But as God hath distributed to every man, as the Lord hath called everyone, so let him walk. And so ordain I in all churches.

18 Is any man called being circumcised? let him not become uncircumcised. Is any called in

uncircumcision? let him not be circumcised.

19 Circumcision is nothing, and uncircumcision is nothing, but the keeping of the commandments of God.

20 Let every man abide in the same calling wherein he was called.

21 Art thou called *being* a servant? care not for it: but if thou mayest be made free, use *it* rather.

22 For he that is called in the Lord, *being* a servant, is the Lord's freeman: likewise also he that is called, *being* free, is Christ's servant.

23 Ye are bought with a price; be not ye the servants of men.

24 Brethren, let every man, wherein he is called, therein abide with God.

25 Now concerning virgins I have no commandment of the Lord: yet I give my judgment, as one that hath obtained mercy of the Lord to be faithful.

26 I suppose therefore that this is good for the present distress, *I say*, that *it is* good for a man so to be.

27 Art thou bound unto a wife? seek not to be loosed. Art thou loosed from a wife? seek not a wife

28 But and if thou marry, thou hast not sinned; and if a virgin marry, she hath not sinned. Nevertheless such shall have trouble in the flesh: but I spare you.

29 But this I say, brethren, the time *is* short: it remaineth, that both they that have wives be as though they had none;

30 And they that weep, as though they wept not; and they that rejoice, as though they rejoiced not; and they that buy, as though they possessed not;

31 And they that use this world, as not abusing *it:* for the fashion of this world passeth away.

32 But I would have you without carefulness. He that is unmarried careth for the things that belong to the Lord, how he may please the Lord:

33 But he that is married careth for the things that are of the world, how he may please *his* wife.

34 There is difference *also* between a wife and a virgin. The unmarried woman careth for the things of the Lord, that she may be holy both in body and in spirit: but she that is married careth for the things of the world, how she may please *her* husband.

35 And this I speak for your own profit; not that I may cast a snare upon you; but for that which is comely, and that ye may attend upon the Lord without distraction.

36 But if any man think that he behaveth himself uncomely toward his virgin, if she pass the flower of *her* age, and need so require, let him do what he will, he sinneth not: let them marry.

37 Nevertheless he that standeth steadfast in his heart, having no necessity, but hath power over his own will, and hath so decreed in his heart that he will keep his virgin, doeth well.

38 So then he that giveth *her* in marriage doeth well; but he that giveth *her* not in marriage doeth better.

39 The wife is bound by the law as long as her husband liveth; but if her husband be dead, she is at liberty to be married to whom she will; only in the Lord.

40 But she is happier if she so abide, after my judgment: and I think also that I have the Spirit of God.

8 Now as touching things offered unto idols, we know that we all have knowledge. Knowledge puffeth up, but charity edifieth.

2 And if any man think that he knoweth any thing, he knoweth nothing yet as he ought to know.

3 But if any man love God, the same is known of him.

4 As concerning therefore the eating of those things that are offered in sacrifice unto idols, we know that an idol *is* nothing in the world, and that *there is* none other God but one.

5 For though there be that are called gods, whether in heaven or in earth, (as there be gods many, and lords many,)

6 But to us *there is but* one God, the Father, of whom *are* all things, and we in him; and one Lord Je′sus Christ, by whom *are* all things, and we by him.

7 Howbeit *there is* not in every man that knowledge: for some with conscience of the idol unto this hour eat *it* as a thing offered unto an idol; and their conscience being weak is defiled.

8 But meat commendeth us not to God: for neither, if we eat, are we the better; neither, if we eat not, are we the worse.

9 But take heed lest by any means this liberty of yours become a stumblingblock to them that are weak.

10 For if any man see thee which hast knowledge sit at meat in the idol's temple, shall not the conscience of him which is weak be emboldened to eat those things which are offered to idols;

11 And through thy knowledge shall the weak brother perish, for whom Christ died?

12 But when ye sin so against the brethren, and wound their weak conscience, ye sin against Christ.

13 Wherefore, if meat make my brother to offend, I will eat no flesh while the world standeth, lest I make my brother to offend.

9 Am I not an apostle? am I not free? have I not seen Je′sus Christ our Lord? are not ye my work in the Lord?

2 If I be not an apostle unto others, yet doubtless I am to you: for the seal of mine apostleship are ye in the Lord.

3 Mine answer to them that do examine me is this,

4 Have we not power to eat and to drink?

5 Have we not power to lead about a sister, a wife, as well as

other apostles, and *as* the brethren, and of the Lord, and Ce'phas?

6 Or I only and Bar'na-bas, have not we power to forbear working?

7 Who goeth a warfare anytime at his own charges? who planteth a vineyard, and eateth not of the fruit thereof? or who feedeth a flock, and eateth not of the milk of the flock?

8 Say I these things as a man? or saith not the law the same also?

9 For it is written in the law of Mo'ses, Thou shalt not muzzle the mouth of the ox that treadeth out the corn. Doth God take care for oxen?

10 Or saith he it altogether for our sakes? For our sakes, no doubt, *this* is written: that he that ploweth should plow in hope; and that he that thresheth in hope should be partaker of his hope.

11 If we have sown unto you spiritual things, *is it* a great thing if we shall reap your carnal things?

12 If others be partakers of *this* power over you, *are* not we rather? Nevertheless we have not used this power; but suffer all things, lest we should hinder the gospel of Christ.

13 Do ye not know that they which minister about holy things live *of the things* of the temple? and they which wait at the altar are partakers with the altar?

14 Even so hath the Lord ordained that they which preach the gospel should live of the gospel.

15 But I have used none of these things: neither have I written these things, that it should be so done unto me: for *it were* better for me to die, than that any man should make my glorying void.

16 For though I preach the gospel, I have nothing to glory of: for necessity is laid upon me; yea, woe is unto me, if I preach not the gospel!

17 For if I do this thing willingly, I have a reward: but if against my will, a dispensation *of the gospel* is committed unto me.

18 What is my reward then? *Verily* that, when I preach gospel, I may make the gospel of Christ without charge, that I abuse not my power in the gospel.

19 For though I be free from all *men*, yet have I made myself servant unto all, that I might gain the more.

20 And unto the Jews I became as a Jew, that I might gain the Jews; to them that are under the law, as under the law, that I might gain them that are under the law;

21 To them that are without law, as without law, (being not without law to God, but under the law to Christ,) that I might gain them that are without law.

22 To the weak became I as weak, that I might gain the weak: I am made all things to all *men*, that I might by all means save some.

23 And this I do for the gospel's

sake, that I might be partaker thereof with *you.*

24 Know ye not that they which run in a race run all, but one receiveth the prize? So run, that ye may obtain.

25 And every man that striveth for the mastery is temperate in all things. Now they *do it* to obtain a corruptible crown; but we an incorruptible.

26 I therefore so run, not as uncertainly; so fight I, not as one that beateth the air:

27 But I keep under my body, and bring *it* into subjection: lest that by any means, when I have preached to others, I myself should be a castaway.

10 Moreover, brethren, I would not that ye should be ignorant, how that all our fathers were under the cloud, and all passed through the sea;

2 And were all baptized unto Mo'ses in the cloud and in the sea;

3 And did all eat the same spiritual meat;

4 And did all drink the same spiritual drink: for they drank of that spiritual Rock that followed them: and that Rock was Christ.

5 But with many of them God was not well pleased: for they were overthrown in the wilderness.

6 Now these things were our examples, to the intent we should not lust after evil things, as they also lusted.

7 Neither be ye idolaters, as *were* some of them; as it is written, The people sat down to eat and drink, and rose up to play.

8 Neither let us commit fornication, as some of them committed, and fell in one day three and twenty thousand.

9 Neither let us tempt Christ, as some of them also tempted, and were destroyed of serpents.

10 Neither murmur ye, as some of them also murmured, and were destroyed of the destroyer.

11 Now all these things happened unto them for examples: and they are written for our admonition, upon whom the ends of the world are come.

12 Wherefore let him that thinketh he standeth take heed lest he fall.

13 There hath no temptation taken you but such as is common to man: but God *is* faithful, who will not suffer you to be tempted above that ye are able; but will with the temptation also make a way to escape, that ye may be able to bear *it.*

14 Wherefore, my dearly beloved, flee from idolatry.

15 I speak as to wise men; judge ye what I say.

16 The cup of blessing which we bless, is it not the communion of the blood of Christ? The bread which we break, is it not the communion of the body of Christ?

17 For we *being* many are one bread, *and* one body: for we are all partakers of that one bread.

18 Behold Is'ra-el after the flesh: are not they which eat of

the sacrifices partakers of the altar?

19 What say I then? that the idol is any thing, or that which is offered in sacrifice to idols is any thing?

20 But *I say*, that the things which the Gen'tiles sacrifice, they sacrifice to devils, and not to God: and I would not that ye should have fellowship with devils.

21 Ye cannot drink the cup of the Lord, and the cup of devils: ye cannot be partakers of the Lord's table, and of the table of devils.

22 Do we provoke the Lord to jealousy? are we stronger than he?

23 All things are lawful for me, but all things are not expedient: all things are lawful for me, but all things edify not.

24 Let no man seek his own, but every man another's *wealth*.

25 Whatsoever is sold in the shambles, *that* eat, asking no question for conscience sake:

26 For the earth *is* the Lord's, and the fullness thereof.

27 If any of them that believe not bid you *to a feast*, and ye be disposed to go; whatsoever is set before you, eat, asking no question for conscience sake.

28 But if any man say unto you, This is offered in sacrifice unto idols, eat not for his sake that showed it, and for conscience sake: for the earth *is* the Lord's, and the fullness thereof.

29 Conscience, I say, not thine own, but of the other: for why is

my liberty judged of another *man's* conscience?

30 For if I by grace be a partaker, why am I evil spoken of for that for which I give thanks?

31 Whether therefore ye eat, or drink, or whatsoever ye do, do all to the glory of God.

32 Give none offense, neither to the Jews, nor to the Gen'tiles, nor to the church of God:

33 Even as I please all *men* in all *things*, not seeking mine own profit, but the *profit* of many, that they may be saved.

11 Be ye followers of me, even as I also *am* of Christ.

2 Now I praise you, brethren, that ye remember me in all things, and keep the ordinances, as I delivered *them* to you.

3 But I would have you know, that the head of every man is Christ; and the head of the woman *is* the man; and the head of Christ *is* God.

4 Every man praying or prophesying, having his head covered, dishonoreth his head.

5 But every woman that prayeth or prophesieth with *her* head uncovered dishonoreth her head: for that is even all one as if she were shaven.

6 For if the woman be not covered, let her also be shorn: but if it be a shame for a woman to be shorn or shaven, let her be covered.

7 For a man indeed ought not to cover *his* head, forasmuch as he is the image and glory of God: but the woman is the glory of the man.

8 For the man is not of the woman; but the woman of the man.

9 Neither was the man created for the woman; but the woman for the man.

10 For this cause ought the woman to have power on *her* head because of the angels.

11 Nevertheless neither is the man without the woman, neither the woman without the man, in the Lord.

12 For as the woman *is* of the man, even so *is* the man also by the woman; but all things of God.

13 Judge in yourselves: is it comely that a woman pray unto God uncovered?

14 Doth not even nature itself teach you, that, if a man have long hair, it is a shame unto him?

15 But if a woman have long hair, it is a glory to her: for *her* hair is given her for a covering.

16 But if any man seem to be contentious, we have no such custom, neither the churches of God.

17 Now in this that I declare *unto you* I praise *you* not, that ye come together not for the better, but for the worse.

18 For first of all, when ye come together in the church, I hear that there be divisions among you; and I partly believe it.

19 For there must be also heresies among you, that they which are approved may be made manifest among you.

20 When ye come together

therefore into one place, *this* is not to eat the Lord's supper.

21 For in eating everyone taketh before *other* his own supper: and one is hungry, and another is drunken.

22 What? have ye not houses to eat and to drink in? or despise ye the church of God, and shame them that have not? What shall I say to you? shall I praise *you* in this? I praise *you* not.

23 For I have received of the Lord that which also I delivered unto you, That the Lord Je'sus the *same* night in which he was betrayed took bread:

24 And when he had given thanks, he brake *it*, and said, Take, eat: this is my body, which is broken for you: this do in remembrance of me.

25 After the same manner also *he took* the cup, when he had supped, saying, This cup is the new testament in my blood: this do ye, as oft as ye drink *it*, in remembrance of me.

26 For as often as ye eat this bread, and drink this cup, ye do show the Lord's death till he come.

27 Wherefore whosoever shall eat this bread, and drink *this* cup of the Lord, unworthily, shall be guilty of the body and blood of the Lord.

28 But let a man examine himself, and so let him eat of *that* bread, and drink of *that* cup.

29 For he that eateth and drinketh unworthily, eateth and drinketh damnation to himself, not discerning the Lord's body.

30 For this cause many *are* weak and sickly among you, and many sleep.

31 For if we would judge ourselves, we should not be judged.

32 But when we are judged, we are chastened of the Lord, that we should not be condemned with the world.

33 Wherefore, my brethren, when ye come together to eat, tarry one for another.

34 And if any man hunger, let him eat at home; that ye come not together unto condemnation. And the rest will I set in order when I come.

12 Now concerning spiritual gifts, brethren, I would not have you ignorant.

2 Ye know that ye were Gen'-tiles, carried away unto these dumb idols, even as ye were led.

3 Wherefore I give you to understand, that no man speaking by the Spirit of God calleth Je'-sus accursed: and *that* no man can say that Je'sus is the Lord, but by the Ho'ly Ghost.

4 Now there are diversities of gifts, but the same Spirit.

5 And there are differences of administrations, but the same Lord.

6 And there are diversities of operations, but it is the same God which worketh all in all.

7 But the manifestation of the Spirit is given to every man to profit withal.

8 For to one is given by the Spirit the word of wisdom; to another the word of knowledge by the same Spirit;

9 To another faith by the same Spirit; to another the gifts of healing by the same Spirit;

10 To another the working of miracles; to another prophecy; to another discerning of spirits; to another *divers* kinds of tongues; to another the interpretation of tongues:

11 But all these worketh one and the selfsame Spirit, dividing to every man severally as he will.

12 For as the body is one, and hath many members, and all the members of that one body, being many, are one body: so also *is* Christ.

13 For by one Spirit are we all baptized into one body, whether *we be* Jews or Gen'tiles, whether *we be* bond or free; and have been all made to drink into one Spirit.

14 For the body is not one member, but many.

15 If the foot shall say, Because I am not the hand, I am not of the body; is it therefore not of the body?

16 And if the ear shall say, Because I am not the eye, I am not of the body; is it therefore not of the body?

17 If the whole body *were* an eye, where *were* the hearing? If the whole *were* hearing, where *were* the smelling?

18 But now hath God set the members everyone of them in the body, as it hath pleased him.

19 And if they were all one member, where *were* the body?

20 But now *are they* many members, yet but one body.

21 And the eye cannot say unto

the hand, I have no need of thee: nor again the head to the feet, I have no need of you.

22 Nay, much more those members of the body, which seem to be more feeble, are necessary:

23 And those *members* of the body, which we think to be less honorable, upon these we bestow more abundant honor; and our uncomely *parts* have more abundant comeliness.

24 For our comely *parts* have no need: but God hath tempered the body together, having given more abundant honor to that *part* which lacked:

25 That there should be no schism in the body; but *that* the members should have the same care one for another.

26 And whether one member suffer, all the members suffer with it; or one member be honored, all the members rejoice with it.

27 Now ye are the body of Christ, and members in particular.

28 And God hath set some in the church, first apostles, secondarily prophets, thirdly teachers, after that miracles, then gifts of healings, helps, governments, diversities of tongues.

29 *Are* all apostles? *are* all prophets? *are* all teachers? *are* all workers of miracles?

30 Have all the gifts of healing? do all speak with tongues? do all interpret?

31 But covet earnestly the best gifts: and yet show I unto you a more excellent way.

13 Though I speak with the tongues of men and of angels, and have not charity, I am become *as* sounding brass, or a tinkling cymbal.

2 And though I have *the gift of* prophecy, and understand all mysteries, and all knowledge; and though I have all faith, so that I could remove mountains, and have not charity, I am nothing.

3 And though I bestow all my goods to feed *the poor,* and though I give my body to be burned, and have not charity, it profiteth me nothing.

4 Charity suffereth long, *and* is kind; charity envieth not; charity vaunteth not itself, is not puffed up,

5 Doth not behave itself unseemly, seeketh not her own, is not easily provoked, thinketh no evil;

6 Rejoiceth not in iniquity, but rejoiceth in the truth;

7 Beareth all things, believeth all things, hopeth all things, endureth all things.

8 Charity never faileth: but whether *there be* prophecies, they shall fail; whether *there be* tongues, they shall cease; whether *there be* knowledge, it shall vanish away.

9 For we know in part, and we prophesy in part.

10 But when that which is perfect is come, then that which is in part shall be done away.

11 When I was a child, I spake as a child, I understood as a child, I thought as a child: but

when I became a man, I put away childish things.

12 For now we see through a glass, darkly; but then face to face: now I know in part; but then shall I know even as also I am known.

13 And now abideth faith, hope, charity, these three; but the greatest of these is charity.

14 Follow after charity, and desire spiritual gifts, but rather that ye may prophesy.

2 For he that speaketh in an unknown tongue speaketh not unto men, but unto God: for no man understandeth him; howbeit in the spirit he speaketh mysteries.

3 But he that prophesieth speaketh unto men to edification, and exhortation, and comfort.

4 He that speaketh in an unknown tongue edifieth himself; but he that prophesieth edifieth the church.

5 I would that ye all spake with tongues, but rather that ye prophesied: for greater is he that prophesieth than he that speaketh with tongues, except he interpret, that the church may receive edifying.

6 Now, brethren, if I come unto you speaking with tongues, what shall I profit you, except I shall speak to you either by revelation, or by knowledge, or by prophesying, or by doctrine?

7 And even things without life giving sound, whether pipe or harp, except they give a distinction in the sounds, how shall it be known what is piped or harped?

8 For if the trumpet give an uncertain sound, who shall prepare himself to the battle?

9 So likewise ye, except ye utter by the tongue words easy to be understood, how shall it be known what is spoken? for ye shall speak into the air.

10 There are, it may be, so many kinds of voices in the world, and none of them is without signification.

11 Therefore if I know not the meaning of the voice, I shall be unto him that speaketh a barbarian, and he that speaketh shall be a barbarian unto me.

12 Even so ye, forasmuch as ye are zealous of spiritual gifts, seek that ye may excel to the edifying of the church.

13 Wherefore let him that speaketh in an unknown tongue pray that he may interpret.

14 For if I pray in an unknown tongue, my spirit prayeth, but my understanding is unfruitful.

15 What is it then? I will pray with the spirit, and I will pray with the understanding also: I will sing with the spirit, and I will sing with the understanding also.

16 Else when thou shalt bless with the spirit, how shall he that occupieth the room of the unlearned say Amen at thy giving of thanks, seeing he understandeth not what thou sayest?

17 For thou verily givest thanks well, but the other is not edified.

18 I thank my God, I speak with tongues more than ye all:

19 Yet in the church I had

rather speak five words with my understanding, that *by my voice* I might teach others also, than ten thousand words in an *unknown* tongue.

20 Brethren, be not children in understanding: howbeit in malice be ye children, but in understanding be men.

21 In the law it is written, With *men of* other tongues and other lips will I speak unto this people; and yet for all that will they not hear me, saith the Lord.

22 Wherefore tongues are for a sign, not to them that believe, but to them that believe not: but prophesying *serveth* not for them that believe not, but for them which believe.

23 If therefore the whole church be come together into one place, and all speak with tongues, and there come in *those that are* unlearned, or unbelievers, will they not say that ye are mad?

24 But if all prophesy, and there come in one that believeth not, or *one* unlearned, he is convinced of all, he is judged of all:

25 And thus are the secrets of his heart made manifest; and so falling down on *his* face he will worship God, and report that God is in you of a truth.

26 How is it then, brethren? when ye come together, every one of you hath a psalm, hath a doctrine, hath a tongue, hath a revelation, hath an interpretation. Let all things be done unto edifying.

27 If any man speak in an *unknown* tongue, *let it be* by two, or at the most *by* three, and *that* by course; and let one interpret.

28 But if there be no interpreter, let him keep silence in the church; and let him speak to himself, and to God.

29 Let the prophets speak two or three, and let the other judge.

30 If *anything* be revealed to another that sitteth by, let the first hold his peace.

31 For ye may all prophesy one by one, that all may learn, and all may be comforted.

32 And the spirits of the prophets are subject to the prophets.

33 For God is not *the author* of confusion, but of peace, as in all churches of the saints.

34 Let your women keep silence in the churches: for it is not permitted unto them to speak; but *they are commanded* to be under obedience, as also saith the law.

35 And if they will learn anything, let them ask their husbands at home: for it is a shame for women to speak in the church.

36 What? came the word of God out from you? or came it unto you only?

37 If any man think himself to be a prophet, or spiritual, let him acknowledge that the things that I write unto you are the commandments of the Lord.

38 But if any man be ignorant, let him be ignorant.

39 Wherefore, brethren, covet to prophesy, and forbid not to speak with tongues.

40 Let all things be done decently and in order.

15 Moreover, brethren, I declare unto you the gospel which I preached unto you, which also ye have received, and wherein ye stand;

2 By which also ye are saved, if ye keep in memory what I preached unto you, unless ye have believed in vain.

3 For I delivered unto you first of all that which I also received, how that Christ died for our sins according to the scriptures;

4 And that he was buried, and that he rose again the third day according to the scriptures:

5 And that he was seen of Ce'-phas, then of the twelve:

6 After that, he was seen of above five hundred brethren at once; of whom the greater part remain unto this present, but some are fallen asleep.

7 After that, he was seen of James; then of all the apostles.

8 And last of all he was seen of me also, as of one born out of due time.

9 For I am the least of the apostles, that am not meet to be called an apostle, because I persecuted the church of God.

10 But by the grace of God I am what I am: and his grace which was bestowed upon me was not in vain; but I labored more abundantly than they all: yet not I, but the grace of God which was with me.

11 Therefore whether it were I or they, so we preach, and so ye believed.

12 Now if Christ be preached that he rose from the dead, how say some among you that there is no resurrection of the dead?

13 But if there be no resurrection of the dead, then is Christ not risen:

14 And if Christ be not risen, then is our preaching vain, and your faith is also vain.

15 Yea, and we are found false witnesses of God; because we have testified of God that he raised up Christ: whom he raised not up, if so be that the dead rise not.

16 For if the dead rise not, then is not Christ raised:

17 And if Christ be not raised, your faith is vain; ye are yet in your sins.

18 Then they also which are fallen asleep in Christ are perished.

19 If in this life only we have hope in Christ, we are of all men most miserable.

20 But now is Christ risen from the dead, and become the firstfruits of them that slept.

21 For since by man came death, by man came also the resurrection of the dead.

22 For as in Ad'am all die, even so in Christ shall all be made alive.

23 But every man in his own order: Christ the firstfruits; afterward they that are Christ's at his coming.

24 Then cometh the end, when he shall have delivered up the kingdom to God, even the Father; when he shall have put down all rule and all authority and power.

25 For he must reign, till he hath put all enemies under his feet.

26 The last enemy *that* shall be destroyed *is* death.

27 For he hath put all things under his feet. But when he saith all things are put under *him, it is* manifest that he is excepted, which did put all things under him.

28 And when all things shall be subdued unto him, then shall the Son also himself be subject unto him that put all things under him, that God may be all in all.

29 Else what shall they do which are baptized for the dead, if the dead rise not at all? why are they then baptized for the dead?

30 And why stand we in jeopardy every hour?

31 I protest by your rejoicing which I have in Christ Je'sus our Lord, I die daily.

32 If after the manner of men I have fought with beasts at Eph'-e·sus, what advantageth it me, if the dead rise not? let us eat and drink; for tomorrow we die.

33 Be not deceived: evil communications corrupt good manners.

34 Awake to righteousness, and sin not; for some have not the knowledge of God: I speak *this* to your shame.

35 But some *man* will say, How are the dead raised up? and with what body do they come?

36 *Thou* fool, that which thou sowest is not quickened, except it die:

37 And that which thou sowest, thou sowest not that body that shall be, but bare grain, it may chance of wheat, or of some other *grain:*

38 But God giveth it a body as it hath pleased him, and to every seed his own body.

39 All flesh *is* not the same flesh: but *there is* one *kind* of flesh of men, another flesh of beasts, another of fishes, *and* another of birds.

40 *There are* also celestial bodies, and bodies terrestrial: but the glory of the celestial *is* one, and the *glory* of the terrestrial *is* another.

41 *There is* one glory of the sun, and another glory of the moon, and another glory of the stars: for *one* star differeth from *another* star in glory.

42 So also *is* the resurrection of the dead. It is sown in corruption; it is raised in incorruption:

43 It is sown in dishonour; it is raised in glory: it is sown in weakness; it is raised in power:

44 It is sown a natural body; it is raised a spiritual body. There is a natural body, and there is a spiritual body.

45 And so it is written, The first man Ad'am was made a living soul; the last Ad'am *was made* a quickening spirit.

46 Howbeit that *was* not first which is spiritual, but that which is natural; and afterward that which is spiritual.

47 The first man *is* of the earth, earthy: the second man *is* the Lord from heaven.

48 As *is* the earthy, such *are*

they also that are earthy: and as *is* the heavenly, such *are* they also that are heavenly.

49 And as we have borne the image of the earthy, we shall also bear the image of the heavenly.

50 Now this I say, brethren, that flesh and blood cannot inherit the kingdom of God; neither doth corruption inherit incorruption.

51 Behold, I show you a mystery; We shall not all sleep, but we shall all be changed,

52 In a moment, in the twinkling of an eye, at the last trump: for the trumpet shall sound, and the dead shall be raised incorruptible, and we shall be changed.

53 For this corruptible must put on incorruption, and this mortal *must* put on immortality.

54 So when this corruptible shall have put on incorruption, and this mortal shall have put on immortality, then shall be brought to pass the saying that is written, Death is swallowed up in victory.

55 O death, where *is* thy sting? O grave, where *is* thy victory?

56 The sting of death *is* sin; and the strength of sin *is* the law.

57 But thanks *be* to God, which giveth us the victory through our Lord Je′sus Christ.

58 Therefore, my beloved brethren, be ye stedfast, unmovable, always abounding in the work of the Lord, forasmuch as ye know that your labor is not in vain in the Lord.

16 Now concerning the collection for the saints, as I have given order to the churches of Ga·la′ti·a, even so do ye.

2 Upon the first *day* of the week let every one of you lay by him in store, as God hath prospered him, that there be no gatherings when I come.

3 And when I come, whomsoever ye shall approve by *your* letters, them will I send to bring your liberality unto Je·ru′sa·lem.

4 And if it be meet that I go also, they shall go with me.

5 Now I will come unto you, when I shall pass through Mac·e·do′ni·a: for I do pass through Mac·e·do′ni·a.

6 And it may be that I will abide, yea, and winter with you, that ye may bring me on my journey whithersoever I go.

7 For I will not see you now by the way; but I trust to tarry a while with you, if the Lord permit.

8 But I will tarry at Eph′e·sus until Pen′te·cost.

9 For a great door and effectual is opened unto me, and *there are* many adversaries.

10 Now if Ti·mo′the·us come, see that he may be with you without fear: for he worketh the work of the Lord, as I also *do*.

11 Let no man therefore despise him: but conduct him forth in peace, that he may come unto me: for I look for him with the brethren.

12 As touching *our* brother

A-pol'los, I greatly desired him to come unto you with the brethren: but his will was not at all to come at this time; but he will come when he shall have convenient time.

13 Watch ye, stand fast in the faith, quit you like men, be strong.

14 Let all your things be done with charity.

15 I beseech you, brethren, (ye know the house of Steph'a-nas, that it is the firstfruits of A-cha'ia, and *that* they have addicted themselves to the ministry of the saints,)

16 That ye submit yourselves unto such, and to everyone that helpeth with *us*, and laboreth.

17 I am glad of the coming of Steph'a-nas and For-tu-na'tus and A-cha'i-cus: for that which was lacking on your part they have supplied.

18 For they have refreshed my spirit and yours: therefore acknowledge ye them that are such.

19 The churches of A'sia salute you. A'qui-la and Pris-cil'la salute you much in the Lord, with the church that is in their house.

20 All the brethren greet you. Greet ye one another with an holy kiss.

21 The salutation of *me* Paul with mine own hand.

22 If any man love not the Lord Je'sus Christ, let him be An-ath'-e-ma Mar'an-a'tha.

23 The grace of our Lord Je'sus Christ *be* with you.

24 My love *be* with you all in Christ Je'sus. Amen.

2 CORINTHIANS

1 Paul, an apostle of Je'sus Christ by the will of God, and Tim'o-thy *our* brother, unto the church of God which is at Cor'inth, with all the saints which are in all A-cha'ia:

2 Grace *be* to you and peace from God our Father, and *from* the Lord Je'sus Christ.

3 Blessed *be* God, even the Father of our Lord Je'sus Christ, the Father of mercies, and the God of all comfort;

4 Who comforteth us in all our tribulation, that we may be able to comfort them which are in

any trouble, by the comfort wherewith we ourselves are comforted of God.

5 For as the sufferings of Christ abound in us, so our consolation also aboundeth by Christ.

6 And whether we be afflicted, *it is* for your consolation and salvation, which is effectual in the enduring of the same sufferings which we also suffer: or whether we be comforted, *it is* for your consolation and salvation.

7 And our hope of you *is* steadfast, knowing, that as ye are

partakers of the sufferings, so *shall ye be* also of the consolation.

8 For we would not, brethren, have you ignorant of our trouble which came to us in A'si.a, that we were pressed out of measure, above strength, insomuch that we despaired even of life:

9 But we had the sentence of death in ourselves, that we should not trust in ourselves, but in God which raiseth the dead:

10 Who delivered us from so great a death, and doth deliver: in whom we trust that he will yet deliver *us;*

11 Ye also helping together by prayer for us, that for the gift *bestowed* upon us by the means of many persons thanks may be given by many on our behalf.

12 For our rejoicing is this, the testimony of our conscience, that in simplicity and godly sincerity, not with fleshly wisdom, but by the grace of God, we have had our conversation in the world, and more abundantly to you-ward.

13 For we write none other things unto you, than what ye read or acknowledge; and I trust ye shall acknowledge even to the end;

14 As also ye have acknowledged us in part, that we are your rejoicing, even as ye also *are* ours in the day of the Lord Je'sus.

15 And in this confidence I was minded to come unto you before, that ye might have a second benefit;

16 And to pass by you into Mac·e·do'ni·a, and to come again out of Mac·e·do'ni·a unto you, and of you to be brought on my way toward Ju·dæ'a.

17 When I therefore was thus minded, did I use lightness? or the things that I purpose, do I purpose according to the flesh, that with me there should be yea, yea, and nay, nay?

18 But *as* God *is* true, our word toward you was not yea and nay.

19 For the Son of God, Je'sus Christ, who was preached among you by us, *even* by me and Sil·va'nus and Ti·mo'the·us, was not yea and nay, but in him was yea.

20 For all the promises of God in him *are* yea, and in him Amen, unto the glory of God by us.

21 Now he which stablisheth us with you in Christ, and hath anointed us, *is* God;

22 Who hath also sealed us, and given the earnest of the Spirit in our hearts.

23 Moreover I call God for a record upon my soul, that to spare you I came not as yet unto Cor'inth.

24 Not for that we have dominion over your faith, but are helpers of your joy: for by faith ye stand.

2 But I determined this with myself, that I would not come again to you in heaviness.

2 For if I make you sorry, who is he then that maketh me glad, but the same which is made sorry by me?

3 And I wrote this same unto you, lest, when I came, I should have sorrow from them of whom I ought to rejoice; having confidence in you all, that my joy is *the joy* of you all.

4 For out of much affliction and anguish of heart I wrote unto you with many tears; not that ye should be grieved, but that ye might know the love which I have more abundantly unto you.

5 But if any have caused grief, he hath not grieved me, but in part: that I may not overcharge you all.

6 Sufficient to such a man *is* this punishment, which *was in-*flicted of many.

7 So that contrariwise ye *ought* rather to forgive *him*, and comfort *him*, lest perhaps such a one should be swallowed up with overmuch sorrow.

8 Wherefore I beseech you that ye would confirm *your* love toward him.

9 For to this end also did I write, that I might know the proof of you, whether ye be obedient in all things.

10 To whom ye forgive anything, I *forgive* also: for if I forgave anything, to whom I forgave *it*, for your sakes *forgave I it* in the person of Christ;

11 Lest Sa′tan should get an advantage of us: for we are not ignorant of his devices.

12 Furthermore, when I came to Tro′as to *preach* Christ's gospel, and a door was opened unto me of the Lord,

13 I had no rest in my spirit, because I found not Ti′tus my brother: but taking my leave of them, I went from thence into Mac·e·do′ni·a.

14 Now thanks *be* unto God, which always causeth us to triumph in Christ, and maketh manifest the savor of his knowledge by us in every place.

15 For we are unto God a sweet savor of Christ, in them that are saved, and in them that perish:

16 To the one *we are* the savor of death unto death; and to the other the savor of life unto life. And who *is* sufficient for these things?

17 For we are not as many, which corrupt the word of God: but as of sincerity, but as of God, in the sight of God speak we in Christ.

3 Do we begin again to commend ourselves? or need we, as some *others*, epistles of commendation to you, or *letters* of commendation from you?

2 Ye are our epistle written in our hearts, known and read of all men:

3 *Forasmuch as ye are* manifestly declared to be the epistle of Christ ministered by us, written not with ink, but with the Spirit of the living God; not in tables of stone, but in fleshy tables of the heart.

4 And such trust have we through Christ to God-ward:

5 Not that we are sufficient of ourselves to think anything as of ourselves; but our sufficiency *is* of God;

6 Who also hath made us able ministers of the new testament;

not of the letter, but of the spirit: for the letter killeth, but the spirit giveth life.

7 But if the ministration of death, written *and* engraven in stones, was glorious, so that the children of Is'ra-el could not steadfastly behold the face of Mo'ses for the glory of his countenance; which *glory* was to be done away:

8 How shall not the ministration of the spirit be rather glorious?

9 For if the ministration of condemnation *be* glory, much more doth the ministration of righteousness exceed in glory.

10 For even that which was made glorious had no glory in this respect, by reason of the glory that excelleth.

11 For if that which is done away *was* glorious, much more that which remaineth *is* glorious.

12 Seeing then that we have such hope, we use great plainness of speech:

13 And not as Mo'ses, *which* put a veil over his face, that the children of Is'ra-el could not steadfastly look to the end of that which is abolished:

14 But their minds were blinded: for until this day remaineth the same veil untaken away in the reading of the old testament; which *veil* is done away in Christ.

15 But even unto this day, when Mo'ses is read, the veil is upon their heart.

16 Nevertheless when it shall turn to the Lord, the veil shall be taken away.

17 Now the Lord is that Spirit: and where the Spirit of the Lord *is*, there *is* liberty.

18 But we all, with open face beholding as in a glass the glory of the Lord, are changed into the same image from glory to glory, *even* as by the Spirit of the Lord.

4 Therefore seeing we have this ministry, as we have received mercy, we faint not;

2 But we have renounced the hidden things of dishonesty, not walking in craftiness, nor handling the word of God deceitfully; but by manifestation of the truth commending ourselves to every man's conscience in the sight of God.

3 But if our gospel be hid, it is hid to them that are lost:

4 In whom the god of this world hath blinded the minds of them which believe not, lest the light of the glorious gospel of Christ, who is the image of God, should shine unto them.

5 For we preach not ourselves, but Christ Je'sus the Lord; and ourselves your servants for Je'sus' sake.

6 For God, who commanded the light to shine out of darkness, hath shined in our hearts, to *give* the light of the knowledge of the glory of God in the face of Je'sus Christ.

7 But we have this treasure in earthen vessels, that the excellency of the power may be of God, and not of us.

8 *We are* troubled on every

side, yet not distressed; *we are* perplexed, but not in despair;

9 Persecuted, but not forsaken; cast down, but not destroyed;

10 Always bearing about in the body the dying of the Lord Je'sus, that the life also of Je'sus might be made manifest in our body.

11 For we which live are always delivered unto death for Je'sus' sake, that the life also of Je'sus might be made manifest in our mortal flesh.

12 So then death worketh in us, but life in you.

13 We having the same spirit of faith, according as it is written, I believed, and therefore have I spoken; we also believe, and therefore speak;

14 Knowing that he which raised up the Lord Je'sus shall raise up us also by Je'sus, and shall present *us* with you.

15 For all things *are* for your sakes, that the abundant grace might through the thanksgiving of many redound to the glory of God.

16 For which cause we faint not; but though our outward man perish, yet the inward *man* is renewed day by day.

17 For our light affliction, which is but for a moment, worketh for us a far more exceeding *and* eternal weight of glory;

18 While we look not at the things which are seen, but at the things which are not seen: for the things which are seen *are* temporal; but the things which are not seen *are* eternal.

5 For we know that if our earthly house of *this* tabernacle were dissolved, we have a building of God, an house not made with hands, eternal in the heavens.

2 For in this we groan, earnestly desiring to be clothed upon with our house which is from heaven:

3 If so be that being clothed we shall not be found naked.

4 For we that are in *this* tabernacle do groan, being burdened: not for that we would be unclothed, but clothed upon, that mortality might be swallowed up of life.

5 Now he that hath wrought us for the selfsame thing *is* God, who also hath given unto us the earnest of the Spirit.

6 Therefore *we are* always confident, knowing that, whilst we are at home in the body, we are absent from the Lord:

7 (For we walk by faith, not by sight:)

8 We are confident, *I say*, and willing rather to be absent from the body, and to be present with the Lord.

9 Wherefore we labor, that, whether present or absent, we may be accepted of him.

10 For we must all appear before the judgment seat of Christ; that everyone may receive the things *done in his* body, according to that he hath done, whether *it be* good or bad.

11 Knowing therefore the terror of the Lord, we persuade men; but we are made manifest unto God; and I trust also are

made manifest in your consciences.

12 For we commend not ourselves again unto you, but give you occasion to glory on our behalf, that ye may have somewhat to answer them which glory in appearance, and not in heart.

13 For whether we be beside ourselves, *it is* to God: or whether we be sober, *it is* for your cause.

14 For the love of Christ constraineth us; because we thus judge, that if one died for all, then were all dead:

15 And *that* he died for all, that they which live should not henceforth live unto themselves, but unto him which died for them, and rose again.

16 Wherefore henceforth know we no man after the flesh: yea, though we have known Christ after the flesh, yet now henceforth know we *him* no more.

17 Therefore if any man *be* in Christ, *he is* a new creature: old things are passed away; behold, all things are become new.

18 And all things *are* of God, who hath reconciled us to himself by Je′sus Christ, and hath given to us the ministry of reconciliation;

19 To wit, that God was in Christ, reconciling the world unto himself, not imputing their trespasses unto them; and hath committed unto us the word of reconciliation.

20 Now then we are ambassadors for Christ, as though God did beseech *you* by us: we pray

you in Christ's stead, be ye reconciled to God.

21 For he hath made him *to be* sin for us, who knew no sin; that we might be made the righteousness of God in him.

6 We then, *as* workers together *with him,* beseech *you* also that ye receive not the grace of God in vain.

2 (For he saith, I have heard thee in a time accepted, and in the day of salvation have I succored thee: behold, now *is* the accepted time, behold, now *is* the day of salvation.)

3 Giving no offense in any thing, that the ministry be not blamed:

4 But in all *things* approving ourselves as the ministers of God, in much patience, in afflictions, in necessities, in distresses,

5 In stripes, in imprisonments, in tumults, in labors, in watchings, in fastings;

6 By pureness, by knowledge, by longsuffering, by kindness, by the Ho′ly Ghost, by love unfeigned,

7 By the word of truth, by the power of God, by the armor of righteousness on the right hand and on the left,

8 By honor and dishonor, by evil report and good report: as deceivers, and *yet* true;

9 As unknown, and *yet* well-known; as dying, and, behold, we live; as chastened, and not killed;

10 As sorrowful, yet always rejoicing; as poor, yet making

many rich; as having nothing, and *yet* possessing all things.

11 O *ye* Co-rin'thi-ans, our mouth is open unto you, our heart is enlarged.

12 Ye are not straitened in us, but ye are straitened in your own bowels.

13 Now for a recompense in the same, (I speak as unto *my* children,) be ye also enlarged.

14 Be ye not unequally yoked together with unbelievers: for what fellowship hath righteousness with unrighteousness? and what communion hath light with darkness?

15 And what concord hath Christ with Be'li-al? or what part hath he that believeth with an infidel?

16 And what agreement hath the temple of God with idols? for ye are the temple of the living God; as God hath said, I will dwell in them, and walk in *them*; and I will be their God, and they shall be my people.

17 Wherefore come out from among them, and be ye separate, saith the Lord, and touch not the unclean *thing*; and I will receive you,

18 And will be a Father unto you, and ye shall be my sons and daughters, saith the Lord Almighty.

7 Having therefore these promises, dearly beloved, let us cleanse ourselves from all filthiness of the flesh and spirit, perfecting holiness in the fear of God.

2 Receive us; we have wronged no man, we have corrupted no man, we have defrauded no man.

3 I speak not *this* to condemn *you:* for I have said before, that ye are in our hearts to die and live with *you.*

4 Great *is* my boldness of speech toward you, great *is* my glorying of you: I am filled with comfort, I am exceeding joyful in all our tribulation.

5 For, when we were come into Mac-e-do'ni-a, our flesh had no rest, but we were troubled on every side; without *were* fightings, within *were* fears.

6 Nevertheless God, that comforteth those that are cast down, comforted us by the coming of Ti'tus;

7 And not by his coming only, but by the consolation wherewith he was comforted in you, when he told us your earnest desire, your mourning, your fervent mind toward me; so that I rejoiced the more.

8 For though I made you sorry with a letter, I do not repent, though I did repent: for I perceive that the same epistle hath made you sorry, though *it were* but for a season.

9 Now I rejoice, not that ye were made sorry, but that ye sorrowed to repentance: for ye were made sorry after a godly manner, that ye might receive damage by us in nothing.

10 For godly sorrow worketh repentance to salvation not to be repented of: but the sorrow of the world worketh death.

11 For behold this selfsame thing, that ye sorrowed after a

godly sort, what carefulness it wrought in you, yea, *what* clearing of yourselves, yea, *what* indignation, yea, *what* fear, yea, *what* vehement desire, yea, *what* zeal, yea, *what* revenge! In all *things* ye have approved yourselves to be clear in this matter.

12 Wherefore, though I wrote unto you, *I did it* not for his cause that had done the wrong, nor for his cause that suffered wrong, but that our care for you in the sight of God might appear unto you.

13 Therefore we were comforted in your comfort: yea, and exceedingly the more joyed we for the joy of Ti'tus, because his spirit was refreshed by you all.

14 For if I have boasted any thing to him of you, I am not ashamed; but as we spake all things to you in truth, even so our boasting, which *I made* before Ti'tus, is found a truth.

15 And his inward affection is more abundant toward you, whilst he remembereth the obedience of you all, how with fear and trembling ye received him.

16 I rejoice therefore that I have confidence in you in all *things.*

8 Moreover, brethren, we do you to wit of the grace of God bestowed on the churches of Mac-e-do'ni-a;

2 How that in a great trial of affliction the abundance of their joy and their deep poverty abounded unto the riches of their liberality.

3 For to *their* power, I bear

record, yea, and beyond *their* power *they were* willing of themselves;

4 Praying us with much entreaty that we would receive the gift, and *take upon us* the fellowship of the ministering to the saints.

5 And *this they did,* not as we hoped, but first gave their own selves to the Lord, and unto us by the will of God.

6 Insomuch that we desired Ti'tus, that as he had begun, so he would also finish in you the same grace also.

7 Therefore, as ye abound in every *thing,* in faith, and utterance, and knowledge, and *in* all diligence, and *in* your love to us, *see* that ye abound in this grace also.

8 I speak not by commandment, but by occasion of the forwardness of others, and to prove the sincerity of your love.

9 For ye know the grace of our Lord Je'sus Christ, that, though he was rich, yet for your sakes he became poor, that ye through his poverty might be rich.

10 And herein I give *my* advice: for this is expedient for you, who have begun before, not only to do, but also to be forward a year ago.

11 Now therefore perform the doing *of it;* that as *there was* a readiness to will, so *there may be* a performance also out of that which ye have.

12 For if there be first a willing mind, *it is* accepted according to that a man hath, *and* not according to that he hath not.

13 For *I mean* not that other men be eased, and ye burdened:
14 But by an equality, *that* now at this time your abundance *may be a supply* for their want, that their abundance also may be *a supply* for your want: that there may be equality:
15 As it is written, He that *had gathered* much had nothing over; and he that *had gathered* little had no lack.
16 But thanks *be* to God, which put the same earnest care into the heart of Ti'tus for you.
17 For indeed he accepted the exhortation; but being more forward, of his own accord he went unto you.
18 And we have sent with him the brother, whose praise *is* in the gospel throughout all the churches;
19 And not *that* only, but who was also chosen of the churches to travel with us with this grace, which is administered by us to the glory of the same Lord, and *declaration of* your ready mind:
20 Avoiding this, that no man should blame us in this abundance which is administered by us:
21 Providing for honest things, not only in the sight of the Lord, but also in the sight of men.
22 And we have sent with them our brother, whom we have oftentimes proved diligent in many things, but now much more diligent, upon the great confidence which *I have* in you.
23 Whether *any do* inquire of Ti'tus, *he is* my partner and fellow helper concerning you:

or our brethren *be inquired of, they are* the messengers of the churches, *and* the glory of Christ.
24 Wherefore show ye to them, and before the churches, the proof of your love, and of our boasting on your behalf.

9 For as touching the ministering to the saints, it is superfluous for me to write to you:
2 For I know the forwardness of your mind, for which I boast of you to them of Mac·e·do'ni·a, that A·cha'ia was ready a year ago; and your zeal hath provoked very many.
3 Yet have I sent the brethren, lest our boasting of you should be in vain in this behalf; that, as I said, ye may be ready:
4 Lest haply if they of Mac·e·do'ni·a come with me, and find you unprepared, we (that we say not, ye) should be ashamed in this same confident boasting.
5 Therefore I thought it necessary to exhort the brethren, that they would go before unto you, and make up beforehand your bounty, whereof ye had notice before, that the same might be ready, as *a matter of* bounty, and not as *of* covetousness.
6 But this *I say,* He which soweth sparingly shall reap also sparingly; and he which soweth bountifully shall reap also bountifully.
7 Every man according as he purposeth in his heart, *so let him give*; not grudgingly, or of necessity: for God loveth a cheerful giver.
8 And God *is* able to make all

grace abound toward you; that ye, always having all sufficiency in all *things*, may abound to every good work:

9 (As it is written, He hath dispersed abroad; he hath given to the poor: his righteousness remaineth forever.

10 Now he that ministereth seed to the sower both minister bread for *your* food, and multiply your seed sown, and increase the fruits of your righteousness;)

11 Being enriched in every thing to all bountifulness, which causeth through us thanksgiving to God.

12 For the administration of this service not only supplieth the want of the saints, but is abundant also by many thanksgivings unto God;

13 Whiles by the experiment of this ministration they glorify God for your professed subjection unto the gospel of Christ, and for *your* liberal distribution unto them, and unto all *men;*

14 And by their prayer for you, which long after you for the exceeding grace of God in you.

15 Thanks *be* unto God for his unspeakable gift.

10 Now I Paul myself beseech you by the meekness and gentleness of Christ, who in presence *am* base among you, but being absent am bold toward you:

2 But I beseech *you,* that I may not be bold when I am present with that confidence, wherewith I think to be bold against

some, which think of us as if we walked according to the flesh.

3 For though we walk in the flesh, we do not war after the flesh:

4 (For the weapons of our warfare *are* not carnal, but mighty through God to the pulling down of strongholds;)

5 Casting down imaginations, and every high thing that exalteth itself against the knowledge of God, and bringing into captivity every thought to the obedience of Christ;

6 And having in a readiness to revenge all disobedience, when your obedience is fulfilled.

7 Do ye look on things after the outward appearance? If any man trust to himself that he is Christ's, let him of himself think this *again,* that, as he *is* Christ's, even so *are* we Christ's.

8 For though I should boast somewhat more of our authority, which the Lord hath given us for edification, and not for your destruction, I should not be ashamed:

9 That I may not seem as if I would terrify you by letters.

10 For *his* letters, say they, *are* weighty and powerful; but *his* bodily presence *is* weak, and *his* speech contemptible.

11 Let such an one think this, that, such as we are in word by letters when we are absent, such *will we be* also in deed when we are present.

12 For we dare not make ourselves of the number, or compare ourselves with some that

commend themselves: but they measuring themselves by themselves, and comparing themselves among themselves, are not wise.

13 But we will not boast of things without *our* measure, but according to the measure of the rule which God hath distributed to us, a measure to reach even unto you.

14 For we stretch not ourselves beyond *our* measure, as though we reached not unto you: for we are come as far as to you also in *preaching* the gospel of Christ:

15 Not boasting of things without *our* measure, *that is,* of other men's labors; but having hope, when your faith is increased, that we shall be enlarged by you according to our rule abundantly,

16 To preach the gospel in the *regions* beyond you, *and* not to boast in another man's line of things made ready to our hand.

17 But he that glorieth, let him glory in the Lord.

18 For not he that commendeth himself is approved, but whom the Lord commendeth.

11 Would to God ye could bear with me a little in *my* folly: and indeed bear with me.

2 For I am jealous over you with godly jealousy: for I have espoused you to one husband, that I may present *you* as a chaste virgin to Christ.

3 But I fear, lest by any means, as the serpent beguiled Eve through his subtlety, so your minds should be corrupted from the simplicity that is in Christ.

4 For if he that cometh preacheth another Je′sus, whom we have not preached, or *if* ye receive another spirit, which ye have not received, or another gospel, which ye have not accepted, ye might well bear with *him.*

5 For I suppose I was not a whit behind the very chiefest apostles.

6 But though *I be* rude in speech, yet not in knowledge; but we have been thoroughly made manifest among you in all things.

7 Have I committed an offense in abasing myself that ye might be exalted, because I have preached to you the gospel of God freely?

8 I robbed other churches, taking wages *of them,* to do you service.

9 And when I was present with you, and wanted, I was chargeable to no man: for that which was lacking to me the brethren which came from Mac·e·do′ni·a supplied: and in all *things* I have kept myself from being burdensome unto you, and *so* will I keep *myself.*

10 As the truth of Christ is in me, no man shall stop me of this boasting in the regions of A·cha′ia.

11 Wherefore? because I love you not? God knoweth.

12 But what I do, that I will do, that I may cut off occasion from them which desire occasion; that wherein they glory, they may be found even as we.

13 For such *are* false apostles,

deceitful workers, transforming themselves into the apostles of Christ.

14 And no marvel; for Sa'tan himself is transformed into an angel of light.

15 Therefore *it is* no great thing if his ministers also be transformed as the ministers of righteousness; whose end shall be according to their works.

16 I say again, Let no man think me a fool; if otherwise, yet as a fool receive me, that I may boast myself a little.

17 That which I speak, I speak *it* not after the Lord, but as it were foolishly, in this confidence of boasting.

18 Seeing that many glory after the flesh, I will glory also.

19 For ye suffer fools gladly, seeing ye *yourselves* are wise.

20 For ye suffer, if a man bring you into bondage, if a man devour *you*, if a man take *of you*, if a man exalt himself, if a man smite you on the face.

21 I speak as concerning reproach, as though we had been weak. Howbeit whereinsoever any is bold, (I speak foolishly,) I am bold also.

22 Are they He'brews? so *am* I. Are they Is'ra-el-ites? so *am* I. Are they the seed of A'bra-ham? so *am* I.

23 Are they ministers of Christ? (I speak as a fool) I *am* more; in labors more abundant, in stripes above measure, in prisons more frequent, in deaths oft.

24 Of the Jews five times received I forty *stripes* save one.

25 Thrice was I beaten with rods, once was I stoned, thrice I suffered shipwreck, a night and a day I have been in the deep;

26 *In* journeyings often, *in* perils of waters, *in* perils of robbers, *in* perils by mine own countrymen, *in* perils by the heathen, *in* perils in the city, *in* perils in the wilderness, *in* perils in the sea, *in* perils among false brethren;

27 In weariness and painfulness, in watchings often, in hunger and thirst, in fastings often, in cold and nakedness.

28 Beside those things that are without, that which cometh upon me daily, the care of all the churches.

29 Who is weak, and I am not weak? who is offended, and I burn not?

30 If I must needs glory, I will glory of the things which concern mine infirmities.

31 The God and Father of our Lord Je'sus Christ, which is blessed for evermore, knoweth that I lie not.

32 In Da-mas'cus the governor under Ar'e-tas the king kept the city of the Dam'as-cenes with a garrison, desirous to apprehend me:

33 And through a window in a basket was I let down by the wall, and escaped his hands.

12 It is not expedient for me doubtless to glory, I will come to visions and revelations of the Lord.

2 I knew a man in Christ above fourteen years ago, (whether in the body, I cannot tell; or whether out of the body, I can-

not tell: God knoweth;) such an one caught up to the third heaven.

3 And I knew such a man, (whether in the body, or out of the body, I cannot tell: God knoweth;)

4 How that he was caught up into paradise, and heard unspeakable words, which it is not lawful for a man to utter.

5 Of such an one will I glory: yet of myself I will not glory, but in mine infirmities.

6 For though I would desire to glory, I shall not be a fool; for I will say the truth: but *now* I forbear, lest any man should think of me above that which he seeth me *to be,* or *that* he heareth of me.

7 And lest I should be exalted above measure through the abundance of the revelations, there was given to me a thorn in the flesh, the messenger of Sa'-tan to buffet me, lest I should be exalted above measure.

8 For this thing I besought the Lord thrice, that it might depart from me.

9 And he said unto me, My grace is sufficient for thee: for my strength is made perfect in weakness. Most gladly therefore will I rather glory in my infirmities, that the power of Christ may rest upon me.

10 Therefore I take pleasure in infirmities, in reproaches, in necessities, in persecutions, in distresses for Christ's sake: for when I am weak, then am I strong.

11 I am become a fool in glory-ing; ye have compelled me: for I ought to have been commended of you: for in nothing am I behind the very chiefest apostles, though I be nothing.

12 Truly the signs of an apostle were wrought among you in all patience, in signs, and wonders, and mighty deeds.

13 For what is it wherein ye were inferior to other churches, except *it be* that I myself was not burdensome to you? forgive me this wrong.

14 Behold, the third time I am ready to come to you; and I will not be burdensome to you: for I seek not yours, but you: for the children ought not to lay up for the parents, but the parents for the children.

15 And I will very gladly spend and be spent for you; though the more abundantly I love you, the less I be loved.

16 But be it so, I did not burden you: nevertheless, being crafty, I caught you with guile.

17 Did I make a gain of you by any of them whom I sent unto you?

18 I desired Ti'tus, and with *him* I sent a brother. Did Ti'tus make a gain of you? walked we not in the same spirit? *walked we* not in the same steps?

19 Again, think ye that we excuse ourselves unto you? we speak before God in Christ: but *we do* all things, dearly beloved, for your edifying.

20 For I fear, lest, when I come, I shall not find you such as I would, and *that* I shall be found unto you such as ye

would not: lest *there be* debates, envyings, wraths, strifes, backbitings, whisperings, swellings, tumults:

21 And lest, when I come again, my God will humble me among you, and *that* I shall bewail many which have sinned already, and have not repented of the uncleanness and fornication and lasciviousness which they have committed.

13 This *is* the third *time* I am coming to you. In the mouth of two or three witnesses shall every word be established.

2 I told you before, and foretell you, as if I were present, the second time; and being absent now I write to them which heretofore have sinned, and to all other, that, if I come again, I will not spare:

3 Since ye seek a proof of Christ speaking in me, which to you ward is not weak, but is mighty in you.

4 For though he was crucified through weakness, yet he liveth by the power of God. For we also are weak in him, but we shall live with him by the power of God toward you.

5 Examine yourselves, whether ye be in the faith; prove your own selves. Know ye not your own selves, how that Je′sus Christ is in you, except ye be reprobates?

6 But I trust that ye shall know that we are not reprobates.

7 Now I pray to God that ye do no evil; not that we should appear approved, but that ye should do that which is honest, though we be as reprobates.

8 For we can do nothing against the truth, but for the truth.

9 For we are glad, when we are weak, and ye are strong: and this also we wish, *even* your perfection.

10 Therefore I write these things being absent, lest being present I should use sharpness, according to the power which the Lord hath given me to edification, and not to destruction.

11 Finally, brethren, farewell. Be perfect, be of good comfort, be of one mind, live in peace; and the God of love and peace shall be with you.

12 Greet one another with an holy kiss.

13 All the saints salute you.

14 The grace of the Lord Je′sus Christ, and the love of God, and the communion of the Ho′ly Ghost, *be* with you all. Amen.

GALATIANS

1 Paul, an apostle, (not of men, neither by man, but by Je'sus Christ, and God the Father, who raised him from the dead;)

2 And all the brethren which are with me, unto the churches of Ga·la'ti·a;

3 Grace *be* to you and peace from God the Father, and *from* our Lord Je'sus Christ,

4 Who gave himself for our sins, that he might deliver us from this present evil world, according to the will of God and our Father:

5 To whom *be* glory forever and ever. Amen.

6 I marvel that ye are so soon removed from him that called you into the grace of Christ unto another gospel:

7 Which is not another; but there be some that trouble you, and would pervert the gospel of Christ.

8 But though we, or an angel from heaven, preach any other gospel unto you than that which we have preached unto you, let him be accursed.

9 As we said before, so say I now again, If any *man* preach any other gospel unto you than that ye have received, let him be accursed.

10 For do I now persuade men, or God? or do I seek to please men? for if I yet pleased men, I should not be the servant of Christ.

11 But I certify you, brethren, that the gospel which was preached of me is not after man.

12 For I neither received it of man, neither was I taught *it,* but by the revelation of Je'sus Christ.

13 For ye have heard of my conversation in time past in the Jews' religion, how that beyond measure I persecuted the church of God, and wasted it:

14 And profited in the Jews' religion above many my equals in mine own nation, being more exceedingly zealous of the traditions of my fathers.

15 But when it pleased God, who separated me from my mother's womb, and called *me* by his grace,

16 To reveal his Son in me, that I might preach him among the heathen; immediately I conferred not with flesh and blood:

17 Neither went I up to Je·ru'sa·lem to them which were apostles before me; but I went into A·ra'bi·a, and returned again unto Da·mas'cus.

18 Then after three years I went up to Je·ru'sa·lem to see Pe'ter, and abode with him fifteen days.

19 But other of the apostles saw I none, save James the Lord's brother.

20 Now the things which I write unto you, behold, before God, I lie not.

21 Afterwards I came into the regions of Syr'i·a and Ci·li'ci·a;

22 And was unknown by face unto the churches of Ju-dæ´a which were in Christ:

23 But they had heard only, That he which persecuted us in times past now preacheth the faith which once he destroyed.

24 And they glorified God in me.

2 Then fourteen years after I went up again to Je-ru´sa-lem with Bar´na-bas, and took Ti´tus with me also.

2 And I went up by revelation, and communicated unto them that gospel which I preach among the Gen´tiles, but privately to them which were of reputation, lest by any means I should run, or had run, in vain.

3 But neither Ti´tus, who was with me, being a Greek, was compelled to be circumcised:

4 And that because of false brethren unawares brought in, who came in privily to spy out our liberty which we have in Christ Je´sus, that they might bring us into bondage:

5 To whom we gave place by subjection, no, not for an hour; that the truth of the gospel might continue with you:

6 But of these who seemed to be somewhat, (whatsoever they were, it maketh no matter to me: God accepteth no man's person:) for they who seemed to be somewhat in conference added nothing to me:

7 But contrariwise, when they saw that the gospel of the uncircumcision was committed unto me, as the gospel of the circumcision was unto Pe´ter;

8 (For he that wrought effectually in Pe´ter to the apostleship of the circumcision, the same was mighty in me toward the Gen´tiles:)

9 And when James, Ce´phas, and John, who seemed to be pillars, perceived the grace that was given unto me, they gave to me and Bar´na-bas the right hands of fellowship; that we should go unto the heathen, and they unto the circumcision.

10 Only they would that we should remember the poor; the same which I also was forward to do.

11 But when Pe´ter was come to An´ti-och, I withstood him to the face, because he was to be blamed.

12 For before that certain came from James, he did eat with the Gen´tiles: but when they were come, he withdrew and separated himself, fearing them which were of the circumcision.

13 And the other Jews dissembled likewise with him; insomuch that Bar´na-bas also was carried away with their dissimulation.

14 But when I saw that they walked not uprightly according to the truth of the gospel, I said unto Pe´ter before them all, If thou, being a Jew, livest after the manner of Gen´tiles, and not as do the Jews, why compellest thou the Gen´tiles to live as do the Jews?

15 We who are Jews by nature, and not sinners of the Gen´tiles,

16 Knowing that a man is not justified by the works of the

law, but by the faith of Je'sus Christ, even we have believed in Je'sus Christ, that we might be justified by the faith of Christ, and not by the works of the law: for by the works of the law shall no flesh be justified.

17 But if, while we seek to be justified by Christ, we ourselves also are found sinners, *is* therefore Christ the minister of sin? God forbid.

18 For if I build again the things which I destroyed, I make myself a transgressor.

19 For I through the law am dead to the law, that I might live unto God.

20 I am crucified with Christ: nevertheless I live; yet not I, but Christ liveth in me: and the life which I now live in the flesh I live by the faith of the Son of God, who loved me, and gave himself for me.

21 I do not frustrate the grace of God: for if righteousness *come* by the law, then Christ is dead in vain.

3 O foolish Ga-la'tians, who hath bewitched you, that ye should not obey the truth, before whose eyes Je'sus Christ hath been evidently set forth, crucified among you?

2 This only would I learn of you, Received ye the Spirit by the works of the law, or by the hearing of faith?

3 Are ye so foolish? having begun in the Spirit, are ye now made perfect by the flesh?

4 Have ye suffered so many things in vain? if *it be* yet in vain.

5 He therefore that ministereth to you the Spirit, and worketh miracles among you, *doeth he it* by the works of the law, or by the hearing of faith?

6 Even as A'bra-ham believed God, and it was accounted to him for righteousness.

7 Know ye therefore that they which are of faith, the same are the children of A'bra-ham.

8 And the scripture, foreseeing that God would justify the heathen through faith, preached before the gospel unto A'bra-ham, *saying*, In thee shall all nations be blessed.

9 So then they which be of faith are blessed with faithful A'bra-ham.

10 For as many as are of the works of the law are under the curse: for it is written, Cursed *is* everyone that continueth not in all things which are written in the book of the law to do them.

11 But that no man is justified by the law in the sight of God, *it is* evident: for, The just shall live by faith.

12 And the law is not of faith: but, The man that doeth them shall live in them.

13 Christ hath redeemed us from the curse of the law, being made a curse for us: for it is written, Cursed *is* everyone that hangeth on a tree:

14 That the blessing of A'bra-ham might come on the Gen'-tiles through Je'sus Christ; that we might receive the promise of the Spirit through faith.

15 Brethren, I speak after the

manner of men; Though *it be* but a man's covenant, yet *if it be* confirmed, no man disannulleth, or addeth thereto.

16 Now to A'bra-ham and his seed were the promises made. He saith not, And to seeds, as of many; but as of one, And to thy seed, which is Christ.

17 And this I say, *that* the covenant, that was confirmed before of God in Christ, the law, which was four hundred and thirty years after, cannot disannul, that it should make the promise of none effect.

18 For if the inheritance be of the law, *it is* no more of promise: but God gave it to A'bra-ham by promise.

19 Wherefore then *serveth* the law? It was added because of transgressions, till the seed should come to whom the promise was made; *and it was* ordained by angels in the hand of a mediator.

20 Now a mediator is not *a mediator* of one, but God is one.

21 *Is* the law then against the promises of God? God forbid: for if there had been a law given which could have given life, verily righteousness should have been by the law.

22 But the scripture hath concluded all under sin, that the promise by faith of Je'sus Christ might be given to them that believe.

23 But before faith came, we were kept under the law, shut up unto the faith which should afterward be revealed.

24 Wherefore the law was our schoolmaster *to bring us* unto Christ, that we might be justified by faith.

25 But after that faith is come, we are no longer under a schoolmaster.

26 For ye are all the children of God by faith in Christ Je'sus.

27 For as many of you as have been baptized into Christ have put on Christ.

28 There is neither Jew nor Greek, there is neither bond nor free, there is neither male nor female: for ye are all one in Christ Je'sus.

29 And if ye *be* Christ's, then are ye A'bra-ham's seed, and heirs according to the promise.

4 Now I say, *That* the heir, as long as he is a child, differeth nothing from a servant, though he be lord of all;

2 But is under tutors and governors until the time appointed of the father.

3 Even so we, when we were children, were in bondage under the elements of the world:

4 But when the fulness of the time was come, God sent forth his Son, made of a woman, made under the law,

5 To redeem them that were under the law, that we might receive the adoption of sons.

6 And because ye are sons, God hath sent forth the Spirit of his Son into your hearts, crying, Ab'ba, Father.

7 Wherefore thou art no more a servant, but a son; and if a son, then an heir of God through Christ.

8 Howbeit then, when ye knew

not God, ye did service unto them which by nature are no gods.

9 But now, after that ye have known God, or rather are known of God, how turn ye again to the weak and beggarly elements, whereunto ye desire again to be in bondage?

10 Ye observe days, and months, and times, and years.

11 I am afraid of you, lest I have bestowed upon you labor in vain.

12 Brethren, I beseech you, be as I *am*; for I *am* as ye *are*: ye have not injured me at all.

13 Ye know how through infirmity of the flesh I preached the gospel unto you at the first.

14 And my temptation which was in my flesh ye despised not, nor rejected; but received me as an angel of God, *even* as Christ Je'sus.

15 Where is then the blessedness ye spake of? for I bear you record, that, if *it had been* possible, ye would have plucked out your own eyes, and have given them to me.

16 Am I therefore become your enemy, because I tell you the truth?

17 They zealously affect you, *but* not well; yea, they would exclude you, that ye might affect them.

18 But *it is* good to be zealously affected always in *a* good *thing*, and not only when I am present with you.

19 My little children, of whom I travail in birth again until Christ be formed in you,

20 I desire to be present with you now, and to change my voice; for I stand in doubt of you.

21 Tell me, ye that desire to be under the law, do ye not hear the law?

22 For it is written, that A'braham had two sons, the one by a bondmaid, the other by a freewoman.

23 But he *who was* of the bondwoman was born after the flesh; but he of the freewoman *was* by promise.

24 Which things are an allegory: for these are the two covenants; the one from the mount Si'nai, which gendereth to bondage, which is Ha'gar.

25 For this Ha'gar is mount Si'nai in A·ra'bi·a, and answereth to Je·ru'sa·lem which now is, and is in bondage with her children.

26 But Je·ru'sa·lem which is above is free, which is the mother of us all.

27 For it is written, Rejoice, *thou* barren that bearest not; break forth and cry, thou that travailest not: for the desolate hath many more children than she which hath an husband.

28 Now we, brethren, as I'saac was, are the children of promise.

29 But as then he that was born after the flesh persecuted him *that was born* after the Spirit, even so *it is* now.

30 Nevertheless what saith the scripture? Cast out the bondwoman and her son: for the son of the bondwoman shall not be

heir with the son of the free-woman.

31 So then, brethren, we are not children of the bondwoman, but of the free.

5 Stand fast therefore in the liberty wherewith Christ hath made us free, and be not entangled again with the yoke of bondage.

2 Behold, I Paul say unto you, that if ye be circumcised, Christ shall profit you nothing.

3 For I testify again to every man that is circumcised, that he is a debtor to do the whole law.

4 Christ is become of no effect unto you, whosoever of you are justified by the law; ye are fallen from grace.

5 For we through the Spirit wait for the hope of righteousness by faith.

6 For in Je'sus Christ neither circumcision availeth anything, nor uncircumcision; but faith which worketh by love.

7 Ye did run well; who did hinder you that ye should not obey the truth?

8 This persuasion *cometh* not of him that calleth you.

9 A little leaven leaveneth the whole lump.

10 I have confidence in you through the Lord, that ye will be none otherwise minded: but he that troubleth you shall bear his judgment, whosoever he be.

11 And I, brethren, if I yet preach circumcision, why do I yet suffer persecution? then is the offense of the cross ceased.

12 I would they were even cut off which trouble you.

13 For, brethren, ye have been called unto liberty; only *use* not liberty for an occasion to the flesh, but by love serve one another.

14 For all the law is fulfilled in one word, *even* in this; Thou shalt love thy neighbor as thyself.

15 But if ye bite and devour one another, take heed that ye be not consumed one of another.

16 *This* I say then, Walk in the Spirit, and ye shall not fulfil the lust of the flesh.

17 For the flesh lusteth against the Spirit, and the Spirit against the flesh: and these are contrary the one to the other: so that ye cannot do the things that ye would.

18 But if ye be led of the Spirit, ye are not under the law.

19 Now the works of the flesh are manifest, which are *these;* Adultery, fornication, uncleanness, lasciviousness,

20 Idolatry, witchcraft, hatred, variance, emulations, wrath, strife, seditions, heresies,

21 Envyings, murders, drunkenness, revelings, and such like: of the which I tell you before, as I have also told *you* in time past, that they which do such things shall not inherit the kingdom of God.

22 But the fruit of the Spirit is love, joy, peace, longsuffering, gentleness, goodness, faith,

23 Meekness, temperance: against such there is no law.

24 And they that are Christ's

have crucified the flesh with the affections and lusts.

25 If we live in the Spirit, let us also walk in the Spirit.

26 Let us not be desirous of vainglory, provoking one another, envying one another.

6 Brethren, if a man be overtaken in a fault, ye which are spiritual, restore such an one in the spirit of meekness; considering thyself, lest thou also be tempted.

2 Bear ye one another's burdens, and so fulfill the law of Christ.

3 For if a man think himself to be something, when he is nothing, he deceiveth himself.

4 But let every man prove his own work, and then shall he have rejoicing in himself alone, and not in another.

5 For every man shall bear his own burden.

6 Let him that is taught in the word communicate unto him that teacheth in all good things.

7 Be not deceived; God is not mocked: for whatsoever a man soweth, that shall he also reap.

8 For he that soweth to his flesh shall of the flesh reap corruption; but he that soweth to the Spirit shall of the Spirit reap life everlasting.

9 And let us not be weary in well-doing: for in due season we shall reap, if we faint not.

10 As we have therefore opportunity, let us do good unto all *men*, especially unto them who are of the household of faith.

11 Ye see how large a letter I have written unto you with mine own hand.

12 As many as desire to make a fair show in the flesh, they constrain you to be circumcised; only lest they should suffer persecution for the cross of Christ.

13 For neither they themselves who are circumcised keep the law; but desire to have you circumcised, that they may glory in your flesh.

14 But God forbid that I should glory, save in the cross of our Lord Je'sus Christ, by whom the world is crucified unto me, and I unto the world.

15 For in Christ Je'sus neither circumcision availeth anything, nor uncircumcision, but a new creature.

16 And as many as walk according to this rule, peace *be* on them, and mercy, and upon the Is'ra-el of God.

17 From henceforth let no man trouble me: for I bear in my body the marks of the Lord Je'sus.

18 Brethren, the grace of our Lord Je'sus Christ *be* with your spirit. Amen.

EPHESIANS

1 Paul, an apostle of Je'sus Christ by the will of God, to the saints which are at Eph'e-sus, and to the faithful in Christ Je'sus:

2 Grace be to you, and peace, from God our Father, and from the Lord Je'sus Christ.

3 Blessed be the God and Father of our Lord Je'sus Christ, who hath blessed us with all spiritual blessings in heavenly places in Christ:

4 According as he hath chosen us in him before the foundation of the world, that we should be holy and without blame before him in love:

5 Having predestinated us unto the adoption of children by Je'sus Christ to himself, according to the good pleasure of his will,

6 To the praise of the glory of his grace, wherein he hath made us accepted in the beloved.

7 In whom we have redemption through his blood, the forgiveness of sins, according to the riches of his grace;

8 Wherein he hath abounded toward us in all wisdom and prudence;

9 Having made known unto us the mystery of his will, according to his good pleasure which he hath purposed in himself:

10 That in the dispensation of the fullness of times he might gather together in one all things in Christ, both which are in heaven, and which are on earth; even in him:

11 In whom also we have obtained an inheritance, being predestinated according to the purpose of him who worketh all things after the counsel of his own will:

12 That we should be to the praise of his glory, who first trusted in Christ.

13 In whom ye also trusted, after that ye heard the word of truth, the gospel of your salvation: in whom also after that ye believed, ye were sealed with that holy Spirit of promise,

14 Which is the earnest of our inheritance until the redemption of the purchased possession, unto the praise of his glory.

15 Wherefore I also, after I heard of your faith in the Lord Je'sus, and love unto all the saints,

16 Cease not to give thanks for you, making mention of you in my prayers;

17 That the God of our Lord Je'sus Christ, the Father of glory, may give unto you the spirit of wisdom and revelation in the knowledge of him;

18 The eyes of your understanding being enlightened; that ye may know what is the hope of his calling, and what the riches of the glory of his inheritance in the saints,

19 And what is the exceeding

greatness of his power to us-ward who believe, according to the working of his mighty power,

20 Which he wrought in Christ, when he raised him from the dead, and set *him* at his own right hand in the heavenly *places*,

21 Far above all principality, and power, and might, and dominion, and every name that is named, not only in this world, but also in that which is to come:

22 And hath put all *things* under his feet, and gave him *to be* the head over all *things* to the church,

23 Which is his body, the fulness of him that filleth all in all.

2 And you *hath he quickened,* who were dead in trespasses and sins;

2 Wherein in time past ye walked according to the course of this world, according to the prince of the power of the air, the spirit that now worketh in the children of disobedience:

3 Among whom also we all had our conversation in times past in the lusts of our flesh, fulfilling the desires of the flesh and of the mind; and were by nature the children of wrath, even as others.

4 But God, who is rich in mercy, for his great love wherewith he loved us,

5 Even when we were dead in sins, hath quickened us together with Christ, (by grace ye are saved;)

6 And hath raised *us* up together, and made *us* sit together in heavenly *places* in Christ Je'sus:

7 That in the ages to come he might show the exceeding riches of his grace in *his* kindness toward us through Christ Je'sus.

8 For by grace are ye saved through faith; and that not of yourselves: *it is* the gift of God:

9 Not of works, lest any man should boast.

10 For we are his workmanship, created in Christ Je'sus unto good works, which God hath before ordained that we should walk in them.

11 Wherefore remember, that ye *being* in time past Gen'tiles in the flesh, who are called Uncircumcision by that which is called the Circumcision in the flesh made by hands;

12 That at that time ye were without Christ, being aliens from the commonwealth of Is'-ra-el, and strangers from the covenants of promise, having no hope, and without God in the world:

13 But now in Christ Je'sus ye who sometimes were far off are made nigh by the blood of Christ.

14 For he is our peace, who hath made both one, and hath broken down the middle wall of partition *between us;*

15 Having abolished in his flesh the enmity, *even* the law of commandments *contained* in ordinances; for to make in himself of twain one new man, *so* making peace;

16 And that he might reconcile both unto God in one body by the cross, having slain the enmity thereby:

17 And came and preached peace to you which were afar off, and to them that were nigh.

18 For through him we both have access by one Spirit unto the Father.

19 Now therefore ye are no more strangers and foreigners, but fellow citizens with the saints, and of the household of God;

20 And are built upon the foundation of the apostles and prophets, and Je'sus Christ himself being the chief corner *stone;*

21 In whom all the building fitly framed together groweth unto an holy temple in the Lord:

22 In whom ye also are builded together for an habitation of God through the Spirit.

3 For this cause I Paul, the prisoner of Je'sus Christ for you Gen'tiles,

2 If ye have heard of the dispensation of the grace of God which is given me to you-ward:

3 How that by revelation he made known unto me the mystery; (as I wrote afore in few words,

4 Whereby, when ye read, ye may understand my knowledge in the mystery of Christ)

5 Which in other ages was not made known unto the sons of men, as it is now revealed unto his holy apostles and prophets by the Spirit;

6 That the Gen'tiles should be fellow heirs, and of the same body, and partakers of his promise in Christ by the gospel:

7 Whereof I was made a minister, according to the gift of the grace of God given unto me by the effectual working of his power.

8 Unto me, who am less than the least of all saints, is this grace given, that I should preach among the Gen'tiles the unsearchable riches of Christ;

9 And to make all *men* see what *is* the fellowship of the mystery, which from the beginning of the world hath been hid in God, who created all things by Je'sus Christ:

10 To the intent that now unto the principalities and powers in heavenly *places* might be known by the church the manifold wisdom of God,

11 According to the eternal purpose which he purposed in Christ Je'sus our Lord:

12 In whom we have boldness and access with confidence by the faith of him.

13 Wherefore I desire that ye faint not at my tribulations for you, which is your glory.

14 For this cause I bow my knees unto the Father of our Lord Je'sus Christ,

15 Of whom the whole family in heaven and earth is named,

16 That he would grant you, according to the riches of his glory, to be strengthened with might by his Spirit in the inner man;

17 That Christ may dwell in your hearts by faith; that ye,

being rooted and grounded in love,

18 May be able to comprehend with all saints what *is* the breadth, and length, and depth, and height;

19 And to know the love of Christ, which passeth knowledge, that ye might be filled with all the fullness of God.

20 Now unto him that is able to do exceeding abundantly above all that we ask or think, according to the power that worketh in us,

21 Unto him *be* glory in the church by Christ Je'sus throughout all ages, world without end. Amen.

4 I therefore, the prisoner of the Lord, beseech you that ye walk worthy of the vocation wherewith ye are called,

2 With all lowliness and meekness, with longsuffering, forbearing one another in love;

3 Endeavoring to keep the unity of the Spirit in the bond of peace.

4 *There is* one body, and one Spirit, even as ye are called in one hope of your calling;

5 One Lord, one faith, one baptism,

6 One God and Father of all, who *is* above all, and through all, and in you all.

7 But unto everyone of us is given grace according to the measure of the gift of Christ.

8 Wherefore he saith, When he ascended up on high, he led captivity captive, and gave gifts unto men.

9 (Now that he ascended, what is it but that he also descended first into the lower parts of the earth?

10 He that descended is the same also that ascended up far above all heavens, that he might fill all things.)

11 And he gave some, apostles; and some, prophets; and some, evangelists; and some, pastors and teachers;

12 For the perfecting of the saints, for the work of the ministry, for the edifying of the body of Christ:

13 Till we all come in the unity of the faith, and of the knowledge of the Son of God, unto a perfect man, unto the measure of the stature of the fullness of Christ:

14 That we *henceforth* be no more children, tossed to and fro, and carried about with every wind of doctrine, by the sleight of men, *and* cunning craftiness, whereby they lie in wait to deceive;

15 But speaking the truth in love, may grow up into him in all things, which is the head, *even* Christ:

16 From whom the whole body fitly joined together and compacted by that which every joint supplieth, according to the effectual working in the measure of every part, maketh increase of the body unto the edifying of itself in love.

17 This I say therefore, and testify in the Lord, that ye henceforth walk not as other Gen'tiles walk, in the vanity of their mind,

18 Having the understanding darkened, being alienated from the life of God through the ignorance that is in them, because of the blindness of their heart:

19 Who being past feeling have given themselves over unto lasciviousness, to work all uncleanness with greediness.

20 But ye have not so learned Christ;

21 If so be that ye have heard him, and have been taught by him, as the truth is in Je'sus:

22 That ye put off concerning the former conversation the old man, which is corrupt according to the deceitful lusts;

23 And be renewed in the spirit of your mind;

24 And that ye put on the new man, which after God is created in righteousness and true holiness.

25 Wherefore putting away lying, speak every man truth with his neighbor: for we are members one of another.

26 Be ye angry, and sin not: let not the sun go down upon your wrath:

27 Neither give place to the devil.

28 Let him that stole steal no more: but rather let him labor, working with *his* hands the thing which is good, that he may have to give to him that needeth.

29 Let no corrupt communication proceed out of your mouth, but that which is good, that it may minister grace unto the hearers.

30 And grieve not the holy Spirit of God, whereby ye are sealed unto the day of redemption.

31 Let all bitterness, and wrath, and anger, and clamor, and evil speaking, be put away from you, with all malice:

32 And be ye kind one to another, tenderhearted, forgiving one another, even as God for Christ's sake hath forgiven you.

5 Be ye therefore followers of God, as dear children;

2 And walk in love, as Christ also hath loved us, and hath given himself for us an offering and a sacrifice to God for a sweet-smelling savor.

3 But fornication, and all uncleanness, or covetousness, let it not be once named among you, as becometh saints;

4 Neither filthiness, nor foolish talking, nor jesting, which are not convenient: but rather giving of thanks.

5 For this ye know, that no whoremonger, nor unclean person, nor covetous man, who is an idolater, hath any inheritance in the kingdom of Christ and of God.

6 Let no man deceive you with vain words: for because of these things cometh the wrath of God upon the children of disobedience.

7 Be not ye therefore partakers with them.

8 For ye were sometimes darkness, but now *are ye* light in the Lord: walk as children of light:

9 (For the fruit of the Spirit *is* in all goodness and righteousness and truth;)

10 Proving what is acceptable unto the Lord.

11 And have no fellowship with the unfruitful works of darkness, but rather reprove *them.*

12 For it is a shame even to speak of those things which are done of them in secret.

13 But all things that are reproved are made manifest by the light: for whatsoever doth make manifest is light.

14 Wherefore he saith, Awake thou that sleepest, and arise from the dead, and Christ shall give thee light.

15 See then that ye walk circumspectly, not as fools, but as wise,

16 Redeeming the time, because the days are evil.

17 Wherefore be ye not unwise, but understanding what the will of the Lord *is.*

18 And be not drunk with wine, wherein is excess; but be filled with the Spirit;

19 Speaking to yourselves in psalms and hymns and spiritual songs, singing and making melody in your heart to the Lord;

20 Giving thanks always for all things unto God and the Father in the name of our Lord Je'sus Christ;

21 Submitting yourselves one to another in the fear of God.

22 Wives, submit yourselves unto your own husbands, as unto the Lord.

23 For the husband is the head of the wife, even as Christ is the head of the church: and he is the savior of the body.

24 Therefore as the church is subject unto Christ, so *let* the wives *be* to their own husbands in everything.

25 Husbands, love your wives, even as Christ also loved the church, and gave himself for it;

26 That he might sanctify and cleanse it with the washing of water by the word,

27 That he might present it to himself a glorious church, not having spot, or wrinkle, or any such thing; but that it should be holy and without blemish.

28 So ought men to love their wives as their own bodies. He that loveth his wife loveth himself.

29 For no man ever yet hated his own flesh; but nourisheth and cherisheth it, even as the Lord the church:

30 For we are members of his body, of his flesh, and of his bones.

31 For this cause shall a man leave his father and mother, and shall be joined unto his wife, and they two shall be one flesh.

32 This is a great mystery: but I speak concerning Christ and the church.

33 Nevertheless let everyone of you in particular so love his wife even as himself; and the wife *see* that she reverence *her* husband.

6 Children, obey your parents in the Lord: for this is right.

2 Honor thy father and thy mother; which is the first commandment with promise;

3 That it may be well with

thee, and thou mayest live long on the earth.

4 And, ye fathers, provoke not your children to wrath: but bring them up in the nurture and admonition of the Lord.

5 Servants, be obedient to them that are *your* masters according to the flesh, with fear and trembling, in singleness of your heart, as unto Christ;

6 Not with eye-service, as menpleasers; but as the servants of Christ, doing the will of God from the heart;

7 With good will doing service, as to the Lord, and not to men:

8 Knowing that whatsoever good thing any man doeth, the same shall he receive of the Lord, whether *he be* bond or free.

9 And, ye masters, do the same things unto them, forbearing threatening: knowing that your Master also is in heaven; neither is there respect of persons with him.

10 Finally, my brethren, be strong in the Lord, and in the power of his might.

11 Put on the whole armor of God, that ye may be able to stand against the wiles of the devil.

12 For we wrestle not against flesh and blood, but against principalities, against powers, against the rulers of the darkness of this world, against spiritual wickedness in high *places.*

13 Wherefore take unto you the whole armor of God, that ye may be able to withstand in the evil day, and having done all, to stand.

14 Stand therefore, having your loins girt about with truth, and having on the breastplate of righteousness;

15 And your feet shod with the preparation of the gospel of peace;

16 Above all, taking the shield of faith, wherewith ye shall be able to quench all the fiery darts of the wicked.

17 And take the helmet of salvation, and the sword of the Spirit, which is the word of God:

18 Praying always with all prayer and supplication in the Spirit, and watching thereunto with all perseverance and supplication for all saints;

19 And for me, that utterance may be given unto me, that I may open my mouth boldly, to make known the mystery of the gospel,

20 For which I am an ambassador in bonds: that therein I may speak boldly, as I ought to speak.

21 But that ye also may know my affairs, *and* how I do, Tych'i-cus, a beloved brother and faithful minister in the Lord, shall make known to you all things:

22 Whom I have sent unto you for the same purpose, that ye might know our affairs, and *that* he might comfort your hearts.

23 Peace *be* to the brethren, and love with faith, from God the Father and the Lord Je'sus Christ.

24 Grace *be* with all them that love our Lord Je'sus Christ in sincerity. Amen.

PHILIPPIANS

1 Paul and Ti-mo'the-us, the servants of Je'sus Christ, to all the saints in Christ Je'sus which are at Phi-lip'pi, with the bishops and deacons:

2 Grace *be* unto you, and peace, from God our Father, and *from* the Lord Je'sus Christ.

3 I thank my God upon every remembrance of you,

4 Always in every prayer of mine for you all making request with joy,

5 For your fellowship in the gospel from the first day until now;

6 Being confident of this very thing, that he which hath begun a good work in you will perform *it* until the day of Je'sus Christ:

7 Even as it is meet for me to think this of you all, because I have you in my heart; inasmuch as both in my bonds, and in the defense and confirmation of the gospel, ye all are partakers of my grace.

8 For God is my record, how greatly I long after you all in the bowels of Je'sus Christ.

9 And this I pray, that your love may abound yet more and more in knowledge and *in* all judgment;

10 That ye may approve things that are excellent; that ye may be sincere and without offense till the day of Christ;

11 Being filled with the fruits of righteousness, which are by Je'sus Christ, unto the glory and praise of God.

12 But I would ye should understand, brethren, that the things *which happened* unto me have fallen out rather unto the furtherance of the gospel;

13 So that my bonds in Christ are manifest in all the palace, and in all other *places;*

14 And many of the brethren in the Lord, waxing confident by my bonds, are much more bold to speak the word without fear.

15 Some indeed preach Christ even of envy and strife; and some also of good will:

16 The one preach Christ of contention, not sincerely, supposing to add affliction to my bonds:

17 But the other of love, knowing that I am set for the defense of the gospel.

18 What then? notwithstanding, every way, whether in pretense, or in truth, Christ is preached; and I therein do rejoice, yea, and will rejoice.

19 For I know that this shall turn to my salvation through your prayer, and the supply of the Spirit of Je'sus Christ,

20 According to my earnest expectation and *my* hope, that in nothing I shall be ashamed, but *that* with all boldness, as always, *so* now also Christ shall be magnified in my body,

whether *it be* by life, or by death.

21 For to me to live *is* Christ, and to die *is* gain.

22 But if I live in the flesh, this *is* the fruit of my labor: yet what I shall choose I wot not.

23 For I am in a strait betwixt two, having a desire to depart, and to be with Christ; which is far better:

24 Nevertheless to abide in the flesh *is* more needful for you.

25 And having this confidence, I know that I shall abide and continue with you all for your furtherance and joy of faith;

26 That your rejoicing may be more abundant in Je'sus Christ for me by my coming to you again.

27 Only let your conversation be as it becometh the gospel of Christ: that whether I come and see you, or else be absent, I may hear of your affairs, that ye stand fast in one spirit, with one mind striving together for the faith of the gospel;

28 And in nothing terrified by your adversaries: which is to them an evident token of perdition, but to you of salvation, and that of God.

29 For unto you it is given in the behalf of Christ, not only to believe on him, but also to suffer for his sake;

30 Having the same conflict which ye saw in me, and now hear *to be* in me.

2 If *there* be therefore any consolation in Christ, if any comfort of love, if any fellowship of the Spirit, if any bowels and mercies,

2 Fulfil ye my joy, that ye be likeminded, having the same love, *being* of one accord, of one mind.

3 *Let* nothing *be done* through strife or vainglory; but in lowliness of mind let each esteem other better than themselves.

4 Look not every man on his own things, but every man also on the things of others.

5 Let this mind be in you, which was also in Christ Je'sus:

6 Who, being in the form of God, thought it not robbery to be equal with God:

7 But made himself of no reputation, and took upon him the form of a servant, and was made in the likeness of men:

8 And being found in fashion as a man, he humbled himself, and became obedient unto death, even the death of the cross.

9 Wherefore God also hath highly exalted him, and given him a name which is above every name:

10 That at the name of Je'sus every knee should bow, of *things* in heaven, and *things* in earth, and *things* under the earth;

11 And *that* every tongue should confess that Je'sus Christ *is* Lord, to the glory of God the Father.

12 Wherefore, my beloved, as ye have always obeyed, not as in my presence only, but now much more in my absence, work out your own salvation with fear and trembling.

13 For it is God which worketh in you both to will and to do of *his* good pleasure.

14 Do all things without murmurings and disputings:

15 That ye may be blameless and harmless, the sons of God, without rebuke, in the midst of a crooked and perverse nation, among whom ye shine as lights in the world;

16 Holding forth the word of life; that I may rejoice in the day of Christ, that I have not run in vain, neither labored in vain.

17 Yea, and if I be offered upon the sacrifice and service of your faith, I joy, and rejoice with you all.

18 For the same cause also do ye joy, and rejoice with me.

19 But I trust in the Lord Je′sus to send Ti-mo′the-us shortly unto you, that I also may be of good comfort, when I know your state.

20 For I have no man likeminded, who will naturally care for your state.

21 For all seek their own, not the things which are Je′sus Christ's.

22 But ye know the proof of him, that, as a son with the father, he hath served with me in the gospel.

23 Him therefore I hope to send presently, so soon as I shall see how it will go with me.

24 But I trust in the Lord that I also myself shall come shortly.

25 Yet I supposed it necessary to send to you E-paph-ro-di′tus, my brother, and companion in labor, and fellow soldier, but

your messenger, and he that ministered to my wants.

26 For he longed after you all, and was full of heaviness, because that ye had heard that he had been sick.

27 For indeed he was sick nigh unto death: but God had mercy on him; and not on him only, but on me also, lest I should have sorrow upon sorrow.

28 I sent him therefore the more carefully, that, when ye see him again, ye may rejoice, and that I may be the less sorrowful.

29 Receive him therefore in the Lord with all gladness; and hold such in reputation:

30 Because for the work of Christ he was nigh unto death, not regarding his life, to supply your lack of service toward me.

3 Finally, my brethren, rejoice in the Lord. To write the same things to you, to me indeed *is* not grievous, but for you *it is* safe.

2 Beware of dogs, beware of evil workers, beware of the concision.

3 For we are the circumcision, which worship God in the spirit, and rejoice in Christ Je′sus, and have no confidence in the flesh.

4 Though I might also have confidence in the flesh. If any other man thinketh that he hath whereof he might trust in the flesh, I more:

5 Circumcised the eighth day, of the stock of Is′ra-el, *of* the tribe of Ben′ja-min, an He′brew

of the He'brews; as touching the law, a Phar'i see;

6 Concerning zeal, persecuting the church; touching the righteousness which is in the law, blameless.

7 But what things were gain to me, those I counted loss for Christ.

8 Yea doubtless, and I count all things *but* loss for the excellency of the knowledge of Christ Je'sus my Lord: for whom I have suffered the loss of all things, and do count them *but* dung, that I may win Christ,

9 And be found in him, not having mine own righteousness, which is of the law, but that which is through the faith of Christ, the righteousness which is of God by faith:

10 That I may know him, and the power of his resurrection, and the fellowship of his sufferings, being made conformable unto his death;

11 If by any means I might attain unto the resurrection of the dead.

12 Not as though I had already attained, either were already perfect: but I follow after, if that I may apprehend that for which also I am apprehended of Christ Je'sus.

13 Brethren, I count not myself to have apprehended: but *this* one thing I *do,* forgetting those things which are behind, and reaching forth unto those things which are before,

14 I press toward the mark for the prize of the high calling of God in Christ Je'sus.

15 Let us therefore, as many as be perfect, be thus minded: and if in anything ye be otherwise minded, God shall reveal even this unto you.

16 Nevertheless, whereto we have already attained, let us walk by the same rule, let us mind the same thing.

17 Brethren, be followers together of me, and mark them which walk so as ye have us for an example.

18 (For many walk, of whom I have told you often, and now tell you even weeping, *that they are* the enemies of the cross of Christ:

19 Whose end *is* destruction, whose God *is their* belly, and *whose* glory *is* in their shame, who mind earthly things.)

20 For our conversation is in heaven; from whence also we look for the Savior, the Lord Je'-sus Christ:

21 Who shall change our vile body, that it may be fashioned like unto his glorious body, according to the working whereby he is able even to subdue all things unto himself.

4 Therefore, my brethren dearly beloved and longed for, my joy and crown, so stand fast in the Lord, *my* dearly beloved.

2 I beseech Eu-o'di-as, and beseech Syn'ty-che, that they be of the same mind in the Lord.

3 And I entreat thee also, true yokefellow, help those women which labored with me in the gospel, with Clem'ent also, and *with* other my fellow laborers,

whose names *are* in the book of life.

4 Rejoice in the Lord always: *and* again I say, Rejoice.

5 Let your moderation be known unto all men. The Lord *is* at hand.

6 Be careful for nothing; but in everything by prayer and supplication with thanksgiving let your requests be made known unto God.

7 And the peace of God, which passeth all understanding, shall keep your hearts and minds through Christ Je'sus.

8 Finally, brethren, whatsoever things are true, whatsoever things *are* honest, whatsoever things *are* just, whatsoever things *are* pure, whatsoever things *are* lovely, whatsoever things *are* of good report; if *there be* any virtue, and if *there be* any praise, think on these things.

9 Those things, which ye have both learned, and received, and heard, and seen in me, do: and the God of peace shall be with you.

10 But I rejoiced in the Lord greatly, that now at the last your care of me hath flourished again; wherein ye were also careful, but ye lacked opportunity.

11 Not that I speak in respect of want: for I have learned, in whatsoever state I am, *therewith* to be content.

12 I know both how to be abased, and I know how to abound: everywhere and in all things I am instructed both to be full and to be hungry, both to abound and to suffer need.

13 I can do all things through Christ which strengtheneth me.

14 Notwithstanding ye have well-done, that ye did communicate with my affliction.

15 Now ye Phi-lip'pi-ans know also, that in the beginning of the gospel, when I departed from Mac-e-do'ni-a, no church communicated with me as concerning giving and receiving, but ye only.

16 For even in Thes-sa-lo-ni'ca ye sent once and again unto my necessity.

17 Not because I desire a gift: but I desire fruit that may abound to your account.

18 But I have all, and abound: I am full, having received of E-paph-ro-di'tus the things *which were sent* from you, an odor of a sweet smell, a sacrifice acceptable, well-pleasing to God.

19 But my God shall supply all your need according to his riches in glory by Christ Je'sus.

20 Now unto God and our Father *be* glory forever and ever. Amen.

21 Salute every saint in Christ Je'sus. The brethren which are with me greet you.

22 All the saints salute you, chiefly they that are of Cæ'sar's household.

23 The grace of our Lord Je'sus Christ *be* with you all. Amen.

COLOSSIANS

1 Paul, an apostle of Je'sus Christ by the will of God, and Ti-mo'the-us *our* brother,

2 To the saints and faithful brethren in Christ which are at Co-los'se: Grace *be* unto you, and peace, from God our Father and the Lord Je'sus Christ.

3 We give thanks to God and the Father of our Lord Je'sus Christ, praying always for you,

4 Since we heard of your faith in Christ Je'sus, and of the love *which ye have* to all the saints,

5 For the hope which is laid up for you in heaven, whereof ye heard before in the word of the truth of the gospel;

6 Which is come unto you, as *it is* in all the world; and bringeth forth fruit, as *it doth* also in you, since the day ye heard *of it*, and knew the grace of God in truth:

7 As ye also learned of Ep'a-phras our dear fellow servant, who is for you a faithful minister of Christ;

8 Who also declared unto us your love in the Spirit.

9 For this cause we also, since the day we heard *it*, do not cease to pray for you, and to desire that ye might be filled with the knowledge of his will in all wisdom and spiritual understanding;

10 That ye might walk worthy of the Lord unto all pleasing, being fruitful in every good work, and increasing in the knowledge of God;

11 Strengthened with all might, according to his glorious power, unto all patience and longsuffering with joyfulness;

12 Giving thanks unto the Father, which hath made us meet to be partakers of the inheritance of the saints in light:

13 Who hath delivered us from the power of darkness, and hath translated *us* into the kingdom of his dear Son:

14 In whom we have redemption through his blood, *even* the forgiveness of sins:

15 Who is the image of the invisible God, the firstborn of every creature:

16 For by him were all things created, that are in heaven, and that are in earth, visible and invisible, whether *they be* thrones, or dominions, or principalities, or powers: all things were created by him, and for him:

17 And he is before all things, and by him all things consist.

18 And he is the head of the body, the church: who is the beginning, the firstborn from the dead; that in all *things* he might have the preeminence.

19 For it pleased *the Father* that in him should all fullness dwell;

20 And, having made peace through the blood of his cross, by him to reconcile all things unto himself; by him, *I say*, whether *they be* things in earth, or things in heaven.

21 And you, that were sometime alienated and enemies in *your* mind by wicked works, yet now hath he reconciled

22 In the body of his flesh through death, to present you holy and unblamable and unreprovable in his sight:

23 If ye continue in the faith grounded and settled, and *be* not moved away from the hope of the gospel, which ye have heard, *and* which was preached to every creature which is under heaven; whereof I Paul am made a minister;

24 Who now rejoice in my sufferings for you, and fill up that which is behind of the afflictions of Christ in my flesh for his body's sake, which is the church:

25 Whereof I am made a minister, according to the dispensation of God which is given to me for you, to fulfill the word of God;

26 *Even* the mystery which hath been hid from ages and from generations, but now is made manifest to his saints:

27 To whom God would make known what *is* the riches of the glory of this mystery among the Gen'tiles; which is Christ in you, the hope of glory:

28 Whom we preach, warning every man, and teaching every man in all wisdom; that we may present every man perfect in Christ Je'sus:

29 Whereunto I also labor, striving according to his working, which worketh in me mightily.

2 For I would that ye knew what great conflict I have for you, and *for* them at La-od-i-ce'a, and *for* as many as have not seen my face in the flesh;

2 That their hearts might be comforted, being knit together in love, and unto all riches of the full assurance of understanding, to the acknowledgement of the mystery of God, and of the Father, and of Christ;

3 In whom are hid all the treasures of wisdom and knowledge.

4 And this I say, lest any man should beguile you with enticing words.

5 For though I be absent in the flesh, yet am I with you in the spirit, joying and beholding your order, and the stedfastness of your faith in Christ.

6 As ye have therefore received Christ Je'sus the Lord, *so* walk ye in him:

7 Rooted and built up in him, and stablished in the faith, as ye have been taught, abounding therein with thanksgiving.

8 Beware lest any man spoil you through philosophy and vain deceit, after the tradition of men, after the rudiments of the world, and not after Christ.

9 For in him dwelleth all the fullness of the Godhead bodily.

10 And ye are complete in him, which is the head of all principality and power:

11 In whom also ye are circumcised with the circumcision made without hands, in putting off the body of the sins of the

flesh by the circumcision of Christ:

12 Buried with him in baptism, wherein also ye are risen with *him* through the faith of the operation of God, who hath raised him from the dead.

13 And you, being dead in your sins and the uncircumcision of your flesh, hath he quickened together with him, having forgiven you all trespasses;

14 Blotting out the handwriting of ordinances that was against us, which was contrary to us, and took it out of the way, nailing it to his cross;

15 *And* having spoiled principalities and powers, he made a show of them openly, triumphing over them in it.

16 Let no man therefore judge you in meat, or in drink, or in respect of an holy day, or of the new moon, or of the sabbath *days*:

17 Which are a shadow of things to come; but the body *is* of Christ.

18 Let no man beguile you of your reward in a voluntary humility and worshipping of angels, intruding into those things which he hath not seen, vainly puffed up by his fleshly mind,

19 And not holding the Head, from which all the body by joints and bands having nourishment ministered, and knit together, increaseth with the increase of God.

20 Wherefore if ye be dead with Christ from the rudiments of the world, why, as though living in the world, are ye subject to ordinances,

21 (Touch not; taste not; handle not;

22 Which all are to perish with the using;) after the commandments and doctrines of men?

23 Which things have indeed a show of wisdom in will-worship, and humility, and neglecting of the body; not in any honor to the satisfying of the flesh.

3 If ye then be risen with Christ, seek those things which are above, where Christ sitteth on the right hand of God.

2 Set your affection on things above, not on things on the earth.

3 For ye are dead, and your life is hid with Christ in God.

4 When Christ, *who is* our life, shall appear, then shall ye also appear with him in glory.

5 Mortify therefore your members which are upon the earth; fornication, uncleanness, inordinate affection, evil concupiscence, and covetousness, which is idolatry:

6 For which things' sake the wrath of God cometh on the children of disobedience:

7 In the which ye also walked some time, when ye lived in them.

8 But now ye also put off all these; anger, wrath, malice, blasphemy, filthy communication out of your mouth.

9 Lie not one to another, seeing that ye have put off the old man with his deeds;

10 And have put on the new *man*, which is renewed in

knowledge after the image of him that created him;

11 Where there is neither Greek nor Jew, circumcision nor uncircumcision, Bar-ba'ri-an, Scyth'i-an, bond nor free: but Christ is all, and in all.

12 Put on therefore, as the elect of God, holy and beloved, bowels of mercies, kindness, humbleness of mind, meekness, longsuffering;

13 Forbearing one another, and forgiving one another, if any man have a quarrel against any: even as Christ forgave you, so also do ye.

14 And above all these things put on charity, which is the bond of perfectness.

15 And let the peace of God rule in your hearts, to the which also ye are called in one body; and be ye thankful.

16 Let the word of Christ dwell in you richly in all wisdom; teaching and admonishing one another in psalms and hymns and spiritual songs, singing with grace in your hearts to the Lord.

17 And whatsoever ye do in word or deed, do all in the name of the Lord Je'sus, giving thanks to God and the Father by him.

18 Wives, submit yourselves unto your own husbands, as it is fit in the Lord.

19 Husbands, love your wives, and be not bitter against them.

20 Children, obey your parents in all things: for this is well pleasing unto the Lord.

21 Fathers, provoke not your children to anger, lest they be discouraged.

22 Servants, obey in all things your masters according to the flesh; not with eye-service, as menpleasers; but in singleness of heart, fearing God:

23 And whatsoever ye do, do it heartily, as to the Lord, and not unto men;

24 Knowing that of the Lord ye shall receive the reward of the inheritance: for ye serve the Lord Christ.

25 But he that doeth wrong shall receive for the wrong which he hath done: and there is no respect of persons.

4 Masters, give unto your servants that which is just and equal; knowing that ye also have a Master in heaven.

2 Continue in prayer, and watch in the same with thanksgiving;

3 Withal praying also for us, that God would open unto us a door of utterance, to speak the mystery of Christ, for which I am also in bonds:

4 That I may make it manifest, as I ought to speak.

5 Walk in wisdom toward them that are without, redeeming the time.

6 Let your speech be always with grace, seasoned with salt, that ye may know how ye ought to answer every man.

7 All my state shall Tych'i-cus declare unto you, who is a beloved brother, and a faithful minister and fellow servant in the Lord:

8 Whom I have sent unto you

for the same purpose, that he might know your estate, and comfort your hearts;

9 With O·nes'i·mus, a faithful and beloved brother, who is *one* of you. They shall make known unto you all things which *are* done here.

10 Ar·is·tar'chus my fellow prisoner saluteth you, and Mar'cus, sister's son to Bar'na·bas, (touching whom ye received commandments: if he come unto you, receive him;)

11 And Je'sus, which is called Jus'tus, who *are* of the circumcision. These only *are my* fellow workers unto the kingdom of God, which have been a comfort unto me.

12 Ep'a·phras, who is *one* of you, a servant of Christ, saluteth you, always laboring fervently for you in prayers, that ye may stand perfect and complete in all the will of God.

13 For I bear him record, that he hath a great zeal for you, and them *that are* in La·od·i·ce'a, and them in Hi·e·rap'o·lis.

14 Luke, the beloved physician, and De'mas, greet you.

15 Salute the brethren which are in La·od·i·ce'a, and Nym'-phas, and the church which is in his house.

16 And when this epistle is read among you, cause that it be read also in the church of the La·od·i·ce'ans; and that ye likewise read the *epistle* from La·od·i·ce'a.

17 And say to Ar·chip'pus, Take heed to the ministry which thou hast received in the Lord, that thou fulfill it.

18 The salutation by the hand of me Paul. Remember my bonds. Grace *be* with you. Amen.

1 THESSALONIANS

1 Paul, and Sil·va'nus, and Ti·mo'the·us, unto the church of the Thes·sa·lo'ni·ans *which is* in God the Father and *in* the Lord Je'sus Christ: Grace *be* unto you, and peace, from God our Father, and the Lord Je'sus Christ.

2 We give thanks to God always for you all, making mention of you in our prayers;

3 Remembering without ceasing your work of faith, and labor of love, and patience of hope in our Lord Je'sus Christ, in the sight of God and our Father;

4 Knowing, brethren beloved, your election of God.

5 For our gospel came not unto you in word only, but also in power, and in the Ho'ly Ghost, and in much assurance; as ye know what manner of men we were among you for your sake.

6 And ye became followers of us, and of the Lord, having

received the word in much affliction, with joy of the Ho'ly
Ghost:

7 So that ye were examples to
all that believe in Mac-e-do'ni-a
and A-cha'ia.

8 For from you sounded out the
word of the Lord not only in
Mac-e-do'ni-a and A-cha'ia, but
also in every place your faith to
God-ward is spread abroad; so
that we need not to speak any
thing.

9 For they themselves show of
us what manner of entering in
we had unto you, and how ye
turned to God from idols to
serve the living and true God;

10 And to wait for his Son from
heaven, whom he raised from
the dead, *even* Je'sus, which
delivered us from the wrath to
come.

2 For yourselves, brethren,
know our entrance in unto
you, that it was not in vain:

2 But even after that we had
suffered before, and were shamefully entreated, as ye know, at
Phi-lip'pi, we were bold in our
God to speak unto you the gospel
of God with much contention.

3 For our exhortation *was* not
of deceit, nor of uncleanness,
nor in guile:

4 But as we were allowed of
God to be put in trust with the
gospel, even so we speak; not as
pleasing men, but God, which
trieth our hearts.

5 For neither at anytime used
we flattering words, as ye know,
nor *is* a cloak of covetousness;
God *is* witness:

6 Nor of men sought we glory,
neither of you, nor *yet* of others,
when we might have been burdensome, as the apostles of
Christ.

7 But we were gentle among
you, even as a nurse cherisheth
her children:

8 So being affectionately desirous of you, we were willing to
have imparted unto you, not the
gospel of God only, but also our
own souls, because ye were
dear unto you.

9 For ye remember, brethren,
our labor and travail: for laboring night and day, because we
would not be chargeable unto
any of you, we preached unto
you the gospel of God.

10 Ye *are* witnesses, and God
also, how holily and justly and
unblamably we behaved ourselves among you that believe:

11 As ye know how we ex-
horted and comforted and
charged every one of you, as a
father *doth* his children,

12 That ye would walk worthy
of God, who hath called you
unto his kingdom and glory.

13 For this cause also thank we
God without ceasing, because,
when ye received the word of
God which ye heard of us, ye
received *it* not *as* the word of
men, but as it is in truth, the
word of God, which effectually
worketh also in you that believe.

14 For ye, brethren, became
followers of the churches of
God which in Ju-dæ'a are in
Christ Je'sus: for ye also have
suffered like things of your own

countrymen, even as they *have* of the Jews:

15 Who both killed the Lord Je'sus, and their own prophets, and have persecuted us; and they please not God, and are contrary to all men:

16 Forbidding us to speak to the Gen'tiles that they might be saved, to fill up their sins always: for the wrath is come upon them to the uttermost.

17 But we, brethren, being taken from you for a short time in presence, not in heart, endeavored the more abundantly to see your face with great desire.

18 Wherefore we would have come unto you, even I Paul, once and again; but Sa'tan hindered us.

19 For what *is* our hope, or joy, or crown of rejoicing? *Are* not even ye in the presence of our Lord Je'sus Christ at his coming?

20 For ye are our glory and joy.

3 Wherefore when we could no longer forbear, we thought it good to be left at Ath'ens alone;

2 And sent Ti mo'the-us, our brother, and minister of God, and our fellow laborer in the gospel of Christ, to establish you, and to comfort you concerning your faith:

3 That no man should be moved by these afflictions: for yourselves know that we are appointed thereunto.

4 For verily, when we were with you, we told you before that we should suffer tribula-

tion; even as it came to pass, and ye know.

5 For this cause, when I could no longer forbear, I sent to know your faith, lest by some means the tempter have tempted you, and our labor be in vain.

6 But now when Ti mo'the-us came from you unto us, and brought us good tidings of your faith and charity, and that ye have good remembrance of us always, desiring greatly to see us, as we also *to see* you:

7 Therefore, brethren, we were comforted over you in all our affliction and distress by your faith:

8 For now we live, if ye stand fast in the Lord.

9 For what thanks can we render to God again for you, for all the joy wherewith we joy for your sakes before our God;

10 Night and day praying exceedingly that we might see your face, and might perfect that which is lacking in your faith?

11 Now God himself and our Father, and our Lord Je'sus Christ, direct our way unto you.

12 And the Lord make you to increase and abound in love one toward another, and toward all men, even as we *do* toward you:

13 To the end he may stablish your hearts unblamable in holiness before God, even our Father, at the coming of our Lord Je'sus Christ with all his saints.

4 Furthermore then we beseech you, brethren, and exhort *you* by the Lord Je'sus, that as ye have received of us how ye ought to walk and to please God, *so* ye would abound more and more.

2 For ye know what commandments we gave you by the Lord Je'sus.

3 For this is the will of God, *even* your sanctification, that ye should abstain from fornication:

4 That every one of you should know how to possess his vessel in sanctification and honor;

5 Not in the lust of concupiscence, even as the Gen'tiles which know not God:

6 That no *man* go beyond and defraud his brother in *any* matter: because that the Lord *is* the avenger of all such, as we also have forewarned you and testified.

7 For God hath not called us unto uncleanness, but unto holiness.

8 He therefore that despiseth, despiseth not man, but God, who hath also given unto us his holy Spirit.

9 But as touching brotherly love ye need not that I write unto you: for ye yourselves are taught of God to love one another.

10 And indeed ye do it toward all the brethren which are in all Mac-e-do'ni-a: but we beseech you, brethren, that ye increase more and more;

11 And that ye study to be quiet, and to do your own business, and to work with your own hands, as we commanded you;

12 That ye may walk honestly toward them that are without, and *that* ye may have lack of nothing.

13 But I would not have you to be ignorant, brethren, concerning them which are asleep, that ye sorrow not, even as others which have no hope.

14 For if we believe that Je'sus died and rose again, even so them also which sleep in Je'sus will God bring with him.

15 For this we say unto you by the word of the Lord, that we which are alive *and* remain unto the coming of the Lord shall not prevent them which are asleep.

16 For the Lord himself shall descend from heaven with a shout, with the voice of the archangel, and with the trump of God: and the dead in Christ shall rise first:

17 Then we which are alive *and* remain shall be caught up together with them in the clouds, to meet the Lord in the air: and so shall we ever be with the Lord.

18 Wherefore comfort one another with these words.

5 But of the times and the seasons, brethren, ye have no need that I write unto you.

2 For yourselves know perfectly that the day of the Lord so cometh as a thief in the night.

3 For when they shall say, Peace and safety; then sudden destruction cometh upon them, as travail upon a woman with child; and they shall not escape.

4 But ye, brethren, are not in

darkness, that that day should overtake you as a thief.

5 Ye are all the children of light, and the children of the day: we are not of the night, nor of darkness.

6 Therefore let us not sleep, as *do* others; but let us watch and be sober.

7 For they that sleep sleep in the night; and they that be drunken are drunken in the night.

8 But let us, who are of the day, be sober, putting on the breastplate of faith and love; and for an helmet, the hope of salvation.

9 For God hath not appointed us to wrath, but to obtain salvation by our Lord Je´sus Christ,

10 Who died for us, that, whether we wake or sleep, we should live together with him.

11 Wherefore comfort yourselves together, and edify one another, even as also ye do.

12 And we beseech you, brethren, to know them which labor among you, and are over you in the Lord, and admonish you;

13 And to esteem them very highly in love for their work's sake. *And* be at peace among yourselves.

14 Now we exhort you, breth-

ren, warn them that are unruly, comfort the feebleminded, support the weak, be patient toward all *men*.

15 See that none render evil for evil unto any *man*; but ever follow that which is good, both among yourselves, and to all *men*.

16 Rejoice evermore.

17 Pray without ceasing.

18 In everything give thanks: for this is the will of God in Christ Je´sus concerning you.

19 Quench not the Spirit.

20 Despise not prophesyings.

21 Prove all things; hold fast that which is good.

22 Abstain from all appearance of evil.

23 And the very God of peace sanctify you wholly; and *I pray God* your whole spirit and soul and body be preserved blameless unto the coming of our Lord Je´sus Christ.

24 Faithful *is* he that calleth you, who also will do *it*.

25 Brethren, pray for us.

26 Greet all the brethren with an holy kiss.

27 I charge you by the Lord that this epistle be read unto all the holy brethren.

28 The grace of our Lord Je´sus Christ *be* with you. Amen.

2 THESSALONIANS

1 Paul, and Sil-va'nus, and Ti-mo'the-us, unto the church of the Thes-sa-lo'ni-ans in God our Father and the Lord Je'sus Christ:

2 Grace unto you, and peace, from God our Father and the Lord Je'sus Christ.

3 We are bound to thank God always for you, brethren, as it is meet, because that your faith groweth exceedingly, and the charity of every one of you all toward each other aboundeth;

4 So that we ourselves glory in you in the churches of God for your patience and faith in all your persecutions and tribulations that ye endure:

5 Which is a manifest token of the righteous judgment of God, that ye may be counted worthy of the kingdom of God, for which ye also suffer:

6 Seeing it is a righteous thing with God to recompense tribulation to them that trouble you;

7 And to you who are troubled rest with us, when the Lord Je'sus shall be revealed from heaven with his mighty angels,

8 In flaming fire taking vengeance on them that know not God, and that obey not the gospel of our Lord Je'sus Christ:

9 Who shall be punished with everlasting destruction from the presence of the Lord, and from the glory of his power;

10 When he shall come to be glorified in his saints, and to be admired in all them that believe (because our testimony among you was believed) in that day.

11 Wherefore also we pray always for you, that our God would count you worthy of this calling, and fulfil all the good pleasure of his goodness, and the work of faith with power:

12 That the name of our Lord Je'sus Christ may be glorified in you, and ye in him, according to the grace of our God and the Lord Je'sus Christ.

2 Now we beseech you, brethren, by the coming of our Lord Je'sus Christ, and by our gathering together unto him,

2 That ye be not soon shaken in mind, or be troubled, neither by spirit, nor by word, nor by letter as from us, as that the day of Christ is at hand.

3 Let no man deceive you by any means: for that day shall not come, except there come a falling away first, and that man of sin be revealed, the son of perdition;

4 Who opposeth and exalteth himself above all that is called God, or that is worshipped; so that he as God sitteth in the temple of God, showing himself that he is God.

5 Remember ye not, that, when I was yet with you, I told you these things?

6 And now ye know what withholdeth that he might be revealed in his time.